**Praise for** *The Best ...*

'One of those books that makes you reassess
how you live your own life. Deeply moving
but ultimately uplifting'
Katie Fforde

'Wise, moving and heart-warming –
this is Lucy Diamond at her very best'
Rosie Walsh

'You'll laugh as often as you cry'
*Sunday Express*

'This is a masterpiece. An absolutely beautiful book'
Milly Johnson

'Wise and wonderful. No-one does real life
better than Lucy Diamond'
Veronica Henry

'Have the tissues at the ready for this poignant,
yet uplifting and comforting read'
*My Weekly*

'This book touched my heart'
Sarah Morgan

# The Best Days of Our Lives

*Novels*

Any Way You Want Me
Over You
Hens Reunited
Sweet Temptation
The Beach Café
Summer With My Sister
Me and Mr Jones
One Night in Italy
The Year of Taking Chances
Summer at Shell Cottage
The Secrets of Happiness
The House of New Beginnings
On a Beautiful Day
Something to Tell You
An Almost Perfect Holiday
The Promise
Anything Could Happen

*Novellas*

A Baby at the Beach Café

*Ebook Novellas*

Christmas at the Beach Café
Christmas Gifts at the Beach Café

# Lucy Diamond

# The Best Days of Our Lives

QUERCUS

First published in Great Britain in 2023 by Quercus Editions Ltd
This paperback edition first published in 2023 by

**QUERCUS**

Quercus Editions Ltd
Carmelite House
50 Victoria Embankment
London EC4Y 0DZ

An Hachette UK company

A CIP catalogue record for this book is available
from the British Library

PB ISBN 978 1 52942 042 5
EBOOK ISBN 978 1 52942 039 5

10 9 8 7 6 5 4 3 2 1

Typeset by CC Book Production
Printed and bound in Great Britain by Clays Ltd, Elcograf S.p.A.

MIX
Paper | Supporting
responsible forestry
FSC® C104740
www.fsc.org

Papers used by Quercus are from well-managed forests and other responsible sources.

# The Best Days
# of Our Lives

# Prologue

Everything could change so much in a year. Twelve months ago today, on her thirty-fourth birthday, Leni had woken up to the sound of Adam clattering around in the kitchen of their Ealing flat, making her a surprise breakfast. Things weren't perfect between them, sure – they were rowing on and off, both stressing about whether or not their final round of IVF would work – but he'd put in the effort with poached eggs, coffee and orange juice at least. He'd even gone out to the garden in his boxers to snip a couple of white shrub roses to slot into a glass of water, their velvety perfumed heads nodding from the tray as he re-entered the bedroom with a cheery 'Happy birthday!' He was trying, in other words – they both were – and as she saw him there in the doorway, giving it his best shot in the role of loving husband, she thought, *Okay, we can do this. We're going to be all right*.

A year on, and she was starting the day in a different bedroom, in a smaller, cheaper flat all alone, unless you included her ginger rescue cat, Hamish. So far his sum contribution to festivities had been a dead mouse on the kitchen floor that

1

morning, a gift she could have done without. 'I appreciate the effort, Haymo,' she said, picking up the stiff little corpse with a piece of kitchen roll, feeling a pang for its delicate pink feet. 'But, you know, sometimes less is more, mate, do you hear me?'

She pushed open the back door; mid-May and it was unseasonably warm. A cabbage-white butterfly fluttered in jerky zigzags across the garden and the sight of its papery wings beating felt like an encouragement. Keep going, she reminded herself, the sunshine falling benevolent and golden against her bare legs. Keep flying. Her family were coming to celebrate with her today, and they would fill the place with laughter and chat; they would eat and drink and reminisce. The comforting weight of familiarity and belonging would settle upon her, the layers of so many other birthdays and good times from years gone by. Here you are. These are your people. They've got your back, remember?

'This is where it all turns around,' she pep-talked herself, heading for the shower. 'Life begins at thirty-five.' And who knew, by this time next year, she could be madly in love with a handsome prince, radiant with a surprise pregnancy ('It was meant to be!') and looking forward to a whole new wonderful chapter. There was a happy-ever-after out there somewhere, Leni was certain of it.

'Ta-dah! Have you got any candles, Len?'

It was a few hours later and Alice was in the kitchen holding a plate where she'd arranged the mini brownies into a chocolate rockery. They looked about as dry and hard as real rocks, Leni thought, glancing round from where she was

2

carving the roast chicken. *I'll bring cake, obviously!* Alice had said during the week, because she was the best baker in the family and prided herself on her birthday bakes. Last year, for example, she'd appeared with an incredible chocolate and hazelnut meringue creation, and the year before, the most heavenly devil's food cake with a praline topping. The vision of her sister, apron on, whipping up some new chocolatey masterpiece for her had sparked a little match inside Leni, the small act of love a welcome light in the darkness. But then Alice had arrived with a plastic box of supermarket-branded brownies and excuses about being *just so insanely busy at work*, and the bright flickering flame inside her had promptly been snuffed out.

It didn't matter, she told herself. There were more important things than cake. Anyway – silver lining – at least Alice hadn't brought Noah with her. Apparently he'd come down with another of his migraines; it was uncanny how they always struck whenever he had to do something on Alice's behalf.

'Cake candles? No, sorry,' she replied, dismembering the bronzed chicken legs. When she and Adam split up, he'd stayed on in the Ealing flat and she'd been the one to move out, which meant that all of the vaguely useless detritus you accumulated through years of marriage – spare batteries and cake candles and Sellotape – had stayed put in the bottom kitchen drawer of their old place. For Leni to have packed and taken any of it would have seemed petty, but now, as a consequence, she kept being reminded of all that she'd once had and then lost.

'Uh-oh,' came Molly's voice from across the room. *A*

3

*compact through-plan living space*, the estate agent had called it, when Leni was trailing around west London looking at the scant few one-bedroom flats affordable on a divorced teacher's budget. Translated, this meant the kitchen had a sofa and telly at one end, which was where Will, her brother, was currently sitting with his giggling, hair-flicking girlfriend, Molly. It was the first time Leni had met her – Will seemed to operate a revolving-door policy with his love life – but the couple were apparently at the surgically attached stage. Molly had been perched on Will's lap since they arrived, while he looked permanently dazed with lust. 'Is that a *chicken*?' the hair-flicker asked now in a slightly too loud whisper. 'Babe, you did tell your sister I was vegetarian, didn't you?'

Leni's jaw clenched, her hand tightening on the knife because no, obviously Will hadn't told her anything of the sort. 'There are plenty of vegetables,' she said brightly without turning round. It was the voice she used with her class of nine-year-olds – cheery but firm. *We're not going to make a silly fuss about this, are we?* She tried to catch Alice's eye – the two of them had form when it came to post-match analyses of Will's girlfriends, and she could already imagine her sister's wicked, wide-eyed 'Is that a *chicken*?' impression, complete with all the mannerisms – but Alice was preoccupied, peering into cupboards. 'How about some icing sugar?' she was asking. 'Edible glitter?'

The doorbell rang at that moment, thankfully, and Leni escaped the room, head jangling, feeling as if everything was out of kilter today, as if she couldn't quite align herself with the happy mood of togetherness previously envisaged. It had only been a few months since her divorce and she still felt so depleted and fragile; she wasn't sure she could remember how to behave like the person they expected her to be any more. Was she acting too uptight? Should she try harder to care about the edible glitter situation? Yesterday's strange encounter flashed back into her head – the man who'd done a double take on hearing her name. *Coincidence!* he'd said, blinking and staring at her in an unnervingly intent way. *I used to know a Leni McKenzie.*

*Yeah, tell me about it*, she thought to herself now. *I wish she'd hurry up and come back.*

'Happy birthday, darling! So sorry we're late. Traffic was appalling and then it took us forever to find a parking space. But here we are at last!'

Here they were indeed, nearly two hours late – Leni's mum, Belinda, and her partner, Ray. Wearing a yellow silk shirt with lots of necklaces, Belinda had brought cellophane-wrapped peonies that rustled against Leni's back as she enfolded her in a perfumed hug. Despite everything, Leni sank gratefully into her mum's warmth, already looking forward to telling her about yesterday's unexpected twist. *You'll never guess who turned up at work!* she imagined herself saying, anticipating the way her mum's eyes would flick open a little wider, the laugh that would bubble up in her throat. Belinda loved surprises.

That could wait though; right now her mum was disentangling herself, necklaces jingling, with the air of a woman who wanted to get on with the day. 'Any word from your dad? Is he joining us?' she asked, giving Leni a beady look.

'Nope, nothing.' Leni hugged Ray, who, as usual, was wearing a long-sleeved T-shirt with some obscure band name on the front, plus jeans. Years ago, he'd worked in the music industry, getting himself into all kinds of trouble in the process. He'd left the business and retrained as a landscape architect, but still dressed as if he were on his way to a gig. These days he got his kicks through more acceptable hazardous activities: hang-gliding and snowboarding – sometimes even persuading Belinda to join him, much to Leni and Alice's hilarity. (Belinda trussed up in a bungee harness was an image that Leni still returned to if ever she needed cheering up; she would prob-ably still be cackling about her mother's expression of deep discomfort on her deathbed.)

'I invited him but I'm assuming he's forgotten,' she went on, deliberately airy so as to prevent any actual feelings slipping out. Her dad, honestly: there was a therapist's case study in human form if ever you needed one. You'd think after all these years, with one new wife after another briefly appearing as bit parts in the Tony McKenzie show, the rest of the family would be immune to his abominable disregard for them, but the lapses still stung. *Do you think you have daddy issues?* Adam had once asked her and she'd laughed her head off, before pretending to frown. 'Daddy ... Wait, I'm sure I've heard that word somewhere before. Remind me what it means again?'

'Not even a text?' Belinda looked exasperated as they went through to join the others. There was an immediate clatter as Hamish took one look at Ray and scuttled through the cat flap, ears back. Having been brought to the animal shelter as an underweight stray, he took against some men on sight.

'No,' she confirmed curtly, and the edge in her voice must have cut through to Alice, mid glitter-mission, because her sister promptly darted her a quick sidelong glance and came to the rescue.

'Mum! Ray! We were starting to think you'd been abducted,' she said. Crossing the room to hug them both, she touched Leni's arm in passing to let her know she was taking this one on. 'Shall I dish up the veg, Len?'

'Oh darling, you've already cooked!' Belinda cried, seeing the chicken on the side, the pans of vegetables bubbling on the hob. 'I thought I was going to do that for you?'

'Well, yeah, so did I, two hours ago, Mum,' Leni said, hoping she sounded jokey rather than plain old annoyed. Belinda was the most generous person in the world with her offers but you couldn't always guarantee them actually coming good on the day. *Plan B for Belinda!* she and Alice often said to one another. 'I thought I should get on with it.'

'On your birthday, though – oh, now I feel awful!' Belinda said, putting a hand up to her face.

A year ago, Leni might have assured her that it didn't matter, but do you know what? Today, it was starting to feel as if it did. It mattered that she'd heard Molly murmur pityingly to Will, 'She's thirty-five and still single? In this poky flat? I think I'd rather kill myself,' when they thought Leni couldn't hear. The crap brownies mattered, as did her dad's disinterest. Any minute now, Belinda would announce news of her latest friend to become a grandmother and Leni wouldn't be able to stop herself from screaming. Watch out, everyone, if the carving knife was in her hand at the time. That yellow silk shirt of her mum's would need some specialist attention at the dry-cleaners for starters.

Deep breaths, she ordered herself. Calm, kind thoughts. 'Who wants a drink?' she asked, opening the fridge to pull out a misted green bottle of Prosecco. The soft pop of the cork, the first cold mouthful could not come soon enough, she reflected darkly. She registered a momentary ache as she remembered previous birthdays where Adam had stepped up as entertainment manager, splashing out on champagne. He'd cook something flamboyant and showy that always drew admiration and compliments, mix cocktails (the more outrageous the better), and make everyone laugh, charming the room like the charisma-bomb he was. Although being married to a charisma-bomb had its downsides too, of course. You could quickly tire of having random women hanging on your husband's every word, for instance. She certainly didn't miss finding their phone numbers stuffed in his pocket, the paranoia that snaked in whenever he was unexpectedly late home. Also, while she was on the subject, show-off cooking was all well and good, but if Adam had bothered to check in with her first, she'd have chosen good old roast chicken every time.

But that was in the past now, she reminded herself. He had a new partner's family to dazzle these days, didn't he? Besides, that handsome prince who was due to appear in Leni's life any day now would not only be an absolute ace in the kitchen, he'd be modest about it too. Charming without being an egomaniac. Imagine!

'Anyone for fizz?' she said brightly.

'Bubbles!' cried Molly as if she were five. 'Yes, please!'

'Lovely,' added Belinda, bustling over to tend to the abandoned chicken. 'Let me get on with this while you pour.'

'Is everyone having a glass?' Leni asked, counting out flutes. Ray didn't drink these days, but Will, Molly and Belinda all replied yes. Alice, meanwhile, was at the sink, filling a tumbler with water.

'I'm fine with this, thanks,' she said, her long chestnut hair falling in front of her face, perhaps so that she didn't have to meet Leni's eye.

'Oh.' Leni's hand suddenly felt clammy on the bottle, her stomach turning over as her mind leapt ahead. The moment of solidarity she'd just felt with her sister seemed to blister, vanishing in the next second. Was Alice saying ... ? Did this mean ... ? The air seized in Leni's lungs as she tried to catch her breath. Alice was wearing pale blue cropped chino-type trousers with a black silky short-sleeved blouse, and Leni found herself peering covertly at her sister's body, wondering if her belly looked a bit rounder than usual, if her loose top was in fact hiding something.

Oh God. She didn't think she could bear it if Alice was having a baby. She might actually drop dead with envy and bitterness, after everything that had happened. She would cover up, of course, put on a good show – *oh wow! Exciting!* – because she knew all the right things to say by now. She'd be the best aunty-to-be ever too – she'd buy the cute little outfits and remember to check in after Alice's scans, conjuring up expressions of delight and wonder, clapping a hand to her heart, and then she'd go home and weep into her sofa, bilious with jealousy.

Leni popped the cork from the bottleneck, but no longer felt so steady on her feet while such unsisterly thoughts were pushing to the forefront of her mind. Was Alice seriously going to have a baby with that idiot Noah? Back in the day, the two sisters had entertained a long-running narrative that they'd marry a prince and a baron and live in neighbouring castles. Prince Antonio, Leni had christened her imaginary future husband at the time, although he'd also been Prince Brad, Prince Keanu and Prince Idris in later conversations, depending on who she was into. 'And Baron . . . Darren,' Alice had quipped, only for the name to stick throughout the years that followed. Couldn't Alice hang out a *bit* longer for the dashing, castle-owning Baron Darren of her dreams, instead of settling for good-looking but shallow Noah?

Belinda, sawing at the chicken breast, did not seem to notice the unspoken frisson between her daughters. Leni was surprised she hadn't pounced upon Alice's uncharacteristic booze refusal with a hopeful gleam in her eye. She had knitted a small white baby hat when Leni and Adam started IVF, and crocheted a little yellow jacket second time around. Then their last attempt had come to nothing, and her woollen production line ground to a halt, along with their optimism. Maybe Alice could give their mother what she wanted, because Leni had failed and failed again.

*Come on. Keep it together. Happy families, remember.* Glad for an excuse to hide her face, she crouched at the cupboard to retrieve her nicest plates – the set that Adam had bought her for Christmas three years ago, crackle-effect porcelain in turquoise, plum and emerald shades – but her fingers were trembling. Perhaps the glass of Prosecco she'd just thrown back in a single, despairing gulp had affected her coordination, or maybe her hands were a bit sweaty, but as she stood up, then attempted to squeeze around Ray, draining the peas at the sink, she lurched sideways and somehow lost her grip on the stack of plates, which went crashing to the floor.

'Oh God!' she wailed as they smashed into pieces. 'Oh *no.*'

It was only *crockery*, she scolded herself later on when the six of them were finally squeezed around the small table for lunch, the food dished out on to the four plain white plates she had bought for everyday use, plus a couple of plastic camping plates she'd unearthed to make up the numbers. Worse things could and did happen. She might be able to glue the pieces back together, she thought, drinking more wine and trying valiantly to engage with the conversation. Trying to smile. But in the moment after they'd fallen from her grasp, smashing into so many bright broken shards on her kitchen floor, she had sunk to her knees beside them and burst into tears – for the plates, for her marriage, for her whole life.

When so many things were broken, how on earth did you go about sticking them back together again?

# Chapter One

Years earlier, when Alice was eight years old, she'd had flute lessons at primary school for a while. Three of them from her class were taught in a group – her, Joe McPhee and Becky Braithwaite – but for some reason, the teacher, Mrs Janson, singled out Alice for a new nickname every week. 'Shorty,' Mrs Janson called her, probably because she was smaller than Joe and Becky; a summer baby yet to catch her peers up in height. 'Titch.' Alice tried to laugh along each time but couldn't ignore the uneasy feeling at the bottom of her tummy. It was confusing. Thus far in life, grown-ups had been mostly kind to her. In fact, until now, she'd go as far as to say that grown-ups had been pretty firm about not calling other people names. So how come this lady was allowed to? Had Alice done something wrong?

Her sister Leni was in the last year of primary school at this point. Year 6 pupils were given extra responsibilities – collecting class registers, running errands and delivering cups of tea or coffee to school visitors. 'Life skills,' the head-teacher called it, but everyone knew it was free skivvying. By coincidence, Leni was on duty this particular day, and appeared in the music room, carefully balancing a cup of coffee on a tray, just as Mrs Janson was saying, 'Oh dear, never mind, Joe,' after he'd mangled an easy scale. 'Let's see if the dwarf can manage it.'

Up until this moment, Alice had been smiling with excitement to see her sister, but when Mrs Janson's words filtered through to her – *the dwarf?!* – she was immediately consumed by a massive wave of embarrassment. She swung her gaze away, but not before she saw Leni's eyebrows shoot up in surprise. Heat flared in Alice's cheeks as she raised the flute to her lips, unable to concentrate until she'd heard the clink of the coffee cup being set down, then the soft closing of the door as Leni left.

'Does she always talk to you like that?' Leni asked that evening. The two girls were in their shared bedroom, with Leni sprawled out on her bed, admiring her non-bitten fingernails. Their mum, Belinda, had said that if Leni could stop biting her nails for a whole month, she would buy her a pot of nail varnish as a reward. There were still ten days to go but Leni, confident of success, was already in a delicious dilemma about which shade to choose, having pretty much committed to memory the entire range of options at the big Boots in town.

'Who?'

'That horrible flute teacher, calling you a dwarf. How mean!'

Alice, on the bed across the room with a comic, twiddled one of her bunches around her finger and said nothing for a moment. She'd managed to put the mortifying scene out of her head but now it leaped up once more: her teacher's sharp voice and cold blue eyes, the awkward giggles from Joe and Becky, the conviction that Alice must be a bad person who deserved the name-calling. 'I dunno,' she mumbled.

'Does Mum know she's nasty to you?' her sister persisted, chin pointy, eyes fierce; a face that said *Don't try and fob me off with a lie now.*

Alice shook her head. Belinda had a short fuse and, in hindsight, good reason to be irritable, when things had been chaotic at home for as long as Alice could remember: that horrible year after Will was born, for starters, when he was in and out of hospital with bronchiolitis and breathing difficulties, with Alice and Leni both having to stay with Janet-next-door when he was really poorly. Then their dad had moved out, initially with talk about a new job a long way away but then not reappearing for seemingly months on end. Belinda had started to say, 'Look, I don't *know*, all right?' in answer to questions about when he'd be back, with enough exasperation that even a small person could sense there might be an issue.

'No,' Alice replied, then glared at her sister with sudden suspicion. 'Don't *you* tell her,' she said, not wanting to be at the centre of any drama. Somehow it would end up being Alice's fault, she knew already. 'You won't, will you?'

Leni was back to admiring her stubby but unbitten nails. 'I'm thinking Mauve Shimmer,' she announced, wiggling her fingers with anticipation. 'Or maybe Coral Kisses. Oh, how am I going to decide?'

A week later, and it was time for another flute lesson. The door opened as usual halfway through, for the arrival of a

Year 6 pupil bearing a coffee for Mrs Janson – but to Alice's surprise, it was Leni again. This was unexpected, as was the strange expression on her sister's face: a sort of gleeful triumph, her mouth twitching in a way that made Alice think she was trying to suppress a laugh.

Minutes later, with Mrs Janson midway through her coffee, Alice realised why. 'Ugh,' spluttered the teacher, only to choke and fish about in her mouth with a look of abject horror.

'What *is* that?' cried Becky Braithwaite, eyes goggling at the small white crescent plucked from her teacher's mouth. 'Is that a *fingernail*, Miss?'

Mrs Janson looked completely ashen. 'Excuse me a minute,' she said, grabbing the cup and fleeing the room.

It turned out there were *ten* small, jagged fingernails in the coffee, bitten quickly off and added to the drink en route to the music room. '*And* a bit of spit too,' Leni said carelessly that afternoon once they were back home. 'Helena McKenzie, what on earth were you *thinking*?' Belinda had exploded, pink in the cheeks, having been called away from work to learn of this crime. 'Well, you can forget that nail varnish now, young lady. And you can forget about going round to Victoria's party at the weekend too. Fingernails in a teacher's coffee, indeed. You're in so much trouble, I can hardly even *look* at you right now!'

Leni was sanguine about the punishments – 'Vicky's already said she'll rearrange the party for when I can come, I don't care,' she told her sister with a lofty shrug – but Alice knew that the withdrawal of nail varnish rights was an absolute stinger.

The first chance she got, dragging around town with her

mum and Will some weekends later, Alice seized the opportunity to sidle back to the make-up shelves while Belinda dithered over nit shampoo brands then queued up to ask the pharmacist about cough medicine. Mauve Shimmer – straight up her right coat sleeve. Coral Kisses – straight up her left. Her heart thudded like a jackhammer as they eventually departed the shop. By then, she'd managed to secrete the two small bottles in the depths of her duffel coat pockets, all the while expecting the accusatory 'Oi!' of a security guard to boom after her. None came. She'd done it. *You see off my mean flute teacher for me, I'll shoplift nail varnish for you*, she thought, picturing the look of delight that she knew would dawn across Leni's face when Alice revealed her stolen booty. It seemed a pretty good deal, frankly.

*And totally worth it, too, for my brilliant, loyal sister*, she typed now, reading back through the words of her story once more before pressing *Post* and sitting back with a small sigh. It was a Sunday evening in December, five and a half months after the accident, and Alice was hunched in bed with her laptop, its screen casting blue light on to her face while a belligerent wind outside rattled the window in its frame. The memorial page was her online sanctuary, a place to which she returned frequently with updates or photos, and she loved scrolling through other people's fondly remembered stories. It was a comfort to retreat into nostalgia when real life kept tripping her up with horrible surprises. Tomorrow, for instance, she would almost certainly be called in for a little chat with her boss, following the debacle with Nicholas Pearce on Friday evening and ...

*Don't*, she ordered herself before any bad thoughts could take root. *Don't think about that*. She refreshed the screen instead, where comments were already appearing beneath her new post.

*She was the best, wasn't she? RIP.*

*Love this story, Alice. Can totally imagine her doing this. Hope you're okay.*

*Oh Leni, we all miss you so much.*

'I'm sorry, Alice,' said Rupert the next day, after he had, as expected, requested a quick word with her in his office. The grim set to his mouth signalled that the quick word would not be about a pay rise nor her fantastic work. (It probably wouldn't even be quick, Alice registered with an inner groan.) 'But the phone call from Nicholas Pearce was the final straw. I'm afraid this conversation will be minuted as a verbal warning about your misconduct. This can never happen again, do you understand?'

Leni had once confided in Alice that whenever people said fatuous things like 'Do you understand?' or 'Are you listening to me?' her instinct was to reply in the negative, if only to annoy them even more. Sitting in her boss's office now, facetiousness didn't seem a great option to Alice though. 'What, so you're saying you're taking his side over mine?' she asked, trying to choke back the *Are you fucking kidding me?* boiling within her. 'Even though he thought it was fair game to fondle my leg in a bar, and then follow me to the bus stop? When I'd made it clear that was not appropriate?'

Rupert was a successful, charming man, used to being

adored by clients and staff alike. He liked to boast that he'd dreamed up his award-winning marketing and communications agency on the back of a fag packet, but that was yet another example of his own-brand spin; Alice knew for a fact he'd relied heavily on family wealth and some very well-connected friends in the early days. Whatever – it sounded good, and she of all people understood the sheen that a slick of marketing gloss could bring. Except when it turned out that Rupert was *all* gloss, and slippery as hell with it. 'And you think him behaving that way is okay, do you?' she burst out.

'Of *course* it's not okay,' he replied, dark eyebrows sliding together. He tapped a silver pen on the desk for good measure and the tinny noise was so irritating, Alice felt like snatching it off him. Maybe even whacking him over the head with it for good measure. 'But by the sound of it, you completely overreacted. Swearing at him in a bar—'

'His hand was halfway up my thigh!'

'And pushing him in the street like some kind of oik—'

'I was scared for my own *safety*!'

'You're lucky he's not pressing charges for assault, you know. Very lucky.'

'Lucky?' Alice's voice rose almost to a screech. She'd plunge that silver pen into his eyeball in a minute. 'I didn't *assault* him. Jesus! I wish I bloody *had* assaulted him, and he'd have had it coming to him too, the dirty old pervert, I—'

'Alice—'

'And you're disciplining *me*, like this is somehow *my* fault? When I was just trying to do my *job*?'

'ALICE.' He was thundering now and she broke off, clutching

18

her hands together in the vain hope she might stop them from shaking. How she wished her fingernail assassin sister could burst into the room and come to her rescue. Even appear as a ghostly apparition just to frighten the bejeezus out of him. No such luck. 'That's not the only problem, though, is it?' Rupert went on. 'I might have been prepared to overlook this whole disgraceful business were it not for the fact that you've not been yourself for some months now. Many months.'

Alice hung her head. Here we go. 'It's not like I haven't had good reason,' she muttered, face blazing. *Sure, drag me into it*, she imagined Leni drawling, one eyebrow raised sardonically. *Get that excuse on his table, see if that shuts him up for a minute. There must be some perks to having a dead sister, right?*

'Absolutely,' he said, his tone softening a fraction. Not enough to change tack though. 'We're all aware that you've had a very difficult time. However.'

Oh Christ. She did not want to listen to the 'However'. She was still reeling from his dismissal of her defence just now, furious that he didn't seem able to understand how awful the encounter had been. She and Nicholas Pearce were in the bar together, supposedly to go through a few final details of the contract he was poised to sign with the agency, only for her to feel sinking dismay when she realised his actual agenda. Rupert didn't get it because he'd never had to deal with such a situation, presumably; he'd always been respected, valued for his work, taken at face value. Did he really not see that it was different for women?

'I have caught up on all the days I missed,' she said haltingly, wanting to pre-empt whatever criticism was coming next. 'I have worked so hard on the Red Lobster campaign; Edie and I smashed it at the presentation last week. Yes, I've had a difficult time, but I'm turning a corner now, I'm on the way up again.'

She crossed her fingers under the desk because saying she was on the way up was a massive exaggeration but, you know, marketing. She could gild a lily with the best of them.

'The thing is though, Alice,' he went on, 'this has come after months of poor time-keeping, unreliability, outbursts in meetings. And we've all been very patient with you but there comes a point when enough is enough. I'm wondering if perhaps you should take a bit more time off. Possibly look into some anger management sessions.'

Alice swallowed hard. The clock on the wall seemed to be ticking particularly loudly all of a sudden. Her skin felt sticky, her throat dry; her breath was shallow in her lungs as if she was on the verge of a panic attack. *Alice, you're, like, mentally unhinged*, Noah had shouted the day he finished with her. He'd actually put his hands up in the air as if she were a wild animal, saying he couldn't cope with the drama any more, he was sick of it. Now here was her boss intimating pretty much the same thing. *We've all been very patient with you*, as if the whole office had been bitching about her. They could sod off too, she thought in a new explosion of fury.

'Do you know what,' she said, the words spilling out of her before she even knew what they might be, 'I quit.' She got to her feet, sweat prickling in the small of her back despite it being December and Rupert ever-stingy about the office heating setting. 'I don't want to work here any more.'

'Alice—' He was doing that weary, patronising sigh that her dad sometimes used to adopt, as if she was a silly little girl. This alone was enough to make her double down on her impulse decision.

'I've got some holiday left and it's Christmas coming up,' she said. 'I'm not staying where I don't feel valued. Shove your anger management sessions – and find someone else to do your shit job while you're at it.' And then she was storming out of there, only stopping to grab her bag and coat, barging past her wide-eyed colleagues, some of whom called after her in concern – *Alice, are you okay?*

Erupting into the freezing Soho street, she half expected buildings to be collapsing around her, fires to be blazing in cars, the ground shifting beneath her feet, because that was how it felt: as if the world was ending. Leni, Noah, now her job . . . all of those solid structures in her life, everything she'd treasured six months ago, had crumbled to rubble. She put her arms around herself for a brief moment, tried to banish forever the image of Rupert's supercilious face, and stumbled blindly along the street, unsure where she was going or even what she might do next. 'Fuck,' she said aloud and then, for good measure, yelled at the top of her voice. 'FUCK!'

# Chapter Two

'You know, I think you might have been all right if you hadn't said the "shit job" bit,' Lou ventured that evening, a mixture of side-eye and sympathy.

'You could probably still go back if you sent a grovelling email,' Celeste added. The three of them were squeezed around a corner table in the Queen and Compass, Alice's local pub, and she was starting to wish she'd suggested a different venue, seeing as the house band were in tonight and their set list was resolutely festive. They'd already murdered Mariah Carey's 'All I Want for Christmas', and were now trying to persuade the clientele to join in with a headbanging cover of 'Last Christmas'. 'This is a really bad time of year to lose your job, for one thing.'

These were Alice's two best friends and she was grateful to them for dropping everything in order to come out with her in commiseration, but if they thought for a minute she was regretful or about to beg for her old job back, they had completely missed the point. 'It's not gonna happen,' she said. 'Me grovelling or going back. And it's January in a few weeks anyway – I thought that was meant to be the perfect time for a new start. That's what all the adverts say.'

'True,' Lou conceded. 'Have you got anything in mind?'

'Well, first up: getting absolutely hammered,' Alice replied, raising her glass in the air with a bravado she didn't quite feel. Lou had bought them all Christmas-themed cocktails in an attempt to bolster spirits, and Alice's so-called Jingle Juice Punch had come complete with a candy-cane-striped straw plus a liberal helping of cranberries. The lead singer of the band gave a drawn-out, many-syllabled flourish to the word 'special' just then, complete with an enthusiastic drum roll from the drummer to end the song, and Alice joined in with the half-hearted applause. 'Cheers.'

She slugged back her drink, catching a tiny private look exchanged between her friends as she set the glass down. 'In the meantime,' Celeste said in a bright voice, 'we've been thinking. We know you've had a shit time of it this year, but how about us making some plans together for the next one, to keep us all going? Only I've had a few ideas – like organising some nights out? Booking in a weekend away?'

'And I was wondering about us starting a fitness challenge together,' Lou said, ignoring the look of horror that appeared immediately on Alice's face. 'Like – every month, we try a different activity. Kick-boxing or climbing or—'

'There's a women's cycling group in Hackney I keep hearing about,' Celeste put in.

'Yeah! Or go old-school and join a netball club. It could be fun! What do you think, Alice?'

What did Alice think? She thought the word 'fun' was

doing a lot of heavy lifting in that sentence, for one thing. And while she knew her friends were trying to gee her up, she'd have preferred to spend longer on the 'weekend away' option rather than the dismal image of sporting a polyester netball bib on a rainy winter's evening. 'Mmm, maybe,' she said unconvincingly, then pretended she needed the loo so that she could escape before anyone pinned her down with actual arrangements.

Inside the safety of a toilet cubicle, she leaned against the wall, the alcohol racing hectically through her bloodstream. The situation didn't seem quite real yet; it felt like a fever-dream, her storming out of the ReImagine office building, the door closing behind her. What had she done? 'You've lost it, Alice,' she remembered Noah saying, the words still smarting a full two months after they'd split up. 'You're, like, mentally unhinged. This is doing my head in, I don't want to be with you any more.'

Gorgeous, sexy, utterly shallow Noah, who'd moved in with her, holidayed with her, with whom she'd idly discussed a future, babies, commitment, before the world spun off its axis and everything went dark. Had he ever meant a word of it? Because he'd been so spectacularly shit when Leni died and Alice broke into a million tiny pieces; he could hardly scramble out of the relationship quick enough. *I could have told you he was no Baron Darren*, she'd imagined Leni intoning, while her friends had similar comments to make. 'Absolute wanker,' they chorused as one, swooping in with wine and Marks and Spencer trifle, plus a side helping of venom. 'You're better off without him. Forget him!'

To be fair to Noah, she *had* kind of lost the plot back then. If Alice had seen a woman at the side of a busy street on a dark evening, yelling incoherently, before stumbling into the road and almost getting herself killed amidst a blare of horns, the word 'unhinged' might have come to her own lips. What was more, if she'd been the one driving the car forced to swerve around a drunk woman falling into the path of traffic, she would definitely have called the police and reported this dangerous behaviour – for the woman's own safety. But at the time, Alice hadn't been thinking in rational terms. She'd been so overcome by rage, she'd felt compelled to stand at that particular spot in Shepherd's Bush, shouting her sister's name so that it would be heard, it would be known. So that nobody would forget her. 'What about planting a tree instead, love, have you thought about that?' the tired-looking police-woman asked, as Alice was bundled into the back of the cop car. 'That's what most people do and it's a lot less dramatic, on the whole.'

*I'm wondering if perhaps you should take a bit more time off. Possibly look into some anger management sessions*, she heard Rupert say again, and an unwanted image came to her: of her standing in the shadowy driveway of a house, an egg in her hand – and then a man appearing out of the darkness, striding towards her. *Don't you ever come here again*, he'd warned, his angular face half lit by the streetlights, his body taut like a boxer, everything about him a threat. She hadn't cared a bit though, because yeah, she was angry. You bet she bloody was.

There was a loud knock just then and she reoriented herself

with a start: pub toilet, the faint sounds of a grungy 'Santa Baby' cover drifting under the door. 'Alice? Are you all right in there?' she heard.

Lou, come to get her. No doubt they'd been fretting at the table following her departure. *Is she okay? Should we check on her, do you think?* Her friends, doing their best to haul her up from rock bottom with their plans and solidarity. *Exercise is good for mental health, isn't it?* they'd have said, cooking up schemes beforehand of how they could help her.

Then Alice remembered the way Lou and Celeste had glanced at one another when they thought she wasn't looking, and wondered if they, like Noah, thought she was unhinged, but were too nice to say so. Oh God. She'd already lost so much this year. She couldn't lose them on top of everything else.

'I'll be right there,' she called back, doing her best to sound cheery. *Come on, Alice*, she ordered herself, with a flashback to how she'd sat at the funeral, hands twisted in her lap, tears streaming down her face, vowing *I'll live for both of us from now on, Leni. I promise you I will.*

*Yeah, right*, she imagined Leni saying drily now, giving her a ghostly nudge. *And you sitting in the pub bogs feeling sorry for yourself is your idea of living for us both, is it? Sheesh! Don't bother on my account, will you?*

She pulled a face at the idea of her big sister bossing her around from beyond the grave, but all the same, she had a point. *That's my girl*, said Leni minutes later as she got to her feet and returned to her friends. *Up and at 'em, Alice!*

★

A subdued Christmas passed, the first without Leni, and Alice hunkered down with her mum and Ray at the old family home in Oxford. Together they limped through the days, propped up by plentiful carbohydrates, back-to-back old films and too much alcohol, plus Ray's insistence on dragging them out for regular walks as if they were dogs, like it or not. The year was almost over, Alice consoled herself as she returned to London with a Tupperware box of mince pies and the dazzled feeling of having been indoors for too long. Once home, she gamely put on a party dress for New Year's Eve and knocked back cocktails with her friends, trying to ignore the empty feeling inside. Next year would be better. It had to be.

January began and she fixed up some temporary work so as to keep the wolf from the mortgage payments, before returning once more to her mum's house with a stressful task looming: that of helping to sort through Leni's belongings that had been stowed up in the loft. Belinda had decided to sell up and move on, and they could put off this onerous challenge no longer.

Alice forced herself to take a calming yogic breath as her mum hauled down the concertina loft ladder first thing. It was only *stuff*, after all, she thought. Tonight, once they'd got through this, they would drink a toast to Leni and no doubt both cry a bit, but there would be a new layer of relief bedding down in the background too, because the dreaded task would be behind them by then. *It's going to be a tough day but think of the closure*, Celeste had texted that morning. Lou, meanwhile, had sent details of a Park Run on Saturday, which Alice was pretending not to have seen. That was for Future Alice to deal with, she decided, climbing the cold metal steps.

'All right?' came her mother's voice as Alice reached the top and crawled on to the dusty loft carpet. Unsurprisingly, Belinda was anxious about injury or worse befalling another member of the family. Between the time it had taken Alice to leave her flat that morning and reach Oxford approximately an hour and forty-five minutes later, Belinda had sent seven texts, including travel updates, weather updates, advice about pulling over for a break if she felt tired, plus the unhelpful worry that Alice hadn't checked her tyres lately. 'I'd be more likely to die trying to read your flipping texts on the motorway than any weather-related problem,' Alice had grumbled on arrival, but hugged her nonetheless.

Shuffling bent-backed to the pile of boxes and bin bags in the centre of the attic space, she wished for the hundredth time that her mum hadn't chosen now as the time to pack up and move house. Look at any bereavement leaflet or website, and the advice was stark: avoid making big decisions within the first year. Admittedly, Alice could hardly talk, seeing as she'd split up with Noah and impulsively quit her job, but Belinda had comprehensively outdone her. First, she'd taken early retirement from her social work job, and now she was overhauling the family home to put it on the market, which meant a bulk-buy order of magnolia paint plus countless trips to the dump. The plan was for her and Ray to buy a house in the countryside to run as a bed and breakfast, but Alice couldn't help having a few misgivings. Surely that was far too many life changes in quick succession, on top of the loss of a daughter?

'I just want to keep busy,' Belinda said mutinously whenever Alice tried to persuade her to slow down. 'Being in this house makes me sad, Alice. Every single day, I'm reminded of what I've lost. And I can't keep living like that. For my own sanity, my own peace, I need a fresh start.'

Fair enough. Leni's death had thrown everything up in the air; it was like stepping into a new room and being unable to turn back. Their family had altered forever, the great chasm of loss rupturing their lives. Will had left the country, relinquishing himself to a non-stop hedonistic lifestyle. Tony was feathering the nest for family number two, and Belinda was a paint-speckled whirlwind of decluttering. They'd all pinballed away from one another, Alice thought ruefully, her breath drifting in puffs on the freezing air like small ghosts as she picked up the first box. She wondered if they'd ever find their way back.

After Leni died, Tony had borrowed a transit van to drive down to her Ealing flat to clear out her belongings. Will had helped, the two of them returning with bin bags of clothing, and boxes of hastily packed possessions, plus Leni's cat Hamish, hissing and spitting from inside a borrowed cat carrier. Hamish had initially stayed with Belinda and Ray, but when they began redecorating last autumn, he became stressed at this further upheaval and took to peeing everywhere. With Noah's fur allergy ruling out Alice taking him in, and Will already far away in Thailand, everyone had hoped Tony and his partner Jackie might rehome the poor creature. Only ten years older than Alice, Jackie was something impressive in the financial world and owned a fabulous architect-designed barn conversion with a big garden, perfect for a cat – or so you'd think. But apparently she'd refused point-blank to take him. 'Probably too worried about getting fur on her designer clothes,' Belinda had snarked to Alice at the time.

Hamish might have gone but Leni's other belongings remained, and Alice worked steadily to pass them down to Belinda, box by box, bag by bag. She felt proprietorial about the contents – determined to sort everything as Leni would have wanted her to – as well as kind of curious too. Back on Leni's birthday, the two sisters had fallen out and, for one reason or another – a week-long hen do abroad for Leni during the May half-term, the fortnight's holiday taken by Alice and Noah in early June, general busyness – they had never seen each other again. It had haunted Alice ever since that she'd missed out on the last six weeks of her sister's life. Might there be some clues to that time within these boxes and bags?

'Any secrets in here, Len?' she murmured aloud, hauling the biggest box of all along the old carpet. 'What am I going to find out, hey?'

The box was heavy and she banged it clumsily against the top of the ladder, apologising under her breath in the next minute. After Leni and Adam had split up, Alice had helped Leni move into her new flat, lugging these same possessions into and then out of the van they'd hired, both of them determinedly cheerful. 'Oi, mind the heirlooms,' Leni had said whenever Alice took a speed bump too quickly. If Leni was watching her now, she'd be tutting and moaning about her precious 'heirlooms', Alice knew it. The thought made her smile, just a little bit. 'Yeah, yeah, all right,' she told her. 'I'm doing my best, okay?'

Down below, Belinda had carried everything through to Will's old bedroom. It had once been Alice's room, decades ago, but she'd moved in to share with Leni when their new brother came along, and she had only a few dim memories of this being her space: waking up with a nosebleed one morning, the shock of scarlet blood across the pillow; the toadstool-shaped nightlight she'd had that shone a soft pink glow through the darkness; her dad's weight at the end of the bed as he told her stories when he got in from work. Since then, the room had been home to model train tracks, toy dinosaurs and a glow-in-the-dark solar system dangling from the ceiling, all the way through to posters of pouting pin-up models and a strong smell of cheap spray deodorant and hair gel. These days, it housed Belinda's overflow wardrobe, Ray's surfboards, and a fold-up exercise bike that still had the instructions taped to the saddle, bought presumably in a short-lived flush of self-improvement. Also, as of this morning, the full collection of Leni's belongings. Alice knelt beside her mum, feeling a quickening grip of dread take hold inside her. They were doing this. *Here goes.*

'Shall we start with the clothes?' Belinda suggested, untying the handles of a bin bag. 'Might be more straightforward.' Then she stopped, a nervous look flitting across her face, still clutching the top of the bag. She was wearing mascara and sparkly gold eyeshadow, as well as a traffic-stopping pink lipstick, but all of a sudden it was as if she'd shrivelled beneath her armour. 'Okay. We're going to get a blast of Leni's perfume, I bet, just as soon as I open this properly, and it'll probably set us both off. So brace yourself, all right? This will be tough.'

Alice nodded, steeling herself. 'Rip off that plaster, Mum.'

Belinda was right about the unmistakable fragrance rising from the clothes. The scent of her sister's favourite woody perfume practically cracked Alice's heart in two. For a moment it was as if Leni was present in the room with them, about to tell a joke or funny story. Both Alice and Belinda made laugh–cry sounds as they absorbed the shock, then, after a deep breath, they settled into a routine, distributing the bag's contents between three piles: Keep, Charity Shop, Chuck. Leni had always been tiny, two sizes slimmer than Alice at the time of her death, and so there were few clothes that Alice could fit into, which simplified what to keep. Plus, aside from all of her primary-school-teacher work clothes, Leni had hung on to a lot of her former art-student wardrobe; a style all of her own. Fake-fur jackets, plasticky-looking trousers, a healthy selection of neon items, a lot of tartan and at least seven skinny black polo-neck jumpers. Into the charity-shop mountain they went.

Glancing over at her mum, she saw Belinda delve into one of the bags with a little cry, then retrieve some woollen baby clothes – a pale lemon jacket with round buttons, a tiny white hat. Alice felt a lump in her throat as Belinda pressed them wordlessly against her cheek, pain etched across her features. Clothes for a baby that wasn't to be. 'Are you okay?' she asked, reaching over to put a hand on her mum's arm. Stupid question.

Belinda exhaled, lowering the jacket and hat from her face although she didn't let go of them immediately. 'I'm okay,' she replied with a watery smile. 'Let's keep going.'

Having eventually worked through the clothes, Alice took some photos of them. Then, while her mum went to make a phone call, she added them to the online memorial page she'd set up for Leni. *These are bringing back some memories today . . .* she typed beneath the images. *I'd love to see any photos you might have of Leni wearing her wackier outfits. Please share! One of the things I miss is arranging to meet her for a drink, arriving before her (always) and looking out for her, wondering what she would turn up in! PS This particular collection will be heading to the Oxford charity shops soon, but shout if you spot something you'd like as a memento.*

What next? With her mum still out of the room, she reached for a carrier bag stuffed with papers, wondering if it contained something that would help in her quest for answers. Taking a deep breath, she tipped the contents on the floor, lightly sorting through them with her fingertips. Letters, loose photographs, birthday cards, a folder marked 'Lesson Plans' . . . Then her heart accelerated at the sight of a small pocket diary with a soft grey cover and the year stamped in gold foil in the top corner. Leni's *diary* – jackpot. What might she find inside?

# Chapter Three

Before Alice had a chance to open the diary, she heard her mum's returning footsteps and instinct told her to stuff the little book into the back pocket of her jeans. Guilt pounded through her along with a shot of adrenalin as Belinda reappeared and Alice picked up a couple of old utility bills and pretended to be checking the dates. 'These have been paid, I'll start a recycling pile,' she announced, fakely efficient. She wasn't even sure why she'd hidden the diary like that; she just knew she wanted it to be her own private discovery, something of her sister's that she could pore over in peace without her mum's involvement. Was that bad? Was it mean of her not to share?

'This looks a bit more complicated than clothes,' Belinda commented, kneeling down on the other side of the papers with an apprehensive expression. She pounced on a pencil drawing amidst the paperwork. 'Oh, look! A drawing of the cat. She was so creative, wasn't she?'

Her eyes were faraway, and Alice experienced a jealous little stab inside at the adoring expression on her face. Mums weren't supposed to have favourites, of course, but Alice had long suspected that Leni was Belinda's number-one daughter, the golden girl, while Alice had always struggled to keep up. Back when she'd been seven or eight, she'd kept getting nosebleeds, but the family doctor had dismissed the problem, telling Belinda, 'It's psychological, in my opinion. Attention-seeking', as if Alice was so desperate to catch her mother's eye that she could produce blood at will, like some kind of witch.

'Yes,' she agreed now, wondering what it said about her when, even after her sister's death, she still felt a twinge of envy at any praise sent in Leni's direction. She touched her nose surreptitiously, half expecting it to start gushing blood again. Was she horrifically insecure or merely needy? And why hadn't she grown out of feeling this way?

Belinda put the drawing to one side and picked up a notebook, flicking through its pages uncertainly. 'She said we shouldn't hang on to everything,' she commented, then pulled herself up short. 'I mean ...'

She had turned a strange shade of puce, Alice noticed, but perhaps that was from the emotion. 'I talk to her,' Belinda blurted out in the next moment, fiddling with the binding of the notebook. 'I talk to Leni.'

'So do I,' Alice replied, with feeling. 'All the time. Every day.' Often quite exasperatedly, admittedly – *Why didn't you get that bloody bike sorted out? How could you have been so stupid?* – but frequently she would come across something during the day – a snippet of tabloid gossip about an old soap star they'd both fancied, or a new series of a TV drama they'd been equally mad about – and she'd want to share it with her sister. 'I nearly messaged her only this morning. It must be a muscle-memory thing.'

'No, but ...' Belinda hesitated. She seemed embarrassed for some reason. Confessional, even. 'I mean, I *really* talk to her. And she replies.'

'Mum, it's fine to talk to her. I think it would be weirder if you didn't. Whatever helps, right?' Alice picked up a sheaf of old Christmas cards and put them in a pile to be recycled. 'I have spent entire evenings rereading stupid text conversations I had with Leni and laughing till I cried. The therapist I spoke to said that was healthy, part of processing what happened. We're just working through stuff, that's all. And talking is better than ...' Now it was her turn to stumble gruffly over her words. 'You know, being angry and behaving like an idiot.'

Belinda reached over and squeezed her hand. 'Don't be hard on yourself. You loved her, that's all. And she loves you.'

The use of the present tense was jarring but Alice decided not to comment. Maybe this was a coping mechanism, a means of keeping Leni alive, she reasoned. And if it helped, where was the harm?

She picked up a large brown envelope, oddly light, and peeped inside to find a handful of peacock feathers, still somehow sellotaped to a piece of bamboo. 'Oh my God,' she said, as a hundred memories tumbled dizzily into her mind. 'Mum, look!'

Belinda put a hand on her heart, eyes damp. 'The Flying Beauties,' she said, with a noise that could equally have been a sob or a laugh.

'Flying Beauties forever,' Alice replied, emotions in tumult.

She felt as if she'd been flung back in time as she touched the frondy edges of the feathers. 'Oh gosh, Mum, I can't believe it.'

'It was that summer Will was born, wasn't it?' Belinda said.

Yes, it was the summer Will was born. Alice and Leni had been packed off to stay with their maternal grandparents in Dorset, so that their parents could have some respite during the school holidays. The two girls always shared a bunk bed there and spent ages one day playing birds and jumping off the top bunk on to a pile of duvets and pillows beneath, flapping their arms and trying to fly.

'I think I really did fly a *bit* just then. Did you see?' eight-year-old Leni would say each time she collapsed into the soft squish of bedding. 'I'm definitely getting better at it.'

Soon, bunk beds were not their only take-off point. They leaped from the tops of walls and from their grandparents' stairs. They jumped from some of the big rocks down at the beach too, their bare feet curling around the hard ridges until, with a bend of the knees and a yell of 'Lift off!' they would take flight for a split second of exhilaration before the inevitable sandy landing.

Then came the thrilling moment of discovering Grandma's battered old peacock-feather fan when poking around her bedroom one day. 'Wings!' cried Leni, her face lighting up. 'This could make the prettiest wings in the world!'

Grandma was a kind-hearted sort who recognised a passion in a small girl, and knew to take it seriously. 'What a good idea!' she said when Leni went to her, brandishing the fan, and asked if they could please cut it up to make wings please please please. Grandma carefully snipped the feathers free from their bindings, then taped them to chopped-down bamboo sticks, requisitioned from Grandad's shed.

'Now, no funny business with these, my beauties,' she warned, handing over a pair of 'wings' to Alice then a pair to Leni. 'Your mum will have my guts for garters if any bones are broken, okay?'

Alice could remember even now the updraught of air that came through the trembling, vibrant feathers with their beautiful, mysterious-looking 'eyes' at the end; how convinced she had been that, if she just tried hard enough, she'd soon be soaring off the ground.

'We're *flying* beauties now,' Leni cried, swishing and swooshing with such gusto that the pages of Grandad's newspaper, perched on the kitchen table, lifted and fell with a flutter, as if they too were possessed with the exuberance of new-found flight.

'We're the flying beauties!' Alice, nearly six, had echoed, in thrall as ever to her sister's leadership.

The Flying Beauties became their favourite game that summer. Their peacock-feather wings were too precious to take on the beach or out along the coastal path, Grandma decreed, but they were permitted around the garden and throughout the house, and the long, sunny afternoons rang with cries of 'I'm flying!' and 'Flying Beauties forever!', soft thumps of landing and whoops of delight. It had felt so glorious, so free after an intense period at home where Mum or Dad – often both of them – kept dashing away to the hospital, looking strained. Not listening properly whenever Alice or Leni tried to tell them interesting things about school. Arguing in low voices – not always that low, actually – when they thought the girls were asleep. Here at Grandma's, the two of them were the centre of the world; they were showered with love. They were the Flying Beauties. Who could ask for more?

It had continued as a shared thread between the sisters from then on. As teenagers, Leni made them both matching T-shirts one Christmas with the logo FLYING BEAUTIES FOREVER! painted above an elegant silhouette of a peacock feather. The following year, Alice was browsing a vintage jewellery stall in the covered market when she came across a bangle with a stone that shimmered iridescent green and blue, and knew instantly that Leni would get the reference. Sometimes when drunk or merely sentimental, they'd end up clinking glasses and chorusing, 'Flying Beauties forever,' like an incantation, and the connection between them would be forged all over again, shining and true, as sure as a bird in flight.

She had no idea what had happened to her peacock-feather 'wings' made so many summers ago, but somehow or other, careless, erratic Leni had managed to hang on to one of hers for all this time. Here it was, as vivid as ever, despite the prolonged thrashing about it had suffered in the name of attempted launches. Alice touched a fingertip to the delicate feather ends then pressed it to her face. 'Thank you for my heirloom, Leni,' she said under her breath, unwilling to set it down again for fear that it might dematerialise before her eyes. But it was real, a dusty weight in her hand, battered yet still shimmering. A talisman sent to help Alice through today?

★

After lunch, Alice was relieved when one of her mum's neighbours popped round to ask a favour. She wasted no time in heading back upstairs alone to open the diary, with a jolt of anticipation. The little book was laid out with a week per double page, plus a box marked 'Notes' in the bottom right-hand corner. The size meant it was for arrangements rather than any confessional outpourings, but the mere sight of her sister's neat handwriting charting term dates and weekend plans was oddly comforting. She flipped to mid-August and saw 'Alice's birthday' written with a heart penned beside the words, and couldn't immediately drag her eyes away from that small symbol of love. It was only the sight of the emptiness around it in the diary, blank pages she hadn't lived long enough to fill, that gave Alice an ache inside.

She leafed back slowly to Leni's birthday, the last time she'd seen her sister, squirming as she did whenever she thought about that day. Everything had gone wrong – Belinda arriving late, Tony forgetting completely, the plates smashing – and of course Alice and Leni had had that horrible argument. *Everyone here 12 o'c!* Leni had written and Alice cringed at that jaunty exclamation mark when it had not turned out to be an exclamation-mark kind of day.

Moving on, some of the entries afterwards were obvious – the hen do break to Valencia during half-term, dinner with her friend Francesca 7 p.m., for instance – while others were more cryptic. *T 7.30 p.m.!!!* baffled her – who was 'T'? she wondered, until she realised that the same entry, minus the exclamation marks, appeared every Tuesday evening throughout June and into July. A recurring appointment, but what for? Did 'T' stand for 'therapist', maybe? she wondered, biting her lip. Leni hadn't exactly been happy the last time Alice had seen her. She continued turning the pages, noticing *Josh 8 p.m.* had been written in on a Friday in early June and a couple more times in the weeks that followed, on a Saturday morning and a Tuesday evening. She frowned, unable to place a Josh in her sister's life. Was he a new friend? A *date*?

Her fingers shook as she reached the last week in June when Leni had died. The accident had been on a Thursday evening, and Alice's heart almost stopped when she saw written there, on that fateful day, *A!! 8 p.m.* Did 'A' stand for Alice? she mused, putting a hand to her chest and feeling her heart thud beneath the skin. Leni had tried ringing her that night, after all, but Alice hadn't answered. She felt sick with the idea that Leni might have been cycling over to hers, maybe with some kind of peace offering in mind, only to be killed before she even got there. Was this something else to feel guilty about?

'Another tea?' Belinda called up the stairs at that moment, making Alice jump.

'Please!' she called back, still staring at her sister's cryptic note. Maybe the 'A' her sister had written didn't stand for Alice at all, but 'Adam', her ex-husband, she reasoned – although would Leni really have put in exclamation marks after his initial, when the two of them had parted on such bad terms? Then she noticed an address had been jotted in the 'Notes' section at the bottom right of the page: 62 Cherry Grove, W12. A Shepherd's Bush postcode, she registered, feeling her skin prickle. Leni had been killed in Shepherd's Bush. Was

Cherry Grove where she'd been heading that night? And who was the mysterious 'A' she was going to meet there?

Someone must know, she figured, as the handwritten words refused to divulge their secrets. She could ask Leni's friends, maybe see if one of them lived on Cherry Grove or knew who did. Putting down the diary, she typed the road name into her phone, staring at it on the map, then zoomed in to the street numbers. 62 was larger than the adjoining buildings and as she zoomed in even closer, a link appeared: Cherry House. Clicking on it took her to the web page of a community centre with listings for a Brownies group, pensioner breakfasts, toddler mornings, infant ballet classes . . . *Hire this space!* read a banner along the bottom of the screen. Maybe someone – the mysterious 'A'? – had booked the venue for a birthday party? A supper club? She'd be able to find out, she was sure, and was struck in the next moment by how important it felt to her to unravel this mystery, to discover everything about the last weeks of Leni's life she'd missed out on.

Returning the diary to her back pocket, she abandoned the paperwork for the time being and opened a nearby box instead. She unpacked various novels and cookery books, stacking them in wobbling towers on the carpet. Then she stopped, her breath catching in her throat as she peeled away a newspaper wrapping, to discover Leni's gorgeous, colourful plates inside, the plates she'd dropped so spectacularly on her birthday last year.

Lifting them carefully out, she wondered why Will – if it had been him who'd put them in the box – hadn't simply dumped the whole stack in the bin. Perhaps he'd recognised them from that day, too, and felt the same guilt that she did on seeing them again. The plates were nearly all either cracked or chipped or, in some cases, broken into sharp, glinting pieces, but Leni had kept them, presumably wanting to fix them at some point, or perhaps because they had been given to her by Adam, and it would have pained her to lose them entirely.

Gently she ran her finger along one of the broken pieces, a lavender colour with a pearlescent lustre. She remembered an article she'd read online about a Japanese tradition of repairing broken pots, highlighting their fractures and scars with golden glue to make the object more beautiful than ever; shattered but mended. Would she ever feel shattered but mended? Maybe painstakingly repairing Leni's crockery would patch her up a little bit, she thought, carefully rewrapping the broken plates and setting them aside. It was definitely worth a go.

Okay. Good progress. Was that everything sorted out from this particular box? She peered inside to see that the only thing left was a magazine. No, a brochure, she realised, lifting it out and reading the words *Your Family With Our Help* below a picture of a woman holding a tiny baby to her chest. The IVF clinic, she guessed, until she saw, in smaller lettering, the words *Specialist International Adoption Agency* and nearly dropped the thing. What the hell? Leni and Adam had not been able to get pregnant, despite their best attempts, but Alice wasn't aware that they'd considered adopting. Why hadn't Leni told her?

She heard footsteps coming up the stairs just then and instinctively stuffed the brochure into an empty bag. Her mum had been so upset when Leni's IVF failed each time, Alice didn't want to raise the spectre of another possible grandchild she'd been denied. Also, she didn't think she could bear it, if this was something Belinda knew about and she didn't. She returned to the paperwork, trying to look busy as her mum re-entered the room.

'Sorry about that,' Belinda said, carrying a tray of tea things. 'I've brought cake too, to keep us going.' She set the tray down on a dusty weights bench. 'Flapjack? Swiss roll? Bit of both?'

'Flapjack, please,' Alice said, picking up a scrap of paper with a name and phone number scrawled on it, then putting it down again uncertainly, before doing the same with a letter from someone she'd never heard of. What was she supposed to do with them? There were so many tiny jigsaw pieces to a life, she thought, suddenly overwhelmed.

'Everything all right?' her mum asked, turning with a mug of tea and a flapjack on a plate. 'Other than the obvious?'

'It's just ...' Alice broke off, gesturing to the papers in front of her. 'I don't know what's important and what's not. There's a letter here from someone called Cathie – no idea. A phone number of someone called Graham – no idea. And I don't – oh!'

Belinda's hand must have wobbled or maybe the mug was too full, because in the next moment, hot tea went splashing everywhere. 'Oh dear,' she said, setting down the mug and snatching up the sodden papers. 'I didn't scald you, did I? Sorry, I'm so clumsy.'

'I'm fine, Mum, don't worry,' Alice said, but her mum seemed really stressed, an expression of what could only be described as anguish on her face. 'It doesn't matter, I'm sure,' she called after her as Belinda hurried out of the room, saying something about getting kitchen roll and that she'd be back in a minute.

Alice watched her go, frowning. Maybe Belinda's emotions were getting to her, because in Alice's eyes, that had seemed a massive overreaction. She hadn't seen her looking so panicked since ... well, since that weird moment on Leni's birthday, come to think of it. Biting into the soft, buttery flapjack, Alice took herself back to that afternoon: how she'd gone out into the garden after lunch, only to find her mum and Leni deep in private conversation, voices low. She'd forgotten until now that, right before they noticed her there, Belinda's face had become stricken. Frightened, almost. What had Leni said to her to make her look like that?

The flapjack was sticking to her gums; its sweetness suddenly made her feel nauseous. Today had already prompted so many unsettling questions about her sister, she wasn't sure if she could cope with any more mysteries. Did she even want to know Leni's secrets?

Belinda returned, pink in the face, with two squares of kitchen roll, still clucking about how clumsy she was. Alice couldn't stop herself. 'Mum – do you remember, back on Leni's birthday, you two were having a chat outside in the garden at one point, and I walked out and interrupted you,' she blurted out. 'I was just wondering, what were you talking about? Only—'

'Nothing,' Belinda said quickly, before Alice had even finished the sentence. 'I mean – I can't remember. We talked about lots of things.'

'Yes, but ...' Alice saw it again in her head: the shaken

expression on her mum's face. Real alarm in her eyes, mirroring the alarm she'd seen two minutes ago. 'You looked really rattled. Did she upset you? I'm not being nosey, but ...' She *was* being nosey, obviously, but whatever. 'If you want to talk about ... anything, then ...'

'Honestly, darling, I'm not sure what you mean,' Belinda said. 'You know what my memory's like!' She flashed Alice a smile that wasn't wholly convincing. 'Shall we crack on? Where are we up to?'

'Sure,' said Alice. But for the rest of the afternoon, she couldn't help glancing sidelong at her now and then. She didn't want to accuse her mum of lying, but it was clear that she knew exactly the moment Alice was referencing, only, for whatever reason, didn't want to discuss it. Had her mum and sister kept a secret from her, Alice wondered, her frown deepening. What did Belinda know that Alice didn't?

# Chapter Four

*Leni McKenzie memorial page*

*Leni and I went to Glastonbury one summer and, slightly worse for wear, we tried to blag our way into the backstage VIP area. Leni gave the security guys on the gate a very convincing story that we were backing singers for Elvis Costello, and all was going pretty well, I thought, until one of the security team, clearly not buying it for a second, asked us to give him a song. God knows why, but Leni launched straight into 'When the Red, Red Robin' at the top of her voice, shimmying and bopping like there was no tomorrow, with me joining in a beat or two behind. The security guy burst out laughing, as did everyone else around him – including a couple of guys from the Kaiser Chiefs who had just arrived and proceeded to JOIN IN. Needless to say, we failed in our mission, but I think everyone who heard the performance enjoyed it in a so-bad-it's-good way.*

*Leni, you were such fun to be with. I'll miss you forever. Love, Suze*

'Hey! You! Flip-flop guy!'

Will didn't pay any attention to the shouts at first because there were always people shouting on Chaweng beach – noisy games of frisbee or beach tennis, as well as calls from the other sales people as they trudged along the hot sand, announcing they had sarongs to sell, goggles, bat and ball sets, fresh fruit. Flip-flops too, sometimes. On this particular day, his head was buzzing with a combination of dazzling sun and too much weed the previous evening, plus a bad night's sleep, and he was trying to zone out all unnecessary noise. It was taking a lot of his energy to conjure up the big smiles and charm he was currently displaying to the pasty-white couple spread out on two beach towels, in the hope of flogging them some crap sunglasses.

'I've got homage Armani, Dior, Pilot, Ray-Bans,' he said, crouching down to set out the cellophane-wrapped glasses before them. His golden rule: get enough stuff out and on to their space until it was impossible for them to ignore you. Also, say the word 'homage' really quick at the start of the list of designer names and hope that they didn't know what it meant or assumed it was merely another cool brand. You're not just a pretty face, he'd sometimes say to himself in the small bathroom mirror of his flat. Sometimes he'd even point his index fingers at his tanned reflection in a gameshow-host sort of way. *You da man.*

'I like the ones you're wearing,' the woman said to him now, in a tone flirty enough that her boyfriend shot her a peeved look. The two of them were English, which was always a good way in; he'd already flattered the bloke by asking him about the football back home, even though Will had access to a hacked Sky Sports subscription and kept up with the Premier League as if it were his own personal religion.

'These?' He waggled them up and down on the bridge of his nose without removing them – nobody needed to see quite how bloodshot his eyes were in the bright Koh Samui sunshine. 'Good old Tom Ford – I've got some ladies' styles here if you want a look?' He rummaged through his bag to produce a selection. Of course they weren't actual Tom Fords, neither his pair nor the ones he was touting. If you looked closely at the branding, you could see an 'E' at the end of the surname, but whatever. 'These green ones are cool,' he said. 'Oh, and these ones with the gold bar across are really stylish, I think. I've only got one pair left of those.' Another lie – he had approximately forty of them back at the flat, cellophane-wrapped in a pile of boxes from the wholesaler. She wasn't to know that though.

'Hey! Flip-flop guy! I'm talking to you!'

He registered the voice – loud, female, Scottish – with a prickle of unease, but decided not to turn around just in case 'flip-flop guy' turned out to be aimed at him. He *had* been selling a lot of flip-flops and other footwear recently, as it happened, the cheapest and possibly worst sandals ever manufactured; all designer imitations that would last about as long as the buyer's holiday. But there were loads of other sellers on this beach, he reminded himself. The shouts were probably for someone else altogether.

Meanwhile, the woman on the towel sat up, sucking in her white tummy self-consciously as she leaned over, squinting at the goods on offer. 'I'm such a klutz, I managed to sit on my sunglasses on the plane before we'd even taken off,' she confessed, pulling a face. 'Brand new as well, I'd literally just bought them in the airport.' She was sweet, Will thought, with her long blonde hair piled up in a topknot on her head, and a snub nose, and now – *yes, get in* – she was reaching out for the pair he'd mentioned as being stylish. Of course she was. Because he was brilliant at selling this shit. 'Mind if I try these on?'

He gave the gallant spreading of hands he'd perfected. 'Be my guest,' he said. 'I've got a mirror here, so you can take a look.'

'Excuse me,' came the voice again, more strident this time. 'Hi! Remember me?'

He turned to see a red-haired, freckled woman in a pale blue bikini standing before him, an angry look on her face. 'Er . . .' He did, in fact, remember her, because she had really amazing legs and great hair, but this probably wasn't the moment to reference her assets, he decided. Especially as she seemed pretty riled up right now.

'Well, I remember *you*,' she went on before he had the chance to say anything else. 'I remember you flogging me a pair of crummy knock-off Havaianas two days ago, and guess what? They've fallen apart already. I want my money back.' She glanced down at the blonde woman who was about to open the cellophane-wrapped sunglasses. 'Don't bother, love,' she advised her. 'They'll be shite as well, I bet.'

'Hey!' Now Will was annoyed. Having been on the verge of a sale – the Tom Ford(e)s were practically chosen and paid for – it was highly irritating to be interrupted in this way.

Especially as it was mid-afternoon now and he was yet to sell a single sodding thing so far today. 'Do you mind? I'm in the middle of—'

But the woman on the towel had already put the sunglasses back down and reached over to pick up her book. 'I'll give them a miss, thanks,' she said, with a new, chilly edge to her voice.

'Yeah, we're all right for sunglasses, cheers, mate,' her boyfriend said, rolling over on to his front and shutting his eyes as if the matter was closed.

'Wise move,' the red-haired woman told them. Even the way she was standing was aggressive, Will thought crossly: chin jutting, chest forward, legs planted in the sand as if braced for imminent combat.

He ignored her. 'Well, thanks anyway,' he said to the couple, leaning down to pick up the unwanted sunglasses littering their towels. The blood rushed to his head and weariness overtook him, coupled with a strong surge of pissed-off-ness. He was sick of these whining tourists. What did they expect when they bought something from a beach seller – that they would get a guarantee and printed receipt? In their dreams. The Scottish woman, meanwhile, was still griping on, however hard he tried to block her out.

'I mean, I guessed they were knock-off from the price, but come on, the strap broke that same night, the first time I'd actually worn them,' she complained shrilly. 'The first bloody time! It's all just landfill, the shite you're selling, isn't it? Absolute rubbish. Aren't you ashamed of yourself?'

He stuffed the final pairs of sunglasses into his bag, heaved it on his shoulder and strode past her without replying. The sun slammed down on him with dizzying intensity, and he felt dehydrated and empty; he hadn't been able to face breakfast first thing but now he regretted not trying harder to force something into his stomach. *Aren't you ashamed of yourself?* Yes, he was, more than she would ever know, but not about anything as trivial as a pair of effing flip-flops.

'Hey!'

Oh great, now she was following him across the sand. This was the last thing he wanted, a beach-wide public scene with her loudly berating him, as well as his stock. If she kept this up much longer, he could kiss goodbye to customers on this patch, that was for sure. Did he even have the energy to try again somewhere else though? He should have guessed that today would turn out to be difficult, having woken up that morning to find a message from Alice: *Did Leni ever mention a place called Cherry House to you? I think she was going there the day she died.* Will had flinched because he had been trying very hard not to think about the day Leni died. Or anything to do with home, for that matter.

He whirled around. 'What do you want?'

She was right there at his shoulder, her forehead a bit sweaty where she'd matched him stride for stride. The sun shone into her face and she put up a hand to shield her eyes. 'What do you *think* I want? I already told you. A refund and an apology is the least you owe me, for starters.'

What a buzzkill this woman was. And she was on *holiday*, for heaven's sake. Did she not have better things to do with her time? He heaved a sigh. Might as well get this over with.

'Okay,' he said flatly. 'I'm sorry your shoe broke.' Then he shrugged. 'As for a refund ... do you have the item in question with you?'

'Do I have ... ?' Incredulity spread across her face. 'Are you kidding me?' She made a show of patting herself down as if checking for pockets. Given that she was practically naked apart from the bikini, this was actually quite enjoyable, although Will did his best to maintain neutrality. 'No, funnily enough, I'm not carrying around a broken *flip-flop* on the off-chance of seeing you again,' she went on scathingly and he jerked his gaze back up to her face. 'But I'm hardly gonna lie about that, am I?'

He gave another shrug, as if to question her honesty. How should he know? Then he said, somewhat sanctimoniously, 'I'm afraid I can't issue you a refund without evidence,' which had her rolling her eyes. *Yeah, well, up yours, Ginger,* he thought. *You started this.* 'There are some very dodgy people around here,' he went on for good measure. 'I'd love to believe you, but ...'

She snorted with derision. 'Oh *please*. Spare me,' she said. 'The only dodgy person around here is you, you total chancer. God! What a cheek. Like I'd keep a useless, broken shoe, my arse. It went straight in the bin, obviously. Where the rest of your tat ought to be shoved.'

He assumed a bland, polite expression which he hoped she would find deeply irritating. 'Sorry. Nothing I can do, then. Company rules, you see,' he said, even though they both knew very well that there was no company and there were no rules. 'Very nice to meet you, anyway. Enjoy your holiday!'

He loved saying that. *Enjoy your holiday!* – one, because it was ever so slightly patronising, and two, because it underlined the fact that he was not a holidaymaker like the rest of them, he had climbed above that lowly position to acquire new status as a local. Someone who lived and worked here on Koh Samui, paradise island. Admittedly, he didn't love the fact that he heard her say, loud and clear, 'Bellend,' in response as he walked away, but whatever. Who cared? He never had to see her again, after all. She'd be getting on a plane home in a matter of days, and good riddance to her, frankly.

Having walked a safe distance away, he risked a glance over his shoulder to see that, yes, good, she was currently stomping off in the opposite direction, shoulders tight, bottom wiggling with indignation. Farewell forever, he thought, before scanning the horizon for suitable mugs who might want to buy a pair of knock-off sunglasses. Please, for the love of God, let there be someone gullible enough soon.

Aha. His gaze landed on two lads with white torsos and legs that showed they were newly arrived. Even better, one was lying on an Arsenal beach towel, the other West Ham. Jackpot. 'Afternoon, fellas,' he began, arriving beside them. 'Cor, bit of a result for West Ham at the weekend, wasn't it?' Cue a friendly grin that said, *I'm one of you, boys*. Then he plunged a hand into his bag and pulled out the fake Dior, fake Prada, fake Balenciaga, holding them up like cards in a magic trick. 'I've got some cracking gear here, if you're interested?'

Later that day, over in Oxford, Belinda was sitting in the driver's seat of her car, engine off, down at the quiet end of the

Park and Ride car park. A small white knitted baby hat sat in her lap – she had taken to using it as a phone case since discovering it in Leni's possessions the week before last – and her phone was pressed to her ear because the connection with Apolline was often a bit on the iffy side. She had wondered previously if Apolline was even in the UK, as she claimed, but it seemed rude to ask, as if she was accusing the other woman of lying. Mind you, the hotline was expensive enough that she might as well have been in Australia or some other faraway place, but what price could you put on your own daughter's words from the other side? These calls were worth every penny.

'I see,' she said now as Apolline described at length how at peace Leni said she was, how she wanted for nothing. She often said this sort of thing, but Belinda never minded because it was so soothing to hear. Sometimes she closed her eyes in rapture as if listening to a beautiful symphony on the radio rather than a woman's slow, breathy voice. She had been so anxious the first time they had connected that Leni might not even want to speak to her. 'Is she ... angry with me?' she had asked tremulously, almost unable to speak with relief when Apolline assured her no. *Thank God. Oh, thank God*, she had thought, tears careering down her face. It had been such a weight off her mind.

A car manoeuvred into the parking space next to hers and a man got out, slamming his door unnecessarily hard and making Belinda jump. This wasn't the optimum place for a phone call to commune with one's deceased daughter, but you could sit here for up to an hour without having to buy a ticket, which was rare in Oxford. Plus she was sick of Ray making little comments about her phone calls at home. This was the alternative: telling him she was running an errand (you wouldn't believe how many trips to the dump she'd had to invent) and then parking up here, dialling with breathless urgency to reconnect.

It wasn't always possible to hear from Leni. According to Apolline, newly liberated souls (as she termed them) were unpredictable, temperamental entities; they could be hard to pin down for communication purposes. 'Sounds like Leni,' Belinda had remarked wryly on hearing this. Sometimes Apolline was able to channel other spirits who had interesting things to say, often words of wisdom for her. Her dad had once appeared, offering his thoughts on her boiler, of all things (which was so typical of him, Belinda had felt the most enormous lump in her throat). At other times, Apolline herself was the one to advise her and listen to her problems. It had been Apolline, actually, who'd floated the idea of moving house. 'Free yourself from the past,' she'd said, and the phrase had cemented itself into Belinda's mind with such certainty that the suggestion turned quickly from mere syllables in the air into physical actions, a plan set in motion.

When Belinda first broached the subject of a house move with Ray, explaining that she needed to free herself from the past, he'd agreed and said he understood, only for her to then make the mistake of admitting that the idea – and those exact words, for that matter – had come from Apolline. She'd told him this because she wanted to impress on him how wise Apolline was, how sensitive to Belinda's feelings, but found herself wishing, almost immediately, that she'd kept quiet. Another time, she'd know better. Ray had made it clear from the start that he was dubious about the whole idea of a clairvoyant hotline ('There are a lot of scams out there, that's all I'm saying'), but he became so scathing during this particular discussion that they ended up having a blazing row, culminating with her bursting into tears and not speaking to him for the rest of the day. 'Apolline? I bet that's not even her name. A tenner says she's really called Pauline,' he scoffed.

Since then they'd made up but he'd remained resistant to accepting Apolline as the pillar of support she had become in Belinda's life. 'What about talking to a counsellor instead?' he suggested a few times. 'You can get free ones on the NHS, you know. Maybe mention it to the GP next time you have an appointment?'

She didn't want to take up NHS resources though, not when Apolline offered her something that no health service ever could: the voice of her daughter reassuring her that she was okay. Well – obviously Leni was not really okay, seeing as she was still dead, but according to Apolline, she had accepted this new state of affairs and was in no pain or distress. Even better, the minefield conversation the two of them had had back on Leni's birthday had never been resurrected. Did this mean her daughter had gone to her grave without knowing the full story? Oh gosh, she hoped so. When Belinda had spotted that bit of paper with Graham's number on it in Leni's belongings the other week, her heart had nearly stopped. Why had Graham given Leni his number? What had he *told* her? Thank goodness she'd had the presence of mind to whisk the paper away from Alice so swiftly.

The nicest thing about these conversations was that Leni seemed far more loving in death than she had been in real life. Way more affectionate! Having Apolline pass on 'She adores you and says you are her rock' was incredibly gratifying, especially when you compared it to the way Leni had lost it on her last birthday, wailing amidst a sea of broken crockery, shouting, *What is wrong with this bloody family? Why are we so shit?* (The scene, needless to say, had cut Belinda to the quick. Having worked all her life in social care, she knew that theirs had been a good family compared to some she'd had to look after. There wasn't anything fundamentally wrong with the McKenzies. Was there?)

'The spirits are telling me that they've sent people to help your other children,' Apolline said now in her soft, sweet voice.

'Oh! That's kind. Who?' Belinda asked in reply. Alice had looked so pale and drawn the other week, but she'd started a new temporary job now at least, which would keep her busy. As for Will, although he talked a good talk on the phone, Belinda couldn't help but wonder if he was telling her everything.

'People who will show them a path through the darkness,' came Apolline's cryptic response. She could be a little *too* mysterious at times, Belinda thought. It was the one frustrating aspect of these phone calls. If only her guide could be slightly more exact, give a touch more detail – dates, names, places, that sort of thing – Belinda would really appreciate it. But then again, it probably wasn't very zen to badger the spirits for specifics, was it? To whip out her diary and demand extra. And she didn't want to annoy Apolline.

She jumped again as a woman in a mustard-yellow coat got

out of the neighbouring car and started yelling across the car park to the door-slamming man that he'd left his phone on the seat, and wouldn't he need it to buy the ticket? Belinda blinked away a rush of exasperation – couldn't a person take an important call in peace any more? She'd deliberately parked at this end of the car park because it was hardly ever used! – before tuning back in to Apolline, who was urging Belinda to pay attention to her dreams this week, as she would be sent an important message.

'What sort of message?' she asked, stroking the neat stitches of the white knitted hat. The hope that had gone into those stitches! The grandmotherly love! She tried not to think about the baby that should have been wearing it, had life turned out differently, but it was hard to banish the rosy-cheeked cherub of her imagination. The grandchild that had never quite appeared.

'A symbol to interpret, a sign of change,' Apolline told her with typical opacity and Belinda sighed in the torment of anticipation.

*A symbol to interpret in dream*, she jotted in her notebook so that she wouldn't forget. With regret, she saw that her time was nearly up. In two minutes she would have to end the call and leave the car park before she was issued with a fine for overstaying. 'I've got to go,' she said unhappily, already feeling an ache at the thought of saying goodbye once more. With Apolline her only remaining link to Leni, it always wrenched her heart to break the connection. 'Please tell her I love her, won't you? Always have, always will.'

'She knows that, Belinda,' Apolline assured her. 'She knows it deep in her soul, and the knowledge comforts her.'

A sob burst from Belinda's throat because, at the end of the day, this was all she'd ever wanted. 'Thank you,' she managed to say before the timer on her phone gave a warning beep. 'Thank you, Apolline. I'll talk to you soon.'

She draped her arms over the top of the steering wheel and rested her head there for a few moments, tears sinking into her coat sleeves as the usual wave of emotion rolled through her like a breaker on to shore. Until last year, the worst thing ever to happen to Belinda was Tony leaving her and the children high and dry. But you could get over a failed marriage in time; you could rebuild yourself, fall in love again. How did you ever get over losing your own child?

She became aware of a light tapping at the window and jerked out of her position, startled to see the woman in the mustard coat standing there, mouthing ARE YOU OKAY?

Belinda nodded weakly, gave her a thumbs up and then started the engine and shoved the gearstick into reverse. Her would-be Good Samaritan gave an audible yelp and had to leap out of the way to avoid a potential foot crushing, but Belinda didn't stop. Back to the grindstone of the house-clearing and painting; she had approximately one million small jobs to complete before the first of their estate agent appointments tomorrow. But Leni loved her, and that was enough for now. Certainly, enough to see her safely home and through Ray's suspicious glances and the rest of the day. Until the next phone call and the next assurances, anyway.

# Chapter Five

*Leni McKenzie memorial page*

*My favourite Leni story was when we were both in a club one night and she persuaded a couple of blokes she could read palms. Before we knew it, there was a massive queue of people lined up with their hands out, wanting theirs done! Was it true about her looking at the palm of one particularly hot guy and telling him that his luck was in that night, especially when it came to a woman with long brown hair and a black dress? 'Wow — coincidence!' she said, looking down at herself and pantomiming surprise. Well, he ended up coming back to our flat, so judge for yourself!*

*God, I miss you, Leni. RIP you beautiful woman.*

*Francesca*

'Here we are,' Alice slurred, slotting her door key into the lock. The crop-haired man was standing very close behind her and a warning bell rang in her head momentarily: *you don't know him, you're completely hammered, this could be a really bad idea.*

But she ignored it – she just wanted a bit of fun for a change, all right? – and asked, 'You coming in, then?'

'Sure,' the man said. She couldn't remember his name, was that terrible? Had he even told her? She couldn't recall how they'd got talking in the first place, come to think of it. She'd met up with one of Leni's friends, Francesca, in a pub near St Paul's because Francesca worked around there too, and then when she left – too early – Alice didn't feel like going straight home. He'd caught her eye across the room and the next thing she knew, he was sidling over with his smile and chat, buying them more drinks and then . . . Well, to cut a long story short, here she was letting him into her flat, and here they were kissing in the hall before she'd even had a chance to put the light on.

He was a good kisser, the man with no name; sexy and passionate, his hands expertly peeling off her clothes, the two of them laughing together as they staggered into her living room. 'You are so hot,' he said thickly into her ear, pausing to retrieve a condom from his pocket (a bad sign, surely, she registered distantly) but then they were kissing again, standing in the middle of the room, and she felt shivery all over from wanting him. He didn't know Sad Alice, he had no idea about Mad Alice – and how bloody lovely that was, how utterly refreshing, she thought, to meet someone who wasn't aware of the massive airport trolley of baggage she'd been carting around with her for the last six months. He thought she was hot, and that was all he needed to know right now. That was enough.

As for her, she was so pissed she couldn't remember anything he'd told her about himself, but he was considerate enough to check, *Is this okay?* a couple of times, at least, before he pushed her roughly over the table in the living room and rammed into her from behind. The force was enough to send a pile of paperwork — Leni's paperwork, yet to be fully dealt with — cascading to the floor and Alice cringed, feeling disrespectful. *Well, that's just charming*, she imagined Leni deadpanning in her head. *Don't let me stand in the way of your animal passion, you hussy.* Alice sent up a mental apology to her sister, but a minute or two later it was over anyway and he'd collapsed on top of her, his body fever-hot against hers, his breath juddering into her hair. Human contact, she thought wistfully, before he withdrew and fiddled about getting the condom off.

'You all right?' he asked afterwards when she remained there motionless. 'Sorry about the—' He bent down to gather the scattered papers, and she yanked up her knickers and helped him.

'Whoa — adoption certificate?' he exclaimed in the next moment. 'Who's Hamish, your kid?'

She shook her head weakly. 'No. A cat. My sister's cat.' She jabbed at the paper. 'See that, where it says "West London Animal Shelter"? Bit of a clue for you there. They don't tend to give out kids as well. Not unless you pay extra.'

He didn't respond to her sarcasm, putting the pile of papers back in a neat stack on the table. 'Oh, right,' was all he said. Then an awkward silence fell, where neither of them quite knew what to do. She thought about offering him a drink but couldn't be bothered. *Go away now, please.*

'Well,' she said brightly, in the end. 'Nice to meet you, er—'

'Darren,' he said. 'It's Darren.'

She almost laughed. Baron Darren? Had Leni pulled some heavenly strings to send along her handsome husband-to-be? 'Delighted to meet you,' she said, mouth twitching. 'Tell me, do you have a castle, Darren?'

'A what?'

'Never mind.' Of course he didn't. 'Well … thanks?' she said, gesturing rudely to the door.

'Bye, then,' he said, taking the hint and going.

She sank into the sofa as she heard the door close behind him. 'That was unexpected,' she said into the emptiness, still feeling a bit giggly about the whole business. Not-a-Baron Darren … well, there were worse ways to spend an evening.

Not that she'd intended any kind of passion when she'd left work to meet Francesca earlier. Francesca and Leni had become friends when they did their postgraduate teaching course together and she'd got in touch after Alice's Facebook post about Leni's clothes, to ask if she could have a rust-coloured jumper of hers that she'd always loved. Sorting through her sister's possessions, Alice had found a book of Francesca's too, and so they'd met up for the handover and a chat. Half-Italian with a cloud of dark curls and a sweet round face, Francesca was warm and bubbly, hugging Alice and then pressing the jumper to her face and saying she'd think of Leni every time she wore it.

'Francesca, does this address mean anything to you?' Alice remembered to ask. She had brought Leni's little grey diary with her and held it open between them, pointing out the note from Leni's final week. 'Only I'm trying to fill in the blanks of what Leni was up to, when she was alive. We'd fallen out, you see, and I feel as if I missed out on that whole time.' Her voice shook, not least because she hadn't got very far with her investigations. Will hadn't replied to the message she'd sent but that wasn't a surprise, he never wanted to talk about Leni. Nor had she got any further with the other mysteries thrown up by the diary: where Leni was going on Tuesday nights (*T 7.30,* regular as clockwork), who 'A' was that Leni had gone to meet on the day of her death, the identity of 'Josh'. . .

Francesca shook her head blankly. 'No idea, sorry,' she said. 'But I can ask around.' The smile left her face. 'I feel bad too for not seeing more of her last summer. I was so caught up in the kids; Greta was only six months then, I wasn't getting out much at all. The last time I saw her . . .' She leafed back through the pages of Leni's diary until she came to one with her name on. 'Yes – dinner at our favourite Chinese place, that's right. If I'd known then that I wouldn't see her again . . .' Her eyes filled with sudden tears; she looked distraught. 'God. I have the horrible feeling I just talked about the kids, baby stuff, you know. Me, me, me. Because Leni was such a good listener, wasn't she? I wish I could have . . .' She put the diary gently back down on the table, her mouth buckling with sadness. 'I should have listened more to her while I had the chance.'

Alice nodded. 'Same.' She tried again. 'How about this guy – Josh, 8 p.m.?' she asked, finding the page. 'She met him a couple of other times too. Was she dating, do you think? Oh, and did she ever talk to you about trying for adoption?'

But Francesca couldn't answer any of her questions, grimacing apologetically and blaming 'baby brain', and before long saying she should go home to help her husband with bedtime. As well as the swirl of confusion inside her head, Alice had also felt a pang for her sister that so many of her friends seemed to have babies and children, when she hadn't been able to. It must have chipped away at her a little whenever there was a happy announcement made, or the detailing of domestic arrangements, knowing that she had to keep up a smile of feigned delight or understanding each time.

As the other woman got up, putting on her coat and saying how lovely it had been to catch up, it was all Alice could do not to grab her hand and force her to stay, begging her for more memories and stories. But then they were hugging goodbye and Francesca was gone. Was it any wonder Alice had ordered herself another drink to blot out her dismay at this non-starter? Was it any wonder that when the crop-haired man – not-Baron Darren – approached her, she was all too willing to be sweet-talked and distracted?

Standing in the middle of an upmarket babywear shop the following day, surrounded by overpriced prams with stupid names, Tony McKenzie could feel his irritation levels rise past 'Bit Annoyed', exceed 'Pretty Fed Up Now' and continue on, all the way up to 'For the Love of God, Get Me Out of Here Before I Lose My Mind'. Lullabies tinkled from the speakers overhead; you had to pity the poor bastards working in here, having 'Row, Row, Row Your Boat' on a loop. Give it another few minutes and he'd be smashing the music player with his own bare hands. Besides, if the lullabies were meant to soothe the customers' offspring, it wasn't working. One small girl in a padded turquoise coat was yelling on the floor, face puce, in the midst of a full-blown tantrum. Tony was this close to doing the same, to be honest. Christ, this was awful. This was so bloody awful.

He would be sixty next year, astonishingly. Every time the thought crossed his mind, it landed with a thud of shock. In his head, he was still mid-thirties, king of the castle, but in a real-life twist, not only was he nearly sixty, he was also about to become a dad again for the fourth time. Would the baby make him feel even older, or would he experience a new surge of life as a consequence? He hoped fervently for the latter, needless to say. He'd always been a handsome man, tall and lean with thick hair and twinkly blue eyes, and he'd traded on his looks shamelessly, talking his way in and out of all sorts of shenanigans. These days, his hair was starting to thin and he was having to put brightening drops in his eyes, and, perhaps most alarming of all, women had started looking straight through him, as if his charisma had exceeded its sell-by date.

It made it even worse, being here with so many young couples, excitement shining out of their faces. He had a creeping dread that, any minute now, somebody would assume he was a grandad, not a father-to-be, and he'd be forced to storm out of the place in a massive huff. Actually, that wouldn't be so bad, he conceded; he could recover from the ordeal with a large coffee downstairs, let Jackie take care of all the decision-making alone.

'Which one do you think, then, Tony?' she asked at that moment and he blinked, aware that he had totally zoned out of the store assistant's pram-versus-buggy patter for the last few minutes. Possibly longer. Hours, days could have trickled by for all he knew.

'Um,' he said blankly, staring around in the hope that, subconsciously, he somehow might have gleaned enough information to form an opinion on this, the biggest purchase of the trip. But no. His mind hummed like an empty fridge. 'Well . . . what do *you* think?' he hedged in the end.

She narrowed her eyes at him and he knew she had seen right through him. A highly successful company director, Jackie was as sharp as a gleaming new tomato knife, and often about as cutting, too. Would she be kind and overlook his lapse in concentration though, or mercilessly hang him out to dry? 'In terms of what Fern here was saying about considering a single-to-double,' she replied, eyes boring into his, 'would you be for or against?'

Shit. What the hell was she talking about? He chanced his arm. 'Er . . . for?'

She burst out laughing – which was better, at least, than a sharp dig in the ribs. *'Really?'* She shook her head. 'You have no idea what I mean, do you?'

He glanced down at the carpet which was printed, rather nauseatingly, with a repeating pattern of storks carrying nappy-slung cherubs. 'No,' he confessed. 'Must admit, I drifted off a bit towards the end there.'

'Time for your afternoon nap, is it?' Jackie teased, which annoyed him because he wasn't *that* old, for goodness' sake. Even if he did often enjoy a quiet forty winks around this time of day, if work was on the slow side. 'Okay, well, for your information, a single-to-double pushchair is one that can be adapted for when you have your next baby.'

'Your *next* baby?' he spluttered. 'What, you mean—?'

'*I* don't want another baby after this one,' she said. (Thank heavens.) 'But you apparently do, if you want us to consider that kind of kit.'

The assistant was smirking. Jackie apparently found this hilarious too. He gave them both a tired smile. 'Okay, ha ha, very good.' Time to remind them he knew a thing or two about vehicles. 'So. We need good suspension. Comfort for the baby. Decent tyres. A model that can be folded up and down quickly, preferably one-handed. If there's a removable car-seat element – all the better,' he reeled off briskly. Then he paused, enjoying their startled expressions – expressions which said, *Oh, okay, maybe he does know what he's talking about after all. Maybe we should stop patronising him now.* 'We'll have one like that, please,' he summed up to the assistant. 'My girlfriend can choose the colour. What?' he added, as Jackie pulled a face. 'Look, I have done this before, remember. Three times over. I'm not a complete novice, whatever you think.'

Jackie exchanged glances with the assistant. 'That's me told,' she said. And then, perhaps resentful of Tony's reference to his other children (it was the only area of their lives in which he could pull rank, the only thing he had done already that she hadn't), she added, 'Okay, he's bored, let's cut to the chase, then. We'll take the Cosy Kanga all-terrain travel system in the navy, please. With the matching changing bag.'

A thrilled light flashed through the assistant's eyes (shit, it must have been a very expensive choice) then she bowed her head subserviently. 'Of course. Excellent,' she replied, adding to the list she was compiling on an electronic tablet.

Tony leaned over so that his mouth was in the warm space of Jackie's neck. 'You are so sexy when you bark out orders like that,' he murmured into her skin.

Jackie yanked her head around to give him a withering look. She was statuesque and well-groomed – glossy brown hair, French-manicured nails, perfect make-up – and Tony knew that her friends privately (some not so privately) wondered what she was doing with him, a car salesman in his late fifties who'd already been around the block a few times. To be fair, sometimes he wondered the same. The two of them had met at a race day at Newbury – she was there because she loved horses, he was there because he loved a day out betting with his mates. She was great fun, he made her laugh, they'd had a bit to drink and really hit it off. Things progressed from there, although faster than either of them had anticipated, what with the accidental pregnancy. 'Looks like you're moving in with me,' she'd said at the time, 'seeing as I don't fancy living in your gaff, no offence.' Before he knew it, he was waking up every day in her very expensive barn conversion, all moody lighting and gleaming surfaces, enjoying the monsoon shower, the designer farmhouse kitchen with underfloor heating, the remote-controlled security gates that made him feel like a celebrity every time he approached. There were worse places to find yourself, he'd figured.

'In your dreams, mate,' she said from the side of her mouth now. '"Sexy" will be a distant memory for you, if you don't pull your finger out and take more of an interest in our baby's future, do you hear me?'

'I *am* interested in our—' he began protesting, only for her to raise an eyebrow and keep talking over the top of him.

'Good, because that means all the boring shit too. Like shopping for the right gear.' She lavished another smile on the assistant before asking, 'What next, then, Fern? Things for the bathroom, is it?' She elbowed Tony in a friendlier manner. 'Come on, indulge me. I'm only doing this once and it's a big deal for me.'

'I know. Sorry. And it's a big deal for me, too,' he replied, which was true at least. He had worked out that Jackie and he must have conceived pretty much the day that Leni had died, and the realisation had come with an enormous weight of conflicting emotions that he was still struggling to come to terms with. Was this some kind of redemption? A second chance to get fatherhood right?

Alice had been scathing when he had – admittedly fool-ishly – mentioned the timing of the conception. 'One in, one out, is that what you're saying?' she'd asked angrily. 'Dad. Please tell me you are not suggesting this baby will compensate in any way for Leni dying. This is not a like-for-like replacement situation here, do you hear me?'

Oh, he heard her all right, loud and clear. The whole of the east London café where he'd taken her for lunch had probably heard her too, because there seemed to be one heck of a lot of angry vegans giving him dirty looks after that. As for telling Will over a video call there was a new half-sibling on the way, that hadn't been exactly cheering either; his son looking very much as if he was grimacing with revulsion. Tony tried to console himself later that the screen *had* been pixelated due to wi-fi issues, but it was a tough sell.

Both conversations had left him disconcerted. No parent wanted to feel waves of contempt from their own children. 'Give them time, they're still cut up about their sister,' Jackie had said, which was decent of her, when both Alice and Will had snubbed her attempts to sympathise at the funeral. 'They'll love their little half-sister or -brother once they meet them. Come on – with our combination of genes? Who wouldn't?'

Over in a different area of the store, they now had to choose between pastel-coloured infant bathtubs, and giant sponges, and soft little hooded towels with cute animal ears. He and Belinda hadn't bothered with any of this sort of paraphernalia when Leni was born – they hadn't been able to afford a cot for six months; they'd had her in bed with them the whole time. Why did every single life experience get turned into one massive shopping expedition? *Duh ... it's called capitalism, Tone,* he heard Leni say sarcastically in his head and had to hide a smile. She and Alice had gone through a stage in their teens when they both called him 'Tony' or 'Tone' because ... well, he wasn't entirely sure. He hoped it was merely teenage affectation, their efforts to be cool, rather than the pair of them making a point about him not earning the name 'Dad' any more. (*Was* that what they'd meant?)

'Lilac or aquamarine?' Jackie was asking, a changing mat in each hand.

Uncaring, he pointed at the blue one. Then, trying to show willing, he grabbed a yellow plastic duck. 'Ah – here's an essential,' he said, and in the next moment was hurtled right back to the tiny flat he and Belinda had bought just off the Cowley Road – their starter home. There he was, young and dashing, kneeling at the side of the bath with his shirtsleeves rolled up, one arm around baby Leni's back as she sat there, a similar duck bobbing in the water before her. 'Duck!' she had said, her very first word, and he and Belinda had stared at each other, eyes wide. Their baby was a genius! The cleverest baby ever! 'I thought she was about to throw it at me for a moment,' he remembered quipping. 'I took "Duck!" as an instruction,' and they'd both laughed, and it had felt such a moment of togetherness for the three of them. Such joy. He couldn't quite believe he would be doing all of that again.

'Panda or fox?' Jackie asked, thrusting two hooded towels under his nose. 'Aren't they sweet? Should we get both, do you think?'

'Panda,' he replied. 'Adorable.'

For all his avowed wisdom at having done this before, for all the shocked delight that had rushed through him when Jackie broke the news, it was becoming impossible to ignore the doubts simultaneously doubling and mutating inside him like a virus, now that they were here, buying stuff, making it real. And it wasn't as if they'd planned things this way. In fact, Alice's first response on hearing about the pregnancy back in November had been a scornful laugh. 'Oh dear. A mistake, I take it?'

Thank you, Alice. Astute as ever.

He picked up a packet of white flannels, remembering the harrowing days and nights in the parent and baby intensive care unit when Will had been in and out of hospital throughout his first year. He was too tiny and weak to be bathed like ordinary babies, so they'd sponged him down with warm wet flannels, section by section, whenever he needed to be washed. Tony's back had ached as he leaned over the unit, carefully cleaning the creases in his son's small neck, his face, his bottom, and the memory made him feel sad that he could have cared for Will with such tender love and devotion then, only for the connection between them to break like a cheap necklace chain, for the links to drop away.

Blinking, he returned to the pastel surroundings of the store and reached for Jackie's hand, forcing himself to pay attention to what Fern was saying. He *would* get it right for this baby, he vowed, squeezing his girlfriend's fingers when she glanced over at him in surprise. (His *partner's* fingers, he reminded himself in the next moment, because Jackie had complained previously that whenever he called her his girlfriend, it made her feel as if they were fifteen.)

If you're going to do something, do it properly, his own dad had been fond of saying. No cutting corners or shortcuts. Sure, he was usually referring to DIY jobs – cleaning and repairing surfaces before slapping on a new coat of paint, that sort of thing – but his words came back to Tony now. If he was so set on being a good father this time around, maybe he should get in some practice beforehand, try again with his other children. Make an effort, if they'd let him. It wasn't too late to offer some fatherly love where it was needed, surely? A bit of friendly advice and encouragement.

Three months and counting, he calculated as they selected

a white baby bath and a massive sponge in the shape of a whale and a set of toiletries in lavender-coloured bottles. Three months to roll up his sleeves and make an effort. He might have been the one to leave the family back in the day, but what if he could reunite them all? Bring them back together? He'd prove that he was a good person, a good father, and he'd start by doing his best to repair the fractures and fault lines within family number one. He could do this for the McKenzies, couldn't he?

# Chapter Six

*Dad created group 'McKenzies Together'*
   *Dad added you*
   *Dad is typing . . .*
   Will frowned down at his phone, both at the unexpected sight of his father's name appearing there in his messages – this in itself a rarity – and the fact that he had apparently started a new family group chat called McKenzies Together, consisting, astonishingly, of Will, Alice and both parents. 'Seriously?' he muttered in disbelief. You had to laugh, honestly. Did his dad have any idea that there was a word 'irony' in existence? Since when had Tony McKenzie ever felt a shred of togetherness with the rest of them? Maybe the imminent arrival of child number four had prompted a late-onset midlife crisis (another one). Or maybe he'd been caught up in a sentimental moment, and would go on to delete the group in later regret.

   His dad was apparently still typing and Will turned his phone over on the table, not wanting to wait for the message. He would read it some other time, he decided. He certainly wouldn't expend any energy hoping that this was a sea change in his father, because he'd been there, worn the disappointment too many times. *You know Dad left because you were such a nightmare when you were born, don't you?* Leni had once said to him in a vile teenage mood. She'd muttered an apology later but he'd only been eight, and that sort of thing stuck with you. He shook his head, as if trying to dislodge the memory from his mind before it could totally harsh his mellow.

Exist in the moment, he reminded himself, and right now he was sitting at a rickety wooden table in his favourite rustic beach bar, a cold bottle of Singha in front of him. He also had a perfect view of the sea, which was starting to turn flamingo pink with bronze highlights as the sun descended steadily towards it. With half an hour to kill before he met Juno, a friend who happened to sell the best grass on Koh Samui, he planned to sit here, exhale slowly and watch the waves rush in and out again, as the sky filled with deepening colours. Breathe out the stress of the last few days, which had not exactly been the best of his life. For one thing, he hadn't sold as many sunglasses as he'd hoped, and he was wondering if he'd lost his edge. He'd certainly lost his motivation to get out there every day, pandering to holidaymakers as they said no to him and no again. It hadn't bothered him at first because work had been such a small element of his life compared to the parties, the scene, the casual friendships and even-more-casual sex, but the fewer items he sold, the less money he had, and the less money he had, the more he found himself obsessing over it. Meanwhile, the boxes of souvenirs, bought with such optimism back when he'd decided to just not go home, to try and make a living here, were still piled up in his flat, reminding him of his shortcomings.

He frowned again, taking a long cool glug of the beer, the alcohol sinking soothingly through his system. He was just a bit flat, that was all, he told himself. He'd be back in his groove within a few days, for sure. Absolutely.

A group of young people were heading out for a sunset paddleboard trip, he noticed, watching them stride across the sand together in their boardshorts and swimsuits, along with a guy lugging down a wheeled rack of boards. In the next moment, he felt a pang for his old sixth-form mates back home and missed feeling part of something bigger. Missed being among people who got him.

'Oh my *God*,' he heard then, followed by swift footsteps and a loud rubbery slap as a broken black flip-flop was slammed down on the table in front of him. And there was the red-haired Scottish woman again, looking insufferably pleased with herself. '*Voilà,*' she said, as if she'd just performed a magic trick, then held out her hand. 'My refund, please.'

So much for this being a relaxing half hour gazing at the waves. He stared in disbelief from the shoe up to the woman's triumphant face. Seriously? he thought. What was wrong with people? 'Wow,' he said sarcastically, feeling very much like hurling the flip-flop into the sand at their feet. 'You must feel so vindicated. For what, a few quid? Well done. Great.'

If anything, she seemed disappointed that he wasn't about to engage in combat, her big moment ruined as he dug into his pocket for his wallet, then dumped some money on the table without another word. *There. You won. Happy now?* his expression said, with a hefty side order of disdain.

'Thank you,' she said, stuffing the cash into a zip-up money belt around her waist. No blue bikini tonight, she was wearing denim shorts and a pale pink off-the-shoulder top with floaty sleeves. She picked up the shoe somewhat self-consciously. 'No hard feelings,' she added when he didn't respond.

He gave a snort. 'Getting that flip-flop out of the bin and carrying it around with you was clearly so worth it,' he commented without looking at her. 'I'm thrilled for you.'

She left without another word, and he drained the rest of his beer in a single exasperated gulp, feeling as if the peace he'd enjoyed at the start of the bottle had now deserted him. Just to top everything off, a message came through from Juno: she'd been waylaid, sorry, hon, could they rearrange? *Love you*, she signed off and he felt nauseous all of a sudden, sick of people he barely knew bandying that phrase around as if it was a mere pleasantry. And calling him 'hon' like they were old friends rather than two relative strangers who'd got stoned together a few times at beach parties. *You don't know me*, he felt like replying. Nobody knew him – that was the point.

He stared bleakly out at the idyllic beach scene before him, noticing the coral tones of the sky as the sun slid ever lower, the silhouetted palm trees, their leaves like dark feathers. The paddleboarders were out on the water, drifting serenely through the sunset colours. It was the sort of paradise image you'd see on postcards in the souvenir shops, but all he could think about was his small, empty flat awaiting him a few streets away. Now that he'd been denied the prospect of being able to smoke a numbing spliff to take the edge off his day, he couldn't face returning to its quiet, to the accusing sight of all those boxes full of stuff he was yet to sell. If he hadn't necked the rest of his beer so quickly, he could have lingered over it for another half an hour, but he couldn't really afford to buy a second one in this pricey tourist bar. Damn it. Now what?

His phone vibrated with the arrival of his dad's inaugural group chat message.

**Dad:** *Hi all. Losing Leni has made me realise we only have a limited number of days together – and I want to make them count. We're still Leni's family members, aren't we – can we try to support one another through this difficult time? I know I haven't been good at this in the past but I want to do better. Maybe talking to each other here might help?*

Will rolled his eyes. 'Oh my God,' he muttered under his breath. Had the old man lost the plot? There was more.

*Yes, I'm starting a new family with Jackie but you guys are still so important to me. You're family number one – the originals! Can we coalesce around our grief and offer mutual support? I'm here if so. Love Tony/Dad x*

Jesus. Whatever had possessed Tony McKenzie to start pontificating about family matters in this vein, like he had any right? Why did he think anyone needed *his* support at this precise moment in time? He was no dad to Will – he never had been. It wasn't until his mum started seeing Ray that Will had realised just what having a father figure in your life really meant. Ray had taken him rock-climbing and paddle-boarding with a bunch of his ageing but surprisingly cool mates; he'd helped Will find his apprenticeship and driven him to Swindon for the interview. He'd traipsed round rental properties with him, dealt with a dodgy landlord when Will felt too intimidated ... Where had his real dad been all this time? Not there, anyway.

He put the phone down and cradled his head in his hands as a sudden wave of melancholy washed through him. It was all closing in around him: his own uselessness, his dwindling funds, the shadow of real life back home looming larger at the corner of his eye with every passing day.

*Can I ask you a favour, Will?* he heard Leni ask in his head, words which had tormented him since the bombshell of her death, and he swallowed hard, conscious of all the guilt and regret he'd been pushing down this whole time, aware that it could come rearing back up any second to consume him again. Don't think about that, he ordered himself fiercely. Do not go there.

There was a soft throat-clearing behind him and then a new bottle of Singha was set down on the table, like a mirage, its neck frosted with condensation. He looked round and saw the Scottish woman there again, looking sheepish this time. A slight, dark-haired woman with a nose ring stood behind her, arms folded in a meaningful sort of way. 'Sorry,' the Scottish woman said, sounding and looking astonishingly meek compared with earlier. 'My friend has been very clear that I acted like a total dick just now. Have a beer with my apologies.'

Will glanced from the Scottish woman to her friend but this didn't seem to be a wind-up.

'You looked a wee bit down in the dumps, if you don't mind me saying,' added the dark-haired friend. 'Isla here's terrible for grinding men into despair. Don't worry, I've put her in her place on your behalf.'

Not a wind-up. Not a trick. He had a lump in his throat at this startling turn of events. At the beer he'd wished for having manifested before him so unexpectedly. 'Thank you,' he croaked. And then, because they were still hovering and he noticed they had their own drinks in hand, he rallied himself. Made an effort to resurrect the last dregs of his charisma. Maybe this was the distraction he needed to see him through this lonely evening. 'Would you like to join me?'

# Chapter Seven

*Leni McKenzie memorial page*

*One of my favourite memories of Leni is back when we were ten
years old, and went to a Brownie camp together. An older girl from
a different Brownie pack kept picking on Alice, Leni's sister, and
obviously Leni was determined to get her back for it. But how?
We were all out in the woods for various activities and games when
Leni became very thoughtful, and I guessed she was hatching a plan.
That evening, she told the most blood-curdling ghost story about a
forest monster made of branches and owls' beaks who loved to eat
little girls ... and you could always tell who it was going to kill that
night because they'd find three sticks beneath their pillow. Later, a
great scream went up when we went back to our beds because, you
guessed it, the bully had just discovered three sticks under her pillow
and was crying so much, her parents had to be called to take her
home. As an adult now, I hope the girl wasn't traumatised for too
long but as a kid, I just thought it was the funniest thing ever!*

   *Danielle*

*

Like her brother, Alice had been taken aback to see the messages from their dad in the new so-called McKenzies Together chat group. *WTF???* she messaged Will with several eye-rolling emojis. *Is this some kind of joke?*

*He'll get bored of it soon*, he'd replied. *Let's ignore him and hopefully he'll go away.* Belinda similarly didn't sound in any great hurry to fall in with her ex-husband's new idea. 'That old leopard will never change his spots,' she said dismissively when Alice mentioned the subject on the phone. 'He was probably drunk and maudlin when he wrote that. Take no notice, it won't mean anything.'

So far, none of them had replied to Tony's initial message and Alice felt paralysed by indecision. On one hand, wasn't this what she'd always wanted – for her dad to reach out with fatherly concern? But then again, after all the times he'd let them down, choosing other women over his 'first family', as he put it, forgetting important events in their lives ... wasn't it already too late? The other day at work, a girl had been regaling the office with how her dad had grilled her boyfriend on meeting him for the first time. 'How much are you earning?' the dad wanted to know, gimlet-eyed. 'What car are you driving? So what makes you think you're good enough for my daughter?' *It was so embarrassing!* she'd cried, clapping her hands to her face as the office erupted in laughter, but all Alice could feel was a twist of envy that her dad had never bothered to meet *her* boyfriends over the years, let alone pepper them with questions to see if they made the grade.

It was complicated, she thought, emerging from Shepherd's Bush tube station on Saturday morning. Life was far too bloody complicated. Although maybe today she'd be able to resolve one of the mysteries that had floated into her consciousness following the discovery of Leni's diary. She paused to check the map on her phone, then headed off along the green. *Cherry Grove, here I come.*

The road was a fast-moving river of traffic, the pavement almost as full, with people hurrying along in their winter coats and scarves: parents holding hands with dawdling children, clusters of track-suited youths with huge white trainers and loud voices, tired-faced women in headscarves lugging bags of shopping. Food smells drifted out from the takeaways – fried chicken, doughnuts, curry spices – and Alice's stomach flipped over with a rush of nausea to be back here, so near the place where her sister had died. She hadn't returned to this part of London since the dark nights of the previous autumn when she'd caused such a scene she'd ended up in the back of a police car. She pushed the memory away, striding determinedly on.

Alice hadn't been able to get very far finding out more about Cherry House. She'd called the number on the website a couple of times and emailed to ask if they had any details about who'd booked the venue for the June day when Leni had (possibly) been heading there, but she'd had no response. *A!! 8 p.m.* was all that was written in her diary that day, and Alice had combed through her sister's social media friends and contacts for people whose names began with 'A', only to draw a blank each time. *Adam, sorry for the random question, but I don't suppose you had made arrangements to meet Leni on the day she died?* she'd messaged her former brother-in-law, but he'd replied in the negative too. If only Leni's phone was available to pore over, it would have been so much easier to piece together her last movements, but that wasn't an option either. The phone had bounced out into the road when Leni was hit by the car, only to be found much later, run over by another vehicle and completely destroyed.

Maybe it wasn't a person she was going to meet. Turning off the main road on to Cherry Grove, Alice remembered the adoption brochure she'd found at the bottom of one of Leni's boxes. Could 'A' stand for 'adoption group'? Aerobics class? Amateur dramatics club? She bit her lip uncertainly. Surely Leni wouldn't have added two exclamation marks if she was going to an aerobics class?

She was getting nearer. 84, 82, 80, she counted, walking past the houses. She could see a red-brick building ahead, different to the Victorian terraced houses she was currently passing, and quickened her step. There it was. She imagined a receptionist behind a desk, tapping away at a keyboard, pot plants set around her. Soft music playing. The receptionist would be calm, helpful. 'You've been trying to call? So sorry, we've had connection issues,' she'd say apologetically. 'But you want some information on a date last June? Of course, let me see ...' And then she'd click a few keys, perhaps squint at the screen a little (the receptionist in her imagination had been meaning to book an optician's appointment) before her face cleared. 'Ah, yes. Of course,' she'd say. And then ...

Alice broke out of her reverie as she arrived at the hall, only to be greeted in the doorway by three little girls in Brownie uniforms. CHERRY GROVE BROWNIES BRING AND BUY SALE, read a hand-painted sign behind them.

'It's 50p to come in,' the tallest Brownie told her, shaking a biscuit tin that jangled with coins.

'Ah,' said Alice. 'Actually, I just wanted to—' There was a woman in a bright pink hair wrap sitting beyond the Brownies, presumably stationed to help out if need be, and Alice looked over the girls' heads, trying to catch her attention. 'Excuse me!' Unfortunately the woman seemed glued to something on her phone and didn't raise her head. 'Could I talk to that lady there, please?' Alice asked the girls.

'That costs 50p as well,' giggled the smallest Brownie, who had red curly hair and a riot of freckles.

'Florence! No, it doesn't!' scolded the middle Brownie crossly. She also had red hair but it was tamed into two neat plaits. Sisters? Alice wondered, remembering with a pang the message someone had left on Leni's memorial page, about the two of them at Brownie camp with Leni coming to her rescue once again. 'She's only six, she shouldn't even *be* here, but Mum said—'

'We've got lots of nice stalls,' the tallest Brownie wheedled, elbowing the other two. Clearly she was the entrepreneur of the group. 'There are clothes and baby things and cakes. I made some of the cakes,' she added, like that might be the clincher.

Browbeaten, Alice got out her purse. 'Fine. 50p,' she said, putting it into the tin, telling herself it would be money well spent if she came away with any answers.

Having finally been allowed over the threshold, it was clear there was no receptionist, so Alice approached the woman in the pink hair wrap. 'Hi. Do you work here?'

The woman had humorous brown eyes and a dimple in her left cheek. 'Me? No! I'm just helping out. Keeping an eye on these monkeys,' she said, raising her gaze from her phone screen.

'Ah, okay. Is there anyone here who might be able to help with a question about booking the hall, do you know?' Alice tried next. 'A booking from last year, I mean; I don't want to make one myself.'

The woman looked blank. 'Sorry, I've got no idea. You could ask Brown Owl, I suppose? I think she's on the tombola. Tall lady. Fluffy blonde hair.' She put her hand up in a confidential manner. 'Been channelling Stalin all morning but don't tell her I said that.'

Recounting this story to her friends Lou and Celeste the following day, Alice was greeted with gales of laughter at this point. 'Intrigue at the Brownies' Bring and Buy Sale,' Lou gurgled. 'This story is taking us to some wild places, Alice.'

'Please tell me the Stalinesque Brown Owl was worth your 50p,' Celeste added, panting slightly. The three of them were jogging very slowly around Victoria Park with the promise of lunch at a dumpling place afterwards; a compromise from Lou's original Park Run suggestion that Alice had vetoed as too ambitious. It had been raining all night and the ground was pocked with puddles reflecting the grey sky, while over on the sodden grass, blackbirds pecked industriously for worms.

'Brown Owl was singularly unhelpful,' she replied, clutching her side where she was getting a stitch. 'I'd even say she got quite arsey with me for interrupting her very important tombola work.' She spoke the words lightly to disguise how deflated she'd felt, standing there in the packed hall, full of excited girls and their parents, stalls laden with second-hand children's books, Brownie-made arts and crafts ('Come and get your home-made pencil cases!') and various bits of pre-loved baby equipment.

'Bummer,' said Lou. 'How frustrating.'

'Yeah. I found a noticeboard with a couple of numbers and a different email address, so I've sent off an enquiry about the date, which is a start. Oh, and the other thing ...' They swerved to one side to make way for a group of mums wielding buggies with gigantic all-terrain wheels. 'Well, it wasn't an entirely wasted trip.'

She'd been about to leave, she told them, when her eye was caught by a stall selling home-made cushions with appliqued felt designs – a red house, a blue rabbit, an orange cat – and the latter had reminded her of Hamish, Leni's old cat, and of finding his adoption certificate the other night, after her encounter with sexy Darren. (No, she hadn't told her friends about sexy Darren. Would they make a fuss about her drinking alone and taking home random men for casual sex? You bet. Did she need that in her life? Definitely not.)

'So on my way home, I thought I'd see if I could find out what had happened to Hamish. You know, in the hope he'd been adopted by a lovely new family,' she went on, dodging to avoid a runaway toddler in a red puffa jacket who was bearing down on a nervous pigeon.

Alice still felt bad for not being able to take Hamish in

when he'd needed rehoming, little knowing that Noah and his fur allergy would be moving out of her flat anyway mere months later. Sitting there on the swaying overground train, she'd looked up the Oxford cats' home where her mum had eventually left him and her heart sank with sorrow to see that he was still there, glowering from the web page, no doubt having put off every prospective cat-seeker with his slit-eyed unfriendliness. Oh, Hamish. You deserved better than this, she thought disconsolately. Unless ...

An idea had struck her like a ray of sunshine beaming through thick cloud and she'd sat up a little straighter. She had space now in her life for a pet to love, didn't she? Her sister's pet ... what if she was the one to give him his forever home? It would be something really good she could do for him – and for Leni too. Surely this was meant to be? (*Of course it's meant to be!* she imagined Leni crying in frustration at her slow-wittedness. *Just get on the ruddy phone already, will you?*)

The idea had taken hold all the way home and she found herself dialling the number of the rescue centre as soon as she got in her front door, before she'd even taken off her coat. The woman who answered didn't soft-soap Alice about what she might be letting herself in for. 'We tried him with one family before Christmas but his fur started falling out – with stress, we think – and then there were a couple of biting incidents which meant they changed their minds about having him.' She also seemed dubious about someone from London adopting a cat from them – 'We like to do home visits, you see, to make sure you have a suitable place for our animals' – but when Alice explained the situation, only just managing not to cry, and promised she would do everything she could to make him feel loved and safe, the woman softened.

'Bless you, darling,' she said. 'Leave it with me and I'll see what I can do.'

'Oh my God!' cried Lou on hearing this. They were passing a group of lads having a kickabout and the cheer that went up as one of them scored sounded as if they too approved of the story. 'So what happens now?'

'I've had to send them photos of the flat and garden to prove I can give him a safe new home,' Alice replied, panting with the exertion of trying to jog *and* talk. 'And I've filled in an application form and sent that off too. Now I just have to wait.' She was too out of breath to tell them how, unlocking the back door to the garden to take pictures, she'd been ashamed to realise that it was the first time she'd been out there in months. But as she tidied up a little, appreciating the waxy white snowdrops gleaming in the small flowerbed and remembering how the honeysuckle always smelled so beautiful in summertime, she had felt the first faint glimmerings of hope. *This could be a nice space for Hamish, and for her too,* she thought. It might be midwinter now, but on warm days, the garden became a real suntrap; he could stretch out on the cobbles and catch some rays while she perched on the deckchair with a good book. She would fit a cat flap so that he could come and go as he pleased. And on cold evenings, they could curl up together, cosy and warm. Forget all those clichés about spinsters and their moggies, she was up for it.

'Well, fingers – and paws – crossed,' Celeste said. 'I'm totally here for this love story.'

91

'Me too,' said Alice. If she could bring Hamish back into the McKenzie fold, it would feel like a connection across the void, a shining new link minted with her sister, spanning then to now. *Darren picking up the adoption paper, the ginger cat cushion at the Brownie fair . . . maybe a pattern was emerging,* she thought hopefully. Was this Leni's way of leaving her a breadcrumb trail showing her how to get through this, how to live?

# Chapter Eight

*Leni McKenzie memorial page*

*I met Leni at uni and some of my funniest memories ever are from when we shared a flat in Wavertree. One hot June day, we were trying and failing to revise for our second-year exams when an ice cream van trundled along the street. I don't know how, but Leni talked the ice cream man into letting us help him because we needed 'work experience for our careers'. 'Have a break, I'll make you a coffee,' she told him. 'We'll serve your customers.' He must have been mad – or maybe he just hated the job – but anyway he agreed and we both ended up in the van for over an hour, serving terrible ice creams to the Wavertree kids. Much more fun than revision!*

*I still think of Leni and smile every time I hear an ice cream van. I think I probably always will.*

*Maxine*

Ray pulled on the handbrake and they sat motionless for a moment, staring at the house in front of them. 'Well,' he said unnecessarily. 'And wow. Bloody hell. Here we are, your ladyship.'

Here they were indeed. Outside a double-fronted Cotswold stone farmhouse, way out in the sticks, with a crescent-shaped gravel drive and planters either side of the door. Belinda gulped. Despite the weeks they'd spent clearing out and painting, all the trips to and from the storage centre and the dump, she hadn't quite believed in what they were doing. Now, belatedly, the magnitude of their plans was hitting home and the reality seemed ... well, pretty daunting. 'Are you sure we can afford this?' she asked eventually, her voice a croak.

'With the money from my flat, and what we'll hopefully get from your house, plus a fair wind behind us, just about,' he replied, reaching over and patting her leg. 'Don't be fooled by first appearances, by the way. When I booked the appointment, the estate agent himself warned me that it would need a hell of a lot of TLC to make it habitable for us, let alone any paying guests.' He nudged her across the handbrake when she didn't reply. 'You do still want this, don't you?'

She tried to say yes but the word wouldn't fall easily from her tongue. They had talked endlessly about their shared pipe dream of running a B. & B.: creating a beautiful, comfortable haven for a stream of interesting guests. Ray was keen to offer bespoke experiences to the guests – quad-biking and falconry and kayaking; he had all sorts of ideas. Now that they were here though, presented with a version of that dream in actual bricks and mortar, she felt paralysed with uncertainty. *Did* she want to do this? Had she ever wanted this, or had it been a suggestion that she'd seized upon, clung to as a way out?

Her own hesitation made her feel such an idiot after all the work they'd done together to reach this point, not to mention all the couples who had already come traipsing round their spotless house flicking glances into every corner. It was as if she'd been joining in a game all along, a lovely distracting game of make-believe that she hadn't quite expected to turn into anything more.

'Yes,' she managed to say at last, but there was a quaver in her voice that he must have heard too. 'But ...' It was so quiet here. Only the sound of the birds, and the wind in the trees. The nearest neighbours were a few minutes' walk away and the centre of the village half a mile. She had lived in her home for three decades and her entire life was centred on that street, that postcode. All her friends were nearby, she had her routines, her favourite shops and pubs, walks on Port Meadow ... 'It's just ... I feel a bit weird,' she confessed.

She looked at the house again, this time taking in more of the details. There was a beautiful stone portico around the doorway, its roof carved in the shape of a seashell; a stained-glass fanlight above the white-painted door; two twisting red-brick chimneys on the roof. First impressions – it was undeniably beautiful, however crumbly the inside might turn out to be. A hundred times fancier than anywhere she'd ever lived before. The driveway, for starters – imagine never having to parallel park on her narrow street any more. Sometimes you could be tootling around for ten minutes or more, looking for a space to squeeze into. And yet, according to Ray's calculations, that daily irritation could be removed. Oxford house prices were insane, but even so, she was astonished to realise that her small three-bedroom terraced house had gone up in value enough over the years for them to even consider a place like this.

'You *are* allowed to be happy again,' Ray reminded her gently and she flashed him a grateful smile.

'I know,' she said, pulling herself together. 'I'm just being silly. Come on, let's go and look around.'

She'd met Ray soon after Will had left for university, nine years ago. The noisy, busy family home now an echoing empty nest, she hadn't known what to do with herself. 'You're free, lucky you,' sighed her sister Carolyn, who'd had children much later than Belinda, and was still stuck in the routine of swimming lessons and gym kit and pet hamsters that either escaped or died. Friends whose houses were now similarly depleted all seemed to be booking themselves holidays and relishing the independence that came with having newly dispatched their offspring. 'It's our time now!' was the gleeful catchphrase among them.

Belinda, meanwhile, had gone through something of a crisis of confidence. After twenty-plus years, certain of her place as a mum at the centre of her family, it was unsettling to find herself relegated to a lower priority in her children's lives. No longer needed in the same way, no longer the lynchpin keeping them all together. She still had work, sure, but coming home to a cold, dark house each night felt so dispiriting, she sometimes felt very much like turning round and going straight back out again. And it was all very well for her friends to gallivant about, but most of them were settled in couples, which made the whole experience easier and more fun to navigate. Who did Belinda have to gallivant with? Were the best days of her life already over?

In the end, it had been a friend, Kath, who rescued her from total stagnation by throwing a wild house party for her fiftieth and inviting everyone she knew. And this happened to include Ray, an old mate of Kath's husband from the days when they'd both been roadies together. That night, Ray had made Belinda laugh again for what felt like the first time in weeks, with some of his tall stories about life on the road. He was funny, charming and unconventional, and although he had a pretty wild hinterland – addiction demons, and a marriage and family life that he'd destroyed (his words) due to his own selfish behaviour – he was twelve years clean at that point and great company.

Sod's law, of course, Will dropped out of university after a single term – 'Just full of snobby arseholes from private schools' – and so he was home again anyway, but by then she and Ray were an item, and she had a new spring in her step. Belinda had previously led something of a conventional life – she'd married young, and then had the dual responsibilities of children and work to keep her busy – but Ray brought an extra spice to her life, opened her eyes to new thrills that the world had to offer. He took her to festivals (and seemed to know *everyone* backstage), they travelled around India together – he even taught her how to surf one summer in Cornwall.

So *this* is living, she kept finding herself thinking, fizzing with reinvention.

Almost a decade later, here they were, planning to throw in their lots together in the name of a whole new joint adventure. Maybe even based around this very house they'd parked in front of – if it didn't fall down before then, obviously. She eyed it with new wariness. It wouldn't fall down, would it? There were so many accidents that could happen at any moment. Maybe they'd be better off with a new-build after all?

Before she could suggest this to Ray, the estate agent pulled up beside them in a smart racing-green Mini and hopped out, a whirl of energy, brandishing keys and a rather dog-eared brochure. According to Ray's intel, the house had been on the market for eight months already, long enough for the estate agent to have honed his spiel about 'potential' and 'transformation' plus a hastily mumbled – and ominous – warning about not touching any of the wiring: *it's probably safe but best not to chance it*. Oh heavens, thought Belinda, who'd always been a dreamy toucher of things, the sort of person who'd trail her fingertips absent-mindedly along walls and surfaces without even knowing she was doing so. 'Let's hope we get out of here alive,' Ray said, taking Belinda's hand as they crossed the threshold. 'You don't need *all* your limbs, do you?'

Inside, the house smelled of damp and neglect, there were cobwebs in the corners, dust everywhere, and interesting-looking mould creeping up the wall of the downstairs loo. Bare wires sprouted alarmingly from ceilings and occasion-ally from what once had been light switches on the walls. Faded wallpaper bubbled and peeled around the living-room hearth, a withered brown sprig of holly lay forlornly on the mantelpiece, a relic from a Christmas long before, while the carpet throughout had seen better days. The kitchen looked about twenty years out of date, and without needing to touch anything (no thanks) Belinda knew that every surface would be coated with a disgusting sticky film. Meanwhile, outside, the garden was positively jungly, with long grass invading what was left of the flowerbeds, bindweed strangling elderly rose bushes and the flagstones of the patio covered in moss.

'Well, it's a mess, all right,' Ray said cheerfully as they stood there on the grimy old patio. As someone who'd had his name down on the local allotment list for almost three years, Belinda knew he would already be thinking about vegetable plots and a greenhouse and a proper lawn with stripes. 'But there's definitely potential. This must have been the most glorious house in its heyday, don't you think? Imagine the parties!' He whistled under his breath, shaking his head. Then, when she made no immediate reply, he prompted, 'What *do* you think?'

Above them, the milky white clouds parted and Belinda turned her face to the weak winter sun, grateful for its benevolent warmth. She could hear birds singing, the distant rumble of a tractor, a breeze soughing through the bare branches of the old cherry tree nearby. She thought again of the large quiet rooms they'd walked through; their generous sizes, the big windows with their views out on to the Oxfordshire countryside. Yes, the house was rundown, but it was gorgeous. Its walls whispered to her temptingly about all the good times it had seen, and her imagination obligingly filled in the gaps to conjure up colourful images of decadence and beauty.

They'd have to roll up their sleeves and work harder than ever before, but ...

Her stomach cramped as she thought again of the memories she would be leaving behind. Christmas dinners and birthday parties in the kitchen. All of those broken nights with babies, nursing them in the bedroom as the sun sent the first rays of pink morning light beneath the curtains. The walks to school. The trick-or-treating along the street. The washing machine forever rumbling through school uniform and PE kits and bedding ... *You know you're not meant to make any big life decisions in the first year after a bereavement*, she heard Alice chide again in her head, and bit her lip that she could have dismissed her daughter's advice so breezily. Might they be making a mistake after all?

'Bel?' prompted Ray, still looking at her expectantly. 'So I was thinking we could run the zip wire from the attic window down to the back wall there ... Maybe turn the garden into a mountain bike circuit ... Nope. You're not listening, are you?'

Something even more serious had occurred to her. What did Leni think of this place? And Apolline? Would she still be able to speak to Leni here? *She keeps mentioning a man*, Apolline had said the other day and Belinda's heart had almost stopped. *A name beginning with G, perhaps?*

'I ... I ...' she stuttered now, aware of Ray's eyes on her. The thing was, she felt unable to give a proper opinion without the soothing tones of Apolline steering her in one direction or another. How could she make such a massive decision without guidance? 'I think I'd like to speak to a ... a friend,' she stammered, unable to look him in the eye any more.

His sigh sounded very much like one of exasperation. 'Don't I count? I'm right here. Can't you talk to me? I won't even charge you a premium hotline rate.'

She flushed. 'Yes, but I need . . . I'm not sure . . .' She broke off because she couldn't bear the irritated stiffness of his body language, the resignation now on his face.

'You're talking about your psychic pal, I take it,' he said stonily and she hung her head. 'Bel – this has got to stop. This is holding you back, can't you see? She's not good for you. I dread to think how much money you've already wasted calling her.'

'It's *not* holding me back! And it's not a waste! How can you say that? She means everything to me!' Her voice was more passionate than she intended and the sound seemed to reverberate off the stone wall behind them.

'And that, right there, is the problem,' he replied, folding his arms. Ray was not the argumentative type, but today she had the feeling he was digging in mulishly for the long haul, that he was not about to back down. Well, so be it, she thought, hackles rising in self-defence. Because neither was she. 'These phone calls have become a problem,' he went on. 'You must know, deep down, that it's a scam. You must do. None of it is real. She's a charlatan, this woman, she's preying on your unhappiness. And at what price, eh?'

Belinda gasped as if he'd hit her. 'She is *not*! She's my friend! Our calls are the most precious thing in my life because through her I can talk to Leni again.' Her voice shook. 'How can I give that up? How?'

She was starting to feel hysterical, which was not helped

by Ray taking hold of her arms. 'Listen to me,' he said. 'Leni's gone. I know it's awful. I know it's the worst thing ever. But—'

'How are we doing, then?' Of course the estate agent had to pick that moment to walk out of the kitchen door towards them, his eager face drooping as soon as he realised he'd interrupted an emotional scene. 'Ah. Sorry. I'll … I'll give you a few minutes,' he said, backing away immediately, hands raised.

'It's fine, you don't need to,' Belinda said heavily, wrenching herself from Ray's grasp. 'We don't want the house. It's a no.'

'We – wait. We haven't even talked about it yet,' Ray protested, but she was walking blindly past him by then, past the startled-looking estate agent too and back into the cold damp air of the house, feeling overwhelmed by everything. 'Bel!' he shouted after her, hurrying to catch her up. 'Wait!'

# Chapter Nine

*McKenzies Together group*

*Saturday*
*Hi all, hope everyone has nice plans for the weekend. Am attaching some of my favourite photos of Leni. I love the one with her gappy teeth! Take care of yourselves. Love Dad/Tony x 10.17*

*Sunday*
*Happy Sunday, everyone! What are you all up to? Anyone fancy a chat later? Love Dad/Tony x 15.43*

*Monday*
*How are you all doing? I've been reading up on grief and keep seeing that talking can really help – to a counsellor or a bereavement group. What do you think? Maybe we should all give that a go? 09.27*
**Will:** *You first then, Dad 18.50*

'He was only nineteen; he'd barely started his life. Everything was ahead of him: falling in love, finishing university, travelling with friends, his first proper job ...' The blonde woman's voice wobbled. You could tell she was trying her hardest not to cry. *Christ*, thought Tony, shifting uncomfortably on his seat, wondering if it would be too obvious for him to make an excuse to leave the first chance he got.

'As far as I knew, he'd never even smoked a cigarette before, let alone tried drugs,' the blonde went on. 'And to think of him there, all alone, in his final few moments ...' Her shoulders heaved. 'The post-mortem said ...' She broke down and beside her, a young woman with short pink hair reached out and put a hand gently on her back as she sobbed. 'The post-mortem said his organs failed. He must have been in absolute agony.'

Tony bowed his head so that he didn't have to witness the woman's distress with his eyes as well as his ears. This was *horrific*. Pretty much on a par with having his fingernails ripped out one by one. Whatever had made him think that coming here, to the east Oxford bereavement support group, would be a good idea? Already he had sat through so much suffering, so many tragic tales of loss. It was deeply disturbing, being this close to raw grief and heartbreak. He thought longingly of the Champions League match taking place right now, wishing he could check the score on his phone. Not because he was totally callous – more as a temporary, necessary reprieve from the misery currently sweeping through this chilly village hall; so that he could be reminded that life went on at European football grounds and elsewhere, that other people were still happy and excited and enjoying themselves.

'You, going to a support group? Wow, that's ... good. That's really good, Tony,' Jackie had said in surprise when he announced his whereabouts for that evening. Admittedly, he'd surprised himself with the decision, but after days of silence on the group chat – you could practically see the tumbleweed rolling across the screen – he'd been so pleased to get a response from Will, even a sardonic, challenging one, he hadn't felt able to fudge the issue. Meanwhile Alice was yet to reply to any of his messages, and as for Belinda ...

He sighed to himself, remembering her expression when he'd seen her the other day: shock, guilt and finally dislike crossing her face within a single second. The whole thing had been discomfiting, frankly. He'd popped into town on his lunch break and was walking up the high street when he glimpsed her through the window of a café, sitting there on her phone. In the past he might have glanced across and kept on walking, but in the spirit of McKenzies Together, he knocked on the window instead and gave a friendly wave when she looked up. Sod it, he thought. They had once been married and the best of friends; they had children together. Whatever had gone wrong between them in the past, didn't he owe it to what was left of their family – and to Leni – to be civil and pleasant now?

She didn't seem to agree, shaking her head at him when he gestured that he would come in and then looking extremely fed up when he arrived beside her table. 'I'm on the *phone*!' she hissed, clutching her mobile protectively to her chest. 'Is it important?'

'Well ... no, I ...' His good intentions shrivelled away. 'I just thought I'd say hello, that's all.'

'Right. Hello,' she replied, pretty rudely, on reflection. Then she turned away, pressing the phone to her ear once more. 'Hi. Sorry about that,' he heard her say. 'Carry on.'

That might have been that, him sent packing and sloping back out again, but then he heard her asking in a low voice, 'Has Leni told you anything else?' which stopped him in his tracks. His heart thudded, his skin prickled; for a stupid, wild moment he found himself wondering if he'd been mistaken and Leni was actually still alive, before catching on to himself. *Idiot. You went to her funeral.* He must have misheard.

Something prevented him from walking any further though. He dropped down, pretending to retie his shoelace, ears on stalks to hear more. Belinda gave a little chuckle. 'Well, she *would* say that,' she said happily. 'One thing you should know about Leni, she loves to wind me up.'

A silver-haired woman on the table nearby shot Tony a disapproving look as if she'd seen right through him, crouching there with his fake shoelace problem. He got reluctantly to his feet, keen not to be confronted in case it alerted Belinda's attention. Could there be another Leni in her life? he mused on his way out. Unless he'd heard wrong and she'd said 'Penny' or 'Nelly' or some other similar-sounding name. It was possible, he supposed.

Anyway, he would keep on trying with Belinda and his children, he'd vowed – hence him being here at this bereavement group meeting, having a very uncomfortable time. When he'd suggested talking to a counsellor or group to the rest of the family, he'd intended his advice to be gratefully picked up by *them*, rather than thrown back at him, but never mind.

The blonde woman was now shuddering to a tearful halt, poor thing. Looking at her made Tony feel as if he in comparison was a weak imitation of a grieving parent, as if he hadn't loved his own daughter adequately, as if his heart wasn't big enough to contain the equivalent depths of feeling. Nor would he ever be able to unload his feelings like that to a room full of strangers with such unflinching honesty. It was as if she had peeled open the layers of her skin to reveal her heart, stuttering valiantly along, despite everything.

'Thank you for sharing, Ellen,' the group leader, Monica, said gently. Monica was tall and rather headmistress-like, nearing retirement age, with a kind but firm manner. Her bespectacled gaze roamed the circle of grievers and then – horror of horrors – stopped at Tony. 'Tony, is it? Would you like to say anything this evening?'

Tony swallowed, under pressure. 'Oh,' he mumbled, floundering for words as he stared down at the beige lino floor. 'Er ...'

'It's completely up to you,' Monica told him, pushing her glasses a little further up her nose. She had bobbed, greying hair and wore a smart navy skirt with a mustard blouse which was adorned by a big amethyst brooch. His mind wanted to lead him off on a tangent about brooches and how you never really saw people wearing them any more but he dragged himself reluctantly back to the room.

'Um. Not today,' he muttered, embarrassed. 'Thank you though.' He could feel everyone looking at him, wondering what his story might be, and his cheeks began heating up under their collective gaze. 'I'm ... I'm still coming to terms with ... the situation,' he said awkwardly after a moment, which earned him a few nods of understanding at least.

'That's fine. We're here when you feel like speaking – and for when you'd rather listen, too,' Monica said. Then she turned to the rotund man with a cast on his ankle who was perspiring under the light, even though it was a freezing January evening and most people still had their coats on. 'Gary? How are you this week? Do you want to talk to the group?'

Gary's mouth was trembling and he passed a hand over his face as if overcome, but then nodded and began. He was a newly widowed dad to three children and spoke eloquently of the guilt he felt at being the parent who'd survived, as well as the dread that he was letting down his sons and daughter on all counts.

Jesus, Tony thought, sinking lower in his seat. This got worse and worse. He was actually starting to feel tearful himself, listening to Gary berate himself for crying in front of his kids, for not knowing the right things to say to them, for feeling as if he was getting everything wrong, every day. Tony was not proud of the heady jag of relief that came when Monica said, a short while later, that they would have to finish now for the evening, but honestly, he wasn't sure he could sit there any longer and be part of this man's unhappiness. Thank heavens for that.

Monica was still talking: if anyone wanted to continue the conversation, they could move next door, to the Four Oaks pub, she told them. 'Although, remember, alcohol is not always your friend when you're fragile,' she added as some of the group got to their feet, looking more cheerful. 'Soft drinks *are* available and are, in my opinion, the advisable choice during difficult periods.'

Tony, meanwhile, could hardly make for the exit fast enough. But his swift getaway was snatched from his grasp when a young woman fell purposefully into step with him.

'I know it's hard, on your first time,' she said, zipping up her silver padded coat as she walked. It was the pink-haired woman – not much older than a girl, really; she had the youthful bloom of someone still in their twenties. 'I was the same, the first few weeks I was here. Didn't trust myself to speak in case I lost it. But it does make you feel better, if you can get stuff off your chest. Everyone's lovely, as I'm sure you noticed.'

He gave her a brief, tight-lipped smile, not really wanting to get into conversation. He didn't feel like admitting that the problem was not that he was worried he'd 'lose it', as she'd said, more that the evening had left him feeling emotionally unqualified from start to finish. He was a middle-aged, pretty old-fashioned bloke at the end of the day – pouring his heart out to strangers was not what he did. Besides, what if the others judged him for not having been much of a dad in the first place?

'Yes, they seemed nice enough,' he responded blandly, longing to be in the sanctuary of his car by now, 5 Live providing football updates, his hands on the wheel as he sped away from this place forever. 'I'd better go – I think my parking ticket's about to run out. Nice to meet you.'

She opened her mouth as if there was more to discuss, but he didn't give her the chance to say another word, calling

'Goodbye!' and striding quickly out into the street. Instantly, he felt like a wanker for doing so. She was young and only trying to be friendly, after all. Presumably while still dealing with her own bereavement on top of everything else.

God. How come when he tried to do something good he ended up making a prick of himself? Even the bit about the parking ticket was a lie. 'Sometimes I wonder if you're actually human,' his second wife Isabelle had shouted at him shortly before their marriage broke down irreparably. She was half Spanish and a dancer, and he'd been bewitched by her passion and tempestuousness, until both of those personality traits rebounded on him, and not in a good way. 'Do you *have* any feelings in there, or are you merely selfish bullshit through and through?'

He had reached his car by now and slunk into the driver's seat, exhaling with his eyes shut for a few moments. *No*, he told the Isabelle of his memory. *I am not entirely made of selfish bullshit.* Then, as if to prove it, he reached for his phone. 'Call Alice, please,' he requested, glad that Jackie wasn't there to tease him for it. *It's not a person, you don't have to be polite to your phone!* she hooted whenever she caught him out. Tony had been brought up to mind his P's and Q's ('McKenzies have manners!'), and privately thought barking orders at technology was the beginning of the end for civilisation.

'Hi Dad,' Alice said, sounding surprised. Perhaps a little suspicious. 'Are you okay?'

'Yeah. I just …' He ducked his head away as he saw a couple of people from the group walking by – a couple whose severely disabled son had died at the age of two, seven years earlier. *We're having another baby but we're both very scared*, the woman had said, eyes filming over with unshed tears. Tony blinked their faces away and forced himself to continue. 'Well, I just thought I'd ring for a chat.' Even to his own ears, his words sounded implausible. He tried to think when he'd last called her like this. Christmas, maybe?

He braced himself for a sarcastic reply – *Wow, I'm honoured* or something similar – but none came. If anything she sounded a bit flat. 'Okay,' she said uncertainly. 'So ... how are you?'

'I've had better evenings,' he replied. 'I took my own advice tonight and went to talk about my feelings at a bereavement support group,' he went on. 'Although ironically I didn't say a word. Sat there feeling depressed about everything. God knows why anyone thinks these things help. Everyone there was crying their eyes out. It was awful, Alice. Terrible. We must never take my advice seriously, ever again. I mean it. I know nothing.'

She laughed – politely, perhaps, but the sound lit a tiny flame inside him nonetheless. 'Oh dear.'

'Exactly. A spectacular own goal.' His thoughts flicked back to that evening's football – he still hadn't checked the scores – and then he had to hunt around his mind for something else to say because suddenly, already, it felt as if the conversation had lost momentum. 'How's work?' he said, cringing as he did so, because it felt like all those awkward weekend dad *How's school?* conversations he'd attempted back when the children were little and he'd moved out.

'Fine,' Alice mumbled, just as she and her siblings had always done to the *How's school* question. Then she must have changed her mind, because she added, 'Actually no, it's really boring and tedious. I'm temping at the moment, it's not great.'

'Oh,' he said, wrong-footed. The last he'd heard she'd been working for a glamorous-sounding marketing agency in London, and absolutely loved it. 'What happened to your other job? Fancied a change, or ... ?'

'Something like that,' she muttered in a way that didn't invite further discussion.

'Right,' he said, frowning. 'And how are you ... in yourself? I mean, with everything, you know ...' He grimaced, hating feeling so tongue-tied with his own daughter. At work, he could schmooze anyone into a sale, but when it came to actual sincerity, the right words seemed to slide out of reach.

'Well ... Not great, to be honest,' she said. 'But I've been sorting through some of Leni's things, which makes me feel closer to her, at least. Mum and I started a few weeks ago and I've taken the rest of her stuff back to my flat to finish.'

'That's good,' he said heartily, putting her on speakerphone and starting the car. 'There's something comforting about doing useful tasks like that; I remember me and your uncles sorting out Grandad's house after he died.' His parents had passed away one after the other, as neat and punctual in death as they had been in life, and he found himself back there momentarily, standing with his brothers in the living room of that small Kidlington semi, confronted by the accumulation of two lifetimes: the soft, faded armchairs, the prickly hearthside rug they'd wrestled on as boys, the yellowing paperbacks in the bookshelves constructed by his dad. 'It's not an easy job, I know. So please don't feel you have to do it alone. You've got me, remember, keen and eager to offer my services.'

There was a small pause and then she said, 'I'm finding it quite emotional, actually. I'm trying to do right by her – you know, make sure everything goes to a good home. Giving her stuff to her friends, which has been really nice, especially hearing their memories of her.' He heard her sigh. 'But it's made me realise there was a lot I didn't know about her, which makes me feel sad.'

He felt the weight of her grief compound his own mood. 'Same,' he said, his voice catching on the word. He drove past the pink-haired woman just then, walking with her head down, looking completely miserable, and felt a further wrench of guilt that he'd been so quick to shake her off. 'You always think there's more time, don't you? All the time in the world to tie up loose ends, say sorry, make amends. But …'

'Mmm,' Alice said, with rather an edge to her voice. 'Anyway, talking of things going to a good home – or at least a new one,' she went on with determined-sounding brightness, 'I'm adopting her cat. Remember Hamish?'

'The ginger savage who scratched your brother's arm to pieces? Oh yeah. Yowled the entire van journey back up the M40.' The full meaning of her words belatedly sank in. 'So you're having him, are you?'

'That's what I said. Picking him up after work tomorrow. The start of a beautiful new relationship, I hope.'

'Oh, Ali, that's lovely. Really lovely. Leni would have been so chuffed. I felt bad that, you know, we didn't step up for him at the time, but …'

'Mmm,' she said again, before he could launch into excuses. Another little cut, right there. 'How's Jackie?'

'Jackie's fine. We're starting antenatal classes next week,' he said. A black BMW was coming towards him and his fingers tightened automatically on the wheel. It had been a BMW that had knocked Leni down that night, and for a while he'd found himself obsessively calculating the driver's braking capacity, wondering darkly about the state of his tyre treads. He still detested BMWs and their drivers. 'Screw you,' he said under his breath, like he did whenever he saw one.

'Pardon?'

'Sorry – not you. Um. Yes, so antenatal classes, everything's getting real now. I'm a bit nervous, Ali, about going through it all again.'

'Going through it all again? What do you mean – whether you'll stay the course this time?'

He winced at her iciness and scrambled to clarify. 'I mean – the sleepless nights, the anxiety about every little rash and cough and whether or not they're still breathing ...'

'Dad – you know Leni was desperate for a baby, don't you?' she interrupted angrily. '*Desperate*. She and Adam tried and tried and tried. She was even considering adoption at the end, I think. So for you to be moaning about feeling anxious, when you're so bloody lucky that you can apparently produce babies at the drop of a hat, without even trying—'

Oh God.

'– Then it's kind of bad taste, don't you think? But maybe that's part of the problem – that you *don't* think. Anyway, I'd better go. Thanks for ringing, okay? Bye.'

*Phone disconnected*, the automated voice told him through the speaker and he gave a groan of frustration before tooting a dawdling Volvo in front, out of sheer irritation. Damn it, he was trying, all right? He was doing his best. As for Leni being 'desperate' for a baby, that wasn't the sort of thing daughters talked to their dads about, was it? How was he supposed to know?

Except she might have confided in him, if he'd been there to listen, he reminded himself. If they'd had a decent father-daughter relationship to start with. And now she was gone and it was too late, and he was left feeling like a failure, neither liked nor trusted by any of his kids. Or even his ex-wife, he thought, remembering their strange exchange the other day. Then he felt like kicking himself for not having mentioned it to Alice while he had the chance. Although she'd probably have torn a strip off him for that too: criticised him for eavesdropping, saying it was none of his business who Belinda spoke to or about.

Tony sighed again and thumped the steering wheel miserably, overwhelmed with self-recrimination. He had to do better for the new baby, he told himself. He could do it, couldn't he?

# Chapter Ten

*Alice:* Dad rang me last night – really pissed me off tbh. Going on about sorting through Grandad's things after he died, like that's in any way the same as me sorting through Leni's stuff! So insensitive!!

*Belinda:* That man has absolutely no idea sometimes [angry-face emoji, dagger emoji]

*Belinda:* Also – is it too much for you? Don't feel you have to do everything yourself, darling [heart emoji]

*Alice:* It's fine, Mum. I want to do it, if that doesn't sound weird. Just got fed up with Dad making it about himself as usual. Talk later? Going out with the girls tonight but could ring you afterwards?

*Belinda:* Sounds good. Have fun! Love you [clinking-glasses emoji, heart emoji]

'So how's it working out with your new feline flatmate?' Lou asked, a forkful of chicken jalfrezi halfway to her mouth. 'I bet he's glad to be back in a home again, after the rescue centre.'

Alice pulled a face. 'You'd think so, wouldn't you?' she said drily. Was it too soon to admit that she was already wondering if she'd made a terrible mistake in adopting Hamish? So far he'd repeatedly peed in a corner of the bedroom despite his clean new litter tray, he'd sharpened his claws on the sofa (her only decent bit of furniture) and he'd turned his nose up at the food she set down, the bed she'd bought him, the love she kept trying to offer. It was Saturday evening now, two days since she'd gone to pick him up, and frankly she was relieved to be out with her friends in their favourite Hackney curry house rather than feeling bad about her inability to make Hamish happy. 'It's early days, I guess,' she added with a shrug.

'Yeah,' said Celeste. 'It's going to be a slow-burn, this relationship, I reckon. You're at the awkward stage now – all covert glances and shyness – but give it time, and he'll be venturing over for affection. Dinner. A bit of a cuddle on the sofa. Then, before you know it, he'll be in your bed every night, hogging all the space.' She pulled a face. 'Or is that just me and my love life I'm talking about?'

They laughed, and Alice felt a rush of gratitude that the two of them had insisted on her coming out tonight, with Celeste even driving over to give her a lift when she'd initially made an excuse about being too tired.

It turned out that chat, delicious curry and background sitar music was the holiday from real life she needed. Lou had surprised everyone with a cool new fringe ('Are you sure it's not too short?') and cracked them up with stories about her boyfriend's eccentric family. Meanwhile, Celeste, who worked as the events manager for a wine company, always had juicy anecdotes about badly behaved partygoers. Thank God for friends.

'And what else is happening with you, Alice?' Lou prompted during a conversational lull. 'Have you got any further with your investigations?'

'With Cherry House? Not really,' she replied. She'd had a dream last night that she was lost in a high-hedged maze, calling Leni's name, disoriented and alone. *Where are you?* she kept yelling. *I can't find you!* Her search for answers was proving similarly hopeless. 'I finally got through to the person who runs the bookings for the place, but there's no regular booking for Thursday nights at eight o'clock. Leni had put 8 p.m. in her diary,' she added, seeing their uncomprehending looks. 'And it was a Thursday when – you know.'

'Right,' said Celeste sympathetically, tearing off a piece of naan bread.

'A local junior orchestra book the space from 6.30 to 7.45 on Thursdays, apparently, and then there's a choir that meets at 8.30, but nothing in between. So I think the address must be a red herring, unless this "A" Leni wrote down was, like, a junior saxophonist called Albert or a soprano called Amaryllis, maybe.' She shrugged, disappointed that she didn't have more to report. That she seemed to have hit a brick wall in her investigations. *I can't find you!* she heard herself shout once more in her dream.

Lou and Celeste exchanged a look. 'Must be frustrating,' Lou said after a moment. 'But ...' She hesitated and Alice steeled herself for what might be coming. 'Maybe you could ... let it go? Sorry, I'm not being flippant,' she added hastily. 'I'm really, really not. I know how much you wished you could have been with her in those last few weeks, but ...'

She was floundering, so Celeste stepped in to help. 'But at the end of the day, you were thick as thieves for all of those months and years beforehand, right? So ...'

Alice stared down at her plate as Celeste left her sentence unfinished. They didn't get it. 'It matters to me,' she said quietly, flashing back to the argument they'd had on Leni's birthday, the last time she'd seen her sister alive. It transpired that Leni had read far more into Alice's refusal of a glass of fizz than she should have done, and later, when everyone else had gone home, she had lashed out, drunk and nasty with it.

'I don't think you and Noah should have a kid' was her opening salvo. By then, the sunny May day had sweated into a heavy, oppressive afternoon and Leni was fiddling about opening windows while Alice finished the washing-up.

*'What?'* Alice wasn't sure she'd heard correctly at first. She put the last wine glass in the drying rack and turned, looking around for a tea towel to dry her wet hands.

'You, not drinking earlier. Is that what it's about? *Let's have a baby!* Well, it's a bad idea for you two, that's all. If you ask my opinion.' Leni's chin was up in that defiant way she had, but usually Leni's defiance was aimed at other people, not Alice. It was horrible, Alice thought shakily, to find herself in the firing line. 'He's just another Tony McKenzie, can't you see? A man-child who won't stay with you. Don't saddle yourself with him *and* a kid, whatever you do.'

Alice felt as if she'd been slapped by her sister's presumptions, not least because they were all wrong. 'I wasn't asking

119

your opinion,' she said in reply, wiping her hands on her trousers for want of anything else. Leni was not herself, sure, but Alice had done nothing to deserve this. She thought longingly of the street outside, the walk to the tube station and home. Get me out of here already. 'Right. Well, if that's everything, I—'

'Why aren't you being honest with me? Worried I might cry or something? Tell me the truth!'

'Stop being so paranoid! I'm not hiding anything,' Alice snapped, irritation rising. 'We're not trying for a baby. But even if we *were*, it wouldn't be up to you to grant me approval or police the whole thing, like you seem to think. Because it would be none of your goddamn business.' Sod off, she felt like saying as she walked stiffly over to pick up her bag. Why couldn't Alice and her boyfriend make their own decisions without consulting her? The truth was, yes, they had occasionally talked about babies, but only in that idle, dreamy way that couples did after a while. 'I've got a hangover, that's all,' she added. 'That's why I didn't want a drink today. So you can take your little paranoid theories and shove them.'

That might have been it, a quick stride to the front door and then across the threshold and out, but Leni hadn't finished yet. 'Yeah, whatever, I was only thinking of you,' she called down the hall. 'Because Noah's not good enough for you, Alice.'

'Well, I like him, all right?' Alice was unable to suppress her anger. Just because Leni was the older sister, it didn't give her the right to toss her opinions about like this. Not good enough for you, indeed. What about all the dodgy boyfriends Leni had had before she married Adam? 'I *love* him. We're happy together. Just because you're still moping around, doesn't mean I can't be happy!'

'When are you going to grow up though? What do you know about adult life? Nothing, because you're still acting like a teenager, passively letting stuff happen to you; you've never had the bottle to commit to anything. Lucky you! You get to be the younger sister who keeps screwing up while I'm—'

Alice was out of the house by then and didn't hear any more. What the hell? she raged to herself, all the way to the tube station. What the actual fuck?

*Sorry*, Leni had texted a few days later. *I didn't mean the things I said, I was drunk and horrible. Forgive me?*

But Alice had found it hard to move past the vicious words because she knew Leni *had* meant them at the time, that they clearly contained some knotty truth at their centre. She'd always basked in her sister's approval and love, but now ... now she didn't feel Leni had her back in quite the same way.

*Sure*, she eventually replied, but a coolness had set in by then. They had texted a few more times but hadn't seen one another again. How Alice wished she could have picked up that last phone call. Why, oh why had she listened to Noah when he said, 'Hurry up, babe, we're going to be late. Call her back some other time'?

It had plagued her ever since, wondering what Leni would have said. Was she lonely? Unhappy? In need of a friend? If Alice could have just answered her phone and said, 'I'm sorry too, let's not argue again, come out with us tonight,' Noah might have had a sulk – he had been saying for months that Leni took advantage of Alice's kind heart – but they would all still be alive, wouldn't they? Leni would be alive. Why had Alice been so selfish, so small-minded as to refuse her own sister that small act of charity?

'Most people find it easier to be angry rather than sad,' the policewoman had commented to Alice back in October, driving her home in the police car, after picking her up for 'making a public nuisance of herself' on the street. Despite the woman's stern manner, Alice could detect a certain gruff kindness too – the officer herself had lost her brother two years ago, it turned out, and she understood the pain. What was more, she was right. Sadness was bloody awful. It never went away! At least with anger you could burn off your feelings with an explosive blow-up now and then.

'Sorry,' Lou said now because obviously some of Alice's painful memories were showing on her face. 'I didn't mean – I wasn't saying—'

'I just want to know where she was going that night,' Alice said flatly, and tipped the rest of her beer down her throat. 'It feels important, like finding out might bring me closer to her.'

'We understand,' Celeste said, taking her hand and squeezing it. 'And if there's anything we can do ...'

'Thanks,' Alice said, and then changed the subject, asking Lou about a work conference she'd been dreading. But as her friend launched into the story, she found it impossible to concentrate because her thoughts were sliding back down into the bad place again, remembering the coroner's inquest, how they'd seen the grainy CCTV images of Leni losing control of her bike and then the car ploughing straight into her.

Callum Ferguson, the driver was called: a stocky, grey-haired man in his late fifties, a plumber on his way home from fixing a leaking shower. He'd held a full clean driving licence for almost forty years, without so much as a speeding fine to show for himself. 'She came from out of nowhere,' he said, wringing his hands. 'There was nothing I could do.' He'd been exonerated, with the coroner saying Ferguson had been put in an impossible situation. The announcement of the conclusion had him breaking down in tears, putting big meaty hands up to his eyes, shoulders shaking.

Alice had watched, unmoved. Not good enough, she thought, anger stoking ever hotter in her inner furnace. This changed nothing – he'd still killed Leni with his massive, dangerous car. It was all his fault!

In hindsight, she was not proud of her behaviour over the weeks and months that followed, but it was as if she couldn't stop herself. She tracked down Callum Ferguson to a terraced house in Perivale, then made a point of going round there whenever possible and throwing an egg at the front window. Yes, it was petty. No, it didn't change anything. But God, it was satisfying to throw something hard and see it smash, to cause someone else pain for a change.

One night she turned up as usual though, only for a wiry young man to step out of the shadows and approach her before she could make her move. 'Throw another egg at my parents' house and you'll have me to deal with,' he said, his voice soft with menace.

'Your dad killed my sister,' was all Alice could say in response, trembling with heightened emotion. 'A fucking egg on his house is the last thing he should be worried about.'

He took another step towards her, jabbing a finger. 'Your *sister* has destroyed my *dad*,' he said and she could see it then, the flash of pain across his face, an agony she recognised. 'He's catatonic in there. Signed off work with depression. It's completely ruined his life. So think about that for a minute, will you? It wasn't his fault. The best driver in the world couldn't have done anything differently. *It wasn't his fault.*'

He was yelling at her by then, his face colouring below the yellow glow of the streetlight, and Alice's hand had tightened inadvertently around the egg she was holding ready, feeling it break stickily between her fingers. *He's lying, don't listen,* she told herself shakily, driving away afterwards. *We're the ones suffering, not them!* But his angry words rang in her head for days afterwards.

'Anyone fancy dessert?' Celeste said at that moment and Alice blinked, realising that she had been miles away. Somehow or other she'd finished her plate of food having barely tasted it.

'You all right, Alice?' asked Lou as if reading her mind. 'You went a bit quiet there.'

'I'm fine,' she said, then screwed up her face because she'd always been a terrible liar and she was remembering the egg crumpling within her palm, the slimy liquid dripping on the ground. 'Well – not really,' she admitted in the next breath. 'But ... you know. Hanging on in there.'

She was aiming at jokey but it must have come out sounding downbeat because the two of them looked concerned and Lou promptly grabbed her hand across the table. 'Oh, lovely,' she said. 'It will stop feeling so painful one day.'

124

'We're right with you in the meantime,' said Celeste. 'Good times ahead.'

'And I bet that if Leni has any say in the matter, something really great is just around the corner for you,' Lou added. Alice's phone beeped with a notification a split second later and they all laughed. 'There it is now,' she said.

Smiling faintly, Alice glanced at her phone, only to almost hyperventilate with shock. 'Oh my God,' she said, staring at the screen and reading the message again. A little laugh escaped her throat. 'No way.'

'What? Is this the something great that Leni's sent your way?' Lou asked.

A thrill ricocheted through Alice. *Leni, was that really you?* she thought, half amused, half excited. 'You're never going to believe this,' she said.

# Chapter Eleven

*McKenzies Together group*

*Tuesday*
*How are we all doing? Everyone bearing up? Love Dad/Tony 12.23*

Hurtling through the air, high above the treetops, Will felt a scream rip from his lungs as he plunged down the cable, adrenalin shooting wildly around his body as if he'd had a close encounter with death. Ironically, he couldn't remember when he'd last felt so alive. SMILE – YOU'RE IN PARADISE! read a sign at the end of the zip line, presumably for a photo-sale opportunity, but he didn't need any reminding because he was already smiling like a total idiot. 'Whoaaaa,' he exclaimed, arms and legs turning to jelly as he made it on to the landing jetty where a young Thai man stepped forward to unclip him.

'You like, huh? You scream?'

Will laughed, a little shamefacedly. 'Yes, I like,' he replied, his heart still thumping. 'And yes, I scream.'

He waited at the viewing deck for Isla to descend, her legs bent at the knee, her red hair streaming out from beneath the safety helmet, her shrieks even more piercing than his had been. She and Meg had persuaded him to join them on a safari trip, taking in waterfalls, jungle, golden-roofed Buddhist temples, and this, a fifty-mile-an-hour zip line that had been the biggest thrill he'd had for months. 'Why don't you come with us? You can take a day out of your busy schedule, surely?' Isla had said, tongue-in-cheek, that first evening they'd got chatting in the bar. 'Even Jeff Bezos has a *bit* of downtime now and then.'

He'd demurred at first, wanting to give the impression that he didn't have time for tourist frivolities – and also because he wasn't sure he liked her taking the piss out of him. When pushed though, he'd had to admit that no, he hadn't been on any of the jungle safari tours advertised everywhere to holidaymakers. 'And you've been here, what, six months, did you say? You're a slave to the nine-to-five, you. All those tourists to fleece, eh?'

Meg had been somewhat softer in her approach. 'Say yes, come with us,' she'd coaxed. 'You know what they say about all work and no play ...'

He'd hesitated just long enough for Isla to tease him again. 'Meg, don't badger the lad! Those flip-flops won't sell themselves!' at which point he'd laughingly admitted defeat. Why shouldn't he have a bit of fun? Besides, there was something about Isla that he found very appealing. She was stunning, for one thing, and he liked her fiery spirit – at least, he did now that she was no longer shouting at him. Born and raised in Stirling, she'd trained as a paramedic and was soon to be moving to Aberdeen with a new job. In the meantime, she was taking a month-long break to have some adventures around Thailand. As for Meg, she was a chef en route to Australia, armed with a year's work visa, in the pursuit of new kitchen experiences and fun. After some beach time in Koh Samui and Koh Phangan, they were planning to head up to Chiang Mai to go trekking, explore Bangkok and then – 'Well, whatever takes our fancy, basically,' Isla had shrugged. 'Before Meg heads down under and I fly home again in February, to sicken the rest of Scotland with my incredible tan.'

'How's that going so far?' he'd teased, with a pointed look at her milk-white skin, to which she'd scowled, pretending affront.

Meg was still thinking about their itinerary. 'Any tips you can give us for travel would be great – any cool places you've been to, or stayed in, anything that's a real must-see,' she'd said that evening in the beach bar. By now they'd decided to order cocktails and Will felt obliged to buy a round, wincing at the marked-up tourist prices as he did so. Oh well, he thought. He'd redouble his beach-selling efforts in the morning.

'Um,' he'd said, busying himself by prodding a juicy slice of orange with the end of his straw. 'Well ... yeah, Chiang Mai is a big tourist spot,' he blustered. 'You can go elephant trekking there, and that.'

'You've been, have you?' asked Isla. 'Where did you stay, can you remember?'

'Um ...' The thing was, he hadn't actually been to Chiang Mai. He hadn't, in fact, been anywhere other than Koh Samui since he'd left the UK, but if he admitted this, they might think he was a bit of a loser. People packed so much into their holidays, didn't they – boat trips, snorkelling, trekking, everything ticked off at an exhausting pace ... Will was in no rush. Of course he wanted to go to all of these places – and he would, definitely. He just hadn't got round to it yet. 'I can't remember, sorry,' he replied, then decided to change the subject. 'So you're a chef, that's cool,' he said to Meg. 'Have you got a job arranged in Australia, or are you planning to rock up and see what happens?'

Meg launched into a long story about the gorgeous but snooty hotel she'd been working in in St Andrews, and how strange it was to be out of Scotland this January, and not cooking up Burns Night dinners for pissed hotel guests.

Isla had been quiet throughout this, although Will caught her looking at him quizzically now and then. 'And how about you?' she'd asked.

'What do you mean, how about me?' he replied. 'I'm flip-flop guy, I thought you knew that? I'm Mr Koh Samui beach bum.'

'No, I mean – after this. Other than this. What does British Will get up to? Or does your flip-flop empire stretch all the way around the world?'

British Will ... Right. Was it overly dramatic to say that the words struck an instant sensation of dread into his bloodstream? It was like thinking back to someone you'd met a long time ago, barely able to recall their features any more. 'British Will ...' He broke off and looked down at himself in his sun-bleached singlet, his board shorts, his sandy grey

Converse with the rip on one toe. It was so long since he'd even dressed as his old self, it was hard to imagine his tanned legs clad once more in jeans, a pair of spotless designer trainers on his feet. 'I used to work in engineering,' he said eventually, aware that this might sound boring to them, compared to their more adventurous lives. 'For a construction company near Swindon.' He gave a self-conscious laugh and spread his hands wide. 'Now it all makes sense, right? Who'd want to go back to that?'

They'd laughed in response, as he'd intended them to, but Isla had given him another of her glances, as if trying to figure him out, and he'd quailed a little beneath her gaze, braced for another personal question. It hadn't come and he was relieved at the time, although afterwards he'd wondered if it was a bad sign, that she hadn't wanted to find out anything else. Because there *was* more to him than his job, he felt like saying. He wasn't just a nerd with a calculator and graph paper; he did have a personality, mates, family, actual interests. Well, before he left them all behind, that was. Not the personality, obviously. He hadn't left his personality behind. Had he?

Back at the zip-wire viewing platform, Isla was taking off her helmet and shaking out her hair as she walked towards him now. 'Wow! That's got my heart pumping all right. I feel as if I could do anything.' She grinned at him, rummaging in a pouch attached round her middle for her phone. 'Come on, let's take a photo while we're still sparkly-eyed and euphoric.'

He liked the way she took the lead, he thought, making his way over. He could just imagine her in a crisp, green paramedic's uniform, issuing firm instructions, calmly taking control of a situation. *You can take control of my situation any time, darling*, he might have said back in the UK if he'd met her in a bar. (*Ugh, cringe, Will*, his sisters piped up in his head, pulling faces as if they were about to throw up.) Something told him Isla was the sort of woman who'd wet herself laughing at such a cheesy line anyway, he thought, standing beside her as she reached out a long freckled arm before them and snapped a few photos.

'There,' she said, showing him a picture of the two of them, heads close together, both looking dazzled and – yes, actually pretty euphoric – in front of the dense green jungle, with Meg just visible in the background, skimming down the cable. 'One for the grandchildren. Well – not *our* grandchildren, obviously ...' she laughed, as he gave an involuntary jerk of surprise. 'I just meant ...' Her cheeks had turned rosy pink with a blush; it was the first time she'd seemed wrong-footed since their paths had crossed. Interesting. 'Ach, you know what I meant. Anyway, here's Meg. Meg!'

The moment was over because then Meg was being unclipped and staggering towards them, beaming and hoicking her shorts out of her bum, exclaiming hoarse-voiced how she'd started to think she'd have a wedgie for the rest of her life what with the G-force. Then Isla was replying, 'Ah yes, that well-known medical phenomenon, the G-force wedgie – you wouldn't believe the number of times we paramedics have been called out to deal with this predicament,' and Will laughed alongside them. But he hadn't imagined it, he was sure; that frisson between them, that wordless exchange. That sudden rosy blush on Isla's face as if she maybe liked him too.

He came to his senses soon afterwards as they headed back towards their safari jeep, ready to take their seats for the next leg of the journey. So what if he and Isla liked each other? It wasn't as if anything would happen. She and Meg would be leaving Koh Samui soon for the rest of their adventures, like all the other women he'd met so far. And there had been plenty of other women, let's face it: tipsy and sunburned, in their little sundresses and shorts and bikinis, looking for something to spice up their holiday. He'd been happy to go along with it when they started coming on to him, ending up in their hotel rooms, or on the beach, once even around the back of a bar, the two of them propped against kegs of lager, the air fragrant with the stink of stale alcohol and drains.

None of it had meant anything, for either party. But with Isla ... she was different. Funny. Feisty, in the way that Leni had been, he realised, before he could hold back the thought. Damn it. Too late. Now his sister's face had floated up into his head and he was remembering that last phone call – *Can I ask you a favour, Will?* – and his equilibrium was in danger of shattering to pieces. Don't think about that. Don't think at all, in fact.

He pulled his sunglasses over his eyes even though the jeep windows were tinted, and sighed, wondering if he'd ever be able to travel far enough to rid himself of the shadows that dogged him. If he'd ever stop hearing his sister's last request – and if he'd ever forgive himself for what he had said in reply.

# Chapter Twelve

*Leni McKenzie memorial page*

*Sorry I'm late to this, I've only just heard the news. I imagine Leni's family and friends must be devastated. I knew Leni as a teenager and into my twenties. She was such a fun person to be around. One of my proudest memories was when she anointed my shoulders with a peacock feather and told me I was an honorary Flying Beauty along with her and Alice. Apparently this was a very exclusive club! Leni, I will do my best to keep flying, but the world is definitely a greyer and less beautiful place without your peacock-bright presence.*

  *Jacob*

The post had come in moments after Lou had said that thing in the curry house about Leni sending her something great, and Alice couldn't help but see this as the mother of all signs. Jacob Murray, holy moly: only her sixth-form boyfriend and one-time light of her life for the three happy years they'd spent together, right until he was offered a place to study at

Harvard that he couldn't turn down. The distance between them had proved too much within a few months – she became jealous and insecure, struggling to remember how to study up in York after their gap year travelling together, while he seemed perplexed by her sudden transatlantic neediness. She'd been one for self-sabotage even then and, anticipating that he'd soon move on to some rich, tanned American girl (who ~~wouldn't~~ prefer a Harvard super-brain?), she pre-empted the inevitable heartache by ending it that Christmas, telling herself it was a mercy killing that would save a lot of anguish in the long run. Years had gone by since then; they'd both lived their separate lives – the last she'd heard about him, he was living in Gothenburg with his molecular biologist wife and little boy (how come everyone except her seemed to have got their shit together?) – but she'd always felt a residual fondness towards him, not least because, unlike other boyfriends she'd gone on to have, he'd never done her wrong. And now here he was, popping up unexpectedly, just when she needed something good to happen.

A swift foray into Jacob's social media profile revealed that he was no longer in Sweden but living in London. Alice felt herself seized by the compulsion to see him again. Think of the stories he might have about Leni that she had forgotten! She had met up with a couple of her sister's friends now, in order to pass on clothes or other items they had asked for, and been gifted in return with anecdotes and reminiscences about her sister, new knowledge she hadn't been aware of before this time. She still hadn't got to the bottom of Leni's cryptic diary entries, but there had been the occasional throwaway remark – *We used to go to this Greek restaurant together in Soho* or *We always seemed to end up in this one cocktail bar in Farringdon on the espresso martinis* – and she'd found herself making mental notes. She too would go to that particular Greek restaurant, she decided privately. She too would seek out the cocktail bar in Farringdon. She'd even force herself to drink an espresso martini, despite disliking coffee, because it would make her feel closer to her sister. At Leni's funeral, she'd sat there vowing, *I will live for both of us now*, but she hadn't exactly followed through on her promise. Yet. Maybe this could be a way for her to honour Leni and break out of her usual routines though? By visiting Leni's old haunts, maybe even fulfilling things her sister always wanted to do and never had the chance to?

So far she hadn't mentioned such intentions to any of her friends – they were encouraging her to stop immersing herself in the past and instead look ahead, suggesting new restaurants, Pilates sessions (February's fitness challenge), tickets for a film that was getting great reviews. Jacob might understand though, especially as an honorary Flying Beauties member himself. They could chat about old times together – there were sure to be parties, nights out, stupid obsessions the three of them had shared that Alice had forgotten about. If Jacob could shed any light whatsoever on them, so much the better.

*Hi!* she messaged him on Sunday, unable to fake nonchalance or even try. This was someone who'd held her hair back as she vomited up cider and black at countless teenage parties, after all; someone who'd let her dance on his shoulders to the Flaming Lips at Glastonbury, bellowing along the words to 'Do You Realize??'; someone she'd swum with underwater on the Great Barrier Reef, gleefully pointing out the octopus and colourful fish to one another; the smart, gorgeous boy she'd fallen in love with under the glitterball at the Year 12 Christmas disco. She'd never been cool or nonchalant and he of all people knew that. *Lovely to see your name! Flying Beauties forever etc,* she typed. *And you're in London! Fancy meeting up for a drink and reminiscing?* He didn't reply immediately as she'd hoped, and he still hadn't by the next morning. Her earlier optimism had all but evaporated by the time she arrived at work. She'd probably been too keen, freaked him out. Perhaps his wife had seen the message, got the wrong idea and deleted it without telling him. Maybe he'd only left his original message on the memorial page to be polite and couldn't care less about Alice, still hated her in fact for dumping him on Christmas Eve back in the day.

The maternity cover job she'd taken on largely consisted of administrative duties for the loss adjustment team of a large insurance firm – typing correspondence, processing claims, managing files and looking after the diaries of more important people – and there was always plenty to do, which helped the days speed by at least. Sage and Golding was an old-fashioned, traditional company and although coming in on a temporary basis was exactly what she'd needed, buying herself time while she got her act together, she was already looking forward to working somewhere more creative again. She had the feeling that Sage and Golding traded heavily on their history as one of the oldest insurance providers and seemed to take it for granted that they were safe, snuggled into their strong market position for all eternity. Alice was no expert on the world of insurance, but even she knew there were shiny new companies appearing every year, specifically targeting a younger demographic. It was a mistake for a firm to rely so much on its past performance, surely?

Also, while she was on the subject of dinosaurs, she couldn't help thinking that whoever was running their comms department needed dragging into the twenty-first century. This boring leaflet, that dreary print ad . . . it was as if nobody cared enough to put together a proper campaign strategy. As for their social media, it was abysmal – completely unengaging and clearly very low on the company priorities. God, she missed working at ReImagine, she thought for the millionth time, as she began typing another letter. Why hadn't she merely put up and shut up, done her best to ignore Rupert's poor management decisions and carry on, rather than resign on the spot like a massive drama queen?

'Um . . . Alison, is it?' came a voice just then, interrupting her thoughts. 'Could you take the minutes for our morning meeting, darling? Ruth's off sick.'

Alice looked up to see Stuart, one of the team leaders, at her desk. He was in his fifties, overweight and apparently so uninterested in anyone below management level that he couldn't be bothered to remember their names. 'It's Alice,' she said, grabbing her notebook and pen. 'And Rosalind, for that matter. Yes, I could take the minutes.'

He wasn't listening, however; he was already walking off down the corridor, his back fat rolling beneath his jacket. 'It's room seven,' he called over his shoulder. 'Starting now.'

Alice saved the file of correspondence she'd been working on, tried to suppress the snarl inside her and rolled her eyes at Tina, one of the PAs who sat nearby.

'I love it when he talks dirty to us,' Tina said, pulling a face in response.

Alice snorted a laugh, grateful for the solidarity, and set off for the meeting, hoping it wouldn't take up too much of her time. She wrinkled her nose, hoping too that she wouldn't be sat anywhere near Stuart, whose sour, sweaty smell lingered pungently in his wake. Then her phone beeped and it was a message from Jacob.

*Alice! Great to hear from you, although I'm sorry it's under these circumstances. Would love to reminisce. I'm now working at UCL so anywhere in central London is easy for me. Want to suggest somewhere? Dinner? Pint?*

She stopped in the corridor, the opening guitar chords of 'Do You Realize??' strumming in her head, certain that if she didn't reply to Jacob's message before the meeting, she'd be completely unable to think straight for its entirety, let alone take any minutes for sweaty Stuart and his squad.

*There's a nice Greek restaurant in Soho,* she found herself typing. *Dimitris on Berwick Street? When are you free?*

Then she walked in, only for her smile to vanish abruptly in the next second. Because sitting there at the meeting table, in a smart charcoal suit and gold tie, was the man with close-cropped hair she'd met in the bar after work the week before. Darren, the man she'd taken home and had sex with over her living-room table.

She went hot and cold all over to see him again so

unexpectedly – the perils of drinking in the pub nearest to your office, she realised, stricken – and dropped her pen in a fluster. Taking a seat at the far end of the table, she ducked her head so that her hair swung forward, hoping that he might not recognise her – please God, let him not recognise her. So Darren worked at Sage and Golding too – oh help. Better start praying for the quickest meeting in history, she thought, heart thudding.

# Chapter Thirteen

*McKenzies Together group*

*Saturday*
**Tony**: *Happy weekend, all. What have you got planned? Jackie and I are going to a friend's housewarming tonight and then Sunday lunch with her folks tomorrow. How about you guys? Love Dad/ Tony x 08.45*
**Will:** *Dad, you don't have to sign off at the end of every message – we know it's you [eye-roll emoji]*

*Sunday*
**Alice:** *Hi all, here's a pic of Hamish snoozing. Look at those magnificent whiskers! I think we're starting to get the hang of this cohabiting business x 10.22*
**Tony:** *What a hunk!! Glad for you both. Have a good day, everyone xxx 10.25*

*Monday*
**Tony:** *Morning all. Hope you had good weekends. I was going*

# HE CRASHED ME SO I CRASHED HIM BACK

## Mark Bechtel

The True Story of the Year the King, Jaws, Earnhardt,
and the Rest of NASCAR's Feudin', Fightin' Good Ol' Boys Put
Stock Car Racing on the Map

Little, Brown and Company

NEW YORK   BOSTON   LONDON

For my parents

Little, Brown and Company
Hachette Book Group
237 Park Avenue, New York, NY 10017
www.hachettebookgroup.com

First Edition: February 2010

Little, Brown and Company is a division of Hachette Book Group, Inc. The Little, Brown name and logo are trademarks of Hachette Book Group, Inc.

Library of Congress Cataloging-in-Publication Data
Bechtel, Mark.
    He crashed me so I crashed him back : the true story of the year the King, Jaws, Earnhardt, and the rest of NASCAR's feudin', fightin' good ol' boys put stock car racing on the map /
Mark Bechtel. — 1st ed.
        p. cm.
    Includes bibliographical references and index.
    ISBN 978-0-316-03402-9
    1. NASCAR (Association) — History.    2. Stock car racing — United States — History.
    3. Stock car drivers — United States.    I. Title.
    GV1029.9.S74B44 2010
    796.720973 — dc22                                                        2009031952

10 9 8 7 6 5 4 3 2 1

RRD-IN

Printed in the United States of America

# *Contents*

# CONTENTS

# *Introduction*

NOBODY STOOD out more than the guy in the nice loafers and the suit. In addition to his sharp threads, he was carrying an eel skin briefcase as he slogged through the muddy infield at the half-mile racetrack in Richmond, Virginia. He was from the *New York Daily News*. This wasn't the kind of place he was used to.

The small band of writers who did this every week, who covered NASCAR for a living, were all thinking the same thing: *What is everyone doing here?* There were plenty of other stories out there. Some kid named Bird was finally getting a national audience in the first round of the NCAA basketball tournament. Spring training was under way, and Pete Rose was no longer a Red. Yet the press box at the Richmond Fairgrounds Raceway was overflowing. For a stock car race.

Why?

It all started with a fight.

And it wasn't even a good one.

A few punches were thrown, but mostly it was two men — two exhausted, middle-aged men — grabbing each other. Looking back on it years later, driver Buddy Baker said, "It was more of a slow waltz. If I ever get beat up, I wanna be beat up like that." Indeed, the enduring image of the fracas is of a man in a blue and white jumpsuit grabbing the foot of a man in a white and blue jumpsuit. It looked like Evel Knievel was being mugged by an Evel Knievel impersonator.

Still, it was a fight, and who doesn't love one of those?

Because of the melee, and the last-lap wreck that triggered it, the 1979 Daytona 500 got the kind of national play normally reserved for Super Bowls and All-Star Games, even in cities, such as New York, that were remote outposts in the stock car racing universe. It helped that the people across the country were a captive audience. It snowed everywhere that day. It snowed in Cleveland, Chicago, New York, and Detroit. A lot. It snowed in Atlanta and Charlotte. Not quite as much, but hard enough to put the locals off their game. It even snowed in the Sahara.* So millions of people who normally wouldn't be watching TV on a Sunday afternoon were, save for the heartiest of sledders and snowman builders, confined to their couches. And in those pre-cable days, the choices were slim. ABC showed local programming. NBC had a college basketball game. CBS showed the race live from start to finish, something no one had ever tried before.

Ten million people watched it.

They were mesmerized by what they saw. The speed! The crashes! The fighting! The sideburns! And then at the next race it happened again. Another wreck, same drivers. No fight this time, but plenty of racers who lost cars were talking like they'd be up for one, which was why Richmond was packed. They were anticipating round three.

The writers who didn't feel like cramming into the tiny press box spilled out into the pits, where it wasn't hard to tell the racing beat

---

*For the first time in recorded history. It snowed so hard for half an hour in Algeria that traffic stopped.

regulars from the interlopers. The newbies were the ones who were wearing nice shoes, looked afraid to touch anything, and jumped every time someone revved an engine. The whole scene — the carpetbaggers coming in to gawk at the feudin' good ol' boys — left the locals amused. Bill Millsaps of the *Richmond Times-Dispatch* wrote: "The grist of the mass media, publications like the *Washington Post, Washington Star, New York Daily News* and *Time* magazine are sending staff writers down here to mix with us fried-chicken-eating rednecks to discover what all the cursing is about."

But saying that NASCAR was discovered in the spring of 1979 is like saying that America was discovered in the fall of 1492. Stock car racing and the New World were both around — and, the natives would likely argue, doing just fine — long before the outsiders showed up. But stock car racing was chiefly a southern phenomenon, born on the winding Appalachian roads where bootleggers souped up their family sedans so they could outrun the revenuers. It was the one sport southerners could call their own. Until the 1960s there were no NFL, NBA, or major league baseball teams south of Washington, DC. There was racing in the North, to be sure, but if a driver wanted to see how he measured up against the best, he would have to move down south.

For years sports pages and magazines all but ignored stock car racing. Sure, a few names were universally familiar to casual sports fans. Richard Petty was recognizable to anyone who had ever seen an STP ad. And Cale Yarborough was on the cover of *Sports Illustrated* in 1977. But it's safe to say that Benny Parsons or Buddy Baker could walk down Fifth Avenue without fear of having his shirt torn by a pack of rabid fans. When NASCAR did get some coverage, the tone tended to be patronizing to the serious fan or the story read as if the author had stumbled upon a bizarre religious ritual in some faraway country. (A *People* magazine story reported, "Not so long ago, most of the big name racers on the stock-car circuit were just redneck grease monkeys who liked courting death at high speed.") Even the greatest piece of journalism ever composed about NASCAR—Tom Wolfe's 1965 *Esquire* story "The Last American Hero Is Junior Johnson. Yes!"—loses some of its bite when stripped of the details that were scandalous revelations in the halls of the Hearst Building but were nothing new south of the Mason-Dixon Line, where almost everyone knew someone who ran a 'shine still on the side.

And then the fight happened.

Virtually every list of the greatest or most seminal moments in NASCAR history is topped by the Daytona brawl. "It's astronomical how many tickets they've sold and how much money they've made because of that fight," said Donnie Allison, whose wreck with Cale Yarborough triggered it. Thirty years later, the sport's growth is undeniable. Those 10 million people who watched the 1979 Daytona 500 on TV? That's what the average weekly race draws. The 500 now pulls in 20 million viewers. Races are held everywhere from the rolling wine country of Northern California to the hills of central New Hampshire. The drivers are rock stars. Their fiercely loyal fans sustain an economy that puts the GDP of many developed nations to shame. Souvenir trucks carry shirts, hats, and every imaginable trinket for every driver. Junior Johnson has his own brand of pork rinds. Barbecue aficionados with especially discerning palates can argue over which sauce is best: Tony Stewart's Smoke barbecue sauce or Mario Batali's NASCAR-branded sauce. Harlequin has a line of NASCAR-themed bodice rippers.

Attributing all of that growth to one moment, though, to pin it all on one fight, is a little too simple, a little too neat. Many of the writers who had descended upon the Fairgrounds Raceway in Richmond would be back to covering the NCAA tournament or spring training within the week. The heartland's infatuation with NASCAR would, like the snow that still blanketed much of the country, start to melt away. No, NASCAR's growth was an achingly slow process that, like any extended period of growth in nature, was made possible by a nurturing environment. And in 1979 the world was finally ready for NASCAR.

# INTRODUCTION

There was a Georgian in the White House and southern culture was suddenly intriguing to the Yankees who had forever dissed it. In other words, there were cowboy hats *everywhere*. The post-Watergate distrust of government was giving way to a new, more rally-round-the-flag vibe, one that meshed perfectly with the unabashed patriotism on display at NASCAR races. The sporting landscape was changing as well. Teams and leagues were discovering that they could build around larger-than-life personalities, and NASCAR was discovering that it had a rookie driver who fit the profile. The notion of what could sensibly be broadcast on television was being challenged by the emergence of cable stations.

It all made 1979 the most significant year in the history of stock car racing. When it was over, the sport had taken its first steps on the journey from regional curiosity to national phenomenon.

# HE CRASHED ME SO I CRASHED HIM BACK

## Chapter One

# Something Borrowed, Something Blue

**Sunday, February 4**
**High Point, North Carolina**

The BRIDE looked stunning, wearing an immaculate gown that Irish nuns had spent nine months crocheting. The groom looked like he was auditioning to be a *Welcome Back, Kotter* extra: a gangly teenager with a frizzy perm. If he thought his mustache made him look more grown-up than he was, he couldn't have been more wrong.

Nonetheless, the guests who packed Kepley's Barn—the biggest party venue this side of Greensboro—all seemed to agree that they made quite the handsome couple. She was Pattie Huffman, a school-teacher from High Point. He was Kyle Petty, a recent graduate of the high school just up the road in Randleman. His status as the only son of Richard Petty, stock car racing's reigning king, made their wedding the social event of the season, which explained why all nine hundred seats were filled and there were people standing in the balcony.

The resemblance between the groom and his father, who was standing beside him as his best man, was uncanny. From the back of the barn, the only discernible difference a squinting guest could make out between the two was that one of them — the groom — was holding a top hat. They were both wearing identical long-tailed tuxes and had the same curly hair, the same mustache, and the same tall, angular build — a natural frame for a growing young man like Kyle, but one that made a forty-two-year-old, normally hearty man like Richard appear gaunt. And they were both wearing the same wide, aw-shucks grin. That was something the King hadn't had much reason to do recently.

Richard Petty had been driving a race car since ten days after his twenty-first birthday. His first race at NASCAR's highest level was in Toronto in 1958. He was knocked out by his father, Lee — a three-time NASCAR champion — who put him into the fence on his way to Victory Lane. "Daddy and Cotton Owens were racing for the lead halfway through the race," Richard recalled fifty years later. "They came up to lap me, and Daddy thought I was in the way, so he hit me."

Lee loved his son. He also loved a good payday.

The winner's share that day in Toronto was $575, which Lee Petty and his cronies didn't consider to be too bad for a few hours of work. But Richard was young, and he looked at things differently, more optimistically. Where the old guard saw racing the family sedan as a hobby — albeit one they took very seriously — Richard saw it as something that could one day allow him to make a nice living. But for that to happen, there had to be a demand from fans. For a demand to be created, there had to be awareness. And for that reason he had been talking about driving a race car since about eleven days after his twenty-first birthday.

Talking came naturally to Richard Petty. He was a southern gentleman, blessed with a gift for making people feel at ease, and he peppered his speech with enough "YouknowwhatImean?'s" and "Seehere's" to make his interviews feel as informal as a couple of old friends discussing a hunting dog or a tractor on the front porch. He'd hold court on the pit wall, talking to anyone with a notebook, discussing the track, his car, or them cats he raced against. (Everyone, it seemed, was a "cat.") He was good-looking and bright, and whatever he might lack in book smarts he more than made up for in charm and an ability to think on his feet. In 1978, a racing observer described the difference between Petty and David Pearson, his main rival of the day: "The reason David doesn't say much is that he's worried about his lack of education. He'd be mortified, for instance, if somebody asked him, 'How would you compare your driving as art next to Michelangelo's?' Richard would make a joke out of not knowing it. He'd say, 'Oh, you mean Joe Michelangelo what paints the track billboards?' And that would be that." Petty was so fond of the fourth estate that he joined it: throughout the 1970s he wrote a regular column for *Stock Car Racing* magazine.*

As giving as he was with the press, Petty was even more generous with fans, who almost universally adored him — rare in a sport in which spectators take almost as much delight in booing drivers as they do in cheering for them. (Some adored him so much that they took advantage of a magazine offer to buy one square inch of the Petty compound in Level Cross, North Carolina, for $2.) No one who asked for an autograph came away unsatisfied, unless the person violated his one rule: "I do draw the line at some things, like folks following me into the bathroom or into the shower when I'm changing out of my uniform." Petty was one of the rare individuals — the president of the United States and Santa Claus also come to mind — who was recognizable enough that he'd receive mail even if it didn't have an address, as one young

---

* If the occasional literary reference he dropped was any indication, he knew good and well who Michelangelo was. "A few hundred years ago, some cat got famous in the field of literature with something he called Pepys Diary," he wrote in October 1979. "Seems his name was Sam Pepys and the hour by hour timetable of his days brought home the way folks lived during that time in merry old England." If it broke no other journalistic ground, it was probably the first time anyone had ever referred to Samuel Pepys — or any other Restoration period Englishman, for that matter — as a "cat" in print.

autograph seeker from the West Coast found out when he glued a picture of the King and his car to an envelope in lieu of a name or address and promptly received a picture adorned with the royal signature.

And when Petty gave an autograph, he didn't just scribble his name. No, his signature was an ornate collection of loops and lines that took several seconds to compose, the product of an Oriental handwriting class he had taken at King's Business College in Charlotte. Lee Petty had insisted that Richard go to business school because he knew that he would eventually take control of Petty Enterprises, the race team Lee had started at the family farm in Level Cross in 1949. Petty Enterprises didn't start as a huge operation. Lee drove, and his two preteen sons — Richard and his older brother, Maurice, who'd come to be known as "Chief" — were his crew. But by 1979 it had grown substantially. Chief was still there, building the engines. Richard's cousin Dale Inman was the crew chief. And there were a couple of dozen mechanics, fabricators, and engineers on the payroll.

Spending two decades being everything to everyone — driver, businessman, spokesman, face of his sport — had taken its toll, which is why Richard looked so frail at his son's wedding. Two months earlier, in December, he'd had nearly half of his stomach removed because of ulcers. "He internalizes a lot, so he's always had stomach trouble," says Kyle. Richard's agita was part of the Pettys' daily routine and an occasional source of amusement for Kyle. The family lived a hundred yards from Kyle's grandparents, Lee and Elizabeth. "At night," Kyle recalled years later, "my father would eat supper, and at about eight thirty or nine o'clock he'd say, 'I need some stomach pills. Run over to your grandaddy's house and get some.' They were these little pink pills or these little white pills, like Zantac or something. And I'd say, 'All right. Here's what I'm gonna do. Time me. Let's see how quick I can run over to his house, get a pill, and run back.'"

After the first race of the 1976 season, Richard developed what he called a "bellyache." Doctors told him that he had the beginnings of an ulcer and that he should take it easy and stay away from the race shop. Petty decided that the best way to remove the temptation to work was by checking himself into the hospital. "They put me in the hospital like some folks get put in jail," he said. Unable to bear the tedium, he returned to the track without missing a race. But by the end of 1978, the problem could no longer be ignored. After he returned from a cruise with his wife, Lynda, he had a three-hour procedure to remove scar tissue left by an ulcer. He was supposed to spend two or three days in the hospital, but his recovery turned into an ordeal. Petty spent twelve days in the hospital, suffering nearly constant nausea as his stomach failed to function properly. As the start of the racing season approached, Richard insisted he was fine, and no one in the Petty clan made too much of it. "We're a strange family," says Kyle. "We don't worry about each other. I don't know how to explain that. When anything happens, as long as you're walkin' and talkin', we figure you're all right. You may be slower, you may not be moving as fast, you may not be exactly 100 percent, but you're all right and that's the main thing."

The guys in the shop — who had seen Richard survive some truly horrific crashes, including one that sent him over the wall at Daytona and into the parking lot — were the same way. "It's like the old Monty Python movie where the guy's cut into pieces and just the head is still talking," says Steve Hmiel, who was a mechanic on the team. "Richard could do that. We all thought so much of Richard — they can do whatever they want to him, he's still going to be the King."

To an outsider raised in a less macho world, it was easy to see how serious the situation at the Petty household really was. And it was made even more serious when Lynda had to have an operation of her own. Things were so dicey that Kyle's fiancée moved in to help take care of his younger sisters, Lisa and Rebecca.

Petty's doctors advised him not to race in the first event of the 1979 season, at the road course in Riverside, California, on January 14. "Richard thinks he's Superman," one of his doctors told a Florida newspaper. "And he has been a remarkable patient. But he's putting himself under great stress. That was a serious operation, and it's asking too much of the body to come back this quick." Petty predictably ignored those orders, but the team arranged for Oregon driver Hershel McGriff to be on hand and relieve Petty at some point during the 312-mile race just in case. It wasn't necessary: Petty's engine blew up after just fourteen laps. He finished thirty-second, a terrible result—but the kind that was becoming all too familiar. NASCAR's King hadn't won a race since the middle of 1977.

In his first eighteen and a half seasons—from that day in Toronto when his own father wrecked him through that last win in the summer of '77—Richard Petty won 185 races, more than twice as many as any other driver except David Pearson (who had won 103). Whether that made him the best driver in the sport is a question that is still debated. It was no secret that Petty Enterprises turned out the best cars, and Petty had the wherewithal to run every race in an era when most drivers picked and chose a limited number of events. He won everywhere, from the most hallowed tracks (he had won the Daytona 500 five times) to the most rinky-dink bullrings (his 1962 win in Huntsville, Alabama, featured only sixteen cars and was over in fifty-four minutes). His six championships were twice as many as Pearson's, although Pearson ran a full season only five times in his career.

For years Petty's stiffest competition came from two teams: Wood Brothers, a Virginia outfit whose driver through most of the 1970s was Pearson, and Junior Johnson, the old moonshine hauler whose driver, Cale Yarborough, won the NASCAR Grand National* title in 1976, '77, and '78. Like Petty Enterprises, the Woods and Johnson ran down-home operations—the Wood boys up in the Blue Ridge Mountains and

---

*At the time, the highest level of NASCAR racing, what's now known as the Sprint Cup, was called the Grand National Series. The rung beneath it on the NASCAR ladder, what's now known as the Nationwide Series, was called the Sportsman division.

Johnson from his farm in Yadkin County, about seventy miles north of Charlotte. But in the mid-1970s the sport began to see a new kind of team, backed by outsiders with deep pockets—most notably DiGard, an outfit fronted by Bill Gardner, a Connecticut real estate maven. His driver was the brash young Darrell Waltrip, who was hated by many drivers and most fans for being unbearably cocky and having fancy hair that never seemed to get messed up. During Petty's winless 1978 season, Yarborough, Pearson, and Waltrip combined to win twenty of the thirty races, and Bobby Allison took another five.

But Petty's problems ran deeper than increasingly stout competition. For years Petty had been racing Dodges, but after going twelve months without winning a race, he switched to Chevrolets in the middle of the 1978 season. It was a big deal. Even though the invention of those stickers of Calvin from *Calvin and Hobbes* pissing on a Ford or Chevy logo was still years away, stock car fans were still intensely loyal to their brands. Their opinions of the products coming out of Detroit were strongly shaped by how the cars performed on the track. "Win on Sunday; sell on Monday" had been the factories' mantra for years. So when someone of Petty's stature began entertaining notions of switching models, as he first did in 1977, it raised eyebrows. *Auto Racing Digest* devoted its September 1977 cover to the question "Should Richard Petty Have Switched to Chevy?" When he made the move, *Stock Car Racing* gave the story five pages. And in early 1980 STP released a sixty-four-page comic book, with art by *Batman* creator Bob Kane, that devoted an entire page to the switch. In one frame a sober-looking man in a fedora is reading a newspaper with the banner headline PETTY SWITCHES CARS. His son, with a tear in his eye, says, "*Sob*. Is it true, Daddy?" "I'm afraid so, son!" comes the grave reply.

Switching cars, let alone makes, was uncommon at a time when drivers stuck with rides as long as they could—partly because there was no need to fix something that wasn't broken, and partly because new cars were expensive. Waltrip won the Riverside season opener in a two-year-old Chevy he called Wanda; her stablemate was a four-year-old named Bertha. When Petty abandoned his Dodges, it meant starting from scratch with Chevrolets. Nowadays, the size and shape of virtually every part of a car is dictated by NASCAR. Thirty years ago, there were only a few templates, so while the cars were supposed to resemble actual street models, a clever crew chief could manipulate the body in scores of different ways to make it sleeker—and faster. Petty's team knew none of those tricks, at least not for a Chevy.

After the fiasco in Riverside, Petty had a month to prepare for the next race: the Daytona 500, easily the biggest event on the thirty-one-race schedule. He decided to build a Chevy Caprice and took the car to the two-and-a-half-mile superspeedway shortly after New Year's to test it. "We came down and ran like a box of rocks," says Kyle. Petty decided to scrap the Caprice and run an Oldsmobile, which was the preferred ride for the rest of the drivers in the General Motors stable. The problem was, everyone loved their Oldses so much that no one would sell Petty a body, so over the next couple of weeks Kyle, Steve Hmiel, and another mechanic, Richie Barsz, built an Oldsmobile from scratch, working fourteen-hour days all month.

The uncertainty that hung over the team also caught the attention of Petty's chief sponsor, STP. The oil and gas treatment company had come on board in 1972 and immediately became NASCAR's most high-profile sponsor. Until that time, all of the Pettys' cars had been a shade of robin-egg blue that became so iconic that it was patented as Petty Blue.* When STP first expressed an interest in sponsoring Petty, the major sticking point had been what color to paint the car—Petty Blue or STP red. "I don't give a damn what color Petty likes," said STP

---

* Richard and Maurice stumbled upon the color in 1959. They were repainting a car but didn't have enough white or blue paint to handle the entire job, so they dumped the two partial cans into one tub. Lee raved about the final robin-egg blue product, but his sons hadn't written down the formula they used, so they had to go back and tinker with the ratio until they found the right mix.

president Andy Granatelli, a short, round, pushy Chicagoan who was used to getting his way.* "I happen to like red." Negotiations lasted two days; at one point, crayons were broken out. "I offered him $50,000 finally to paint it all red," Granatelli said, "and, by God, he wouldn't." Petty finally left to go to the track for the first race of the season, leaving Chief at STP headquarters in Chicago to bicker about swatches. He and Granatelli came to a compromise: blue on top, red on the sides. It quickly became auto racing's most recognizable paint scheme.

As these were the days before extensive TV coverage, the only guaranteed exposure for a sponsor came in Victory Lane. And as Richard Petty seemed to have forgotten how to get there, STP cut back its financial commitment; instead of a large logo on the hood, there would be only a small one on the rear quarter panels. The car was almost entirely blue, a fact that wasn't lost on the crew members, who had a large chunk of their salaries paid, at least indirectly, by money from STP. Says Hmiel, "I don't think people realized how close we were to not having the funding we needed."

Even Petty's wife couldn't ignore what was happening. Lynda opened an antique store. "With Richard on a losing streak," she said, "I figured somebody should start making some money."

If all of that—the surgery, the losing streak, the loss of sponsorship money, the sight of his wife selling tchotchkes—wasn't enough to tie what was left of Richard Petty's stomach in knots, he had one other thing to deal with: his son was getting into the family business.

In one of his *Stock Car Racing* columns, Petty wrote that as he was sorting through his mail, "I could hardly believe the percentage of

---

*When Petty won the 1973 Daytona 500, Granatelli barged into Victory Lane with a guest, Jordan's King Hussein, in tow ("How'd ya like it, King?" Granatelli asked him), then proceeded to pour champagne on himself and grab the microphone from Petty so that he could deliver his own remarks.

questions from young fellas, plus an increasing number of gals. They wanted me to tell 'em how to break into the racing business. In response to all of them, one more time around, my best answer is a simple negative: 'Don't.' I can't think of a tougher road to set out on." Richard had always wanted Kyle to go to college. Lynda had a more specific vision for her son: she wanted him to be a pharmacist. "She just thought that when she was growing up, the pharmacy in Randleman was the coolest place in the world," says Kyle.

Ken Squier, who had been calling races on the radio since the early 1970s, remembers playing basketball one night at the Petty house when Kyle was eleven or twelve. After Kyle went inside, Squier asked Richard, "So, is he gonna be a racer?"

Petty said, "You know, when I grew up, my dad wouldn't let me have a car until I was twenty-one. Then I could make my decision as to what I wanted to do. That's all I've ever done was cars. You know, Kyle has got so many things he can do. He can go to college, he loves music, so I don't know if he's gonna race or not." Then he paused and added, "You know, once you make up your mind in life what you want to do, you got your whole life to do it, so there ain't no sense in hurrying."

So, just as his father had done with him, Richard did his best to keep Kyle out of the driver's seat. The only time Kyle drove a race car as a kid was when he was fourteen. Richard and Kyle were in Georgia, selling Chrysler Kit Cars—basically, a Petty Enterprises race car in a box. Richard let Kyle take a finished car out onto a half-mile track, with strict orders to keep it in low gear and with the understanding that if he wrecked it, it would be the last race car he ever crashed.

Kyle had plenty of things to keep him busy. He played guitar—and he did it very well. ("He borrowed one from somebody and spent two afternoons alone in his bedroom," his grandfather Lee boasted. "The third day he was playing the thing well enough to make you want to tap your foot.") He looked after horses on the family farm. When he got to Randleman High, he lettered in golf, basketball, and football. He was a good enough quarterback to attract the attention of a few colleges: Georgia Tech, East Carolina, and some smaller schools near home. But Kyle just didn't see the use in going to school, not when he knew that he was going to end up doing what his father and grandfather had done. He'd always hung around the race shop, at first sweeping the floor or helping clean up, and as he got older he became friendly with some of the younger crew members, including Hmiel, a twenty-five-year-old sharp-tongued Yankee from upstate New York, and Barsz, who was thirty-six but didn't always act it.

Barsz was a Chicagoan who went to work for Holman Moody, the Charlotte-based outfit that built the cars for the Ford factory teams, shortly after he got out of the army in 1964. Freed from the rigors of service life, Barsz embraced his inner hippie, which made him stand out at the track. By the time he latched on with the Pettys in 1970, he says, "I had hair longer than Jesus Christ, and I protested everything."* He used nylon rope as a makeshift headband, and when it frayed, it made his hair look twice as long. The only way NASCAR officials would let him into the garage was if Richard came out to the gate and personally walked him in.†

At first Hmiel and Barsz would help Kyle work on his minibike. "We weren't supposed to do that because we weren't supposed to fool around with any of the stuff in the machine shop, so we'd do it at lunchtime when nobody was looking," says Barsz. They were then told to teach Kyle to be a mechanic by having him build kit cars. Kyle was a typical teen—"pretty wild in the street," says Barsz—and he had a tendency to wander off in search of something more exciting than welding. Barsz joked that they should weld a piece of pipe

---

* The long hair could occasionally be problematic. "You roll over it with a creeper, and it'll make you tear up," remembers Barsz.
† For a straitlaced organization, the Pettys employed a fair number of counterculture types. In the early '70s, they painted peace signs on the headrests in their race cars. No one seemed to mind the long hair or the Fu Manchu—Richard even grew one—except Lynda, who, according to Barsz, "got mad because we hated Jesus."

around his ankle and attach a cylinder head on a chain to it. "That way," says Barsz, "when Kyle would run off, you could at least see his tracks." But eventually he became pretty handy with a wrench. He fixed up a '69 Dodge Charger and sold it to a guy, who then proceeded to lead half a dozen state troopers on a chase at 140 miles per hour. "They couldn't catch him," Kyle beamed as he recounted the story. By the time he was in high school, he'd become such a valuable member of his father's crew that a team member would be charged with the task of hanging around Friday night and waiting for Kyle's football game to end, then driving with him to whatever track his father was racing at.

In the summer of '78, right around the time he graduated from high school, Kyle did an interview with Squier in which he declared his intention to drive. It aired when the family was in Daytona for the Fourth of July Firecracker 400. Richard saw it on TV at the hotel and was more than a little surprised. He found his son at a Coke machine out by the pool. The King took Kyle to an umbrella-covered table and sat him down. He pulled out a pouch of Red Man.

"Want a chew?"

"You know I don't chew."

"Well, I thought maybe you'd changed your mind about that, too."

Over the course of their talk, during which Richard smoked a cigar on top of his chew, Kyle explained that he didn't want to take a football scholarship away from another kid when racing was what he really wanted to do. Swayed by his son's argument, Richard tapped his ashes into his spit cup, got up, and said, "Oh, boy."

"It's not that bad, is it, Daddy? I mean, being a race car driver?"

"It's not the drivin' part. I gotta go tell your mother. That's the hard part."

Later in the year, after Lynda had reluctantly been sold on the idea, the King came up with a plan for Kyle. He gave him one of the old Dodge Magnums he had ditched, the one he had driven to a fourth-place finish at the Firecracker 400 in Daytona, and made Hmiel Kyle's crew chief. Newspapermen would have a field day writing that Kyle had been born with a "silver steering wheel to grasp," which stood out in a sport in which most competitors wore their past hardships like an oil- and sweat-stained badge. *(You had to steal an engine for your first car? Hell, my first car didn't even have an engine. That's how poor I was!)* But Richard made it clear that there would be no handouts; Kyle was going to have to make a go of it on his own. Everyone's first priority — including Kyle's — would still be the King's car.

That meant any work done on Kyle's car was OT. But that wasn't a problem. "It seems like everybody has a story about how hard it was coming up," says Hmiel. "Then Kyle comes along, and he's the one kid who does have everything given to him. But nobody resented him. He was just a cool kid, a really cool guy. He was real self-deprecating, too. It was a perfect opportunity for him to be a spoiled brat, and he didn't act like one. We all wanted to help him. It wasn't, *Oh my God, the boss's kid wants to start driving a race car. Ugh. More work for us.* It was, *Man, let's stay late tonight and get Kyle's car going.*"

Kyle's first race would be a 200-miler in the ARCA Series — a series for late-model cars that was similar to the Grand National circuit, but with a lot less prestige and a lot less prize money. It was a curious choice for a debut. The race was in Daytona a week before the 500. Daytona is radically different from most other tracks — two and a half miles with incredibly steep banking, which meant that you could just about run an entire race without taking the gas off the floor. It's not the kind of place where a novice can ease his way into things. "Here's the way I'm looking at it," Richard explained. "If a man's got twenty years of experience on short tracks, makes no difference. When he gets to Daytona, he's a rookie. He's got to learn about running 180 to190 miles per hour. He's got to learn about drafting. He's got to learn about crosswinds. What he has learned on a half-mile dirt or a quarter-mile asphalt [track] is good for nothing. And the future of Grand National racing is the superspeedways. That's where the money is. That's where the television's going to be. That's where the sponsors want to be. And that's where you want to be."

The first time Kyle got behind the wheel on a track — for real, not some low-speed excursion around a short track in Atlanta — was at a test session in Daytona on January 24. Goodyear had already booked the track for a motorcycle tire test that day, so Kyle could use the track only when Motorcycle Hall of Fame rider Kenny Roberts was between runs.

Before he took his car out, Kyle rode around the track in a van with his father, who drove and pointed out the preferred line and the tricky parts — most notably the fourth turn, which, because of the D shape of the tri-oval track, wasn't as sharp as the others. The finish line was just past it, and more than one race at Daytona had been decided by a driver making a bold move, or a stupid mistake, coming off of Turn 4. After the tour was over, Richard took Kyle's car out for a few laps to make sure it was running okay. Then he turned it over to the kid and went to watch with Hmiel from on top of a truck.

Kyle turned a few cautious laps at 155 miles per hour, then pulled into the pits. Feeling a little more confident, he went back out and hit 165. Then, feeling a lot more confident, he dropped the hammer. Richard looked at his stopwatch: Kyle had run a lap at 179 miles per hour. He hightailed it off the truck, yelling, "Get that kid off the racetrack! He's running too fast for his experience!"

The next afternoon, with one day of experience under his belt, Kyle ran ten consistent laps between 185 and 186 miles per hour. His top speed for the day was 187 — faster than his dad had ever driven the same Dodge at Daytona. (In the King's defense, the track had been repaved over the winter, which made it a little faster.) Then Richard took his Oldsmobile out so the two could run a few laps together and Kyle could see what it was like to drive in traffic. "I noticed he didn't get too close behind me," Richard said later.

It was a hell of a crash course — sticking a newbie behind the wheel of a ridiculously fast car on a track where nine drivers had been killed in the twenty years since it had opened. "It's more bizarre to me thirty years later than it was at the time," recalls Kyle. "At the time I just assumed it was normal. Looking back on it, I'm thinking, *My God, that was wrong*." Coming through things unscathed would have been impressive enough, but his times had everyone excited. Just about everyone. "I had to break the news gently to Lynda," Richard told a writer. "I told her by phone that Kyle had run 154. She said that wasn't too bad, not too fast. Then I told her he had run 160...and 179...and 184...and 187. She had a fit and reminded me that I'd promised not to allow him off the apron of the track."

Lest his son think that a couple of hot laps in a test session made him a big-time driver, Richard had Kyle tow the Dodge back to Level Cross by himself, a menial task that ate up most of Thursday night. When he got up Friday morning, his hometown paper, the *High Point Enterprise,* had a story about his test session under the headline KYLE's RUNS AT DAYTONA AMAZING. He couldn't help but be optimistic about his first race. But before he hit the track again, he had another big event to prepare for.

Even by high school BMOC standards, Kyle Petty had done pretty well for himself. Before his new bride became a teacher, she had been a model. They had met two years earlier, when he was sixteen. She was eight years older.

The wedding was a lovely ceremony. The service was performed by Colonel Doug Carty. The music, which included "The Wedding Song," the Lord's Prayer, and the Everly Brothers' "Devoted to You," was performed by the colonel's wife, Mausty.* The seven bridesmaids wore calico dresses and wide-brimmed hats, looking as if they were, in the words of the bride, "dressed like Holly Hobbie dolls."

At the reception, the guests ate barbecue and danced to music provided by some of Kyle's high school friends. When it was time for the bride and groom to run the rice gauntlet, they made their way into an almost–Petty Blue Rolls-Royce Silver Shadow II limousine — worth sixty-six grand and on loan from a local dealer — with a bouquet across its hood. They were driven to the airport, where they flew to Florida for their honeymoon. Their destination wasn't uncommon for young North Carolina newlyweds, but their itinerary was. Instead of lounging on the sand, they'd spend most of their time at the track, where the young groom would do what his grandfather and father had done before him: make a name for himself on stock car racing's biggest stage.

---

* The Cartys would have a son, Austin, who'd grow up to be a contestant on *Survivor: Panama,* bringing him a level of notoriety rarely seen by non-racing High Pointers.

## Chapter Two

# Birthplace of Speed

**Sunday, February 4**
**Daytona Beach, Florida**

As THE Petty nuptials were wrapping up, another star-studded event of interest to the racing community was drawing to a close, this one five hundred miles to the south: the 24 Hours of Daytona. The endurance challenge kicked off Speedweeks, a fortnight of racing at Daytona International Speedway that would culminate with the 500 on February 18. The participants were driving sports cars — Porsches, Ferraris, Corvettes, and the like — and they generally weren't as recognizable, in the States at least, as the NASCAR boys who would pull into Daytona later in the week or the drivers who competed in the Indianapolis 500. But in 1979, for the third year in a row, the field included one driver everyone knew: Paul Newman.*

---

*Newman's presence as a driver for a Porsche team with Dick Barbour and Brian Redman was big news, overshadowing the race itself. The front page of Saturday's

Newman had been bitten by the racing bug when working on the 1969 movie *Winning,* in which he played a hotshot who wins both the Indy 500 and Joanne Woodward. He started racing sports cars in 1972, and by the mid-'70s he was good enough to be taken seriously at major competitions. So it was only natural that he'd eventually wind up in Daytona Beach.

In Daytona Beach driving fast is about the most natural thing a person can do. It's almost as if God created the town specifically for that purpose. The sand on central Florida's Atlantic coast comes from the shell of the coquina clam, unique to the area, and the fine, round grains naturally pack themselves into a surface that is as hard as asphalt. The city was incorporated in 1876, and it—along with Ormond Beach, its neighbor to the south—quickly became a choice destination for wintering northerners, thanks in large part to the lavish Ormond Hotel. After its expansion in 1890, the hotel was the largest wooden structure in the United States. It featured eleven miles of corridors, four hundred bedrooms, and a dining room that seated three hundred. It sat on eighty acres covered with palm trees (owner Henry Flagler removed the indigenous pines, as they were not exotic enough), and the grounds stretched from the Halifax River all the way to the Atlantic. If guests tired of the hotel's orchestra, seawater swimming pool, archery contests, dog shows, and silent movies, they could enjoy the beach, riding their bikes up and down the sand without leaving a hint of a tire mark, or taking a ride in a carriage and trying to talk over the clatter of the horses' hooves, which was so loud it sounded as if they were trotting on bricks.

---

*Daytona Beach Morning Journal* carried a story with the headline EVERYONE KNOWS PAUL NEWMAN'S HERE BUT 24 HOURS OF DAYTONA — WHAT? Most of the local mallgoers quoted in the *Journal* story were unclear on the specifics. "I know this one is at night," one helpfully pointed out. The piece ran above a picture of a bubbly Kyle and Pattie Petty and a story noting that former Sex Pistols bassist Sid Vicious had died of a heroin overdose after likely killing his new bride.

The ultimate mode of beach transportation, though, was the automobile. At the turn of the century, finding a decent place to drive one's car was a chore. Asphalt had yet to be perfected, and with dirt roads one never knew what one was getting. Daytona's beach, however, was perfectly smooth and required neither construction nor upkeep. One paper wrote, "Surely it must have been made for the automobile for regardless of weather conditions, there is no dust, no mud, tires are never heated owing to the moisture and an exploded tire is unknown. Here, too, the great dangers of road racing are eliminated, and man can never build a road so hard and smooth. Repairs are unnecessary, as twice every twenty-four hours it is entirely rebuilt by the tides."

Driving at the turn of the century, before Henry Ford began producing cars the average person could afford, was a pastime of the rich. The hoi polloi were often confounded by the horseless carriage. One newspaper account noted that a car owner in Daytona "had many queer experiences with the native crackers, who at the time were very much opposed to these 'new-fangled machines.'" The "crackers," however, warmed to them when they realized just how it cool it was to watch them roar up and down the beach.

Racing was already in vogue overseas, and like so many continental fads, it was quickly adopted by well-to-do Americans. "Automobilism is the enthusiasm of the day throughout Europe," the *Times-Democrat* of Lima, Ohio, noted in 1901. "All the world loves a race and is ready to apotheosize the winner of it." The first apotheosizing in Daytona took place in March 1903, in a hastily arranged event thrown together after the owners of the Ormond Hotel agreed to foot the bill, figuring it would help drum up winter business.\* The three-day event featured a handful of races involving cars and motorcycles, mostly against

---

\* There's an oft-told story about a 1902 race between auto barons Ransom Olds and Alexander Winton, in which they finished side by side at 57 miles per hour and, being perfect gentlemen, called it a tie. If it sounds too good to be true, that's because it probably is. No account of the race exists in either newspapers of the day or in Olds's biography.

the clock.* Media coverage of the carnival was spotty. AUTOS FLEW AT DAYTONA was the headline of the *Atlanta Constitution*'s story, which, at about one inch, was significantly shorter than the item next to it detailing the stomach contents of a recently deceased insane asylum patient.†

On the Florida coast, though, the races were an unquestioned hit. Locals with cars would drive them onto the beach and park facing the ocean, watching as the racers rolled by. Some arrived in chauffeured tricycles with one wheel in the back and two in the front, the space between being wide enough to hold a spectator. Others walked. No matter how they got there, they contributed to the festive atmosphere, forging a bond that is as strong as ever today: the union of racing and partying. The crowd was certainly not as rough as those you'll see in the infield of a race today, as many of the attendees were well-bred guests of the hotel, with names — Astor, Vanderbilt, Ford — that brought to mind brandy, cigars, and staterooms. In other words, no one was shouting "Remove your corset" or "Show us thy bosom, my good lady." But they had a good time nonetheless.

When the second Winter Speed Carnival was held, in 1904, it was a bona fide social event. The Atlanta paper noted in its Savannah Society News section that a "Mr. and Mrs. E. E. Theus left last week for Daytona to attend the automobile races." The *New York Times* reported that in Palm Beach "after the Ormond races, large dinners will be given at which New Yorkers will be prominent. Many of the automobilists will come down from the races, and they will add speed to the Palm Beach pace, making the first week of February very lively." But the races really arrived in 1905, when the *Atlanta Constitution* sent Isma Dooly, the South's foremost society editor, to write a column

---

* Alexander Winton, an automobile manufacturer from Cleveland, came the closest to breaking the most esteemed record, the one-mile timed run. At 52⅕ seconds, he was three-fifths of a second too slow.

† Included in the six pounds of junk doctors pulled out: a four-inch metal spike, twenty-seven buttons, and more than three hundred nails.

unimaginatively titled "International Automobile Races As Viewed By A Woman." In addition to marveling at the foliage and the blue sky that "subdues one into an eloquent silence and creates a longing for the talent of the painter and the expression of the poet," Ms. Dooly described the well-to-do being ferried from their yachts onto the beach and up to the clubhouse, "the social rendezvous of automobilists and an excellent point from which to view the racing machines pass on the broad expanse of white beach one after another."

Dooly also witnessed firsthand a less seemly side of racing. Frank Croker, the son of a Tammany Hall politician, crashed into the ocean when he swerved to avoid a bicyclist. His car flipped into the surf, and he and his mechanic were killed, becoming the first—but certainly not last—men to die while in search of speed in Daytona. Dooly wrote:

*Not even the tragic death of young Frank Croker more than momentarily subdued the enthusiastic interest of the hundreds of people assembled more than ten days ago at the Daytona-Ormond track for the automobile races that were held there the past week. There were expressions of sadness on all sides, that the calamity had occurred, but almost at the moment the sympathy was expressed there were cries of "Here he comes," and groups of people stood aghast as automobile drivers of world-wide fame came dashing along the beach, recklessly unmindful of the awful warning given them in the death of their comrade but a few hours before.*

In subsequent years, interest in beach racing slowly began to wane. The millionaires whose deep pockets made the beach races possible had a new toy to play with: the airplane. As the number of participants declined, the event became less of a moneymaker for Daytona Beach and Ormond Beach, and the cities gradually withdrew their support. Bureaucratic haggling over who had the right to sanction the races also hastened the demise of the Winter Speed Carnival, but the coup de grâce came in 1911, when the Indianapolis Motor Speedway opened its doors, bringing about the dawn of a new kind of racing in the United States.

Daytona's first golden age was over. It would take only one man to bring about a second.

By the late 1920s, keeping up with the technology necessary to even approach the land speed record made racing even more of a rich man's game than it had been two decades earlier. And Malcolm Campbell was a rich man. All you really need to know about Campbell is that his grandfather founded a diamond business and his estate in Surrey had its own nine-hole golf course. Schooled in France and Germany, the exceedingly well-bred Campbell cut a dashing figure. He was ruggedly handsome and, like Paul Newman, possessed what the morning editor of the London *Daily Herald* called "those piercing blue eyes, characteristic of lovers of speed." He was extremely fit; when he came to Daytona for the first time in 1928 as a forty-three-year-old, he could have easily passed for thirty. He had a hint of a Scottish burr, and his genial nature—one profile asserted that he knew "as many Scotch jokes as [Scottish entertainer] Harry Lauder, and can tell them delightfully"—made it hard not to love him.

When he was a kid, Campbell had been stopped by a bobby for riding a bicycle down a hill at 27 miles per hour, "to the confusion and terror of two elderly ladies." He was hauled in front of a magistrate, who gave him a 30-shilling fine and the following admonishment: "Malcolm Campbell, you have endangered life and property on the public highway. You drove this machine of yours at a totally unnecessary speed. If you come before us again, we will take a much more serious view of the matter. We hope this will be a lesson to you not to travel so fast in the future."

But Campbell was a recidivist—a serial speeder. He dabbled in racing while he worked as an insurance underwriter. His early career was interrupted by World War I, during which he served in the Royal Automobile Club, but after the armistice his day job became a thing of the past. Campbell set the land speed record at Pendine Sands in Wales in 1924 and again in 1927 in his car *Bluebird,* which was the name he gave to all his vehicles.* The mark lasted only a month before Sir Henry Segrave broke it at Daytona, which prompted Campbell to make his next attempt in Florida. He and his fellow Briton swapped the record until Segrave retired in 1929 to focus on the water speed record. At that point, with his only human competition gone, Campbell's opponent became a number: 300 miles per hour.

Campbell was often asked why he did what he did. On one occasion, he insisted that he was trying to make the world a better place, one blazing run at a time. He said that he raced "to explore every means likely to help scientists, metallurgists and engineers to make rapid transport cheaper and safer; to uphold national prestige and to provide scientists with data which might help in spheres quite apart from motoring."† Another time, he said, "If I break my neck then I'm unlucky. It's just a great adventure." Such derring-do made Campbell the most popular sportsman in England and a bona fide celebrity on both sides of the Atlantic. His every move was documented by the press, which would make for some racy reading when he and his wife divorced in 1940. Sir Malcolm accused Lady Campbell of having several affairs, and she, according to the *New York Daily News,* "charged that she had heard him invite their [grown] son Donald to go along on a tour of the more gilded bagnios. She added that Sir Malcolm had boasted how he had seduced the waitress who had served lunch to his son at a Mayfair bunshop."‡

---

* They were named after Maurice Maeterlinck's play *The Blue Bird,* which is about a boy and a girl seeking the bluebird of happiness.

† Actually, airplane mechanics worked on the car, and the technology they perfected on the beach was used in planes during the Battle of Britain.

‡ "Bagnio" is a fancy word for a brothel. Although it sounds like a euphemism for a house of ill repute, "Mayfair bunshop" literally means a shop in the town of Mayfair where buns were sold. And the next time someone tells you that people's unhealthy obsession with the private lives of famous people is a new phenomenon, remember that this story was on the front page of a New York newspaper in 1940.

Like any good immensely loaded daredevil, Campbell indulged in some seriously cool hobbies. In fact, he was something of a real-life Indiana Jones. In December 1931, nine months after he upped the land speed record to 245.73 miles per hour, Campbell went treasure hunting on Cocos, an island four hundred miles off the coast of Colombia. Club Med it was not: a month earlier three shipwrecked Americans had been rescued there after what one paper called "six months of Crusoe-like existence." Undaunted—and with the full backing of the Colombian government, which provided locals to serve as guides—Campbell went to Cocos in search of what he called "the richest and most authentic pirate treasures in the world," booty he estimated at being worth £12 million (somewhere around $1.3 billion today). Campbell said that he had received a clue from someone associated with an old Spanish pirate that was supposed to lead to a large rock that hid the entrance of the treasure cave. Alas, he and his men couldn't contend with the scorching heat, the steep hills, the prickly underbrush, and the "millions of beastly little insects" that "stung and irritated like the deuce." Campbell came home empty-handed. Three years later, while searching for Captain Kidd's treasure in Southwestern Africa, Campbell's plane crashed, leaving him stranded alone for forty hours in an area that was home to many leopards. When one happened upon him while he slept, Sir Malcolm scared it away with his flashlight.

But that was nothing compared to what happened to him following a plane crash in the Sahara in 1930. There he was held captive for several days by the indigenous Riffs in the hills of northern Morocco. Campbell hadn't been in search of treasure. Rather, he had taken his plane up over the desert so that he could scout for a better place to race *Bluebird*. He was getting worried that he was approaching the maximum speed possible in Florida. It took him nearly six miles to get *Bluebird* up to speed and six more to slow her down; soon there just wouldn't be enough sand in Daytona. Convinced that the Sahara wasn't the answer, Campbell trained his eyes west. By 1934 he had all but settled on the Bonneville Salt Flats, the dried-up bed of a lake that in prehistoric times had covered most of what is now Utah. But before he abandoned Daytona, he wanted to give the beach one last chance, in the spring of 1935.

The quest was plagued with problems from the outset. Campbell could never get the beach quite smooth enough. At night mules would pull scrapers over the course to try to smooth and level it out, the beach being lit by torches as the animals made their way across the sand. Though still not entirely satisfied with the course, Campbell grew tired of waiting, and on the morning of March 7, the siren atop the Orange Avenue Fire Station sounded, putting the town on notice that a run was imminent. A crowd of 50,000 made its the way to the beach, packing the grandstand on the Measured Mile. Those who couldn't find seats sat on the dunes or stood along the thirteen-mile route, their cars parked at odd angles wherever they could find a spot.

*Bluebird* could be heard before she could be seen. Then, trailing the roar, a small dot approached. By the time the spectators were able to make her out, she had disappeared in a cloud of sand. Campbell's speed on the first pass was 330 miles per hour, but for the record to be official he had to make another pass in the opposite direction within an hour, and the average of the two runs would stand as his time. As he exited the speed trap on the return run, he bit a small bump in the sand and skidded sideways through the Measured Mile. He was able to wrestle *Bluebird* under control and bring the car to a stop, its tires torn to shreds. Leaning up against the car, he related the near catastrophe to the press as nonchalantly as he might talk about his dozen Alsatians. "When the *Bluebird* hit it she shook her head sort of like a fish after a strike and headed for the soft sand," he said. "In my heart I thought I was done for." He had beaten his existing world record but hadn't come close to the magic number of 300. Campbell dismissed the run as "a picayune world's record of 276 miles per hour." That time, combined with the near-death experience, convinced him that he'd never reach his goal in Florida. His next attempt, later that summer, would take place in Utah.

The Bonneville Salt Flats were two hundred square miles of rock-hard ground three feet thick, caked hard by the desert sun and as smooth as marble. If you tried to drive a metal stake into the ground, the stake would bend. There was minimal skidding, and the salt actually cooled the car's tires. Up to that point in time, the Flats had been used for closed-track records; there were two circular tracks, of 10 and 12½ miles. For Campbell, a special 13-mile open course was laid out from north to south (so that he wouldn't have to drive into the sun), parallel to the Western Union Pacific tracks.

As Campbell made his way to the States that summer in typical luxury—he booked a stateroom on the Cunard White Star liner *Majestic*—he was not sure what to expect. When asked by Arthur Daley of the *New York Times* whether he thought he would reach 300 miles per hour, Sir Malcolm stated, with typical English understatement, "I'm none too sanguine about it." Down in Florida, his fans followed his exploits closely and with mixed emotions. Campbell was a favorite son of Daytona, and the affection went both ways. (He would later call the city his "second home.") But the locals knew that if Utah proved to be as fast as Campbell suspected it to be, he'd relocate his efforts to the desert, and they'd likely never see him behind the wheel of *Bluebird* again. So as much as they embraced Campbell, they could be forgiven for hoping he'd come up short.

On September 3, Campbell made his run. A nine-inch-wide black line had been laid down to guide him. His "good lads," as he always called his crew, shoved off the 28½-foot *Bluebird,* and the 2,500-horsepower machine began making its way across the seemingly endless field of white. Campbell described the sensation: "I could not see the line more than 100 yards ahead. I could see the earth was round, for the black line I was straddling seemed to go up to the horizon, and I had the same impression the early mariners had. When I met the horizon that was the end of the earth, I must be flying into space." When he had completed both runs, he was given his speed: 299.875 miles per hour, agonizingly close but short. Four hours later he was informed that there had been a timing error. His speed had actually been 301.33. "The news comes somewhat flat," said Campbell, his buzz nearly killed, "but I am glad to hear it."

Sensing that their status in the racing world was slipping away, as it had twenty-five years earlier, the Daytona Beach city fathers offered $10,000 to anyone who could do what Campbell couldn't: hit 300 miles per hour on the beach. The move smacked of desperation: who was going to be motivated by a $10,000 bounty when it had cost Campbell a million dollars to get his *Bluebird* past the magic number in Utah? Henry McLemore, the Daytona Beach correspondent for United Press International (UPI), wrote in December 1935:

> *There are citizens here who will tell you that Campbell never drove on the beach while it was at its best. My answer to that is, if you can't get the best beach in as many tries as Campbell made, then there isn't any beach. This isn't meant as a slur on this city's beach. Certainly, it must be the greatest in the world. But it is asking too much of nature to provide 14 miles of absolutely level land. It seems to me that Daytona Beach should be satisfied with having the finest beach for bathing and pleasure car driving in the world, and let somebody else have the speed records.*

And that's what happened. Never again would a record fall on the beach. But Campbell's departure didn't end the natives' quest for speed. It just made them realize that they didn't need to rely on outsiders to provide it. They could race themselves, but they needed someone to provide a little order.

When Malcolm Campbell set that last, "picayune" record in Daytona Beach in the spring of 1935, not everyone shared in his disappointment. Among the gearheads who witnessed the historic run was a bearish service station operator who was new to town. His name was Bill France, and he was mesmerized by what he saw.

Born in Horse Pasture, Virginia, France grew up in Washington, DC. His father was a bank teller who was confounded by his son's interest in cars, which France said he developed when he was "knee-high to a hubcap." The young France would sneak out in the family's Model T and take it to a speedway in Laurel, Maryland. "My dad," he said later, "never could figure out why his tires were wearing out so quickly." He met a pretty nursing student named Anne at a dance in December 1930, and they were married by the next summer. In October 1934, in the middle of the Depression, Bill and Anne loaded their one-year-old son, Bill Jr., and all their possessions into the family car, a 1928 Hupmobile Century Six, and drove south for Miami. France had $100 to his name. As they are with many larger-than-life figures, stories about France tend to be embellished. The most oft-told version of the tale of the Frances' settling in Daytona holds that the Hupmobile serendipitously broke down in town, as if the racing gods reached down and cracked its head gasket. In reality, France just wanted to have a look at the beach he had heard so much about. The empty, placid beach was inviting, so he took his family for a swim and fell in love with the place.

France got a job as a mechanic at the Daytona Motor Company, a car dealership, but shortly after he saw Campbell's last run up and down the Measured Mile, he became motivated to devote more time to racing. He bought a service station so he could be his own boss. "Business was not too good at first," France said. "So I had plenty of time to fish and race. Not bad."

France was typical of a new kind of racer emerging in Daytona: mechanically inclined men who were not especially rich and, with Campbell and his *Bluebird* three thousand miles away, who now had to make their own fun. They raced their own cars, as France put it, "mostly for fun and a little money." But they weren't racing against the clock; they were racing against each other.

In need of a tourist attraction, the city of Daytona Beach staged a race on a makeshift oval track in 1936. Parallel one-and-a-half-mile straightaways—one on the beach, the other on Highway A1A, which ran alongside it—were connected by slightly banked turns. Twenty-seven drivers turned up, including big names such as Indy 500 champ "Wild Bill" Cummings, who was drawn by the $5,000 purse, and locals such as France. The race illustrated the difficulty in staging a race on a beach. The sand that remained pristine when one car made a couple of passes over it displayed a tendency to rut when twenty-seven cars turned lap after lap in the same groove. Tow trucks dotted the course, pulling out cars that got stuck in the sand. To make matters worse, the tide came in earlier than expected, threatening to immerse the makeshift parking lot on the beach, so officials called the race early. The city lost $22,000 on the day.

The local Elks lodge took over the race the next year. Adding clay to the sand in the turns solved the rut problem, but despite the fact that the payout was significantly smaller than the year before—bar owner Smokey Purser got $43.56 for winning—the race again lost money, and the Elks cut their ties.

But France still thought that, done right, a race on the beach could be a winning proposition. He decided to call a well-known promoter who lived in Orange City Beach, which was near Daytona but still far enough away to be a toll call. France didn't have a quarter, so he called collect. The promoter refused to accept the charges, so France decided he'd promote the race himself. With a friend, France convinced the city to let him promote two races in 1938. For the first they charged 50 cents admission and ended up making $200 after expenses. So they doubled the price for the second and still drew roughly the same size crowd. Their take was $2,000. "It taught me a lesson," France said years later. "We had undersold the product the first time out. I never forgot that lesson."

As he learned more about the racing game, France started putting on more and more races in the area. At that time it seemed that most promoters were interested primarily in figuring out how to rip off the drivers and the track owners simultaneously. Stories of slick con men absconding with promised purses were the norm. But France was a forward-thinking man; he realized there was more money to be made in the long run by doing things legitimately than by scamming people for a few bucks here and there.

Of course, France wasn't the only person who realized that it might be a good idea—and a potentially lucrative one—to centralize the process of promoting races. One advantage France had over other promoters was that he had done some racing himself, which gave him a measure of credibility with the drivers. Another advantage was that he was huge, which made pretty much everyone else listen to what he had to say. France stood about six feet four inches tall and weighed around 220 pounds. (Years later *Sports Illustrated* would call him the "Cadillac-size Billy Rose of the racetrack world.") Most of the time, he was a charming southern gentleman, winning over friends and strangers alike with reasoned speech laced with the Virginia drawl he never quite lost. If he had to, though, "Big Bill" could play the heavy. "The fact that he's not by nature a good compromiser worked to his advantage in the early days," said Humpy Wheeler, a longtime race promoter and former president of Lowe's Motor Speedway outside Charlotte. "He was tough, with a one-track mind when it counted." (In the 1960s, not long after France took on the Teamsters and won, he heard the song "My Way," and it quickly became his favorite.)

After World War II, France opened a lounge in Daytona Beach's Streamline Hotel, where racers would come in and swap stories about racing or their favorite tricks for outrunning the cops while hauling moonshine into the small hours of the morning. (Anyone who admitted to throwing a glass jar out the window was considered bush league. The true artists would do things such as inject fluid into their exhaust systems to create a smoke screen.) On December 14, 1947, France welcomed more than two dozen drivers to the lounge for a meeting, with the goal of forming a unified body to promote stock car racing. At 1:00 p.m., once the room was sufficiently smoke-filled for the wheeling and dealing that was about to take place, the meeting convened.

Over the next four days, France solidified his position as the ultimate authority in the stock car universe, and he did so by convincing everyone else that it was in their best interest to endow him with that power. It was a neat trick, one that showed how savvy a negotiator France was. But if it seems slightly underhanded, it wasn't. France was genuinely convinced that the best way to run the operation was to limit the number of voices that were heard. "We had made a study of every racing organization that had ever come along," said Bill Tuthill, France's right-hand man. "I told Bill that the democratic method, where the board voted on everything, had never worked." So France and Tuthill had the body set up as a private corporation. France had been liberal in sending out the invitations; he knew that to get his new organization to work, he was going to have to get every promoter — not just the ones he was friendly with — on board. When rival promoters started clamoring for, say, bylaws to be written, France and Tuthill shut them up by forming a bunch of committees and putting them to work. Tuthill called it "a ruse to get some of the guys out of our hair." France appointed Tuthill chairman, and Tuthill in turn nominated France as president. He was voted in after he delivered the opening remarks, and he would run the National Association for Stock Car Auto Racing (NASCAR) for a quarter of a century before ceding control to his son Bill Jr.* He set up shop in a $40-a-month, second-floor walk-up office in the Selden Bank Building in Daytona Beach.

The early days of France's reign — when the fledgling organization was most in danger of coming apart — were remarkably smooth, because France kept his constituents happy. He improved payouts and safety, and perhaps more important, he didn't skim any cash. It helped that France always remembered his place: a southern man can do few

---

*Deciding on a name had been a tedious process. NASCAR originally lost out to the National Stock Car Racing Association, or NSCRA, because it sounded too much like "Nash car." But when it was discovered that an NSCRA already existed in Georgia, the previous vote was disregarded, and NASCAR was chosen instead.

things worse, at least in racing circles, than put on airs. Bill France's home number was always listed in the Ormond Beach phone book, even as the sport began its explosion in the late 1970s and '80s. France also went to great lengths to honor the sport's history and heritage, although he was never so sentimental that his judgment was clouded: he bought Malcolm Campbell's *Bluebird* but kept it locked up out of sight in the warehouse of a Daytona moving company.

As NASCAR took hold in the Southeast, France began thinking about what he could do to improve its status in his hometown. The beach course was becoming increasingly problematic. Hotels were moving farther down the beach, gradually encroaching on the course. And although there was something appealingly rustic about holding an event al fresco, having to deal with the tides was becoming a major headache. In 1949 France started talking with the city about building something bigger and more permanent. He had his eye on a piece of land just west of the airport. The city talked about issuing bonds but dragged its feet, so France set about scrounging up the money himself. The track, designed by Charles Moneypenny, was a marvel. It was two and a half miles, the same size as Indianapolis, but whereas Indy was flat and shaped like a rectangle with rounded corners, Daytona was banked at 33 degrees in the turns and 18 degrees in the tri-oval. At that point the fastest track in the world was Monza, a bowl-shaped oval outside Milan, Italy. France had Moneypenny design Daytona with consistent banking so there would be more than one groove and side-by-side racing would be possible. In addition to the main track, Moneypenny's design included a road course on the infield and a lake that would be large enough to stage boat races. (The void for the lake was created when the dirt was taken away to construct the banked turns.) The original plan called for a football field between pit road and the start/finish line. *Sports Illustrated* marveled that Daytona International Speedway was "one of the most ambitiously conceived racing plans ever blueprinted, and one of the

fastest, with a projected average lap speed for *stock cars* of 125 mph."
(Their emphasis.)

Another Bill France story that may or may not be embellished holds
that in the mid-1950s he went to the Indy 500 and was tossed out of
the pits for not having the proper credentials. Whether or not that actually happened, there's little doubt that France—who enjoyed one-
upmanship as much as the next guy—had his eye on Indy when he
built his track. "Absolutely, unquestionably, Indy was the Genesis of
the Daytona 500," says Humpy Wheeler. "The old story about not giving credentials in Indianapolis, if that's true, that was a terrible mistake, because it ended up costing them a premier spot in the U.S. for
motorsports. He built Daytona to be faster than Indianapolis."

The track was a source of pride for the locals. "If it is not the fastest in
the world," Ken Rudeen wrote in *Sports Illustrated,* "a lot of citizens will
have to eat their hats." The first race on the track was held in February
1959, in front of 41,000 fans. Although the speeds were a touch slower
than at Indy, no one felt compelled to eat his chapeau, because the track
produced a remarkable show. Johnny Beauchamp was declared the winner of the first Daytona 500, but many observers thought that Lee Petty
had beaten him to the stripe. It took three days of looking at photos and
newsreel footage before France declared Petty the winner by two feet.

Speedweek became plural in 1964 when France added a fourteen-
hour race. In typical fashion, he one-upped Sebring, also in Florida,
which had been home to the longest endurance race in the United
States, at twelve hours. In 1966 the Daytona race became a daylong affair, the equal of Le Mans. To mark the occasion, Bill France put track
workers in Charles de Gaulle caps and had signs printed in French:
drivers were directed to *les pits*.

The transition from the beach to the track was complete. France
had given the sport a signature event and a home worthy of it—a place
where drivers could fly without being at the mercy of the tides or the
wind or the sand.

# Chapter Three

# The Good Ol' Boys

**Thursday, February 8**
**Drawing for the Busch Clash**

THE GRAND National drivers had been off for nearly a month since their first race, Darrell Waltrip's win on the road course at Riverside. As they descended on Daytona and took over the hotel rooms of the sports car set,* the first substantial task for many of them was something most had plenty of practice doing: grabbing an ice-cold beer. It was a made-for-media dog-and-pony show to determine the starting order for the newest Speedweeks event: the Busch Clash, an all-star race for the nine drivers who'd won pole positions the year before.

---

\* After his engine blew up in the 24-hour race, Paul Newman couldn't get out of town without suffering one last indignity. ARCA car owner Sap Parker checked into the suite that Newman and Joanne Woodward had stayed in and reported to the *Daytona Beach News-Journal*, "Had to wait five hours for them to check out Monday. Talked to the maid that cleaned their room and Newman gave her a little trinket that must have cost two dollars when they checked out. Here's a poor little country girl, got two kids and he gives her that. I'd thought he'd at least give her $100. Hell, I gave her $50 today. I'm just a crazy Kentucky hillbilly, but damn proud."

The Clash was a fifty-mile sprint with unheard-of stakes. First prize was $50,000, more than every race except Daytona, and second paid $18,000—an obscene amount of money for twenty minutes of work, especially considering that in the 1978 season, ten of the thirty Grand National races paid their winners less than eighteen grand. The huge difference between the payout for first and second had most everyone convinced that all hell was going to break loose. "Nobody's going to be giving any breaks," said Buddy Baker. "For $50,000, you might see a tiny hole and try to go through it." In the garage, betting pools were set up, with action offered not only on who would win but also on how many cars would be taken out in wrecks. The starting order would be determined by drawing lots: specifically, cans of Busch beer with numbers on them.

If it sounds like something a fan would dream up, it was. Monty Roberts, the marketing director for Busch beer, got the idea in 1978 while mingling with the hoi polloi at a race in Charlotte. "I like to talk to fans—you know, find out what kind of beer they like to drink, what they are interested in—and they said we should run some sort of special race to really find out who is the best," he explained. Roberts was pushing the envelope for sponsor involvement. These were the days before most big businesses recognized the potential appeal of having a stock car racer as a spokesman—which is to say, the days before drivers' suits looked like patchwork logo quilts. Of course, there were sponsors in the sport. Companies such as STP, Gatorade, and Holly Farms paid money to get their names on cars, a few races had title sponsors, and Winston had been paying big money to sponsor the Grand National season points race since 1971. But this wasn't a case of a company latching onto a popular existing event. This was a company paying to rent a track and stage its own show, an exhibition that didn't affect the driver standings at all. The kind of people who now complain that postrace interviews sound like recitations of the automotive section of the Yellow Pages might have looked at the event with a cynical eye, but at the time it was hard to find anyone who wasn't in love with the idea. "This is completely upstaging the Daytona 500," said Benny Parsons, who had won two poles and three races in 1978. "Back home in North Carolina, this is all people can talk about."

Virtually every big-name driver was in the field. Most of the attention was focused on two: Bobby Allison, the defending Daytona 500 champ, and Cale Yarborough, who had won three straight NASCAR titles — in Allison's old ride.

Richard Petty may have been the King, but Cale Yarborough was the driver with the most regal lifestyle. He designed his 7,000-square-foot house in Sardis, South Carolina, himself, sparing no expense. Adjoining the master bedroom was a sauna and a whirlpool, and Yarborough put a tennis court and a swimming pool on the grounds. Out front was a landing strip for his two airplanes, and on the roof were three 60-foot TV antennas, all pointed in different directions so that he could pick up signals from Columbia, Florence, and Charleston. ("We're a television family," his wife, Betty Jo, explained.) The house was brown brick, very long and low to the ground. Yarborough was the first to admit that the row of columns out front made the place look kind of like a motel.

Yarborough was "the Baron of Florence County." In and around Sardis and Timmonsville, the small town seven miles up the road where he had been born thirty-nine years earlier, he owned a couple of dry cleaners, a Goodyear tire shop, a carpet-yarning factory, and a feed and fertilizer store. His 1,000-acre farm in Timmonsville contained substantial lumber reserves — not to mention its own church — and was worth upwards of $1.5 million.

Still, at the end of every day, Yarborough made sure to take the loose change from his pockets and put it in a homemade piggy bank — a ten-gallon milk jar with a slotted lid welded in place. He liked having a reminder that he hadn't always been so flush.

Yarborough's father died in a plane crash when he was eleven, leaving his mother to run the family's tobacco farm, cotton gin, and country store. "I never went hungry," he said. "But we sure weren't rich, and I can remember when we didn't have any electricity, running water, or indoor toilet." Yarborough found the time to do a little racing, first in soap box derby cars and then in hot rods. In the fall of 1957, when he was eighteen—three years younger than NASCAR's minimum age requirement—Yarborough and a couple of pals took a car to nearby Darlington, at that point the largest track on the NASCAR circuit, to race in the Southern 500. They had no idea what they were getting themselves into. By the time they got the car past the NASCAR inspectors, they had missed qualifying. But the rules were fairly lax in those days, and they were still allowed to enter at the back of the fifty-car field.

Yarborough had come armed with a fake birth certificate, but the chief steward, Johnny Bruner, wasn't fooled. He pulled Yarborough out of the car and told him to get lost. Yarborough's older friend got behind the wheel until Bruner left, at which point Yarborough got back in. The race started with Yarborough driving, but he had violated the first rule of remaining inconspicuous: he was wearing a bright red shirt. Bruner noticed it and ordered the car into the pits, where he oversaw another driver change. A few laps later, Yarborough's friend pitted, and they switched positions again. Bruner caught him again. This time Bruner put Yarborough in his own car and drove Cale outside the track. Yarborough, however, had plenty of experience sneaking into Darlington. As Bruner sat in traffic trying to get back into the infield, Yarborough slithered through the fence and into his race car. When Bruner got back inside the track, he noticed the red shirt again. This time he walked onto the middle of the front straightaway and stepped in front of the Pontiac, directing it into the pits like a traffic cop. "He wouldn't even let me drive around and come in the pits," said Yarborough. "He stands there and makes me back up against all them cars back to the pit entrance."

Perhaps realizing they were beaten, NASCAR officials soon lowered its minimum age to eighteen, allowing Yarborough to run the occasional race without resorting to identity theft. He wasn't a full-timer; he figured the real money was in poultry farming. But the turkey market crashed in '63, costing him $30,000 and plunging him into a period of his life that could have supplied the plot of a very bad country song—a time of terrible living conditions (a ten-by-fifty-foot trailer), worse luck (a turkey market crash?), and abject poverty.

In 1964 a track promoter in Savannah, Georgia, called Yarborough and told him he had found him a ride if he could be there the next day. Yarborough cashed a check for his last $10, packed his pregnant wife and some sandwiches into his car, and headed off. They were more than halfway there when Yarborough got pulled over for doing 40 in a 35 mile per hour zone. The fine was—you guessed it—$10. Now completely broke, Yarborough continued along until it dawned on him that the road he was on led to a 50-cent toll bridge. Betty Jo, pregnant and hungry (those sandwiches were long gone), started crying as Yarborough tried to figure out how they were going to get across. "Then I remembered that when you wash a car and pull the backseat out, sometimes you find money that has fallen out of people's pockets," he said. So Yarborough pulled out the seat, and he and Betty Jo scrounged up 37 cents. He explained his situation to the toll taker, promising to pay the last 13 cents on his way back to South Carolina. The toll taker—moved by Yarborough's situation, or at least recognizing the makings of a good story when he saw one—waved them through, and Yarborough made it to the track, where, of course, his engine blew before the race began. That meant no prize money, which meant Yarborough had to bum twenty bucks to get home. But he did stop to pay the toll taker his 13 cents. "He is still there," Yarborough said a few years later. "I often stop and talk with him when I cross."

Not long after—apparently figuring that he had already survived the worst that racing could throw at him—Yarborough turned his attention to driving full-time. He worked his way up from a shop hand at Holman Moody, the Charlotte outfit that built race cars for Ford, and by June 1965 he had won his first NASCAR race, in Valdosta, Georgia. He won the Daytona 500 for the first time in 1968, driving a Ford for the Wood Brothers team. But after the 1970 season, Ford pulled out of stock car racing. The turkey fiasco still fresh in his mind, Yarborough was worried that without the backing of a factory, stock cars wouldn't offer the kind of financial security he needed—especially since he had just become the proud owner of a $300,000 mortgage on the farm in Timmonsville. "Everything I had made I had invested, and I had obligations I had to meet," he said. He accepted an offer from Gene White to drive in the open-wheel USAC series.

Yarborough had already had a brief dalliance with Indy cars. It hadn't gone well. He'd made it thirty yards in the 1966 Indianapolis 500 before a wreck ended his day. The next year he got arrested after scuffling with an Indianapolis sheriff's deputy at a motel, then wrecked his race car as he drove it onto the track for the first practice session. After his crew replaced the nose cone, Yarborough finally made it safely onto the track, only to be fined $25 by the stewards for running through a yellow light to get there.

Signing the deal with White meant that Yarborough would drive the entire 1971 season on a team with Lloyd Ruby, a quiet Texan whose open-wheel experience made him the operation's focus. Yarborough struggled driving on the flatter tracks, and he didn't like playing second fiddle to Ruby. ("Cale didn't have second-rate equipment, but he did have second-rate help," his crew chief confessed.) After two lackluster seasons Yarborough was ready to return to stock cars.

Many owners were excited by that news—in particular, Junior Johnson.

While Yarborough was plotting his return in late 1972, Junior Johnson was trying to figure out how to handle an increasingly pressing personnel problem—namely, that his driver, Bobby Allison, was a pain in his ass. Johnson was an old-school racer, a moonshiner who had perfected his trade running moonshine in the woods of North Carolina. Johnson could drive a car—on a racetrack or a winding mountain road—arguably better than any man before or since.* His exploits have been documented in print (Tom Wolfe's story "The Last American Hero Is Junior Johnson. Yes!") and on celluloid (the 1973 Jeff Bridges movie *The Last American Hero*). He's credited with inventing the bootleg turn—a full-speed, 180-degree spin used to avoid the revenuers—and he took great pride in the fact that the cops never caught him hauling 'shine. He only got busted when federal agents snuck up on him one morning as he stoked the family still in Wilkes County, North Carolina. That was in 1956, the year after Johnson had won five races and been NASCAR's rookie of the year. He spent eleven months in federal prison in Chillicothe, Ohio, and returned to the track in 1958. Nine years later he quit driving at age thirty-five because, he said, winning had become too easy for him.

Looking for a new challenge, Johnson began fielding cars for other drivers. He'd done all right with Lee Roy Yarbrough, but things really got interesting for him when he hired Allison in 1972—in no small part because Allison came with a handsome dowry of $85,000, courtesy of Coca-Cola, which sponsored his car. Allison was so excited at the prospect of driving for Johnson that he kicked in fifteen grand of his own money to satisfy Johnson's request for an even $100,000.

But the relationship never had a chance. Junior Johnson liked things done his way, and as the man who signed the checks, he had no qualms about exercising his authority. And Allison had problems with authority. Big problems.

The roots of Bobby Allison's attitude toward The Man could be traced back to his first boss in the racing game, Carl Kiekhaefer. Kiekhaefer

---

* In 1998 *Sports Illustrated* named him the best driver of NASCAR's first fifty years.

had made his fortune by founding Mercury Marine, which made out-board motors. When Allison finished high school, his uncle had, at his mother Kitty's insistence, gotten him a job testing motors in Wisconsin, which was a dream gig* for Allison, who had grown up toying with cars and engines at the junkyard his father owned. Eventually, he crossed paths with the boss. "Kiekhaefer had some sort of a deal where little people annoyed him," says Allison. That was a problem: at the time Allison was five feet four inches tall and weighed maybe 110 pounds. "I was very timid in nature—a wimp," Allison says. "I didn't go for any of that he-man stuff."

Kiekhaefer had the two things any good despot needs: power and a burly, imposing physique with which to flaunt it. (For good measure, he also had one of the vilest mouths in the Midwest. And the cigars he was always chewing made nice props, too.) Kiekhaefer saw racing as a way to promote his motor company, but he insisted that the operation people saw was first-rate. His racing crews had pressed uniforms; his cars had shiny paint jobs, and they were carried to the track in trucks. That was unheard-of in the mid-1950s. So unheard-of, in fact, that no one made trucks designed for that purpose. Kiekhaefer's boys used the same trucks they used to haul boat motors, so the tail ends of the race cars would always stick out.

Allison got his break when Kiekhaefer sent him on an errand to the race shop in Charlotte and told him to wait there for a company truck to take him back to Wisconsin. Running the shop was Ray Fox, who'd go on to become a legendary engine builder but at that point would

---

*Except for the time he flipped a boat and nearly died of exposure. Allison was in the lake for exactly thirty-five minutes, which he knew because his watch froze as soon as he hit the water. He eventually got out and made his way to a nearby house. The woman who lived there put him in some dry clothes belonging to her husband and took him to the ER—where her husband worked. After she explained what an eighteen-year-old kid was doing in his clothes, he fixed Allison up and sent him on his way.

have been happy just to find some good help. Allison approached him and notified him that he was, under the boss's orders, around until his ride arrived.

"Well, okay," said Fox. "Are you a good mechanic?"

"Yeah, I'm a mechanic," said Allison. "Why?"

"A lot of these people here, Kiekhaefer went up to them and said, 'You go to my race shop in Charlotte or you're fired.' So they're here, but they don't work. I need to get a car ready for tomorrow night's race. Will you work on it for me?"

Allison jumped at the chance. Fox gave him a checklist and some tools and pointed him toward the car. Four hours later Allison returned. "What's next?" he asked.

"Are you done already?"

"Well, I did what you had on the sheet…"

"Did you do it right?"

"Well, I did it like the sheet said to do it."

"Man, I gotta keep you here. Here, come on, get on this second car."

Fox convinced Kiekhaefer to let him hang on to Allison. The living conditions in Charlotte weren't ideal: Kiekhaefer put twenty-one young employees up in a three-bedroom house with one bathroom. "You had to take a number to get in the bathroom, and if you weren't done in two minutes, you got thrown out," says Allison. But Allison didn't care. He was living the life—working on cars and going to races. "I was there June and July and went to eighteen races," he says. "I never saw a car besides the Kiekhaefer car win the race."

Then Kiekhaefer's temper reared its head. Carl Kiekhaefer loved to fire people. He loved to fire people so much that he even tried to fire people who didn't work for him. On one occasion he spotted a guy standing around the shop, not doing much of anything. Enraged that someone was loafing in his presence, Kiekhaefer asked him how much he made, gave him a week's severance, and told him to get out of the shop. Needless to say, the delivery man happily took the cash and went back to his own job.

Allison's demise came about when Kiekhaefer saw Allison and three of his pals hanging out near the time clock. He accused one of them, a kid named Willard Stubby, of milking the clock. He flew into a rage that ended with him calling Stubby every name in the book and firing all three of Allison's friends, who were more expendable than Allison. Enraged, Allison quit on the spot, which made Kiekhaefer even more irate. Kiekhaefer jumped into his Chrysler Imperial, and Allison and his friends knew what was coming next: Kiekhaefer was going to lock them out of the house and hold their belongings ransom. "But I knew a shortcut," says Allison. They were just coming out of the house with their things when Kiekhaefer showed up, skidding onto the front lawn, which had just been re-sodded. As he stood on the torn-up lawn, shaking his fist at Allison and his friends, they hightailed it back to Wisconsin. Without a job to keep him there, Allison decided to go home to Miami.

The irony of Allison's exile in Wisconsin was that the whole reason his mother had sent him away in the first place was that she was concerned he was spending too much time racing. She had no idea that sending him to Kiekhaefer would be like sending a chocoholic to live with an uncle in Hershey, Pennsylvania.

Allison had first started racing when he was fourteen, because it was one of the few sports a one-hundred-pound kid could compete in and not be at a disadvantage. When some friends discovered a paved quarter-mile track at an old deserted amusement park just off the Tamiami Trail, they'd sneak onto it at night and race their jalopies, using only their headlights to illuminate the course. The thrill of beating his friends gradually subsided, and Allison started looking for better venues and better wheels. As the manager of the Archbishop Curley High School football team, Allison befriended Fran Curci, the best player on the team and owner of the coolest car, a decked-out '38 Chevy coupe that he had painted blue and yellow.* Allison liked the looks of it and the way it ran, so he sold his Harley and gave Curci the proceeds, $40, in exchange for the car. (He didn't miss the Harley much, since he had to have someone else ride it with him as ballast.) He took his new car to Hialeah Speedway and won his third race — and $8, less 50 cents for the pit pass.

Not long after, Kitty shipped her boy off to Wisconsin. Says Allison, "She called Aunt Patty and Uncle Jimmy and said, 'We gotta get Bobby away from this racetrack.'" When Allison returned following his blowup with Kiekhaefer, Kitty, realizing that subterfuge wasn't going to work, chose a more direct approach in her efforts to derail her son's career. She simply forbade it, telling him that he couldn't live in her house if he was racing. Allison was sharing his dismay with the boyfriend of one of his sisters when the two hatched a plan: the boyfriend, Bob Sundman, would give Allison his ID, allowing him to race under an alias. To make the ruse a little tougher to spot, a sympathetic pit steward changed the name to Sunderman on the entry forms. It worked for a little while: Allison had nine brothers and sisters, so it was tough for Pop and Kitty to keep an eye on them at all times. But Pop eventually caught on when he realized that the exploits of this Sunderman character he was reading so much about in the newspaper tended to coincide with periods of time when his son was out of the house. When Kitty and Pop saw the lengths their son was willing to go to drive, they relented, and when he informed them in 1959 that he was going to go racing in Alabama, where the purses were richer, they even suggested that he take his brother Donnie with him.

The Allisons' Alabama odyssey was, like so many other great journeys, undertaken because a guy was chasing a girl. The guy was Gil

---

*Curci went on to become the first All-American quarterback at the University of Miami. He also coached the Hurricanes and led Kentucky to its only two SEC championships, in 1976 and '77.

Hearne, a pal of Bobby's from Florida. He and another friend had taken their car up to Georgia and Tennessee, ostensibly to go racing, but in reality they were trying to find a girl Hearne was interested in whose family had supposedly moved to Tennessee. They made a trip back to Florida and told Allison that he should come with them to Alabama because there was a lot more money to be made at the tracks up north. They were right. "The first place we went was Montgomery," remembers Allison. "We saw this beautiful half-mile paved track, and a man comes walking out and says, 'We race here tomorrow night. Tonight we race at Dixie Speedway in Midfield. That way, one hundred miles.' So we get to Dixie, and I run fifth in the heat race, fifth in the semi, and fifth in the feature. I go to the pay window, and I tell Donnie, 'I'll get our couple bucks, and we'll go get a hamburger and sleep in the truck on the way back to Montgomery.' I go to the pay window, and the guy gives me $135! The stack of money looked *that* high. I went down the steps from the pay shack and said to Donnie, 'We've died and gone to heaven. Look at all this money!' So we went and had a $1.99 special steak at Miss Mary's Drive-in, and we slept in a $2 hotel room."

Hearne, by the way, found the girl. Her family was living in a little place on a peach orchard outside Chattanooga. That came in handy when there was racing nearby. "They let us camp out in their peach orchard," says Allison. "That's where I worked on my car."

The Allison boys—they eventually were joined by their wives and brother Eddie—set up shop in Hueytown, a small town a few miles west of Birmingham. Bobby and Donnie won enough races at local tracks in the Southeast to support the Alabama Gang, as they came to be known. Bobby won the national modified-special championship in 1962 and '63 and the modified title in 1964 and '65. He made the decision to move up from the minors to Grand National racing, securing a ride with Betty Lilly, the invalid wife of a Georgia realtor. In the end, it would only give Allison more reason to be skeptical of working for someone else. Despite Mrs. Lilly's assurances that Allison would be given whatever he needed, she decided the stock car game was too rich for her blood and pulled out after just eleven races — and four blown engines.

Allison decided to stay in Grand National as his own boss. He bought a '64 Chevelle and spent sixteen days with Donnie, Eddie, and a friend named Chuck Looney getting the car into shape. His fourth race in the Chevelle was on July 10, 1966, in Bridgehampton, New York. Allison's engine blew up eleven laps into the race, leaving him with nothing under his hood for a race two days later at Oxford Plains Speedway in Maine. So he drove to Maine, found a Chevy dealer, and asked if the dealer had any cheap engines lying around. The dealer told him he had one that had come out of a car a customer had returned — because the engine didn't work. Unable to afford anything else, Allison bought the busted engine, convinced the dealer to let him use one of the dealership's bays, and spent the whole night rebuilding it, with help from Looney and a NASCAR PR man.

The next day Allison put the car on the pole and lapped the field, winning his first Grand National race. He won again four days later in Islip, New York, but again only after getting a little help from his friends. Two days after the win in Maine, Allison was involved in a wreck at Fonda Speedway in upstate New York. Luckily, he had a cousin who owned a body shop in New Jersey, so he took the Chevelle to him and went to work. Another rookie driver, James Hylton, who was an excellent body man, lent a hand as well. Hylton's generosity ended up costing him: he finished second to Allison in Islip. Had he not spent his spare time helping Allison, he would have won his first Grand National race.

But Allison and Hylton were both independent drivers, making do without the support of the factories. There was a camaraderie, an us-against-them vibe that made the independents band together, traveling in a caravan, sharing shop space and tools, even forming one over-the-wall crew to pit all of their cars, since they couldn't afford their own full crews. It was a classic case of small-market teams versus large-market teams. They were the Royals and the Twins. The Pettys and Wood Brothers were the Yankees and the Red Sox. Allison didn't mind, at least not at first, because he was winning races—three in 1966 and six in '67—and he answered to no one. It meant a hectic schedule. While the Curtis Turners of the world (he was driving for Junior Johnson at the time) could turn their busted-up cars over to their crews between races, Allison's crew was pretty much the guy in the mirror. *Sports Illustrated* documented how frenetic his rookie season was:

> *In the space of two weeks last month—before and after the National 500 at Charlotte—Bobby was disturbed because he couldn't discover the cause of an unexpected blown engine, could not obtain vital parts for another engine he was rebuilding, had wiped out his racing budget to pay another parts bill, had been ridiculously overcharged at a Charlotte motel, had learned that [his wife] Judy was expecting Junior Allison No. 4, and had driven 650 miles to Martinsville for the privilege of tangling with Lee Roy Yarbrough.*

Allison's success on the track paled in comparison to Petty's, who won twenty-seven times in 1967, including ten in a row, two of the safest records in sports. Finishing behind the Chrysler-supported number 43 week in and week out made the chip on Allison's shoulder grow. He also wasn't crazy about the way the Pettys threw their weight around. In Peter Golenbock's book *Miracle,* Allison recounts an incident in Birmingham in 1967 when Firestone brought the wrong tires to the track. Allison had a bunch of good tires at his shop in Hueytown, so he sent someone to pick them up. Suddenly, his lap times were a second faster than anyone else's, so Petty had a Firestone rep confiscate Allison's tires for Petty's own use. Allison switched to Goodyears and won the race.

The rivalry grew more intense. In November 1967 Allison and Petty swapped the lead all afternoon at the half-mile speedway in Weaverville, North Carolina. Allison won the race with a late pass that came after he knocked Petty out of the way, which led to a near brawl between their pit crews following the race. The next summer the cars came together again in a race on Long Island. Petty wound up with a bent fender that knocked him out of contention. After the race Dale Inman and Maurice Petty went after Allison. Someone kicked him in the back (Allison thought it was Inman), and the melee grew to include Allison's cousin and aunt, whom he described as "a big woman with a big pocketbook." "I guess it was a blowoff of one of those things that happens over time," Chief explained at the time. "You might say we settled an old score."

The feud simmered for years, and it grew to include the drivers' fans. "When we were running against Allison at those short tracks, with fifty laps to go we'd have the trailer ramps down, because you knew there was going to be a fight after the race," remembers Petty crew member Richie Barsz. "You wanted to get your shit loaded. When they turned the fans loose out of the stands, you had so many people who pulled for Allison, that if you didn't fight the Allisons, you'd slap a couple of the fans. They get in your face and spit on you. That just didn't work well. I'm Polish; it don't matter to me. Someone would get up in your face and say, 'That goddamn Petty,' and that's all it took. They just got it. Most of the time you dropped something on them, like a jack or a tool or something, because if you blatantly just punched them, then NASCAR was all over you. But if you stumbled with your hands full, they wouldn't say anything." * A few years — and several

---

* Fans weren't the only ones who could be felled by equipment. "Same thing with reporters," says Barsz. "If they got in your way, the first thing you'd do is encircle their feet with the air hose, so when you had a pit stop, you'd jerk their feet out from under them."

more run-ins—after the Long Island brawl, Petty and Allison dented each other's sheet metal repeatedly late in a race in North Wilkesboro, North Carolina. It was their third dustup in a month. "He could have put me in the boondocks," said an irate Petty, who won the race. In Victory Lane, a drunken Allison fan hopped the fence and made a run at Petty, only to be stopped by Chief, who grabbed his brother's helmet and hit the intruder over the head.

The battles with the Pettys—not so much the fighting aunts or the fans getting popped with racing equipment, but the struggle of trying to compete with a team that had more backing and more pull—finally wore on Allison to the point that he decided to hook up with a factory-backed team. He drove for Holman Moody in 1971, but the team no longer had the resources to race in '72, so Allison took his Coke money and agreed to drive for Junior Johnson. It was the beginning of a not-so-beautiful relationship. Oh, they got results. That wasn't the problem. Allison won ten races and finished second twelve times in thirty-one starts in '72, finishing just behind Petty in the championship race. Their record together is all the more amazing considering they amassed it without speaking to each other for much of the year. Johnson had always set up his own cars when he was driving, which sometimes meant doing things idiosyncratically—such as attaching the track bar to the left frame, when everyone else in the world hooked it to the right. It had always worked out well for Johnson when he was behind the wheel, so he didn't see a need to alter his ways just because Allison thought it needed to be changed. It got to the point where Johnson only spoke to Allison through Herb Nab, the crew chief. The situation came to a head in August, when Allison, Johnson, and Nab were standing around the car. When Allison suggested a chassis adjustment, Johnson told Nab to tell Allison—who was standing a few feet away—that they weren't going to make it. Allison's response: "Herb, tell Junior to kiss my ass."

Allison had muscled up since his high school days.

After the season, when Johnson found out that Cale Yarborough was available, he called up Allison early one morning and said that he needed to know whether Allison wanted to return in '73 because he had a chance to "get the best driver in NASCAR right now." Allison was groggy, but he still knew when he was being insulted.

"Get him," he said, and hung up the phone.

As odd a couple as Allison and Johnson were, Yarborough and Johnson seemed made for each other. Yarborough was, like Johnson, a strong, rugged, outdoorsy type, a real man's man. Not that Allison was still a wimp. He had driven through some incredible injuries, and never backed down from a fight. But he wasn't the kind of fella who would be the subject of a magazine profile detailing his nocturnal varmint-hunting habits, as Johnson later was in the the summer of 1979, when *Stock Car Racing* ran a piece called COON HUNTIN' WITH JR. JOHNSON.*

The first sign that Yarborough and Johnson had a lot in common came in 1966, when Johnson gave Yarborough a bear as a gift and Yarborough didn't think it the least bit strange. Yarborough named her Susie. "The bear is a good conversation piece," he said, but she also played another role: occasional wrestling partner. It just seemed like the thing a man should do with his ursine pet. "Any time you raise a bear," he said, "you're probably going to wind up doing some bear wrestling."

Yarborough's menagerie also included, at one point, a lion, and in addition to grappling with Susie, he was fond of tangling with snakes and alligators. There was something very Bunyanesque about him. As a young man, he'd jump off ninety-foot cypress trees into swimming holes, and he once parachuted out of an airplane without so much as a lesson. (He missed his target by two miles and wound up on top of a

---

* "I enjoy hearing the dog run and tree," he said. "A good dog in the field is one of the finest artists in anything."

dentist's office.) That was just the way Yarborough was—impulsive, fearless, and not always as responsible as the situation might call for. Back in the mid-1960s Yarborough and Wib Weatherly pooled their money and bought a Piper J-4 airplane. When they took it out for its maiden flight, they decided that Yarborough would handle the take-off and then turn the controls over to Wib. Once they got airborne, Yarborough kept offering the stick to Weatherly, who kept declining. "Naw, Cale, you're doing just fine," he'd say. As the needle on the fuel gauge got closer to "E," Yarborough got more insistent, but Weatherly wouldn't budge. Finally Yarborough blurted out the truth: he'd never flown a plane before. Weatherly then one-upped him: not only had Wib never flown a plane, but it was only the second time he'd been in one. "Well," Yarborough recounted later, "I brought it in, bouncing all over the place and with Wib's eyes as big as saucers, and the next day I was out there and took off again and practiced landings in this field until I could do it pretty good. Never had a lesson in my life."

Of course, had the plane crashed, Yarborough likely would have walked away from it. The man seemed indestructible. He was five feet seven and 175 pounds, with a broad chest, muscular legs, and cartoon-ishly large forearms. He looked like Popeye with a comb-over. His neck—or whatever it was that his head sat on—was so thick and strong that he never used a neck strap to keep his head upright while racing, although most drivers joked that he didn't need a neck strap because he didn't have a neck. (He also refused to wear a cool suit, which kept the driver's temperature down but added fifty pounds to the car's weight.) He had the perfect build for a fullback. In fact, he had turned down a football scholarship offer from Clemson and played a little semipro ball for the Sumter Generals when it looked like he might not make it as a racer. And he boxed. Very well, in fact. In high school he had been the South Carolina Golden Gloves welterweight champion.

But Johnson didn't jump at the chance to hire Yarborough because he was tough. He jumped at the chance to hire him because Yarborough would get results—"Who's the best driver, that's who you want," Johnson says—and he'd be easy to deal with. Yarborough had plenty of things on his plate—he liked to show his face around his businesses and glad-hand the locals in Timmonsville, and he insisted on answering his own fan mail—so he wasn't going to spend all of his time at the shop looking over Johnson's shoulder. Allison was one of the best all-around mechanic/drivers the sport has ever seen, a masterful tinkerer. He'd sense a problem in the car and set about fixing it. Yarborough was just a great driver. He was happy to get out of the car, say "It was loose" or "It was tight," and leave it at that, confident that Junior and his boys could fix it.

It also helped that Yarborough and Johnson drove the same way—hard. Johnson wanted Yarborough to push the other cars from the time the green flag dropped, the idea being that nobody was going to build a sturdier car than theirs. Yarborough had finished every race in 1977 and all but two in '78. "Our racing philosophy couldn't be more identical," Yarborough said at Daytona in '79. "We both believe in putting the pedal to the floor and keeping it there. Speed is what the sport is all about. We start every race intending to lead every lap we possibly can."

"It's the crew's job to build 'em to stand up to Cale," said Johnson. "We've done okay in that regard."

Since leaving Junior Johnson, Bobby Allison had done slightly less than okay. He'd latched on with Roger Penske, but they'd had a falling out over, among other things, Penske's insistence that Allison drive one of Penske's cars in the Indy 500. So Allison went back to the one owner he truly got along with—himself—and struggled through a winless 1977, his second straight season without a trip to Victory Lane. As it did with Petty, losing literally ate at him. Stomach problems—which he attributed to fatigue, worry, disappointment, and "lack of personal care"—caused Allison to lose fifty pounds and necessitated a short stay at the Mayo Clinic. During Allison's drought, Yarborough won eighteen races and two titles. On his own again, Allison reverted to his me-against-them mode, complaining that NASCAR was turning a blind eye as Johnson and the Pettys skirted the rules. He started calling Johnson's car "the Company Car," and one of the things gnawing at him was seeing Cale Yarborough take it to Victory Lane week after week.

Being a race car driver is a peculiar way to make a living. It's sort of like being a test pilot, in that it requires a man to be able to compartmentalize his feelings and to make peace with the possibility that one day he might not make it home from work. The second he starts thinking about how dangerous his job is, or the first time he sees a bad wreck and thinks, *Shit, that could've been me,* he might as well get out. But whereas a test pilot works all alone up in the sky, pushing the envelope Tom Wolfe wrote about in *The Right Stuff,* a racer risks his neck in close proximity to forty other guys, men who, like himself, are riding on the edge — and who, if they get a little chippy, might kill him. (Not on purpose, of course.) It can make for some interesting interpersonal relationships.

Still, there were plenty of close friendships among drivers, and even when there was a fight, there was a pretty decent chance the combatants would put it behind them over a beer later that night. But in any closed circle, especially one containing so many alpha males, there are going to be personality clashes, petty jealousies, and instances of guys just not being able to stand each other. The drivers, however, couldn't let whatever animosity they might feel toward each other manifest itself on the track. That was just too dangerous. And even off the track, it was easier for them to find a way to get along than to be openly hostile, since for nine months out of the year they traveled to the same small towns, stayed at the same motels, ate at the same diners, and drank at the same bars.

One of the most entertaining examples of driver cooperation occurred in 1975, when Bobby Allison, Buddy Baker, David Pearson, Richard Petty, Darrell Waltrip, and Cale Yarborough got together and recorded the album *NASCAR Goes Country*. It's the kind of recording everybody should listen to once. (And just once.) The Jordanaires, who had backed up Elvis Presley for twenty years, were brought in to sing background vocals, allowing the drivers to more or less speak most of their parts, which is probably a good thing. The album's high point, such as it is, is probably Richard Petty's performance of Roger Miller's "King of the Road," a fitting pairing of singer and subject matter. As for the low point, the less said about Buddy Baker's rendition of "Butterbeans" the better.

The record opens with "Ninety-nine Bottles of Beer (on the Wall)." (Luckily, most of the numbers between zero and ninety-eight were skipped, and the song lasts only three and a half minutes.) Baker handles the first verse, which contains a line about what began as a social event devolving into a brawl. That was especially fitting on a record sung by stock car drivers, because so much of their time was spent with people they were just as likely to take a swing at as to pat on the back. Granted, six race car drivers spending a few days goofing off in a studio wasn't as remarkable an accomplishment as Fleetwood Mac recording *Rumours* at a time when everyone in the band was either cheating on a bandmate or breaking up with one, but there was still plenty of intrigue among the warbling drivers, the kind of lurking-beneath-the-surface tension that permeated the sport. Some of it was rooted in on-track incidents (Allison and Petty). Some of it was born of an intense rivalry (Petty and Pearson). Sometimes it was a case of general principles (no one really cared for Waltrip's mouth, which didn't bother Waltrip, because he didn't care for the old guard). And sometimes it was nothing more than two strong personalities that just seemed destined to butt heads. "Cale and Bobby had trouble," says Junior Johnson. "They were just so competitive. They hated each other."

Bobby Allison's fortunes changed in 1978. He hooked up with owner Bud Moore, a World War II veteran who had been awarded the Bronze

Star for his service during Operation Overlord. Moore didn't sweat the small stuff—landing at Normandy on D-Day will do that to you—and actually welcomed feedback from Allison. They won five races together in '78, including Allison's first Daytona 500, and finished second to Yarborough in points, making Allison—who after thirteen years in the Grand National division was still looking for that elusive season championship—one of the favorites to unseat Yarborough.* Allison didn't help his title hopes in the first race of the '79 season. He had been leading at Riverside with seventeen laps left, but his engine failed, relegating him to nineteenth place. Yarborough finished a comfortable third.

When Allison flew his plane into Daytona, he had a guest: Ken Squier of CBS, who was filming a spot with Allison for the network's coverage of the 500. Allison had been flying for years. He logged an amazing number of hours hopping from short track to short track so that he could race in between Grand National events, but he also enjoyed the serenity that came with being alone in the sky. He told Squier how when he was flying, he liked to reflect on the days when piloting his own plane wasn't an option: "I think about a lot of those times when we spent all night the night after a race getting home, all night the night before qualifying getting to the racetrack, and the times when I really would have loved to have stopped at a motel but couldn't because we didn't have the money."

It hadn't been easy, but he'd come a long way from that abandoned amusement park in Miami to the media center at Daytona, where, on the afternoon of Thursday, February 8, he was preparing to find

---

*NASCAR distributed points roughly the same way in 1979 as it does today. The race winner got 175 points, the next five spots each got five fewer than the previous position (second was 170, third 165, etc.); the five after that decreased by increments of four; and the finishers from eleventh place on decreased by increments of threes. Any driver who led at least one lap got five bonus points, and the driver who led the most laps got five more. The system was often criticized for placing too much emphasis on consistency instead of rewarding wins.

out where he'd start in the Busch Clash, which was, considering the purse and the amount of work involved, the most lucrative race in stock car history. An ice-filled tub of Busch beer was placed in front of the eight drivers, who were wearing matching Busch blazers. (The ninth, Neil Bonnett, was still in Alabama having some dental work done.) As a roomful of writers and photographers looked on, a green flag was dropped, and the drivers grabbed wildly for the cans. Allison drew number 4, while Yarborough, who cut his hand on a can, pulled number 7.

Noticeably absent from the proceedings was Richard Petty, who had failed to sit on a pole during his winless 1978 season and therefore wasn't in the Busch Clash. He wasn't even in Daytona yet. He'd be arriving on Friday, which would give him just enough time to settle in and give his son a last bit of coaching before Kyle's debut.

## Chapter Four

# The Prince

THE JOB of a promoter is to drum up interest in a race and sell as many tickets as possible, and the steady stream of fans coming into the speedway seven days before the Daytona 500 served as proof that Bill France was a very good promoter. Instead of having the field for the 500 set the same way it was everywhere else — give everyone a qualifying lap or two and then order the cars from fastest to slowest — France concocted an elaborate system that increased both track time and ticket sales. Every car ran two laps the Sunday before the race, with the two fastest cars locked in to the front-row spots for the 500. The next twenty-eight spots were set by two 125-mile races held the following Thursday, with the final ten places filled based on drivers' times posted in other qualifying sessions during the week. It was far more complex than it needed to be, but it gave France the chance to sell tickets for the Thursday races, and it gave fans and writers something to pay attention to in the week leading up to the 500.

Sunday began with the qualifying laps at 11:00 a.m., followed by Kyle Petty's debut in the ARCA race, with the Busch Clash closing out the afternoon. The Clash drivers were given the opportunity to qualify first so that their crews would have time to get their cars ready for the race. Lap times had been fast all week during practice, thanks to the track, which had been completely repaved for the first time in its twenty-year history. On Saturday Cale Yarborough had broken his own nine-year-old track record* with a lap of 194.868 miles per hour, despite his insistence that his car was "not running worth a durn." He was even durn worse the next day when, near the end of his first qualifying lap, his engine blew up, sending smoke billowing from his car. Nevertheless, he made it back to the finish line with a speed of 194.321 miles per hour, the fastest up to that point. He stayed on the pole for only ten minutes, when Buddy Baker confirmed his status as the driver to beat. His lap of 196.049 miles per hour obliterated Yarborough's new track record. There were forty-three drivers left to qualify after Baker put up his time, but there was only one with a real chance of catching him: Donnie Allison.

Of all the bad deals in the long and storied history of bad deals — the Red Sox giving up Babe Ruth, the Indians giving up Manhattan — few were worse than the one Donnie Allison made Michael DiProspero and Bill Gardner, two businessmen from Connecticut who were also brothers-in-law. Over pinochle one night at DiProspero's house in the fall of 1972, the talk to turned to cars. DiProspero had a little experience in local short-track racing, and he mentioned that he was thinking of buying a Grand National car and fielding a team the following spring. Gardner had never even seen a race, but he had a sense of adventure and, thanks to his real estate holdings, the means with which

---

*Concerned that cars were traveling too fast, NASCAR mandated smaller, less-powerful engines after the 1970 season to slow them down.

to indulge it. He was on board. The brothers-in-law decided to call their operation DiGard.

DiProspero and Gardner stood out among NASCAR team owners, who were generally not the pinochle-playing types. There was also the matter of DiProspero and Gardner's provenance: they were Yankees in a southern man's sport. But where they truly broke the mold was in the way they questioned the accepted NASCAR way. The owner-driver relationship was historically a simple, informal one, binding only to the extent that a gentleman's handshake was considered such. If a driver wanted to leave, he left. If an owner got sick of his driver, he let him go. DiProspero and Gardner, however, insisted on a formal business arrangement, with written contracts. On the advice of Bobby Allison, who had built a few short-track cars for DiProspero, they hired Donnie Allison for the 1973 season. The deal they struck required Allison to sign over some equipment he had at his shop in Hueytown. In return, he was named president of DiGard as well as the team's driver.

It seemed like a good deal at the time.

Donnie Allison had had a few semi-regular gigs, but for most of his Grand National career he'd been a journeyman. DiGard provided stability. But it was an expansion team, and in its early days it had its share of '62 Mets moments—including ordering the wrong kind of car for its first race. DiGard showed up at the 1973 Daytona 500 with a short-track car, a Chevelle, which was kind of like taking a putter to the first tee at Augusta National. (Allison failed to qualify for the forty-car field.) And when Gardner was scouting territory for a race shop, he looked in Daytona, despite the fact that virtually every team was located within a two-hour drive of Charlotte. "I felt Daytona was the heart of racing," he explained. So he built a state-of-the-art, 20,000-square-foot facility within walking distance of the speedway—then found it was nearly impossible to fill it with workers. Few decent mechanics were going to uproot their families and move to Florida. The location was great for the two races at the speedway but murder for the rest of the season, which was loaded with races in the Carolinas and Virginia. Many weeks the crewmen just crashed at the shop of car builder Robert Gee outside Charlotte to save themselves the fifteen-hour round-trip drive.

The team steadily improved, thanks in no small part to the depth of Gardner's pockets. It brought the right car, a new Chevrolet, to the 1974 Daytona 500, and Allison drove it away from the rest of the field. He had a thirty-eight-second lead with eleven laps left when he ran over some debris and cut both his front tires, allowing Richard Petty to overtake him and win.* Allison came close on several other occasions, but he never took DiProspero and Gardner to Victory Lane. After a fifth-place finish in the 1975 Firecracker 400, the Fourth of July race in Daytona, Gardner summoned Allison to his hundred-foot yacht, *Captiva,* and told Allison he was being let go. "That was a tough decision because Donnie was a great person, a great family guy, and he was a hell of a driver," says Gardner. "But the guys weren't that happy at the time with his performance."

Getting fired is bad. Getting fired by a guy who has called you down to his yacht is worse. But getting fired by a guy who has called you down to his yacht and then informed you that your severance package is going to be $250 is about as bad as it gets. To his credit, Allison talked Gardner up to $500. That was all Allison had to show for his stock and for all that equipment he had signed over. Five hundred bucks. (Allison says it was worth $200,000. Gardner says that's what the gear was valued at, per the contract. "There's always two sides to every story," says Gardner. "It was in the contract, that's what you got paid. It's a way of doing business that nobody had done at the time.")

Gardner hired Darrell Waltrip to replace Allison, who returned to Hueytown and raced a Camaro at local short tracks before latching on

---

* Allison might have had a chance to catch Petty, but the race had been shortened to 450 miles due to the energy crisis.

with Hoss Ellington. Until Ellington started racing, he ran a pipe insulation company and went by his given name, Charles. But he realized that insurance was a lot cheaper for a pipe fitter than a race car driver, so he raced as Hoss. He fit in well with the raucous drivers of the 1960s. Ellington once went on a bender with Coo Coo Marlin and his wife, Eula Faye, the designated driver, near Talladega, Alabama, that ended with Ellington and Marlin getting locked up for being drunk. (It didn't help that Eula Faye, the stone-cold sober one, couldn't figure out how to lower the power windows when they were pulled over.) Ellington woke up in the middle of the night in a pitch-black cell to a loud clanking sound: Marlin was beating a metal cup with his boot in an attempt to fashion a key. He kept at it until Ellington pointed out that maybe they were safer in their cell than outside. "Don't you hear them damn bloodhounds barking?" he said.

Allison was something of a kindred spirit. "Donnie liked to hunt and fish and carry on," says Ellington. "And there ain't nothing wrong with that." Allison never minded that Ellington, who was based in Wilmington, on North Carolina's Atlantic coast, usually ran his car only on superspeedways, which had the biggest purses. But before the start of the 1979 season, Ellington and Allison decided that they were going to run the full schedule. Donnie was excited; it was a chance for him to see how he stacked up and to show that he took racing seriously enough to commit to the grind of going to the track week in and week out. Their year started out well enough, with a fifth-place finish at Riverside. And when they got to Daytona, Allison was consistently one of the fastest cars in practice.

Since he wasn't part of the Busch Clash field, Allison was one of the last cars to make a qualifying run, which put him at a distinct disadvantage. By the time he got on the track, it had gotten significantly warmer, making the surface slicker. And the gentle morning breeze had turned into a strong wind that held the cars up as they made their way down the backstretch. Still, Allison was able to turn the second-fastest lap, guaranteeing himself a front-row starting spot alongside Baker. He had to be delighted that his speed of 194 was almost two miles per hour faster than the time Waltrip posted in his old car.

Satisfied, Donnie cleaned up and headed into the garage to find out whether Richard Petty's boy merited all the attention he was getting.

The roof of the Petty Enterprises van was *the* place to be for the ARCA 200. In addition to Donnie Allison, drivers Neil Bonnett, Buddy Arrington, and Lennie Pond had flocked to higher ground in search of a better vantage point for the race. Cale Yarborough was there, too, but only because his offer to work on Kyle Petty's over-the-wall crew had been gracefully declined. (Yarborough's explanation as to why he was willing to lug tires around during pit stops was simple: "Because I admire the boy's spunk." And he wasn't the only one. Allison also offered his services.) Lee Petty was there, calmly smoking his pipe. Richard Petty was the last to arrive. After giving his son a few last-minute words of encouragement, he hopped on a bike, pedaled through the garage, and joined the party atop the van. Darrell Waltrip, Bobby Allison, and David Pearson watched from the next truck over, and A. J. Foyt was perched on a nearby van, all anxious to see what the kid could do.

While the men congregated in the garage, which was off-limits to the fairer sex, the Petty women gathered at Turn 4 atop an RV owned by Ron Bell, whose Southern Pride Car Wash was one of Kyle's sponsors. Kyle's wife, Pattie, was there, as was his mother, Lynda, and his grandmother Elizabeth. Pattie had already spent plenty of time with Elizabeth; her room at the Hawaiian Inn on the beach—ostensibly her honeymoon suite—adjoined her husband's grandparents' room.

Pattie had entered the NASCAR world two years earlier when she became a "Winston Girl," which one writer described as "those ladies in red shirts and white hotpants who pose beside the red-and-white Winston promotion autos at racetracks while gentleman fans snap pictures and get a peck on the cheek, then mutter happily, 'Ain't she enough to make a man's wife jealous?'" If that was the effect the Winston Girls had on married men, one can only imagine the effect they had on teenage boys, which is what Kyle was when they met. Pattie hadn't taken the job to widen her social circle. (Fraternization with drivers was taboo but certainly not unheard-of.) She was in it strictly for the $88 a day, which went toward putting herself through grad school. She was so set against the idea of hanky-panky that she decided she wouldn't even give the winner a kiss on the cheek. "I will shake hands," she said, "but I will not do that."

Interesting, then, that she ended up marrying the first person she met on the job.

Pattie's introduction to Grand National racing came at Nashville Speedway in the summer of 1977. She was twenty-three and felt completely lost. She vaguely knew about Richard Petty, because she lived in High Point and it was hard to live in High Point and be totally oblivious to the King. She knew of David Pearson, her father's favorite driver. And she knew of another driver in the field that day: Marty Robbins, a country music star who occasionally moonlighted as a racer. Pattie's father had never been crazy about his daughter spending so much time around racetracks, but when he found out that she might be able to meet Marty Robbins — who sang "El Paso," his favorite song — he warmed to the idea. Pattie made it a priority to get her picture taken with Robbins, so she sauntered up to a harmless-looking, frizzy-haired kid with a cast on the leg he had broken playing high school football. Kyle told her he'd be happy to introduce her. Before she knew it, Pattie had her picture. "I was his hero from that point on," she says.

Despite the difference in their ages, Pattie found herself spending more and more time with the friendly kid. She was getting close to Kyle's younger sisters as well; they loved to make trips to Pattie's farm and ride her horses. Things were going swimmingly until Kyle overplayed his hand. "Kyle and I got to be really, really good friends," says Pattie. "Then the next thing you know he's like, I want to marry you."

Cue the freaking-out music.

Pattie's reaction was exactly what one might expect: "I was like, *Okay, I can't see you anymore. Don't come back here. Your mother will have me locked up and put in jail. You're not quite seventeen yet, and I'm twenty-four. This isn't a pretty picture.*"

After a couple of weeks, though, she started to miss him. So she called the Petty house and asked Lynda to send Kyle back down to the farm. They decided that the best course of action was for Pattie to go up to Level Cross and meet the whole Petty clan. She had already won over Kyle's sisters by giving Rebecca a horse. ("You give a four-year-old a pony, and you're set for life," she says.) To their relief, his parents didn't require any grand equine gestures. If anything, Pattie's presence in their living room confirmed what they already suspected about their son. "Believe it or not, he acted more mature then than he does now," says Pattie. "He hung out with older people. He didn't have friends his age. His friends were his dad's crew. His mother said to me one day, 'It never surprised me that he brought home someone who's the same age as the guys he hangs out with.'"

Before Kyle gave her a ring, he gave her a wedding present: a two-year-old filly named Rockell Chick. In August 1978 he told Pattie that if she checked the horse's feed, she'd find another gift. "You might want to go get it before she eats it," he said. Pattie checked as instructed and found a diamond ring. Their engagement official, Kyle took his new fiancée up to the house. "They wanted to know when we were getting married," says Pattie. "His dad said, 'You'll have to get married before racing season starts because I don't have time…'"

So here Pattie was, spending the last day of her honeymoon atop an RV, watching the start of racing season — the ARCA 200, an event that would have attracted virtually no interest had her husband not been in the field. Kyle had run well in practice and qualified on the outside of the front row, which had more to do with what he was driving than how he drove it. The field had a handful of drivers capable of running up front and a whole lot of guys without the experience or the machinery to keep up. Kyle qualified at just under 190 miles per hour, 2 miles per hour behind pole sitter John Rezek; the cars at the back of the pack were a good 40 miles per hour slower.

Despite their lack of star power, the ARCA boys could usually be counted on to put on a pretty good show in Daytona. In 1978 leaders Jim Sauter and Bruce Hill wrecked each other on the last lap, with Sauter hanging on to win the race. But neither driver was in the field in '79. They had been denied entry by ARCA president John Marcum, who wielded the same kind of absolute authority over his series that Bill France had over his, but without France's admirable restraint. Marcum tooled around the Daytona garage in a gold Lincoln Continental, and he had a reputation for going to great — and sometimes questionable — lengths to inject excitement into his races. He would purportedly stand trackside with his houndstooth hat in hand, and if any car got too far out in front, he'd drop the hat — a signal to the flagman to throw the caution flag and bunch up the field.*

Marcum's rationale for keeping Sauter and Hill out was that "they don't normally race with us," but if being an ARCA regular was truly a prerequisite, Kyle Petty shouldn't have been allowed anywhere near the track. That, of course, wasn't going to happen. Hill believed that he and Sauter were being kept out for a more sinister reason: to give Kyle a better chance to win. "Everything was certainly set up that way," Hill

---

* Although phantom cautions are fairly common in NASCAR today, they weren't in the late 1970s, when race officials would just let cars drive away from the pack, no matter how boring a finish that might create. In the 1978 Grand National season, nineteen of the thirty races ended with only one or two cars on the lead lap, and no race finished with more than six.

complained. "The more I think about it, the more it disgusts me. But if I tried to force the issue, I would have difficulty getting past the technical inspectors at NASCAR races."

Marcum did his best to sidestep the controversy. "We got the nicest bunch of cars here this year we've ever had," he said. "All of 'em are independents. Closest thing we got to a factory car is Kyle's. I figured this is his first race and I think we can give him some driving lessons."

If the boy needed lessons, he wasn't going to get them from his father. "I ain't gonna tell you how to drive," Richard told Kyle. "Ain't gonna matter to me if you win or lose." The first part of the statement was far more believable than the second. The only advice Richard gave Kyle was to be patient and use the first couple of laps to get comfortable running in traffic.

Wearing one of his father's old racing suits—he removed the RICHARD portion of the stitching on the chest so it just said PETTY—Kyle slipped behind the wheel of his Dodge. He had painted the car Petty Blue and white, with the logo of his primary sponsor, Valvoline, on the hood and white eagles on the front quarter panels. There was a small Southern Pride Car Wash logo near the rear window. Kyle had encountered ignition problems near the end of Saturday's final practice, but Steve Hmiel and his crew had worked through the night to fix the car, and as it rolled off the starting grid, it was purring.

As the field turned a few warm-up laps behind the pace car, Kyle came to a realization about Daytona: "This is the biggest place in the world until you put multiple cars out there, then it becomes one of the smallest places in the world." Then the pace car pulled onto pit road, and the thirty-one cars bunched up and approached the start/finish line. That brief interval between the time the pace car pulls off the track and the time the green flag drops—transforming a casual Sunday drive into a knuckle whitener—are four or five of the most tension-filled seconds imaginable, so an inexperienced kid could be forgiven for being a little excitable under such conditions. When the green flag flew, Kyle threw his father's advice to take it easy out the window. He tore into the first corner, riding the high line, just like his old man liked to do. As he roared into Turn 2, he got even farther up the track, slapping the wall. "He can't go any higher than that," Richard said to the men on the van. But the contact with the wall didn't slow him down. He got around Rezek and led the pack back to the start/finish line. "If nothing else," his grandfather announced, "he's going to lead at least the first lap."

On the fifteenth lap, Kyle got his first reminder of just how serious the stakes were. Back in the pack, Bobby Fisher got sideways and was broadsided by Marvin Smith and Bobby Davis. Bobby Jacks then hit Davis, and Jacks went flipping through the air. (It wasn't a good lap for Bobbys.) It was a nasty wreck — nasty enough to make Cale Yarborough, who'd seen his share of carnage, let out a long "Wooooo!" on top of the Petty van, where the conversation turned to the effect the accident might have on Kyle's psyche. Richard, who was talking to Kyle over the radio, told him, "Come on back there, and when you get there, slow way, way down." By the time Kyle got around to the site of the wreck, Jacks had scampered from his car — which was on fire and lying on its side — and was sitting on the track with his head down, car parts strewn all over the place. Kyle had been to plenty of races and seen plenty of wrecks, some involving his father, but he'd never before witnessed one as a participant. He handled it without a problem.

The same, unfortunately, could not be said about his ensuing pit stop, the first of his career. Kyle had barely mastered the concept of speeding up; the concept of slowing down was completely foreign to him. He flew into the pits way too fast and almost took out Dale Inman, who was holding the signboard telling him which pit stall was his. (On top of the hauler, Yarborough and Donnie Allison were likely thankful that their offers to work on his crew had been turned down.) As he left the pits, Kyle stalled the engine, leaving him in a situation that called for cool and calm. Instead he screamed, "What gear do I put it in?" and dumped a cup of Gatorade in his lap.

By the time he got the engine refired and left the pits, Kyle had fallen back to tenth place. He worked his way back up near the front and stayed with the leaders despite another near stall in the pits thirty laps later. Watching the kid, the vets atop the Petty Enterprises van couldn't help but feel young again. Allison turned to Yarborough and said, "You know, I wouldn't mind starting all over again. Would you?" Yarborough said nothing, but his wide grin answered the question.

With the exception of the other thirty drivers in the field, and presumably their families, everyone at the speedway was pulling for Kyle, but no one more so than John Marcum, who had visions of front-page stories dancing in his houndstooth-covered head. Alas, as the laps ticked down, it was becoming clear that the car to beat belonged to Phil Finney, a driver from Merritt Island, Florida. Kyle and Marcum needed help from above. With nine laps left, it came.

To hear Kyle tell the story, the help literally came from above. Daytona Speedway is located about two miles inland; its proximity to the beach, along with the lure of Lake Lloyd and the prospect of foraging for food scraps left by infield tailgaters, makes the track a popular hangout for seagulls. Occasionally, there are collisions with the gulls, which is what Petty thought happened. But Finney remembers very well what hit his windshield as it plowed down the backstretch at 185 miles per hour: a small piece of metal about the size of a wallet. NASCAR windshields now are made of Lexan, the same material used in fighter jet canopies. Finney's was made of glass. It cracked, forcing him to pit and relinquish first place to Petty, who had a sizable lead on Rezek. But with seven laps to go, Ramo Stott blew a tire, bringing out the caution flag and allowing Rezek to get back on Kyle's tail for the final restart. "They'll go green for four laps," Lee said. "We'll see what he's learned. See if he's listened."

Richard decided there was nothing he could tell Kyle that would help him in the shoot-out. "It's potluck," he said. "You take what you can get."

Rezek had a strong restart, pulling alongside Kyle, but he couldn't complete the pass and had to back off as they hit the first corner. That's the way it went through the final laps: Rezek making up ground on the straightaways, but Kyle getting through the turns faster.

As Kyle took the white flag, Pattie was jumping up and down, screaming, "Go, Kyle! Go, Kyle! Think about our house payments and the vet bills!" Kyle was still in the lead, but on the last lap at Daytona that wasn't necessarily a good thing. The leader had to run with his foot on the floor at all times. The guy behind him could take advantage of the hole the first car punched through the air. Facing less resistance, he could settle in behind the leader and keep pace without running wide-open. Then, when the time was right, he could pull out, use up that little bit of throttle he had in reserve, and make the pass. It was called the slingshot, and it looked like Kyle was being set up for it. Being in the lead on the last lap at Daytona was such an undesirable position that in the 1974 Firecracker 400, David Pearson had faked a blown engine by taking his foot off the gas on the front stretch and leaving Richard Petty, who was on his bumper, no choice but to go around him. Then he had floored it, caught Petty in the fourth turn, and passed him just before they reached the finish line.

Now, as the cars sped off of Turn 4—the same spot Richard had pointed out to Kyle on their tour of the track three weeks earlier—Kyle did something he hadn't done all day. Instead of staying in the high groove and giving Rezek a chance to get under him, he swung his car down low, near the apron, leaving Rezek only one option: to take the long way and try to pass him high. Rezek got alongside the Dodge one last time, but Kyle beat him to the checkered flag. Had the finish line been farther up the track, the racing world might have been deprived of a storybook ending.

Down at Turn 4, all the Petty women were in tears. In the garage, Richard hopped off the trailer and headed for Victory Lane as the rest of the drivers took turns slapping Lee on the back. "A lot of people are going to be shaking their heads over this day for a long, long time," said Buddy Arrington.

"Whaddya think, Grandpa?" said Donnie Allison.

"Damndest thing I've seen," Lee replied.

"I believe Ol' Richard has just found his successor," Bonnett said.

"Wrong," replied Allison. "Richard had his successor the second that kid was born. I don't want to hear anyone ever tell me again that having a knack for driving can't be traced to heredity."

Down in Victory Lane, Richard was impressed with just about everything his son had done: "He showed a good driving style, but now he's got to learn how to drive a race car. And especially, he's got to learn how to stop one."

Kyle proved to be a natural at the PR side of racing, too. When a photographer asked him to take off his hat, he refused because he wanted to make sure the Valvoline logo got in as many pictures as possible. But lest anyone forget he was new at this, he actually blushed when he was asked if he should be called Prince Kyle. "Aww, no," he said. "Tomorrow I'll be back right where I was before, carrying tires and doing other chores on Daddy's crew."

Someone asked Richard—whose time in qualifying for the 500 that morning had been just eleventh fastest—if he would have done anything differently had he been behind the wheel of the car.

"Yes," the King said. "I probably would have run second."

For all of the buildup leading up to the inaugural Busch Clash—the promise of cars bouncing off one another in a mad dash for cash—Monty Roberts's brainchild turned out to be a ho-hum affair. Granted, anything short of the winner crossing the finish line on his roof was going to suffer for having to follow the Kyle Petty Show, but it would take several cans of Busch beer to convince any fan that what he saw lived up to the billing.

With Donnie Allison out of the field* and Cale Yarborough's engines blowing up on a regular basis, the only driver who had a chance to hang with Buddy Baker was Darrell Waltrip. But for the Clash, the two favorites entered into a nonaggression pact, agreeing to work together to pull away from the field and save any hard racing for the last lap or two.

Getting to the front early was something Baker always tried to do — none of this hang back, stay out of trouble, and make a move late business that Richard Petty and David Pearson were always pulling. Baker's philosophy fit his physique. He was a bear of a man, so big and strong that he looked like he might actually be able to mash the gas a little harder than anyone else. His strategy for the Clash was simple: "I'm gonna get comfortable and put both feet on the floor and see what happens."

That occasionally led to problems — blown engines, crushed fenders, dented bodies. Baker was notoriously tough on his equipment. The joke about him had always been, "Give Buddy an anvil for breakfast, and he'll break it by lunch." Baker also was cursed with horrible luck and an affinity for finding new and interesting ways to lose that would have been funny had they not been so sad. Arguably his best effort in that regard came in 1969, when he lost the Texas 400 by crashing on a caution lap — because he was looking at a sign his crew had made him telling him he had the race sewn up. Daytona had been an especially grim venue for Baker. He had been racing at the track since it opened but had never won. He'd finished second five times in the 500 and had a couple of other tantalizingly close finishes, the most recent in 1978, when he'd blown an engine with four laps left.

But he had every reason to believe that '79 would be different. He joined the team owned by Harry Ranier, a relative newcomer to the game who had deep pockets. Ranier's most significant move was to hire engine

---

* His best qualifying effort in the 1978 season had been second.

builder Waddell Wilson away from L. G. DeWitt's team. Junior Johnson was widely regarded as the best engine man of the day, but a strong case could be made for Wilson. He'd started as a helper in the engine room at Holman Moody in 1963, at the same time Cale Yarborough was sweeping the floors. Holman Moody was a massive operation that supplied equipment to several drivers, so when the engines were built, they were all thrown into a pile and distributed randomly. After Fred Lorenzen lapped the field in the 1965 Daytona 500, he started requesting engines from the same curly-haired kid who had built that one. Before long all the big-name Ford drivers were clamoring for Wilson's handiwork.

With Holman Moody, then later with Wood Brothers and DeWitt, Wilson built the engines that won four Daytona 500s for four different drivers with distinctly different styles. His most impressive win came in 1973, when he built Benny Parsons's motor. Parsons had insisted that Wilson use some drag racing pistons he had been given in California. Wilson said that the engine would blow up in a second, and it did. As they were on a shoestring budget, the only backup engine they had with them in Daytona was one Wilson had thrown together out of pieces from the scrap heap. "I wouldn't have given you $100 for that engine," Wilson says. "I wouldn't have put it in a street car." But it held up through qualifying, practice, and the race.

"He was like the fastest gun in the West," says rival engine builder Lou LaRosa. "The one you're always gunning for. If you beat him, you did something well."

So if anyone could build a motor that was powerful enough to run up front in Daytona but durable enough to stand up to Baker's heavy foot, it was Wilson. And the car that Wilson and crew chief Herb Nab built was sleek, too. The black and gray Oldsmobile rode so low to the ground and blended into the track so well that the other drivers started calling it "the Gray Ghost," because they swore it just appeared out of nowhere on their rear bumpers. "Against the field, that was about as fast a race car as I ever worked on," says Wilson.

Baker, who had drawn the number 3 beer can on Thursday, didn't waste any time showing off the power he had under his hood. He took the lead on the first turn of the second lap, and then, as planned, he and Waltrip hooked up and left the other seven cars behind. As Baker took the white flag, Waltrip was on his bumper, with the battle for third taking place about half a lap behind them.

Baker's car was clearly the class of the field, but like Kyle Petty an hour earlier, he found himself in the unenviable position of having to hold off a slingshot move in the final turn. And also like Petty, Baker protected his position by going low. "They expect you to run up against the wall on the last lap," he said. "But I got down on the apron. That way he couldn't go under me.... When you go in low like that, you are already turned when you get into the corner. The guy behind you, he hasn't turned, and when he goes in, he gets a push in the nose so he can't pass you." For the second time that day, the conventional wisdom had been upended. Maybe taking the lead into the last lap at Daytona wasn't such a bad thing after all.

Baker's $50,000 check brought his take for the day to $56,000. He had won $5,000 for taking the pole in the 500 and an extra grand for breaking the track record. Up to that point, the biggest check he'd cashed in his career had been for $32,300. But when he said that "finally winning here means more than the $50,000," those on hand believed him. In addition to snapping a seventy-race winless streak that stretched back to May 1976, Baker had finally conquered Daytona. "I've been coming here since '59, and now at least I've won something," he said.

As Baker celebrated, the 50,000 fans made their way out of the grandstands and into the parking lots, leaving in their wake piles of empty Busch beer cans. For Kyle Petty, Buddy Baker—and, not least of all, Monty Roberts—it had been a beautiful day.

## Chapter Five

# The Man in the White Hat

**Thursday, February 15**
**125-Mile Qualifying Races**

ALL WEEK Darrell Waltrip had been wearing a white hat. He was hard to miss in it. If the hat couldn't literally hold ten gallons, it at least looked big enough to handle a couple of two-liter bottles of Sun-Drop. If nothing else, it was spacious enough to rest on Waltrip's head without messing up his hair. But more than just a fashion statement, the lid doubled as a metaphorical device. There's a fine line between being the guy people love to hate and being the guy people legitimately loathe, and Waltrip had long ago left that line in his rearview mirror. "When they announced him at the driver introduction, you could almost feel the—I don't know if you could call it hatred—but the vibrations from the fans all saying 'Boo' and stomping their feet," remembers Gary Nelson, one of Waltrip's crew members. It had gotten to the point that he didn't even want to go to driver intros. So he made a conscious effort to remake himself as the good guy, white hat and all. "I'm going to be a nicer fellow," Waltrip said on Wednesday, the day before the twin qualifying races that would set the field for the 500. "I want to prove to everybody that I'm trying to be cooperative."

The "everybody" he was trying to win over could be forgiven if they were skeptical. For years Waltrip had been, in the words of Nelson, "raising the bar for breaking the mold." He was kind of like the protagonist in every movie ever made about racing—the young, brash, fast kid who needed to learn to harness all that energy and respect his elders. Waltrip craved attention, and if he couldn't get it with his driving, he'd get it with his mouth. That's what he had done in Nashville, where his chief competition had come from old schoolers like Coo Coo Marlin and Flookie Buford, good ol' boys who, when talking to reporters, would say things like "Yep, well, we run purty good." With some goading from track promoters, Waltrip assumed the role of the heel, getting in front of the cameras and saying things like "Aw, Flookie Buford's just a backhoe operator." The idea was to get people to recognize him, and it worked. So when he made it to Grand National racing, he started talking about other drivers, other teams, NASCAR— anything that crossed his mind. It was partly for show, but underlying the act was some sincere resentment aimed at the establishment he felt was trying to hold him back. The first time Buddy Baker ever laid eyes on Waltrip was in the early '70s when the unknown kid took the stage at a Q&A at the Hawaiian Inn in Daytona and proclaimed, "I'm the guy that's going to retire Richard Petty." Waltrip later referred to Baker as "a big elephant in a small jungle," and he once called out Junior Johnson's team for not working hard enough.

Needless to say, the subjects of his diatribes were not amused. Johnson shot back, "The trouble with Darrell is that he has hoof in mouth disease, and until he gets a bigger hoof and a smaller mouth, he's got no business talking about us." In 1977 Cale Yarborough dubbed Waltrip "Jaws," partly because Waltrip's aggressive driving left one of Yarborough's cars looking like it had been attacked by a shark, but mostly because Waltrip's jaws always seemed to be on the move. But it was a NASCAR official who probably best summed up the sport's feelings for Waltrip with one slightly haughty sentence: "Darrell's problem is that he just doesn't know his place."

Waltrip wasn't oblivious to the heat from the fans, from his fellow drivers, and from NASCAR. "They want to put a little fear in the new guy," he said in 1977. "It's like prison: when you stop bucking the system, they ease up. Pretty soon they let you get away with candy in your cell. But it's always their ballgame. They only ease up when they want to. If you play by their rules and do everything the way they want you to, you'll never be in trouble."

At first blush, that's an odd sentiment. It's not as if the NASCAR ranks have ever been bursting with corporate types. Historically, they were bootleggers, brawlers, and partyers. There was certainly room in the sport for drivers with personality. Tim Flock raced with a monkey named Jocko Flocko in his car.* "Little Joe" Weatherly drove a rental car into a motel swimming pool. One Sunday morning Curtis Turner landed his airplane on a road so that he could borrow a bottle of whiskey from a friend's house.[†]

But those good ol' boys had the good sense—unlike Waltrip—not to seek out cameras or microphones before putting their large personalities on display. Not that they had much cause to worry about cameras or microphones being around. One year in Riverside, a radio host looking to fill some airtime grabbed Curtis Turner and asked him

---

\* Jocko's career ended after he got out of his seat belt during a race in Raleigh and climbed on Flock, necessitating a pit stop so that Flock's crew could literally get the monkey off his back.

[†] When Turner realized that he had landed adjacent to two churches whose congregations were just getting out, he decided to hightail it out of there. As he taxied down the road and began to lift off, he noticed a traffic light hanging from heavy wires. Knowing he couldn't get in the air fast enough to get over it, he did the next best thing, a maneuver not recommended by most reputable flight instructors. "I had to raise my wheels so's I could fly low enough to get under it," he said.

what he thought of drag racing, since the winter nationals were being held in the area a few weeks later. Turner responded, "Well, I always considered that drag racing was a little like masturbation. It's a little bit of fun, but it ain't much to look at." Not many reporters went looking for quotes from Turner after that, but it didn't bother him at all.

"So many drivers then were smarter than hell, but they lacked education," says Ken Squier. "Curtis was a disaster, and Weatherly, too. Bobby Isaac was the national champion, and I doubt that he could read. He had better answers than anybody, but he wouldn't talk to anyone from the North. He was not about to show his ass to anyone who would embarrass him. He had that pride and respect for himself."

So the press descended on Waltrip, the anti–Bobby Isaac: comfortable in front of the camera, unafraid to throw out a five-syllable word now and again (even if he wasn't always using it properly), and emanating a sense of sophistication rarely seen in the sport, with his Florsheim shoes and Brooks Brothers shirts. "He had a $25 haircut in the days when everybody had $3 haircuts," says Nelson. "Drove the biggest Lincoln he could find. Probably the first driver I know of that bought an airplane but didn't learn how to fly it."

Perhaps the most annoying thing about Waltrip, though, was that he had started winning. When he started driving in the Grand National Series as a twenty-five-year-old in 1972, he was running his own operation and, predictably, struggling. Then he took over Donnie Allison's DiGard ride in the summer of 1975 and won in his eighth start. He'd since won thirteen more races, including six each in 1977 and '78, which just meant more big talk. "He was like Muhammad Ali," remembers Nelson. "He talked big, but then he backed it up on the track. But in the garage area it didn't sit well to have this kid come along and talk about how he was going to kick everyone's ass on Sunday. That made it tough for us in the garage. We were basically living with these other race teams from track to track as we went through the season. You get relationships with these folks. And all of a sudden, they changed when Darrell would piss them off."

Waltrip didn't stop at pissing off other crews. He felt that he was the one putting his neck on the line, and he wasn't about to let some grease monkey ruin his effort. "People point the accusing finger at the driver," Waltrip said. "He's the one who's supposed to have it together. You hate it when your efforts are tarnished because someone lets you down. You hate being handicapped by other people." So he'd see his crew working and would walk by and say, "You're not going to screw up my pit stops again, are you?"

Says Nelson, "His motivational skills weren't quite honed yet."

Waltrip wanted his car running right, and he wanted it—like his uniform, which he insisted be pressed—to look good. The extent of his feedback was often to say, "That's just not gonna work. You gotta repaint that thing." When the car was slow, there were some serious blowups. "He's got a light temper, all right," his former crew chief Jake Elder once said. "He wants to run in the front bad, but Darrell don't quite always understand the circumstances why he's not running in the front. That's when he flies off the handle and throws those temper tantrums." This from a man who once went after one of his crewmen with a jack handle.

For years there had been a revolving door at DiGard. First Waltrip publicly ripped Mario Rossi and then had him fired as his crew chief. After Rossi he went through David Ifft and Darel Dieringer before Buddy Parrott was hired in 1977. Parrott was a card. Like Donnie Allison, he had been a diver when he was younger (he was the North Carolina state champion in high school; Allison was the Florida champ), and like Allison, he enjoyed a good time. Parrott looked forward to trips to Daytona because the hotel he stayed in had a pool that allowed him and Allison to hold impromptu diving competitions. "You've heard of a half gainer?" says Parrott. "My best dive was probably the half goner. I'd be half-gone when I did it."

If Parrott had managed a baseball team, he'd have been what they call a players' manager. "The guys loved him," says Waltrip. "He was a good leader of the team. But working on a car, setting a car up, that didn't interest him. What interested him was running the pits, calling the race on Sunday. And when the cameras were on, Buddy was on. I'll never forget, one of the guys said to me, 'Buddy Parrott, did you know he can't even weld?' It didn't surprise me. He was a Sunday guy." Still, Parrott and Waltrip got along well enough. "We had a lot of fun together," says Waltrip. It helped that Parrott had a very capable supporting cast. As a crew chief, Nelson would win twenty-five races and earn a reputation as one of NASCAR's most creative rule benders, while engine builder Robert Yates won the 1999 championship as an owner.*

The "Waltrip Effect" wasn't lost on other owners. In 1978 Kentucky businessman Harry Ranier began fielding a full-time team, with winless journeyman Lennie Pond behind the wheel. When Ranier saw how Waltrip had elevated a fledgling team to a championship contender, he decided to make a run at him. Waltrip was amenable to the idea. Driving for DiGard was starting to wear on him, and the money Ranier was offering was good. Poaching drivers wasn't uncommon, but Waltrip had signed a deal with Bill Gardner that ran through 1982, and Gardner (who was now running the team with his brother Jim) wasn't about to let him out of it. Waltrip figured that with the Gardners up in Connecticut, his would be the only voice anyone heard, so he started doing what he did best: making outlandish statements, such as calling the Gardners "slave dealers."

Bill Gardner, however, didn't stand by and take it. First, he sent Ranier a cease-and-desist telegram. Then he called a press conference

---

* Nelson, whose roots were in West Coast racing, had been considered for the job as Waltrip's crew chief in 1977, but the driver had nixed the idea. "I didn't like Gary," remembers Waltrip. "He was from California, and when he showed up at DiGard riding a Harley, he had long hair, like a hippie. They wanted him to be my crew chief. I said, 'He ain't working on my car.'"

the morning of the Southern 500 in Darlington to set the record straight about Waltrip's contract status. Realizing he needed his driver at least sort of happy, Gardner sat down with Waltrip and gave him an improved deal for the 1979 season — despite the fact that the driver had yet to win the sport's biggest race or its championship.

It was time to grow a bigger hoof.

Waltrip was one of the few drivers who didn't loathe the Twin 125s. He saw them as a chance to compete: "That's what we're here for, ain't it?" Most of his cohorts — especially the good ones — hated the races, though, primarily because they were being forced to share the track for one hour with some very desperate drivers. "You get seven or eight cars fighting for three or four spots in the field and it will make a guy do things he wouldn't do normally," said Richard Childress. The chief worry was getting caught up in someone else's trouble and wrecking a good Daytona 500 car. "Anytime you get into a car and race something bad can happen," said Richard Petty. "Now how do you suppose a cat is going to feel if he messes up his car in the 125-miler and can't be ready for the 500?"

Petty and Childress were in the first race, which meant they had the unenviable task of chasing Buddy Baker. NASCAR made one concession to the drivers, hoping that something — anything — could be done to take away Baker's advantage: he was required to put bright orange tape on the front of the Gray Ghost so his opponents could at least see the car as it blew past them.

The races were fifty laps each, which meant that every driver would have to make one pit stop for gas. Baker dashed to the front of the field and stayed there comfortably until it was time to refuel, on lap 36. He just needed to top off his tank, but somehow the stop took ten seconds. By the time everyone had finished their stops, Cale Yarborough, whose crew had gassed his car in five seconds, had a lead of 3.2 seconds — a lot of ground at 190 miles per hour. Baker was at the back of a pack with Benny Parsons, Bobby Allison, and Richard Petty. It took him just seven laps to pass all three and hitch himself to Yarborough's bumper. He retook the lead with two laps to go, and Yarborough never had a chance to get it back. It was a dominating performance, with Baker making up half a second per lap in traffic, and one that scared the hell out of every driver who witnessed it.

The field was more level in the second race. Donnie Allison and Darrell Waltrip started on the front row and tried to employ the same strategy Waltrip and Baker had used in the Clash. Instead of fighting each other early, they'd team up and drive away from the pack, then decide it between themselves. But Allison had engine trouble and dropped out with twelve laps to go. Four laps later Tighe Scott cut a tire, bringing out a caution and bunching up the pack for a tight finish. Waltrip was in the lead, and A. J. Foyt, the four-time Indy 500 champ, was second. Foyt was one of the drivers Waltrip got along well with because he, like Waltrip, was an outsider, a Texan who ran only a few NASCAR races a year. As the caution flag flew, he pulled up beside his buddy and gave him a friendly wave — what Waltrip called "one of those I-promise-I-won't-pass-you looks" — suggesting that they should work together at the end. "It showed how much experience I've gotten — I didn't fall for it," Waltrip said later with a laugh. Instead, Foyt tried to get around Waltrip as they headed for Turn 3 for the final time. And just as he made his move, the Daytona crowd saw for the first time a scene that would be repeated over and over for the next two decades: a smirking, mustachioed driver making a wild charge.

Behind Foyt on the final lap was Dale Earnhardt, an unknown twenty-seven-year-old who had run nine races in four seasons. Just as Foyt made his move on Waltrip's high side, Earnhardt shot low. It was a bold move, and it almost paid off. Waltrip moved up the track to block Foyt, allowing Earnhardt to see daylight. That forced Dick Brooks, the fourth-place driver, to make a decision. In the draft at Daytona, one car driving by itself won't go nearly as fast as two or more cars working together. Brooks could either cut low and try to push Earnhardt past Waltrip, or he could go high and hitch himself to Foyt. He chose to go with the veteran, and without drafting help, Earnhardt slid back into fourth.

The move didn't have a big effect on the finish — Waltrip won, Foyt was second, and Earnhardt cost himself one place. But it was a ballsy move, a rookie trying to pass two of the best drivers on the track with one move. Earnhardt pulled into the garage, hopped out of his car, and met the media at Daytona for the first time. The opening question came from Earnhardt himself, who was smiling slyly under his bushy mustache, and it was certainly rhetorical: "How 'bout it, boys? Think I'm gonna make it?"

Richard Petty had little reason to be optimistic. After coming home seventh in the first qualifier, he immediately called a team meeting, at which he made clear that nothing about the car was working. "Richard said the car wasn't handling," said Maurice Petty, "plus it wouldn't run either." He wound up one spot behind Ricky Rudd, a rookie who had never driven on the track before.

But no one was feeling good, not after Baker's display. Waltrip sang the praises of his car, Maybelline, the lone Oldsmobile in his Chevy-heavy stable. "Maybelline is one of the easiest old girls I've seen. She's a pleasure to drive. I told her not to get any bugs on her face." But his cockiness was tempered by a heavy dose of realism; the brashest statement he was willing to make about the 500 was that he and Baker were co-favorites. "But him more than me," Waltrip said, sounding nothing at all like Muhammad Ali.

The general consensus was that it was going to take, as Benny Parsons said, "some kind of miracle" to keep Baker from winning. A few drivers grumbled that he was so fast he had to be cheating, but as he watched NASCAR tear down his car in the postrace inspection, Baker said, "I just want to see all those red faces among people who thought we might be doing something illegal, because that engine is two cubic inches smaller than it's supposed to be." (The ability to get away with cheating was something many crew chiefs and engine builders wore as a badge of honor, but Waddell Wilson swore that every engine he built was legal.) Yarborough tried to remain optimistic, positing that when Wilson put a more durable race engine in the Gray Ghost, it would bring Baker back to the pack. "Only bad thing about that," said Baker, "is Waddell tells me the one we're going to put in is better than the one we're taking out."

The hardest thing for Baker to do was not to get his hopes up. "I'm going to the golf course before I get a big head," he said. "Some pals can't wait to get me over to Indigo Country Club. They know I've got a little money now, and they're circling like vultures." But after years of heartbreak at Daytona, it was hard for him to think that trouble wouldn't somehow find him. "I don't know how many parts there are in a race car, but I do know that at any time the smallest thing can put you out of a race. I just hope I can run as good as this car's been running."

## Chapter Six

# On the Air

OF ALL the accents in the drawl-laden Babel that was the garage at Daytona International Speedway, the most unique probably belonged to David Hobbs. Born in Royal Leamington Spa, England, Hobbs hit all of his g's and was one of the few people around whose vocabulary didn't include "y'all." He was a popular interview subject the day before the race, partly because of his résumé—he had experience driving in Formula One, the Indy 500, the Daytona 500, and various sports car series—and partly because he was going to be calling the 500 with Ken Squier. "I think we're going to see a good race," Hobbs told a couple of newspapermen, "if Buddy Baker will take the money CBS is offering him not to run away and keep the show competitive."

They had a laugh, but there was no doubt that CBS was hoping someone would find a way to keep up with Baker, because if he turned the race into a snoozer, the network had no choice but to show the whole dreary thing. It was a novel concept, showing a stock car race from start to finish. Saturday's Sportsman 300 would be a dry run, shot but not aired. On Sunday, though, there would be no safety net, thanks to an audacious deal that had the potential to make or break the man who had agreed to it.

Neal Pilson wanted to go home. He was a thirty-eight-year-old New Yorker in Daytona, a man out of his element, and he had spent several days in intense negotiations with Bill France Jr., which would drain the energy out of even the most vigorous person. In addition to inheriting control of NASCAR and the speedway from his father when Big Bill retired, France had also inherited his dad's prowess at the negotiating table, which Pilson was finding out the hard way as they tried to hammer out a deal to broadcast the 1979 Daytona 500 on CBS. The window in the conference room next to France's office on the second floor of NASCAR's offices at the speedway afforded him a perfect view of the airport, which allowed him to gaze longingly out the window at all the planes that were leaving Daytona without him. He'd see a Delta jet take off, then get up and change his reservation to a later flight, hoping he might make that one.

Pilson had no one to blame but himself. As vice president of business affairs for CBS Sports, he had, with some urging from Ken Squier, convinced his bosses to get into the racing game. It was his idea, and if it didn't work out, it was going to be his ass, so it was in his best interest to stick around and get the best deal he could, no matter how many flights he had to rebook. The negotiations were made especially tough by the fact that what they were talking about doing—scheduling a special program to show a 500-mile NASCAR race live, from start to finish—was unprecedented.

At that time, if you wanted to see a NASCAR race, your choices were limited. You could buy a ticket and go to the track, or you could turn on ABC's *Wide World of Sports* and wait for the car racing segment, which could usually be found somewhere between the barrel racing segment and the Mexican cliff diving segment. The only time a car race was shown from start to finish was on Memorial Day weekend, when ABC would tape the Indianapolis 500 on Sunday afternoon and air it that night. The only nod to Daytona's status as the preeminent stock car event was that the TelePrompTer company would occasionally broadcast the race in theaters on closed circuit, the same way many prizefights were shown.

The thinking behind keeping cars off the air was simple: with three networks and virtually no cable, there simply wasn't room on the airwaves for a three-hour, forty-five-minute block of anything, especially something with as narrow appeal as a stock car race. Then there was the fact that live racing was unpredictable—not always in a good way. In 1970 ABC decided to air the conclusions of a few races live, to capture what it presumed would be some gripping late-lap drama. One of the first races the network tried this on was the Nashville 420, which turned out to be a battle of attrition. By the time ABC returned to the track for that gripping late-lap drama, there were only nine cars running—and none on the same lap. As part of *Wide World of Sports,* ABC also showed one race live in its entirety, the 1971 Greenville 200. The seventy-five-minute snoozer—Bobby Isaac won by two laps—was entirely unmemorable,* and the live racing experiment was soon abandoned.

France, though, thought that his race could be different. Daytona was bigger and faster and less prone to the kind of sheet metal banging that could sideline twenty or twenty-five cars. And he could also trade on the race's status as the Super Bowl of its sport. CBS started warming to the idea primarily because the race took place in the middle of winter, when nothing else was happening. The NFL season was over, baseball's spring training was just getting started, and no one seemed

---

* The broadcast was so unmemorable that it is rarely, if ever, mentioned. Virtually every story of the past thirty years credits the 1979 Daytona 500 as being the first race shown live from flag to flag.

to care that the NBA season was in full swing. Squier had also lobbied Pilson, arguing that there were plenty of race fans out there who had no way of satisfying their racing joneses, because most local tracks weren't open yet.*

In May 1978 CBS made its move. Pilson and Barry Frank, the head of CBS Sports, went to Daytona to meet with France. Squier had already spoken to France and had given Pilson a heads-up that NASCAR's main demand was going to be that the race be aired live. When France asked if CBS would be amenable to doing that, Pilson and Frank looked at each other and said yes. France smiled, and Frank got on a plane for New York, leaving Pilson to work out the details. "Bill said to me, 'You're not leaving here until we get a signed agreement,'" says Pilson. "I was thinking, *When am I ever going to be able to leave?*"

They negotiated in the conference room, writing out provisions that France would have typed up so that Pilson could fax them back to New York. After two days they had an agreement. Then Jim France, Bill's brother and NASCAR's vice president and secretary, came into the room and offered his take: "Wow, I'm not happy with this." So Pilson and Jim went a few rounds of their own, renegotiating the deal. After six hours they settled on an agreement they could both live with. Then Bill Sr. came by to offer his thoughts. He'd been retired for seven years, but he still cut an imposing figure, and Pilson was dreading the latest in the parade of Frances. But Big Bill simply put his hand on Pilson's shoulder and said, "Looks like we have a deal, because I'm really pleased."

It was time to celebrate, which in Daytona meant one thing: Steak n Shake. France picked up the $7 lunch tab. "I told him that was very generous of him," Pilson says. Then he finally got on a plane for home, feeling, in his words, like a "limp dishrag."

---

*Squier could be trusted to speak to the mind-set of the cold-weather race fan. He has run the Thunder Road International SpeedBowl, a quarter-mile oval, in Barre, Vermont, since 1960.

Because it was NASCAR, the contract was only twelve pages long, the closest thing to a handshake deal that Pilson's bosses would stand for. (A standard contract would have run in excess of fifty pages.) The sheer number of concessions Pilson made in those twelve pages are a testament to the Frances' powers of persuasion. Not only was CBS on the hook for the Daytona 500, but Pilson also agreed to show the Talladega 500—which was held at another track owned by the France family—live. CBS would also air the Twin 125s on tape delay. The deal ran for five years and was worth $6 million. "It was," says Pilson, "a lot of money for an event that no one had ever covered live."

CBS sent its top NFL crew, producer Bob Fishman and director Mike Pearl, along with a separate producer for the pits, Bob Stenner. None of them had any experience broadcasting racing, though, and they had a tall order. "We were trying to find this balance between not offending the people who were racing fans, who found it every weekend wherever it was, and trying to educate the people who were not usually watching," says Stenner.

They would cover the race with nine cameras, less than a quarter of the number Fox employs now. There were two on the roof of the press box, one in each of the first three turns, three in the pits, and one hand-held camera behind the wall in Turn 4. The restraining wall was only about four feet high, so the handheld gig was dangerous. Every day cameraman Joe Sokota was sent to his post with a motorcycle helmet and instructions to hit the deck if he thought a runaway car was coming his way. And every day he came back looking like he had spent the afternoon rolling around a junkyard trash heap. "His helmet would be full of dirt and grease, and he couldn't see out of his visor," Fishman recalls. "He'd have little bits of sheet metal in his hair and the back of his neck. I'd say, 'Joe this is insane.' And he'd say, 'No, no, I love it. It's completely safe.'"

Other than dodging debris, the toughest task for Sokota and the other eight cameramen was covering all the action. With more than three dozen cars running around the immense track, there was plenty of action. And not just in the lead pack.

Shortly before 1:00 p.m. the thirty-eight cars in the Sportsman 300 rolled onto the track under dark skies. The race was designed to showcase drivers who raced at short tracks around the country, but there were a few big names in the field. Darrell Waltrip was racing, as were Bobby and Donnie Allison. There was some controversy over the Grand National stars dipping down into the lower ranks, but all three of them had the requisite short-track bona fides.* And no fan who had seen the previous two races was going to complain about the presence of Waltrip and Donnie Allison. They had provided photo finishes each year, with Allison winning in '77 and Waltrip returning the favor the next year.

At the other, shallower end of the talent pool were the small-timers who met the requirements: twenty bucks for a license and a car that could pass inspection. One Sportsman regular was a reverend in the Carolinas who didn't harbor any thoughts of moving up to Grand National, because he refused to race on Sunday. Perhaps the least experienced driver in the field was Don Williams, a ball bearing salesman from Madison, Florida, who hid his racing from his parents and hid the fact that he had a college education from his racing buddies. Like everyone who gets behind the wheel of a race car, Williams was curious about how he'd fare at NASCAR's biggest track against its biggest names. "My life's ambition is to race here," he had told his sisters on a trip to Daytona. His qualifying time of 170.32 miles per hour was more than 20 miles per hour slower than pole sitter Donnie Allison's, but it was fast enough to make his dream come true.

The rain clouds hanging low over the speedway made for an ominous setting, and they would also have a profound effect on strategy. In

---

*Waltrip, for instance, had raced sixty-two times in 1978 and was well on his way to doing the same in '79.

long races, the smart play is usually to lay back and stay out of trouble before making a late move. But the drivers didn't have that luxury, because the weather forecast virtually guaranteed that rain would cut the race short. Everybody's plan was to get to the front quick and hope to be there when the skies opened up.

Donnie Allison led the field to the green flag, and he and Waltrip duked it out for the first couple of laps.

Then all hell broke loose.

One thing scares a driver. Not hitting the wall. Not flipping a car.

Fire.

Crashes are an occupational hazard. They happen so frequently that every driver becomes inured to them. If he doesn't, he is never going to make it. The thing about a wreck is, you hit something—be it a car or a wall—and it's over.

Fire, though, is a different story. When a car goes up in flames, it's just the beginning of the ordeal. And since protecting against injuries in a crash requires a driver to strap himself into his seat very securely, getting out of the car is an elaborate process that involves unhooking several belts, lowering a window net, and climbing out of a very small opening while wearing a bulky suit and a helmet.

Joe Frasson, a journeyman from South Carolina, took more precautions than most. He wore a fire suit and fireproof underwear, and—unlike most drivers of the era, who steered with their bare hands—Frasson wore double-layered Nomex gloves. He entered the Sportsman 300 in a Pontiac, and it was fairly stout.* He had it running in the middle of the pack on the fourth lap, when Freddy Smith's car suddenly swerved up

---

* A few Sportsman drivers used Pontiacs, but the make had been absent from Grand National racing for years. Frasson had tried to bring it back in Charlotte in 1975. When he failed to qualify for the race, he called a press conference, produced a tire iron, and began beating the crap out of the car. "I would like to announce that Pontiac is retiring from racing," he proclaimed.

the track and pinched Frasson into the wall. Smith later said that all he knew was that "something" knocked out his windshield. (Most likely it was debris from an engine that blew in front of him.) After that, Smith swore, he couldn't remember a thing.

What he missed was one of the most spectacular wrecks Daytona had ever seen. The initial contact with Frasson's car caused a small oil fire to start in the Pontiac. Frasson was driving blind—his hood popped up after the collision—so he hit the brakes and did his best to guide the car down to the inside of the track. Just as he was coming to a stop, Del Cowart rear-ended him at about 150 miles per hour, driving Frasson's twenty-two-gallon fuel tank, which was still full, out of the trunk and up into the oil fire. The explosion sent flames dancing fifty feet into the air.

Certain situations in life call for one to keep one's composure and remain cool. This, to Joe Frasson, was not one of those situations. He wanted to get out of the oven he was in as fast as he could. He could barely tell what he was doing—it can be tough to see when your goggles are melting to your face—but he somehow unhooked his safety belts and climbed out of the window, then ran away from the car, trusting that his fellow drivers would be able to avoid him. (They did.)

As Frasson was playing Frogger, the cars behind him were swerving to miss the fireball. Dodging a wreck on a superspeedway is an art form, something that has to be learned. It's a delicate operation. One's first instinct is to stand on the brakes, but with that comes the risk of getting hit from behind. The main idea is to put the trouble in your rearview mirror as quickly as possible. Don Williams had no experience dodging superspeedway wrecks. In fact, he had no experience on pavement or on anything bigger than a half-mile track. What happened when he approached Frasson's roasting Pontiac is unclear, as none of the nine CBS cameras picked it up. Some reports said that Williams hit his brakes and was hit from behind. Others insisted that he selflessly turned his car toward the wall to avoid another car.

However it happened, Williams went into the wall. Hard. The next day the papers would report that a piece of metal had been driven under the visor of his helmet and into his forehead. He was bleeding from both ears and had multiple fractures, including one at the base of his skull. The worst fears of his mother were realized. The day before the race, a friend of Don's had let slip that he was racing. His mother, Robbie, got up at the crack of dawn to get a Jacksonville paper so that she could check the starting lineup. When she saw her son's name, she called his hotel room at 6:00 a.m. to plead with him not to race. The phone just rang and rang. He was already on his way to the track.

As rescue workers pulled Williams from his car, officials put out the red flag, which stopped the race while the mess was cleaned up.*

When the race restarted half an hour later, Bobby and Donnie Allison swapped the lead, but the brothers went out of the race when their engines expired within seven laps of each other. That left Waltrip—who was driving Wanda, the same Chevy that had won the season-opening Grand National race at Riverside—and Dale Earnhardt—who was forcing his way into the spotlight for the second time in three days—as the cars to beat.

Earnhardt took the lead on lap 60—the midpoint of the race, at which point it became official—and stayed there until he had to pit with a flat tire on lap 66. Within minutes a gentle rain began to fall, but it was hard enough to bring the race to a halt and deprive Earnhardt of the chance to catch Waltrip.

After the race Frasson met with reporters, his face covered with burn lotion and most of his bushy beard gone. "I had all my fireproof underwear on, thank goodness," he said. "Everything on my helmet was burned off."

---

* Williams lived for ten years in a near-vegetative state before passing away in May 1989.

\* \* \*

The rain continued throughout the afternoon, and drivers were getting word from back home that the weather in North Carolina was even worse. Cale Yarborough, who had honed his piloting skills significantly since that first flight with Wib Weatherly, had flown to Daytona and came to the realization that he wasn't going to be able to fly back home if the snow that was forecast actually fell. He asked a buddy, Hoss Ellington, for a ride back after the race on Sunday. Ellington said sure. So what if Hoss owned the car Donnie Allison was driving? Cale needed a lift, and Cale was a friend. It didn't make any difference that Yarborough was the opposition.

Back at his hotel on the beach, Allison watched the raindrops pound his window. It had been a bad day all around. First Williams had crashed, then Allison's engine had blown, and then the rain had spoiled what had been shaping up to be a pretty good race. Unlike Bobby, Donnie had a well-earned reputation for having a good time, but the night before an important race he was always serious. And Daytona was as important as it got, the one race big enough to validate a driver's career, to maybe even nudge him out of his brother's shadow. As he took in the storm outside and contemplated what lay ahead of him the next day, he repeated the same four words to himself over and over: "This is not good. This is not good."

## Chapter Seven

# So Fair and Foul a Day

**Sunday, February 18**
**Race Day**

RICHARD PETTY awoke to troubling news. During the night someone had broken into the Petty Enterprises van parked outside his hotel and stolen the CB radio. They had also boosted the fuzz buster, but that wasn't a terrible loss. Given the weather in Daytona on race day, nobody was going to be driving the van very fast.

The rain had continued all through the night, and the gray morning sky didn't bode well. It didn't take much rain to stop the race, and even if the weather miraculously cleared up, there was still the matter of getting the track dried. Not that there was reason to be optimistic that the weather would cooperate. All over the country it seemed as if Mother Nature was hell-bent on showing off her nasty side.

One of the first things a transplanted northerner learns during his first southern winter is that the natives are so ill equipped to function in snow that they descend into a state of near panic at the prospect, let alone the presence, of it. And in most of the South on Sunday morning, there was plenty of snow present. Nine inches blanketed Charlotte, covering roads and race shops, closing businesses, and generally confounding the populace. Edison Searles, who had moved his family to the Queen City from Detroit three months earlier, lamented to the *Charlotte Observer,* "I can deal with the snow, but I can't deal with the city's inability to handle it or the people's inability to drive in it."

In defense of the locals, the storm had arrived with little warning. Two days earlier, temperatures in Charlotte had been up around 70 degrees. The sudden appearance of snow was followed almost immediately by a predictable, comprehensive run on provisions. The manager of one A&P reported, "They're buying out the whole store. I guess they think we're gonna be snowed in for a couple weeks." Shovels were the hottest sellers, though the quantity of booze being stockpiled suggested that a sizable chunk of the city was content to leave the snow clearing to someone else and wait out the blizzard as comfortably as possible. The A&P manager said that he was moving "a lot more beer and wine than milk and bread."

Shoppers aside, most people found the streets of Charlotte almost impossible to navigate. The staff of Town & Country Ford assembled a fleet of half a dozen four-wheel-drive pickup trucks and took to the streets, picking up doctors and hospital staffers and dropping them off at Presbyterian Hospital. A panicking bride-to-be named Debbie Holder called the police and tearfully explained that she had no way of getting to the Carmel Presbyterian Church, where she was supposed to marry Atef Sohl that afternoon. (With the law as her chauffeur, she made it on time, although the flight that was to take her and Sohl to their Hawaiian honeymoon was canceled. The newlyweds were last seen walking hand in hand down a snowy street.)

Atlanta was hit hard, too. The airport was completely shut down for the first time in its history, but the streets were still semi-drivable, which was good news for the enterprising man who put on his snow skis and was photographed being towed down Peachtree Street. Other citizens did their best to enjoy and preserve the novelty of a winter wonderland. Aaron's, a photofinishing store in town, would see a 5,000 percent increase in the number of rolls of film it developed in the week following the storm.

But the farther north one progressed, the more bone-chilling the stories one heard. Washington, DC, saw its heaviest snowfall in fifty years: twenty-three inches, with gusting winds creating drifts as high as five feet. The National Guard was ordered in to clear the streets, fight fires, and drive ambulances. In New York City, which had been on the verge of bankruptcy only two years earlier, Mayor Ed Koch authorized $500,000 in emergency overtime pay for a thousand sanitation workers to drive salt trucks and snowplows to help clear the six inches of snow that fell overnight. Visibility was close to zero, as was the temperature. It was the coldest the city had been in eighty-three years, but it was downright balmy compared to conditions upstate, where the village of Old Forge, in the Adirondacks, had seen an overnight low of 52 below.

In the heartland, temperatures were so low and snowfall levels so high that even the grizzled midwesterner Edison Searles would likely have had trouble dealing with the elements. Four of the five Great Lakes were completely frozen over for the first time in recorded history.* The *Chicago Tribune* couldn't help but take a defeatist tone, suggesting "that perhaps this winter will never end," and so many residents of the Windy City simply abandoned their cars on the snow-covered roads that the city's impound lots couldn't handle them. Overflow vehicles were taken to Comiskey Park, where their owners could pick them up after paying a $45 towing fee.

All over the country, the pressing question on people's minds became: *How am I going to kill a Sunday afternoon if I can't leave the house?*

---

*Lake Ontario, the deepest and fastest moving of the five, was only about 40 percent frozen.

The *Charlotte Observer* ran an article with several ideas for fighting cabin fever, including a recipe for homemade Play-Doh and a suggestion that parents let kids finger-paint using chocolate pudding and a cookie sheet: "They can eat their masterpiece. Also, they can use liquid starch and food coloring, but shouldn't try to eat that."

The paper did concede the obvious: "The old standby, of course, is TV." That was very good news for Neal Pilson and Bill France Jr.

Actually, it was good news for Pilson and France only if they could give their captive audience something to watch. The race was a sellout, which meant that the provisional blackout for the southern states France had insisted upon in his talks with Pilson was lifted. But the weather meant that there were plenty of spare tickets to be had. Outside the track a lanky fifteen-year-old who had driven down from Owensboro, Kentucky, with his family tried unsuccessfully to off-load a pair of primo grandstand tickets he had inherited from some less hearty friends. They had skipped town at the sight of the storm and told the kid he could keep whatever cash he got for the tickets. Alas, Michael Waltrip's quest for "some running-around money" would go unfulfilled. "I never did sell them," remembers Darrell's younger brother.*

In his suite above the track, Neal Pilson was protected from the rain, but he was feeling anything but secure. He had dragged two of his CBS bosses to the event. Gene Jankowski, the head of the CBS Broadcast Group, called Pilson over and said, "Neal, we don't have to pay for this if it rains, right?" Pilson told him that not only would they still have to pay, but they'd have to show the race when it was run—most likely the following afternoon, which would mean paying to keep the production crew in Daytona for another day and preempting the network's popular daytime lineup of *The Young and the Restless, Guiding Light,* and *As*

---

* Don't feel too bad for him. Twenty-two years later Daytona would finally yield that running-around money—$1,331,185—when Michael won the 2001 Daytona 500.

*the World Turns.* Airing a race on a Sunday afternoon when nothing else was on was one thing; depriving America's housewives of the exploits of Julia and Katherine and the rest of the good people of Genoa City was another thing entirely. To make matters worse, Pilson didn't even have a decent backup plan if the race was postponed. Traditionally, the previous year's race would be shown, but the '78 Daytona 500 had been an ABC production. Says Pilson, "Gene kind of gave me a look like, *Well, it's your career. Call us when you get another job.*"

Bill France Jr. and his father were also sweating. They'd gone to great lengths to get the race on TV, to give Americans who wouldn't normally be paying attention their first impression of the sport. And the last thing they needed was for that impression to be of a bunch of guys—most of whom had neither the inclination nor the camera presence to give lengthy interviews—huddling under umbrellas in a garage.

The race was scheduled to start at 12:15 p.m. Shortly before noon Big Bill disappeared. Legend has it that he went onto the roof of the grandstand, held out his arms, and commanded the rain to stop. To this day, when NASCAR types speak of France's reputed supernatural powers, they tend to be dismissive without actually coming out and saying they don't believe in them, the same way that skeptical nine-year-olds hedge their declarations that they don't believe in Santa Claus on the off chance that he really does exist and just happens to be listening.

Whether he made a trip to the rooftop and conversed with the gods is debatable. What is known for certain is that France got into his Cadillac and went for a drive to check on the weather up in Ormond Beach. He gave a walkie-talkie to a NASCAR employee named Jim Bachoven and sent him in the opposite direction.

"Bachy, I've got sunshine over here," France reported.

"Well, I've got some sunshine over here, too," Bachoven responded.

"You bring your sunshine, I'll bring mine and I'll meet you at the tunnel."

NASCAR flagman Chip Warren was listening to the conversation from the flag stand. "I remember that Cadillac coming up out of that tunnel," he said years later. "It was like the sky just opened up and sun started shining. It just sent cold chills all over me. I thought, Man, this guy's got something here."

As the sky lightened, the drivers and teams prepared for the start of the race. The drivers were introduced to the crowd. As Darrell Waltrip's crew busied themselves setting up their pit box, they could tell by the thunderous boos that their driver's name had been called. As Mike Joy, then the track announcer, talked about the bad weather in the rest of the country, Waltrip's crewmen realized what the storm meant. "We knew our parents were all going to be watching back home," says Gary Nelson. "We talked about doing it for them."

Grand marshal Ben Gazzara, still a decade away from his most memorable role as Patrick Swayze's nemesis in *Road House,* gave the command for the drivers to start their engines, and the forty-one cars rolled off pit road.

On millions of couches, millions of snowbound viewers—ranging from hard-core race fans to people who simply weren't interested in watching Jimmy Swaggart or a discussion of the recently begun Islamic Revolution in Iran on *Meet the Press*—flipped on CBS's broadcast. Back in Charlotte, many a fan settled in front of the TV with a copy of the Sunday *Observer,* which featured a lengthy story in the sports section by Tom Higgins titled "A Man Called Cale." In it Yarborough told a story explaining the origin of his determined ways:

*I was in the fourth grade. There was this big ol' boy in my class who had failed a couple grades. For some reason, he didn't like me and he whipped my fanny twice a day—once before the bell rung in the morning and again at recess. I was scared to death of him. It got so bad I'd hide behind a tree 'til classes took up and he had to go in.*

*Then one day he got off the school bus and he had one arm in a cast.*

*He'd fallen off a horse the evening before and broken the arm. Man, I ran out from behind that tree and jumped him.*

*After that, I whipped him every day for a month. When his arm got well I could still whip him. I've never backed down from any sort of challenge since then.*

It wouldn't be long before Yarborough found himself challenged yet again.

Once the prerace pomp died down and the cars took the track at 12:15—right on time—television viewers were treated to fifteen of the most tedious minutes in the history of broadcasting. The track was still damp, and since jet dryers weren't yet in use, the only way to get rid of the moisture was to use the heat from the race cars. That meant starting the 500 with the caution flag out and the cars circling the track behind the pace car at a leisurely 85 miles per hour.

In addition to being boring, the caution laps—which counted toward the 200 that would make up the race—had the potential to wreak havoc. After several circuits, Darrell Waltrip started to feel Maybelline's motor skipping. He hoped the problem was something minor, or at least fixable, like a spark plug. What had actually happened was that one of the lobes on a camshaft had worn down because running so many laps at such a slow speed and on such steep banking had caused the oil to pool away from the cam. It wasn't something that could be easily diagnosed, let alone fixed. The green flag hadn't even dropped, and Waltrip, though he didn't know it, was already at a huge disadvantage: he was running on seven and a half cylinders.

As the yellow-flag laps mounted, NASCAR asked Waltrip to take a run at speed to see if the track was dry enough to race on. It was called being the rabbit, and it meant putting additional strain on the motor.*

---

*In the 1973 Daytona 500, Buddy Baker made a rabbit run. Eight laps from the finish, with Baker leading the race, his engine blew up.

Waltrip, however, was happy to do it. He thought that running a few miles wide-open might clear up whatever was clogging up Maybelline's engine. He completed a lap, then pulled into the pits to talk with a NASCAR official and Buddy Parrott. He had good news for the former, bad news for the latter. The track was fine, but Maybelline wasn't: "The thing was still missing."

Meanwhile, CBS was trying to give viewers something—anything—more interesting to watch than pavement drying. Pit reporter Brock Yates tracked down Baker's crew chief, Herb Nab, who said, "Well, this is the coolest I've ever seen Buddy in my racing career.... Maybe it's because that Spectra Oldsmobile is running so good, the engine performance is good." And in an interview Petty taped before the race aired, the King told Ned Jarrett, "Looks like for me to win I'm going to have to run wide-open every lap and just hope that I can keep up. We're not really running that good, and we're not really running that bad.... We're just going to have to run and try to keep up with the crowd and hope that we get the good breaks and somebody else gets the bad breaks."

When the real racing finally started on lap 17, Donnie Allison blew past Baker to take the lead. Since Baker was physically incapable of laying back or taking it easy, it was a sign that something was wrong with the Gray Ghost. Like Maybelline's, the Ghost's engine was skipping, and it didn't seem to want to get up to power. Earlier Sunday morning Baker's crew had found a loose strut on the back bumper, and before they'd welded it back into place, they'd unplugged the ignition box, which was standard procedure. There was a chance, Baker thought, that the ignition had been reconnected improperly. There was a backup, but changing it required someone to take a wire from the primary ignition box and plug it into the backup. Baker didn't want to make a pit stop while everyone else was racing, so he and his crew decided to ride out the problem and wait for a caution, when the entire field would pit. The Ghost labored along, well back in the pack.

Up front, Donnie and his brother Bobby were leading a seven-car breakaway pack. The brothers had done plenty of racing against each other, most of it on short tracks in and around Alabama during the 1960s. Their relationship was typical of so many sets of brothers who are nearly the same age, characterized first and foremost by a family bond that would never be broken: for years their families lived up the street from each other in Hueytown. But there was definitely a sibling rivalry.

Unlike his older brother, who had been consumed by a desire to race since he was big enough (or almost big enough) to get behind the wheel of a car, Donnie Allison just dabbled in the sport as a kid. He had other things on his mind. He loved horses so much that before he suffered a bad leg injury, his dream was to be a jockey—though given the frame he would grow into, it was probably all for the best that he didn't. He liked to fish, wrestle alligators, dive, swim, and hang out. He'd always been carefree, the mischievous Allison kid. In a big family—Donnie and Bobby had eight brothers and sisters—it's easy to pick up a tag like that but tough to lose it. It ate at Donnie. Even though he spent a lot of time practicing to be a competitive swimmer, his family thought he was just "goofing off at the pool."

Donnie's feelings about driving changed with one fateful conversation when he was eighteen. The brothers tell slightly conflicting versions of the story, but they agree on the relevant facts. One night at Miami's Medley Speedway, Bobby, who was twenty and by then a well-known driver in South Florida, won a heat race and was then coaxed into letting Donnie drive his car in another race before the main event. Fifty years later Bobby's memories of what happened next are still remarkably vivid: "Donnie comes through [turns] three and four, and he gets that thing outta shape. He overcorrects and goes into the wall right where they had had a crash. This guardrail at Medley was made out of railroad rails. This was an iron fence that you should have been able to hit with a semi, but it was beat-up enough that it was beginning to break up a little bit. He hits right at the worst place you can hit this thing, and that car digs in and turns over. I mean, it ripped that car apart. You cannot believe how bad that thing was wrecked." Donnie was okay. His helmet had a nasty dent in it, and he went to the hospital to get checked out, but he was no worse for wear. Bobby, on the other hand, was hot. His car was done for the night, which meant no prize money for the main event. In Bobby's version of the story, the wreck cost him $17.50. In Donnie's, it was $75.

Bobby took the car home to his father's shop and started working on it so that he could race it the next night. Donnie apologized and promised to come by and help with the repairs. Says Bobby, "At about five o'clock, Donnie shows up with his dancing clothes on. He was really big into roller-skating, and he did fancy dance skating. He showed up in his skating outfit. It was fairly plain in today's deal, but it was a shirt with a little extra trim on it, maybe a belt that had some kind of skating emblem on it. Anyway, it was conspicuously not something you would wear to work on a wrecked race car."

Here the brothers' stories again diverge.

Bobby recalls telling his brother, "Get the heck out of here. You will never drive one of my cars again."

Donnie remembers hearing, "You'll never make a race car driver."

Either way, in Donnie's eyes a challenge had been issued.

"At that moment," Donnie said, "my main mission in life became to prove him wrong. He got one of the toughest rivals he'd ever have to race against in his entire career."

It doesn't take much to get a car out of shape at 190 miles per hour. On the thirty-first lap Donnie had the lead in Turn 2, less than a car length ahead of his brother, who was inside him. As they came to the head of the 3,000-foot backstretch, Bobby slid up the track ever so slightly, his right front fender barely clipping Donnie's left rear quarter panel. As Donnie's Oldsmobile began to spin, the nose of Bobby's Ford dug into the driver's side door, lifting three of Donnie's wheels off the ground. For a split second the Olds hung in the air, looking like a C-130 struggling to leave the runway, before it returned to earth. Donnie and Bobby both spun into the infield. Cale Yarborough, who had been right behind Donnie, minding his own business, swerved low to avoid the wreck and also wound up in the infield, which thanks to the rain had the consistency of the Okefenokee Swamp. Today a restraining wall would stop them, but since there were no spectators on the grass, there was no wall, and the three cars started to hydroplane through the field. Bobby didn't stop until he backed into a mound on the bank of Lake Lloyd. Donnie and Yarborough finally came to rest in the marsh and immediately got bogged down.

Two workers pushed Donnie back onto the course, but Yarborough, whose car was only ten feet from the track, couldn't get out of the muck. And once he did, he couldn't get his engine to fire, so he rolled slowly down the backstretch, cars whizzing past, putting him farther and farther behind.

The caution flag the wreck brought out was a welcome sight for Baker and Waltrip, because they could pit and have their engines looked at. Baker brought the Gray Ghost to a stop in his stall, and a crew member reached in, unplugged the ignition box, and jammed the wire into the backup. Or at least he thought he did. When Baker took the Ghost back onto the track, it still wasn't pulling him like it had been all week. He took the car back into the pits, and Waddell Wilson and the crew started replacing other parts — the distributor, spark plugs, anything that might possibly be the problem. Nothing worked. Baker climbed out of the car, his day over, his Daytona drought extended to twenty-one years.

Of all the races he lost at the track, this would be the toughest to accept, especially after what Wilson learned back at the shop in Charlotte the next day. The problem had been the ignition after all. But after the crewman had unplugged the primary system, he had stuck the wire right back into the same faulty box. When Wilson made the switch and started the car, the shop was filled with the sound of a perfectly purring engine.*

---

* As Wilson recounted the story to me, he said, "If we don't screw that up, you don't have a book."

In Waltrip's pit stall, engine builder Robert Yates and Gary Nelson had the hood up, and they were still thinking that Maybelline's problem was a bad spark plug. They decided to change all eight of them, a laborious, time-consuming process under the best of conditions. Most of the plugs were right under the exhaust header, a piece of metal that got roasted by the engine when the car was running. Changing the plugs was Nelson's job, and he had to use his bare hands. He couldn't get at them with a wrench, and there wasn't enough room between the header and the plug for him even to wear gloves. Imagine trying to pick a paper clip off a cookie sheet in a hot oven, and you get an idea what he was up against. Nelson would change one plug, then send Waltrip back out so he wouldn't get lapped. Then they'd bring him back in and change another. Holding up his hands nearly thirty years later, Nelson said, "I really believe you could trace back some of these scars from that day."

Of the wrecked vehicles, Bobby Allison's car had the most obvious damage—a sagging left front fender that gave his Ford a hangdog look, like a seven-year-old who'd been sent to bed without dessert. Donnie had only a dent in his driver's side door, and Yarborough's Olds, which had finally been towed to the pits, had no visible damage. The undercarriage, though, was a mess. "We'd just reach under there and pull out handfuls of mud and grass," says crew member Jeff Hammond. As the crew worked on the car, CBS showed a head shot of Yarborough, grinning his big South Carolina grin. "I'll bet he's not looking like that now," said David Hobbs. "I'll bet he's absolutely fuming in there, because he had nothing to with that accident."

The caution period lasted ten laps, and by the time it was over, Neil Bonnett was in the lead, with A. J. Foyt, Richard Petty, and Waltrip right behind him.

That was about all anyone knew for sure.

Today's NASCAR fan is never starved for information. Leaders, intervals, lap times, pit times, pit windows, even how many rpm a car is turning or how much throttle a driver is using—everything is monitored electronically and disseminated in real time on TV and online. Thirty years ago scoring was far more rudimentary. The only thing anyone kept track of was the number of laps completed: a volunteer would track each car and make a mark on a pad every time it crossed the start/finish line. It invited human error. At the next-to-last race of the 1978 season, the job of scoring Donnie Allison's car for the Dixie 500 in Atlanta was given to a woman who happened to be a die-hard Richard Petty fan. At one point during the race, Allison was in the pits while Petty was making a pass in Turn 2, which excited the scorer so much that she rose to her feet and cheered wildly, oblivious to the fact that Allison had just crossed the start/finish line on pit road. That left Allison officially one lap down.

Petty took the checkered flag, but Allison drove straight to Victory Lane, insisting that his team's unofficial scoring sheets had him completing all 328 laps. At first NASCAR said the race was Petty's. Then after spending several contentious hours poring over scoring sheets and debriefing the involved parties and witnesses—including Bill France Jr.'s fifteen-year-old son, Brian, who was the one who saw the scorer on her feet cheering for Petty—Allison, who had left the track near tears, was declared the winner. *Stock Car Racing* magazine called it "NASCAR's strangest race."

Now, three races later in Daytona, another confusing situation was brewing. The problem this time wasn't the official scoring—NASCAR had credited every driver for the proper number of laps. The problem was getting the information to the TV crew, to fans, and, most important to the teams. Since there were no scoring monitors in the broadcast booth or the pits, the announcers and crews were left to collect their own information. Donnie Allison was one lap down—that much was fairly clear—and his brother was down two. But Yarborough had wallowed in the muck for so long that no one was sure how far behind he had fallen. CBS speculated one or two laps. Allison's crew got its information from a NASCAR official in the pits. Says Hoss Ellington, "He walked up to me and told me that Cale was five laps down."

But Yarborough was much closer than that. He was only three laps back.

The repaved surface at Daytona International Speedway made it possible for just about anyone to tear around the track at mind-numbing speeds. The result was a fast, tightly packed bunch of cars — some being driven by drivers who had no experience driving in a draft or going quite so fast. On lap 55 Bruce Hill got together with Gary Balough, who was making his first Grand National start, coming out of Turn 4, which led David Pearson to collide with rookie Joe Millikan. Behind them cars went skidding all over the track and into the muddy infield. The situation was perhaps summed up best by the droll Englishman David Hobbs, who commented, "Oh, crikey."

Petty's crew got him out of the ensuing round of pit stops first. He was followed by two rookies, Terry Labonte and Geoff Bodine, with another Daytona neophyte, Dale Earnhardt, in fifth. On the restart, the cars that are on the lead lap line up on the outside, while the lapped cars form a line on the inside. Donnie Allison was at the head of that queue, meaning that if he could get in front of Petty and stay there until another caution flag came out, he could then pull around to the back of the lead pack and get his lap back. Petty and the newbies proved no match for Allison. Even with his car banged up from the collision with his brother, Donnie pulled away and remained on the point for nine laps, until Neil Bonnett cut a tire, triggering yet another spectacular crash. As the cars behind Bonnett checked up coming off Turn 4, Harry Gant got nudged from the rear, sending him sliding across four lanes of traffic. He slammed into the inside wall and ricocheted back across the track. Somehow he didn't get hit. His car was crumpled, but Gant walked away from the wreckage.

With Allison back on the lead lap (albeit at the tail end), Benny

Parsons pulled to the front and stayed there for a long stretch, towing Cale Yarborough—who was still three laps down, despite a CBS graphic saying he was one back—away from the rest of the field. At the midway point of the race, Parsons and Yarborough had put five seconds between themselves and the pack. But just as it looked like Parsons might turn the race into a snoozer, his gauges showed that his engine getting too hot. Yarborough got around him, and less than a minute later John Utsman's engine blew up on lap 105, bringing out another caution and allowing Yarborough to make up one of his three laps. As Parsons sat in the pits, his crew trying to diagnose the problem—a leak in the radiator or a cracked head gasket were the primary suspects—Donnie Allison, who had worked his way through traffic, assumed the lead. And Yarborough pulled up alongside him for the restart.

Yarborough tucked in behind Allison and stayed there until lap 121, when the engines of Blackie Wangerin and Dave Marcis blew up. The caution flag came out as Allison and Yarborough were in Turn 3. Thinking that Yarborough was still four laps down, Allison decided not to risk a wreck by racing him hard. He backed off, and Yarborough beat him to the stripe by half a car length. He was only one lap back.

The scene repeated itself on the next restart: Allison and Yarborough pulled away, and on lap 138 Balough's engine let go. Allison and Yarborough were again on the backstretch when the yellow flag dropped, and as they pulled into Turn 3, Yarborough again tried to pass. And again, a misinformed Allison let him go.

Unlike Allison and Ellington, CBS had finally realized that Yarborough was back on the lead lap. Said Ken Squier, "We've seen a lot of tumultuous finishes here at Daytona, but I've got a feeling we're in for one today like we've never seen before."

The hardest thing about winning a 500-mile race, especially at Daytona, is staying out of trouble for three and a half hours. The '79 event was a battle of attrition. Everyone's prerace favorite, Buddy Baker, was out of it before the green flag even dropped. Darrell Waltrip was running on a handicapped engine all day. David Pearson was caught up in someone else's wreck, his day over after fifty-three laps. A flat tire sent Neil Bonnett home early. Parsons had his engine troubles. Bobby Allison, who had caused a wreck and made contact with cars on at least two other occasions, was two laps down. Every lap was just another chance for something bad to happen. A questionable call by his crew kept Dale Earnhardt on the track during the final caution period, so he had to pit under green to refuel on lap 162 — about fifteen laps before the rest of the field came in. He wasn't happy, and he said goodbye to whatever slim chance he had of becoming the first rookie to win the Daytona 500 when he showed his frustration as he pulled out of the pits. "Dale got pissed and went out of the pits really hard," says Lou LaRosa, his engine builder. "He missed a shift and over-revved the motor and broke a rocker arm and a spring." Another upstart who had been strong all day, Tighe Scott, saw his chances evaporate less than twenty-five laps from the end. Scott, a dirt tracker from Pennsylvania who had never even raced on asphalt before he went to Daytona for the first time in 1976, was nonetheless a contender because he was driving an Oldsmobile prepared by Harry Hyde, the inspiration for Robert Duvall's crusty old crew chief in the movie *Days of Thunder*. The car was in the top 5 when Scott brought it onto pit road way too fast. Scott slammed on his brakes, but he hit a giant puddle left by Parsons's crew as they'd tried to keep his engine from overheating. He hydroplaned past his stall and out of contention.

The few cars that had stayed out of trouble didn't look like they had the power to keep up with Donnie Allison and Yarborough. Petty had been lingering near the front all day, but now, twenty laps from the end, when the leaders decided it was time to put the hammer down, the Oldsmobile that Petty's crew had spent all those hours building just got smaller and smaller in the leaders' rearview mirrors.

Allison and Yarborough seemed so evenly matched that as the number of laps remaining dwindled, NASCAR officials decided it would be a good idea to test-fire the photo finish camera. They were almost a second per lap faster than everyone else. It was no coincidence that their machines had been constructed by Junior Johnson and Hoss Ellington, two of the most, shall we say, *creative* car builders of their day.

Cheating has been a part of stock car racing for about as long as there's been stock car racing. At one of the first races Bill France promoted on Daytona Beach, in 1938, Smokey Purser took the checkered flag and kept right on driving up the shore. A couple of officials figured that he must be doing something to his car — or, more likely, undoing something — so they started searching likely hiding spots. They found him at Roy Strange's garage, frantically trying to get his engine back to its intended, legal specifications. Then there was NASCAR's very first race, which produced NASCAR's very first disqualification: Glenn Dunaway was stripped of a win at Charlotte Speedway in 1949 for using an unapproved chassis.

One of the original appeals of stock car racing was that the drivers were in vehicles that might have been — and indeed sometimes were — driven straight from the showroom to the track. A race would be decided by a man, not a machine. But the desire to win often exceeds the desire to keep the playing field level, and when NASCAR gradually instituted rules allowing minor modifications, the result was, predictably, an assault on those regulations. "If you bend the rules, they might crack," says Johnson. "But if you don't go plumb to that crack, you're not gonna win."

Crew chiefs and engine builders wore their ability to approach that cracking point like a badge of honor. Ask Junior Johnson who the best rule bender of his day was, and he immediately says, "I was." Ask him who was second best, and he thinks for a while. "Well, Hoss was pretty good."

Ellington saw getting around the rules as a game. "I like to beat the other guy," he says. "That's always a lot of fun to do that." He had one advantage: he was based in Wilmington, North Carolina, so none of the other teams knew his business. "In Charlotte, everybody knows what's going on," Ellington recalled. "Crew guys would be in the same bars, and someone's going to have a loose tongue. But I was down here by myself." Ellington's rap sheet was as long as a jack handle. In 1976 he built a car that A. J. Foyt put on the pole at Daytona. Bill Gazaway, NASCAR's top cop at the time, thought it was suspicious that Foyt was 2 miles per hour faster on his second qualifying lap than his first, so he ordered the Chevy torn down. After two hours he found what he was looking for: a steel bottle containing nitrous oxide — laughing gas — which, when injected into the intake manifold, provides a brief but potent boost in horsepower.* If anyone was disappointed in Ellington, it was because he had used such a rudimentary, unoriginal cheating device, unlike the Rube Goldberg contraptions he usually came up with.

In 1970 he built what became known as Glotzbach's Gizmo, a small apparatus that looked like a mini–moonshine still attached to Charlie Glotzbach's carburetor. A length of piano wire connected it to a lever in the cockpit. When Glotzbach hit the switch, the Gizmo would allow more air into the carburetor, and the car would take off.† Later in his career Ellington got busted running a line from the carburetor to a small box filled with dry ice, which would cool the gasoline and boost the horsepower. Of course, not all of Ellington's transgressions were his fault. He once bought an engine from another owner and then had it confiscated when it turned out to be illegal. The guy who sold it to him? His old buddy Junior Johnson. "Junior would tell on me, or he'd have Herb Nab do it," says Ellington.

---

* Gazaway also found laughing gas in the car of the second-fastest qualifier, Darrell Waltrip, and Dave Marcis, who qualified third, was caught with an unapproved radiator cover.
† When the Gizmo was discovered, Ellington was summoned to the NASCAR trailer by Gazaway, who had the device on his desk. Ellington decided to play dumb. After Gazaway demonstrated it, Ellington said, "Damn, that's slick. I wouldn't mind having one of those." To which Gazaway said, "You used to have one."

There were plenty of other ways to get around the rules. Darrell Waltrip once put a hunk of lead painted to look like a radio on his front seat as the car went through inspection. After inspection, out came the radio—which no one, presumably, would miss—and suddenly the car was fifty pounds lighter. Johnson's favorite trick was to tinker with the fuel cell. Cars were supposed to hold only twenty-two gallons, but a bigger tank meant fewer pit stops, so a clever crew chief might build an expandable cell or run extra yards of tubing from the tank to the motor. But Johnson was versatile. Listening to him tick off the areas where he bent the rules is like listening to someone read the index of an Auto Shop 101 textbook: "motor, chassis, tires, wheels, transmission, carburetor..."

Asked if they were running anything illegal in '79, Ellington and Johnson both responded with the same *What do you think?* grin.

They weren't the only ones dabbling in the dark arts. Gary Nelson, Waltrip's engineer, thought it would be nice to eavesdrop on NASCAR officials during a race. But he couldn't just buy a programmable scanner. Radios in those days had crystals that had to be set to a specific frequency. Nelson knew that NASCAR had to register its channel with the FCC, and he also knew of a Motorola shop in Charlotte that had a huge book of every licensed frequency in the country. So he went to the shop and convinced the guy behind the counter to look up NASCAR's frequency and build a radio that would allow him to listen in. It wasn't illegal, but it was devious.* And it would let him pick up the unique play-by-play call for the bizarre finish that was to come.

Finding a vantage point at Daytona International Speedway that allows you to see everything is not easy. All over the infield, fans were set

---

* Later in his career Nelson would become so adept at chicanery—he designed a system that would drop buckshot from a car's rails in mid-race to shed weight—that NASCAR, figuring it takes a thief to catch a thief, finally threw up its hands and hired him to police the garage.

up atop cars, trucks, and campers, watching the action on the slice of track in front of them. The Petty women were behind pit road in the vacated Sportsman garage, listening to the race on their car radios and eating food set out on long tables. Terry Labonte, whose clutch gave out, was watching from the back of a wrecker parked on the backstretch. Geoff Bodine, who had led for six laps in his first 500 before his engine expired, was standing on the roof of a car in the infield. And down between Turns 3 and 4, Michael Waltrip was standing with his sister, watching their brother battle Richard Petty and A. J. Foyt for third place. They all adhered to the same routine: they'd look right and see the leaders blaze into view, rotate their heads to the left, crane their necks as they followed the cars until they disappeared from sight, then wait forty seconds and do it all over again on the next lap. The PA system offered some idea of what was happening, but it wasn't always audible over the din of so many engines.

Donnie Allison passed in front of Michael Waltrip for the 199th time, with Cale Yarborough riding in his wake. Twenty seconds later Darrell came by, sandwiched between Petty and Foyt. Michael watched his brother disappear into the dogleg, then turned his attention back to Turn 3 to wait for Allison and Yarborough to make their final appearance. He waited. And waited. And waited some more, like a NASA mission control worker anxiously waiting for an Apollo capsule to return from the dark side of the moon into radio range. Then, finally, some activity. "We could see all the ruckus," says Michael. "But we couldn't see a whole lot of what was going on."

It happened right where Donnie Allison thought it would. Before the race he had taped an interview with CBS in which he'd discussed his endgame strategy: "If it comes down to a last-lap run for the checkered flag, I'm going to do it on the backstretch, because I just don't think we have enough room from the fourth turn to the finish line to beat anybody. The cars are all too equal for that. You have to do it on the backstretch." So he couldn't have been surprised when Yarborough made his move coming out of Turn 2.

Yarborough had been getting anxious. For the past few laps he had noticed Bobby Allison, three laps down, lurking a couple of hundred feet ahead. Yarborough radioed Junior Johnson, telling him he was afraid that Bobby would slow down and run interference for his brother. "You worry about Donnie," Johnson told him. "Bobby ain't nothing you need to be worried about. He ain't a factor. You won't catch him before the race is over."

When they got to the backstretch, Yarborough decided he couldn't wait any longer. He tugged the steering wheel hard to the left and mashed the gas. The Holly Farms Olds started to pick up ground on Allison, who couldn't do much to stop the slingshot except to cut Yarborough off.

No driver likes to throw a block, a defensive maneuver that just ain't racing. "When I was a driver, I would have wrecked everyone who blocked me," says Junior Johnson. "That's not racing. When they block you, they deserve to be wrecked. It's like you're in a fight. You defend yourself. That just didn't happen back in my day. If it did, you were out of there, and it didn't make no difference who you were. Lee Petty, Curtis Turner—you blocked one of them, they'd knock you plumb out of the racetrack. So would I."

But Allison didn't consider what he was doing blocking; he saw it as "protecting his position." He crowded Yarborough down the track, hoping he could hold him off over the mile or so that stood between him and glory. Yarborough, down near the apron, was running out of asphalt. They ran side by side, each waiting for the other to back down in a strange game of chicken. Neither blinked. They touched, sending Yarborough even farther down the apron. Yarborough slid up, and they hit again, harder. The first tap might have been incidental. This one wasn't. "I was going to pass him and win the race," Yarborough said years later, "but he turned left and crashed me. So, hell, I crashed him back. If I wasn't going to get back around, he wasn't either."

Down on pit road, Gary Nelson was listening to Bill Gazaway describe the action on his pirated signal: "Don't chop him off. He's cutting him off! Look out! Oh no!" Allison and Yarborough banged doors a third time, and when they did, the cars locked together and shot up into the outside wall, then slid down the banking to the infield, where they came to a stop.

In the CBS truck, Bob Fishman couldn't believe what he was seeing. The lead camera positioned just past the start/finish line had caught the wreck perfectly, giving him magnificent footage. But now Fishman had a problem. That camera was the only one that could give him a head-on shot of the winner crossing the line. It had to pick up the new leader. Only no one seemed to know where—or even who—the new leader was.

Richard Petty, Darrell Waltrip, and A. J. Foyt were so far behind Allison and Yarborough that they could no longer see them. As the leaders went crashing into the wall, the trio was all the way back between Turns 1 and 2. So when the caution lights came on, they didn't know where the accident was or whom it involved. The crew members they were talking to on the radio were in the pits and couldn't see which cars were in trouble either. The drivers' first instinct when they saw the yellow lights was to lift off the gas. Waltrip remembers: "Richard backed off; I backed off; A.J. backed off. Then we realized—it's the last lap. You race back to the flag. Better get going. So everybody takes off." They stayed in formation down the backstretch, but Foyt—who was used to open-wheel racing, in which there is no racing back to the flag under yellow, and had stayed off the gas the longest—was falling off the pace. When Petty and Waltrip approached Turn 3 and saw Allison and Yarborough in the mud, it finally hit them. They were racing for the win.

In the CBS booth Ken Squier was playing two roles: play-by-play man and spotter. He had picked up Petty as the new leader and was incorporating hints for the cameramen in his call of the race. After a few seconds a camera locked in on a car with the familiar red and blue scheme. Alas, it was Buddy Arrington, who bought much of his equipment from the Pettys and used their colors. "They're still up in Turns 3 and 4," Squier said, his rising voice conveying both his excitement at the events and his dismay at the fact that the camera was still on the wrong car. "The leaders ARE UP IN TURNS 3 AND 4."

Everywhere spectators rose to their feet—even in the press box, where a few writers had climbed onto their desks to see over the standing, screaming crowd in front of them—in anticipation of the finish. (Except for Tom Higgins of the *Charlotte Observer*, who presciently declared, "I don't care about the finish. I want to see the fight!") The lead camera finally picked up the new leaders as they passed an ecstatic Michael Waltrip. They exited Turn 4, and Darrell Waltrip sized up Petty for a slingshot. The King was known to prefer the high line, so Waltrip looked low. But Petty took a cue from an unlikely teacher—his eighteen-year-old son. Just as Kyle had done on the last lap of the ARCA race a week earlier, Richard dropped his car down the track, giving Waltrip no way around him. Unlike Donnie Allison, Petty had slammed the door shut before the guy chasing him was able to get a foot in it. It was a clean move. Waltrip had nowhere to go. The King's forty-five-race losing streak was over.

Petty took one victory lap, then pulled down pit road, where he was met by twenty mechanics in bright red pants and navy blue Petty Enterprises shirts, who turned the Oldsmobile into something resembling an oversize Independence Day parade float. Included in the mob that obstructed Petty's view was a grinning tire carrier whose frizzy hair was jammed under an STP hat.

"Where's Victory Circle?" asked Richard.

"I'll show you," replied Kyle. "I know the way."

## Chapter Eight

# The Fight

IT's NO stretch to say that winning the Daytona 500 changes a driver's life. Wherever he goes, whatever he does, "Daytona 500 Champion" will precede his name the same way "the Godfather of Soul" always prefaces "James Brown" or "Wild" comes before "Bill Hickock." Derrike Cope won two races in his career. So did Gober Sosebee and Emanuel Zervakis. But only Cope won at Daytona, which explains why, of the three drivers, Cope's is the name fans remember. There are also more tangible benefits to winning the race: that oversize novelty check pays a lot of bills, and no sponsor in its right mind is going to distance itself from a Daytona 500 winner.

So Richard Petty drove to Victory Lane, where a cold glass of milk—a nod to his stomach problems, not the traditional Indy 500 victory celebration—and a new beginning were waiting for him. STP would be back, and all the talk that he was washed-up would be silenced. As Petty was driving toward his brighter future, Donnie Allison was getting out of his car on the grass in Turn 3. His dream

*119*

of winning the race that would guarantee he would finally be taken seriously was, like his Oldsmobile, in tatters. Allison had climbed out without trying to refire the engine. Getting the car started and back around to the checkered flag had been a long shot, but given the size of the lead Allison had had on Petty, it was one Hoss Ellington maintains to this day was possible.

Cale Yarborough was pissed, too. Pissed because he thought he had been ganged up on. Pissed about the first wreck. Pissed that, in his mind, both incidents had been caused by Bobby Allison. Just then, the object of his ire came driving up.

Bobby pulled onto the grass to see if his brother needed a lift back to the garage. Donnie waved him off, saying no, he'd make his way back on his own. Yarborough, who had already had a few choice words for Donnie as he sat in his car, approached Bobby's Ford, yelling that he had caused the wreck. A bemused Bobby wondered how he could have caused a wreck he was nowhere near and punctuated his rebuttal by, in his words, "questioning Cale's ancestry." More screaming from Yarborough was met with more familial insults. "That," says Bobby, "did not calm him down any."

Fighting has always been inextricably linked with racing. "It happened all the time on the short tracks, the dirt tracks," says Humpy Wheeler. "I remember operating dirt racetracks back in the '60s and the early '70s, and it was so common for a fight to break out among drivers—on the track after a wreck, in the pits after a wreck, or after the race was over. It was just par for the course. What you would do is try to keep it from becoming a riot, which usually you were successful at. Not all the time."

"One of my earliest memories was of being at a stock car race at a dirt track," says Fox NASCAR analyst Dick Berggren. "The guy that won the race had lost a left front wheel in the process. And somebody argued that therefore he didn't have four-wheel brakes [and should be disqualified]. An argument broke out, and the next thing you knew there were fifty people, all fighting, slinging fists. For me, having been through fight after fight after fight at local short tracks, a fight was never a surprise whatsoever."

One of the best fighters ever to drive a car was Tiny Lund. His nickname was ironic—there was nothing little about him. In 1959 at Lakewood Speedway, a one-mile dirt track south of Atlanta, he tangled with Curtis Turner, who had put Lund into the fence when he couldn't get around his car. Lund was livid. After he pulled his fenders out as best he could, he went back on the track and slowed to a crawl on the front stretch, waiting for Turner. But Curtis was no fool; he refused to go fast enough to let Lund wreck him.

Still thirsty for vengeance, Lund went looking for Turner after the race. He found him washing up at the lake in the track's infield. "I just made a damned run like a bull and grabbed him under one arm, and when I stopped running, we was standing in water up to my chest," Lund remembered years later. "But it was about over his head. Turner was praying. He was scared of water anyway."

"Now, Pops," said Turner, who called everyone Pops.* "What are you getting mad at me for? You know I wouldn't wreck you purposely. You got in my way."

"I didn't get in the way," Lund said. "Goddamn you. You think you can run over everybody."

"You know I wouldn't run over you," Turner said. "We're buddies. We party together. We race together."

"Yeah, but you don't have to fix your goddamned race car. You don't depend on it for a living. That old raggedy race car is all I got. You got that sonofabitch tore up, and now I'm fixing to drown your ass."

---

*Pops was also Turner's nickname, one he acquired for his propensity for popping other drivers on the track.

Turner offered Lund anything he wanted—first-place money, anything. Lund emerged from his red mist long enough to look up and see the people on the shore: "I seen all the people on the bank hollerin' and yellin'—part of 'em to drown him and part of 'em to save him. Shit." Lund loosened his grip on Turner.

A few years later Lund got into it with Lee Petty in Greensboro. Lund's car blew a head gasket, but he was trying to finish as many laps as he could so he could win enough money to get home. Petty, who even then had the best equipment around, had bolts sticking out of his door from where it was bolted shut. Every time Petty would lap Lund's car, he'd give him a good get-out-of-my-way bang. "He had four of those goddamn things," Lund said. "And when he hit a car, it'd be like a can opener."

Back then, drivers were paid on the spot after the race. Most of them put the money to use on the trip home. "So we're in line at the payoff getting our money, and ol' Lee was standing right behind me," said Lund. "We're on a platform, oh, a good fifteen feet in the air. So Lee says, 'Don't you know where to go when you're getting lapped?'"

Lund wasn't in the mood for a lecture. "Goddamn, you don't have to run over me just because you've got enough goddamn sheet metal and parts down there at your place to build more race cars than what there is on the racetrack. You like to tear everyone's car up, but you ain't gonna tear mine up no goddamn more."

Petty, no small man himself, took a swing at Lund. After he got his money—first things first—Lund took off after Petty, who was at the edge of the platform. "I kicked him in the ass, and I mean he took off of there like a big damned bird," said Lund.

From the ground, Petty looked up at Lund. "Is that the way you fight?"

"Hell no," Lund said. "Stay there. I'm coming down." He jumped off and, he recalled later, "commenced to knocking the shit out of him." Soon the Petty boys, Richard and Maurice, showed up along with their cousin Dale Inman, brandishing screwdrivers and pop bottles. Lund had some support—sort of: "Ol' Speedy Thompson, he jumped in there and was gonna help me, but he'd been frog hunting and shot a hole through his toe, and he was on a cane. One of them hit him in the goddamned toe, and he went hobbling off, holding his foot."

Another driver, Jack Smith, arrived, and just when things were about to get really interesting, Lund felt something hit the back of his head. "I seen butterflies and everything," he said. "It was ol' Liz Petty—Lee's wife. She had a pocketbook. I don't know what she had in it, but she was going *Pow! Pow! Pow! Pow!* just wearing my damned head out. And this broke things up."

On another occasion Lee Petty went after Curtis Turner with a tire iron, but that was nothing compared to the time a driver named Bobby Myers brandished a billy club at Turner. Pops pulled out a .32 pistol. "Bobby," he said, "if I was you, I'd lay that club down."

"Curtis, old man," replied Myers, "I'm just lookin' for a place to put it."

Why is brawling a natural by-product of racing? First, consider the obvious answer, courtesy of Richard Petty: "Ever driven a race car?" After three hours of defying death, a man might understandably emerge from his car a little on edge. But there's more to it than that. Formula One racing is just as dangerous, and yet its history, though occasionally colorful, isn't checkered with tales of drivers packing heat. And while A. J. Foyt did his best to bring a rollicking, ass-kicking vibe to U.S. open-wheel racing, it should be noted that the most memorable Indy car fight in recent years was a shriekfest between two female drivers that culminated with Milka Duno throwing a towel at Danica Patrick.

No, stock car racing is different from open-wheel racing because the cultures that gave birth to them are so different. Formula One and, to a slightly lesser extent, Indy car racing have aristocratic roots, bringing to mind dashing continental playboys in leather goggles and silk scarves, the kind of men who were occasionally knighted and could be invited to a dinner party without fear that the good china would be broken, stolen, or used as a spittoon. By contrast, stock car racing sprang up in a hardscrabble part of the United States where rough-and-tumble was the way of life.

James Webb, U.S. senator from Virginia, wrote a very entertaining and informative book in 2004 called *Born Fighting: How the Scots-Irish Shaped America,*\* which argues that the inherent feistiness found in Appalachian culture can be traced back nineteen centuries to the Roman emperor Hadrian. The Romans had been having trouble subduing the local tribes in northern Britain, and after the Ninth Legion was wiped out trying to quell a minor rebellion, Hadrian decided that it might not be such a good idea to keep fighting them. So he ordered his men to pen them in. In A.D. 122 construction began on a fifteen-foot-high wall constructed across the breadth of Great Britain from the North Sea to the Irish Sea, cutting off what is now northern England and Scotland from the rest of the island. In doing so, he made an already clannish people even more isolated.

Beginning in the early eighteenth century, the Scots-Irish began immigrating to America in droves. Being late to the colonial party, they found the good coastal land already snatched up, so they made their way inland, where the land was cheaper and more easily had. By the time the Declaration of Independence was written, a quarter of a million Scots-Irish had settled in America, primarily in the Carolinas and Virginia, where vestiges of the old country are still evident. On the drive east from NASCAR's hub in Charlotte to the Atlantic coast, you pass through Scotland County and see signs for the town of Aberdeen and for St. Andrews Presbyterian College.

---

\* The cover of Webb's book features, among other images, pictures of Ronald Reagan, George Patton, Andrew Jackson, William Wallace, Robert the Bruce, and three stock cars.

Many of the pejoratives used to demean modern-day inhabitants of the area — and a lot of race fans — have their roots in Scotland and Ireland: *redneck* (the Presbyterian followers of King William and Queen Mary in the Battle of the Boyne in 1690 wore red necker-chiefs), *hillbilly* (*billy* being Scottish for friend), and *cracker* (from *craic,* a term still used in Ireland and Scotland for conversation, which begat *cracker,* a term that originally meant someone who boasted or talked too much).*

"Because Hadrian's Wall cut them off, the Scots-Irish developed different, socially, than the English did," says Humpy Wheeler. "And then they had to live off a terrible land. Even today in Scotland, there's nothing there. Sheep and rocks and whiskey. And how the Scots-Irish people — and I'm one of them, so I can talk bad about them — just love misery. They love it. They're followers of misery. The worse it is, the better they are.

"I remember Harry Gant won his first race here in '82. Harry is from Taylorsville, which is right in the semi-hills of North Carolina. In twenty minutes you'd be deep in the mountains, up near Wilkes County. This is a celebration of Harry's first victory. A celebration. I went up there for it, because Harry's a dear friend of mine. They have it at the high school in the gym. It's a dreary January, just one of those depressing days. I walk in there a little bit before it started. The place is packed full of Taylorsvillians plus people from the racing industry. Harry's up on the stage, and the country gentlemen are playing bluegrass music, singing a dour, mournful song, 'Legend of the Rebel Soldier,' which is the saddest song you could possibly sing.† It's about

---

* Of course, etymology is often an inexact science. Alternative theories hold that *redneck* comes from the sunburn patterns prevalent on farmers and that *cracker* comes from the sound made by a slave master's whip.

† He's not exaggerating. The song begins with the soldier lying in a dreary prison and ends with him dying. In between, we learn he left behind a wife and a young daughter. It's not the kind of thing you'd hear Up with People singing.

a Civil War soldier dying in prison up north. It comes from an Irish ballad about a guy dying in Brixton prison. And I'm thinking, *Is this Harry's funeral? Is there anybody in here happy?* I kept looking around, and I couldn't find anybody. It's just the way it is. It was as typical a Scots-Irish thing as I've ever seen in my life, yet it was in celebration of Harry's victory.

"All that led to people that would literally fight at the drop of a hat. Now the kind of fighting they did was primarily with their fists. So, when I was coming up in the '50s, all these mill towns in North and South Carolina, hundreds of them, were populated primarily by Scots-Irish people. In the wintertime, the sport was not basketball, as a lot of people would assume. It was boxing. Every little town had a boxing club. They had tournaments galore. These were Scots-Irish kids fighting Scots-Irish kids. That's what it was. Mean group of people."

So Cale Yarborough, the Timmonsville native, one of those kids who'd boxed competitively in high school, the man who days earlier had related the story of how he'd whipped that fourth-grade bully, approached Bobby Allison's car. With his helmet in hand, he took a swing at Allison, who was still belted into the driver's seat. "Blood was dripping in my lap," says Allison. "I said to myself, 'I gotta get out of this car and handle this right now or run from him the rest of my life.'"

Getting out of a race car is no easy feat, especially not when there's a miffed former Golden Gloves champion standing next to your car waiting to pummel you. But Allison got all his belts undone and slithered out the window in what had to be record time. As is so often the case with fights, what transpired after the punches started flying depends on whom you ask. Allison's standard line is "Cale started beating my fist with his nose. That's my story, and I'm sticking to it." Yarborough says, "I went over and knocked the hell out of Bobby." Donnie said, "Bobby kicked the shit out of him." Truth is, no one walked away much worse for wear—physically at least. At one point Yarborough tried to karate kick Bobby, which is never a good idea in a racing suit. Allison, still wearing his helmet, grabbed Yarborough's leg, and they both wound up on the ground. The Thrilla in Manila it wasn't.

The only thing that truly took a beating was Donnie's reputation, at least among people who didn't follow NASCAR closely but looked at the sports page. Donnie arrived at the melee, helmet in hand. "I have a helmet, too, if you want to fight with helmets," he yelled at Yarborough, who had just used his on Bobby's nose. Unfortunately for Donnie, that's the pose he had assumed in the most famous picture of the fight. Never mind that he never so much as threw a punch; the enduring image is of Donnie looking as if he's about to brain Yarborough with a cheap shot. "If Cale Yarborough would have raised his fist to Donnie, Cale Yarborough wouldn't be here," said the Allisons' brother Eddie, who watched the fight back home in Hueytown. "If Cale had wanted to fight Donnie, Cale would have been dead, and Donnie would be in the penitentiary."

It didn't last long, and by the time CBS cut to it, the skirmish was almost over. Viewers saw less than ten seconds of grappling before track workers pulled the two men apart. But it made for incredible theater. It wasn't so much the action that gripped fans, but the idea that this was how disagreements were dealt with in the racing universe. "For something like that to happen in stock car racing was a common, ordinary, everyday thing almost," says Wheeler. "But to happen on TV in front of the American public just brought out this hidden culture that we had, where you settle things like a man, with your fists. None of this shouting, throwing handkerchiefs at each other. Let's settle it now, like a man."

Word of the fight traveled fast. "As anxious as I was to get to Victory Lane, I was tempted to stop over there after getting the checkered flag and watch them cats go at it," Petty joked. But since no one in the garage actually saw what transpired in Turn 3, it was like a game of telephone. The smart money in the Allison-brother-most-likely-to-get-into-a-fight-on-national-TV pool had always been on Donnie, so most everyone assumed he was one of the combatants. "Donnie was the biggest fighter of them all," says Wheeler. "He was very feisty. If you had one of those 1868 pictures of gold miners in the Yukon wearing tin cloth, Donnie Allison would've been one of them." Even Kitty Allison, Donnie's own mother, was so sure he was at fault that when he showed up in the garage, she began berating him for fighting until he explained to her that it was Bobby.

Bobby was sitting on a bench with his wife, Judy. He was blasé about the fight. "Nothing happened," he said.

"Yarborough said he hit you," a reporter offered.

"He got a little excited," Allison said. "I didn't block anybody. I wasn't even close." Then two of his crew members shooed away the reporters.

Yarborough was stalking through the garage, fists clenched, calling what the Allisons had done — or what he thought they had done — "the worst thing I've ever seen in racing. I had him beat."

Donnie, meanwhile, was in his semitrailer, his face smudged with dirt and his eyes red with rage. When informed of Yarborough's assertion that he had him beat, Allison said, "I'll be damned if he did. He was just going to win the race or else. I was down as low as I could go. And Cale got off in the infield grass and came up and hit me. He wasn't going to give, and I wasn't going to. I figured if I hit that wall hard, he's going to hit it hard, too." As for his role as a bystander in the fight, Allison explained that if he had been as proficient as his brother at getting his belts off, the fight might have ended differently: "He called me those names, and I told him to wait until I was out of the car and he could call me anything he wanted. I'd have beat his brains out."

Bill France told them all to come to his office the next morning. Nobody was going anywhere anyway.

The snow and ice that focused the attention of a captive TV audience on Daytona Beach also made getting out of the city next to impossible for teams, journalists, and fans. Most flights that left from Daytona

Beach went through Atlanta or Charlotte, which meant that most flights were canceled. Dick Berggren, who was covering the 500 for *Stock Car Racing* magazine, was flying to Boston via Charlotte. He and his boss were anxious to get out of the airport, in no small part because his boss was carrying a duffel bag filled with $10,000 in small bills, the proceeds from subscriptions sold to fans during Speedweeks. "If anybody had known how much money he was carrying, he absolutely would have been knocked off," says Berggren.

Among the airline officials milling about the airport was the pilot of Berggren's flight. The writer proposed a novel idea: why not bypass Charlotte and just fly straight to Boston, where the airport was open. These being heady, pre-TSA days, the pilot said he thought it was a great idea. He hollered that anyone in the gate area who wanted to go straight to Boston should get on board.

Most travelers weren't so lucky, but not everyone was in a hurry to get out of Daytona. STP and Petty Enterprises threw a celebratory dinner at Indigo Lakes, the fanciest golf club in the area. Given all that had happened in the past year and a half, it came as no surprise that Richard Petty, who earlier in the day had issued a reminder of just how tough he was, choked up while making a speech. They laughed and celebrated into the night, aware that a long trip back to North Carolina awaited them the next day.

When they got home, they'd find that their sport would never be quite the same.

For the seventh time in as many attempts, Darrell Waltrip left the Daytona 500 without the Harley Earl Award.* But he was a happy

---

\* Earl was a car designer — known as "the Father of the Corvette" and the inventor of tail fins — who served as a NASCAR commissioner in the 1950s. For years the winner had his name engraved on the Harley J. Earl Trophy and was given a smaller wooden trophy, called the Harley Earl Award. Since 1998 the winner has been given a miniature replica of the trophy.

man nonetheless. He'd finished second in a car that had no business finishing second. And it didn't even bother him that one of his many nemeses had won (though it's a pretty safe bet that whoever won would have fallen under the heading of "Waltrip nemesis"). Waltrip didn't want to ascend to the King's throne. He wanted to take it away. Two years earlier he had explained his motivation: "I want to set some records. That's why I'd like to win some more races before those guys retire. Then people won't be able to say I couldn't beat 'em." Waltrip needed a foil. And to get that, he had to hope that Daytona was, in fact, a sign that Petty was rejuvenated. He needed the sleeping giant to wake up and give him a fight.

It was a dangerous thing to wish for.

One of the few people to get back to Charlotte on race day was Humpy Wheeler.* Wheeler was an old track operator, and track operators, like farmers who took cues from the posture of their cows, tended to be avid amateur weathermen. He fancied himself a pretty good prognosticator and felt in his bones that things were going to get nasty in Daytona, so he left town Sunday morning a couple of hours before the race and headed for Charlotte, with a pit stop in St. Augustine so he could to go to Mass. Since Big Bill France's weather mojo trumped Wheeler's intuition, Humpy ended up missing all the excitement at the track, settling for the CBS feed on his car radio. As Bobby Allison and Cale Yarborough were duking it out in Turn 3, Wheeler was in lower South Carolina, dealing with what he says was "a raging snowstorm where there had never been a raging snowstorm before."

But Wheeler made it home on Sunday night and was able to keep his Monday morning appointment to speak at a meeting of the Charlotte

---

* We've talked so much about Humpy that we might as well answer the question that's probably on your mind. He's called Humpy because that was his father's nickname. His father got it for his penchant for smoking Camels.

Rotary Club, an august, archconservative club of downtown business-men. Because nothing stops the Rotary Club, Wheeler found himself playing to a full house of starched gentlemen who had braved the ele-ments just to see him. "There's a bunch of guys who have never ex-pressed any interest in racing whatsoever, and all they could tell me about was the finish at the Daytona 500, which I had not even seen yet," says Wheeler. "I knew that something monumental had happened be-cause these guys were talking about it. You could have finished upside down at the World 600 [at Charlotte Motor Speedway], and they might have said, 'Well I heard you had a good finish.' But they would never talk in detail about it."

The race had received coverage on Sunday night's network news broadcasts, a rarity for a NASCAR event. On NBC Dick Schaap com-mented, "The speed, stakes, and the risks are so great, tempers can and do suddenly flare." The race, he said, "produced an incredibly dramatic finish and an explosion of tempers." Apparently taking his cue from Kitty Allison, Schaap then reported that Donnie Allison had been the one exchanging blows with Yarborough. Over on ABC, Al Ackerman proclaimed that the race had been decided by "a deliberate crash at 200 miles per hour."

Monday's newspapers gave the Daytona 500 unprecedented real es-tate: first page of sports, six columns, above the fold was the norm. And most didn't run pictures of the race winner. They ran pictures of the fighters. Aroused by what they were seeing on their TVs and in their morning papers, people began to clamor for a real, live taste of the action. The phone lines for the ticket office at the Charlotte Motor Speedway (CMS) were jammed even though the World 600 was three months away. "We're getting an unusual number of calls from people who say they've never been to a major race before," the CMS ticket manager said. "But now that they've seen the spectacle at Daytona, they want to see a race in person."

So much ado about scuffling presented Bill France with a dilemma.

As a promoter, he saw the value in any kind of publicity, but as the son of the man who'd founded NASCAR, he didn't want to chuck the hard work his father had put into making the sport respectable in exchange for a short-term bump in media attention and ticket sales. "When you're promoting races or you're running NASCAR, you need to be at the edge of the cliff all the time," says Wheeler. "That's what makes people want to buy tickets. You need to stand at the edge of the cliff; you just don't want to fall off." So France knew he had to do something to counter the impression that he was running an anarchic sport without completely discouraging future acts of lawlessness that might land his drivers' faces on the front page of a sports section or two. Public penalties were rare in NASCAR. Any trouble was usually dealt with behind closed doors, where a stern admonition from France, or from Big Bill before him, to "cut that crap out" usually did the trick. This one was different, though, because the crap had been nationally televised. So France summoned Cale Yarborough and the Allison brothers, plus a track worker who had been in the infield during the fight, to his office on Monday. The drivers repeated the same arguments they had made on Sunday, and then finally, after nearly two weeks in Daytona Beach, they went home.

Hoss Ellington was a man of his word. Cale Yarborough had asked him for a ride home the day before the 500. Ellington's kids often swam and played with Yarborough's at motels on the road, and Hoss's wife was friendly with Betty Jo Yarborough. To Ellington, the fact that Yarborough ran into his driver on the last lap, tore up a $60,000 race car, and cost him the biggest win of his life didn't change the fact that he had made a promise to a friend. Still, he knew giving Yarborough a lift home might not sit well with his driver or his crew, so he made it a point not to hide it from them. "It's a damn shame this wreck happened," Ellington told them after the race, "because I told Cale and Betty Jo I'd take them home."

One crew member threatened to quit, as did Allison. Says Ellington, "I said, 'Well, I feel bad about this, guys, don't get me wrong, but I made a promise before this race even started that I'd take him home. I'm as good as my word. I wasn't in either one of them damn cars. Had nothing to do with that damn wreck. And it ain't got nothing to do with me taking a man and his wife home.'"

After Yarborough finished giving his side of the wreck and fight to France, he and his wife piled into Ellington's van. The trip was awkward, to say the least. Hoss sat up front with a member of his crew, while Cale and Betty Jo sat in the back. Around Savannah, Yarborough said, "Hoss, you want me to drive?"

Says Ellington, "I looked back at him and said, 'Cale *can* you drive?'" Eventually, he relented and gave Yarborough the wheel, but he made sure to point out the ice on the road: "I told him not to get onto the grass, that he had trouble driving on the grass."

"I don't know whether Hoss changed his mind after that or I changed mine," says Allison, "but things were definitely different between us."

The Kyle fever that had a hold on so much of the stock car community continued unabated even after Petty returned to his job as tire carrier and gopher on his father's team. The ABC News national broadcast following the Daytona 500 briefly mentioned Richard's win and then devoted several minutes to a feature on Kyle. "Maybe I'm bragging a bit," Lee Petty told Al Ackerman, "but he's a chip off the ol' block. In fact, he's got the second chip. I've taken the first chip with Richard, and Richard chipped him off."

Lee then suggested that his grandson retire and become "the only undefeated race car driver in the world." Kyle, looking a bit uncomfortable in a blazer, said, "I don't think I want to do that."

So what did Kyle want to do? Well, he wanted to make a name for himself, but he was smart enough to know that wasn't going to happen.

"I want to race as Kyle Petty if everybody will allow me, not as Richard Petty's son," he said. "As far as all the assets I have, my situation is ideal. Being Richard Petty's son is not ideal. From the identity standpoint, I'd be better off as Kyle Jones. But I like being Richard Petty's son."

What Kyle wanted to do was largely a moot point anyway, since as long as he was a part of Petty Enterprises, his fate rested with Richard and Lee. The King's win in the 500 was vital: STP would be back on the hood for the next race, and any worries the crewmen had about their jobs or their paychecks were allayed. And the win rejuvenated Petty. No one was talking about how frail he looked or whether he'd make it through the year in one piece. He'd driven a grueling 500-mile race against the strongest field ever assembled and come out on top. But he was forty-one and clearly on the downhill side of his career, which made Kyle's win so significant for the operation. There was a successor in place, one who looked just like his old man, talked just like his old man, and, thank God, drove just like his old man.

For the ARCA race, Kyle — who, like Richard twenty years earlier, had started going to business school three nights a week — negotiated his own sponsorship deal with Valvoline. He clearly wasn't going to need to rely on his entrepreneurial skills going forward. Finding a sponsor was going to be as easy as answering the phone when it rang. "With 10 laps to go in [the ARCA] race, two potential sponsors were already talking," reported Petty Enterprises business manager Bill Frazier. "When I got back to the motel, I had a bunch of telephone messages that resulted in at least four more legitimate offers." The most fervent suitor was STP, which was anxious to get Kyle into the fold and to sever his association with Valvoline, one of its chief rivals. "Once the Pettys decide which way Kyle is going, they have promised us first crack at sponsoring him," an STP exec told the *Atlanta Constitution*. "I don't know when that will be — a week, a month or whenever. But we will be ready."

And it wasn't just sponsors doing the wooing. Promoters were dying to have the Kyle Show come to their tracks. Rockingham, North Carolina, which was host to a Grand National race on March 11, and Atlanta, which had one the following week, both made pitches to Richard. Humpy Wheeler wanted him for the World 600 on Memorial Day weekend, so much so that he was willing to pony up $25,000. "Some guy in California even wanted Kyle to drive a Corvette in a race there," Frazier said.

Richard was reluctant to rush Kyle into a Grand National car, not because it wasn't safe, but because it wasn't cheap. "If a sponsor will come up with $200[,000] or $300,000, we will build Kyle his own race car," Richard said. "But if that doesn't work out, I might even farm him out for a few races. If someone comes up with enough money to run a NASCAR.Grand National or an ARCA race or any type of race, then we will look at it."

It's easy to be cynical about the way Kyle was being shopped, but he was in an unprecedented situation. Drivers simply didn't enter the sport to that kind of fanfare. It didn't happen that way. "You may be talking about a $10 million man," Buddy Baker said. "The Pettys are handling him just like a Sugar Ray Leonard."

Of course, Sugar Ray Leonard had almost as much experience behind the wheel as Kyle, and that was going to have to be addressed at some point. "It will take four or five years for Kyle to be a steady Grand National contender," Junior Johnson said. "When he goes to Darlington and some other tracks, he is going to find a whole new deal. Take Darrell Waltrip. People forget that Darrell had years of short-track experience before going Grand National, and it took him three or four years to make it then. If Petty doesn't run the short tracks, he never will be an effective driver. Racing who he did and racing against the Pearsons, the Yarboroughs, the Bakers, the Allisons, and, well, his daddy, you are talking about two different worlds."

Johnson was right, and Richard knew it. Following his son's win he said, "Kyle has won a trophy, kissed a beauty queen, and met the press. Now he has to learn how to drive a race car." They could have sent him out to compete in some more ARCA races or on any one of the short tracks in the Carolinas, where he could get the seat time he needed. But the lure was too great. Not the money — though the $25,000 was nice — but the lure of believing that he was *that* naturally gifted, that he could repeat what he had done at Daytona.

They took Humpy's deal. Kyle's second race would be the World 600 in May.

On Bill France's agenda Tuesday, the day after he sent the combatants home, was watching videotape of the race and fight, which was a much bigger production than it sounds. No one in the NASCAR offices had a VCR, so France and Bill Gazaway had to go across International Speedway Boulevard to the offices of the Motor Racing Network, where they set up a makeshift screening room in the office of broadcaster Jack Arute. "He was trying to be serious, but he couldn't help himself," says Arute. "He was smiling, because he knew it was something people were going to talk about."

The punishments were handed down that evening. All three drivers would be fined $6,000, with the proviso that $1,000 would be returned following each of the next five races so long as they kept out of trouble. It was a cagey move by France. Six thousand bucks was a lot of money — half the Daytona 500 field made less than that in the race — so he gave the appearance of coming down hard on the ruffians. But by giving most of the money back, France was ultimately administering little more than a slap on the wrist.

Had France stopped there, the issue might have died. But he and Gazaway ruled in no uncertain terms that the wreck was Donnie Allison's fault. "In reviewing the television tapes, Donnie Allison went down onto the apron, resulting in Yarborough's car going into the grass. In doing so, Donnie Allison acted in a manner contrary to the best interests of the sport," Gazaway said. "Again, a race leader cannot run anywhere he pleases on the race track." Allison was given six months' probation. The additional penalty, coupled with having a very big finger pointed at him, didn't sit well with Donnie or with his brother. "It's unreal," Bobby said. "I am shocked by the amount of the fines and the unfairness of the whole thing. I don't see how Donnie can be blamed for the wreck. He was leading the race and can use up all the track he wants. He didn't have to give anything to Yarborough, and didn't, but Cale just ran over him."

Bo Grady, a friend of Donnie's who worked on his short-track car, was the most indignant member of the Allison camp. "I'm not believing that," he said. "Six months' probation? You don't get that for killing someone."

Yarborough, meanwhile, felt vindicated. The way he saw it, he was being fined solely for the fight, and a thousand bucks was pretty good value for getting a pop at Bobby Allison. "I'm glad NASCAR has taken its stand," he said. "I think they clarified it pretty well. It's always been a gentleman's agreement that you can use all the racetrack you want when you are out front, but you don't ever leave a man without an escape route. When a man gets alongside you, you don't try to put him out of the racetrack. That's what happened to me. If I had been behind him, he could have gone anywhere he wanted. I would have finished second. But I got beside Donnie fair and square. He moved down on me and I moved down with him as far as I could go. My left side tires were off the track and I was running the left side on the dirt when he finally hit me the first time. We were side-by-side then....When he saw me down low, here he came with me. I went low as far as I could go, and I wasn't about to drive out in Lake Lloyd."

His ruling handed down, France, a man whose word on a subject was usually the last, considered the matter closed. Asked if he was worried about the wreck, the fight, or both spilling over into subsequent races, he said, "It better not. It was a big race, and those guys came down here to race...and they carried it one step beyond. It's over now....We do not anticipate any more trouble."

But not even Bill France always got what he anticipated.

## Chapter Nine

# Round Two

**Sunday, March 4**
**Race 3: Carolina 500**
**Rockingham, North Carolina**

THANKS TO the weather—perhaps Big Bill France climbed on top of a press box and prayed for a storm—the second race on the 1979 schedule, the Richmond 500, was snowed out and rescheduled for the open week following the Carolina 500. That meant the fight would remain topic A for seven more days, providing the kind of buildup that Don King would have loved.* Indeed, spectators heading into Rockingham were greeted by a billboard that read, WELCOME, RACE FANS, TO ROUND TWO.

---

\* At the first Daytona 500, Big Bill France and his cronies learned that a little controversy goes a long way in keeping a story alive. At that race, in 1959, Johnny Beauchamp and Lee Petty crossed the finish line in such close proximity that it was virtually impossible for the naked eye to separate them. Beauchamp was declared the winner, but Petty drove his car to Victory Lane. France issued a nationwide call for any photos or film that might shed some light on the matter to be sent to the NASCAR offices. They spent three days—perhaps dragging their feet a little to keep the story in the sports pages—poring over the evidence before reversing themselves and declaring Petty the winner.

The Rock was a tough track to drive. Originally built as a flat one-mile track in the mid-1960s, it had been reconfigured as a banked, D-shaped tri-oval. Because of the high sand content in the soil in that part of North Carolina, the asphalt used to pave the track was especially gritty, and it ate up tires. Rockingham stood in sharp contrast to Daytona — in terms of both the track and the surrounding town. Rockingham is a tiny burg of less than 10,000 people about halfway between Charlotte and Fayetteville, down near the South Carolina border. Which is to say, it's in the middle of nowhere. The closest thing to a tourist destination is Pinehurst No. 2, the golf course twenty-five miles up the road that has hosted two U.S. Opens and a Ryder Cup. So during their stay in Rockingham, drivers had to make their own fun. One way they did that was to roast one of their own the week of the spring race, and in 1979 it was Buddy Baker's turn to sit on the dais.

It wasn't easy to find someone who didn't like Baker, so a large crowd of fans and drivers showed up, including both Allison brothers and Cale Yarborough.* Two of Baker's friends, Buck Brigance and Jim Hester, were dressed as mountain men, replete with overalls, floppy hats, and shotguns, to keep order and stand guard over the guest of honor in case he decided to make a run for it. Yarborough took the stage, eyed the shotgun-toting hillbillies, and said, "Where were you guys when I needed you in Daytona?" He then surveyed the room and cast his eye on the Allisons, who were sitting in the front row. "You know," Yarborough said, "looking out and seeing Bobby and Donnie in the audience, I have something I'd like to do before I get to Mr. Baker. I would like to apologize to the Allisons for the fight. It was an unfair fight. I used both hands."

---

* Being a straight-out-of-central-casting gentle giant, Baker was a fine roast target. To a point. Steve Waid of *Grand National Scene* was supposed to hit Baker in the face with a lemon meringue pie. Waid's pal Tom Higgins of the *Charlotte Observer* told him, "Unless you want to be embarrassed, you better leave that pie the way it is." Waid wisely took his advice.

With that, the brothers shot out of their seats, and for a brief second it looked like everyone in the auditorium was going to find out the hard way whether or not the hillbillies' shotguns were indeed loaded. But none of the combatants could keep a straight face, and everyone had a good laugh, making it clear that although no one should expect the Allisons and Yarborough to become fast friends, they could certainly put any residual resentment over what happened at Daytona behind them. The détente continued when Donnie Allison was seen having a beer with Busch Clash mastermind Monty Roberts, whose status as an employee of the company that sponsored Yarborough's car should have made him the enemy. "We have disagreements," Monty said, "but we are friends."

When qualifying started at 3:00 p.m. on Thursday, Bill Gazaway was noticeably absent. Earlier that afternoon NASCAR's director of competition had abruptly left the track and hopped on a private plane bound for Daytona.

Bobby Allison turned the fastest lap, followed by his brother and Yarborough, meaning they would start the race in the exact same positions they'd been in when Bobby triggered the wreck that sent them all sliding through the muck in Daytona. Buddy Baker was fourth. "What a hell of a place to begin the race," he said. "It's like having a choice between smoking a cigar in a dynamite factory or carrying a tube of nitroglycerin on a roller coaster. You could get blown away either way." Baker's tongue was in his cheek, but the light mood in the garage didn't last long. Shortly after qualifying ended, the reason for Gazaway's absence became apparent. NASCAR was announcing a change in the penalties.

As promised, the Allisons had lodged a formal appeal of the sanctions Bill France had handed down. They were given a hearing on February 26 at a motel near the Atlanta airport. The night before, Donnie Allison received a cryptic phone call. A man who refused to identify himself told him that NASCAR was in possession of a video-tape of the wreck shot by a Florida TV station. The footage, shot from a different angle than the CBS race coverage, seemed to back Allison's claim that Yarborough had initiated the contact. "Make them show you the tapes," the caller told Allison. "Make them show you the tapes."*

The hearing was held in front of a three-man committee comprising NASCAR field director Lance Childress, Riverside Raceway president Les Richter, and president of Dover Downs International Speedway John Riddle. The first order of business was to discuss the penalties for the wreck. Since Bobby was only appealing a penalty for fighting, he excused himself. The mood in the room was informal; no lawyers were present, and the proceedings were not recorded.

The VCR was cranked up, and just as Donnie's Deep Throat had told him, one of the tapes showed Yarborough turning into Allison while he was still on the track, which seemed to contradict his argument that he had been forced down onto the apron before there was any contact. "Why haven't we seen this before?" Childress asked. If the footage didn't completely exonerate Allison, it certainly implicated Yarborough. After an hour and ten minutes, Allison was excused. The committee members shut off the VCR, had lunch, and talked things over. Says Riddle, "It was obvious that the only real solution was to cut the baby in half." Allison's six-month probation was chopped to three, and Yarborough was given a three-month probation of his own.[†]

"I thought we did well," says Riddle, "because they were all mad at me."

\*    \*    \*

---

\* Allison still doesn't know who the caller was. For a time he suspected it was Jack Arute, which makes sense, as Arute was in the room when France and Gazaway looked over the videotapes. However, to this day Arute denies making the call.

[†] Bobby, who spent only ten minutes in front of the panel, lost his appeal. He never had much of a chance, given that the whole world had seen pictures and/or video of him fighting Yarborough.

The wreck and fight in Daytona offered NASCAR fans a chance to live up to their reputation for unmatched loyalty and zeal. *Stock Car Racing* got an unprecedented amount of mail, as did *Grand National Scene*. One reader called Donnie's actions "disgusting," but most agreed with the Canadian gent who distilled the wreck and NASCAR's decision to penalize Allison down to two words: "pure bullshit." No one was entirely certain how fans were going to treat the drivers, especially after a few prerace cocktails. The depths to which a drunken sports fan could fall had been demonstrated the night a week earlier when someone had chucked a liquor bottle onto the court during the ACC basketball tournament in Greensboro. To be safe, L. G. DeWitt, the president of the Rock, hired extra police to sit in the grandstands and observe the crowd of 44,000—a speedway record—with binoculars from towers.

Reaction to the drivers as they were introduced was mixed. Yarborough was booed, and the Allisons were cheered, but the ovation they got was no match for the one reserved for the grand marshal, Kyle Petty. He performed his duties—riding around the track in the back of a convertible in an STP jacket, while looking mildly embarrassed at the fuss being made over him—then made his way to the pits, where he became likely the first grand marshal in the history of the esteemed position to perform menial tasks such as carrying tires during the race. His dad, who had seen plenty of fenders banged in his day, wasn't sure what to expect when the green flag flew. "There'll be no love taps out there," Richard said. "There'll either be a whole lot or nothing."

There was a whole lot.

The Carolina 500 consisted of 392 laps. Nine of them were peaceful. Yarborough pulled into the lead almost immediately, but going into Turn 3 on the tenth lap, Donnie got inside him. The roles were reversed from the last lap at Daytona, but the result was the same: Yarborough moved down and hit Allison, and both cars ended up in the fence. This time they weren't a mile in front of their closest pursuers. The wreck touched off a pileup that collected several of the fastest cars: Petty, Darrell Waltrip, Buddy Baker, Dale Earnhardt, and Ricky Rudd. Neil Bonnett, who was driving a second Hoss Ellington car, couldn't avoid the mess either, meaning that in the last ten laps of Grand National racing, Hoss had seen three of his cars totaled in wrecks involving Yarborough.

Allison and Yarborough both had the same initial reaction, one shaped by the fact that they were on probation and they wanted to see their $1,000 checks again: *Hey, man, it was an accident*. If anyone was in the right, it was Allison, who was minding his own business when Yarborough hit him. But controversy of any sort was the last thing he needed, and he wasn't about to start pointing fingers. Instead, he was content to write it off as just one of them racing deals.* He found a phone in the garage and called Bill Gazaway, who was up in the tower, to tell him it was an accident. Allison's car was done, but Yarborough's was fixable. He blew an engine fifty laps later, and as he watched his crew put a new motor in the Oldsmobile, he echoed Allison's sentiment that there was no malicious intent. "What happened was totally unrelated to anything else that has happened between us," he said. Allison's final assessment was: "I don't blame Cale for anything. We just went slidin' and everybody ran over everybody. There's no hard feelings."

He was clearly speaking for himself.

The fact that Allison and Yarborough swore that they didn't mean to take out most of the contenders provided little solace to Baker and Bonnett, who both ended up in the hospital getting foot X-rays. In the ambulance on the way to the hospital, they tried to reconstruct

---

* The NASCAR phrase "Just one of them racing deals" translates roughly to "Shit happens." The word "deal" itself has no set definition. It can be used to describe just about any noun. In rare cases, it actually means a business agreement, an explanation of which might begin, "The deal with that deal..." Usually, though, it means "that thing." On one memorable occasion, it was used in place of "hot dog cart." A few crewmen were screwing around with half a stick of dynamite and happened upon a cart in the middle of a field. When explaining what happened next, one of the crewmen told me, "We lit it and threw it up under that deal."

the origin of the wreck, but neither had seen much except tire smoke. Others, though, had no trouble identifying the culprit. Petty sounded like he was trying to tie what was left of his stomach in knots, his syrupy voice wavering with rage. "If they keep driving like that much longer, I'm gonna start fighting," he said. "Donnie got under Cale. Outmaneuvered him. Then Cale turned left—and Donnie was sittin' there. Deliberate? Yeah. He had control of the steering wheel. How deliberate I don't know. It was a misjudgment in driving, and I made one too, for being so close. They should put 'em on top of the trucks and let 'em watch other people show 'em how it's done." He might not even have been the hottest Petty. Maurice got into an altercation with Bill Gazaway's brother Joe, a NASCAR official, in the pits following the wreck, which led to a two-week suspension. "Chief just pushed the wrong cat," said Richard later. "That's all."

But the most enraged driver had to be Waltrip, whose white hat was nowhere to be seen. As he watched his crew give Wanda the mother of all nose jobs (they performed a hoodectomy and removed the front fender, too), he looked like he would have gone after Yarborough if the opportunity had presented iteself. "It was the stupidest thing I ever saw. He drove over the man's hood is what he did," Waltrip said. "They ought to pull his butt out of the car and beat the hell out of him.... There should be one driver on probation after today, and it ain't Donnie Allison. The other one ought to be up there," he said, pointing at the stands, "learning how to drive."

One of the few fast cars to get through the wreck unscathed was Bobby Allison's. When he saw his brother and Yarborough start to spin, Allison took his Ford down onto the grass and floored it. David Pearson also made it through safely and led for 119 laps, but he blew an engine just past the halfway point. Three laps later Allison took the lead from Benny Parsons and looked like he was going to drive away from what was left of the field. But there was one driver hanging around who had a car that was strong enough to keep up with Allison: rookie Joe Millikan, a former floor sweeper at Petty Enterprises.

Millikan was a well-fed twenty-nine-year-old who wasn't used to wrestling a Grand National car for almost four hours. "My back was killing me, and I wasn't doing the car justice," he'd say later. Luckily for him, thanks to round two there were plenty of guys in the garage with nothing to do. Around lap 240 Millikan got out of his Chevy during a pit stop and turned it over to a relief driver: his old boss, Richard Petty.* The King had just about everything he needed to reel in Allison—a solid car and years of experience on the track. Although he'd already shipped his gear back to Level Cross, he had Buddy Baker's helmet and one of Millikan's old uniforms. But he didn't have his shoes.

The evolution of the driver over the past three decades has been pronounced. He's become less shaggy, more presentable to sponsors, and, for the most part, more at ease in front of a camera. His sunglasses have become much fancier, his caps are less boxy, and his helmet no longer looks like something the Great Gazoo would wear. But perhaps the most notable advance has been on his feet. Drivers today wear state-of-the-art kicks designed specifically for racing. They're heat-resistant but thin enough to let the driver feel the pedals, and only a handful of companies make them. Petty and his cronies, though, had to look no further than the local Payless to get their gear. They drove in everything from Hush Puppies (Bobby Allison) to Converse running shoes (Yarborough) to wing tips (Dave Marcis). Dale Earnhardt wore snappy yellow and blue sneakers that matched his uniform, while Neil Bonnett drove in casual shoes with thick soles that looked like something he stole from his grandfather's closet. "I don't just wear them to race," Bonnett said. "I wear them everywhere except to church." He loved them so much he bought them in bulk

---

* The driver who starts the race is the one who gets the points and the check.

at a discount store near his home in Hueytown. David Pearson raced in a pair of $60 patent leather loafers he had originally intended to wear as dress shoes, only to discover he didn't like the color. They had replaced a pair of alligator loafers he'd worn in 116 straight races; Pearson had resoled the right one fifty times before his wife finally had them pewtered.*

The key was to find something with a thick enough sole to keep the right foot—the one that works the gas—from blistering. Benny Parsons wore work boots; he gave tennis shoes a try but wound up with a blister on his heel the size of his fist. Petty also drove in work books, and to give himself added protection, he glued rubber to the right sole. But he had sent the boots home with the rest of his stuff after the crash, meaning that when he got into Millikan's car, he was wearing his cowboy boots.

Petty was two laps behind Bobby Allison when he took over, but he got one back when Allison ran out of gas. Allison's radio wasn't working—he wasn't aware that it was Petty chasing him now, not Millikan—and he missed the sign Bud Moore put out telling him it was time to pit. Allison had to coast all the way around the track. Petty got around Allison again to get back onto the lead lap and was closing in on him when the discomfort in his feet became unbearable. "I wasn't used to the car," he said. "I got blisters on my hands and on the heels of my feet because I had to drive in my street boots....I would have stayed in the car, but I couldn't see hurting myself with someone else's car." With thirteen miles left, he got out of the car, and Millikan got back in. The driver change did away with any chance that Allison would be caught. "I really do think if I hadn't made the stop to get Joe back in the car, we could have beaten Allison," Petty said. Instead, Millikan was denied the chance to become the first rookie since 1974 to be credited with a win.

Talk in the garage after the race, however, had nothing to do with

---

* Not bronzed. Pewtered.

Allison's victory, Millikan's aching back, or the King's toasted feet. The story was what had happened on the tenth lap. Petty, who finished thirty-second, was among the many who believed that suspensions were in order, but he realized it was unlikely that NASCAR would keep two of its most popular drivers — both of whom had loyal sponsors — away from the track. "Suspensions? Yeah, why not? But NASCAR officials didn't see it," he said with a wink. "Know what I mean?"

He was right. Bill Gazaway said that he wasn't even going to look at film of the incident "unless I happen to be watching TV and it comes on."

### Standings After the Carolina 500

| | | |
|---|---|---|
| 1. | Darrell Waltrip | 472 |
| 2. | Cale Yarborough | 444 |
| 3. | Bobby Allison | 431 |
| 4. | Donnie Allison | 398 |
| 5. | D. K. Ulrich | 395 |
| | ... | |
| 13. | Richard Petty | 314 |

## Chapter Ten

# Round Three

*Sunday, March 11*
**Race 4: Richmond 400**
**Richmond, Virginia**

BEFORE HE flew to Richmond, Bobby Allison made a quick stop in Atlanta to appear at a press conference alongside Zell Miller, whose duties as lieutenant governor included officially designating the week of the upcoming Atlanta 500 as "Race Days" in Georgia. Donnie Allison was noticeably missing from the festivities. He had previous engagements, but his absence gave birth to rumors that he was lying low because he feared for his safety. The *Atlanta Constitution* broke a story earlier in the week that he had received a warning in the mail, scrawled on tablet paper, from a Cale Yarborough fan, whose lack of social graces was matched only by his lack of command of the English language: "You'd better look out for a Coke bottle through your winshield or somthing like that when you race at Atlanta." The missive bore an Atlanta postmark.

Ed Hinton of the *Atlanta Journal* had been approached with the story of the letter by the promoter of the Atlanta International Raceway, who

Shortly after announcing he was leaving Chevy in the summer of 1978, Richard Petty—in a rare mustache-free phase—posed with a handful of other American icons. (Dozier Mobley/Getty Images)

Bobby Allison with fellow racing enthusiast Paul Newman at the final race of the 1978 season, in Ontario, California. The actor's presence at Speedweeks the following spring—he and his Porsche team retired early in the 24 Hours of Daytona with a blown engine—brought an uncharacteristic amount of attention to the endurance race. (Dozier Mobley/Getty Images)

Dale Earnhardt first made his mark on NASCAR at Speedweeks in 1979. His gumption and his family roots meant he was embraced by his fellow drivers, including Bobby Allison. Not all of them were convinced he was destined for greatness, though. Says Darrell Waltrip: "If you looked at him and said, 'Will this guy ever make it?' You'd probably have said, 'Nah, I don't know. Questionable.'" (Dozier Mobley/Getty Images)

The Petty clan celebrates Kyle's win in the ARCA 200. Kyle and Pattie are flanked by Kyle's grandparents *(left)* and parents *(right)*. After the race the honeymoon was over — literally — for Kyle, and it was back to work... (Courtesy of the Richard Petty Museum)

...lugging tires for his dad's race team. (Kyle is at the front right of the car holding two tires.) Notice the one-tone paint scheme Petty used in Daytona after STP cut back its sponsorship. (RacingOne/Getty Images)

The team that dominated NASCAR in the mid- to late 1970s: Junior Johnson's boys, with Cale Yarborough behind the wheel, won three straight championships from 1976 to 1978. Johnson is at the center in the heavy coat, obscuring the white pants and white T-shirt outfit he was known for, and Yarborough is on the far right in one of his many big hats. Third from the right is Jeff Hammond, who would later become Darrell Waltrip's crew chief and a TV analyst for Fox. (Dozier Mobley)

Fun-loving Donnie Allison, who became serious about driving the night his brother told him he'd "never make a race car driver." The 1979 Daytona 500 was Donnie's best chance to emerge from Bobby's shadow. (Dozier Mobley/Getty Images)

Donnie's dream went up in smoke on the last lap of the 500. As a huge television audience looked on, he and Yarborough banged on each other down the backstretch, eventually winding up in the fence near Turn 3. (Ric Feld/AP)

It wasn't graceful, but it caught people's attention. After the wreck, Bobby Allison stopped in to check on his brother. One thing led to another, and Bobby and Yarborough engaged in the fisticuffs seen round the world. (Ric Feld/AP)

Yarborough and Donnie Allison certainly didn't look like enemies when they sat down together at Richmond after round two. The talk centered mostly on hunting—Yarborough said he'd consider giving Allison a coon dog—and it succeeded in smoothing things over. The Richmond race went off without incident. (RacingOne/Getty Images)

Dale Earnhardt's first win came less than a month after the hiring of Suitcase Jake Elder *(left)* as his crew chief. Elder's advice to Earnhardt at Bristol, site of the win: "Stick with me, and we'll both be wearing diamonds as big as horse turds." (Dozier Mobley/Getty Images)

By midsummer, Earnhardt's working-class ruggedness had won over a whole new set of fans. But his season wasn't without a major bump. This picture was taken at Pocono just before the Coca-Cola 500, during which a nasty wreck left him briefly convinced he was dead. (Dozier Mobley/Getty Images)

Buddy Baker's Gray Ghost got sideways and triggered the Big One during the Winston 500 in Talladega. The wreck led to one of the season's stranger scenes: Cale Yarborough dragging himself to Dave Marcis's window and asking Marcis to check to see if Yarborough's legs were still attached. They were. (Dozier Mobley)

NASCAR's preeminent showman, Humpy Wheeler, brought everything from dancing bears to a re-creation of the invasion of Grenada to his track. Here, Wheeler *(left)* escorts Elizabeth Taylor and her then-husband, Senator John Warner. (Bryant McMurray)

Bobby Allison on a Sunday drive, with Cale Yarborough and Darrell Waltrip in pursuit. (Dozier Mobley)

Filling in for an injured Dale Earnhardt, David Pearson returned to the site of his earlier fiasco and stood on the gas with his Hush Puppies at the Southern 500. The win was the 104th of his career. Darrell Waltrip had the car to beat but got greedy and wrecked it. "That," Waltrip said years later, "started our trouble." (Dozier Mobley)

Things only got worse for DW at North Wilkesboro, when Bobby Allison (15) hooked his rear bumper and spun him into the wall. (Bryant McMurray)

Like father, like son. With STP back in the fold, Petty Enterprises sent two cars out for five races in 1979: Richard's familiar number 43, and Kyle's nearly identical 42. (Dozier Mobley)

The final stop of the season, in Ontario, California, was a one-race shootout between Waltrip and Petty for the championship. (Dozier Mobley)

claimed that he had found it in the garbage near Hoss Ellington's garage stall in Rockingham. Finding the whole story a little too neat—the promoter of an Atlanta track fortuitously finding a letter postmarked in Atlanta two weeks before a race in Atlanta—Hinton had passed.* But after the story broke, Hinton contacted Donnie, who denied that he was hiding. "I don't know where they get those stories—in the bars, or where," he said. "But as for any of that business about that letter keeping me out of Atlanta, that's a bunch of bull. I don't want a bottle through my windshield or Bobby's or Cale's or anybody else's. And I'll tell you what: If something is thrown at any of us, and we find out who it is, Cale and Bobby and I are all going to be fighting—but not against each other. We'll be on the same side."

Donnie knew that bad blood was nothing new in NASCAR. For proof of that, he only had to look as far as his brother, who had spent the better part of a decade cleaning Petty Blue paint out of dents in his fenders. But that rivalry, like most, simmered. It didn't rear its head every week, because you couldn't just put someone into the fence every time you got mad at him. The sport was described by Petty as "a live-and-let-live kind of deal." Said the King, "I'd hate to see us get to the place where if I crash you last week, it's for sure you're going to crash me this week." But that's exactly what fans were banking on, and that's exactly why the press box was flooded with out-of-towners. Bloodlust had gripped the sport. Papers in Houston and Jacksonville didn't send writers to see if Waltrip would hold on to his slim lead in the points race. They sent them to see if Donnie was going to get back at Cale for getting back at Donnie. And Richmond was a good place for it to happen. Banging was inevitable. The track is barely half a mile long and not especially wide, meaning that even if a driver decides he wants to steer clear of conflict, there's little room to hide. Said Bobby Allison, "Every time we go to Richmond we're wary of tempers flaring."

Only one driver was even remotely happy that the ill will was still

---

* "If you were writing a novel and you wanted a death threat from a Georgia redneck, that would be the letter," says Hinton.

lingering in the air: Darrell Waltrip. On his last trip to Richmond, in the fall of 1978, he had spun out leader Neil Bonnett nine laps from the end of the Capital City 400 and gone on to win. Bonnett had responded by ramming Wanda on pit road after the race and then trying to get at Waltrip in Victory Lane. NASCAR gave both drivers thirty days' probation, but Waltrip paid a far more severe price than Bonnett in the court of public opinion. He was booed lustily after the race, and the incident was routinely held up by Waltrip haters as further evidence of his moral turpitude. But no one was looking to dredge up that old story, not with the prospect of round three. "It's a hell of a break for me," Waltrip said. "I wasn't really looking forward to coming here."

Eager though he was to have things return to normal, Cale Yarborough wasn't about to hold his tongue. If anything, on Friday he seemed to be spoiling for a fight. He had been given a stall in the corner of the garage, isolated from everyone else, meaning that if he wanted casual chatter without having to walk across the garage to seek it out, he was going to have to settle for his crewmen or members of the press, several of whom were lurking near his car. As he talked to a couple of reporters, he took exception to the way his fellow drivers had reacted to the "racing incident" he had triggered the previous Sunday. In a clipped voice he said, "What happened at Rockingham could have happened to anybody. The real problem at Rockingham was two big mouths that started more trouble than anything else—Jaws One and Jaws Two."

He was referring to Petty, who didn't appreciate being dissed (or lumped in with Waltrip, for that matter). "Consider the source," Petty said. "Consider the source."

The back-and-forth only whetted the appetites of the fans. One Richmond writer suggested that tickets would be "as hard to come by as gold-filled chickens' teeth." Track officials announced that they were releasing 8,000 tickets on Saturday morning at 8:00. By 7:00 people were already lined up in the snow waiting for a crack at them. They might not have been so eager to brave the elements had they known that there was a movement afoot to bring the feud to an end through diplomacy. With some coaxing from Hoss Ellington, who was perhaps the most innocent victim in the whole wreckfest,* Donnie and Yarborough finally sat down face-to-face. For thirty minutes they hung out in the back of the NASCAR trailer. When they emerged, they were all smiles. "We talked about what good friends we've been all these years," Yarborough said. "We talked about everything—about bird hunting, deer hunting, coon hunting, about what a good pair of coon dogs I've got. It turns out Donnie doesn't have a good coon dog. I just might give him one."

But if the main combatants had agreed to a truce, word of the cease-fire didn't make it to the front. Junior Johnson was in the garage launching broadsides at Petty and Waltrip, who he felt had gone too far with their rebukes of Yarborough in Rockingham. Johnson claimed that Waltrip had "wrecked himself" by trying to speed through the crash instead of avoiding it. And he used an old defense attorney's trick to paint the King as an unreliable witness. "Petty's not god," Johnson said. "He's just another race car driver. He lied about Donnie getting alongside Cale in the first turn [at Rockingham]. He didn't get under him until they were going into three. A man that would tell a lie about one thing would tell a lie about another."[†]

Yarborough and Donnie planned to celebrate the thaw in their relations by having dinner together Saturday night, but their racing responsibilities forced them to cancel. When Allison finally left the track, he seemed also to leave behind the sense of peace that had been forged there. When he got back to the Holiday Inn, he began to agonize. The knock on Donnie had always been that he wasn't like Bobby, that he wasn't intense enough, that he didn't care enough about racing to put

---

* The value of his cars torn up in the two wrecks was around $120,000, and the damage to the second car from the Rockingham wreck kept him from being able to enter Neil Bonnett in the March 18 Atlanta race, as he had planned to do.
† Johnson also accused Waltrip's owner, Bill Gardner, of instructing Waltrip to wreck Yarborough in Rockingham after Wanda was repaired.

himself in the Mayo Clinic with stomach problems. But Donnie was fine with that. He believed there was more to life than racing, that it wasn't a life-or-death proposition. And now, wouldn't you know it, that's just what everyone seemed hell-bent on making it—literally, if the yokel letter writer from Atlanta was to be taken seriously.

He decided he had to talk to someone. He picked Hinton, who, as a writer, was the closest thing to a neutral party he was going to find. As Hinton headed into the Holiday Inn, Allison emerged from the shadows. "I don't know what to do," Allison said softly. "I've never been through anything like this before in my life. I don't know how to handle this."

"It'll die down," Hinton told him. "Everybody will go away as soon as you don't wreck each other."

Allison seemed relieved, but he was understandably still a little freaked about what might happen the next day.

Nothing happened.

Okay, stuff happened. But it wasn't the kind of stuff that was going to please sports editors, and it certainly wasn't the kind of stuff that was going to please the fans who were freezing their asses off in the hope that there might be some carnage in the offing. It snowed again Sunday morning and didn't stop until two hours before the green flag. In a repeat of Rockingham, the Allisons were cheered during driver introductions, while the three-time defending champ was given the Waltrip treatment. The race started under gray skies, as pole sitter Bobby Allison pulled away from the pack. Yarborough, who started ninth, was playing it safe and stroking. "I wanted to stay out of the crowd and take no chances of getting into any more trouble like that, and then make my move when the field got strung out and the traffic was thinner," he said. And Donnie Allison, who started eleventh, had handling problems from the start. His brother put him a lap down early in the race, and Yarborough got around him shortly thereafter. The pass was clean and uneventful, as Donnie, realizing he was no match for the leaders, pulled to the side and let Yarborough go.

And that's when people started leaving.

To the chagrin of many, the Richmond 400 was, according to Petty, "the cleanest race I ever saw." There were two caution periods for a total of ten laps. The first yellow came out on the second lap, when Dale Earnhardt hit a slick patch and spun, and the second flew when Baxter Price spun just after the midway point. There was one lead change in the race that was the result of a pass, not a pit stop: Yarborough got around Bobby on lap 225, and he gradually built a comfortable lead, winning by a cozy six-second margin. The closest thing to drama came with three laps left when Waltrip, who was one lap down, tapped Yarborough's bumper while fighting off Benny Parsons for third place. "He almost spun me out," said Yarborough. "I don't know what his problem is."

After the race, Bobby stood in the muddy infield talking to the press. One of the newbie reporters pointed out that it had been an exceptionally clean race. "Does that disappoint you?" Allison shot back. Yarborough was also short with the media. "Now I mean this," he said. "This press conference is going to be the last time I'm going to say anything about all that other mess. So there's no use in people asking me anymore. Like I told Bobby and Donnie, as far as I'm concerned, it's like all that stuff never happened." Yarborough was then asked by one of the regular beat writers what he thought of all the new faces in the press box. "I hope," Yarborough said, "that they'll now become interested in racing."

### Standings After the Richmond 400

| | | |
|---|---|---|
| 1. | Darrell Waltrip | 637 |
| 2. | Cale Yarborough | 624 |
| 3. | Bobby Allison | 611 |
| 4. | Donnie Allison | 536 |
| 5. | Joe Millikan | 530 |
| | ... | |
| 10. | Richard Petty | 469 |

## Chapter Eleven

# Wild and Young, Crazy and Dumb

ITS PEACE seemingly restored after Richmond, NASCAR moved the following week to Atlanta and then to North Wilkesboro, North Carolina, where Bobby Allison beat Richard Petty in a race that was, like every other sporting event that weekend, overshadowed by what was happening in Salt Lake City. On Saturday, March 24, in the first of the day's two NCAA basketball national semifinals, Michigan State sophomore Magic Johnson put up a triple double (29 points, 10 rebounds, 10 assists) in the Spartans' 101–67 undressing of the tournament's hopelessly overmatched Cinderella team, Penn. The Michigan State fans at the Special Events Center were so dismissive of the Quakers that they spent much of the game taunting fans of undefeated Indiana State, which was playing DePaul in the second game. "We want the Bird!" the Spartan fans chanted, to which the Sycamore fans responded, "You'll get the Bird!" (Many, with one finger, gave the State fans another kind of bird as well.) They all got their wish. Playing with a broken left thumb, Larry Bird had 35 points, 16 boards, and 9 assists in a 76–74 win, booking Indiana State's spot in Monday's championship game.

If the fans were thrilled about the prospect of a Bird-Magic matchup in the final, the people who inhabited the Manhattan offices of the National Basketball Association were ecstatic. The NBA was in trouble, and the Fifth Avenue suits knew it. The league had already decided to hire an outside PR firm — necessitating the quadrupling of the NBA's meager PR budget of $125,000 — to deal with a litany of image problems, many of which had been spelled out the week after the Daytona 500 in a *Sports Illustrated* story titled "There's an Ill Wind Blowing for the NBA." Attendance in the big four markets — New York, Los Angeles, Chicago, and Philadelphia — was down from the previous season by an average of 24 percent. Jerry West, the coach of the Lakers — one of the league's best teams — lamented, "People I talk to around Los Angeles all tell me that there isn't a great deal of interest in either the Lakers or the NBA." And national TV ratings, never too good to begin with, were off by 26 percent. "Those twin indicators of public appeal — attendance and television ratings," wrote *SI*, "are disappointing, raising serious questions about the future of the sport."

The playoffs were just around the corner, but instead of drumming up interest in the NBA, the advent of the postseason only invited more criticism. At the start of the 1979 playoffs, the *Charlotte Observer* ran a column by *New York Daily News* columnist Mike Lupica* under the headline NBA'S PLAYOFFS BEGIN, BUT DOES ANYONE CARE? The piece centered on a ho-hum Friday night game between the Lakers and the Seattle SuperSonics aired by CBS — a game the network's Charlotte affiliate did not, as was its policy, broadcast. That was nothing new. The CBS affiliate in Atlanta, home to an NBA team since 1968, hadn't shown NBA games for five years.

In a way, the NBA had the same problem as NASCAR in the late 1970s: when it came to TV, it was largely relegated to the land of misfit sporting events. "CBS has been properly criticized for treating its telecasts as little more than a bridge between a refrigerator race and a golf tournament," wrote *SI*. Indeed, when CBS wasn't showing NBA

---

*In his pre-TV, pre-novel days, Lupica was something of a boy wonder in the newspaper business. In 1977, at age twenty-five, he had become the youngest sports columnist for a New York paper. That didn't stop the *Observer* from mistakenly calling him *Ron* Lupica in the byline.

Finals games on tape delay, the network was often trying to force the NBA to alter its schedule to allow more popular sports to be shown in choice time slots. As a result, Game 3 of the 1976 NBA Finals in Phoenix between the Suns and the Boston Celtics tipped off at 10:30 on a Sunday morning so that CBS could show the Kemper Open golf tournament in its entirety. Still, the outrage in Phoenix was mild at best, and it came mostly from members of the clergy.

But unlike NASCAR, the NBA had occasionally enjoyed prime-time exposure, and when it did, the results were abysmal. In the fall of 1978 *Variety* published the ratings of the 730 shows that appeared in prime time from September 1, 1977, through August 31, 1978. Four of the top five were sporting events, led by the Super Bowl. The highest-rated NBA broadcast, the deciding sixth game of the Celtics-Suns series, was tied for 442nd with *Peter Lundy and the Medicine Hat Stallion* (Leif Garrett as a Pony Express rider in pre–Civil War Nebraska), *The Hostage Heart* (terrorists in the OR!), and *Country Night of Stars* (Eddy Arnold!).

College basketball had proven only slightly less unappealing to television viewers. The 1978 NCAA title game between Duke and Kentucky was tied for 216th with *The Laughing Policeman, Battle of the Network Stars,* and *Hanna-Barbera's All-Star Comedy Ice Revue.* But the Magic-Bird game changed all that, even though as a game, it was nothing special. Bird was frustrated by his thumb injury and a stifling Michigan State matchup zone. He finished just 7 of 21 from the floor, and the Spartans were never really threatened in a 75–64 win. But the meeting of the sport's two brightest stars still pulled a 24.1 rating and a 38 share, numbers that had never been approached before and haven't been since.

That's just what the NBA was banking on. In May, Magic declared himself eligible for the 1979 draft under the league's hardship rule and was subsequently taken by the Lakers with the first pick. Bird's rights had been shrewdly snapped up by the Celtics a year earlier, meaning that they'd both be in the league in the fall of '79, which is why the NBA was optimistic that people might actually start paying attention to pro basketball.* In his column ripping the playoffs, Lupica wrote: "Hopefully this will be the last NBA season to be covered with such tedium and disgust. Players like Larry Bird and 'Magic' Johnson…can begin to change things next season. But for now, the NBA playoffs, once so special, are nothing more than a sideshow for a faltering circus. The circus will still be playing in June. By then, no one outside of two cities will care."

Marketing players is nothing new. There have always been superstars. But in the late 1970s and early '80s, they became something bigger. They became personalities. The biggest sports star in the mid-'70s was probably Cincinnati Reds third baseman Pete Rose. When would a kid in Topeka ever see Pete Rose play, let alone listen to him talk? Sure, he'd hear about him. But actually lay eyes on him? The All-Star Game. Maybe once or twice a season on *Monday Night Baseball*. The playoffs, if the Reds had a good year. Past that, Rose was just a face on a baseball card, a guy to be read about in the sports pages, that dude who warbled embarrassingly alongside Vic Tayback in a commercial for Aqua Velva.

But the '80s brought about new means by which Rose and his cohorts could infiltrate their fans' lives. Cable TV meant a wider audience for games and highlights. In 1982 *USA Today* hit the shelves. Computers meant players had their own personalized video games, such as Dr. J and Larry Bird Go One on One. Magic and Bird had their Converse Weapon deals; Jordan shilled his Air Jordans. And the process fed on itself. The more we saw of Bird—hey, there he is selling Chardon jeans or playing H-O-R-S-E with Michael Jordan in a McDonald's commercial—the more famous he got, which meant we saw even more of him. Being a superstar was no longer the pinnacle of athletic achievement. No, in the 1980s you had to be a megastar.

---

*LA got the pick from New Orleans as compensation for the Jazz signing Gail Goodrich in 1976 and then won a coin toss with the Bulls for the top pick overall. Boston was able to draft Bird with the sixth pick of the '78 draft because of the NBA's arcane "junior eligible" rule, which was taken off the books shortly after the Celtics landed Bird.

No sport thrived more in that new era than pro basketball, which rode Bird and Magic—and Jordan a few years later—to unprecedented heights. In 1979 just six of the NBA's twenty-two teams averaged 12,000 fans per game, and the average attendance was 10,756. In 1989 twenty-one of twenty-five teams were pulling in 12,000 people a game, and the average had climbed to 15,073, an increase of 42 percent—by far the largest increase of the four major sports.* As for the second indicator of public appeal, TV ratings, the NBA was the only sport to see its viewership rise between 1979 and 1984. Which explains why CBS, which nearly dropped the NBA in 1978 in the middle of a contract that paid the NBA $11 million a season, signed a four-year, $173 million deal with the league seven years later.

Of course, all that success can't be laid at the Converse-clad feet of Bird and Magic. But the NBA's growth showed that hitching its star to larger-than-life personalities—especially Bird, who gave the NBA what it so sorely needed, a Great White Hope that its fans could relate to[†]—was a viable growth model, especially if the sport in question had a lot of room to grow.

A sport like NASCAR.

There was remarkable overlap in the life stories of Larry Joe Bird and Ralph Dale Earnhardt. Many of the similarities were superficial: The sandy hair. The beady blue eyes. The mustache. The twang in the voice.

---

*Baseball attendance rose by 27 percent over the same period, the NHL was up by 17 percent, and the NFL held steady.

[†] The subject of race in the NBA wasn't danced around by blacks or whites. "This is something we must no longer whisper about," Denver general manager Carl Scheer told *Sports Illustrated* in 1978. "It's definitely a problem and we, the owners, created it. People see our players as being overpaid and underworked, and the majority of them are black." His sentiments were echoed by Seattle forward Paul Silas, a black player who was the president of the NBA Players Association: "It is a fact that white people in general look disfavorably upon blacks who are making astronomical amounts of money if it appears they are not working hard for that money."

The *I'm having the time of my life because I'm so damn good at what I do* smirk. But their paths to stardom also had a lot of similar landmarks.

Bird was a self-described "hick from French Lick," a factory town in southwestern Indiana, a place where everyone was obsessed with one sport—basketball. His early life had been bumpy. He'd had a difficult relationship with his father, a Korean War vet who had killed himself when he couldn't adjust to life back in the States. Then he'd married early and dropped out of college for a year, which he spent working as a garbageman.

Earnhardt was a "linthead." That's what everyone from Kannapolis, North Carolina, was called, on account of the Cannon textile mill that dominated the town's otherwise unremarkable skyline. Without the mill, there wouldn't have been a Kannapolis. It was carved out of what had been a cotton plantation northeast of Charlotte in the first decade of the twentieth century by James William Cannon, who needed a place to house his workers and their families. Cannon-opolis, as it was originally called, was organized in a series of grids, with the street names in each grid sharing a theme. Earnhardt's family lived in an area known as Car Town, at the corner of Sedan and Coach.

If basketball was made for Indiana, short-track auto racing was made for North Carolina. The soil—a thick red clay that packed just right—made a perfect racing surface. Tracks sprang up all over the Charlotte area, where every neighborhood had at least one or two shade-tree mechanics who turned wrenches on their cars after work or on the weekend. Ralph Earnhardt was one, at least until he quit his job at the mill and started racing full-time in cars he built in the cinder block shop in his backyard. His middle young 'un, as Dale's mother called him, was Ralph's biggest fan, and Dale often found himself drifting into the same kind of dazes that made Larry Bird such an average student. "I can remember being in school," Dale said in 1979, "counting the seconds ticking off the clock until class was over and I could go home and help him in the racing shop."

\*　　\*　　\*

Ralph Earnhardt was a stoic man, described by one friend as "taciturn to a fault."* He was devoted to his family, so much so that he passed on a Grand National career in favor of dirt tracking in the Carolinas so he wouldn't have to be away from his wife, Martha, and their three kids. And he steadfastly refused to put the family in debt by borrowing money to fund his racing. That necessitated a conservative on-track style. He'd lay back and keep his car out of trouble, not showing his hand until he absolutely had to. It kept the repair bills down, and it won him a lot of races to boot: he was the 1956 NASCAR Sportsman champion. As good as he was at driving a car, Ralph might have been even better at putting one together.† "He never worked on the car at the track," says Humpy Wheeler. "He was always perfectly prepared. Everyone else would be working, and Ralph would be leaning against his car, smoking a cigarette."

Eventually, Dale got sick of counting down the seconds left in the school day, so he dropped out at fourteen. "It was the only thing I ever let my daddy down over," Earnhardt said in 1987. "He wanted me to finish. It was the only thing he ever pleaded with me to do. But I was so hardheaded. For about a year and a half after that, we didn't have a close relationship."

He got a job as a mechanic at Punch's Wheel Shop in Concord, a gig he gave up in 1973, when he was twenty-two, to have a go at a racing career. When Earnhardt handed in his notice, Punch Whitaker's immortal reply was "You're going to starve, boy." In retrospect, ol' Punch was wide of the mark. But for a while it looked like he had gauged the situation perfectly. Dale was, by his own admission, "wild and crazy, young and dumb." His favorite movie was *Animal House,* which apparently inspired

---

* Ralph was played by J. K. Simmons in *3,* the ESPN movie about Dale's life, which pretty much tells you all you need to know about Ralph.

† He built cars for other drivers, too, most of whom were racers. "Ralph was well-known for building engines for cars that would transport liquids other than gasoline," said his friend Marshall Brooks.

Earnhardt as much as it entertained him. To wit: One late night Earnhardt and a friend, a motorcycle shop owner named Marshall Brooks, were cruising Kannapolis in a truck that Brooks used to haul bikes. The truck had a loudspeaker, the kind of toy that made Earnhardt's eyes light up. He suggested that they go and harass his brother-in-law. They parked outside the house and ordered the inhabitants to come out with their hands over their heads, but they got no reaction. Dejected, Brooks took Earnhardt home, but as he made his way back to his place, he noticed several flashing lights in his rearview mirror. The house hadn't belonged to Earnhardt's brother-in-law after all, but rather to Clifford Cook, a lawman who was none too amused. With some sweet-talking, Brooks was able to convince Cook not to haul him down to the slammer. Brooks confronted Earnhardt over the prank the next day. "He was sitting on the floor in the middle of the shop," said Brooks. "When he saw me pull up, I saw him cock his head sideways, and that little grin came out. He thought it was the funniest thing in the world."

So it should come as little surprise to learn that Earnhardt had been married at seventeen, divorced at nineteen, and remarried at twenty. By the time he quit Punch's shop, he already had three kids. A fourth, Dale Jr., would be born within a year, and his second marriage would end shortly thereafter. His family, he said, "probably should have been on welfare.... For our family cars, we drove old junk Chevelles, anything we could get for $200."

As his career progressed, Dale and his father slowly reconciled, largely through time spent together in the shop. Ralph began playing an active role in Dale's blossoming driving career. They built a go-kart, and Dale started driving on dirt. Then on September 26, 1973, Ralph died.

As Dale Earnhardt became more famous, the circumstances surrounding his father's death were romanticized. The most common story to evolve was that he was tuning a carburetor in the backyard when he suffered a massive heart attack. In some versions of the tale,

Dale was the one who found the body. In reality, Ralph had a heart attack, and Martha found him on the kitchen floor. Dale was gutted. "I didn't know which way to turn, what to do, where to go for help and advice," Dale said in 1979. "I was helpless. I tried to go hunting. I couldn't. Everywhere I looked, there he stood, gun in hand. I sold his bird dogs." When he was working on his car, he found himself talking to Ralph, asking how to fix that carburetor or what gear he should be using. "Sometimes, late at night, I would sit down and cry for an hour without stopping," he said.

After Ralph died, Martha gave Dale his cars. And at that point, there was no more wavering about how committed Dale was to racing. He was in it for good. "Daddy had begun to help me," Earnhardt said in 1987. "Then he died. It left me in a situation where I had to make it on my own. I'd give up everything I got if he were still alive, but I don't think I'd be where I am if he hadn't died."

Ralph's death pushed Dale into a world he was destined to conquer, but one he might not have seemed ready for at the time. He didn't look like he belonged. For starters, there was his getup. Says Darrell Waltrip, "Dale was always saying, 'I need to get a break. I need to get a break. I got to get off these dirt tracks. I can't ever make it if I just run dirt. I don't want to end up like all these other guys, spending my whole life running on short tracks and dirt tracks. I want to be out there with you.' I kind of looked at him like, *Good luck*. Because he was rough. He had a scruffy old mustache, and he always had on a dirty T-shirt and a pair of high-water pants, a pair of Hush Puppies. Always wanting to borrow something. If you looked at him and said, 'Will this guy ever make it?' You'd probably have said, 'Nah, I don't know. Questionable.'"

Lou LaRosa, who'd later build engines for Earnhardt, remembers seeing him drive at Metrolina Speedway in Charlotte. "He was no great driver," says LaRosa. "He wasn't a superstar. Only time you heard of Dale is when he flipped the son of a bitch in Atlanta."

The son of a bitch in question was a Chevrolet belonging to man named Johnny Ray. They hooked up right around the time Earnhardt was at his lowest. He'd wrecked everything his dad had left him and was forced to go to Robert Gee, his second ex–father-in-law, with his hat in hand.* Gee put him to work in his shop, doing things like painting cars orange in an unventilated room. Earnhardt would leave at the end of the day looking like the world's most avid University of Tennessee fan, but in exchange for the work, Gee let Earnhardt drive his Sportsman car.

Late in 1976 Gee convinced Ray to put Earnhardt in a Grand National car for the fall race in Atlanta. Aware that Earnhardt's reputation might kill the deal, Gee agreed to fix any damage Earnhardt might do to the car. Waltrip kept his car at Gee's shop, and Gee told him about the arrangement. "I said, 'Well, you might as well get ready to be fixing that thing, because you know Dale is going to tear it up,'" says Waltrip. "Because he was reckless. He just drove like an idiot — run over people, run over anything. He had one speed, and it was like a bull in a china shop. No finesse. Just throw it in there and hope it sticks.

"So anyway, at Atlanta, I come off of Turn 2, the caution lights come on, and I see a car flying through the air, bouncing, rolling, tumbling down the back straightaway. Get down there, and guess who it was: Earnhardt, in Johnny Ray's car. Tore it all to pieces. Totaled it." The wreck was so bad that Richard Petty radioed to his crew, "I think they just killed Ralph Earnhardt's boy."

Earnhardt's driving style had just as much to do with his situation as it did with his naturally aggressive personality. Stroking in a one-time deal wasn't going to do him any good. He needed to get noticed, and being conservative wasn't going to do that. But if you put him in a situation where he didn't feel like he had to drive the wheels off the car, he could put his natural gifts on display. One day in 1978 NASCAR

---

* Gee was Dale Earnhardt Jr.'s grandfather; his daughter Brenda is Junior's mom.

historian Greg Fielden was watching him turn practice laps at Myrtle Beach Speedway, a little old oval with ivy on the wall. Every time Earnhardt went past Fielden, he'd clip a piece of ivy. The groove wasn't that close to the wall; Earnhardt was just doing it for practice, or fun. Awed by the display of precision, Fielden asked, "Are they paying you to clip that ivy off the wall?" Then, says Fielden, "he gave me that possum-eating shit grin and said, 'You noticed that, huh?'"

As freakishly gifted as he was, Earnhardt never forgot who he was. Bird was the same way, which went a long way toward explaining his popularity. When he was presented with the 1984 NBA Most Valuable Player Award at a black-tie affair, Bird accepted it in a bowling shirt. A 1981 *Sports Illustrated* profile noted that aside from basketball, "the rest of his pleasure comes from winning, mowing his lawn, drinking beer, hunting squirrels, fishing, playing golf, and being with friends and family." The same could be said about Earnhardt, except he was partial to chopping wood, not mowing the lawn, and his preferred quarry was deer, not squirrels. He was easy to relate to. People wanted to be like him, the guy who drove his car hard and reckless and knocked the hell out of whoever got in his way. "You have a tremendous amount of transference at the racetrack," says Humpy Wheeler. "People subconsciously become the driver of that car. And here's a kid who came from the bottom, worked hard for everything he got, and didn't have any airs about him. Truck drivers, dockworkers, welders, and shrimp-boat captains loved that. He was everything they dreamed about being."

So all those fans sat in the stands worshipping him because he seemed like the kind of guy they could kick back and go hunting with. And he was. Late in the '79 season, he was driving a beat-up Chevy pickup truck in Charlotte when he saw something in the back of the truck in front of him that piqued his interest: a big, dead deer. He followed the driver to a gas station, then approached him. "I see you've got blood on your shoes," he said. "You either been fighting or hunting." Earnhardt then demanded that the stranger, Frankie Fraley, take him hunting the next morning and show him where he'd bagged the buck.

He and Fraley eventually became such good friends that Earnhardt made Fraley join his race team, even though Fraley, who built mobile homes and raised dairy cows, hated racing. The lengths to which Earnhardt would go to hunt were astonishing. Stalking a stranger on the road was nothing. He'd come to Fraley's at three in the morning to help him milk the cows so he'd have time to hunt. "He'd show up in the milk barn with donuts and Coke," says Fraley. "He'd say, 'We're not having milk.'"

One year Fraley held a dirt bike race on his property, and he got Earnhardt to come out and serve as the honorary starter. Earnhardt waved the flag and then hopped on a four-wheeler, telling Fraley he wanted to go find a good vantage point to watch the race. When it ended two hours later, Earnhardt was nowhere to be seen. Trophies were handed out. No Earnhardt. Finally, around dusk, he appeared, carrying a rifle. Despite the fact that it was a Sunday, which meant no hunting, he thought the race might provide him with an opportunity too good to pass up. "I thought those motorcycles running around would run some deer across," he said.

"Whatever he was doing," says Fraley, "he'd be thinking about hunting."

And God help the man who went hunting or fishing without Earnhardt. In 1989 Neil Bonnett broke his sternum, so he sat out the fall race in Charlotte. Bonnett and Fraley decided to take advantage of Bonnett's time off by launching a boat on the pond on Earnhardt's property and doing some fishing. When Earnhardt got home from the track, he was incensed that his friends were having fun without him. He demonstrated his displeasure by firing several shots across their bow with a high-powered rifle.

That was Earnhardt. Just a guy who'd rather be hunting.

He had the makeup to be NASCAR's megastar, its Bird, and the time was right. But there was one more thing. He had to start winning.

## Chapter Twelve

# Diamonds As Big As Horse Turds

**Sunday, April 1**
**Race 7: Southeastern 500**
**Bristol, Tennessee**

DALE EARNHARDT's 1979 ride was procured at the end of a very strange 1978. In May he made his fifth career Grand National start, in Will Cronkrite's car in the World 600 in Charlotte. Earnhardt hadn't been Cronkrite's first choice. Humpy Wheeler, always looking for a way to drum up publicity at his home track, convinced Cronkrite to give the seat to Willy T. Ribbs, a twenty-three-year-old Californian who happened to be black, which made him something of a novelty in NASCAR. Ribbs certainly had the bona fides—he'd cut his teeth driving in Europe, where he'd won the Formula Ford series championship in his first year. He also shared Wheeler's knack for promotion, possibly to a fault, which became apparent two days after Wheeler introduced him to the press as "what we promoters have been waiting for since Wendell Scott."*

---

*Scott remains to this day the only black driver to win a Grand National race. His life story was told in the 1977 film *Greased Lightning,* with Richard Pryor as Scott.

Late in the evening, Ribbs was spotted by the Charlotte cops going the wrong way down a one-way street in a Charlotte Motor Speedway pace car. His racer's instincts getting the better of him, Ribbs tried to outrun the police and wound up near Queens College, in an upscale part of town. He ditched the car and hightailed it into a gym, where he picked up a basketball and was casually working on his jump shot when the cops happened upon him. Ribbs insisted that he was a student, a defense that might have flown better had Queens College not been an all-girls school that was, in the words of one of the arresting officers, "lily white." When Ribbs was booked, he didn't call a lawyer or Wheeler. No, he called a writer, Tom Higgins of the *Charlotte Observer*. "I'm fine," he told Higgins. "I just thought you'd like to know about me getting nabbed."

A few weeks later Ribbs was a no-show at a couple of practice sessions, and Wheeler and Cronkrite pulled the plug on the experiment. "There could be rednecks with deer rifles out in that infield," Wheeler told Ribbs. Cronkrite gave the ride to Earnhardt, who finished a creditable seventeenth—ahead of both cars entered by Rod Osterlund.

Osterlund was yet another owner with deep pockets who was new to the game. He was from Northern California, where he'd made his fortune in real estate. Like Bill Gardner's pinochle game, Osterlund's introduction to racing was nontraditional. His daughter Lana went to high school with three guys—Dave D'Ambrosio, Jeff Prescott, and Doug Richert—who liked to work on cars and race them at tracks in the San Jose area. "He got interested in who his daughter was hanging out with," says D'Ambrosio. "Then got interested in the racing part of it."

Osterlund wasn't the kind of man who half-assed things. Before long he decided that he wanted to build a real team, one that could be competitive at the sport's highest level. In the summer of 1977 he decided to move the operation, including Richert and D'Ambrosio, to North Carolina. So what if they were still in high school. "Our parents saw how dedicated we were to it, and there was a lot of infrastructure," says D'Ambrosio. "It was the same group we had been running with for the last three or four years. There was a comfort level involved. Rod made sure we were taken care of." They loaded up a truck and trekked across the country, with Richert celebrating his seventeenth birthday on the highway in the middle of Texas. Osterlund also brought along Roland Wlodyka, a thirty-eight-year-old contractor who had done some work for Osterlund and also did a little driving. When they arrived in Charlotte, D'Ambrosio and Richert moved into a fifth-wheel trailer parked at an amusement park near the South Carolina state line. After six months they moved it to the parking lot outside the shop, which was near the Charlotte Motor Speedway. "We'd get up, go have breakfast at the Pit Stop Grill, come back across the street, work, work, work, then go back to the trailer and go back to sleep," says D'Ambrosio. "We didn't make any money—I think it was $123 a week—but everything was paid for."

Osterlund's ownership style was Steinbrenneresque: he had a checkbook and a pen, and he wasn't afraid to use them. He built a shop; poached some talent from DiGard, including Nick Ollila; and hired veteran engine builder Ducky Newman and his protégé, Long Island native Lou LaRosa. The team manager was Wlodyka, whose brashness would make him Billy Martin in this New York Yankees analogy. "Roland had a Northern California smart-ass attitude, like he was trying to convert the good ol' boy network," says Ollila. "He assumed they were all stupid and since they spoke with a southern drawl they couldn't add or subtract, and therefore he was going to be smarter than them. He alienated so many people. He would say it to people's faces, the Pettys and the Pearsons: 'You guys are a bunch of dumb-ass rednecks.'"

Wlodyka also drove for a spell, and he spread about as much joy on the track as he did in the garage. He didn't have much experience, but that didn't bother him. "Roland was braver than Dick Tracy," says LaRosa. "Not a great driver, but fearless." When it became apparent late in the 1977 season that there was more to driving than possessing a square-jawed resolve, Osterlund hired Dave Marcis, an old schooler from Wisconsin who was best known for finishing second in points in 1975 and for driving in wing tips.*

In the eyes of Osterlund and Wlodyka, at least, Marcis's problem was that he wasn't enough like Dick Tracy. Marcis was getting decent results—he finished the '78 season with twenty-four top 10s in thirty starts—but he wasn't winning any races. (Even in his best season, when he finished runner-up to Petty in '75, he won only once.) Osterlund began making noise about dropping him for the '79 season. He took a list of potential replacements to Cale Yarborough in the fall of '78 and asked him whom he should hire. Osterlund might have been hoping that Yarborough would say, "Hell, I'll race for you." Instead, Yarborough picked the most inexperienced driver on the list: Ralph Earnhardt's boy.

Dale Earnhardt had another benefactor, longtime family friend Humpy Wheeler. Wheeler leaned on Osterlund to give Earnhardt a shot. That might have been enough to convince Osterlund, but just to be safe, Wheeler relied on something that tends to be more effective than a persuasive argument: cash. Five grand got Earnhardt a seat in a second Osterlund car in the November Atlanta race, the next-to-last event of the season.

But first Wheeler wanted to get Earnhardt in the Sportsman race at Charlotte in October. Osterlund relented, putting him in a car that Marcis had totaled a few weeks earlier in Darlington. "It was twisted every which way," says LaRosa. Richert, working with brothers Jim and Bill Delaney, took the frame off the junk heap and fashioned the mangled Grand National vehicle into a Sportsman car; LaRosa built the engine. Earnhardt finished second and would have won were it not for problems with the clutch.

Marcis couldn't help but notice the attention being lavished on

---

* Not necessarily in that order.

Earnhardt. "I think the jealousy was there already, or the animosity," says LaRosa. Late in the Atlanta race, Marcis, who was making his 310th career start, gave Earnhardt a rap. The rookie code held that Earnhardt take the contact and like it, but Earnhardt wasn't the type to stand on ceremony. He popped the veteran back. If Marcis was expecting Osterlund to reprimand Earnhardt, he was disappointed. After the race no one said a word about the contact. Marcis finished the race third, one spot ahead of Earnhardt, but he didn't need any help reading the writing on the wall. He drove the season finale, then quit. Earnhardt would be Osterlund's driver in 1979.

Hiring Earnhardt guaranteed one thing: Osterlund and Wlodyka wouldn't be able to complain that their driver wasn't aggressive enough. In January of '79 they took a car to Daytona for testing. It was a Buick with a square back, which made it about 4 miles per hour slower than the Oldsmobiles most drivers were using. But the idea was that it would handle better in the draft, which would make up for the lack of pure speed. After a few practice runs by himself, Earnhardt was disgusted with the results. LaRosa tried to tell him that he shouldn't worry, that when he ran with other cars, his times would pick up. Earnhardt was having none of it. "Put a smaller spoiler on it," he said.* Still slow. So the spoiler got gradually smaller, until Earnhardt finally told LaRosa to take the damn thing off.

"Dale, you can't run without a spoiler," LaRosa told him.

"Who's driving the son of a bitch, me or you?" Earnhardt said.

Off came the spoiler.

"He went through the tri-oval about sideways," remembers LaRosa. "You heard the engine roar, then get quiet when he came off the gas. He came into the pits white as a ghost and said, 'Put the spoiler back on.'"

---

* A spoiler is a metal strip on the trunk that keeps the back end of the car on the track. A small spoiler reduces drag and makes the car faster, but it does so at the expense of stability.

Earnhardt obviously had the nerve, and he had the desire. He was driving well in spells, but his aggressiveness was leading to a lot of mistakes. He slipped the clutch and broke the transmission in Riverside. He got pissed at his crew, revved his motor, and broke the engine in Daytona. He ran too hard on a slick track and spun out on the second lap in Richmond. He ran out of gas in Atlanta. And he was used to driving a Sportsman car, which was lighter and handled differently than a Grand National car.

Yeah, he had the nerve, and he had the desire. What he needed was someone to guide him through this new world.

If there was ever a car whisperer, it was Jake Elder. "Suitcase Jake," he was called, on account of his penchant for blowing into town, instantly improving the fortunes of a race team, and then leaving as suddenly as he had arrived. He was shrouded in an air of mystery, and not just because of his peripatetic ways. Elder had a third-grade education and was illiterate, which ruled out keeping notes on setups. Instead, he carried two tape measures—one for short tracks, one for longer tracks. On the side opposite the ruler he made a series of marks with a felt-tip pen that corresponded with various points on the car. No one was sure exactly how the system worked, but Elder would unroll the tape measure, hold it up against the car, and tinker with the body a little. The end result would be a perfect setup. Elder had a few other tricks. Like every crew chief, he'd lie down on a creeper and slide under the car to check out the setup. Unlike every other crew chief, he'd then slide under an adjacent car and check out *its* setup. Then another, and another, as far down the garage as he could make it until someone noticed him.

"Jake was a simple man," says LaRosa. "If he told you something, it was true. He didn't get paid to read or write. He got paid to make that race car go fast." And he did. Elder won championships with David Pearson in 1968 and '69, but he was best known for mentoring green drivers.

"The reason I had success early on is that Jake could make a car drive right," says Darrell Waltrip, who worked with Elder in the mid-1970s. "I've driven cars that didn't drive right. That just scares the hell out of you. You don't know if it's you, you don't know if it's the car, or you just don't know if you can't do this. Because if you've never been in a car that drives right, you say, 'Man, this is scaring the hell out of me. I can't do this. These things will hurt you. I'm going to wreck this thing.' And that's what Jake could do for everybody that he ever worked with: when you got in that car and you went around the racetrack, you drove the car — the car didn't drive you. I'd get in some other people's cars, and man they'd dart and dive all over the place — scare the heck out of you. And I'd say, 'Forget speed — the car's not going to go fast if you can't drive it. But you can really drive it fast if it handles right and drives right.'

"And that was what he was good at. Could he do anything else? No. But he could look at a race car and tell you what was wrong with it. He could look at the suspension, or he could look at the toe, or he could look at the body — he just had a sense about him. He knew a race car from one end to the other."

In December 1978 Osterlund announced that he had hired Elder, but as was Suitcase Jake's wont, he backed out of the deal the same day and took a job under Herb Nab on Buddy Baker's crew. He reconsidered in the spring of '79, dumping Nab and signing with Osterlund. When the deal was announced in Atlanta, Elder showed that he hadn't moved past his fear of commitment. "I made a mistake [in December], now I want to give Osterlund a shot," Elder said. "If after two months we can't get along, then I'll leave."

Even a two-month marriage seemed optimistic. Working for Osterlund — who was based in California and traveled to only about a quarter of the races — really meant working for Wlodyka, which was proving to be a less-than-attractive proposition. Marcis laid into Wlodyka after he quit, and Ducky Newman had harsh words for the operation when he jumped ship in January to go build engines for Benny Parsons. "The money was better, but the real reason I decided to leave Osterlund is because I couldn't get along with Roland," said Newman. "If we'd had a good crew chief things might have been different."

In the other corner was Elder, himself a perennial no-hoper in the Boss of the Year competition. "Oh, man, he was a nut," says Waltrip. "He had to do it all himself. And that's probably some of that insecurity from not being able to read or write. He couldn't work with people. He had to do it himself. He didn't want anybody helping him. He didn't trust anybody, for one thing. He worked himself to death, because that's all he knew how to do. He couldn't communicate with other people because he didn't know how. He had paychecks in his pocket from when he worked at Holman Moody that he had never cashed."

"Jake could be psychotic at times," says Ollila. "Then the next day we'd be at the Derita Grille, eating lunch together like nothing had happened." Those meals were occasionally eventful. "We'd be at the restaurant, and we'd have our menus out," says Ollila. "I knew he couldn't read. He'd look at me and say, 'What are you going to get?' So I'd point at something I knew he hated, like liver and onions, and say, 'I'm going to get that.' So when the waitress would come, he'd point to that. Then his dinner would come, and he'd say, 'Damn you, you know I hate that shit. Why'd you point that out?'"

Elder's my-way-or-the-highway routine might not have flown with the crew, but it worked wonders with the drivers. Earnhardt — whose nickname early in his career was Ironhead, a play on his father's nickname, Ironheart — occasionally tried to buck him, and when he did, Elder wasted little time forcefully reminding "the boy," as he called him, that he was the boss. But for the most part, they worked well together. In their second race, Earnhardt finished a career-best fourth at North Wilkesboro. Says LaRosa, "If you ask me the one thing that made Dale — Jake Elder settled his ass down and helped refine him as a driver. He was going to be a good driver no matter what, but Jake helped him hurry up and get there sooner."

Waltrip puts it more simply: "Jake made my career, and he made Dale's, too."

There was a palpable sense of inevitability lingering over the Earnhardt team in the garage the day before the Southeastern 500. The writers who followed the circuit were by now pretty sure that Earnhardt had the talent and the equipment to win a race—even though no rookie had done so since 1974—so they started paying attention to him. Gene Granger of *Grand National Scene* was hanging around the Earnhardt stall, observing the ball breaking (Ollila was taking heat for being Swedish) and pondering aloud what it would be like when Earnhardt won a race: "He'll be saying, 'I'm not going to talk to you. You haven't written anything about me.' I'll bet he'll crack up the press."

If he was going to win, Bristol was as good a place as any to start. It's barely half a mile long, and it's banked more steeply than Daytona—36 degrees—so it rewards a driver who can bang a little and isn't afraid to stand on the gas. Buddy Baker qualified on the pole for the 500-lapper, but when he and Yarborough took each other out—Yarborough's third wreck in seven races—it became a two-car race for the final 235 laps: Earnhardt and Waltrip. Neither could get around the other when the green flag was out, so when the yellow flag came out on lap 473, both men knew that whoever got out of the pits first was going to win. It was Earnhardt. With each lap he pulled away a little more from Waltrip, who got a bad set of tires. "I really had to make an effort not to let myself get over-anxious," Earnhardt said. "The last 15 laps, I worked to make every corner count."

The win changed a lot of lives. As payment for various bets, Earnhardt shaved his mustache, and Doug Richert quit smoking. But more significantly, it put the team in NASCAR's Winner's Circle program, which meant they'd get a bigger chunk of the purses for the rest of '79 and all of '80. So while the oversize check Earnhardt received in Victory Lane was for just $19,800, the win was worth, all told, around $200,000. "When we qualified ninth for this race, we didn't win tires or nothing," said Elder. "Now we can go out and buy all we need."

There was no reason to think this wasn't the start of something big. "Stick with me," Elder told Earnhardt after the race, "and we'll both be wearing diamonds as big as horse turds."

### Standings After the Southeastern 500

| | | |
|---|---|---|
| 1. | Bobby Allison | 1,146 |
| 2. | Darrell Waltrip | 1,132 |
| 3. | Cale Yarborough | 1,028 |
| 4. | Benny Parsons | 978 |
| 5. | Dale Earnhardt | 975 |
| | ... | |
| 8. | Richard Petty | 939 |

## Chapter Thirteen

# Pearson's Kerfuffle

DARLINGTON IS located a few miles north of Florence, South Carolina. To get there from Charlotte, you drive south for about an hour and a half on Highway 151, a road named in different places for two local major league baseball players: Bobo Newsom and Van Lingle Mungo.* The pace of life was pretty slow. In setting the scene for the Rebel 500, ABC's Jim McKay said of Darlington, "Population 7,500. They grow tobacco and cotton and soybeans around here, and on Saturdays some of the good ol' boys go down to the barbershop to watch some haircuts."

---

*Mungo and Newsom, who had two of the greatest names in baseball history, both played for the Brooklyn Dodgers in the 1930s, but they never overlapped. Newsom is best known for being a four-time All-Star. Mungo is best known for being smuggled out of Cuba in a laundry cart by Dodgers officials after he was caught in flagrante delicto with a dancer by her butcher knife–wielding husband.

The idea for putting a superspeedway in such a rustic setting first came to Harold Brasington, a local businessman and occasional driver, in 1933 after he returned from Indianapolis, where he watched Louis Meyer win the Indy 500. Not surprisingly, Brasington had a little trouble getting the project off the ground. Given the ramshackle state of stock car racing at the time, there was no way to justify building a huge track in rural South Carolina in the middle of the Depression. But after the war—and after Bill France Sr. brought some order to the sport—Brasington finally pushed forward with his plan. He purchased some land from a poker buddy, Sherman Ramsey, who sold it with one caveat: that the minnow pond on the corner of the property not be disturbed.

When baseball stadiums were built in the early part of the twentieth century, they tended to be constructed in developed areas, leaving their architects at the mercy of existing streets and buildings. Hence the ridiculously odd shape of, say, Cleveland's League Park* and the nooks and crannies of Boston's Fenway Park. Ramsey's request left Brasington in a similar bind, so one end of the track had to be narrower than the other. The result was a quirky racetrack with character and a charm sorely lacking in so many of the cookie-cutter tracks that have sprung up over the past fifteen years.

Getting Darlington Raceway built was no easy task. Brasington did much of the work himself, bulldozing the dirt into mounds for the banked turns. He worked around the clock and even on Sundays, which, according to one local, "brought rebuke from his church." Unbowed by the congregation's collective stink eye, Brasington finished his mile-and-a-quarter, 25-degree-banked, egg-shaped track in 1950, and the first race was held on Labor Day. Seventy-five drivers showed up, and not one of them knew what they were getting into. Up to that point, NASCAR had run twenty races; eighteen had been

---

* The right field fence was just 290 feet from home plate, but it was 461 feet to center field.

on paved tracks, and only the two Daytona Beach races had been on a course of more than a mile. A steep, long, asphalt track was new on all three counts. The biggest problem presented by Brasington's beast—which would soon earn the ominous appellations "the Track Too Tough to Tame" and "the Lady in Black"*—was tire wear. For years "grand theft Goodyear" was a Darlington tradition: desperate crew members would head into the infield mid-race and pinch tires from spectators' cars. (The trick was to find a spectator who had already passed out; they put up the least fight.) The inaugural 400-lap race was won by Johnny Mantz, an Indy car driver who equipped his 1950 Plymouth with harder truck tires. Mantz was slow—he started forty-third—but he avoided the blowouts that plagued every other car in the field. He won by 9 laps and led for the final 351.

The other thing that made Darlington such a challenge was its racing groove. The track was narrow, and the fastest line required that a driver scrape up against the wall coming out of Turn 4, which left the car with a "Darlington stripe" on the passenger side door.† "I put more effort into doing well here than I do anywhere else because it's always considered to be a drivers' racetrack," Darrell Waltrip told ABC before the Rebel 500. "You feel like, *If I'm going to be a great race car driver or if I am of great race driver quality, then I have to excel at Darlington.*" And Waltrip had excelled: he had a win and four runner-up finishes at the track heading into 1979.

With just over 100 of the 367 laps remaining in the Rebel 500, only three cars were on the lead lap: Waltrip, Richard Petty, and pole sitter Donnie Allison. There hadn't been many wrecks, but in her typical fashion, the

---

* For years drivers had to watch a movie before they could race on the track. The flick was similar in tone and production values to those gorefests they show in drivers ed. "They showed about a hundred wrecks," says Ricky Rudd.
† The track was reconfigured in 1997. What are now Turns 1 and 2 were then Turns 3 and 4.

Lady in Black found other ways to vex the big names. Bobby Allison cut four tires before his engine finally blew after 246 laps, relegating him to a twenty-sixth-place finish. Cale Yarborough kept running out of gas and was three laps down. And David Pearson cut a tire and went a lap down, but his car was still strong. He was hanging with the leaders, trying to force his way back onto the lead lap. Pearson was in a frantic duel with Yarborough's lapped car. A wreck looked inevitable, but Pearson finally got around Yarborough, prompting Jackie Stewart, the three-time Formula One champ who was calling the race for ABC's *Wide World of Sports* with McKay, to drop some Scottish lingo on his viewers: "I'm afraid Cale's got himself passed by David Pearson there in that little kerfuffle."

"Would you care to explain that Scottish expression you just gave us?" asked McKay. "A kerfuffle, my boy?"

"A kerfuffle is much the same as getting your foot in the wrong side of the bed when you're trying to get out in the morning. A kerfuffle is a Scottish habit. And James, a lot of things have happened over in this country that the Scots have been a part of."

For Pearson, the kerfuffles were only beginning.

David Pearson was cool. Really cool, in just about every way you could imagine. He looked cool: he was well over six feet tall, was part Cherokee, and had rugged good looks, so he could tick the boxes next to tall, dark, *and* handsome. He acted cool—so cool that you tended to forget he was a forty-four-year-old grandfather. He smoked cigarettes, and even if you don't buy that smoking makes a man look cool, you have to agree that smoking *while driving a race car* does, at least a little. Pearson insisted that his car have a working lighter, lest he crave a butt during a caution period.

Most of all, though, Pearson was cool under pressure.

On the last lap of the 1976 Daytona 500—which until 1979 had set the standard for final-lap hijinks in a major race—he passed

Richard Petty for the lead heading into Turn 3, only to have Petty retake it coming off Turn 4. Petty, however, had to dip down low to get around Pearson, and he couldn't hold the line. His right rear fishtailed, tapping Pearson's front left and sending Pearson into the wall and down into the infield. Petty then overcorrected, which sent him nose-first into the fence and back down the track as well. He wound up one hundred yards ahead of Pearson's car, spitting distance from the finish line. But Petty stalled in the wreck and couldn't get his engine refired. Pearson had the presence of mind to mash the gas and the clutch as soon as he started spinning, so his engine never stopped. When his mangled Plymouth settled, he dropped it into first gear and sputtered across the finish line, taking the checkered flag at 30 miles per hour.

Throughout the entire episode, Pearson was on the radio with one of his crewmen, Eddie Wood, giving him a play-by-play: "I got him," followed a few seconds later by "He's under me," and then "We hit." Then, as his car was still spinning backward, Pearson asked Wood, "Where's Richard?" the same way he might have asked where his pack of smokes was. And to talk to Wood, Pearson had to key a switch on his shoulder harness, which meant he was wrestling the car to a stop, keeping the engine running, and getting it back into gear with one hand. It was like smoking, drinking a cup of coffee, and doing a crossword puzzle all at once.

"He wasn't excited; he wasn't angry," says Wood. "He was just matter-of-fact. *Where's Richard?* I told him Richard was stuck, and he said, 'I'm coming.' So I look up, and here he comes."

Pearson was Petty's greatest rival, the Salieri to his Mozart—just as talented but constantly overshadowed. Pearson didn't seek out the press, because he didn't want his lack of education to show. Born in Spartanburg, South Carolina, he dropped out of high school at sixteen to start working at the local mill, where both his parents worked the second shift. He liked to tell people that he got his education at

WMU, Whitney Mill University, with a degree in "skinning quills, pushing a broom and running an elevator."

If Pearson was self-conscious around strangers, he made up for it when surrounded by friends. He had a wry sense of humor that occasionally bordered on sadistic. Jack Arute once interviewed Pearson at a benefit race. When asked what charity he was racing for, Pearson said, "Well, Jackie, as a result of being around you so much during the past few years, I think I'm going to give what I win to The School for Mentally Retarded Announcers." He was a good-natured ballbuster and an inveterate prankster, with a special knack for automotive mischief. While riding shotgun with Whit Collins, the director of racing operations for his sponsor, Purolator, Pearson hammered Collins about how dirty his car was. Collins finally took the bait and pulled it into a car wash—at which point Pearson lowered the driver's side window, soaking Collins. Pearson was laughing so hard he couldn't get the window back up. On another occasion, he was riding with a friend who was pulled over for going 87 miles an hour. When the police officer approached the car, Pearson feigned relief and told him, "I'm glad you stopped us. I've been trying to get him to slow down ever since we left Savannah." The cop wrote a ticket, which carried a fine, but Pearson's flustered buddy was $10 short. "Shoot, lock him up if he can't pay the fine, officer," Pearson said. "I'll go on without him. A man that wants to drive like he does ought to carry enough money to pay the consequences, don't you think?"

Early in 1978 he bought a sixty-eight-acre farm outside Spartanburg that came with an old country store, which Pearson converted into a trophy room/clubhouse. Busch gave pole winners beer taps as prizes, and Pearson put his in his rumpus room. "I don't drink beer," he said, "but a lot of my buddies do, and that'll be a good place for them to sort of drop by and hang around." His mother, Lennie, lived nearby, in a house around the corner from the mill, and in Jim Hunter's 1980 biography of Pearson, *21 Forever,* the Silver Fox reported, "Miss Lennie is just as apt to get a switch after me today as she was back when I was growing up."

She had ample cause to, as Pearson's love of mischief dated back to childhood. He also loved racing and was able to combine his two loves one year in the soap box derby, when he won, but he was disqualified for having illegal steel-geared wheels. When he was working at the mill, he still made time to work on a car in the garage under "Miss Lennie's" house, using parts scavenged from the junkyard. He raced a little around Spartanburg and finally made the jump to Grand National cars at age twenty-five, in 1960, even though he didn't really want to. Two locals had started a David Pearson fan club and went on the radio to raise money for his racing expenses. "I didn't have any choice but to go along with it," Pearson said. "I didn't know who to give the money back to."

He ended up being named Rookie of the Year — he put his '59 Chevy on the pole in Sumter, South Carolina, and nearly won the race, one of his three top 5 finishes — but he collected only $5,030. Pearson ran a few races at the start of the 1960 season, but he was in danger of going bust until he got an offer to drive a car in Charlotte prepared by Ray Fox, one of the best wrenches in the game. Fox, like Bobby Allison, had had a brief but successful run working for Carl Kiekhaefer. In 1956, his only year with Kiekhaefer, Fox's cars won twenty-two of twenty-six races and he was named NASCAR's Mechanic of the Year. Pearson jumped at the offer. For once in his life, he was in a ride that allowed him to be patient, but he inexplicably drove like a madman. Starting from the third spot, he took Fox's Pontiac down onto the dirt apron in the first turn of the first lap of the 600-mile race to get past pole sitter Richard Petty. Driving the car like he stole it wasn't a sound game plan, but it worked. Pearson pulled away from the field, building up a four-lap lead, which came in handy when he blew a tire as he took the white flag. Pearson pulled down onto the apron and tooled around the track at 40 miles per hour, winning by two laps over Fireball Roberts. Pearson's take was $12,000. The next day he paid $5,000 in cash for the house he and his wife, Helen, had been renting.

He beat Fireball again at Daytona that July, which caught the attention of Cotton Owens, who gave him a full-time ride. Pearson won the 1966 championship with Owens, then moved to Holman Moody, where he won two more.* He left Holman Moody shortly after Ford pulled out of the sport in 1971, and in '72 he latched on with Wood Brothers. He won the pole at Darlington his first day in the car and lapped the field in the Rebel 400 that Sunday.

Glen Wood's early biography mirrors David Pearson's, with one difference. Like Pearson, Wood was from a small southern town: Stuart, Virginia, a sleepy hamlet of less than 1,000 people named for a Confederate general that to this day is twenty-five miles from the nearest McDonald's. Like Pearson, he quit school at age sixteen to work in a mill, in Wood's case a lumber mill, which gave him the nickname "the Old Woodchopper." Like Pearson, Wood dabbled in cars whenever he could and was mesmerized by the speed demons who came to the tracks near his home. Wood's favorite was Curtis Turner; whenever Pops was nearby, Wood would drive the lumber truck to the track to watch him. And like Pearson, Wood eventually started racing his own car, taking it to local tracks and struggling through some lean times. Wood's first race was in 1950 at the Morris Speedway, between Stuart and Martinsville. He crashed out of the heat race and tore up his '38 Ford. Unbeknownst to him, the housing bent and broke the axle, which busted the gas spout. Wood finally realized something was wrong when, as he towed the car home to Stuart, the Ford burst into flames. Wood had to pull the tow chain apart with his bare hands.

---

* For a variety of reasons, Pearson ran only four full seasons in his career. He won the title in three of them.

"We couldn't afford to lose both cars, or we would have been walking home," he said.

That one difference between Pearson and Wood was a big one. Whereas Pearson had the requisite need for speed, Wood, in his own words, was "not what you call a speed demon. I just don't like fast driving that much." Which, no matter how you cut it, is kind of a problem for a race car driver. Still, Wood averaged half a dozen starts a year and won four times before getting out of the car for good in 1964 and focusing his attention on running the team.

Wood Brothers was a loose collection of family members — Glen, his brothers Leonard and Delano, his sons Eddie and Len — and a few locals, most of whom were moonlighting. Scheduling was always a problem — they were at the mercy of one guy's cotton crop — and without the resources to run a full schedule, the Woods usually limited themselves to about twenty-two races a year. Although they'd never won a championship, they came into the 1979 season with eighty-two wins, more than any other team except Petty Enterprises.* Glen was the face of the operation, but Leonard was the brains.

Leonard Wood was one part Robert Carradine in *Revenge of the Nerds,* one part David Carradine in *Kung Fu,*† and one part MacGyver. His tall, angular frame and his horn-rimmed glasses made him one of the most recognizable men in the garage, and he also stood out as one of the more introspective, cerebral people in the sport. He worked on every aspect of the race car — the engine, the chassis, the body, the tires — and he did so tirelessly in the cinder block shop the Woods built on the banks of Poorhouse Creek.‡ (Unless it was Sunday. A

---

* Pearson's 1973 season, his second with the Woods, was ridiculous. He won eleven times in eighteen starts, including one stretch where he won nine of ten and came in second in the one race he didn't win. But since he sat out ten races, he finished thirteenth in the points standings.

† The contemplative part. Leonard didn't go around kicking people.

‡ The shop's proximity to the creek led to a problem: water moccasins. A particularly large one was once discovered in the dyno shop. Leonard originally thought it was an air hose.

devout Presbyterian, Leonard avoided working on Sunday whenever possible.) He once worked straight through dinner — which his wife, Betty Mae, put on the table every night at six o'clock sharp — because his watch had stopped and he somehow missed the fact that the sun had gone down. (Betty Mae finally called him at seven.) When he wasn't working on a car, chances are he was thinking about working on a car. "He thinks all the time, except maybe when he's asleep," Pearson once said of Leonard. The most widely told story about Leonard was that he actually kicked a crewman out of the hotel room they were sharing because the poor guy's presence interfered with Leonard's ability to think.

"I can't ever remember racing when my mind wasn't on it at least 50 percent, trying to come up with a new way to run better or figure out how somebody else is beating you," Leonard said in 1974. "I think if you concentrate on what you're doing hard enough, you can come up with something better than those who don't concentrate at all. I don't know how much thought the others put into it, but I put a lot."

Most people in the sport dreaded the cross-country hauls to California. Wood loved them, though, because the open road was a great place to be alone with his thoughts — so long as someone else was behind the wheel. "I have asked some of the boys to drive the tow truck at a time when I had a lot of thinking to do," he said. "When I'm trying to come up with something on the race car or the engine, I can't concentrate and drive at the same time. Take those trips to Riverside, California. That's about three days of thinking right there."*

Wood had been thinking about cars for most of his life. He spent

---

* The thinking paid off: the Woods won seven times with twenty-four top 5 finishes in forty-three starts at Riverside.

much of his time in school drawing cars or carving them out of wood blocks and selling them to his classmates for 50 cents. (The cars had seats, metallic paint jobs, and hood emblems — always Ford.) He built a foot-long '49 Ford with a working steel suspension, and his prized creation was a go-kart with a washing machine motor that he built when he was fourteen. It could go 30 miles per hour, and Wood hung on to it well into adulthood because, he said, "I'm right proud of it."

He began working on race cars a year later, when Glen started driving. (Leonard never considered getting behind the wheel. "I've always felt driving was too dangerous," he said.) His career was interrupted in 1957, when he was drafted into the army and sent to serve a two-year hitch in Germany, building transmissions for military vehicles. Bored with the challenge that presented, Wood set to building a working model of an Indy car. Powered by a model airplane engine, the eighteen-inch, ten-pound car was hooked up to a cable and ran in circles, but the bumpy ground caused it to jump all over the place. So Wood found a German cobbler, got some sole rubber, and fashioned a set of springs. "I'd trim the rubber out perfectly round and glue two pieces together for one wheel," he explained. "I put them together with metal discs and inserted ball bearings." The car ran so fast that the sole rubber couldn't take it: the springs tore apart, flew through the air, and hit an officer.

Leonard was always on the lookout for anything that would give him even the slightest advantage — like pit stops. Most Grand National teams paid little attention to them, which made no sense to Leonard, given how much time cars spent getting serviced. So he set about speeding up the entire process — choreographing the movements of the crew members to avoid collisions and improving the tools his team used. He built a jack that could get the car off the ground faster, he improved the pneumatic wrenches used to change tires, and he rounded the studs on the tires so the nuts could be threaded faster. The Wood crew became so quick that Ford sent them to Indianapolis in '65 to work in the pits for Jimmy Clark, a Scot who was driving for

Lotus-Ford.* It was an interesting meeting of brogue and drawl. The Woods were apprehensive — "Well, you don't just walk in and start pitting another fellow's car. I mean, you just don't do that...giving orders," Leonard said — but everyone got along swimmingly. Clark's two pit stops lasted 44.5 seconds, the fastest stops Indy had ever seen, and he won by two laps.

By the 1970s the Woods had sliced even more time off a pit stop. In 1977 the *Washington Post Magazine* raved, "They make a practice, even an art, of fueling their race car, changing two tires, wiping the windshield and sending the driver on his way with a drink of water and a kind word — all in fifteen seconds or less." During one memorable stop — one that lasted 12.7 seconds — Leonard, who changed the front tires, left a thumbnail under the front fender. That didn't bother him. To the Woods, pit stops were a matter of pride.

On lap 302 of the Rebel 500, Neil Bonnett hit the wall, bringing out a yellow flag and the final round of pit stops in the 367-lap race. Pearson was still a lap down, which meant he was going to have to beat the leader, Waltrip, out of the pits to have any real chance of winning the race. He pulled the Mercury onto pit road, and the elaborate dance began. Delano Wood was the first over the wall, carrying the jack out into the middle of the pit so he'd be in position to hoist the right side into the air as soon as Pearson stopped. Delano furiously pumped the jack, and once the car was off the ground, the tire changers removed the spent right tires, and two new Goodyears went on in their place. Then Delano dropped the jack, and Pearson took off, which created a problem: it was supposed to be a four-tire change. Pearson never saw

---

*It wasn't the only time Ford sent the Woods on the road. In 1966 Glen went to the 24 Hours of Le Mans as a guest of the factory. Fearing escargots, pâté, and any other food he didn't see in the diners of Stuart, Glen took his own grub to France: pork and beans and Fritos.

the crewman loosen the lugs on the left side because Glen, who had come over the wall to clean the windshield, blocked his view. Pearson made it to the end of pit road before the left-side tires came off and the car came to a halt, sparks flying from its undercarriage. One tire went bounding through the pits and almost brained Hoss Ellington, who didn't see it coming but heard it as it whizzed past his ear. Pearson tried to move the car, but when he hit the gas, the one rear wheel just spun in place. In the booth Jackie Stewart had worked himself into a right lather: "This is the Wood Brothers, perhaps the most experienced pit crew in the world! Something has very, very strangely happened to the car of the great-grandfather of motor racing, David Pearson. The Silver Fox is now spinning his wheels, literally, as, my goodness, two wheels have fallen off!"

A few laps later Pearson, who had already changed out of his racing suit and into a smart maroon shirt, explained what had happened to ABC's Chris Economaki: "I didn't know they was gonna change all four tires. Of course they usually tell me, but that time I guess I was so interested in beating Darrell out of the pits that I didn't hear them. When they let the jack down, that's the signal to go.... They were hollering for me to *whoa*. I thought they were saying *go*."

At that point a light rain began to fall in Darlington, which brought out a caution flag and allowed everyone to catch their breath, while giving Jim McKay an opportunity to display his marvelous gift for extemporization. "Gee," he said to Stewart, "we got up this morning, it was beautiful, someone said zero chance of rain. And it began to change, slowly, but then I guess there was a reason Mr. Shakespeare from your island, Jackie, referred to this month as capricious April."* Then McKay finished his riff with an announcement that succinctly

---

*It was T. S. Eliot, not Shakespeare, and he called April cruel, not capricious. But cut McKay some slack. Most NASCAR press boxes don't keep a copy of *Bartlett's* on hand.

illustrated where, to ABC, NASCAR stood in the sporting spectrum: "We're going to stand by here, see what happens. Right now we're going to go back to the Oriental world of self-defense," at which point the picture cut to a martial arts ring behind a title card that read: THE FELT FORUM, WORLD PROFESSIONAL KARATE CHAMPIONSHIP, MIDDLEWEIGHT DIVISION, LOUIS NEGLIA VS. BUTCH BELL.

When the rain let up and ABC returned from the kicking, there were thirty-nine laps to go and three cars on the lead lap: Waltrip, Petty, and Donnie Allison. The possibility of more showers meant that every lap had to be run all out, because in the event of rain, the winner was going to be whoever was out in front when the skies opened up. With nine laps left, another tire got loose on the track, this one from the car of Butch Hartman, who happened to be driving down the front stretch at the time. That brought out the yellow flag and set up the most frenetic trophy dash the Lady in Black had ever seen.

The green came out with five laps to go and Waltrip in front. Petty got around him in Turn 3 as the cars made the gentlest of contact, and the King held the lead for the next lap. Three to go. Waltrip got inside Petty just past the start/finish line, but Petty regained it going into Turn 3, only to see Waltrip pull back to the inside and go to the front in Turn 4. Petty, unbowed, nipped in front of Waltrip at the start/finish line. To make things even more interesting, Allison materialized out of nowhere to make it three-wide down the front stretch. Officially, since Petty led when the lap started as well as when it finished, there was no lead change. In reality, the lead had switched hands four times in thirty-three seconds. Two to go. No passes. Last lap. Waltrip got inside Petty in Turn 1, then Petty got him back at the end of the backstretch by driving hard into Turn 3. He didn't know it, but he was playing right into Waltrip's hands.

Before Waltrip became a regular on the Grand National circuit, his home track was Nashville Speedway. As it was at Darlington, the natural line at Nashville was up around the wall. "It was a very similar banking kind of track, where you ran in low, went up and almost touched the fence, and then came off the corner," says Waltrip. "I would run a different groove than anyone else, and it scared the hell out of them, because I'd go in and drive underneath them in the middle of the corner. Well, you're not supposed to be able to do that. But I'd just always had a knack for cutting a car under and getting by a guy."

So Waltrip made his pet move. He jerked the wheel hard—it wasn't so much a lane change he was making as it was a left turn—taking Wanda across Allison's grille and inside Petty. You make that move on Van Lingle Mungo Boulevard, and you'll find yourself pleading with a South Carolina state trooper not to write you a ticket. Somehow Waltrip made it stick. Allison was able to get next to Petty and engage him in a battle for second, which gave Waltrip a relatively easy ride to the checkered flag, after seven lead changes in the final three laps.

Upstairs, the Wee Scot, who had seen his share of races, was breathless. "I can't remember ever seeing the end of a motor race, Jim, being as exciting as that!" said Stewart. "Never have I seen a finish with so many passes on such a short track in such a short time."

Waltrip was giddy, as he had every right to be. He had outdueled the King, who several years earlier had put Waltrip in his place by saying, "When he wins at Darlington, then he'll be a real race car driver." And he'd done it cleanly. "Our cars got together a few times there near the end," Waltrip said. "But when they did, he'd wave at me and I'd wave at him, and we'd go at it again."

After he had finished his postrace interviews, Waltrip made his way back up to the press box. Surveying the moonlit track, he raised his arms and serenaded the Lady in Black: "I'll see you in my dreams."

Before he left the track, Pearson talked to Leonard Wood. Neither man mentioned what had happened in the pits. They agreed to talk early in the week about their next race, in Martinsville. The incident would provide some laughs, giving what is still one of Waltrip's favorite gags: singing "You picked a fine time to leave me, loose wheel" to the tune of Kenny Rogers's *Lucille*. But there was also something slightly moribund about it. It wasn't quite Willie Mays fumbling around in center field, but it was unsettling to see Pearson screwing up such a basic task in front of a national TV audience. "I just hope he doesn't let this thing force him to retire," said Petty. "He's not washed-up or through by any means."

Three days later Pearson got a phone call from Glen. He was fired.

### Standings After the CRC Chemicals Rebel 500

1. Darrell Waltrip     1,317
2. Bobby Allison       1,236
3. Cale Yarborough     1,178
4. Donnie Allison      1,142
5. Benny Parsons       1,138
6. Richard Petty       1,114

## Chapter Fourteen

# Old Chow Mein

**Sunday, May 6**
**Race 10: Winston 500**
**Talladega, Alabama**

LIMOUSINES ARE a rare sight in a NASCAR garage—the preferred mode of transportation being more Schwinn than Rolls—so when a stretch job pulled into the Talladega Superspeedway as teams prepared for practice, heads turned. It rolled to a stop near the Wood Brothers stall, and after a minute one of the back doors opened. Out popped David Pearson. The newly unemployed Silver Fox surveyed the bemused faces in the garage and asked with a sly grin, "Now, does this look like I'm doing too bad?"

Pearson had flown himself to Talladega in his Aztec—in addition to a country store, the farm in Spartanburg had an airstrip—and two friends had surprised him with the flashy ground transportation. One of the first people to greet Pearson's limo was Leonard Wood. The two had a friendly chat, and although it was clear that Pearson was serious when he said he bore no ill will toward the Woods, as details of their parting emerged, it became clear that the divorce had been messy.

The day after the Darlington fiasco, Pearson had talked to Glen Wood, who'd complained that the driver wasn't trying hard enough. "I told him he had lost some of his enthusiasm," Wood said a few days later. "He was laying back more so than before. He said he wasn't afraid of the car. In my opinion, he is afraid of the car at Talladega and Daytona. When I was racing and they went to the big tracks, I no longer cared to run up front so I quit driving.... He twice quit at Talladega, and last year part of the crew almost quit because of the way he was driving. When he got a lap or two down he'd quit. Races are won from that far back all the time." Wood also criticized Pearson's driving in the '79 Daytona 500, in which he'd been caught up in a wreck while running far back in the field: "You can't win if you don't stand on it." Pearson didn't appreciate the lecture—"I'm too old to be treated like a kid," he said—and when one of Wood's business partners called later that day, Pearson told him how close he had come to quitting while being reamed out by Wood. That revelation got back to Wood, and it sealed Pearson's fate. Wood called two days later and cut him loose.

Pearson and the Woods had been together since 1972—a remarkably long NASCAR marriage—so they were due for a change. Animosity had been building through the early part of the year. In Bristol Pearson suggested that the Wood Brothers pit crew wasn't as fast or consistent as advertised. There was bickering in Atlanta, when Pearson told some writers that "Leonard wouldn't admit it if he makes a mistake." His brother took umbrage at that. "Leonard works around the clock," Glen said. "You know David was always one of the first to leave the track. Instead of working out the problem, he'd say, 'We'll get it tomorrow.'"

After Glen Wood let him go, Pearson was hounded everywhere he went by well-wishers: the regulars at Jimmy's Restaurant in Spartanburg, the guy who sold him a new lawn mower. All had the same question: "What are you going to do now?" Pearson's standard answer was that he didn't know, and he wasn't going to rush into anything. Pearson was only forty-four, certainly not over-the-hill. He had options. Short-track owners were offering show money, and Humpy Wheeler was desperate to get him in the field for the World 600 on Memorial Day — in part because he wanted a strong field, and in part because he was sitting on fifty billboards touting Pearson that had been ordered months earlier.* Pearson had a shop out behind Miss Lennie's house where he worked on his Ford Fairlane. Until the right Grand National offer came along, he was content to bide his time racing it on short tracks near home, which meant he'd have more time to spend with his wife, Helen, and his peach trees, his three-acre lake, his new lawn mower, and his loyal German shepherd, Bullet. "I want to keep racing, but not in junk," he said. "I may be done. I don't know right now. If a good offer came along, I'd be interested in talking about it. But I won't go looking for a ride, and any ride I take would have to be a good one."

Pearson wasn't the only one goofing around in a fancy mode of transportation. Following Saturday's final practice session, the press box was full of writers slaving over their copy for the Sunday papers. The box provided an excellent view of the airfield beyond the backstretch, which is where all eyes turned when the din of a small plane became audible over the clacking of typewriter keys. The scribes watched with an increasing sense of dread as the Aerostar rose from the runway and made a line right at them. Just when it looked like it might be time to dive under a desk, the plane rose and cleared the roof by a hundred feet, though it seemed like ten. "Who the hell was that?" one frazzled writer asked.

"That was an Alabama kamikaze pilot on his 150th mission," said one who'd seen a similar stunt before.

It was Bobby Allison.

Confronted the next day, Allison admitted to being an Alabama

---

* Pearson was in the midst of an incredible streak: he'd won the pole for eleven straight races at Charlotte Motor Speedway. Wheeler's billboards read: BUSCH PUSH FOR THE POLE: CAN CALE BEAT THE SILVER FOX?

kamikaze pilot. "Yep. That's me. Old Chow Mein," he said, also confessing to some strange flying habits in his younger days. "Maybe we'd throw a cat out with a parachute tied on its back. One of them even came home, parachute and all. But most found new homes."*

Old Chow Mein was taking the Aerostar on a quick hop to Birmingham, where his eighteen-year-old son, Davey, was racing that night in a Chevy Nova he had built from the shell of a car his uncle Donnie had given him. Davey took his first checkered flag, and the next morning in the garage Bobby was showing the kid off like the proud papa he was. It was just another sign that Allison's luck was changing. For once he was catching breaks. Despite all the banging he'd done at Daytona, he'd still finished eleventh. Then he'd avoided the carnage and won in Rockingham. Three weeks later, at North Wilkesboro, his suspension had broken as he took the checkered flag, causing his right front tire to fold back under the car. After a victory lap accompanied by sparks and smoke, Allison had to ditch the car in the pits and walk to Victory Lane. It was the kind of thing that, two years earlier when he had been mired in a sixty-six-race winless streak, would have happened with five laps to go. Through nine races in '79 he had two wins and three second-place finishes, and that elusive first championship seemed a real possibility.

Allison had every reason to expect he'd be strong at Talladega, too. Until the wreck he'd caused took him out of contention in the 500, he had been pretty stout at Daytona, and Talladega is a similar course, just a little bigger. The track has a checkered history, and the fact that it is located on land that once belonged to Creek Indians has led to the birth of some rather wild explanations for all the bad mojo. Some say it can be traced to a Creek chief who was killed in a horse racing accident, while others claim a disgruntled medicine man placed a hex on the land while being driven out by white men. Another tale holds that the curse dates to 1813, when Andrew Jackson boldly put down

---

*PETA wasn't founded until 1980.

an Indian uprising in the area. And some — obviously influenced by *The Amityville Horror, Poltergeist,* and too many episodes of *Scooby-Doo* — believe that the track's woes are the result of its being built on an ancient burial ground.

Hokum or not, there was no arguing the fact that some weird stuff had gone down at Talladega. Located fifty miles east of Birmingham, the track was built by Big Bill France on what had once been an air force landing field, a bit of trivia that was eventually incorporated into the track's supernatural backstory: the military, the story goes, had to shut the place down because planes kept crashing with no explanation. The 2.66-mile tri-oval opened in the fall of 1969, and it quickly became apparent that the track had been born under a bad sign. The steep banking — 33 degrees in the turns — led to speeds that taxed both the drivers (they were nearly blacking out from the g-forces) and the cars (the tires would blow apart after four or five laps). Bobby Allison suggested to France that to maintain a safe speed, the drivers should start on foot, but then he reconsidered. "I take that back," Allison said. "The track is so rough we'd probably trip and fall before we got to the first turn." A short-lived drivers union had been formed that August,* and Talladega provided the Professional Drivers Association (PDA) with a cause to take up. Richard Petty called a meeting of the PDA, and when Big Bill France tried to follow, Cale Yarborough blocked his path and reminded him what "drivers only" meant. After discussing their options — risking their lives, driving at slower speeds, or going home — the union members decided to walk. In an effort to prove that they were overreacting, the fifty-nine-year-old France got behind the

---

* A few years earlier Curtis Turner had tried to unionize the drivers. Turner went into debt building the track at Charlotte and tried to arrange a loan from the Teamsters in exchange for getting his fellow drivers to join that union. Bill France Sr. vowed that he would "plow up my racetrack and plant corn on the infield before I'll let the Teamsters union or any other union tell me how to run my business." France also decreed that no union driver would ever compete in a NASCAR race, a policy he said he'd enforce "with a pistol."

wheel of a car and turned a few laps himself. He filled out the field for the race with lower-level journeymen, and caution flags were thrown every twenty-five laps so they could change tires.

That was nothing compared to the string of oddities that plagued the place in the next decade. Larry Smith, the 1972 Rookie of the Year, was killed in an innocuous-looking crash in '73, supposedly because he had cut the lining out of his helmet so it would fit over his long hair. The next year, several cars were found to have been sabotaged—sugar was put in gas tanks, tires were cut, brake lines were severed—in the middle of the night before the race. In the spring of '75, Richard Petty's brother-in-law Randy Owens died when a pressurized water tank exploded in the pits. That fall, Grant Adcox withdrew from the Talladega 500 after his crew chief died of a heart attack in the garage. His spot in the field was given to the first alternate, Tiny Lund, who was fatally injured in a fiery crash on the seventh lap. And in 1977 the mother of driver David Sisco was killed in the infield when she was struck by the mirror of a passing truck.

The creepiest incident, though, didn't involve death or mayhem. In 1973 Bobby Isaac, who had won the championship in 1970, was cruising down the backstretch when a voice told him to "get the hell out of the car." Isaac, not unreasonably, pulled into the pits, got out of the car, and announced he was quitting, effective immediately.

Although race car drivers are a superstitious lot, most of them tend to brush the curse aside. Bobby Allison scoffed that Talladega was nothing compared to the eerie sixteen-room house he'd lived in as a kid: it was haunted, it had secret passageways and a mysterious room hidden behind a false wall, and none of his friends would come over to play. Petty admitted to having once been scared by ghost stories told by his uncle Roy, but, he said, "when I grew up that stuff quit bothering me." And Waltrip rationalized, "Heck, man, it's so frightening in my car that a ghost wouldn't dare hang around."

Even without otherworldly interference, Talladega is a scary place. The cars draft in tight packs at high speed; if one gets out of shape, there's not much time for the others to react. A field-thinning, multicar wreck has become such a common occurrence that it's been given its own name: the Big One. Since drivers are usually a lot more cautious in the early laps, the Big One usually comes late in the race.

But not always.

As requests went, this one was pretty odd. Four laps into the Winston 500, Dave Marcis was sitting behind the wheel of his Chevrolet, minding his own business and pondering the wreck he had just been involved in, when a face appeared in the driver's side window. It was Cale Yarborough. He was hysterical, and he had a question. Would Marcis mind looking to see if Yarborough's legs were still attached to the rest of his body?

The trouble had started when Buddy Baker had cut a right rear tire and got sideways, triggering a massive chain reaction. Yarborough was in Baker's wake and ended up airborne for what he said seemed like "several minutes" before touching down and sliding over the infield grass. When the car came to rest next to Marcis's, Yarborough got out to inspect the damage. But just because he had stopped moving didn't mean the wreck was over. D. K. Ulrich* was running way back in the pack, and as he came around to the front stretch where the Big One had started, he ran over some debris and flattened all four of his tires. Here's the thing about 33-degree banking: if you're not going fast, you'll slide down the track, and if you have four flat tires, you're not going to go fast. So no matter how hard Ulrich yanked the wheel to the right, his car kept sliding down toward the infield. It collided with Marcis's car, which slid into Yarborough and pinned his legs between his car's left front wheel and Marcis's bumper. After a few seconds Yarborough was able to slither free, but he couldn't feel his legs — and

---

*Yes, D. K. Ulrich is related to Skeet Ulrich. He's the actor's stepfather. Skeet, who briefly worked on D.K.'s team as a teen, is also Ricky Rudd's nephew.

he certainly wasn't going to look down, lest he be confronted with the sight of a couple of stumps where the tree trunks that had carried him on so many wild adventures had been. "I just knew they were cut off," Yarborough said. He was more scared than he'd ever been, which, given the fact that his life up to that point had been one near-death experience after another — the pilot-less plane ride with Wib Weatherly, the bear wrestling, the failed parachutes, the lightning strikes, barring Big Bill France from that drivers' meeting — was saying something.

Marcis was stunned and a little confused by Yarborough's request, and when he finally figured out what Cale was talking about, he assured Yarborough that he was still in one piece and stayed with him until the ambulance arrived. Yarborough was taken to the infield medical center, where he convalesced for an hour and a half before limping out under his own power. But his day was over, and so was any notion he was entertaining of winning a fourth straight championship. He had the skills; he had the car; he just didn't have the luck. In ten races he had wrecked four times, run out of gas at least half a dozen times, and been roughed up by a former water boy — one whose supply of good fortune seemed limitless.

Bobby Allison had no right to escape the Big One, but he did his best Moses imitation and emerged unscathed. "There were four or five cars wrecking in front of me and four or five wrecking behind me," he said. "Then, suddenly, I had a nice wide-open channel right through the middle when a couple cars went high and a couple went low. The Good Lord drove the car for me."

The man upstairs had no such love for contenders Richard Petty, Darrell Waltrip, Dale Earnhardt, and Benny Parsons, though. They were among the seventeen cars that got caught up in the wreck. Earnhardt's car was bent so badly that it wouldn't fit on the truck. When Nick Ollila went to the truck to get a cutting torch, Jake Elder flew into a rage. "Jake got so upset because we were going to have to cut the car, he picked up a jack handle and was going to hit me over the head with it," says Ollila. "The truck driver grabbed him and dragged him off to the side and held him down."

Petty and Waltrip were able to continue, but only after their crews had refashioned new noses for their cars out of duct tape. Donnie Allison, always a threat on a superspeedway, fell a lap down getting his car repaired and dropped out for good when his engine gave out. That meant that Bobby had only one car to be concerned about: the one being driven by his protégé.

Firing David Pearson in the middle of the season left the Wood Brothers with little time to find a replacement. Since the season had already started, they weren't going to lure a big name away from an established operation. The best available man was Neil Bonnett.

Bonnett was from Birmingham, where he had worked as a union pipe fitter, a job that entailed walking a six-inch beam fifteen stories above city streets. He eventually came to the realization that if he was going to have a job that required him to risk life and limb, he should at least pick one that was a little more fun. He'd been dabbling in short-track racing and decided that if he was going to be serious about it, he needed to go where the action was: Hueytown. Bobby Allison was happy to let Bonnett help out around the shop. The two were similar — pragmatic and cerebral, with a quick wit and a quick temper. Allison flew the Aerostar all over the country to race at small tracks in between Grand National events, but he still couldn't make every event he wanted to. When he had to turn down promoters, he sent Bonnett in his place.

Bonnett ran a few Grand National races in his own car before Nord Krauskopf, who'd won the '70 championship with Bobby Isaac, hired him in '77 to drive a car with Harry Hyde as the crew chief. But halfway through the season, Krauskopf pulled out of racing. Hyde was able to convince his old — and rich — friend Jim Stacy to buy out Krauskopf. Stacy pumped a quarter of a million dollars into the operation, and Bonnett put the car on the pole for Stacy's first race.

Of all the flush new owners, Stacy was easily the most mysterious.

Kentucky-bred but based in Scottsdale, Arizona, he was an eighth-grade dropout who had owned his own construction company at nineteen, building tunnels, bridges, roads, and dams. He smoked fat cigars, so they called him "Boss Hogg" when he was in the garage, which wasn't often. "He does most of his business from an airplane," one team member noted. And sometimes those business dealings were shady. In November 1978 he was mired in a lawsuit concerning a loan— unrelated to racing—that required him to appear in court in Concord, North Carolina. Two Cabarrus County sheriff's deputies were having breakfast at Stacy's hotel, the Holiday Inn. As they walked through the parking lot to their car, they stopped to admire Stacy's Cadillac limo. Then one of them noticed something odd: wires under the car. Taking a closer look, they discovered eight sticks of dynamite—each eight inches long and two inches in diameter—connected by wires to the battery and the exhaust pipe, so that when the car moved, the dynamite would go off. A bomb squad from Fort Bragg dismantled the bomb and detonated the blasting caps in an empty field near the hotel. "I feel fine, because it didn't work," said Stacy, who vowed to keep using the limo.

As deep as his pockets were, Stacy didn't realize how expensive racing could be. Bonnett was running well—he won two races in 1977 and had seven top 5s in '78—but he wasn't always getting paid on time, and the team fell apart after the '79 Daytona 500.* Rescued by the Woods, Bonnett found himself in the awkward position of succeeding a living legend. He said all the right things—"I'm the weak link in this chain. I'm a new driver in a new car, and I'm not David Pearson"—but comparisons were inevitable, especially at Talladega, one of the tracks that led to Pearson's falling-out with the Woods. If there was any doubt that the car Leonard Wood prepared was strong enough to run up front at a superspeedway, it was done away with

---

*Stacy was last seen in 2002 trying to turn Elvis Presley's Circle G Ranch into a $500 million Elvis theme park and convention center.

when Bonnett put the Purolator Mercury on the inside of row two. He made it through the Big One scratch-free, and with forty laps left he had opened up a fifteen-second lead on Bobby Allison.

Then his engine blew up. "Boy, that was fun while it lasted," he said.

With Bonnett gone, Allison could have stopped for some barbecue and still won with ease. He won by nearly two laps over Waltrip, who expended so much energy wrestling his jerry-rigged car that he took his postrace Gatorade with a straight oxygen chaser. "The car drove like a tank after the crash," he said. Like Wanda, the nicest thing anyone could say about Petty's car after the wreck was that it was drivable. But the King latched onto the bumper of Buddy Arrington, who was driving an old Petty Enterprises Dodge, and was pulled to a fourth-place finish.

After the race Allison returned to the scene of Saturday's aerial crime, the press box. With his son Davey by his side, he joked, "It's also especially nice to win this one because now I can go home tonight and not be the only winner in the house."

As Allison walked down the stairs of the press box, his path was blocked by two kids. One handed him a program, which Allison grabbed and began to autograph. As he signed his name, he said something, and when he didn't receive a reply, he looked up to see the boy saying something to his friend in sign language. Without saying another word, Allison returned the program and, realizing the boy's friend didn't have anything for him to autograph, took off his hat, signed it, and put it on the kid's head. Allison had seen his son win his first race, made two fans for life, and inched closer to Waltrip. It was the end of a very good weekend.

## Standings After the Winston 500

1. Darrell Waltrip          1,662
2. Bobby Allison           1,581
3. Richard Petty           1,459
4. Joe Millikan            1,397
5. Cale Yarborough         1,377

## Chapter Fifteen

# Bring on the Dancing Bears

**Sunday, May 27**
**Race 13: World 600**
**Concord, North Carolina**

IT HAD been more than three months since Kyle Petty had driven a race car. The Kylemania that had gripped the stock car world had waned in his absence but not completely subsided, which was why, on the morning of May 15, a crowd—writers and photographers included—assembled at Charlotte Motor Speedway to watch one of the most boring aspects of stock car racing: practice. CMS is a mile-and-a-half oval located just north of town. It's fast, but not nearly as fast as Daytona, which meant that for the first time in his driving career, young Mr. Petty was going to have to do something other than put the gas on the floor and keep it there.

Since winning his first race in Daytona, Petty had returned to his relatively mundane life. In April, *People* magazine did a short feature on him, becoming approximately the 2,143rd publication to call him "a chip off the old engine block." Past that, there was little glamour. He and Pattie were living at the farm outside Level Cross. She was still teaching school, and he was drawing a meager check as a mechanic on his father's team. Their most substantial source of income came from the Southern Pride Car Wash that Ron Bell had given them as part of a sponsorship deal. Once a month they'd go into town and pick up their cut. In quarters.

Kyle was still driving his father's old Dodges, but unlike the car he'd taken to Victory Lane in Daytona, they weren't navy blue, there was no eagle on them, and Valvoline's name was nowhere to be seen. The cars were Petty Blue and STP red—a provision of the lifetime deal he had signed with his dad's sponsor. Kyle would pull into the pits, and Richard—shirtless in the heat, wearing a white cowboy hat and sunglasses, and chomping on a small cigar—would stick his head in the window and give a few pointers. On his eighth lap Kyle tapped the wall in Turn 2. On his twenty-fifth, he hit the wall hard coming off Turn 4. "Came in way too low," said his father, watching from pit road. Kyle tried to spin it down onto the grass, but he overcorrected and ended up in the wall. As Richard casually walked across the grass that separates the pits from the track, Kyle waved that he was okay.

The car was a different story. Richard thought it severely damaged, so they loaded it up and made the two-hour drive back to Level Cross. He wasn't optimistic that the Dodge could be fixed quickly; the King's Grand National effort was still priority one, and Petty, who had five races in five weeks, was in the thick of the points race. He was in no position to divert any resources to Kyle's car. But back at the compound, Steve Hmiel and Robin Pemberton were able to get the car repaired, so they took it back to Charlotte the next morning.

Richard watched the second session with Humpy Wheeler, who was a close friend of the family and also wanted to check on his investment. From their bench in the garage, they watched Kyle until he got through the first turn, at which point they lost visual contact. But they had both been around the track enough to be able to tell what was going on by the sound. Things got quiet, which meant he was out of gas. Then a squeal. "We knew he was sideways," remembers Wheeler. "Then things got quiet, and that's when you really know something bad's going to happen. And then we heard the boom."

Petty looked at Humpy matter-of-factly and said, "Well, let's go see how bad it was." They got in a car and drove over.

"It was a hell of a wreck," says Wheeler. "The car was busted in half. He lost it coming out of two and hit the inside wall backwards, something you don't want to do." Kyle had skidded about 750 feet, backed into a steel gate, taken a two-foot chunk out of a concrete retaining wall, flown 150 feet through the air, and had his fuel tank ripped out of the car and go flying down the track. Pattie got the news as she taught at Hasty Elementary School, but aside from a banged-up knee, Kyle was fine. The car, however, was totaled, and any notion the Pettys or Humpy had about Kyle driving in the World 600 was forgotten. "Sure, it takes a load off me for the 600," said Richard. "I'd have been thinking about Kyle and looking for him, no doubt about it."

A few days later things got worse for Humpy. His deal to get David Pearson into the field fell through. Wheeler had convinced Hoss Ellington to prepare a second car and settled on an appearance fee with Pearson. But when Wheeler found out that he wasn't getting an exclusive engagement — Pearson was racing in a short-track race at nearby Concord Speedway the night before the 600 — he substantially cut back his offer, and Pearson backed out.

Racing at Charlotte meant being at home all week, which meant one thing: parties. The most legendary bashes were thrown in the 1960s by Curtis Turner, who'd have a couple of hundred folks out to his sprawling ranch house. Pops's bar was lit by fluorescent lights, which cast everything — including the paintings of nude women on the wall — in a purple glow, and he had not one but two jukeboxes to keep the music — mostly country, with the occasional Motown hit thrown in — pumping until the sun came up.

The social event of race week '79 wasn't nearly as debauched, but it was a good time nonetheless. It was a party in honor of Dale Earnhardt at Sgt. Pepper's lounge in Kannapolis. About two hundred people showed up on Thursday night for what Benny Phillips of the *High Point Enterprise* described as "a promenade of life, a celebration, a roof-raising and the office Christmas party mixed and stirred well." Earnhardt had done his part to fatten the Sarge's coffers when he was younger — "You could tell by the way he knew his way around," noted Phillips — but he returned a different man. Even those who swore they'd never doubted that he'd make it — like his mother, Martha, who was on hand — had to be surprised at how quickly he'd made the transformation from hungry struggler to consistent check casher. Since the win at Bristol, he'd had an eighth-place finish at Martinsville, a fourth at Dover, and a fifth at Nashville. Now he was coming back to a track he was familiar with. He failed to qualify in the first round, when the top 15 spots were set, but in the second round on Thursday afternoon he had the fastest time — and second-fastest overall — meaning that he would start sixteenth. Earnhardt told the well-wishers at Sgt. Pepper's, "We're flying now. We're ready for Sunday, and I don't think it will take me long to work my way to the front." It was hard not to believe him.

Relatively early in the evening, the bash ground to a halt. The lights came up, the music stopped, and the pouring of drinks was halted. After asking for a moment of silence for his father, Earnhardt received a plaque from the city fathers. Then he proposed a toast. "Most of all I want to thank my mother and sisters, especially my mother, for sticking behind me through the tough times before I got to where I am today," he said. "Martha Earnhardt, my mother, is the greatest supporter a son could have." The partygoers gave her a standing ovation, and then the lights went back down, the music started back up, the booze flowed, and the party continued well on into the night.

The biggest race in the United States in 1979 took place, as it had since 1911, at the Indianapolis Motor Speedway on the Sunday before Memorial Day—the same day Humpy Wheeler held his 600-miler. Indy had the advantage of years of tradition and a field full of names that were familiar to even casual fans thanks to ABC's tape-delayed prime-time broadcast, which had given birth to a holiday weekend tradition—trying to make it through the day without finding out who won the race, so the show would not be spoiled.

But the champ car world wasn't without its problems. In 1978 Dan Gurney had sent a state-of-the-sport report to his fellow team owners. The missive, which became known as the Gurney White Paper, laid out a series of grievances with the United States Auto Club (USAC), which sanctioned open-wheel racing in the States. Purses were too small, the promotion was too passive, and the owners didn't have enough say in matters that concerned them. "USAC for instance negotiates with TV as though it had the TV rights which in fact, if it came to a showdown, would turn out to be ours. (The car owners and teams)," Gurney wrote. He suggested the owners band together into something they'd call CART (Championship Auto Racing Teams), which would share power with the USAC. The USAC, not surprisingly, said, in effect, *Thanks, but we're going to go ahead and hold on to our power.* So a handful of teams went ahead and formed CART and put together their own schedule for 1979. But they also planned on running at Indianapolis, which was still a USAC-sanctioned event. In his white paper Gurney wrote, "It appears that a 'show down' with the Indianapolis Motor Speedway is or should be the first target. They are the ones who can afford it."

He got his showdown, all right. The USAC promptly rejected the 1979 Indy 500 entries of six CART teams. CART took the USAC to court, arguing that it was violating the Sherman Antitrust Act, and successfully won a temporary restraining order allowing the six to compete. But that was just the beginning of the farce. After the first of the two weekends of qualifying, the USAC "clarified" a rule dealing with the cars' engines, which prompted the owners of eight cars that failed to qualify to protest, on the grounds that the clarification essentially meant that the qualifying had been held under two different sets of rules. And to top it all off, an owner named Wayne Woodward filed a suit after his car was disqualified because he'd broken a rule having to do with a turbocharger inlet pop-off valve. All thirty-three drivers who qualified were served subpoenas to testify, and some of them were not happy about it. A. J. Foyt told the deputy who served him exactly where he could shove the papers, and Danny Ongais nearly ran his server over with a bicycle. Judge Michael T. Dugan II issued bench warrants for the pair. Ongais quickly showed up, apologized, and was sent on his way. Foyt, however, had gone to Louisville for a day at the horse races. His lawyer called him at Churchill Downs and told him to get back to Indy if he valued his freedom.

In a bizarre hearing Foyt, who'd never been the apologizing type, told Dugan what was on his mind. "Well, I don't have much to say," Foyt told the judge. "But when you are in a group of people and somebody shoves a bunch of papers in your face, you ought to know who they are. I don't appreciate it at all." After Foyt told Dugan that he didn't feel he had done anything wrong, Dugan threatened to hold him in contempt. "Mr. Foyt, do you understand that you are subject to the same service and process like any other ordinary citizen here in Marion County?" Dugan said.

"Right, your honor," Foyt said. "But, you know, I come here to race, not to be served subpoenas." Satisfied that Foyt wasn't going to get any more remorseful than that, Dugan cut the Texan loose. Woodward was denied his motion to stop the race, an extra round of qualifying was added for the disputed cars, and the Indy 500 eventually went off as scheduled and without incident.

But the whole episode exposed a fundamental weakness in open-wheel racing: it was run in a way that fostered bickering. The Indy debacle made a pretty strong case that Big Bill France had been right when he and Bill Tuthill had decided back in 1947 that the best way to run a racing series was to set it up as a dictatorship. Yes, the country had been founded on the principle that all voices should be heard. But when it came to running a racing series, sometimes you needed a guy who wasn't afraid to announce to dissenters that he had a gun and knew how to use it, as France had done when the Teamsters had tried to move in back in 1961. No one ever threw the Sherman Antitrust Act in the face of someone like that.

The litigation also underscored the extent to which the Indy 500 dominated the open-wheel landscape. It was so much more significant than any other race that whoever controlled Indy effectively controlled the sport. It didn't take a Machiavellian mind to see how one might stage a power play: use the 500 to hold everyone else hostage. That's precisely what happened in 1994, when Tony George, whose family controlled the speedway, announced that anyone who wanted to run in the Indy 500 had to do so under his new rules. He formed his own circuit, the Indy Racing League, which competed directly with CART. The schism doomed open-wheel racing, which was having enough trouble surviving in its battle against an increasingly popular NASCAR when it was unified. As a sport divided, it stood no chance.

While the Indy boys were dodging subpoenas and explaining themselves to judges, the Grand National crew was preparing for plenty of good fun in Charlotte. A race at Humpy Wheeler's track was always an event, a chance for Wheeler, who had gotten his start as a promoter at age nine when he'd sold tickets to a bicycle race, to demonstrate his Barnumesque bent. There was nothing he wouldn't try once in the name of entertainment. One year a writer in the press box made a snide crack that the only thing missing from the show was dancing bears. The next year? You'd better believe there were dancing bears.

Wheeler's best-known production was at the fall race in 1977, which was run not long after Cale Yarborough gave Darrell Waltrip the nickname "Jaws" following a run-in during the Southern 500. To commemorate the feud, Wheeler commissioned a friend who was a commercial fisherman in South Carolina to catch a shark. The guy showed up with a 150-pound blacktip, which Wheeler hung from the back of a wrecker. At the time Yarborough was sponsored by Holly Farms chicken, so Wheeler put a dead, bloody chicken in the shark's mouth, drove it around the track, and parked it in the garage. The crowd loved it. Those within smelling distance were less amused.

Wheeler's shows didn't always go off without a hitch. One year, during a tribute to America's farmers, a goat got loose on pit road. And at the fall race in 1986, Wheeler decided to break the record for the world's largest marching band. He assembled 5,000 high schoolers in heavy wool suits, but—just as it did at Daytona on the morning of the 500 in 1979—his internal weather radar let him down. A warm front came in, forcing the kids to march in 85-degree heat. They set off in opposite directions and were supposed to meet at the start/finish line. About halfway a few dropped from the heat. Wheeler's producer asked him what they should do. "The show must go on," said Wheeler. Then a few more dropped. Then a dozen. Then came a new order: "The show must be stopped!" A hundred of them were treated at the infield medical center.

The '79 festivities were tame by comparison. Willie Nelson was the grand marshal, and the three-hour prerace production featured skydivers, hang gliders, cloggers, disco dancers, and—because no Wheeler show was complete without some sort of pyrotechnic display and/or show of force—artillery fire.

Another Charlotte tradition was the candy-apple red and white Wood Brothers Mercury sitting on the pole. David Pearson had put it there twelve races in a row at the track, and Neil Bonnett, who had won at Dover the week before, made it thirteen. Richard Petty started second, and defending World 600 champion Darrell Waltrip, who had had engine trouble in Dover and surrendered the points lead to Bobby Allison, was third. But one of the strongest cars in the early part of the race was Donnie Allison's. He and Hoss Ellington had shelved their plans to run a full slate and compete for the championship after ten races. The stress on a small operation of getting a car ready every week proved too difficult. As Petty was showing, a win in the Daytona 500 was the kind of thing that could kick a team to life, which Ellington's crew desperately needed. And the driver-owner relationship was still strained over Hoss's post-Daytona chauffeur routine. Donnie took the Chevy to the lead seventy-six laps in, but for the third straight race he blew an engine.

The first 341 laps of the 400-lap race featured sixty lead changes, but as the field was culled, Waltrip emerged as the driver to beat. He took the lead with 59 laps left, leaving Earnhardt and Petty to engage in a furious battle for second that thrilled the baking spectators almost as much as it thrilled Waltrip, who was able to stretch his lead to a comfortable five seconds as Earnhardt and Petty fought each other. If Earnhardt's car looked like it was being driven by a man who was holding on for dear life, that's because it was. As the race passed the four-hour mark, Earnhardt couldn't keep his Oldsmobile down on the low groove. He simply didn't have the strength. He could barely keep his head up; other drivers noticed he looked like a bobblehead doll. "That's a pretty good sign when someone has about had it," said Yarborough.

Petty, by contrast, was putting to rest any notion that his stomach ailment was going to cause him any lingering problems. He was clearheaded enough to formulate a strategy and physically strong enough to put his car in a position to carry it out. The plan he came up with was to do to Earnhardt what Waltrip had done to him in Darlington. He was going to let Earnhardt take his car high up into Turn 3 on the last lap and then make a hard left and cut underneath him. It worked like a charm, and he edged Earnhardt to the line for second. "You can say we're never too old to learn something in this business," said Petty.

With his win, Waltrip regained the points lead, thanks to Bobby Allison's engine troubles and twenty-second-place finish. Petty had also sent notice that he was going to be a factor in the championship race. But all anyone wanted to talk about was the guy who came in third—his rivals included. Petty hopped out of his car, went straight to Earnhardt's blue and yellow Oldsmobile, stuck his head in the window, and said, "Where you been, boy?" Buddy Parrott, Waltrip's crew chief, stomped his foot on the pavement in the garage and said, "That boy there is as tough as this asphalt right here." Even Waltrip, who enjoyed few things more than talking about himself, couldn't help but yield the spotlight. "When all the others go by the wayside, he'll be the one I have to fight," he said.

In the garage Martha Earnhardt watched her son, surrounded by a throng of a hundred bodies. A few were media members, but most were autograph seekers. "I never thought it would be like this so soon," Earnhardt said. "I was absolutely awed by the crowd when I was introduced before the race. I think all of my hometown was here. We didn't win, but I think they know we were here."

Oh, they knew. A movement was clearly under way. Earnhardt's win at Bristol had been historic, but it was something most fans had only heard about; they hadn't seen it. But this performance, this duel with the winningest stock car driver who ever lived, happened in front of thousands of people. So what if he didn't win? He showed that he could hang, that he belonged. Martha watched as the throng fussed over her son. "I think Ralph really believed someday Dale would do something like he did today," she said. "In fact, a lot of times I wonder that Ralph might well know what's going on."

## Standings After the World 600

| | | |
|---|---|---|
| 1. | Darrell Waltrip | 2,066 |
| 2. | Bobby Allison | 2,013 |
| 3. | Cale Yarborough | 1,897 |
| 4. | Richard Petty | 1,887 |
| 5. | Dale Earnhardt | 1,756 |

# Chapter Sixteen

# Gassed

As HE watched the mangled car of rookie Gene Rutherford being towed through the Daytona Speedway garage after qualifying for the Firecracker 400, Richard Petty couldn't help himself. "Hey," he called out. "Is Kyle driving for you boys, too?" After the wall-kissing session in Charlotte, the Pettys decided that the best course of action for Kyle's Grand National career was to have him stick to what he knew: Daytona. He entered another one of the cars from Richard's suddenly dwindling stable of old Dodges in the Firecracker 400, the track's annual Fourth of July race. The car was painted blue and red, with Lee Petty's old number, 42, stenciled on the side. That came courtesy of Marty Robbins, who was turning out to be quite a pal to Kyle. First he'd put in a solid wingman performance when Kyle had brought Pattie to meet him in Nashville a few years earlier, and now he was letting Kyle race with his grandfather's old number.*

Kyle practiced okay, turning laps within 1 mile per hour of his dad. But when it came time to qualify, the results were all too familiar: he got the car too high, didn't back off, spun it out, and put it into the wall. Richard consoled Kyle, telling him how he had wrecked so frequently when he was starting out that he carried a hammer under his seat so that when he crashed, he could jump out and break something on the car to make it look like it wasn't his fault. He also told him to load the car up and send it home. "You have just earned yourself a place on my pit crew come Wednesday," the King said.

If there was an upside to it all, it was that Richard no longer had to consider the question of what to do with all those leftover Dodges he had lying around. "It doesn't look like we're going to have to worry about that any longer," he said. "Kyle has pretty well taken care of the Dodge crop."

The latest crash was frustrating, but Kyle had made progress since Charlotte. Richard had realized that more than anything, Kyle needed seat time, so he'd sent him to an ARCA race at the five-eighths-mile Nashville Speedway in early June. Lanny Hester, the track promoter, was elated to welcome Kyle. His nineteenth birthday was on Saturday, June 2, the day before the race, and Pattie and his mother, Lynda, flew in for a party thrown by Hester at the track that afternoon. Hester had arranged for a car for Kyle to drive, but when he took it on the track for shakedown, the brake pedal fell off—never a good sign. After consulting with Richard, who was in College Station, Texas, for the Grand National race, Kyle informed Hester that he was going to pass on the ride and go back to Randleman. It proved to be a wise choice; the guy who ended up driving the car hit the wall after the gas pedal stuck.†

---

* Robbins, a pretty fair superspeedway driver—he finished fifth at Michigan International Speedway in 1974—took number 36.
† The clutch worked fine, though.

A week later Kyle was at the road course in Riverside, California, for a 200-mile Grand American race run the same day as the Grand National NAPA Riverside 400. He was in a '78 Pontiac owned by a couple of locals and sponsored by a towing company. This time all the pedals worked. Kyle qualified twelfth and got up to fourth place before he noticed transmission fluid in the cockpit. Pretty soon he couldn't shift out of third gear, and he had to purposely spin the car out to slow it down. His day was over. "I was driving it," Kyle said. "I guess I was responsible for what happened to it." Still, it was another decent performance on a long track. The time had come to get him some real Saturday night short-track experience.

Bub Moody was having a good time exercising his authority. The chief steward of Caraway Speedway was standing in the back of a pickup truck, addressing the field for the night's 100-lap main event — a field that, in addition to Kyle Petty, included future NASCAR drivers Sam Ard, Jimmy Hensley, and Morgan Shepherd.* Bub spoke passionately in a slow, deep drawl that one onlooker said brought to mind "a combination Barney Fife/worked-up camp meeting evangelist." This particular sermon focused on conflict resolution: "If there's a protest after any of these races, I don't want nobody bringing any woman they might have in the pits with 'em along to the hearing afterward. All of us hear enough of that female chin music at home and I ain't gonna listen to none of it from the sidelines tonight."

It was June 23, an off weekend for the Grand National circuit, so Richard Petty was on hand, soaking in the fumes and waxing nostalgic. "The sights, the sounds the scents are all the same," he said. "Racing on this scale is still pretty rustic. And still a lot of good fun."

---

*Ard was the 1983 and 1984 Busch Series champ, Hensley was the 1992 Rookie of the Year, and Shepherd became the second-oldest race winner in 1993, when he won the last of his four races at age fifty-one.

The last race of the night didn't go green until 10:30. Kyle, who qualified seventh in a Nova, was spun out on the fourth lap by another newbie, Harry Lee Hill. The car was still drivable, but the contact left him a lap down. Fifteen laps later, Kyle mixed it up with Satch Worley on a restart. Kyle maintained that Worley got too high and came down on top of him, but the vet — who backed into the inside retaining wall, ending his night — wasn't having any of that. "The biggest thing that happened is he's racing in the wrong class," said Worley. "Beginners should start at the beginning and not in this class of racing. I had been watching him, and he was all over the track. I was running with the leaders, and he wasn't going anywhere. It sure messed up my car, and it's one of those things that sometimes happen in racing. But the point is, he is not gifted enough to be running in our division. He's being put out there."

Kyle realized that there were going to be drivers who resented him. They were racing for their dinner money, while he was getting guaranteed show money from the promoter, meaning he'd outearn most of them no matter how he drove. Lee would go along on most trips, his job being to make sure the promoter didn't back out of the deal. They wouldn't unload the car until the dough had been handed over to him. It was usually a thousand dollars, and Lee liked it in a sandwich bag or an envelope for easy handling. If they were slow producing it, Lee would make the whole gang — Kyle, Pattie, Steve Hmiel, and Robin Pemberton — sit on the truck until they got paid.

Lee Petty loved his grandson. He also loved a good payday.

"When we went to a short track, especially a dirt track, the locals weren't thrilled," says Hmiel. "It was like, *This kid's getting a lot of deal money. This kid's coming in here with his big truck*. So the dirt racing, they'd certainly run into you. Kyle did a good job with it all. I don't know that the other team people were ever our friends, but he did a great job with the crowd." And he was getting experience. Even if it wasn't in top-notch equipment — "The car was junk," says Pattie — he was at least turning some laps. But he was still a long way from where he wanted to be.

Despite the return of all the major players from the Daytona 500, the Firecracker 400 played to a much smaller crowd. Only about 35,000 fans were on hand for the race. For one thing, Independence Day fell on a Wednesday. For another, even though the race started at 10:30 in the morning, it was hotter than hell in Daytona—104 degrees on the track when the green flag flew.

What was really keeping people away, though, was the fear that they'd get stranded on the highway. The country was in the midst of its second energy crisis of the decade. Americans had long been warned about their dependence on foreign oil, but the release of the movie *The China Syndrome* in March, followed twelve days later by the meltdown at the Three Mile Island nuclear facility in Pennsylvania, pretty much cooled people to the notion of alternative fuel sources for a while. But the summer of '79 was not a good time to be at the mercy of oil producers. The Iranian Revolution, which came on top of strikes by the country's oil workers in late 1978, put a huge dent in supply. The United States was used to importing 750,000 barrels a day from Iran, but the country had cut its production to 250,000 barrels a day by early 1979. The shortage left motorists on edge. OUT OF GAS — WILL ROGERS NEVER MET AN ARAB, read one sign at a station in Iowa. Long lines at the pump led to measures such as even/odd-day rationing based on license plate numbers. Some areas instituted maximum purchases—sometimes as low as $3—while others allowed refills only on tanks that were at least half-empty, to keep away "tank toppers." The situation was so bad by late June that Congress considered shutting down all gas pumps the weekend before the Fourth. Things weren't terrible around Daytona; the speedway released a list of twenty-four area stations that would have gas. But the trick was getting there from someplace like, say, Birmingham, when virtually every station in Alabama was closed.

And even if fans could get gas, a trip on the interstate wasn't exactly a Sunday drive, thanks to a wildcat strike of independent truckers, who were protesting escalating diesel fuel prices, the 55 mile per hour speed limit, and restrictive weight limits on their loads. The strikers were serious about keeping trucks off the road — windshields were busted; trucks were firebombed — and they didn't care about collateral damage. Sniper fire at moving rigs killed a trucker in Alabama and wounded a fourteen-year-old boy in Arkansas. Nails sprinkled on heavily traveled roads had caused huge traffic jams in Alabama and North Carolina. National Guardsmen were called out in at least ten states, and three states, including Florida, declared a state of emergency.

As the nation's highways were turning into the Thunderdome, President Jimmy Carter was in Tokyo at an economic summit. He had planned to take a short vacation in Hawaii following its conclusion, but as *Air Force One* left Japan on June 30, Carter received a call from his pollster Patrick Caddell, who briefed him on the deteriorating situation and told him, "You have to come home." Two weeks earlier Carter had concluded negotiations with the Soviet Union on the SALT II arms control treaty, and the previous fall he had brokered the Camp David Accords between Israel and Egypt. But those foreign policy achievements weren't enough to make Americans overlook the fact that they were spending more and more of their time waiting in line for the chance to be gouged for a few gallons of gas. Carter's approval rating was in the low 20s, worse than Richard Nixon's during Watergate. So Carter canceled his vacation and retreated to Camp David, where he began work on a speech on energy — the fifth of his presidency on that topic.

Before long the president realized that there wasn't much he could say that hadn't been said in the previous four talks. "It just seemed to be going nowhere with the public," his wife, Rosalynn, said. Carter changed tacks, broadening the focus of his address. Spurred by a memo from Caddell that described a national "malaise," he invited dozens of Americans from various walks of life—politicians, professors, preachers—to Camp David and sat on the floor taking notes as they told him what they thought was wrong with America. (Arkansas's boyish governor, Bill Clinton, told him, "Mr. President, you are not leading this nation—you're just managing the government.") After more than a week, Carter—over the strenuous objections of Vice President Walter Mondale, who threatened to quit—delivered what became known as his "malaise speech" (though he never uttered the word). He spoke of a threat to the country, one that "is nearly invisible in ordinary ways. It is a crisis of confidence. It is a crisis that strikes at the very heart and soul and spirit of our national will. We can see this crisis in the growing doubt about the meaning of our own lives and in the loss of a unity of purpose for our nation." Carter accepted his share of the blame, but not all of it. "Too many of us now tend to worship self-indulgence and consumption," he said. "Human identity is no longer defined by what one does, but by what one owns."

The speech, more sermon than policy discussion, was initially well received, but within days public opinion turned. There was something to be said for candor, but as it turned out, suggesting to the American people that there was something wrong with them, or that they were in some way responsible for their dire situation, was pushing it. Carter's approval rating edged back downward, and, worse, he was now associated with a message of pessimism—one that would hound him throughout his reelection campaign in 1980.

The good news for Carter was that the public didn't hold him completely responsible for the energy crisis. The weekend before the holiday, the Greater Miami Jaycees held a seven-hour call-in, inviting people to vent about the situation. A spokesman for the Jaycees reported that blame for the shortage was "running about 50-50 between the government and the oil companies." The callers offered a variety of suggestions for keeping consumption down: a four-day workweek, a four-day school week, an investigation into "where the government is hiding the oil," and mandatory jail terms for drivers caught speeding.

That presented NASCAR with a bit of an image problem, as the sport would pretty much cease to exist if speeding were removed. The cars got around four or five miles to the gallon, which hardly sent the message that the sport was doing its part in the conservation campaign. And in a 1976 study of gas-guzzling pastimes, auto racing ranked seventh.* "A man parked in a line waiting to get a limit of 10 gallons of gasoline and listening to a 500-mile race on his radio could begin to hate the sport in a hurry," said Cale Yarborough.

During the previous energy crisis, in 1974, NASCAR had cut the length of all its races by 10 percent. Bill France decided against shortening any races in '79, but the teams wouldn't be guzzling quite as much gas: NASCAR's fuel provider, Union 76, cut its supply by 20 percent from the 1978 season. A few drivers tried to do their part. Richard Petty dispensed advice to motorists via newspaper columnists, telling them that although drafting allowed racers to ease off the throttle, hitching your car to someone's bumper on the interstate was a bad idea. "There are certain race drivers I would not consider drafting with," he said. "I don't know them that well, and I certainly don't know the strangers I'm behind on the highway."

The trick, according to the King, was to apply steady pressure to the accelerator, which made the difference on both the track and the highway. "Smoothness does it," he said. "That's the key to driving race cars faster than the next cat, and smooth driving is the key to more miles per gallon.... The cat who can run three or four extra laps with his car before he has to make a pit stop for gas is the one who's likely to win the race." And, he noted, if you had access to a top-notch racing

---

* The study took into account everything associated with the sport—fuel used by the race cars as well as fans, transporters, etc. Number one on the list, by the way, was vacations.

team, it might be a good idea to have them take a look at your Dodge Dart. "I try not to slow for curves on the racetrack or on the highway," he said. "I have my passenger car set up to handle real good in curves and corners."

Petty's Oldsmobile was handling pretty well at Daytona, but not as well as Buddy Baker's Gray Ghost, which was on the pole for the Firecracker 400, just as it had been for February's 500. And it was beset by ignition problems, just as it had been in February, but this time it was the real deal. Baker dropped out after fifty-seven laps, but at least he could take solace in the fact that he wouldn't have to spend any more time sitting in his car, which was kind of like sitting in a pizza oven. There was no reprieve from the heat. Darrell Waltrip kept sticking his arm out the window in an effort to cool off, but the air he was bringing in was no relief. He said it was like "working around a blast furnace in a steel mill."

The temperature also made it more difficult to draft. A driver couldn't simply tuck in behind a car and stay there, because if he didn't get his nose out into the fresh air, his engine would overheat. The field was strung out, and after Baker dropped out, four drivers began to pull away: Neil Bonnett, Dale Earnhardt, Benny Parsons, and Waltrip.

That Bonnett was still in the race was a sign that it might have been his fate to win. He escaped two major catastrophes in the first ninety laps. Twenty laps into the race a car spun out in front of Waltrip and Bonnett. Waltrip slammed on his brakes, and Bonnett, who was right behind him, had no choice but to get off the gas and veer left. The car did a one-eighty, and Bonnett went sliding down the grass on the backstretch, backward. Eventually, the front end started to come around, and when it did, Bonnett dropped it into third gear and floored it. "One of the damnedest jobs of driving you ever saw," he said. "I had both my eyes closed." His second break came when Bobby Allison T-boned the sliding car of Terry Labonte, sending Labonte's bumper on a journey that took it through the air, onto Bonnett's hood, and off his windshield before it finally flew over his roof. Bonnett never slowed down, and his car suffered no damage.

Any chance Waltrip had of winning was lost when he made a green-flag pit stop just before a caution period, which allowed the leaders to pit under yellow and left Waltrip a lap down. Earnhardt stayed on the lead lap, but, as he did in Charlotte, he had trouble handling the heat. Late in the race he got woozy — "My brain wouldn't work," he said — and brushed the wall, so he wisely backed off. That left Bonnett and Parsons to duel for the win. Bonnett took the lead with twenty-seven laps left and held on to it as he took the white flag. Parsons was trying to set him up for a slingshot pass, but he was slowed down just enough by two packs of slower cars — packs that Bonnett expertly slalomed through — that he was never able to get close enough to make his move.

Bonnett wasn't able to enjoy the spoils of victory, the hugs of one chesty Winston Girl notwithstanding. As he launched into his postrace speech in Victory Lane, the heat finally caught up with him. He turned as white as the one-lap-to-go flag, his legs went rubbery, and he got light-headed. An official took him by the arm and led him to the infirmary by way of the garage, which looked like a triage area. Waltrip — whose fourth-place finish, combined with Allison's early departure, meant that he added 92 points to his lead — was prone on a workbench, his shirt and shoes off and an oxygen mask on his face. Parsons was on the bench next to him. His foot was so badly blistered that when he saw a crewman with an artificial right leg walk by, he said, "That's just what I need now." Chuck Brown sat on the ground with a wet towel on his foot as he pondered his shoe, the sole of which had become a gooey mess.

Waltrip eventually got up and moved into the drivers' locker room, where he promptly submerged himself in a tub of ice water. Nearby Richard Petty, who had finished fifth, was changing. He was one of the few drivers who didn't look like he had just run two marathons in a winter coat. "Boy," Earnhardt said to him, "you're the toughest old man in the world."

### Standings After the Firecracker 400

1. Darrell Waltrip      2,720
2. Bobby Allison      2,587
3. Richard Petty      2,522
4. Cale Yarborough      2,500
5. Dale Earnhardt      2,342

# Chapter Seventeen

# Rising Again

**Monday, July 30**
**Race 19: Coca-Cola 500**
**Long Pond, Pennsylvania**

IF ANYONE could have used some time away from the track, it was Cale Yarborough. Sure, he'd won two races, but all anyone seemed to remember about his season was that he'd fought Bobby Allison and that he'd nearly turned a routine check of his car into an impromptu leg amputation. His twentieth-place finish in the Firecracker 400 left him in fourth place in the standings. Nobody was talking about whether he'd win a fourth straight championship. Now the talk in the garage centered on his relationship with his owner: there were strong rumblings that Yarborough and Junior Johnson were on the outs.

As luck would have it, the schedule offered Yarborough a break. There was only one race, in Nashville, between Daytona and the 500-miler at Pocono International Raceway. Yarborough spent a large chunk of the downtime on a working vacation in Hollywood, where he filmed a cameo for the TV show *The Dukes of Hazzard*. The producers had originally offered the part to Richard Petty, but the King had turned them down. "It's not that I've got something against good ol' boys," Petty said. "I guess I'm still sort of one myself. Their people contacted us, but we couldn't get together on the money." So Yarborough was recruited instead.

The show, which was based on the 1975 movie *Moonrunners,* had made its debut in January 1979 as a midseason replacement on CBS. *Flying High* — a Connie Sellecca vehicle about three flight attendants — tanked, so the network stuck *Dukes* in its Saturday night time slot. The premise was simple: two bootlegging cousins drove around the backwoods of Georgia in a car that had a giant rebel flag painted on the hood. It was a massive hit, proof that the country had, against all odds, become a place where people would rather watch two flannel-wearing southern boys outsmart some really stupid local lawmen than watch Connie Sellecca and two other hot stewardesses do *Charlie's Angels* at 35,000 feet.

America's tastes had certainly changed.

In 1920 H. L. Mencken published an essay called "The Sahara of the Bozart,"* which laid out the curmudgeonly columnist's view of the post–Civil War South: "It is almost as sterile, artistically, intellectually, culturally, as the Sahara Desert. There are single acres in Europe that house more first-rate men than all the states south of the Potomac; there are probably single square miles in America." Mencken went on to decry the "unanimous torpor and doltishness, this curious and almost pathological estrangement from everything that makes for a civilized culture," and suggested that if a tidal wave were to wash the whole region away, no civilized person would notice.

And this from a man who lived in Maryland, just on the other side of the Potomac.

Ouch.

---

* "Bozart" is a play on "beaux arts."

When he wrote the essay, Mencken had never been to the South; a friend and editor told him it would be a good idea to keep it that way for "two or three years." (The reaction in Dixie was predictable. In Arkansas a campaign was undertaken to implore the state's congressional delegation to have Mencken deported.)* When Mencken did venture down south, his firsthand impressions were little better. In 1925, while covering the Scopes monkey trial in rural Tennessee, Mencken referred to the locals as "yokels," "halfwits," and "buffoons" living in a region he dubbed the "Coca-Cola belt."

Not every northerner viewed the South with such unabashed derision, nor did Yankees pay much attention to how life was lived in the Land of Cotton. It's not that southern culture wasn't embraced; it was barely acknowledged, let alone examined. "The American South has existed largely as an imaginary landscape in the nation's popular arts," historian Allison Graham wrote in her essay "The South in Popular Culture." Meaning that in movies, southerners were almost always one-note characters, bumpkins who were generally harmless and maybe good for a laugh. The tendency to oversimplify applied to historical representations as well. Antebellum southerners all seemed to live on plantations where the men wore bolo ties, the women wore hoop skirts, and the slaves wore smiles that were completely at odds with their lot in life.

The picture provided by television wasn't much better. As TV was becoming a viable medium for delivering national news in the 1950s and early '60s, the enduring images coming out of the South were of governors in schoolhouse doors and fire hoses turned on demonstrators. The picture painted of southerners on shows such as *The Beverly Hillbillies* — slack-jawed, unwashed mouth breathers, who, though

---

* The attitude of the Arkansans would eventually shift from hatred to pity. A decade later, when Mencken wrote that Arkansas was the "apex of moronia," the state legislature passed a motion to pray for Mencken's soul. Said an ungrateful and unmoved Mencken, "My only defense is that I didn't make Arkansas the butt of ridicule. God did."

they had no hope of fitting into polite society, were at least harmless, decent people — didn't seem quite so bad.

But as the '60s wore on, the South's image softened. The Civil Rights Act of 1964 and the Voting Rights Act of 1965 went a long way toward eradicating the nastier aspects of southern life. As more blacks registered and voted, a new guard of young, progressive politicians was installed in local offices and statehouses. Race relations in the South, so long the area's chief source of embarrassment, became less volatile, especially when compared to what was happening up north and out west. Riots in Philadelphia and the Watts section of Los Angeles in 1964 and 1965 were followed by troubles in Cleveland, Newark, and especially Detroit, where five days of rioting in the summer of 1967 led to forty-three deaths and two thousand buildings being burned down. The days of Yankees being able to look down their noses at their overall-wearing neighbors were over. The rubes weren't the ones torching their cities; that was happening in places run by what Alabama governor George Wallace called the "pointy-headed intellectuals."

One of the more interesting explanations for the South's progress on race was offered in, of all places, *Ebony,* which devoted an entire 1971 issue to the region and declared that it had cleaned up its ways because it had become "too busy to hate." Indeed, the 1960s and '70s were a time of unprecedented economic development in the South. After decades of seeing its population shrink, the South grew by 12 million people in the '70s, a jump of 21 percent, and the size of its workforce increased by one-third. Attracted by the untapped resources and the mild weather, businesses — some from the North, many from overseas — moved into the Sun Belt. A study in the mid-'70s ranked the states by their business climate: Texas was first, followed by Alabama and Virginia, with both Carolinas and Arkansas also in the top 10. In his 1975 book, *Power Shift,* Kirkpatrick Sale declared that "the pleasant little backwaters and half-grown cities [had changed] into an industrial and financial colossus."

For the first time in more than a hundred years, the South had become a relevant voice in the national discussion. It was forging its own identity and asserting itself, and its contributions to culture — including stock car racing, the one sport it called its own — were being noticed north of the Mason-Dixon Line. It was happening slowly, but it was happening.

Then came the 1976 presidential election.

From its inception, Jimmy Carter's candidacy seemed something of a lark. For starters, he was a southerner, and no one from the Deep South had been so much as nominated by a major party since before the Civil War. And he wasn't even a famous southerner. Unlike George Wallace, whose ultraconservative message found an audience among disenchanted northerners, Carter — a peanut farmer who had in 1970 been elected governor of Georgia — was anonymous outside the Peach State. At the beginning of 1976, his national name recognition was 2 percent.* When he announced to his family that he was running for president, his feisty mother, Lillian, asked, "President of what?"

But as the Carter campaign gained momentum and the prospect of a southern president began to look like a real possibility, the national curiosity about Carter Country turned into a full-blown case of *Hey-look-at-this-itis*. Writers descended on the South. *The New York Times* ran a weeklong series devoted to the South in February 1976. *Time* sent seventy staffers down to Dixie to collect material for an entire issue dedicated to the region — replete with a piece on stock car racing — that ran six weeks before the election.

Carter's victory over Gerald Ford in November of '76 only hastened what one observer dubbed "the Reddening of America." With

---

*Some quick math: Georgia's population was about 4.6 million. The population of the United States was 203 million, meaning about 2.2 percent of Americans lived in Georgia. So a name recognition of 2 percent means that even some people in his own state didn't know who Carter was. And Carter had been on the cover of *Time* in 1971. *That* is anonymity.

one of their own now the most powerful man in the world, "southern-ers no longer felt ashamed of their region, no longer were blackballed as bigoted, retrograde, out of step," historian Bruce Schulman wrote in *The Seventies: The Great Shift in American Culture.* "On the contrary, their culture—at least the Seventies version of it—became increas-ingly popular in the very places where it had been most disdained."

The increase wasn't entirely due to curiosity about the new com-mander in chief. The post-Watergate landscape bred a strong distrust of The Man, and southern culture has long been infused with a rebellious, antiestablishment streak. The new American heroes of the mid-'70s were antiheroes. "The same distrust of the powers that be that under-mined traditional sources of authority and fractured public life also spurred creative, personal, highly charged art that addressed just that discontent," Schulman wrote. "The decade's most potent and memo-rable cultural projects raised an upturned middle finger at conventional sources of authority." That was evident in films featuring morally am-biguous protagonists, such as *Taxi Driver*'s Travis Bickle (played by Robert De Niro) and *Chinatown*'s Jake Gittes (Jack Nicholson). It also showed up on TV. According to Bo Duke, the blond cousin played by John Schneider, the Dukes of Hazzard were raised "never to turn their back on somebody who needs help fighting the system."

But nowhere was the antihero trend more apparent than in music. Spearheaded by Willie Nelson, Waylon Jennings, and Merle Haggard—who wasn't kidding when he sang, "I turned 21 in prison"—the outlaw movement brought country music to a national audience. In 1960 there were eighty radio stations in the United States dedicated to country. By the mid-'70s, there were more than a thousand. *Newsweek* and *Time* ran cover stories on the crossover ap-peal of country artists, whose songs routinely topped both *Billboard*'s Hot 100 and the country chart. (Among the people who were listening to country, according to *Time,* were novelist Kurt Vonnegut Jr. and former Nixon energy czar John Love.) *Newsweek* put Loretta Lynn on the cover. *Time* went for an edgier choice: Haggard, aka California inmate number 845200.

Country—and its equally raffish cousin, southern rock—stood at the opposite end of the musical spectrum from another genre that was introduced to the mainstream in the mid-'70s: disco. Where sports fans came down on that little battle in the summer of 1979 was answered in Chicago two and a half weeks before the Coca-Cola 500 at Pocono. The Chicago White Sox staged a promotion that allowed fans to attend the team's doubleheader against the Detroit Tigers for 98 cents provided that they brought a disco record, which would be placed inside a giant crate in center field and blown up between games. The Sox expected 20,000 people to show up. More than 75,000 did—20,000 more than Comiskey Park's capacity and 60,000 more than were at the Sox game the night before. DJ Steve Dahl, wearing an army helmet, circled the field in a jeep, then detonated the records, which tore the outfield grass to shreds and incited the crowd—which, having spent much of the first game drinking beer and smoking pot, was already good and rowdy—to a full-fledged riot. Shirtless fans poured onto the field, setting bonfires, throwing firecrackers, and hitting each other. "I didn't know people could have such little regard for other people's safety," said White Sox pitcher Ross Baumgarten, who clearly had never listened to Donna Summer's *Bad Girls* from start to finish.

A distinctive southern twang was also heard in movies and on TV. *Smokey and the Bandit* was the fourth-highest grossing movie of 1977 and spawned two sequels and scores of imitations, including *Every Which Way but Loose,* which was the fourth-biggest draw of 1978. The *Alice* spinoff *Flo,* set in a roadhouse in Houston, was the seventh-highest-rated show in 1979–1980 and was responsible for otherwise urbane types going around telling each other to kiss their grits. The following year, *Dallas* and *The Dukes of Hazzard* were numbers one and two in the Nielsen ratings.

"You couldn't do a show like that about people from the North,"

Richard Petty said of *Dukes.* "They don't seem to have as much fun as people down South." Maybe, but it wasn't for a lack of trying. Had H. L. Mencken seen how many northerners were embracing redneck chic, he would have swallowed his cigar. The nation's most visible redneck was Jimmy Carter's brother, Billy, a gas station proprietor who was so fond of beer that he promoted his own brand, Billy Beer.* The First Brother was perhaps the republic's staunchest advocate for what he called "Redneck Power," a phrase that was painted on the hood of his pickup and emblazoned on the shirt he wore when he played in softball games with members of the White House staff, Secret Service, and press corps. Instead of being appalled, people followed Billy's lead, snapping up boots and hats and vests. Ralph Lauren created an entire line of cowboy duds that he couldn't keep on the shelves. "Imagine," Lauren said in February of '79, "it took me 12 years to build a $12 million menswear business. It took me two months to sell almost $30 million in Western wear." Less pricey options were available at Billy Martin's Western Wear, the national chain of boutiques started by the New York Yankees manager in 1978. Even the pointy-headed intellectuals were getting in on it. Hendrik Hertzberg, President Carter's New York–bred, Harvard-educated speechwriter, confessed to the *Washington Post* that he had started wearing cowboy boots because they made him "feel close to being a movie star." Another Beltway consultant raved to the *Post* about his boots, saying that he wore them to fancy dress balls.

And if dressing like a cowboy wasn't enough, one could always pretend to be one. In September 1979, *Esquire* ran Aaron Latham's "The Ballad of the Urban Cowboy: America's Search for True Grit," which chronicled the lives of a group of Texas oil workers who killed their time riding mechanical bulls. It spawned the John Travolta movie *Urban Cowboy,* which in turn inspired countless

---

* Carter pitched the beer by saying, "I had this beer brewed just for me. I think it's the best I've ever tasted. And I've tasted a lot. I think you'll like it, too."

American men to risk doing irreparable damage to their reproductive systems.

So as NASCAR started to come of age in 1979, it did so in a society that had begun to admire people who had dirt under their fingernails, guys who wore cowboy boots and belt buckles and weren't afraid to fight now and again. If Middle America was ready to embrace Bo and Luke Duke, then it sure as hell would be willing to embrace a real bootlegger like Junior Johnson or a real brawling hotfoot like Cale Yarborough.

Or, as Yarborough later put it, "All Yankees, secretly, deep inside their hearts, want to be Rebels."

High on Yarborough's list of shortcomings in the first six months of the 1979 season was that he hadn't won a pole. If he didn't rectify that by the end of the season, the 1980 Busch Clash would be run without the Busch-sponsored car. Yarborough thought he had spared his sponsor that indignity at Pocono when he put up a time that looked unbeatable. But late in Saturday's qualifying, Harry Gant, a thirty-nine-year-old rookie driving a car owned by the proprietor of a Hartford school bus company, nipped him. Unlike almost every other driver in the field, all of whom used Goodyear tires, Gant used a set built by McCreary, a small Pennsylvania operation. No one expected the softer tires to hold up during the race — and they didn't — but Gant didn't care. The bonus for winning the pole, combined with the berth in the 1980 Busch Clash, was worth at least $12,000 to him, which was more than all but the top two finishers in the Pocono race would take home.

Waltrip qualified third in Bertha despite missing most of Friday's practice. He had been playing in a celebrity golf tournament in Chicago, and when he showed up at the airport Friday morning to fly to Pennsylvania, his pilot delivered some bad news: he had somehow locked the keys inside the plane. A locksmith was summoned, but busting into a jet proved a little more delicate than jimmying the door on a '55 Oldsmobile. As the locksmith worked on getting into the plane, Bertha sat in the Pocono garage, all dressed up with no one to take her out. Waltrip finally got to the track with only fifteen minutes left in the five-and-a-half-hour session. He had the good fortune to turn a fast qualifying lap, but his luck ran out in Saturday afternoon's final practice. Bertha's engine blew, and Waltrip couldn't keep the car out of the wall. The damage was too serious to fix in a day, and without a backup car—bringing more than one ride to the track was rare—Waltrip had no choice but to buy his way into the race.

Al Rudd Jr. had been the engine builder for his younger brother, Ricky, but when Ricky left the family operation at the start of 1979 to drive for Junie Donleavy, the Rudd family Chevy was without a driver. Al decided to give it a crack at Pocono, one of the trickier tracks on the circuit. Tucked away in the Pocono Mountains of eastern Pennsylvania—an area known for heart-shaped bath tubs and honeymoon suites—Pocono Raceway is a two-and-a-half-mile triangle, and all three turns are radically different. Finding a setup that works through two is a chore; finding one that works through all three is impossible. But Rudd, who had never driven on a big track in his life, still put up the eighteenth-fastest time. Then after Waltrip put Bertha into the wall during Happy Hour, D.W. came calling. Rudd gave Waltrip his car in exchange for some much-needed cash and engine parts. He also got to keep his motor; Waltrip had Robert Yates put a new one in the loaner.

The race was scheduled for 1:00 p.m. Sunday, but rain pushed it back to Monday. The weather was better, but there were still enough clouds in the sky to pose a threat of rain. With a shortened race a possibility, there was going to be hard racing from the start. And that meant there were going to be wrecks.

Dale Earnhardt thought he was dead. He opened his eyes, felt himself flying, saw the clouds approaching, and connected the dots. Then he saw a helicopter pilot and figured that unless the dress code for angels had been drastically relaxed, he was probably still alive.

Earnhardt was being airlifted to Pocono Hospital. He had been leading the Coca-Cola 500 as it approached the midway point when his right rear tire blew. His car did a one-eighty and smacked the wall on the driver's side. In the days before head restraints, Earnhardt drove with his head cocked to the left, almost like he was trying to look out his window to see what was happening in front of him. When his tire blew, Waltrip was behind him. After the race he said he was pretty sure that Earnhardt's head hit the wall. He was conscious when he was pulled from the car, and when his crew gave him a ball and told him to squeeze it, he was able to. But after a few minutes at the infield care center, it became clear that Earnhardt was going to need more serious medical attention. He was kept in the intensive care unit at Pocono Hospital, but his injuries weren't as bad as feared. He had broken both his shoulder blades.

As expected, no one had wasted any time rushing to the front. As soon as the green flag flew, Waltrip dropped down low and passed eleven cars by the time he exited the first turn on lap 1, moving from nineteenth to eighth in a matter of seconds. The first serious wreck came a lap later, when Al Holbert's car hit the wall, nearly flipped, and burst into flames. Roger Hamby got caught up in it, staggered out of his totaled car, and lay down on the infield grass before being carted off to the infield medical center.

When it wasn't slowed by caution flags—eight, for forty-six laps—the action was intense, with cars at times stacked five-wide on a track with only one real groove. After Earnhardt fell out, it became a three-car race between Yarborough, Petty, and Waltrip. Yarborough went to the point—the fifty-sixth lead change of the race—after a series of green-flag gas-and-go pit stops with about ten laps left. He was pulling away when the yellow came out on lap 196 for Nelson Oswald's blown engine. Waltrip, who was in second place, decided to duck into the pits for tires. The upside was that the fresh rubber would give him a good chance of running down Yarborough on the restart. The downside was that there might not be a restart.

Waltrip took his spot at the end of the line of lead-lap cars, in seventh place, as the field completed lap 197. The track workers were still cleaning up the mess from Oswald's motor. When the pace car crossed the start/finish line after lap 198, it became official: the race was going to finish under caution.* Waltrip's gamble had cost him $8,250 and 19 points, the difference between a second-place finish and seventh. "Cale might have won anyway, but not starting the race back is what made him win," said Waltrip. Still, it seemed like a reasonable risk to take, as Waltrip still left the track with a 209-point lead.

Yarborough won the race with a fast pit stop and a better race strategy. The win was a reminder of just how good Junior Johnson's operation was. It didn't salvage Yarborough's disappointing season, but it did put an end to the speculation that it would be his last with Johnson. "I'm glad I've got all the press here," Yarborough said after the race. "I don't know who started it, but Junior and I have signed with Busch beer for 1980. I'll be driving whatever Junior wants me to."

### Standings After the Coca-Cola 500

| | | |
|---|---|---|
| 1. | Darrell Waltrip | 3,061 |
| 2. | Richard Petty | 2,852 |
| 3. | Cale Yarborough | 2,850 |
| 4. | Bobby Allison | 2,845 |
| 5. | Dale Earnhardt | 2,588 |

---

* The field had to be given a one-lap heads-up before the green flag came back out. In 2004 NASCAR changed its rules to add extra laps—enough to guarantee two green-flag laps—if a race was going to finish under yellow.

## Chapter Eighteen

# The Gatorade Kid

**Sunday, August 5**
**Race 20: Talladega 500**
**Talladega, Alabama**

ASTRONAUTS AND race car drivers have much in common: The love of speed. The ability to stare down danger. The big helmets. The inordinate amount of time spent answering questions from strangers about how they go to the bathroom on the job. Unlike their orbiting brethren, racers aren't fitted with special devices to handle the call of nature. Their trips are substantially shorter, and at least before the development of cockpit cooling systems, they tended to sweat so much that dehydration made it a largely moot point. Still, occasionally a driver needs to make a pit stop, one that has nothing to do with tires or fuel. If he does, he has two choices. One is to hold it in. You can figure out the other one.

This was among the many things on Darrell Waltrip's mind leading up to the Talladega 500. He'd been sick with an intestinal virus since the day after the Pocono race. He was off solid food, had dropped ten pounds, and was subsisting, for the most part, on glucose and Gatorade. His fever spiked at 102, and he suffered from aches, chills, and lower gastrointestinal issues of the type one never wants to be afflicted with, especially if one is going to be buckled into a car for three hours. Waltrip wasn't about to miss the race, though. He said he'd rely on a supply of what he indelicately called "cork stoppers."

Waltrip's access to a bottomless bottle of Gatorade was one of the things that put off other drivers. He'd had a sponsorship agreement, one of NASCAR's most valuable and most visible, with the drink company since 1976. Not every driver knew every detail of how the deal had come about, but most at least knew enough of the keywords — "father-in-law," "fraternity brother," "golf course" — to come to the conclusion that it involved rich people scratching each other's backs. That led to the assumption that Waltrip had had it easy, which went a long way toward explaining why Waltrip was so desperate to stick it to the old guard. Talk of silver spoons put Waltrip on the defensive, and his MO when that happened was to strike back. The funny part of it all was that Waltrip hadn't even had a privileged upbringing. Yes, his father-in-law had money, but that didn't mean he was just going to give it to Darrell.

Frank Rader wasn't at all happy with his daughter Stevie's latest boyfriend. Darrell Waltrip was known all over Owensboro, Kentucky, as a reckless hood-in-training, whose reputation preceded him to the point that he was once arrested for "attempted drag racing." (The cops had staked out a strip, and when Waltrip showed up in a Corvette, they popped him.) Waltrip did everything fast: he held the state record in the 440 for almost ten years. And when he wasn't running track, Waltrip's idea of fun was to goad the cops into chasing him by throwing beer bottles at their black-and-whites. It was just like *The Dukes of Hazzard:* the police would chase Waltrip and his pals all over town, up and down alleys, out on country roads. One memorable adventure ended with Waltrip ditching a car in a cornfield after it had been shot up by an officer with Barney Fife–like aim who had been trying to flatten the tires.* As if Waltrip needed to drive home the point that he was not prime son-in-law material, he once flipped a car while being chased on his way to the Rader house to pick up Stevie for a date.

And then there was the pumpkin incident.

Waltrip drove a '55 Oldsmobile that he had painted blue — by hand, with a paintbrush. He called it the Blue Goose. One night he and five buddies piled into the Goose, drove up to Reid's farm, and stole some of the biggest pumpkins they had ever seen. They took them to the drive-in, where everyone was hanging out, and smashed them in the entrance, creating a patch of orange "ice" that, by the end of the night, had sent three cars sliding into the Wax Works record shop next door.

A little while later, at a stoplight, a kid in the car next to Waltrip's tossed a water balloon at the Blue Goose. Waltrip had wisely held back a pumpkin — because you never know when the situation is going to require a giant gourd. Waltrip tossed the pumpkin at the kid's windshield, thinking it would splatter. Instead, it went through the glass and wound up in the driver's lap. Some might call that overreacting. Waltrip, however, wasn't interested in quibbling about what was or wasn't an appropriate retaliation. "I didn't care about that," he said. "I had lost my school ring throwing that pumpkin, and I was too busy looking for it. You couldn't go steady without it, you know."

Stevie clearly didn't mind a ring with a little pulp in it. She'd always thought Darrell was cute. They started dating in 1968 and were married a year later. "When we decided we were going to get married, her family about disowned her," Waltrip wrote in 1979.

Waltrip was, by the time they married, fairly serious about racing. He fell in love with it when he was six. His parents would let

---

*Waltrip beat the charge because the cops couldn't tell who was driving.

him go to the track with his grandparents only if they asked him, so young Darrell would call his grandmother and gently remind her to call him back with an invitation. When he was twelve, he convinced his dad to buy him a lawn mower and a go-kart. The idea was that he would use the lawn mower to raise enough money to pay his dad back for the go-kart, though no one seems to remember him ever doing that. Past forgiving that debt, there wasn't a whole lot more LeRoy Waltrip could do to help his son's career. His job as a Dr Pepper delivery truck driver didn't provide him with the means to finance a racing operation. The family made the odd sacrifice, but for the most part Darrell was on his own. When he was old enough to drive, he scraped together $500 and bought a '36 Chevy coupe. He didn't have enough of one color paint for the entire car, so he took a page from the Pettys and put everything he had—a little red, some black, and some brown—in one bucket. Richard and Maurice got a beautiful cerulean blue. Darrell got puke brown. "It sort of looked like somebody threw up on it," he said.

He raced at Ellis Speedway outside Owensboro, and when there was nothing left to win there, he and Stevie moved to Franklin, Tennessee, just south of Nashville, where Waltrip dominated at the Fairgrounds Speedway. Frank Rader had finally warmed to Darrell after going to the track with some friends and being pleasantly surprised at how dedicated his son-in-law was. Liking the kid was one thing; bankrolling him was another. Rader set Waltrip up with Terminal Transport, a subsidiary of Texas Gas, but that deal was worth only $25,000. Waltrip owed various creditors three times that much.

He put together a Grand National team, including Jake Elder and Robert Gee, and on occasion he even paid them. But not often. They tried to run a full schedule in 1975, but the debts kept mounting. "I was getting good finishes," he said thirty years later, "but they didn't pay anything. You could finish in the first five or six and you didn't make enough to hardly pay your tire bill. I was in debt over my head, I owed the bank money, I owed Huggins Tire Company money, I owed [parts supplier] Hutch-Pagan money."

Relief came in Daytona. Waltrip passed Donnie Allison on the last lap of the 1975 Firecracker 400, which pushed Bill Gardner over the edge. After the race Gardner summoned Allison to the *Captiva* to give him his pink slip. Gardner and his brother, Jim, decided that if Waltrip could outrun their man in a bad car, he'd be downright dangerous in a good one. Waltrip and Stevie spent a short vacation in Vero Beach after the race, then stopped in at the NASCAR office on their way back to North Carolina to pick up Waltrip's $8,810 check. Someone in the office told Waltrip that Allison had been fired by the Gardners; Waltrip shrugged and got back in the car.

A few hours later the Waltrips made a pit stop. As Darrell was gassing up his car, a familiar face appeared: Jim Gardner. "Funny that I should run into you here," Gardner said. "We've been trying to find you. We want you to drive for our team." Waltrip told him he was committed to his own team, as underfunded as they were. Gardner gave Waltrip his card and told him to think about it. The more Waltrip and Stevie discussed it on the trip home, the more they realized he had to take the Gardners up on their offer. He was just too far in debt. By the time they stopped for dinner, he was pretty well convinced he was going to do it. Then who should appear at the same restaurant but Jim Gardner, whose stalking skills left much to be desired. He tried to pass it off as another coincidental meeting, but Waltrip wasn't fooled. This time he told Gardner he was inclined to accept, and he did, the next day.

While all of this was going on, Bill Stokely was stewing. The head of Stokely–Van Camp, the company that made Gatorade, had just been to the Brickyard for the Indy 500. It hadn't been a pleasant experience. As they had done to Bill France in the 1950s, the stewards had hassled Stokely and his frat brother Dennis Hendrick, a Texas Gas vice president, for not having the proper credentials, despite the fact that Gatorade was paying a lot of money to sponsor Johnny Rutherford's car. Stokely decided if that's how they were going to treat him, he was going home. Not long after that, Hendrick was playing golf with Frank Rader and suggested that Rader should put his son-in-law in touch with Stokely. They talked, and when the meeting was over, Stokely agreed to a $200,000 deal to have Gatorade sponsor Waltrip. "All of my racing career, I've heard people say what a lucky S.O.B. I am," Waltrip said a few years after he signed the deal. "*Everything he's ever had has been handed to him. He was given the Gatorade ride, he was given this or given that.* I wonder if people ever thought how hard I worked and planned to get where I am. I wonder if they thought about some of the turmoil I had to go through."

"If the people who thought we were wealthy could have known how we lived [then]," said Stevie, "they'd have thought we were on welfare." The only way her husband changed after they started to make a little money, she said, was that Darrell didn't "eat as many Rolaids as he used to." He was still eating them, though, and not just at Talladega. His situation—reviled by most fans, disliked by many peers—ate at him. It also motivated him. Probably. It was kind of tough to get a good read on Waltrip. "Darrell is really a complex individual," Stevie said in 1979, after ten years of marriage. "I'm still getting to know him. There are so many different sides."

The field for the Talladega 500 included a couple of moonlighters. David Pearson, who had been tabbed to do commentary for the race alongside Ken Squier on CBS—an interesting call, given Pearson's well-documented skittishness in front of the camera—took Rod Osterlund up on his offer to drive Dale Earnhardt's car while he recuperated from his injuries. And Richard Petty had to find a new front tire carrier after he qualified for the race. Kyle would start a respectable eighteenth, one spot ahead of Bobby Allison.

The two had different expectations. Kyle's was to stay out of trouble and not "mess up anybody." Pearson set the bar higher. His performance at Talladega had been one of the sticking points in his falling-out with Glen Wood, so a strong showing would prove that Pearson still had the necessary nerve and gumption to race at the superspeedways. Driving Earnhardt's car meant that Pearson would be reunited with an old colleague: Jake Elder, his crew chief for two of his championships at Holman Moody. "Jake hasn't changed a bit," Pearson happily reported. "He's still cussing and fuming like he always has."

The forty-one cars rolled off pit road at 1:00 p.m., and Brock Yates of CBS set the scene from the pits: "It's a classic afternoon in the Alabama summertime. Great wads of humidity hanging around us like moist bales of cotton, the horizon covered with marauding thunderheads." Those wads of humidity were bad news for Pearson, whose crew forgot to fill his water jug. Waltrip's support staff was more vigilant. Several of the wives made ice packs and made sure his water jug wasn't dry, while their husbands added more insulation to the car to keep the temperature down inside the cockpit. Waltrip was showing some signs of improvement. After a nearly sleepless night, he had a hamburger the morning of the race and was able to keep it down. But he was still light-headed, so when Donnie Allison fell out of the race with another engine failure, the DiGard crew recruited him to stand by should Waltrip need relief.

The race unfolded without a Big One, but the field was still thinned out by the heat, which put as much strain on the machines as it did on the drivers. Seventeen of the forty-one cars that started, including a slew of favorites, dropped out with motor problems. For the last fifty laps, only Waltrip and Pearson were on the lead lap. But any chance the Silver Fox had of winning was lost when his clutch, which had been replaced that morning, went bad. Without a low gear, Pearson's crew had to push him out of the pits on his last four stops, enabling Waltrip to eventually put him a lap down and cruise to the win.

Richard Petty finished fourth, in a pack of cars two laps down, but he was more interested in his son's finish than his own. He parked next to Kyle's car and asked him, "Hey buddy, how did you do?"

"All right," said Kyle. "But we've got to get more padding in this seat. I wore out my rear end." Kyle finished ninth, seven laps behind Waltrip, but he accomplished what he had set out to do: he stayed out of the way of the faster cars and did some drafting with the slower ones. "The thing that bothered me most about those crashes was the feeling the other drivers would write me off as just another rookie who didn't have what it takes," he said. "I accomplished what I set out to do, and the next time I get into a car for a Grand National, I'll feel a lot better."

On Talladega's spacious infield, two fans hoisted a large banner that read WALTRIP IS NO. 1 E'VILLE, IND., which suggested that his white-hat routine was actually working. (Of course, the fact that the nearest Waltrip fans apparently lived in Indiana said something.) As several bemused fans watched the sign bearers celebrate, Waltrip pulled Maybelline into Victory Lane, took a hit of oxygen, and beckoned Brock Yates to the car so that he could get in a few words before CBS signed off. Spending three hours driving nearly 200 miles per hour was enough to make a healthy man's stomach do backflips, and Waltrip was nowhere near healthy. But he hadn't just survived. He'd won his sixth race and stretched his lead over Petty to 229 points, the biggest it had been at any point in the season. "What Darrell did," said his crew chief, Buddy Parrott, "is another indication of this being our year."

### Standings After the Talladega 500

| | | |
|---|---|---|
| 1. | Darrell Waltrip | 3,246 |
| 2. | Richard Petty | 3,017 |
| 3. | Cale Yarborough | 2,946 |
| 4. | Bobby Allison | 2,924 |
| 5. | Benny Parsons | 2,662 |

## Chapter Nineteen

# The Beginning of the Trouble

*Monday, September 3*
**Race 23: Southern 500**
**Darlington, South Carolina**
*through*
*Sunday, October 14*
**Race 28: Holly Farms 400**
**North Wilkesboro, North Carolina**

SEPTEMBER 3 was Labor Day, and in Bristol, Connecticut, there was plenty of laboring going on. Workers had been building a large structure on Middle Street for five months, and judging by the amount of activity on what was supposed to be a day of rest in their honor, they had a deadline approaching and were nowhere near as close to being finished as they should have been. Painters were at work on the outside of the building, but there was only so much they could do, because the masons were still putting up the walls. As soon as a section was finished, the insulation and drywall guys would start their work, almost before the mortar had dried.

The building, which dwarfed everything else on Middle Street, was to serve as the broadcast center for a cable television network called the Entertainment and Sports Programming Network. Cable TV was a novelty at the time—in 1979 only 16 million American homes had it—so the giant building exuded an air of mystery that became even more pronounced in early August, when the thirty-foot satellite dishes were installed out front. They looked ominously anachronistic, like something out of an H. G. Wells novel. One mayoral candidate insisted that they would fry anything that came near them, leaving the good people of Bristol with a pile of dead, irradiated birds on Middle Street.

ESPN's launch was four days away. The network had been conceived in the summer of 1978 by Bill Rasmussen—who, having just been fired as director of communications for the New England Whalers of the World Hockey Association—had plenty of time on his hands. Rasmussen's original plan was to offer some local college events and maybe some Whalers-related programming to viewers in Connecticut. When he looked into purchasing time on Satcom I, which had been sitting in orbit for three years without doing much of anything, he discovered something odd. A five-hour block under the hourly rate would cost $1,250. The daily rate was $1,143, though that wasn't even on the rate card, because nobody in their right mind would consider trying to fill that much time. But 107 bucks was 107 bucks, so Rasmussen expanded his vision from a few hours here and there in Connecticut to an around-the-clock, coast-to-coast network because it was cheaper that way.

Getty came on board with financial backing later in '78, and in early 1979—a few months before he poached NBC Sports president Chet Simmons—Rasmussen signed a deal with the NCAA to show a wide range of college sports. But he still had a problem. There was no way he was going to be able to fill his calendar, even if he showed the same college soccer and football games over and over, which he did.* Rasmussen plugged gaps with programming such as hurling, Irish cycling, and softball. The first competitive event the network aired after its September 7 launch was a slow-pitch game between the Kentucky Bourbons and the Milwaukee Schlitz, which was, at best, the second-most-intense booze-related rivalry of its day, behind the war waged by the "Less Filling" and "Tastes Great" factions in countless Miller Lite commercials.

The broadcast of the 1979 Daytona 500 is rightly hailed as a watershed moment in NASCAR's history. It showed that racing was a viable TV commodity, but in no way did it trigger a mad rush to acquire the rights to races. Promoters were still left to cut their own deals, and the major networks were still skittish about devoting too much time to racing. Humpy Wheeler tried selling the 1980 World 600 on its own merits. When the networks said no, he tried to make it a more attractive show. He threw out all kinds of ideas. Qualifying. *No thanks.* The Sportsman race. *Pass.* Car jumps. *No dice.* Motorcycle jumps. *Not gonna do it.* "I thought, *What the hell am I going to do with these guys? What do people in New York like?*" says Wheeler. "And I thought, *Taxicabs.* So I said, 'What about the Great American Taxicab Race?' They lit up like a 400-watt bulb. And I'm thinking, *Holy crap, what am I going to do? I made all that up on the spot.*" So Wheeler set about finding cabbies from all over the country to drive their cars through an on-track obstacle course: a tollbooth on the backstretch, a hotel in the first turn.†

But there were only so many gimmicks that were going to lure the networks into showing a race. And that's where ESPN came into play. Rasmussen had everything NASCAR wanted: a medium for getting

---

*In the early days ESPN was on the air for twelve hours a day on weekdays and nineteen on weekends.

† When they ran the race on Memorial Day weekend in 1980, a hack from Indianapolis won. "We dropped the flag," says Wheeler. "The first lap they knocked the tollbooth down. Then they knocked the hotel down. It was the funniest thing you ever saw."

the sport into the homes of sports nuts (who, given a chance, might really like it), a little money to splash around, and no reservations about airing something as arcane as stock car racing. No one at the network was in any position to be picky. No one at the network — or at NASCAR — knew it yet, but the two would spend much of the next two decades helping each other grow.

Of course, in September 1979 Rasmussen had no idea if his channel would even make it. When the videotape machines he'd ordered arrived, there was no place in the incomplete broadcast center for them. So Rasmussen had them delivered to his son's condo, where the editing was done up until launch. Everything got done in time — or close enough to done — and the network hit the airwaves on September 7 as planned. There were glitches, to be sure (the first remote aired had no audio), but all in all things went well. And there was no shortage of events to talk about, the Southern 500 included, on the network's nightly highlight show, *Sports Recap,* which three days later would be rechristened *SportsCenter.*

While ESPN was preparing for its first week of broadcasting, the mainstream media were keeping alive a story that brightened up their dreary summer. In late August a White House press secretary let slip to an Associated Press writer that back in April, President Jimmy Carter had come face-to-face with an angry rabbit while vacationing near his home. The next day the AP ran a story that began: "A 'killer rabbit' attacked President Carter on a recent trip to Plains, Ga., penetrating Secret Service security and forcing the chief executive to beat back the beast with a canoe paddle." Writers had a field day, writing pieces that looked at the incident from every conceivable angle: Did Carter hit the rabbit? Could bunnies swim? Was this the same rabbit from *Monty Python and the Holy Grail?*

Bob Dole — who, based on his sponsorship of an unsuccessful bill advocating rabbits' rights, considered himself the Senate's foremost authority on the critters — said that Carter should apologize for "bashing a bunny in the head with a paddle." Dole said, "I'm sure the rabbit intended the president no harm. In fact, the poor thing was simply doing something a little unusual these days: trying to get aboard the president's boat. Everyone else seems to be jumping ship." The *Washington Post* ran an editorial pondering, "What did Mr. Carter ever do to rabbits?" And on September 3 a group called the Defenders of Wildlife unveiled a seven-point program to protect rabbits and advised the president that in the event of a future attack, his best course of action was to sound bells, rattle pots and pans, or "play recordings of feeding calls of hawks and owls," which no casual boater leaves home without. It was the kind of stuff that's hilarious — unless it's directed at you.

While the president was going about his business as the butt of so many *Paws* jokes, Jaws was feeling good about where he stood. Darrell Waltrip's motivation in the points race was simple. "I wanted to beat Richard because I didn't like Richard," he says. "That was just the underlying fact." It was a chance to get back at Petty for making Waltrip feel like an outsider, for not accepting him. And now that he had a 160-point lead* with eight races to go, it was starting to look like his crew chief had been right when he'd declared that it was his year. Waltrip had already clinched the $10,000 Olsonite Driver of the Year Award. The voting was done quarterly, and he had an insurmountable lead after three quarters. That meant ten grand and a banquet at the 21 Club in Manhattan after the season. In Darlington he was the one being asked to ride in parades and judge the Miss Southern 500 beauty pageant. He felt he could safely start crowing. And that was one thing Darrell Waltrip was very good at. He took aim at the aging Petty, suggesting that he should get a "prescription windshield."

---

*Petty had cut into Waltrip's lead, which had been 229 points after Talladega, by winning the Champion Spark Plug 400 in Michigan, where Waltrip had mechanical problems and finished nineteenth.

Before the Southern 500 — a race held on a day that was insufferably hot — he'd told ABC, "I'm in good shape. I've run hard everywhere I've been this year. I'm going to run hard today. But I know when this five-hundred miles is over, I'll be a worn-out thirty-two-year-old man. I can't imagine being forty-two and going through the same thing." He didn't have to remind anybody that Richard Petty just happened to be forty-two.

But Darlington was something more than a chance for Waltrip to stick it to Petty. David Pearson, another of the old schoolers who didn't care for Waltrip, was still filling in for Dale Earnhardt. He was back at a track where he'd won eight times, and he was in a very strong car. He seemed to be a real threat to win, and talk of that didn't sit well with Waltrip, who felt that he had established himself as the favorite by driving so well in the Rebel 500 in the spring. "So here I've got Richard on the ropes," Waltrip remembers. "Now we're going to Darlington. Well, Pearson's the king of Darlington. So here's another opportunity for me to knock out another big-time racer. I've beat Richard for the championship; they've got Pearson coming in. That's all I heard going into Darlington: 'Aw, Pearson's going to do this, Pearson's going to do that, and Pearson's the king of Darlington.' And I said — typical redneck — 'Yeah, watch this.'

"So sure enough, they drop that green flag, and we took off. We raced all day long, and as the day wore on, my car was just so much better than every other car. I drove Darlington great. I had a great car that day."

Petty didn't, at least not at the outset. After just eighteen laps engine problems forced him behind the wall, where his Chevrolet was descended upon by a dozen guys in matching red pants and blue shirts. They had the hood up for all of three seconds, time enough to switch the ignition box and send him on his way. But the failure of a $125 part put Petty down a lap, which meant that he couldn't drive his usual smooth race. He had to tax himself to get back on the lead lap. And on a sultry South Carolina day, taxing oneself wasn't a good idea. As Waltrip had smugly predicted, the King wilted in the heat. But he was in good company. Bobby Allison got out of his car and was taken to the infield medical center in an ambulance. Ricky Rudd, a whippersnapper of twenty-two, needed a relief driver because, as he confessed to the ABC cameras, he wasn't entirely sure where he was. Donnie Allison, who started on the pole but went out with engine problems, took over for Petty mid-race. Petty got out and collapsed into the arms of a crew member, who laid him on the pavement in the garage. Maurice Petty shooed away onlookers with a broom handle. With his flat cap, his bearish frame, and his thick beard, he looked like Led Zeppelin's notorious manager Peter Grant, keeping groupies off an overworked Robert Plant.

Two drivers were unaffected by the heat: Waltrip and Pearson, whose crew once again forgot to fill his water jug. Waltrip took the lead just past the halfway point and drove away from the pack. He put a lap on every car in the field except one. "Pearson's running second, and I'm determined I'm going to lap him," Waltrip recalls. "I'm slicing through traffic…he's running second, and I'm going to lap him. Buddy [Parrott] and all the guys said, 'Please slow down. Just slow down and ride it out. You've got this thing won.' And I said, 'Shut up and leave me alone. I know what I'm doing.' And sure enough, I lapped him. I mean I just drove by him and left him, and in five laps couldn't even see him."

In the pits Parrott was pleading with him to take it easy. "I was shaking my fist at him," Parrott says. "I was begging him. Please, you got a lap lead on the field. And he'd say, 'Oh, it feels so good. Ohhh, it feels so good.'"

A little too good. "I wanted to lap him again," remembers Waltrip, "because I was that much faster, and it was late in the day, and the longer we ran, the better I got. I was in great shape, and my car handled good, and that's all you needed at Darlington."

Well, that and a brain. And Waltrip's had apparently been under the impression that, this being Labor Day and all, it had the day off.

Waltrip's quest to embarrass Pearson by putting him two laps down ended on lap 298 of 367. "I just kept on going and going and going until I finally drove and turned a little too hard one time and hit the outside wall," says Waltrip. "Bam, bam, bam. I couldn't get it out of the wall; the thing is just eating the wall up. Knocked the right tire off of it. And there I sat, in the infield, wrecked."

Parrott radioed a message: "I said, 'How's it feel now, you…'"

Waltrip made it to the pits, and his crew made a few cursory repairs before rushing him back onto the track. In their haste, they didn't fix the right front suspension, which ten laps later caused the right front tire to go down and put Waltrip into the fence again. This time the crew had to fix the suspension, and by the time Waltrip rejoined the race, he was twelve laps behind Pearson. He finished eleventh. He actually gained 2 points on Petty, who struggled, but had he not thrown away a certain win, he would have picked up 51.

"That," Waltrip said thirty years later, "started our trouble."

After the bad judgment came the bad luck. In the CRC Chemicals 500 in Dover, Delaware, on September 16, both Waltrip and Petty had to deal with flat tires. Waltrip hit the wall and spent an hour in the garage getting repairs. Petty didn't hit anything, and as soon as his tire went down, the yellow flag came out for an unrelated incident, allowing the King to pit without losing a lap. Petty won, Waltrip finished twenty-ninth, and the lead shrank from 187 to 83. Now it was Petty's turn to talk. "I ain't settled into second," he said. "We picked up a hundred points on Darrell. Maybe a couple more licks like that will knock him in the head." Then Petty introduced what would be his main talking point down the stretch—that he had no reason to feel any pressure. "We're going for wins, not the championship," he said. "I've won six championships already, so that deal would mean a lot more to Darrell than it would to me."

The pressure was starting to eat at the entire DiGard outfit. "Darrell was not psychologically prepared to contend for a championship," says Gary Nelson. "Our team was not." As their lead dwindled, they started tinkering with the car more, tried to push the engines harder than they should have. "We were cracking more [cylinder] heads trying to make more power to get back what we had lost," says Nelson. "In those days there were no aluminum heads. They were cast iron, and they would crack if you ported them too much.* But if you ported them, they'd pick up power, so there was a fine line of how much you could port a head and have it last through the race."

They crossed the line in Martinsville the week after the Dover fiasco. The Old Dominion 500 was postponed after Martinsville got hit with five inches of rain.† When they made it up the next day, Waltrip led 184 of the first 275 laps and was out in front when his engine let go. Robert Yates, Nelson, and the rest of the crew reacted heroically, installing a new motor in less than twelve minutes, which most writers claimed was some sort of record. The change happened so fast that one Waltrip fan in the stands went to the bathroom and missed it entirely. When he got back to his seat, another guy told him his driver was now twenty-nine laps down. Thinking he was being messed with—there was no way an engine could be changed that fast—the Waltrip fan called the other guy a liar, which earned him a black eye, a torn shirt, and a cut lip.

While Waltrip was behind the wall getting a new motor, Petty was once again catching a break. He was racing Cale Yarborough for second place when their cars touched. Yarborough broke a ball joint and had to go to the pits for repairs. Petty got stuck on the curb on the inside

---

* Porting a head entails reshaping the intake and/or exhaust ports to make them more efficient—at the risk of damaging them.
† Part of the Wood Brothers shop was washed away. Twenty of their tires were found a mile away.

of the track and had to be pushed free, but his Chevy was unscathed. After the race Yarborough, who came home eighth, blamed the wreck on Petty, who finished second. "I'm sorry I didn't give you just a little more room," Petty told him. "Not much more, just a little bit."

"Where am I supposed to race? I was up on the curb, and I ain't supposed to run on the grass," said Yarborough, who, given his Daytona experience, would know. Some more words were exchanged, and Petty rescinded his apology. "I'm sorry I apologized if that's the way you're going to be about it," he said, and they went their separate ways.

Petty had made up 35 points on Waltrip, who finished eleventh. With five races left, the margin was a very manageable 48 points.

And then came more bad judgment. Waltrip's hubris had done him in at Darlington; at North Wilkesboro on October 14, it was impatience. On lap 310 of 400, Waltrip was racing Bobby Allison for the lead. Waltrip's brand-new Chevy Caprice was the fastest car on the track, but Allison was throwing some good blocks. Frustrated at not being able to get around Allison, Waltrip did what racers do: he used the chrome horn—his front fender. "We nudged ol' Bobby," Parrott recalled thirty years later as he sat in the infield at Daytona. "He'd race you clean, but the one thing you don't do to Bobby Allison, probably even now, is put one little bumper on him. If Bobby Allison was racing today and one of these guys came in and bump drafted him, he would be over there in Lake Lloyd somewhere, swimming."

There was no lake at North Wilkesboro, just a wall. It would have to do. "Bobby, for whatever reason, had gotten upset with me and he didn't like me anymore, and he'd just as soon as wrecked me as look at me," says Waltrip. "I should have been smarter, but I wasn't. So I got to racing him, and he'd bump me and I'd bump him. Bobby was kind of like Dale [Earnhardt]—if you hit me once, I'm going to hit you twice. First thing you know, we come off Turn 4, I start to go by Bobby on the inside, and he clips me."

Allison claimed he didn't do it on purpose, but he hooked Waltrip's car in the right rear. And, says Parrott, "the worst thing you can do in a race car is be hooked in the right rear. And Bobby Allison was a master." Waltrip spun out and hit the fence head-on near the start/finish line. "He stuffed us into the wall and nearly knocked the flag stand down," says Parrott. "The flag guys jumped out of the stand because Darrell was coming up in there." The car bounced off and continued to spin until the passenger side banged the fence. It was a mess. Waltrip got it into the garage, where he remained behind the wheel, a strange combination of pissed and loopy, as his crew tried to get the car fixed. "Why did he do it? Why did he do it? He's been cutting me off all day. I haven't laid a fender on him," he said, his eyes welling with tears.

The nose of the car was knocked in, and the frame needed to be straightened, so Nelson hooked a chain to the front end and attached the other end to the truck the team used to haul its trailer. He told Waltrip to stand on the brake while he floored the truck, which took off in the direction of the fence that kept the fans in the infield out of the garage. Just when it looked like Nelson was going to run over a pack of paying customers, the chain went taut and the truck jerked to a halt, giving the groggy Waltrip another jolt. "Darrell's eyes were kind of rolling around, and all of a sudden that chain got tight and his head hit the headrest," says Nelson. "We told him, 'Uh, Darrell, we got it fixed. Go back out there!'" Bill Gazaway, who was watching from the control tower overlooking the garage, came down to personally raise hell. "You're going to kill somebody!" he bellowed at Nelson.

The repairs took nine minutes, and Waltrip lost twenty-five laps. When he got back on the track, he was looking for revenge. He positioned himself in front of Allison and started running interference. It looked like another wreck was in the offing until NASCAR black-flagged Waltrip. Twice. He finished thirteenth, ten spots behind Petty. The lead was all but gone, a meager 17 points.

As the DiGard team loaded up what was left of the Caprice, someone asked Buddy Parrott if he wanted to take the front bumper, which had been yanked off the car, back to Charlotte. "Hell no," said Parrott. "I want to wrap it around somebody's neck."

### Standings After the Holly Farms 400

| | | |
|---|---|---|
| 1. | Darrell Waltrip | 4,357 |
| 2. | Richard Petty | 4,340 |
| 3. | Bobby Allison | 4,187 |
| 4. | Cale Yarborough | 4,089 |
| 5. | Benny Parsons | 3,813 |

## Chapter Twenty

# Pretty Good Americans

**Sunday, October 21**
**Race 29: American 500**
**Rockingham, North Carolina**
*and*
**Sunday, November 4**
**Race 30: Dixie 500**
**Hampton, Georgia**

RICHARD PETTY left North Wilkesboro enmeshed in the tightest points race in NASCAR history, but before he could consider his strategy for the suddenly relevant final three races of the season, he had to address more pressing concerns. Like figuring out what role he'd play in the selection of the leader of the free world.

Petty had a meeting later in the week with Ronald Reagan, the front-runner for the 1980 Republican presidential nomination. Jimmy Carter had won the 1976 election by holding on to the traditional Democratic power bases: the Northeast and the Solid South. With Carter's approval rating dipping below 30 percent, the GOP sensed he was going to be vulnerable, especially among the hordes of white evangelical southern males who'd helped put him in office. As the Reverend Jerry Falwell explained before the 1980 election, "Carter last time got that vote because he campaigned as a born-again Christian. But this time people will be more concerned about issues than characterizations. Carter has proceeded to undermine the American family." Falwell estimated that there were 3 million to 4 million evangelical voters who could swing either way, many of them southerners. It would be twenty-five years before someone came up with a name for them, but "NASCAR dads" were clearly going to play a role in the 1980 election.

And that's why Dutch was courting Richard and Lynda Petty. They met in a hotel suite and chatted amiably for an hour about their families and their general visions for America. Carter was hip to the importance of the NASCAR set, too. In September 1978 he'd had a slew of them to the White House. Never before had so many cowboy boots trod upon the South Lawn, where the five hundred guests — more than one dressed in a three-piece polyester suit — ate baked southern ham, jalapeño corn bread, and potato salad as Willie Nelson sang "Whiskey River" and "Up Against the Wall, Redneck Mother." During the 1976 campaign, Carter had painted himself as a friend of stock car racing, dropping the green flag at the Atlanta Motor Speedway — where he had been an occasional ticket seller when his peanut crops were poor — and promising to invite the racing community to the White House if elected. On the night he made good on that pledge, though, he was detained by the Middle East peace talks at Camp David. Instead of trying to explain the significance of "tradin' paint" to Menachem Begin and Anwar Sadat and excusing himself from the negotiations, he sent his regrets to the NASCAR dinner. "It would take something of the magnitude of the Camp David summit to keep him away," First Lady Rosalynn Carter told the guests by way of apology.

It was probably just as well, though. Carter could count few support-ers in the very conservative stock car racing circles.* Big Bill France told the *Washington Post* that the only reason he showed up at the White House was that he "got an invitation. I didn't vote for Jimmy Carter in the last election. Frankly, I've always been a [George] Wallace man. If he hadn't been shot, I think we would have been here four years ear-lier." Most of the drivers were similarly underwhelmed by Carter, but they weren't going to let that keep them from visiting the White House. Several went inside and had their pictures taken under the portrait of a president they could admire: the old Scots-Irish man of the people himself, Andrew Jackson. One of the few allies Carter had in the sport was his close friend Cale Yarborough, and he became a Democrat only because his buddy got elected president. Yarborough was a conserva-tive at heart: in 1974 he had become the first Republican commissioner in Florence County, South Carolina, since Reconstruction.

Petty also dabbled in politics. In 1978 he threw his ten-gallon hat in the ring for Randolph County commissioner. The timing was pecu-liar. Petty was in the midst of the worst losing streak of his career, and here he was spending his spare time driving the other GOP candidates around the county in a van, going door-to-door, signing autographs, and discussing pressing issues — taxes, crime, why he'd left Dodge for Chevy — with the voters. But his motives were sincere. Petty first enter-tained the idea of running when the Peacock Massage Salon — home, if the marquee was to be believed, of the "Prettiest Girls in the South" — opened up on Route 220, not far from the Petty compound. Eventually, Petty's platform grew into a sort of Appalachian Village

---

* The same couldn't be said for Billy Carter. The NASCAR dinner marked the first time in well over a year the president's brother had made an appearance at the White House. He was an extremely popular guest with the drivers — primarily because he, like them, looked and felt like an outsider. A reporter asked Billy if he was comfort-able on the South Lawn. "Yes," he told the writer before turning to a friend and stage-whispering, "Shit, no!"

Green Preservation Society. In the King's eyes, the sheriff (a Democrat) and the commissioners (four of five of whom were Democrats) were not adequately protecting the small-town values that made Randleman the kind of place where a man would want to raise a family. As Petty put it simply, "It's the kind of a deal where it's time for a change."

So he occasionally turned his pit wall bull sessions into stump speeches. He referred to the leader of the free world as "Peanut" in public. Before one 1978 race he asserted, "Since Carter came in, the country's just gone *bllllumphhh,*" as his finger made the international symbol for a nosedive. "I'd rather have Ford still in there. We were better off when Nixon was in there." Petty endorsed Jesse Helms in his successful reelection campaign for the U.S. Senate, going so far as to film a commercial for him. The message Petty put out resonated. Despite alienating the Dart-driving segment of the electorate, he easily collected the most votes in the race for county commissioner, and the other two GOP candidates rode his coattails into office.

With unemployment and inflation on the rise, the 1978 elections brought good results for all Republicans. They picked up three seats in the U.S. Senate and fifteen in the House, and with the economy still struggling in the fall of 1979, they had their eyes on the White House, which looked ripe for the picking. *Time* explained the political landscape: "For much of the year, Carter appeared so ineffective a leader that his seeming weakness touched off an unprecedentedly early and crowded scramble to succeed him."

Carter's approval rating had dipped below 30 percent during the summer. "In many respects this would appear to be the worst of times," his domestic adviser, Stuart Eizenstat, wrote to him. "I do not need to detail for you the political damage we are suffering." Eizenstat wrote the note in July; after that things got worse. Following the gas riots and the malaise speech came the killer rabbit. Just as that aquatic fiasco was dying down, on September 15 Carter entered a 10K race at Catoctin Mountain Park near Camp David. Wearing a yellow headband and a T-shirt with the number 39, Carter struggled as he climbed a hill early in the race. "I've got to keep trying," gasped the fifty-four-year-old president, who was sweating profusely. "If I can just make the top, I've got it made." And with that he collapsed into the arms of a Secret Service agent. He was rushed back to Camp David, stripped, covered in cold towels, and given a quart of saline solution intravenously.

There were factors that mitigated the president's apparent wimpiness. The hilly course was brutal, and Carter, a devoted runner who jogged between forty and fifty miles a week and was in very good shape, simply pushed himself too hard as he tried to shave four minutes off his personal-best 10K time of fifty minutes. But it was another PR debacle. The *Washington Post* described him as "ashen" and "in distress." One aide mused, "I suppose this will replace the rabbit stories." Another asked a writer, "Are you going to headline it, 'Carter Drops Out of Race'?"

The crack was a reference to the percolating talk that Carter might not even seek reelection in 1980. Senator Ted Kennedy had already launched a viable campaign to challenge him for the Democratic nomination, and beyond Kennedy—if Carter made it that far—lurked a strong field of Republicans, led by Reagan and John Connally. The former Texas governor, like Reagan, realized the value of an endorsement from someone like Richard Petty, so Connally scheduled his own meeting with the King, in New York on Monday, October 22.

But first Petty had a race to run.

Like the first go-round in Rockingham, the air at the American 500 was charged with the electricity that's generated by the distinct possibility of a fight. This time the combatants weren't Cale Yarborough and Donnie Allison. Neither one of them had much to fight for. Cale was languishing in fourth place, while Donnie had, since abandoning his quest to run the entire schedule, skipped eleven of the last eighteen races. No, this time everyone was watching Darrell Waltrip and Bobby Allison.

The day after their run-in in North Wilkesboro, Waltrip ranted to the *Tennessean,* "It's the worst thing that's ever happened to me in racing. The incident cost me the race, probably the national championship and the best friend I had in auto racing." The possibility of innocent drivers once again losing their cars because of someone else's bad blood at the Rock wasn't lost on the rest of the field. "Everybody's concerned about the potential for problems, even more so than we were here in March," said Benny Parsons.

Allison wasn't apologetic about wrecking Waltrip, and he didn't sound like he was losing any sleep over the damaged state of their relationship. "I feel sorry for him," Allison said. "I think the pressure may be getting to him." Waltrip, meanwhile, dropped the defeatist tone once he got to the track and did his best to chill out. In the garage he put his arm around Petty and told the assembled reporters, "I just wish it was me and him racing each other." Then he went on the attack. "[Allison is] someone to talk about pressure," Waltrip said. "He's 42 years old, almost ready to retire as a driver, and he's never won a Grand National driving title. What can he say about pressure? If I don't win this year, at least I have several years left in which to win it. That's something he can't say."

Petty, meanwhile, just stood there and smiled. Whenever he was asked if the fact that he was now in the running for another championship meant there was any pressure on him, he'd just grin, chew on that thin cigar, and insist he'd never felt pressure in his life. "The way I look at it is that it's the kind of deal where a beagle is running a rabbit," he said. "The rabbit is in the lead, but the pressure is all on him. And if people keep talking about it like they apparently are, I don't see how Darrell and his team can help but to start thinking along those lines. That's just human nature."

Whatever role Petty's mind games played in Waltrip's demise, they would have meant nothing had Petty not backed up his talk with one of the most impressive driving stretches of his career. He'd won more races and sat on more poles before, but never against such deep fields.* Throughout 1979 he had been consistent and stayed out of trouble, and the engines built by his brother, Maurice, had made it to the finish of every race. In years past that probably wouldn't have been enough to win a championship, but the infusion of so many new, well-funded teams placed a premium on consistency. Since his wreck in the first Rockingham race, Petty had finished in the top 5 in twenty of twenty-five races, and he'd been worse than eleventh just once.

Petty qualified seventh in Rockingham, four spots behind Waltrip, and both seemed content with the way their cars were running. The day before the race, Waltrip didn't even take his car onto the track, instead moseying around the garage in an autumnal outfit—brown slacks and a matching brown sweater—and consulting with Buddy Parrott before slipping away. Petty left early in the day as well. One of the few drivers who stuck around was Benny Parsons. He was in the garage because that's where the radio was, and he wanted to listen to the Duke-Maryland football game.

No one suffered for missing practice. Both Petty and Waltrip picked up five bonus points for leading early in the race, and Waltrip led the pack at the halfway point of the 492-lap race. He gave the lead up to Petty on lap 267 and was still running second a few minutes later when race officials noticed small puffs of smoke coming from Waltrip's car. A small crack had developed in the oil pan, sending small drops onto the header. All of the oil burned off before it could get onto the track, but Bill Gazaway and the rest of the officials had no way of knowing that. All they knew was that Waltrip's engine was smoking, which meant it was leaking. On lap 294 they black-flagged Waltrip, forcing him into

---

*Petty won ten straight races in 1967, a mark that hasn't been approached since. Not to belittle the accomplishment, but in only four of those ten races was the field bigger than thirty cars, and David Pearson ran in only three of the ten.

the pits to have the crack repaired. He lost eight laps and any chance he had of winning.

The rest of the race offered spectacular wrecks and even more spectacular racing. A few laps after Waltrip was black-flagged, Harry Gant started to feel a vibration in his Chevrolet. Before he had time to get the car into the pits, his front right tire popped off and bounced over the fence, crushing the roof of a car in the parking lot. That was nothing compared to the carnage on lap 426, when Bobby Allison and Ricky Rudd got together, sending both cars hard into the wall backward. The filler neck on Allison's fuel tank broke, causing a fuel leak that ignited before the car stopped moving. "Did I know I was on fire? Damn right!" Allison said later. "I started getting my straps loose long before the car stopped. I wasn't paying much attention to traffic when I bailed out. I just wanted to get away from the car." A groggy Rudd got out of his car and lay down next to it, unaware that it was also leaking fuel. Allison ran to Rudd and pulled him out of the gas puddle.

As Allison was dragging Rudd to safety, Petty was stuck behind leader Benny Parsons, who had lapped the field. Shortly after the restart, Petty and Yarborough got around Parsons, and eight laps later they got the break they needed when Baxter Price spun out in front of them. Petty and Yarborough were both able to swing inside and avoid hitting him, and the yellow flag allowed them to pull up onto Parsons's bumper for the restart. Petty got around Parsons on lap 445, but Parsons returned the favor the next time around, with Yarborough lingering close by in third. Waltrip, eight laps down, could do nothing but watch and root like hell for anyone but Petty. "I was setting back there yelling, 'Hold him, boys! Hold him!'" Waltrip said. But Petty took the lead for the last time on lap 484 and held off Parsons by a car length, with Yarborough glued to Parsons's back bumper in third. Waltrip came home sixth. Petty, who had come to Rockingham trailing by 17 points, had made up 25. Waltrip was no longer the leader. He was livid after the race, convinced that NASCAR was still punishing him for his late-race obstructing of Allison the week before. "There wasn't any [oil] going on the race track," he said. "NASCAR knew that. What it amounts to is that you get into something one week like the deal at Wilkesboro, and the next week you can expect something like this to happen."

While his conspiracy theory was just that, Waltrip did have legitimate cause to feel that he'd been harshly done by. So no one blamed him when he offered NASCAR a piece of unsolicited advice: "They can take their black flag and do you know what with it."

After a week off, the fun resumed at Atlanta. The Friday night before the race saw the long-awaited premiere of "Dukes Meet Cale Yarborough," Yarborough's small-screen debut. In the episode Yarborough was down the Duke boys' way to practice for the Illinois 500 (or as all the Hazzard County locals called it, the "Illinoise" 500), a race that paid its winner the unheard-of sum of $100,000.* As Waylon Jennings explained in his narration, "Well, it seems Mister Cale Yarborough has been doing a little shade-tree mechanic work. They come up with a real, live thingamajig." The thingamajig in question was a turbocharger, which was activated by a giant red switch on the dash, right next to a giant red flashing light. (Apparently, either the race inspectors in Illinoise were a laissez-faire bunch or they were a bit slow on the uptake.) Rumors of the existence of the thingamajig spread through racing circles and piqued the attention of the rival Jethro brothers, who decided to steal it from Yarborough. The episode ended with Yarborough driving a Dodge Charger — the same make as the Duke boys' General Lee — seven-hundred miles to Illinois and winning the race with it. The plot was preposterous but all in good fun, and it won its time slot handily.

---

*Richard Petty got $73,900 for winning Daytona, the biggest purse of the season.

The following night, as the racers slept, a situation that would dominate the national landscape for the next year was developing half a world away, in Tehran. The day after the American 500 in Rockingham, President Carter had allowed the deposed shah of Iran into the United States to receive treatment for his pancreatic cancer, ratcheting up the already fervent anti-American sentiment in Iran. On the morning of November 4, scores of students overran the U.S. embassy there, originally intending to stage a sit-in and then go home. But as more protesters showed up—they were bused in at one point—the event snowballed. Ayatollah Khomeini went on the radio and issued a call for the students to take over the embassy. Sixty-six hostages were seized. Two weeks later thirteen were let go, but the remaining fifty-three were still being held, and their captors showed no signs of releasing them.*

The immediate reaction in the United States was to unite and offer unconditional support. Although Carter made little progress in procuring the release of the hostages, his approval rating immediately soared to 60 percent. That bump—combined with increased scrutiny of the 1969 Chappaquiddick incident in which Ted Kennedy pleaded guilty to leaving the scene of a car accident in which a female passenger was killed—effectively knocked Kennedy out of the presidential race. But as the hostages remained in captivity ABC started airing a nightly update (which would become *Nightline*), the ongoing crisis became another scarlet W, a symbol of the president's perceived weakness.

The Republicans nominated Reagan at their convention in Detroit in July 1980. Richard Petty spoke on the first night as part of the "Together...A New Beginning" entertainment program that also featured Jimmy Stewart, Donny and Marie Osmond, Wayne

---

*One was released in July 1980, leaving the fifty-two who would remain until the crisis came to its conclusion in January 1981.

Newton, Vicki Lawrence, Michael Landon, Buddy Ebsen, and Lyle Waggoner.* Throughout the fall Reagan hammered Carter on the hostages. Carter's situation wasn't helped by the fact that Election Day was November 4 — the one-year anniversary of the start of the crisis. Still, Carter's pollsters had him ahead by three points until the only debate between the two candidates, on October 28. The next day most major news outlets declared Carter the winner of the debate, but voters saw it differently. "There were two things that signaled Carter's demise," says Craig Shirley, a longtime Republican adviser and the author of *Rendezvous with Destiny,* a book about the 1980 campaign. "One, the debate. Two, the hostage crisis. The American people basically said, 'That's it.' The crisis was the final bit of evidence of the impotence of America and the American government." Reagan won in a landslide. Southern white males — the NASCAR dads who had helped put Carter in the White House — abandoned the president en masse. Sixty percent of them voted for Reagan.

As much as NASCAR had benefited from Carter's election in 1976, it may have benefited even more from his defeat. Dutch was more of a NASCAR kind of guy. One of his speechwriters compared him to a former president: Andrew Jackson, the old Scots-Irish man of the people who had been such a popular photo backdrop during NASCAR's White House visit. And the ideals Reagan preached as he ascended to the presidency meshed perfectly with the ideals the sport prided itself on, ensuring that as NASCAR built on the foundation laid in 1979, it would do so in an atmosphere conducive to acceptance and rapid growth.

On the day of the 1979 Daytona 500, the *Washington Post* had run a long story on NASCAR in which David Pearson had talked politics: "What really gets me hot is welfare, taxes and food stamps. Too many people aren't interested in working because they can do better in the welfare line. The

---

* The program was put together by Mike Curb, a Reagan aide and record producer. He later got into NASCAR as a car owner.

cities, counties and states should get them off their butts and put them to work. The American people's taxes are paying them to sit on their butts." It echoed a statement Richard Petty had made earlier: "Democrats are trying to help too many people who don't want to work for a living just because they were born in America." Virtually every driver had slogged his way to the top on his own. A race wasn't five-on-five, nine-on-nine, or eleven-on-eleven. It was one man working by himself. And anything he was going to get, he was going to get himself. More than any other sport, there were no handouts in auto racing. That by-the-bootstraps work ethic embraced by the drivers dovetailed with the new brand of populism Reagan preached, one that stressed the importance of the individual. "In this present crisis, government is not the solution to our problem; government is the problem," he said in his first inaugural address in January 1981. Any man, he was saying, could thrive on his own with a little hard work.

The second pillar of Reagan's message was that there was nothing wrong with the country. Reagan wouldn't be caught giving a speech suggesting that the people of the Republic were in some way responsible for its shortcomings. Throughout the campaign Reagan spoke of America as a beacon of hope, a world leader, "a shining city on a hill." Displays of patriotism—jingoism, his critics would label it—came into vogue, especially as the cold war escalated in the early 1980s.

The NASCAR family has always been quick to rally round the flag. "All I know," Bill France Jr. said of his customers in February of '79, "is that when we play 'The Star-Spangled Banner,' they all stand up and cheer. They're pretty good Americans." Similarly, whenever anyone asked France's father who NASCAR fans were, he'd tell them, "They're the people who win wars for this country."*

---

*In keeping with that theme, Humpy Wheeler's prerace productions in Charlotte often included military exercises. In 1984 he staged a reenactment of Operation Urgent Fury, the United States' 1983 invasion of Grenada. The show lasted fifteen minutes and featured thatched huts being strafed by planes and palm trees splintered by simulated gunfire.

Reagan's ascension transformed the national mood. His message celebrated the rugged, God-fearing, patriotic individual. And NASCAR
was offering up forty of them on display every weekend.

Petty and Waltrip staged the same production in the days leading up
to the Dixie 500 that they they'd been putting on for weeks: Petty insisting he didn't care about the championship—"If I win it, it'll be
a pure money thing"—and Waltrip defending himself from charges
that he couldn't handle the p word. "I'm not saying the pressure has
gotten to me," Waltrip lectured the media. "You're saying the pressure
has gotten to me." Then, as he walked away, he pointed to Petty and
said, "The King is here. So let this poor second-class SOB change his
clothes."

Atlanta International Raceway is big and fast, the kind of track that
suited Buddy Baker's let-it-all-hang-out style. Baker won his seventh
pole of the season—clinching the $25,000 bonus for winning the most
poles—and then, as he had all year, went out of the race early with
mechanical trouble. Neither of the two title contenders had qualified
well—Petty was thirteenth, one spot ahead of Waltrip—but by lap
64 of 328, Waltrip had taken the lead, which meant a five-point bonus.
Waltrip was again out in front on lap 129 when he ran over some debris in the first turn. As he pulled into the pits to get fresh tires, Dave
Marcis pulled out of his pit stall right in front of him. Waltrip slammed
on his brakes and went skidding sideways past his box.

Backing up in the pits is against the rules, but, like many NASCAR
regulations, there's some wiggle room. Moments earlier Grant Adcox
had thrown his car in reverse and backed up a few feet into his stall,
and the officials in the pits didn't say a word. Adcox—a middle-of-
the-packer making just his sixth start of the year—had little to lose.
Waltrip, however, couldn't afford to chance being black-flagged for
the third race in a row. Forced to make a split-second decision as his
car sat sideways on pit road, he opted to go back onto the track, circle

around—on two flat tires—and enter the pits again. When he exited with new tires, he was two laps down.

Petty had problems of his own. He spun out on lap 208 and had to stop for tires, which left him one lap down. Like Waltrip, he had no chance to win the race. The two of them were now worried about one thing: racing each other. As they waged their personal battle back in the field, Neil Bonnett, Dale Earnhardt, and Cale Yarborough were putting on a show up front. Bonnett had used a soft set of tires to qualify. Rules stipulated that a car had to start the race on the same tires it had used for qualifying, so Bonnett and Wood Brothers were gambling that there would be a caution early in the race and they'd be able to stop and get some better tires on the car. But the race stayed green for 175 laps, and Bonnett got lapped. Once he got fresh rubber, he got back around the leader, Yarborough, as the caution flag came out on lap 199, and sixteen laps later he passed Yarborough again to take the lead. Over the next one hundred laps, Bonnett, Earnhardt, and Yarborough exchanged the lead twelve times. With seventeen to go, Bonnett came to a realization: all this battling was killing his tires. He radioed Eddie Wood that he was going to drop back to third place for a while. "I felt if I could make one more run at 'em, I just might win it," Bonnett said later. "And I knew I had to have cooler tires to do that."

While Bonnett was playing possum, the Petty-Waltrip duel turned on an unexpected alliance. Waltrip had gotten one of his laps back, joining Petty as the only two cars one lap down. Petty was ahead of Waltrip by about two hundred yards when Bobby Allison, who was on the lead lap in fourth place but out of touch with the leaders, pulled up on Waltrip. At a mile and a half, Atlanta isn't as wide-open as Daytona, so drafting is less of a factor. But two cars will run a little faster than one, so Allison, who was trying desperately to run down the top three cars, began towing Waltrip, with whom he was no longer on speaking terms. With nine laps to go, the enemies got around Petty.

Five laps later Bonnett and his cool tires made their move. He whipped around Yarborough and then Earnhardt, and he stayed there as the three came out of the fourth turn on the last lap. Unable to get inside Bonnett, Earnhardt tried to rattle him by passing him on the outside. Earnhardt got alongside Bonnett—two of the sport's rising stars, side by side—but he came up half a car length short. A few seconds later, Waltrip crossed the finish line ahead of Petty. Fifth place was worth 5 points more than sixth, and Waltrip had picked up 5 more points for leading a lap. The 10-point swing put Waltrip 2 points ahead going into the final race. And it wouldn't have happened without Allison. "That's the way the sport is," said Buddy Parrott, who had been apoplectic after Waltrip had overshot his pit stall but was now flashing a wide grin. "One week you're cussing a fella, the next week you want to kiss him."

### Standings After the Dixie 500

1. Darrell Waltrip         4,672
2. Richard Petty           4,670
3. Bobby Allison           4,458
4. Cale Yarborough         4,434
5. Benny Parsons           4,068

## Chapter Twenty-one

# The Shootout

*Sunday, November 18*
Race 31: Los Angeles Times 500
Ontario, California

WITH THE exception of the guy who owned the operation, the DiGard crew wasn't exactly filled with Vegas types. They weren't high rollers, they didn't wear pinky rings, and no one was telling Buddy Parrott that he was so money and he didn't even know it. But there they all were on the Strip, just days before the final race of the season, the one that would decide whether they would complete a historic collapse. DiGard owner Bill Gardner had originally planned the field trip as a precursor to an even bigger celebration, the one that would follow the clinching of the Winston Cup championship, but Darrell Waltrip's October demise gave the getaway more of a condemned-man's-last-meal kind of vibe.

Most of the team members had flown in, but Parrott and his wife couldn't get a flight from Charlotte, so they flew into LA and drove a borrowed Lincoln Continental through the desert. The Lincoln lost a tire along the way, so Parrott had to foot the repair bill, leaving him only $15 to play with at the Sands.

It was tough to glean a portent from the team's performance at the casino. Waltrip stuck to the slots. "He won three or four jackpots," says Gardner. "I thought it was an omen. People go their whole lives and don't win one." The boss was less fortunate. "I watched Bill Gardner lose $50,000," remembers Parrott.* "I had never been to Vegas. I thought it was just a show. He had these chips, and I thought, *It's not real money.*"

Parrott's fifteen bucks didn't last long, but he still had a high time. "Gardner took us out, fed us food that I had never seen before," he says. "Them snails." And Gardner planned on bringing everyone back for another celebration after the Ontario race. He booked a gourmet room at the Sands and planned a menu that would blow Parrott's mind.

All they had to do was win the championship.

The math was simple. Waltrip's lead on Richard Petty was 2 points. The difference between any two spots in the race standings ranged from 3 to 5 points, so whoever had the better day in Ontario would be the Winston Cup champ. It was easily the tightest points race ever; the last time the final race of the season had even mattered in the standings was in 1973.

When Waltrip's team got to Ontario, they discovered that they were staying at the same Holiday Inn as Evel Knievel, who just happened to be defying death in that neck of the woods that weekend. And Knievel was up for some fun: "If you liked Crown Royal, you could drink all the Crown Royal you wanted to," says Parrott. Petty was staying at the Holiday Inn, too, and relations were cordial. Parrott had a long talk in

---

* As is usually the case with casino-related endeavors, no one remembers it quite the same. Gardner says that he thought he came out ahead. Waltrip recalls Gardner losing a hundred grand.

the bar with Petty, who employed Parrott's sister. At the track Petty was still telling anyone who would listen that all the pressure was on Waltrip. "I'm already here," Petty said as he leaned against the back of his hauler, pointing to an imaginary ladder rung with the thin cigar in his hand. "I can't go nowhere else. Pressure? I don't know how to spell the word." And then, after everyone left the hauler, he took a swig of his stomach medicine.

But there was some truth in what Petty was saying. Unlike Waltrip, he had a sparkling résumé to stand on. No one was going to judge him on how he handled the '79 points race, so he had no need to play it close to the vest come race day. He'd caught Waltrip with a stretch of aggressive, carefree racing. "He has been bumping and banging and spinning out, doing everything," Waltrip said in Ontario. "And he has been getting away with it."

The novelty of an important season finale drew a larger-than-usual crowd to the press box, as many of the East Coast papers that normally decided against sending a writer across the country for a meaningless race sent someone to Ontario. The track was a knockoff of the Indianapolis Motor Speedway, a two-and-a-half-mile rectangle with four straights and four very sharp turns. The front stretch and backstretch seemed interminable. You just pointed the car down the track and stood on the gas for twenty seconds. If you needed to fix your hair in the mirror — or, if you were David Pearson, you craved a butt — this was the place for it. The pressing question Ontario presented teams with was how big a gear they should use. A bigger ratio meant more speed — and more risk of a blown engine. Most drivers were using a ratio of 3.64:1. Petty went with 3.70.

Without the luxury of six championship trophies to fall back on, Waltrip had a more difficult decision — one that was made trickier by the fact that Petty's campaign to convince the garage that Waltrip was cracking seemed to be working. Waltrip said, "People have come up to me and put their arm around my shoulder and looked at me with real concern in their faces and said, 'You all right?' I'd like to haul off and deck them when they do that. Richard's using good tactics. They all believe everything Richard says because he's the King. They don't bother him about his feeling any 'p-p-p-pressure.'" The Pettys' mind games weren't all played out through the press. "Lee Petty would come by and talk to Darrell—'How's it going?'" says Gary Nelson. "I can remember Lee standing there talking to Darrell and Darrell thinking this guy's his friend." Waltrip heard through the grapevine that the Pettys were using different spindles in Ontario, so he made the DiGard crew change his, too, an extreme tactic. Nelson never found out for sure who started the spindle rumor, but he's always believed someone in the Petty camp planted the story. "I realized why Petty had won so many championships," says Nelson. "They found certain nerves within a team and jumped on them."

The prerace festivities featured a shoot-out motif, with the two title contenders dressed up as Wild West gunslingers. Waltrip was in a frilly vest that looked like someone's leftover Village People Halloween costume. Petty brought his own accessory to his snappy outfit: an STP Winston Cup champion belt buckle. Their crews dressed up as well, all in western gear, except for Maurice Petty, who was decked out in a set of Union army blues. Before the race Ken Squier, who was doing the tape-delay broadcast for CBS, stood between Petty and Waltrip and asked if they had any thoughts on the race.

"No," said Waltrip with a laugh.

"It's just another race," Petty insisted, and if the mood of his crew—especially his crew chief and cousin, Dale Inman—was any indication, he wasn't feigning insouciance. They seemed more interested in what was happening 2,500 miles away, in Washington, than in Ontario. The Redskins were the closest NFL franchise to the Petty compound, so Richard and Dale had grown up as Washington fans. The Los Angeles Times 500 was taking place the same day as the

Redskins-Cowboys game. First place was on the line in what was an especially tasty edition of the rivalry. Dallas had run up the score the year before, and a few days before the rematch Washington's Diron Talbert had fired up his teammates by getting up at a team meeting and saying of the Cowboys, "Just pretend they're Iranians." All day Inman had been pestering the CBS guys about the Redskins' chances. "I can get more excited about a close ball game, a basketball game or a football game, than I do for the race," Inman said. "Because when the race is real close, I know Richard's putting out all the effort and we've done all we can do for him."

Petty started fifth. Waltrip, whose team had decided not to be too risky with their setup, qualified tenth. Cale Yarborough won the pole — his first of the year, which spared his sponsor, Busch, the embarrassment of having to stage the 1980 Busch Clash without its car in the field — and Kyle Petty qualified twenty-sixth. Petty and Waltrip each picked up 5 points early in the race for leading a lap. Petty took his Chevy to the front on lap 6. Waltrip inherited the lead by staying out an extra lap when the caution flag came out following a John Rezek spinout on lap 9. Waltrip was lingering about half a lap behind the front pack, near the edge of the top 10, when Rezek spun again on lap 41. This time Waltrip was right behind him. The smoke from the spin was heavy, with Rezek lurking in it somewhere, like an iceberg in the fog. Waltrip didn't want to go into the smoke blind, so he spun his car on purpose, looping around Rezek and coming to rest on the grass with the engine still running. The car was clean, but the abrupt stop flat-spotted the tires. Waltrip pulled all the way around and into the pits. "They'll change all four tires on this," the wry Englishman David Hobbs said on the CBS broadcast. "Possibly change the driver's underwear."

It was a hell of a save, but it was followed by another mistake—this one massive—by the DiGard team. Waltrip was about half a lap behind the leaders when he entered the pits. His crew changed the tires and took a long look at the car to make sure they didn't have a repeat of Darlington, when the broken suspension had led to a second flat tire. The only constraint on their time was that they had to get back on the track ahead of the pace car, but that shouldn't have been a problem, since it took the pace car forever to complete a circuit. "That big old racetrack—there ain't no way you lose a lap," says Waltrip. "But we did."

Waltrip was the only car in the lead pack that didn't beat the pace car out of the pits. He pulled in behind it—passing the pace car is a no-no—and was forced to trudge around the track at something near the legal speed limit. The rest of the leaders tore around at racing speed, crossed the start/finish line, and queued up behind him. When the race restarted, Waltrip was the first car in line, but he was actually the last car on the lead lap. It's an oddity in racing, and when it occurs, it confuses everyone, even the drivers. Waltrip, whose radio was down, thought he was leading the race. Only when his communication with Parrott was restored did he find out that he was a lap down. "It was like someone had kicked a ladder out from under me," Waltrip said later.

Hope wasn't lost, though. As Yarborough had shown in Daytona, getting unlapped wasn't impossible. If Waltrip could keep the leader behind him when a yellow flag came out, he'd be back in business. But Benny Parsons blew by him on the restart, and Waltrip didn't have the muscle to pass him back. ("We guessed wrong on the combination," said Parrott.) The only way he was going to regain his lap was if someone gave it to him, and Waltrip wasn't high on anyone's gift list. Every time a caution came out, Parsons raced Waltrip back to the stripe. Parsons said he was doing it because he didn't want to let a car that could possibly win the race back into the mix. Parrott made a couple of trips to Parsons's pit stall to ask for a break, but none was forthcoming. "He didn't want me to win the championship," Waltrip recalled. "I don't think anybody wanted me to win it." Waltrip finally told Parrott, "I don't want to do this, but if that happens again, I'm going to wreck him, because he's doing that on purpose. He knows if I get that lap back, I'll win the championship." But the opportunity never presented itself.

Waltrip's last hope was that Petty would blow up or wreck, which for a while looked entirely possible. Petty had said all along that he was going to race for the win, but that seemed like just another mixed signal meant to screw with Waltrip's head. Apparently he meant it, though. "The champion should be the cat out there running as hard as he can every race he runs," Petty explained later. "I've found out you can get in just as much trouble if you cool it as if you don't. Basically, a cat's better off if he runs hard all day." On lap 75, he brushed the wall hard enough to dent some sheet metal. "The driver just lost it," Petty joked later. He continued to fight for the lead, hard, in the last fifteen laps, giving Inman fits (though he was buoyed by the news that the Redskins were beating the crap out of the Cowboys). In the last laps, when it was apparent he couldn't beat Parsons, Petty finally backed off a little and cruised home in fifth place. Waltrip was eighth, the first car a lap down. Petty won the Winston Cup by 11 points, the narrowest margin in history.

Petty pulled onto pit road, and Inman lowered the window net. Petty braced for an invasion, a hug, a Pepsi bath, something. Instead, Inman screamed, "The Redskins won! The Redskins won!"

"Is that any way to treat a champion, now?" Petty asked.

After the race, the King held court, twirling his little cigar. "Last year was the low ebb of my twenty years in racing, no doubt about it," he said. "From that standpoint, winning the title again is very satisfying." As he considered where he'd come from, he also had to feel pretty good about where Petty Enterprises was going. His front tire changer—Kyle, his heir apparent—came home fourteenth. And they didn't know it yet, but a fourth-generation driver would soon be in the picture. Pattie Petty was pregnant.

Back in the garage, Waltrip—who was expected to attend a joint press conference with Petty—was in no mood to answer questions. He closed the door on his garage stall, emerging after a few minutes only to go directly into the back of the team's hauler to change his clothes.

Only Stevie was granted admittance. They pulled the door of the truck down almost all the way, so the only thing the curious onlookers could see were the green shoes he had put on. A track worker knocked on the truck. "Do you want an escort to the press box?"

"No, thank you," came the reply through the door. "Not today, I think. Please give everybody my regards and regrets."

Waltrip finally emerged, looking like a man who had been stripped of not only his dream but also his fashion sense. His green shoes were complemented by matching pants and a garish purple and white shirt. "I ain't never going to figure it out," he said of the lost lap. "Never. They took it away from me and broke my heart."

He did a few TV interviews, reiterating that he didn't understand what had happened. But he realized that ultimately what had done him in was that he hadn't brought a strong enough car. "I told everybody Richard was coming to race," he said. "Richard always comes to race. We prepared the car more to go five hundred miles than to race."

He sounded ready to do some more finger-pointing, and a writer gave him the perfect opportunity by asking if he was saying that Parrott had made the fateful decision.

Waltrip thought for an instant. "No," he said. "No, it was a unanimous decision."

Another competition was decided in Ontario. Dale Earnhardt finished ninth to sew up the Rookie of the Year title. It had been a foregone conclusion for a couple of weeks that he'd win the award. NASCAR had an elaborate formula that took each rookie's fifteen best results into account, but that was just a guide. The winner was picked by a four-man panel made of the reigning Winston Cup champ, in this case Yarborough, and three NASCAR officials. Not only did Earnhardt have the best results — he finished seventh in the season points race despite missing four races after the wreck at Pocono — but he had clearly shown the most moxie, heart, allure, and every other intangible that would appeal to the voters. Earnhardt had done things no other rookie had done. He'd won races. He'd put a legitimate fear of God into the old pros. He'd inspired fans. He'd started a movement.

Yet as the forces of the racing universe tugged at him, pulling him on the road from simple country boy to icon in a sport America was finally ready to embrace, you wouldn't know it by looking in his garage or his closet. In late October, when it was pretty clear that he was going to win the award, Earnhardt bummed a ride to the shop with Nick Ollila because Earnhardt and his soon-to-be third wife, Teresa, had only one car. "You know, I'm going to win this rookie of the year thing, and they got this banquet in Ontario," Earnhardt said to Ollila. "Have you got a sport coat I could borrow?"*

Now, before he had occasion to wear it, he and the boys were going to do a little less formal celebrating. Earnhardt and Lou LaRosa rode back from the speedway to the hotel in a rental car with Jake Elder. Deeming some sort of trick driving an appropriate way to honor his latest protégé, Elder came flying into the parking lot at about 35 miles per hour and threw the car into reverse. They spun, transmission fluid went everywhere, and the car caught on fire. No one seemed to think it was a big deal. The Rookie of the Year Award meant ten grand to Earnhardt, plus $1,000 for each race he entered in 1980. All told, the thing was worth close to $50,000 — and that was on top of the money from the Winner's Circle program. That was the kind of money that would cover the damages on a rental car. It was almost the kind of money that would buy a man a diamond the size of a horse turd.

They went up on the balcony. LaRosa, the tough Staten Island native, thought about what he and the rugged linthead had accomplished. This was as touchy-feely as it was going to get: "That was great, Dale," LaRosa said, "you being Rookie of the Year."

---

*Ollila obliged. He doesn't remember what it looked like, but, he says, "there was polyester involved in it. Absolutely."

"That don't mean shit to me," Earnhardt said, flashing that Mona Lisa smirk. "I want to be the Winston Cup champion."

### Final 1979 Standings After the Los Angeles Times 500

1. Richard Petty          4,830
2. Darrell Waltrip         4,819
3. Bobby Allison           4,633
4. Cale Yarborough         4,604
5. Benny Parsons           4,256

# Epilogue

DARRELL WALTRIP's refusal to put the blame for his Ontario disaster on his crew might have been a sign that he had turned over a new leaf, become more of a team player.

It might have, but it wasn't.

Shortly after the 1979 season finale, Waltrip convinced Bill Gardner to fire Buddy Parrott as his crew chief. Parrott did not take the news well. "I let everybody know I was going to kick his ass," he says. It didn't take long for word to make its way to Waltrip. He walked into the DiGard shop one fall day, and a worker came up to him and said, "You seen Buddy? He's looking for you. He says he's going to beat the shit out of you."

Waltrip's reaction: "He's a big strong guy. Damn, I hate this."

A few nights later, after dinner and a few beers with a couple of his pals, including Slick Owens, who was also a friend of Parrott's, Waltrip finally decided he'd had enough of looking over his shoulder. "Somebody said something about Buddy, and I said, 'Yeah, I guess I'm going to have to just go over to his house,'" says Waltrip. "They said, 'You can't go over to his house—he'll kill you.' I said, 'Well, riding around worrying about it is about to kill me, so I don't know anything else to do except go over to his house. I got to get this over with.'

"So we did. We drove over to his house and I knocked on the door, and it sort of disarmed him. Because when he saw me, he grabbed me, but he said he had another job offer anyway." *

That offer fell through, though, and when Gardner and Waltrip couldn't decide on a new chief, they hired Parrott back. Waltrip finished fifth in the points in 1980, and it was clear that his time with DiGard was coming to an end. "After we lost that championship in '79, Bill Gardner called me and he said, 'The one thing you'll never have to worry about as long as you drive for me is winning a championship, because I ain't ever going to spend that much money again trying to win a championship. That's the most ridiculous thing I ever did. I'm going to spend money to win races, but I'm not going to get involved in that championship thing anymore.'" After the 1980 season Waltrip paid $300,000 to get out of his contract and sign with Junior Johnson, who was in the market for a new driver because Cale Yarborough had decided that he wanted to drive part-time and signed with M. C. Anderson.

Like much of NASCAR's old guard, Johnson had been on the receiving end of some unwanted Waltrip smack talk in the past, but he had no qualms about kicking in part of the buyout to hire him. "The best driver, that's who you want," Johnson says. "Personality is not a big thing with me because you both have the same desire." The combination of Waltrip's ability and Johnson's know-how proved unbeatable. "All I needed was somebody to tell me what to do," Waltrip says. "When I went to drive for Junior, Junior told me what to do." They won the Winston Cup their first two years together and took it again in 1985.

All the while, Waltrip was gradually gaining acceptance. He still bragged too much and said what was on his mind, no matter how insolent or obnoxious. Sure, he'd egg the crowd on, asking them to

---

* Parrott remembers it slightly differently: Owens called and told him Darrell wanted to get it over with, but in the end Waltrip "was too scared to come over to my house."

boo him in Victory Lane and then telling his sponsor, Mountain Dew, that they had been chanting, "Dew!" But he was winning races and championships, so he didn't need to use his mouth to manufacture any buzz. The press was going to pay attention to him no matter what he said. Waltrip also benefited from having such a popular, likable wife, who had the couple's first daughter in 1987. "Seeing me and Stevie and Jessica in the winner's circle, people saw I had a softer side," he says.*

The defanging of Jaws was completed on May 21, 1989. With $200,000 on the line in the Winston, then the name of the NASCAR all-star race, Rusty Wallace spun Waltrip out with two laps to go and ended up winning. The teams came to blows on pit road after one of Waltrip's crew members kicked Wallace's car as it drove to Victory Lane. Wallace claimed that he'd barely made contact on the track, but Waltrip was suddenly a victim. People actually defended him, advocated for him. It was like Red Sox fans hearing that Bucky Dent's car got totaled and chipping in to buy him a new one.

By that point Waltrip was heading into the downhill side of his career. He won fifty-seven races in the 1980s, just five in the '90s, and none after 1992. He kept driving, though, turning the 2000 season into his own personal victory tour, on which the same fans who had thrown fruit at him fifteen years earlier fattened his wallet by buying everything from hats to Hot Wheels at Kmart, which was his sponsor. Waltrip had become so popular with the masses that when Fox acquired a share of the sport's broadcast rights beginning in 2001, he was the logical choice to become the network's voice of NASCAR.

Under the terms of the television deal that expired after the 2000 season, NASCAR had been paid $100 million a year. The sport had

---

*It also bears mentioning that Waltrip, though certainly obnoxious in his younger days, was always, at heart, a good and decent guy. After Buddy Parrott was fired in 1979 but before he was rehired, he didn't receive a Christmas bonus from the Gardners. Waltrip gave him one. "Biggest one I ever got," says Parrott.

grown gradually as a TV commodity in the 1980s, thanks largely to Bill Rasmussen's creation, ESPN, which had first started showing races in 1981. But the new deal with Fox and NBC was worth more than four times that: $2.47 billion over six years, a staggering sum for a sport that hadn't been deemed viable programming fifteen years earlier. Fox's first race was the 2001 Daytona 500, which provided ample drama: Darrell Waltrip calling the first career win of his little brother, Michael. That should have been the enduring memory of the race, but seconds before Michael crossed the finish line, Dale Earnhardt hit the wall between Turns 3 and 4. It wasn't the kind of spectacular barrel-rolling wreck that leaves observers marveling *I can't believe he survived that* when the driver invariably walks away unscathed. It was a relatively innocuous-looking hit. But it broke Earnhardt's neck, killing him instantly.

If the 1979 season was the start of NASCAR's transformation from a regional curiosity to a major sport, then the beginning of the 2001 TV deal represented the culmination of that evolution. The sport had arrived. Those two events also roughly bookend Earnhardt's career: his rookie season and his last race. The confluence is no accident. Earnhardt, as he told Lou LaRosa he would, won the 1980 Winston Cup title, despite the somewhat predictable departure of Suitcase Jake Elder in the middle of the season. Doug Richert, who was just twenty, took over, and Earnhardt relied on a 148-point lead he'd built up under Elder to hold off Cale Yarborough by 19 points to win the first of his seven championships, which equaled Richard Petty's total.

But it wasn't numbers that made Earnhardt an icon. It was how he did it. The Osterlund team imploded in 1981, and after a few fallow years Earnhardt hooked up with Richard Childress, an independent driver who had just climbed out of the cockpit to focus on being an owner. The two of them built the team that would win Earnhardt's last six titles. It only reinforced the notion that nothing ever came easy to Earnhardt, and it added to the proletarian appeal that had won over all those fans at Charlotte on Memorial Day weekend in 1979. He was one of them, even when he cut his hair and stopped shooting off guns in other people's yards, as he did when he remarried (this time it took) and settled down. He never really settled down on the track, though. As he led the sport to new heights, he picked up the nickname that would stick with him until he died: the Intimidator.

Perhaps the most tragic element of Earnhardt's death was that it came just as he was embarking on a late-career resurgence. Earnhardt's last title came in 1994, and his yearly finishes were getting gradually worse until his youngest son, Dale Jr., made his Winston Cup debut in '99. Having the kid around seemed to spark the old man. He was noticeably peppier, and in Junior's first full season, 2000, Senior finished second in points. He had a legitimate shot at winning his eighth title in 2001, but he never got the chance to topple the King.

Earnhardt's death ignited a fierce debate over safety in the sport. He was the third Winston Cup driver to die in an eight-month period. In July 2000 Kenny Irwin had been killed in practice at the New Hampshire International Speedway, the same track where two months earlier a nineteen-year-old rookie had lost his life in a similar accident. His name was Adam Petty.

When the Petty clan celebrated Richard's 1979 title, Pattie was pregnant with her first child. Eight months later, in the middle of Kyle's second season, she gave birth to Adam. Being pregnant and then a new mother wasn't easy. When Kyle traveled, he usually shared a hotel room with a couple of crew guys, so Pattie couldn't tag along. Kyle drove half of the Grand National schedule in 1980 and a full season in '81. He improved gradually, leading a few races here and there, including the 1984 Firecracker 400 in Daytona.

Just how far stock car racing had come in the first four years of the decade—and just how inextricably linked it was with the patriotic message of President Ronald Reagan—became evident on that Fourth of July afternoon. Reagan, who was running for reelection, chose to spend the most red, white, and blue day of the year at the track, giving the command to start engines from *Air Force One* and then landing on the runway beyond the backstretch shortly after the race began. He was inside the track in time to see Richard Petty's two hundredth — and final — win.

Following the 1984 season Kyle created a stir when he left Petty Enterprises to drive for Wood Brothers. It wasn't unprecedented; the King himself had taken a two-year leave from Petty Enterprises to drive for Mike Curb. But whereas Richard's move had been about hooking up with what he thought would be a more competitive team, Kyle's was about forging his own identity. He'd always viewed the Petty name as a blessing and a curse. No matter what he did, he'd always be "Richard's son." He wanted to see what would happen when his boss wasn't his old man. "When you get out in the real world, it's make-or-break. When you drive for your daddy, he's going to overlook a lot," Kyle said.

The move was also another indication that Kyle was a little bit different. Racing had been his father's life, and his grandfather's, too. But Kyle — the high school basketball and football star, the kid who could pick up a guitar and set a roomful of toes a-tapping without having had so much as one lesson — was destined to develop other interests. It wasn't uncommon; Dale Earnhardt would occasionally have someone fill in for him in practice while he went hunting. What was uncommon was Kyle's preferred diversion: singing.* This wasn't like when his daddy and five of his rivals had caterwauled their way through a bunch of hillbilly standards on a lark. This was real guitar-playin', voice-twangin' Grand Ole Opry stuff. He lost the perm, grew his hair out, got an earring, and started writing songs. It landed him on the

---

*Of course, Kyle's old buddy Marty Robbins did both, but he was always a singer first and a driver second.

2009 he merged with Gillett Evernham Motorsports. Under the new deal — which didn't provide a seat for Kyle, who has turned his attention to announcing — the team is called Richard Petty Motorsports. Petty has little say in how the team is run, but it's his name on the truck, so every week the King is at the track, roaming the garage, taking it all in from behind his sunglasses, calling people from all walks of life "cats," and serving as a reminder of a time when stock car racing was a little rougher and a little more colorful and when its brightest days lay just ahead.

# *Acknowledgments*

Writing a book, as I discovered, can be a laborious, tedious, and grueling process. But it can also be incredibly rewarding, not least because it's something that can't be done alone. A lot of people played a part in this book — some old friends, and some new ones whom I had the pleasure of meeting as this project took shape.

Thanks first to my agent, Scott Waxman, and my editor, Junie Dahn, who were both enthusiastic about the book from the start. Many a brilliant idea of mine has died on the vine (I had that whole teenage vampire idea like twenty years ago. No, really…). But Scott made me keep this one alive, and Junie did a terrific job helping to shape and hone it. (And though he proved tough when he had to be, Junie was refreshingly lax when it came to contractually mandated deadlines. Thanks, man.)

Originally my plan was to focus solely on the 1979 Daytona 500, but the more research I did, the more sprawling the idea became. Zack McMillin was one of the first to encourage me to think big; I'm pretty sure his advice was, "I'd hope to learn more than Cale Yarborough's drafting strategy." For better or worse, that was my mantra for months.

The research process introduced me to several great people. I found a guy on an Internet message board, Jay Coker, who was willing to share his race DVD collection. Thanks for the DVDs and the friendship. Tim

Boyd, a history professor at Vanderbilt, was full of thoughts on how NASCAR fit into American culture in the late 1970s. He suggested working in Disco Demolition Night at Comiskey Park; pretty impressive baseball knowledge for a Brit. Professor Kevin Fontenot at Tulane provided plenty of background on country music, and Bill Malone was helpful as well. Craig Shirley did much to explain how NASCAR and Ronald Reagan were made for each other. And Suzanne Wise at Appalachian State and Frank Barefoot at the Greensboro Library came up huge in providing clips and research materials.

Many drivers, writers, and crewmen shared their memories, and to a man (and woman), they seemed to relish their time in the sport. I hope that enthusiasm comes through in the book. A few of my subjects went above and beyond the call: Junior Johnson (who provided an amazing home-cooked breakfast), Humpy Wheeler, Tighe Scott, James Hylton, Bobby and Donnie Allison, Darrell Waltrip, Neal Pilson, Jim Hunter, and Bill Gardner. Reading old newspaper and magazine stories was almost as much a pleasure as talking to the men who wrote them. Thanks Ed Hinton, Steve Waid, Tom Higgins, Benny Phillips, and Dick Berggren. And special thanks to Ken Squier, who didn't let massive amounts of snow or dental work get in the way of a great talk in Vermont.

One group of interview subjects deserves its own paragraph: the Pettys. Richard, Kyle, and Pattie couldn't have been more helpful or generous with their time. That's the kind of people they are, and it's the kind of person Adam Petty was. After Adam died, his family opened Victory Junction, a camp in Randleman for kids with chronic or serious medical conditions, that had been Adam's dream. And they've broken ground on a second camp in Kansas City. I can't think of a better tribute to Adam. The camp's website is www.victoryjunction.org. It's well worth a look.

Big thanks also to copyeditors Peggy Freudenthal, Marie Salter, and especially Barb Jatkola, whose many catches helped (I hope) prevent me from looking like I failed seventh-grade English.

## ACKNOWLEDGMENTS

Writing a book while holding down a full-time job isn't easy. Thanks to my boss at *Sports Illustrated,* Terry McDonell, for letting me moonlight. Of course, it would have been impossible without someone to pick up my slack, which Steve Cannella did more times than I care to mention. Cannella also was an excellent reader and sounding board. I'd repay him the favor if he ever writes a book. Until then, I'd like to think his reward is that his kids—who are, against all odds, avid NASCAR fans—will find it cool that he helped out a friend who once drank moonshine while discussing tractors with Sterling Marlin's best friend.

You can say what you will about the prose on these pages, but I won't hear a bad word said about the pictures, which are uniformly awesome. Dozier Mobley took many of them (and countless other cool ones not seen here), and Bryant McMurray dug through his old film to come up with some great action. Procuring the shots and the rights to them would have been impossible without Maureen Cavanagh, Mark Mobley, Linda Bonenfant, and Frankie Fraley. (Moe gets top billing for calling with picture info literally hours before giving birth to her third kid. That's dedication, if slightly questionable parenting.)

And finally, like a best cinematography Oscar winner facing the flashing red light and the swelling orchestra music, I come to the rushed laundry list of people who offered everything from advice to encouragement to transcription services to interview assistance to boozy lunches to spare hotel beds. In no particular order, and with fingers crossed that I'm not forgetting anyone, they are: Mark Beech, Lars Anderson, Rich O'Brien, Allison Hobson Falkenberry (and Little Cat), Rebecca Shore, Scott Price, Jon Wertheim, Gabe Miller, Rob Goodman, Rosalind Fournier, Tim Layden, Chris Stone, Jeff Pearlman, Jon Edwards, David Hovis, Grace Paeck, and all the Bechtels and Valentines I know. Couldn't have done it without you.

# Notes on Sources

Virtually all of the events of this book took place more than thirty years ago. That's a pretty long time—too long to expect someone to remember the particulars of, say, the Northwestern Bank 400, which, for most of the men who drove in it, was one of hundreds of races in a decades-long career. Whenever possible, I relied on the memories of the drivers, their crew members, and others in the NASCAR community. Although it was obviously not possible to reconstruct the 1979 season from firsthand observations, the interviews were essential in putting the events of that year in context.

For the forgotten details, I relied on various contemporaneous race accounts. I am very fortunate that a small band of outstanding writers were on the beat in 1979: Dick Berggren and the rest of the staff at *Stock Car Racing* magazine, Tom Higgins of the *Charlotte Observer*, Ed Hinton down in Atlanta, Benny Phillips of the *High Point Enterprise*, and Steve Waid of *Grand National Scene* wrote stories that were not only essential as source material but also a joy to read. Interviews with those five gentlemen also proved to be invaluable.

### Chapter 1: Something Borrowed, Something Blue

Interviews with Richie Barsz, Steve Hmiel, Dale Inman, Robin Pemberton, Kyle Petty, Pattie Petty, Richard Petty, and Ken Squier. Much of the great detail of Kyle's practice runs in Daytona came from stories by Benny Phillips in the *High Point Enterprise*, and *Stock Car Racing* magazine covered the Petty wedding extensively. Richard's recollection of the discussion that he and Kyle had when Kyle decided to become a racer is detailed in his book *King Richard I*.

### Chapter 2: Birthplace of Speed

Loads of books have been written about the history of Daytona. Perhaps the most comprehensive is *Racing on the Rim* by Dick Punnett, which notably debunks the oft-repeated story that the "first race" on the beach in Daytona, between Ransom Olds and Alexander Winton in 1902, ended in a flat-footed tie. A nice story, but as Punnett shows, it never happened. Like Punnett, I stuck with newspaper accounts whenever possible. I did rely on a few books, to gain insight into what Daytona Beach and Ormond Beach were like in the late 1800s and early 1900s. Also, an interview with Bill Tuthill in William Neely's *Daytona U.S.A.* proved to be extremely helpful in understanding Bill France's strategy in the formation of NASCAR, and Brock Yates's profile of France in the June 26, 1978, issue of *Sports Illustrated* was very illuminating.

### Chapter 3: The Good Ol' Boys

Interviews with Bobby Allison, Donnie Allison, Junior Johnson, and Cale Yarborough. (I don't think I've ever met a better storyteller than Bobby Allison. As the epilogue mentions, he can't remember finishing just ahead of his son in the Daytona 500, but trust me, he has no problem remembering the exact paint scheme of his first car.) Yarborough's autobiography, *Cale,* written with William Neely, and a profile by Kim Chapin in *Sports Illustrated* (August 5, 1968) were particularly helpful. Sam Moses's *Sports Illustrated* piece (November 6, 1978) shed much light on Yarborough's day-to-day existence at that time.

### Chapter 4: The Prince

Interviews with Donnie Allison, Buddy Baker, Hoss Ellington, Phil Finney (who ruined the perfectly good story Kyle told about the seagull breaking Finney's windshield by telling the truth about what really happened), Bill Gardner, Steve Hmiel, Dale Inman, Kyle Petty, Pattie Petty, Richard Petty, Lou LaRosa, and Waddell Wilson. Tom Higgins was among those atop the hauler during the ARCA race. His *Observer* story related what the atmosphere was like as the vets watched Kyle race for the first time.

### Chapter 5: The Man in the White Hat

Interviews with Richard Childress, Gary Nelson, Buddy Parrott, Ken Squier, Butch Stevens, and Darrell Waltrip. Ed Hinton still remembers his first encounter with Dale Earnhardt, in the garage after the 125-mile qualifier, a scene he wrote about in his excellent book *Daytona: From the Birth of Speed to the Death of the Man in Black.* In addition to interviews with Waltrip and those who know him, several magazine pieces helped me tell the Waltrip story: Sam Moses's profile in *Sports Illustrated* (October 17, 1977), Steve Waid's pieces in *Grand National Illustrated* (May 1982) and *Grand National Scene* (April 19, 1979), and a piece Waltrip wrote himself for *Stock Car Racing,* titled "How I Made It in Grand National Racing" (December 1979).

### Chapter 6: On the Air

Interviews with Bob Fishman, Neal Pilson, Ken Squier, and Bob Stenner. Ed Hinton followed the story of Don Williams from the day the accident happened, remaining in contact with the family until Williams died ten years later; it appears in great detail in his *Daytona.*

### Chapter 7: So Fair and Foul a Day
### Chapter 8: The Fight

Interviews with Bobby Allison, Donnie Allison, Jack Arute, Buddy Baker, Dick Berggren, Joe Biddle, Geoff Bodine, Richard Childress, Hoss Ellington, Bob Fishman,

Jeff Hammond, Tom Higgins, Ed Hinton, James Hylton, Dale Inman, Junior Johnson, Terry Labonte, Lou LaRosa, Larry McReynolds, Gary Nelson, Buddy Parrott, Kyle Petty, Richard Petty, Benny Phillips, Neal Pilson, Tighe Scott, Ken Squier, Bob Stenner, Steve Waid, Darrell Waltrip, Michael Waltrip, Humpy Wheeler, Waddell Wilson, and Cale Yarborough.

Even now, everyone has a different memory of how far back Cale Yarborough was. Thankfully, the race is now available on DVD. After countless viewings I feel confident that the version of events related here is accurate. In addition to the usual suspects, colorful and comprehensive coverage of Speedweeks was provided by Shav Glick of the *Los Angeles Times* and Godwin Kelly and Joe Biddle of the *Daytona Beach Morning Journal*. Stories of cities coping with the blizzard were all over various local papers. The conversation between Jim Bachoven and Bill France was related in a piece by Rick Houston on NASCAR.com (July 26, 2007). Cale Yarborough's quote, which gave this book its title, is from a 2003 story by Al Pearce in the *Hampton Roads Daily Press*. The details of the Tiny Lund fracases were uncovered in the transcript of an interview he did with *Time* correspondent Anne Constable. And as much as I'd like to, I can't take credit for the theory that the roots of NASCAR boys brawling can be traced to Hadrian's Wall. That one came from Humpy Wheeler, who gave me a copy of James Webb's book *Born Fighting*.

### Chapter 9: Round Two

Interviews with Bobby Allison, Donnie Allison, Buddy Baker, Benny Phillips, Jim Riddle, Steve Waid, Darrell Waltrip, and Cale Yarborough. The idea for the digression on footwear came from a nice offbeat piece in *Grand National Scene*.

### Chapter 10: Round Three

Interviews with Bobby Allison, Donnie Allison, Hoss Ellington, Ed Hinton, and Cale Yarborough.

### Chapter 11: Wild and Young, Crazy and Dumb

Interviews with Marshall Brooks, Frankie Fraley, Lou LaRosa, Gary Nelson, David Stern, Darrell Waltrip, and Humpy Wheeler. In 1979 Stern, now the NBA commissioner, was the league's general counsel. The best source for Larry Bird's early life is *Drive*.

### Chapter 12: Diamonds As Big As Horse Turds

Interviews with Dave D'Ambrosio, Nick Ollila, Darrell Waltrip, Lou LaRosa, and Humpy Wheeler.

### Chapter 13: Pearson's Kerfuffle

Interviews with Hoss Ellington, Darrell Waltrip, Jim Hunter, Gary Nelson, Buddy Parrott, Butch Stevens, Eddie Wood, and Leonard Wood. Hunter is now NASCAR's vice president for corporate communications. In the past he was a race promoter and an author. His book with David Pearson, *21 Forever,* is a great source of information on the Silver Fox. The April 1974 issue of *Stock Car Racing* contains everything a fan could want to know about the Woods.

# NOTES ON SOURCES

### Chapter 14: Old Chow Mein

Interviews with Jeff Hammond, Jim Hunter, Nick Ollila, Leonard Wood, and Cale Yarborough. Benny Phillips spent a lot of time with Pearson after he was fired by Wood Brothers, and he turned out a lengthy, in-depth series of stories.

### Chapter 15: Bring on the Dancing Bears
### Chapter 16: Gassed

Interviews with Steve Hmiel, Robin Pemberton, Kyle Petty, Richard Petty, Pattie Petty, and Humpy Wheeler. The great details of Kyle's first race, including the chief steward's wonderful monologue, came from Tom Higgins.

### Chapter 17: Rising Again

Interviews with Lou LaRosa and Cale Yarborough. Several books provided background on the South and its development, most notably Numan Bartley's *The New South,* Kirkpatrick Sale's *Power Shift,* and Bruce J. Schulman's *The Seventies. Time* magazine's entire September 27, 1976, issue was dedicated to the region, and *Fortune* followed with a lengthy package in June 1977. Peter La Chapelle's *Proud to Be an Okie* and Bill Malone's *Don't Get Above Your Raisin'* were excellent resources for me on southern pop culture and country music, as were cover stories in *Time* (May 6, 1974) and *Newsweek* (June 18, 1973).

### Chapter 18: The Gatorade Kid
### Chapter 19: The Beginning of the Trouble

Interviews with Bill Gardner, Gary Nelson, Buddy Parrott, Richard Petty, Butch Stevens, Darrell Waltrip, and Humpy Wheeler. Bill Rasmussen's memoir, *Sports Junkies Rejoice!* was useful in helping me piece together ESPN's early days, as was a story by William Oscar Johnson in the July 23, 1979, issue of *Sports Illustrated.*

### Chapter 20: Pretty Good Americans

Interview with Craig Shirley. The details of the 1978 White House visit were gleaned largely from the January 1979 issue of *Stock Car Racing* and a *Washington Post Magazine* story by Bill Morris and Joseph P. Duggan, "The Stock-Car Driver as Politician" (April 22, 1979).

### Chapter 21: The Shootout

Interviews with Bill Gardner, Lou LaRosa, Gary Nelson, Nick Ollila, Buddy Parrott, Kyle Petty, Richard Petty, and Darrell Waltrip.

### Epilogue

Interviews with Bobby Allison, Donnie Allison, Dave D'Ambrosio, Hoss Ellington, Lou LaRosa, Kyle Petty, Pattie Petty, and Darrell Waltrip. Bobby Allison spoke about getting back together with his wife at Adam Petty's funeral; the story is told in much greater detail in Peter Golenbock's book *Miracle.*

# *Bibliography*

Allison, Donnie, with Jimmy Creed. *As I Recall…* Champaign, IL: Sports Publishing, 2005.

Bartley, Numan. *The New South, 1945–1980*. Baton Rouge: Louisiana State University Press, 1995.

Bird, Larry, with Bob Ryan. *Drive: The Story of My Life*. New York: Doubleday, 1989.

Booth, Fred. "Early Days in Daytona Beach, Florida: How a City Was Founded." *Journal of the Halifax Historical Society* 1, no. 1 (1951).

Bowden, Mark. *Guests of the Ayatollah*. New York: Atlantic Monthly Press, 2006.

Cardwell, Harold D., Sr. *Daytona Beach: 100 Years of Racing*. Charleston, SC: Arcadia, 2002.

Cardwell, Harold D., Sr., and Priscilla D. Cardwell. *Historic Daytona Beach*. Charleston, SC: Arcadia, 2004.

Chapin, Kim. *Fast as White Lightning*. New York: Dial Press, 1981.

Cobb, James C. "From Muskogee to Luckenbach: Country Music and the 'Southernization' of America." *Journal of Popular Culture* (Winter 1982): 81–91.

Drackett, Phil. *Like Father Like Son: The Story of Malcolm and Donald Campbell*. Brighton, Eng.: Clifton Books, 1969.

Egerton, John. *The Americanization of Dixie: The Southernization of America*. New York: Harper's Magazine Press, 1974.

Evey, Stuart. *Creating an Empire: ESPN*. Chicago: Triumph Books, 2004.

Fielden, Greg. *NASCAR Chronicle*. Lincolnwood, IL: Publications International, 2007.

Gillispie, Thomas G. *Angel in Black: Remembering Dale Earnhardt Sr.* New York: Cumberland House, 2008.

Golenbock, Peter. *Last Lap: The Life and Times of NASCAR's Legendary Heroes*. New York: Hungry Minds, 2001.

———. *Miracle: Bobby Allison and the Amazing Saga of the Alabama Gang*. New York: St. Martin's, 2006.

———. *NASCAR Confidential: Stories of the Men and Women Who Made Stock Car Racing Great*. St. Paul: Motorbooks International, 2003.

Graham, Allison. "The South in Popular Culture." In *A Companion to the Literature and Culture of the American South,* edited by Richard Gray and Owen Robinson, 335–52. Malden, MA: Blackwell, 2004.

Hammond, Jeff, and Geoff Norman. *Real Men Work in the Pits: A Life in NASCAR Racing*. New York: Rodale Books, 2004.

Hinton, Ed. *Daytona: From the Birth of Speed to the Death of the Man in Black*. New York: Warner Books, 2001.

Hunter, Jim, with David Pearson. *21 Forever: The Story of Stock Car Driver David Pearson*. Huntsville, AL: Strode Publishers, 1980.

Jensen, Tom. *Cheating: An Inside Look at the Bad Things Good NASCAR Nextel Cup Racers Do in Pursuit of Speed*. Phoenix: David Bull Publishing, 2004.

Kirby, Jack Temple. *Media-Made Dixie: The South in the American Imagination*. Rev. ed. Athens: University of Georgia Press, 1986.

La Chapelle, Peter. *Proud to Be an Okie: Cultural Politics, Country Music, and Migration to Southern California*. Berkeley: University of California Press, 2007.

Levine, Lee Daniel. *Bird: The Making of an American Sports Legend*. New York: McGraw-Hill, 1988.

Malone, Bill C. *Country Music, U.S.A.* 2nd rev. ed. Austin: University of Texas Press, 2002.

———. *Don't Get Above Your Raisin': Country Music and the Southern Working Class*. Urbana: University of Illinois Press, 2002.

Montville, Leigh. *At the Altar of Speed: The Fast Life and Tragic Death of Dale Earnhardt*. New York: Broadway, 2003.

Neely, William. *Daytona U.S.A.: The Official History of Daytona and Ormond Beach Racing from 1902 to Today's NASCAR Super Speedways*. Tucson, AZ: Aztex, 1979.

Noonan, Peggy. *What I Saw at the Revolution: A Political Life in the Reagan Era*. New York: Random House, 1990.

Petty, Richard, with William Neely. *King Richard I*. New York: Macmillan, 1986.

Punnett, Dick. *Racing on the Rim*. Ormond Beach, FL: Tomoka Press, 2004.

Rasmussen, Bill. *Sports Junkies Rejoice! The Birth of ESPN*. Hartsdale, NY: QV Publishing, 1983.

Sale, Kirkpatrick. *Power Shift: The Rise of the Southern Rim and Its Challenge to the Eastern Establishment*. New York: Random House, 1975.

Schulman, Bruce J. *The Seventies: The Great Shift in American Culture, Society, and Politics*. New York: Da Capo Press, 2002.

Spencer, Donald D. *Elegance on the Halifax: The Story of the Ormond Hotel*. New York: Camelot Publishing, 2000.

Teachout, Terry. *Skeptic: A Life of H. L. Mencken*. New York: HarperCollins, 2002.

Tuthill, William R. *Speed on Sand*. Ormond Beach, FL: Ormond Beach Historical Trust, 1978.

Waltrip, Darrell, with Jade Gurss. *DW: A Lifetime Going Around in Circles*. New York: G. P. Putnam's Sons, 2004.

Webb, James. *Born Fighting: How the Scots-Irish Shaped America*. New York: Broadway, 2005.

Wilson, Charles Reagan, William Ferris, and Ann J. Adadie. *Encyclopedia of Southern Culture*. Chapel Hill: University of North Carolina Press, 1989.

Wilson, Waddell, and Steve Smith. *Racing Engine Preparation*. Salt Lake City: Steve Smith Autosports, 1990.

Yarborough, Cale, and William Neely. *Cale: The Hazardous Life and Times of America's Greatest Stock Car Driver*. New York: Times Books, 1986.

# Index

*through some old family photos again last night – a few attached*
*here! – and found myself thinking ahead to Leni's birthday in May*
*this year. She used to love getting everyone together for the occasion,*
*didn't she? Should we maybe try and do that this time, in her*
*honour? Xxx 08.35*
**Tony:** *PS I know you told me not to sign off, Will, but I like it!*
*So get used to it, kiddo!! Love Dad xxx 08.36*

Belinda cruised to the side of the pool, put her hand against
the wall, then turned and began tanking slowly in the other
direction, twisting her face away as a fast, splashy front-crawl
swimmer passed in the neighbouring lane, showering her with
water. Ray had suggested they take the morning off and go
to the leisure centre together, then have lunch in town. 'It'll
make you feel great for the rest of the day,' he'd told her over
breakfast that morning, talking her into the idea. 'And it's
good for headspace too.'

He was currently upstairs, taking part in a gruelling-
sounding Body Combat class, while Belinda was having a
much more mellow time of it in the water. This was the pool
where she'd taken her children for lessons all those years before,
and now here she was again, creaking along with her rusty
breaststroke, wondering if this was part of Ray's plan to keep
her off her phone whenever possible. If so, the joke was on
him because, rather than this being an exercise in mindfulness
(and exercise, for that matter), all she could think about was
her phone: namely, Tony's latest post on the McKenzie family
group chat.

It had taken the wind out of Belinda's sails, reading the

message while she buttered her toast that morning. Who did her ex-husband think he was, trying to organise something for Leni's birthday when he hadn't even remembered it last year? And had he forgotten that he'd have a newborn baby by then? Probably. It wasn't until she read it again that she realised he was merely asking, rather than organising, but still. It irked her that he had got in first with the subject, months away as it still was, rather than her. 'Honestly,' she'd tutted, stabbing the knife into the marmalade with such violence Ray had looked over from where he was stirring porridge at the hob. 'It's nothing,' she mumbled, because Ray was estranged from his ex-wife and children and she knew he'd give anything to get messages from them, however irritating.

She still hadn't replied to any of Tony's comments but had noticed Alice and Will both tentatively engaging. Despite her initial annoyance with him for corralling them all in this group, she could see that, yes, okay, it might actually turn into something good; a nice place for them to share. Should she respond? Of course she wanted to do something meaningful for Leni's birthday. But what should she say?

Back in the leisure centre, she had notched up another length and felt as if she was hitting her stride, her body finding a rhythm. Turning and pushing off from the edge, she smiled, seeing a group of mums and toddlers walking towards the baby pool for a swimming lesson. Goodness, look at those tiny little bodies, so wriggly and delicious, with their brightly patterned costumes and trunks, neon armbands and life jackets worn like protective armour. Their high-pitched voices were eager and excited, carrying through the warm, chlorine-smelling air.

The mums, by contrast, looked rather less enthusiastic to be there, with their hair tied up in hasty topknots, sporting the large sober-coloured costumes of motherhood. No doubt their heads were crammed full of lists for the rest of the day – meals to be prepared, other children to pick up, what time the car park ticket would run out, and all the rest of it. If she closed her eyes, she could remember that time as if it were yesterday.

The joy on her children's faces when they won their first swimming badges, when they became confident enough to jump in! Not that Leni ever had any qualms about leaping in, out of her depth – one of Belinda's worst motherhood memories had been here at the pool with the girls, aged about four and two, when Leni, seizing a moment while Belinda was wrestling with a locker, had rushed ahead to the water because she simply couldn't wait. Belinda had snatched up Alice and pelted after her, just in time to see a lifeguard hauling Leni out of the shallow end. He'd given Belinda such a ticking off about the dangers of children falling into water unaccompanied, and how important it was that parents did not take their eyes off their toddlers, not even for a second, that Belinda had burst into hot tears. So had Leni. So had Alice, who never wanted to be left out of anything.

Today though, she had no such responsibilities. Now her children were scattered, with messages pinging through on her phone rather than daily physical contact. *Hold each other tight*, Apolline had urged recently. This had been the day in town when she'd sidled into a coffee shop while waiting for Ray at the bank, only for her precious time to be interrupted by Tony, of all people, waving at her through the window like an idiot. She could have slapped him for it! *Leni wants the four of you to be united, to lean on one another during this time*, Apolline had said after Belinda shooed him away, which was ironic, under the circumstances. There had been no further pointed mentions of 'a man' from Leni, at least, she thought, shuddering as she remembered the unnerving conversation the two of them had had on her eldest daughter's last birthday.

'I had the funniest coincidence yesterday, Mum,' she had said, all smiles. This was after lunch, when things had become a little more relaxed, thank goodness. Will and Molly were telling some long story about a night out they'd had in Swindon, while Ray and Alice were making teas and coffees for everyone. Belinda had asked about Leni's garden and Leni had opened the back door for them both to go out there, and, once she'd admired the roses and alliums and lavender, they'd sat at the small white patio table together. Then Leni dropped her bombshell. 'We had an Ofsted inspection at school this week – you'll never guess who the inspector was!'

No, Belinda hadn't guessed. 'Who, darling?' she'd asked, all innocence.

'Our old neighbour – Mr Fenton!' the answer came and Belinda felt her throat tighten immediately, the Prosecco repeating itself in her mouth, sour and vomit-tinged. Graham Fenton? No.

'Oh,' she managed to say, her heart almost thudding through her ribcage. Shit. Was Leni about to say what she thought? Was this the moment where her world came tumbling down? 'Wow!' she added to fill the silence. She hardly dared look at her daughter's face. What kind of judgement might she find there?

'I know! I never would have recognised him,' Leni went on. Her sunglasses hid her eyes but Belinda could see her own self reflected in the brown lenses: scared-looking. Old. 'I introduced myself and I swear he did this double take. *Coincidence!* he said. *I used to know a Leni McKenzie!*'

Who knew what else might have been revealed, if Alice hadn't come walking towards them in the next moment, coffee mugs in hand? Belinda was all too grateful for the interruption. 'Oh, perfect!' she cried, trying to suppress the hysterical note in her voice. 'Come and join us, Alice, you can share my chair,' she added, shifting over. Surely, if Leni had any truly damning accusations, she wouldn't make them with Alice there, she'd figured, adrenalin racing.

She hadn't. Conversation had turned elsewhere. The subject of Mr Fenton – and what else he might have said – remained unfinished and Belinda, to her shame, had never quite been brave enough to bring it up in subsequent phone calls. What did Leni know? The only way she could ever find out now was through Apolline, and she still wasn't sure if she was ready for that.

Don't think about it, she told herself, kicking hard through the water. It's all in the past; let it stay there.

The mums and toddlers were in the baby pool now, singing 'Five Little Ducks' together, the mums swishing their charges through the water to giggles and shrieks. There was one older lady there too, Belinda noticed, a grandma presumably, and she felt such a surge of envy at the woman, she almost forgot to swim. She thought of the knitted yellow baby jacket, the symbol of all her hopes and dreams, now stuffed into a box of keepsakes at the bottom of her wardrobe, never to be worn. Had things been different, she could have been a grandma herself by now, in a swimming pool somewhere with Leni and Adam's wee one, singing her heart out with a similar group. *Five little ducks went swimming one day, Over the hills and far away. Mother Duck said, 'Quack quack quack quack!' But only four little ducks came back.*

Oh gosh, and now Belinda had tears running down her cheeks at the thought of her eldest little duck never coming back. Of Leni swimming away, and her, poor old Mummy Duck, quacking uselessly into the void.

She reached the edge of the pool, intending to turn and continue swimming, but it was as if a switch had been flicked somewhere inside her, because she couldn't stop crying all of a sudden: the tears pouring, a loud sob issuing from her throat. Embarrassed, she put her hands over her face, leaning against the wall trying to get a grip of herself, but the sadness was too deep, the awfulness too overwhelming. On warbled the singers – three little ducks left now – and her grief only intensified. She had lost so much! So much that she could never get back again. It was as if there was a hole in her, a terrible gnawing hole where Leni had been ripped away. The pain was too much today. She couldn't bear it.

There was a tentative tap on her shoulder. 'Can I help you?'

Gulping as she wrestled to stop the tears, she looked up to see a middle-aged woman in the water beside her, pushing a pair of clear goggles up on to her forehead to reveal kind blue eyes. Oh no, and the pretty, young lifeguard seemed to be coming over too, white trainers squeaking across the wet concrete floor, a concerned look on her face. For heaven's sake, Belinda! Of all the places to have a meltdown. 'I'm sorry,' she hiccuped, dashing the tears away with the backs of her hands. 'I'm fine, really. Just having a moment.'

The lifeguard had reached them now and squatted down, her tanned, hairless thighs right in Belinda's eyeline. (Even in the depths of grief, she was able to envy another woman's legs, apparently.) 'Are you all right?' the lifeguard asked. 'Do you want to get out and sit somewhere quiet for a minute? Can I call anyone to come and get you?'

Lifeguards had become a lot nicer since the one who'd bollocked her all those years ago, at least. She shook her head, feeling foolish. Who on earth got undone by a children's song anyway? How mortifying. 'I'm okay,' she said with a final hiccup. 'Sorry. Thank you, both. I think I'll get out now.'

She could feel them watching her all the way back to the changing room entrance. The walk of shame, she thought to herself with a sigh.

Showering afterwards, she felt her equilibrium returning as she rinsed her hair. She felt lighter, even, as if the wave of crying had been cathartic. Not that she was about to tell Ray what had happened, mind. *Can't take you anywhere*, he'd say, hugging her tightly.

Dressed once more, her hair still damp and faintly chlorine-scented, she waited for him in the reception area, noticing as he appeared that he looked rather wild-eyed. 'Wait till you hear who I've just had a call from,' he said, holding up his phone with a stunned expression on his face. 'Ellis!'

*'Ellis?'* she repeated in surprise. 'Gosh! Is he all right? Are *you* all right?'

Ellis was Ray's mysterious son from his first marriage – mysterious to Belinda, at least, because father and son had been estranged for as long as she'd known Ray. When his ex-wife Nicky had eventually tired of her drug-addicted, gambling, irresponsible husband, there had been a messy evacuation of him from the family home, and then she'd upped sticks and taken herself and the children off to her home town of Crickhowell, for the three of them to begin a new life without him. Ray had made financial contributions since then, but otherwise ties had broken down completely. Once he was sober and clean, he'd tried to start over with his kids, but there was a limit to how much repair work he could do, when they steadfastly refused to have anything to do with him. Belinda knew it had broken his heart, even if these days he rarely talked about Ellis and his sister, Rhiannon. They must be in their twenties now, his son and daughter, and Ray had all but given up hope of reconciliation. Until today.

'He's got a job interview in Abingdon next week,' Ray said, as they headed out to the car park. 'Asked if we could meet for a drink while he's over this way. He wants to meet me, Bel!'

'Oh wow, that's brilliant,' she cried, squeezing his hand. He looked dazzled by the news, his face lit up in a way she couldn't remember seeing in a long time. 'Does he want to stay with us while he's in the area?' she added, because oh, this would mean so much to Ray if he could help his son in a practical way: not only with a drink and a chat, but with a bed for the night too.

'I did offer but . . .' Ray's face dropped a little. 'But maybe that was too much for a first time. I think he probably wants an escape route, in case he decides he still hates me after all these years.'

'He won't hate you,' Belinda said staunchly, as they reached the car and Ray unlocked it. 'Because you are a good man, the very best man, Ray, and as soon as Ellis sees you again, he'll realise that. Gosh, this is big! Did he say anything else?'

'Not a lot. He's going to text me a pub where we can meet later on.' He got into the driver's seat and put a hand to his heart briefly before pulling the seat belt across himself. 'I can't believe it. I'm so happy. My boy . . . Honestly, this has made my day.'

She settled herself in the passenger seat and rubbed his arm affectionately. 'What a lovely bit of news. You deserve this.' It had hurt Ray so much to be cut off from his children, rejected time and again. Who would have thought? It just went to show that life – and people – really were full of surprises. And she couldn't help thinking that if his family, seemingly damaged beyond repair, could see their way to reconciliation, however tentative, then maybe . . . might there be hope yet for hers?

She took her phone out to read through Tony's latest group message once more, noticing that a reply from Alice had arrived in the meantime.

## McKenzies Together group

*Alice: We should definitely do something, even if it's just a video call. You know what Leni was like about getting us together – she'd have been pleased to know we were making an effort! It'll be a tough day x 11.13*

Gazing out of the window, half listening as Ray chattered on about Ellis and how he hoped this might be a turning point, Belinda felt torn in two, in regards to her own family situation. If Alice wanted to get together, of course she wouldn't deny her that. She mustn't.

*Hello everyone*, she typed, then took a deep breath. Life was short, wasn't it? she reminded herself. Too short to waste. *I was going to take some flowers to her headstone that day. Then I think I'll cook her favourite dinner (roast chicken – you're all welcome to come over and join me) and have a very large glass of wine. Raise a toast to her. But yes, it would be lovely to see you, either in person or on a call. X*

She read the words through again, considering adding a few of her beloved emojis for good measure, but deciding against it. There was such a thing as being over-friendly, after all. Then she pressed Send.

# Chapter Fourteen

*McKenzies Together group*

*Monday*
**Alice:** *Sounds great, Mum – count me in for roast chicken. Dad? Will? You in for this? X 17.44*
**Tony:** *That's a lovely idea, Belinda. I would like that very much. Will, might you be back by then? Love Dad/Tony xx 19.33*

Tony was glad that Belinda had finally responded to one of his messages on the group chat (at last!) but he hadn't been able to stop thinking about that strange moment when they'd seen one another in town the week before, her shiftiness in the café when he'd interrupted her phone call. Perhaps she was simply displeased to see him, but instinct told him there was something else afoot. It had troubled him, actually. Was his ex-wife all right?

The encounter might have drifted from his mind if he hadn't bumped into Ray a few days later, on a garage forecourt, of all places, filling up their cars beside each other.

They'd exchanged pleasantries – Tony had always rather got on with Ray, whenever Leni had organised one of her family get-togethers – and then, after a moment's deliberation, Tony found himself saying, 'I saw Belinda last week, actually. Is everything okay? Only ...' He hesitated, trying to find the right words. 'She was having a strange phone call. She seemed to be talking about Leni as if she was still alive. Unless I misheard, maybe ...' But he could tell from Ray's face, the way it sagged with dismay, that the other man knew exactly what he was talking about.

'Bloody Apolline,' Ray muttered, busying himself replacing the petrol nozzle in the holder. 'Belinda's got herself involved with some supposed psychic. It's all a massive scam, of course, but this woman has convinced Bel that she can talk to Leni beyond the grave, and keeps apparently passing on messages.' His eyes were dark, his mouth in a grim line. 'She's the one who told Bel to put the house up for sale in the first place, apparently, and now we seem to be house-hunting with this absolute charlatan having a say in which place we buy. I mean ...'

Tony was finding all of this hard to take in. 'Bloody hell,' he commented, realising too late that the petrol nozzle was clicking in his hand where the tank was full. 'Presumably Belinda's paying through the nose for this, too.'

'I dread to think how much,' Ray replied heavily. 'And once the house has been sold, she'll have a huge amount of capital at her disposal too.' He shook his head. 'I hate seeing her taken advantage of like this, but she's refusing to listen.'

He'd changed the subject then, and that had pretty much

been the end of it, but Tony had been mulling over the situation ever since. Should he say something to the kids? Tackle Belinda himself about it? He didn't want to tread on Ray's toes though, nor did he feel comfortable going behind his ex-wife's back. By the time he met Jackie for their first antenatal class that evening, he still didn't have the answer. He'd have to sleep on it, he decided, putting it out of his mind.

'Well, here we all are – welcome!' said Sallyanne, the course leader, beaming around the group. She was in her mid-forties, at a guess, with short yellow hair and large red-rimmed glasses. To Tony's mind, she had the manner of an infant teacher: smiley and enthusiastic on the outside, but with an authoritative firmness which suggested she'd have no qualms about making you miss playtime with your friends if she caught you being naughty.

'It's lovely to see you, our mummies- and daddies-to-be, plus our small growing passengers along for the ride, of course! Mummies, I hope you're all sitting comfortably. Daddies, I hope you're listening hard and ready to take notes if need be. Let's go around the room and introduce ourselves, shall we? I'll start. I'm Sallyanne, a midwife with eighteen years' experience, and so I've seen pretty much everything in my time. Take it from me, you're in for one incredible journey over the next few months, and I feel very privileged to be guiding you through your first steps of this life-changing time.'

Tony's expression might've been neutral, but inside he was fighting the urge to catch the eye of a fellow 'daddy' and pretend to vomit on to the community centre floor. What was it about some of the people working in baby-related professions that compelled them to infantilise and patronise at any opportunity? He felt fidgety already, and he'd only been in the room a matter of minutes.

As if sensing his discomfort – maybe he'd sighed unacceptably loudly – Jackie swung her head towards him, eyes narrowed. It was the expression of someone approaching the end of their patience and he sensed he'd be in for a series of sharp nudges this evening if he didn't watch himself. 'All I want is to meet a few local mums,' she'd said beforehand, when he started protesting about joining her for the class. 'And I know you've done this whole "having kids" thing before, but I haven't, so humour me, okay? Also, not to be rude, but it's been years since you actually witnessed a birth or changed a nappy, so you could do with brushing up on the knowledge. As well as learning how you're going to make the experience as stress-free as possible for me, obviously.'

With those words ringing in his ears – and the threat of upsetting a hormonal woman – he gave her a nervous smile and tried to concentrate on Sallyanne's summary of the forthcoming sessions. Then the door burst open and everyone turned to see a pink-haired woman rush in, hand in hand with a shyly smiling woman wearing denim maternity dungarees.

'Ah! I was wondering what had happened to you two,' Sallyanne said, with a hint of reprimand as she consulted her list. 'You must be Genevieve and Penelope, welcome. As I was saying—'

'Gen and Pen, that's us,' said the pink-haired woman, ushering her partner to a seat, then sitting beside her and taking her hand. 'I'm Gen, this is Pen. Hi, everyone. Sorry we're late.'

Tony, meanwhile, was having a senior moment where he tried to place the pink-haired woman in his memory. Had he met her through work? Then the woman – Gen – clocked him staring at her and he saw recognition dawn on her face. His own brain caught up in the next second. Yes, of course: the cringe-worthy bereavement group he'd attended, never to return. It wasn't a dissimilar set-up to this evening's do, actually, although the chairs here were more comfortable at least and nobody was weeping. Yet. His heart sank as he smiled weakly back at her. Damn it. Oxford was a big enough city that you could usually get away with anonymity when you needed it, but irritatingly, it was also small enough that paths crossed and recrossed more often than you might choose.

Never mind, he told himself. Hopefully Gen would have enough tact not to mention the group here, or make a thing about it. He focussed back on Sallyanne, who was asking the other couples to introduce themselves. 'If you could give us your names and what you're hoping to get out of the course, that would be a wonderful start,' she said. 'I'm here for each and every one of you, so let me know what you'd like addressing: any concerns, confusion, fears. No question is too silly!'

She gestured at the woman at the far end of the semicircle of chairs to begin. This woman, it transpired, was called Alice, and Tony felt a sparking of warmth inside as he always did when he encountered anyone with the same name as one of his children. After his last conversation with his younger daughter had ended so frostily, he'd been trying to think of ways he could make her like him again, suggesting lunch dates at weekends and then, when she didn't seem to be free on any of the days he offered, wondering to Jackie about turning up at her flat as a surprise. *You need to slow down, back off a bit*, Jackie had advised. *You're her dad, not a stalker. Give her some space.* As for Will, Tony didn't seem to be making much progress there either, bar the very occasional group chat message.

'Our next couple, please?'

He jumped back to the room at the prompt, along with a nudge from Jackie.

'I'm Jackie, forty-two, first baby,' she said. 'Absolutely delighted to have reached this point, although I still can't quite believe it's real.' She put a hand on her bump. 'I had sort of thought that ship had sailed, that it wouldn't happen for me, but . . . Well, here we are.'

Everyone was smiling warmly at Jackie. Now it was Tony's turn. 'I'm Tony and I've been here before – I've got three grown-up children,' he said and then broke off as the reality caught up with him. *Make that two*, he corrected himself unhappily. *Neither of whom seem to like me very much.* 'I . . . um . . .' If in doubt, crack a joke, the chimp part of his brain instructed him. 'Well, it was all a bit different in my day, I've got to say,' he went on, taking refuge in glibness. 'Women just got on with the birth, while us blokes had the easy job of standing in the car park, having a fag.'

He was joking – of course he was joking! – and yet the atmosphere changed in an instant, with the previous air of friendliness taking on a distinct tinge of frost.

'Right,' said Sallyanne primly. Oh shit. He'd misjudged the mood; he'd be ordered to sit on the naughty step in a minute.

'Well, I, for one, think it's *good* that we've moved on from those less progressive days, but . . .'

'So do I! I was only having a laugh,' he tried to say, but she was talking over him now, moving on to the next couple, and his excuse petered out. Jackie rolled her eyes at him, looking exasperated, so he was in the doghouse with her, too. Off to a cracking start, Tony.

The evening proceeded with some graphic talk about labour, what it involved, and the options available to the mothers-to-be. Then a weird one-upmanship kicked off, with several of the women saying, rather piously to Tony's ears, that they wanted drug-free births because that seemed more natural and holistic. Which was all very well, sure – and Tony admired their optimism in the face of what was sure to be extreme pain – but in his opinion, there was nothing holistic about women routinely bleeding to death during childbirth in the Middle Ages, for instance. Belinda had agreed with him, he remembered, feeling a burst of solidarity with his ex. 'Why would anyone in their right mind choose to go through hours of agony if they didn't have to?' she'd asked, flummoxed. *Why indeed,* thought Tony.

Still, after his first attempt at humour had bombed so dismally, he wasn't about to disgrace himself further to the group, even when one woman talked eagerly and at length about hypnobirthing and reiki power, and the uplifting play-lists she was already compiling. What did he know? He was a man. He knew nothing, in other words. Nobody would want to hear his opinion: that despite having a rather hazy idea of what reiki meant, he was pretty sure it would be bog-all help when a ten-pound baby was insistently making its painful, bloody exit.

He was on safe ground with Jackie's birth plan at least, because she'd been very clear before now: caesarean, plenty of drugs, job done, get me home. She'd even said the words, 'Just unzip me and get the kid out already,' when speaking to friends about it. But then Sallyanne, going around the parents in turn, asked for Jackie's thoughts on the matter, and Tony, once again, found himself wrong-footed.

'Well, we were previously thinking of a caesarean—' Jackie began.

'Hashtag "unzip me and get the kid out already",' Tony interjected, grinning around the group in the hope of winning back favour.

'— But I'm coming round to the idea of a natural birth,' she went on, which gave him a start. She was? Since when? His surprise must have shown on his face because then she said, 'Tony, I know you think natural births are for masochists, but—'

You could almost hear a pantomime hiss of disapproval sweeping around the group. Oh God. Why did she have to say that, in front of this lot? 'I don't think I actually used the word "masochist",' he retaliated, accidentally catching Reiki Woman's eye and wishing he hadn't. She was practically clenching her fists now, as if tempted to cross the room and poke him in the eye with an incense stick. 'It's just ... Look, I've seen it three times over, remember, and—'

'I thought you were in the car park, having a fag?' one of the women muttered sarcastically.

'And – that was a joke! I'm just saying, it's not a pretty business. Blood everywhere. Screams of agony ...'

'I really don't think—' someone put in sharply, but he was going full throttle now and couldn't stop.

'Total carnage, from start to finish. I mean, my ex-wife, Belinda, she was an absolute trooper, but—'

'What, and I'm not?' Jackie asked, rounding on him, sounding hurt. Oh Christ. This was going from bad to worse.

'No! I mean, yes! Of course you are! I'm just saying—'

Sallyanne came to his rescue – if you could call closing him down with steely authority a rescue, anyway. 'Perhaps that's a conversation to have outside the class,' she said. 'And while all the partners here will have opinions about what *they* think should happen, it's my firm belief that a mother's wish is paramount.'

'Absolutely!' Tony cried, desperate to defend himself. 'I agree! So—'

'Moving on,' Sallyanne said sternly. 'Eve and Nathan, what are your intentions regarding your birth?'

Tony sat there with his head down, feeling Jackie's leg move incrementally away from his, while Eve twittered on about pregnancy yoga and homeopathic bullshit. He wasn't quite sure how it had happened, but in the space of two minutes, he'd managed to antagonise every single person in the room, it seemed. Although ... He risked a glance up to see that pink-haired Gen was giving him an amused look; the only person who didn't hate him, apparently.

Barely able to listen to the other introductions as Sallyanne went around the semicircle, he bristled with the injustice of being misunderstood. They'd all painted him as some oaf now, he reckoned, some chauvinist throwback, when they had no idea how deferential he was to Jackie in the relationship, how much he admired her and marvelled at her. He wished he hadn't blurted out that thing about Belinda though. Jackie was not a fan of Belinda, and he'd almost certainly have to listen to her telling him why this in particular had pissed her off all the way home in the car later.

Once everyone had spoken, Sallyanne announced a tea break – 'And a loo break, obviously – I know *all* about pregnancy bladder issues!' – and everyone started getting up and making conversation with one another. Jackie was immediately grabbed by the reiki woman and a yoga devotee who hustled her away, presumably with intentions of signing her up for natural birth workshops or possibly even staging an intervention to rescue her from her caveman partner. *I know a cry for help when I hear one!* Whatever, thought Tony, getting out his phone and pretending he had an urgent email needing his attention.

'Hi again,' came a voice and he didn't need to look up to know that it was Gen. 'Are you okay?' she asked.

He raised an eyebrow. 'It's a pretty hostile crowd,' he replied drily. 'I'm half expecting to find that a massive bonfire has been built for me in the car park when I try to leave later. Chants of "kill the pig" echoing around the perimeter, pitchforks, that sort of thing.'

She sniggered. 'Bit po-faced, aren't they? Christ! Get a sense of humour, people.' Then she elbowed him. 'Don't worry, the lezzers have got your back. Pen would have come to say hello too but she's queueing for the loo. Says it's her main hobby these days.'

He felt his equilibrium returning a touch with her cheerfulness. 'When is she due?' he inquired politely, because even he knew that this was one of the questions you were meant to ask.

'Star Wars day. May the Fourth be with you? We're hoping for a Wookie.' Then she leaned closer. 'Top tip for you, by the way. Friends of ours went to a class like this in Brighton, and apparently it's one of the ice-breaker things to bond the mums, where they go around and see if the partners have a clue when the due date is. Most of them have no idea and then the mums get to cluck and moan about how hopeless their other halves are. So whatever you do, make sure your due date trips off the tongue, all right? You might even claw back a few brownie points with the mega-mums that way.'

'Blimey, thank you so *much*,' he said, almost dropping his phone in his haste to check his calendar app. This was Premier League information. Absolute gold. 'Ours is April but I have no idea of the day. Let's see . . . ah, the 5th. Got it.' He mimed wiping his brow. 'Thank you, I think you might just have saved my life.'

She grinned at him, then pretended to speak into a walkie-talkie. 'Call off the bonfire. Repeat – call off the bonfire,' and they both laughed, Tony with a slight edge of hysteria. 'Seriously, though, are you okay with this?' she asked. 'I'm finding it a bit of a shocker to get my head around, the whole birth and death thing. You know, what with the bereavement group and all?' She bit her lip. 'That's not me being nosey, I know you didn't want to talk about … about whoever you were grieving. But you're clearly going through a lot right now. As am I.' Her green eyes glistened momentarily and she looked away.

'Yes,' he agreed. 'It's a lot, like you say.' There was a weighty pause, then he found himself helplessly plunging on into it. 'It was my eldest daughter who died, actually, so …' His voice trailed away, his eyes suddenly wet.

'Oh God, Tony, I'm sorry,' she said, horror on her face. 'What an absolute headfuck this must be for you. I can't imagine how—'

'Hello, hello,' came a friendly voice just then, and there was Pen, Genevieve's partner, appearing with paper cups of juice for them all. 'Let's pretend these are really full of wine and see if that helps us get through the rest of this sodding evening,' she said. Pen had long hennaed hair and dimples, and spoke in a Yorkshire accent. Tony liked her immediately.

'Thank you,' he said, taking the drink she passed him. 'Cheers to the pair of you – to all three of you, I should say.' He raised his cup to them, grateful that he hadn't been entirely cold-shouldered by the group. 'A lovely glass of crisp, perfectly chilled Sauvignon blanc,' he said after a mouthful of the lukewarm apple juice. 'Delicious.'

'Do you think you'll go back to the other lot, the bereavement massive?' Gen asked, just as they heard the distant foghorn call of Sallyanne requesting that they reconvene for the second half of the meeting.

'I …' He faltered because he had already scrubbed the so-called other lot from his mind, written off as a bad idea. And

162

yet there was something about Gen that made him reluctant to say no to her. 'I'm not sure.'

'Give it another go,' she urged him. 'Honestly. I was really surprised by how helpful they've been. Going there, talking to other people – it's turned things around for me.'

Tony noticed that Pen had reached down to squeeze Gen's hand, and he felt a pang of envy at their obvious togetherness, especially when he felt he'd only managed to rile his own partner so far. 'Um,' he said, failing to think of an excuse. Damn it. 'Yeah. Sure. I'll give it another go,' he ended up mumbling. Then he glimpsed Jackie approaching, cackling with some new friends she'd made. 'Nice to talk to you both,' he said, as everyone returned to their seats.

In exactly one hour this will be over, he reminded himself. Sixty minutes, and you can get into the car, go home and pour a very large glass of crisp, perfectly chilled Sauvignon blanc for real. In the meantime, he simply needed to smile serenely, agree with everything Jackie said, and reply '5th April' at the right moment. He could manage that, couldn't he?

# Chapter Fifteen

*Leni McKenzie memorial page*

*Leni was two doors down from me in the university halls of residence where we both lived during our first year. I was quite shy and homesick, especially in the first term, and watched in envy as she seemed to flit from party to party, drama to drama. Two months in, my grandma died and I was in bits for ages. Leni made a point of knocking on my door to chat, making me cups of tea (and once, memorably, a really terrible tuna fish curry), and she was not afraid of my sadness. Her kindness meant so much to me. It really helped me through a bad time. Thank you, Leni. You were a good person.*

    *Stephen Teale*

'Hello, stranger,' said Alice when Will answered the phone, and he felt a little jolt at her voice, sounding impossibly close despite the miles between them. 'How's my favourite brother?'

'Great,' he said automatically, lying on his thin mattress watching a cockroach scuttling across the tiled floor. It was early evening but the heat from the day still filled the room like a solid block, despite the efforts of his ceiling fan to stir up a breeze. 'Living the dream – sun, sea, sand, parties: you know how it is . . .'

He heard her laugh. 'Er, no, actually, you wanker,' she replied. 'That sounds very far from my life of freezing London, tube strikes and office knobheads.'

'Sorry, not sorry,' he told her. 'How are you, other than dealing with all of that?'

'I'm okay. Not an angry mess any more,' she said, with a rueful note in her voice. 'I'm still trying to piece together what Leni was doing on that last night, and the weeks before,' she went on, before launching into details about some address in Shepherd's Bush. He shut his eyes, saying *La la la la la* in his head so that he didn't have to think about Leni's last night.

'Oh yeah, and the weirdest thing,' Alice said. 'Did you see the message from Jacob on the memorial page?'

There was no chance he'd have seen a message on the memorial page because he never looked at it. Why would he torture himself like that? 'Jacob – your ex-boyfriend Jacob?' he asked in surprise.

'Yeah! Total blast from the past. We're going out for dinner next week and—'

'Whoa, whoa – what?' Will had always liked Jacob: the big brother he'd never had. Jacob had compiled playlists in an attempt to give the eleven-year-old Will some musical education, and took him to his first Oxford City match when someone he knew had spare tickets, and let him win at arm-wrestling occasionally, even though Will was the puniest boy in his year back then.

'Not like that! He's married with a kid, it's not a date or anything. Anyway, I've got . . . Well, it's complicated,' she added cryptically. Oh God, don't say she'd hooked up with that bellend Noah again, he thought, not daring to ask. He and Leni had been united in their dislike for the slimy weasel-boy, as they'd privately called him. 'No, with Jacob, I'm just tapping him for his Leni memories,' Alice continued. 'Hoping he's got some anecdotes that I've forgotten, that sort of thing.'

And now they'd come full circle again. Will frowned, unable to understand why his sister was apparently so determined to keep putting herself through this shit. He couldn't see the point when it only seemed to make her feel sad and guilty. 'Right,' he said after a moment. 'Um . . . give him my best. Hope you find out what you want.'

'How about you? What are you up to? Have you fallen in love out there? Tell me the juicy bits, liven up my bleak British winter, it's the least you can do.'

'Well . . .' He made the mistake of hesitating and she immediately pounced.

'Ooh! A mysterious pause. That means gossip, I can tell. Okay, I'm making myself comfortable, let's hear the details.'

He rolled his eyes because, despite everything, he missed his sister. He wished he could transport himself to her London flat for the evening – or afternoon, whatever time it was there – and give her a hug, go out for a pint and catch up properly. But how could he? How could he go back and look her in the eye, after what had happened?

'All right. So I met this girl ...'

'I *knew* it! Amazing. Tell me everything.'

Her enthusiasm was infectious and despite his earlier reti-cence, Will found himself warming up. 'Yeah, I'm trying, give us a chance!' he laughed.

'From the very beginning.'

'Okay. From the beginning. Well, you could say, we didn't exactly get off on the right foot. That's a joke, by the way, but you won't find out how it's a joke until a bit later. Anyway ...'

It was nice to talk about Isla. She'd now left Koh Samui, bound for new adventures, and he'd found it hard to stop thinking about her, in part because the last time he'd seen her, everything had gone wrong. He'd blown it.

On the evening in question, he'd been in a funny mood, unexpectedly thrown by two words that had appeared on his phone screen earlier that day: 'roast chicken', part of his mum's debut posting on the family group chat (so she'd cracked at last). The conversation was about how they as a family should get through Leni's birthday in a few months' time, but rather than dwell on the date and its implications, Will's mind had snagged on the tripwire of his mum's roast chicken offer. Suddenly it was all he could think about: the crispy skin of the meat, golden and glistening, with the juicy, succulent flesh beneath. His mum's Sunday dinners were the absolute best: her roast potatoes with the perfect amount of crunch, the gravy in its blue spotted jug, the dishes of vege-tables. He remembered how, on childhood Sundays gone by, the smell would drift up through the house until they were all drawn helplessly towards it, sniffing the air like hungry dogs, offering to set the table in the hope it would speed the process along.

*Leni's favourite*, Belinda had written in her message, but it had always been his favourite too. The dinner that made everything feel a bit better, that eased you towards the upcoming week at school or college with a full, contented stomach. He found himself yearning to be taking a seat at his mum's laden table again, in the cosy, cluttered kitchen, steam on the windows, the radio playing *Sounds of the Seventies*. Thinking about this, and about seeing her again, her cheeks flushed from the heat of the stove, wearing the navy and white striped pinny she'd had for as long as he could remember, made him feel a tearing sensation inside that was almost painful.

'Everything all right, Will? You look miles away.'

He was down at the Elephant Bar at the time, a place he'd taken to frequenting and not simply because it was close to the hotel where Isla and Meg were staying. ('Yeah, yeah, I believe you,' Alice said on hearing this.) Isla had appeared at the table, dumping her bag on the seat beside him as if the two of them were meeting for a date. They weren't, obviously, but he felt a little pinwheel of happiness spin inside him nonetheless, because already the evening had taken a welcome turn for the better.

'Hmm? Oh, hi,' he said, as she sat down. Her hair was in a long plait over one shoulder and she wore a black top that was almost sheer in a certain light, with cut-off jeans and silver low-top Converse. She looked beautiful, in short, and he swallowed, promising himself that he must keep his eyes on her face, rather than getting distracted with the outline beneath her clothes. 'Yeah, I'm fine,' he said, in reply to her question. 'No Meg tonight?'

She waggled an eyebrow. 'Hot date with a guy we met diving earlier. He's an Aussie, from Sydney; he's promised to give her the intel on the restaurant scene out there. Which is kind of a niche chat-up line if you ask me, but it worked for Meg.'

'I see,' he said and then, feeling a stab of envy at the thought of a bunch of handsome blokes chatting them up on this trip, was unable to stop himself from adding, 'There was no one you fancied on the dive, then?'

'Well, it was mostly women, apart from this one particular guy, so . . .' That eyebrow again, so expressive in its flexibility. 'So no. Can I get you a drink? Oh −' she hesitated, 'do you mind me sitting with you, by the way? You're not waiting to meet someone, are you? Got one of your business meetings arranged?'

He laughed, if only because she always looked so chuffed with her own wit whenever she teased him about his work. 'Yeah, it's a global conference tonight. All the big guns flying in for this,' he said, before pulling a face at her. 'Or in the real world, no, I'm not waiting for anyone, and I'd love you to sit with me. I'm fine for a drink, thanks.' He indicated the half-bottle of Singha he'd been stringing out for the last twenty minutes. It was lukewarm by now and less refreshing than it had been, but he was trying to be frugal and make it last as long as possible after another unsuccessful day on his rounds. Nobody wanted to buy a fan or a sarong from him, apparently. Zilch on the sunglasses, also. Had he lost his touch or was it that he'd stopped caring enough about winning over his punters? Maybe it was there in his eyes, the certainty that he considered his products to be pretty shit and not worth anyone's money. Whichever, something had changed to jolt him out of his sales groove into this losing streak. He hoped he could find a way back to profit soon.

*You could always take a sideways step in my direction*, his friend Juno had said the other night, with a meaningful glance. Juno sold weed and pills to holidaymakers and made astronomical profits, but the Thai laws around drug-dealing were so hardcore, Will had always been too intimidated to consider this an option. But if he wanted to stay on the island longer – and he did – then maybe he should think again?

A few minutes later, Isla was back and setting down two hurricane glasses on the table, clinking with ice and some peach-coloured concoction or other. 'Here – I went crazy and got us a cocktail each,' she said when he looked at the glasses, then up at her in surprise. 'I know you said you were okay for a drink, but sod it, it's Monday, everyone needs a drink on Monday, right? And it's my last night here too, so . . . Cheers.'

'Thank you,' he said, touched. 'What is this, by the way? Not some slow poisonous revenge for the mis-sold flip-flop, I take it?'

She laughed. 'If it is, I'm drinking the same, so we'll go down together. It's a Samui Sundowner, apparently. Bottoms up, my friend. Let's get the evening started.'

He asked about the diving trip she'd been on that day and she talked for some time about the turtles, barracuda and stingrays they'd encountered, the incredible visibility. Then she sharpened her gaze and asked in return, 'So go on then, what were you thinking about when I got here? You looked a wee bit sad, you know. Is everything all right?'

He gave her a small smile. 'To be completely honest, I was thinking about my mum's roast chicken,' he confessed.

She laughed. 'Okay! I would not have guessed that.'

'Yeah, bit random,' he agreed, but then faltered, wanting to change the subject before he waded out any further. Since he'd been in Thailand, he hadn't talked to a single person about Leni, about home. It had been a deliberate policy: to detach himself from the mess and sadness by acting like it had never happened. Yet now it was as if home had risen to the surface of his feelings, as if he could no longer put a lid on that night back in June.

'It's a good roast chicken, then, I take it,' she prompted, sipping her drink through a straw, her eyes steady on him.

'It's the best.' He managed another weak smile, desperately wishing they could return to the safer territory of her diving trip because he could feel his usual façade cracking, and he didn't like that at all. 'Anyway, tell me more about—'

'When I first left home for uni, it was my dad's Saturday fried breakfasts I missed the most,' she said at the same time. 'He properly goes for it at the weekend – it's like he's cooking for an army. Eggs, bacon, sausages, beans, mushrooms, piles and piles of toast ... At the start of my first year, I kept waking up on Saturday mornings in my halls of residence with this absolute ache of homesickness. Or maybe an ache of hunger, I don't know. Maybe my stomach was finely tuned to its weekly routine and was like, *Hey, where's my massive fry-up then?*' She laughed, and he noticed the way her eyes crinkled at the edges. She was so pretty. Mesmerisingly so. It was all he could do to stop himself from offering to cook her a fried breakfast right there and then.

'Of course, it wasn't just his fry-ups I missed,' she went on, 'it was him too, but the breakfast was ... I dunno. Symbolic, I guess. Food does that, doesn't it?' She patted her belly with both hands then smiled at him. 'What's your mum like, then? Apart from being a wonder with a roast chicken. You haven't said much about your family.'

The question caught him off guard. 'Oh,' he said. 'She's ...' Then he stopped because the last time he'd seen his mum she'd been crying at the airport and now it was all he could think about. *You will come back, won't you? Please take care of yourself. I can't lose anyone else. Please, I mean it, Will.* 'She's had a rough time,' he blurted out, then felt like kicking himself.

'Sorry to hear that,' Isla said. 'Anything you want to talk about?'

No, definitely not, was his instinct, but there was something about the way she was looking at him, gaze unwavering, chin propped on her palm as if she had all the time in the world to listen, that gave him pause. 'Well—' he said haltingly, because it turned out to be really hard to drag himself away from her periwinkle-blue eyes, impossible to fob her off. 'Actually, my sister died,' he went on before he could help it.

'Oh God!' Her eyebrows signalled how little she'd antici-pated such a bombshell. 'Will, I'm so sorry.'

He looked away, already regretting opening his mouth at all. These were words he hadn't said aloud for so long, for months and months. The last person he must have said them to was his boss when he took some time off work, or maybe one of his mates, who knew the family. *My sister died.* They were terrible words to say. Absolutely awful. And then to have Isla gazing at him with such concern, such empathy, only made him feel a hundred times worse. 'Yeah,' he managed to get out. 'So ...' The rest of the sentence eluded him and he shrugged, trying to throw off the bad feelings churning up his guts. *Can I ask you a favour, Will?* he heard Leni's voice in his head, and emotion surged perilously. 'Let's not talk about it, anyway,' he said, gruffly. 'You're on holiday, it's not exactly holiday chat.'

He sought sanctuary in his drink but could feel her watching him. 'I don't mind,' she said. 'Just because I'm on holiday doesn't mean I've turned into a selfish tosser who doesn't care about anyone else's troubles. It's your call.'

You could tell she was a health professional, he thought, meeting her eyes again. Underneath her tough exterior, she was kind, she was straight with you. 'Tell me about your family,' he said, desperate to switch the spotlight away from himself. 'Do you have brothers and sisters?'

She took the baton and regaled him with tales of her three younger brothers, and soon the atmosphere had lightened once more as he laughed at her stories and felt his turbulent feelings subsiding. Okay. Dodged a bullet. Moving on, he thought, mentally patching up the fractures that had appeared so disconcertingly in his protective shell. Nothing to see here.

They had another round of Sundowners, then ordered plates of noodles and then, because why not, she was on holiday and it was her last night on the island, they ended up in Hush, one of the nightclubs, dancing to old R'n'B under the colourful lights. His body felt loose with alcohol, and the music took hold of him in the best kind of way. How could it be that during the course of a single evening, you could swing from feeling sad to joyful and celebratory? Isla was a good dancer and, in the crush of bodies on the dance floor, he felt alive once more, as if he was in the right place, as if nothing else mattered. What was the point in dwelling on the past? You couldn't change it, however much you'd like to, however hard you wished you could have said to your own sister, *Sure, you can ask me a favour. Yes, I can help.*

Around midnight, Isla professed tiredness and they left, the resort still pumping with music from the surrounding bars and clubs. His senses felt heightened, taking in the distant roar of generators, the Thai boys on their mopeds buzzing through the streets, the smells from the food stalls serving up moonlit curries and satay skewers while stray dogs sniffed around for scraps. Walking along together, he took her hand in his and then, emboldened, pulled her towards him and tried to kiss her, only for her to push him away under a flickering streetlight.

'No,' she said. 'Sorry.'

He felt discomfited, as if he must have misread the signs. 'Oh,' he said. 'That's okay.' Still confused, he added, 'I thought we were getting on?'

'We were,' she said. 'I mean, we are. But—' She shrugged and they went on walking, her face pale in the half darkness.

He had the sinking feeling that he might not want to hear

the rest of that sentence, although a masochistic streak in him prompted her to finish nonetheless. 'But ... ?'

She gave him a rueful smile. 'You're a lovely guy, Will. You're gorgeous and funny and good company. But you play your cards so close to your chest, I still don't have any real idea who you are. I get that you've suffered an enormous tragedy and I'm really sorry for you and your family. But—'

'That's got nothing to do with anything,' he said stubbornly.

'It has, because you're like a closed book, sealed all the way shut,' she replied. There was silence for a moment where he didn't know what to say, then she went on, her tone gentle but still devastating. 'If I kissed you – and don't think I wasn't tempted – I wouldn't know who I'd be kissing.'

He felt himself deflate. There was nothing he could say by way of self-defence because she was right and they both knew it. 'Fair enough,' he replied, trying to let the criticism slide right off him. *Let it go, don't think about it.* There was nothing wrong with being a closed book. 'That's cool.'

'Is it, though? You're happy to be like that? This is you now, forever, is it?'

He felt winded by the criticism in her words. 'Wow,' he said. 'Don't hold back, will you? Say what you really think.'

He must have sounded hurt – he *was* hurt – because now she was grimacing. 'Sorry. Ignore me,' she mumbled. 'I've had too much to drink.' They'd reached the building where she and Meg were staying and she gave him an apprehensive smile. 'Thanks for tonight, I had a great time. All the best, yeah? I hope you find what you're looking for.'

She hoped he'd find what he was looking for? What the

hell was that supposed to mean? 'Right, sure,' he said, none the wiser. He wasn't looking for anything, other than a good time. 'Same to you. Have a nice life.'

Her mouth opened as if she wanted to say something else but he didn't give her the chance, turning away, his hand raised in farewell. 'Night, then,' he said, without looking back.

His eyes stung as he walked back towards the main drag; his mouth trembled as if he wanted to cry. It didn't matter, he told himself fiercely. *She* didn't matter. Who was she? Some girl on holiday. Nobody who could hurt him or leave any kind of trace on him, that was for sure. *You're like a closed book*, he heard her repeat in his head. *You're happy to be like that?*

Yes, he replied, hands knotting into fists, telling himself it was the smoke from a nearby noodle stall making his eyes water. Of course he was happy to be like this. Why wouldn't he be?

He didn't tell Alice the full story, obviously. He sprinkled a little glitter over the details, focussed on the chemistry and banter, kept Leni – and the roast chicken – out of it.

'So ... oh.' She sounded disappointed when he got to the (heavily edited) part about them saying goodbye. 'So that's it? She's gone now? But you're going to stay in touch?'

'Probably not,' he admitted. Isla had made it pretty clear that Beach Bum Will wasn't enough for her, and he knew he couldn't open up his closed book and give her Real Will, tarnished and ugly as that version was. He tried to lighten the mood. 'You know me – easy come, easy go. Loads more tourists arriving every single day.'

'But ...' She sounded confused, as if he'd sold her short on the romantic story she'd been expecting. Understandable. He wasn't sure why he'd even told her now.

'Anyway, I'd better go,' he said, grabbing one of his shoes and throwing it across the room at the cockroach. Too slow; it had run for cover beneath the ancient chest of drawers. 'Good to talk to you, Alice. Bye!'

He hung up before she could ask him anything else or start talking about Leni again, and flopped back on the bed, his eyes shut. *Easy come, easy go*, he reminded himself. *Smile – you're in paradise!*

# Chapter Sixteen

*Alice:* So guess who I'm meeting tonight? Jacob Murray!

*Belinda:* WHAT???!!!! Oh my goodness! Give him my love. Such a lovely boy [heart-eyes emoji, smiling-face emoji, heart emoji]

*Alice:* Don't get too excited, Mum, we're only having a drink and reminiscing about Leni.

*Belinda:* Sounds like a date to me!! [red heart emoji, pink heart emoji, red heart emoji]

*Alice:* It's not a date, he's married with a kid! Friendship only.

*Belinda:* [sad-face emoji, broken-heart emoji]

*Alice:* Talking of dates though, did you ever hear Leni mention someone called Josh? Was she seeing anyone last summer, do you know?

*Belinda:* Josh. Hmmm. That name is ringing a bell but I can't think why. [bell emoji, confused-face emoji] Love you. Have fun tonight! [red heart emoji]

*

*It's complicated*, Alice had told Will in reference to her love life, although other, juicier words had sprung to mind when she walked into the meeting room at work, only to be greeted by her one-night stand, Darren Not-a-Baron, there at the table. Goodness knows how she managed to take any minutes; it had been practically impossible to concentrate. She would never go drinking alone in any bars near work again if this was what happened, she thought, blushing with mortification. The worst thing – the second worst thing – was that he actually looked pretty hot in his dark suit and snazzy tie, which was not the sort of confusion she needed right now.

He, at least, didn't seem to have noticed her. Maybe he was one of those men who saw a woman in a meeting with a notebook and pen, and instantly dismissed her as having no value, no worth within the discussion. Tosser. From the meeting's agenda, she could see that he was an actuary, so would be based in the legal division up on the ninth floor, with no connection to Alice's usual work. If her colleague Rosalind had been in that day to take notes as usual, chances were Alice could have got away with never seeing him again. Her one crumb of comfort throughout the deeply uncomfortable experience was imagining how Leni would have screamed with mirth on hearing the story later on. *Oh my Godddd! Noooo! This is hilarious. So awkward!*

The meeting finally ended and just as she was thinking she'd successfully remained under his radar, they ended up alongside each other in the bottleneck to leave the room. 'Nice to see you again, Alice,' he'd said in a low voice – aargh, excruciating, she was actually *dying* now – and she responded with a sound that was half yelp, half laugh, before escaping quickly through the door and away. Nightmare, she thought with a full-body shudder. Genuine did-that-just-happen nightmare.

Anyway. It was Friday now, and she'd survived the rest of the week without any further sexy-Darren interactions, thank heavens. Dare she say it, office dramas aside, the week had been pretty good. Hamish was definitely getting used to living with her, even if he was yet to permit any strokes or other affectionate moves. He had stopped scuttling under the bed or behind the sofa whenever she came into a room, for one thing, and had filled out a little, no longer appearing quite so scrawny and unkempt. In a sign that he might have accepted her flat as his new home, he had settled on a few preferred spots around the place too. He particularly enjoyed sitting on the kitchen windowsill for garden surveillance sessions, his beautiful orange tail occasionally flicking with interest whenever a bird flew into view.

The cats' home had advised her to keep him indoors for at least three weeks before allowing him to explore outside, but she could tell already he was desperate to bust out of there. Lou, who was good at such things, had promised to come over at the weekend so that she could fit a cat flap before Freedom Day in a week's time, and also, Alice suspected, so that she could get the full low-down on her forthcoming evening with Jacob.

'Meeting up with your first love, oh wow! This is so exciting!' she'd cried when they had met for lunch yesterday. Lou worked for a drugs charity in Holborn, two tube stops away from the Sage and Golding office, and Alice enjoyed escaping to meet her for a break, especially after an interminably dull morning spent wading through a backlog of claims to be processed. 'You know what they say, don't you? About getting straight back on a horse?'

'I will not be getting on any horses, Lou,' Alice said, wishing everyone would stop jumping to the wrong conclusions about this. 'We're—'

'The sex horse, I mean, before you think I'm making Pony Club references.'

'The sex horse?' Alice found herself giggling at the ridiculous, exaggerated winks her friend was now giving her. 'Stop it,' she gurgled. 'You look like you're having a stroke. And no, I'm not having sex with a horse – not for you, not for anyone. Definitely not for the horse.'

'God, I would,' Lou said dreamily, eyes glinting as she bit into her prawn sandwich. 'Where's your sense of adventure, Alice? Come *on*! With Valentine's Day next week, too.' She gestured towards the counter, where a line of scarlet hearts had been strung across the coffee machines like tinsel. Valentine's Day decorations were a *thing* now? No doubt that had been dreamed up in a marketing meeting somewhere, Alice thought, feeling a brief pang for fun creative meetings where the wildest ideas could be bounced around. Nobody would be festooning the walls with Valentine bunting at Sage and Golding any time soon, that was for sure.

'If the thought of a manufactured, commercialised day of so-called romance doesn't make you feel like throwing caution to the wind, or your knickers to the wind, whatever the phrase is, then I don't know what will,' Lou was saying. 'Get with the program, girlfriend.'

Alice snorted. 'Knickers to the wind, indeed. Are we still on horse sex, by the way? I can't keep up.'

'That's what the horse will say,' Lou had sniggered.

Remembering this now, Alice smiled to herself, pulling her coat around her as she exited the tube at Tottenham Court Road and headed towards Berwick Street. She was due to meet Jacob in Dimitris, the Greek restaurant Leni had loved, according to her friend Rosie. What better place for a meeting of the two remaining Flying Beauties? No doubt this was silly of her, but already Alice was feeling a thimbleful of comfort at the thought of sliding on to a banquette that her sister might have sat on, experiencing the exact same view of the street outside that Leni might have enjoyed, lingering over the menu and wondering which dishes had tempted her tastebuds. *Here I am, living for you* and *me, just like I promised*, she would think, breathing in the ambience, silently raising a glass to her sister's memory.

Dimitris was busy when she arrived, the windows steamed up, the tables set with paper tablecloths, bouzouki music playing from a wall-mounted speaker high up in one corner. An aproned waiter was pouring red wine from a carafe for a couple nearby; elsewhere she could smell herbs and tomatoes and grilled cheese. Then she saw Jacob, sitting at a table in the corner frowning at the menu, and her heart stuttered a little, trying to take in his appearance before he could notice she'd arrived. Stupidly, her first thought was that he was a man now, rather than the skinny teenager she'd dated – he looked broader around the shoulders (was he working out?), his cheekbones no longer quite so angular (to be fair, whose were, post-thirty?), and he sported a short, tidy beard that suited him. His dark brown hair was a bit longer than when they'd been together, sitting maybe an inch above his collar now, and he wore a pair of black-framed glasses (since when did he need glasses?). He also had on a rather crumpled grey shirt, the sort that she knew would be soft between her fingers, and she blushed all of a sudden, imagining touching it, before reminding herself, semi-hysterically, how inappropriate that would be. Look at him though, all grown-up and good-looking. It was doing strange things to her.

'Alice McKenzie, oh my God,' he said, getting to his feet when he saw her. There was his lovely wide smile again, the one in all the photos she'd found herself poring over the night before. 'Wow, look at you. Time flies!'

She had wondered beforehand how they might greet one another – a polite kiss on the cheek or just a smile? – but he didn't seem to have any qualms about grabbing her for a hug, and in the next minute she was pressed against his (disarmingly beefy) shoulder with his arms around her. He had always been a good hugger, she thought fleetingly, a montage playing in her head of other embraces – when her gran had died, A-level results day, the night they had to sleep in a train station in India, when she'd never been so grateful for another person's bodily warmth. 'Hello,' she said, suddenly shy as she sat opposite him. 'Thank you so much for this,' she went on, wanting to set the agenda from the start. 'I was so pleased to see your message on the memorial page. Do you know, I'd forgotten that we even made you an honorary Flying Beauty?'

'Forgotten? How dare you,' he joked. 'You can't rewrite history that easily, mate.' Then he looked awkward, as if remembering what this was all about. 'I was so sorry when my mum told me the news. You know she and my dad have moved out of Oxford now? They're down in Paignton, both retired; they love it there. Mum got together with some old friends after Christmas and one of them mentioned Leni.' His gaze was sincere and direct. 'It's just ... You must be devastated. I'm so sorry, Alice. How are you doing? If that's not too inane a question.'

'I'm okay,' she said, because that seemed the safest reply, and because she didn't want to frighten him with confessions of her rock-bottom times. 'Yeah,' she added, more rallyingly. 'So this was one of Leni's favourite restaurants, apparently. I thought it might be nice to come here, in the hope that I'd feel close to her again.'

He nodded, still meeting her gaze. His eyebrows had grown bushier in the last decade, she noted, but his eyes were just how she remembered them – coffee-bean brown and expressive. He had cried that Christmas when they split up, the first time she'd ever seen him like that; his hands curling and uncurling by his sides as if he didn't know what to do with them. 'Sounds a good idea,' he said now and she felt a rush of relief. She knew he'd get it.

They ordered food and launched into nostalgic stories over the bread and dips that the waiter brought, clinking their bottles of Mythos together by way of a toast. Alice had always known Jacob was smart – he had aced his A levels, he'd been awarded that incredible scholarship, he'd gone on to study for a master's and then a doctorate – but she became increasingly grateful for his pin-sharp memory that had captured all sorts of events she'd forgotten. The day in December many years earlier, for instance, when the two of them plus Leni had gone into town together. The trip was ostensibly to do some Christmas shopping, but they'd become cosily ensconced in the Turf Tavern drinking pint after pint (the joys of fake ID). Some time later they re-emerged, ending up drunkenly singing carols alongside the Salvation Army in front of the Mound, before being asked by a French-horn player, pretty forcefully, to sod off. 'Oh my God. Yes! And we ended up giving them all our change because we felt so bad,' Alice cried, helpless with laughter.

'Didn't Leni get the phone number of some guy on the bassoon too?' Jacob asked.

'Sounds about right,' Alice said, shaking her head. Then she caught his eye and felt a swell of happiness inside, remembering them being carefree teenagers together. They'd had so many good times.

They smiled at one another, the memory hanging in the air between them. 'So what are you up to these days?' he asked. 'If that isn't too much of a screeching handbrake turn back from drunken carol-singing.'

Still deep in times gone by, she misunderstood the question. 'Well, I'm sorting through Leni's belongings and catching up with some of her friends to return various bits and bobs,' she replied. 'And I'm trying to make a point of going to places that were important to her. Doing things that she loved. It kind of haunts me that I don't know much about the night she died – how she was feeling, or where she was even going – so I've been trying to piece together what she was doing then, and in the weeks leading up to that day, so that . . .' Jacob was looking at her as if he didn't quite follow and she momentarily lost her thread. 'So that I feel connected to her. It's why I was so keen to meet up with you,' she went on. 'To hear all of your stories. I feel as if I'm collating this mental scrapbook – I want to fill it with everyone's memories, all the snippets of her life.' She could feel tears in her eyes suddenly – oh gosh, she'd got embarrassingly earnest on him now, she hoped he could handle it. Thankfully the waiter arrived to take their empty plates away and the mood was broken.

'Thank you, that was delicious,' Jacob said, and Alice blinked, realising that she'd barely noticed her food again. They'd shared all sorts of little dishes – prawn skewers, calamari, spinach pie – but she'd been so engrossed in Leni stories, it had been as if Leni was there at the table, and she'd felt too happy to care about dinner. Never mind. 'Back to what we were talking about,' Jacob went on, once the table was clear. 'When I asked what were you up to, I meant *you*, *Alice* – you know, for yourself. Where do you work, for instance? Not that I'm not interested in what you're doing for Leni, I mean . . .' he added, perhaps because her face had fallen.

'Oh.' It was as if she'd been jolted out of the warm bubble of nostalgia back into the real world, where Leni was no longer present. Couldn't they have stayed longer in the past? 'Um. I'm just temping at the moment. A maternity cover. I left my old job just before Christmas. Let's not talk about that though,' she said quickly, seeing his eyebrows rise. 'Oh!' she exclaimed as something occurred to her. 'I know what I was going to ask you – do you remember that barbecue at my mum's house the summer after our A levels? Remember those boys who fancied Leni gatecrashed and the shed ended up catching fire?'

He hesitated, like he wanted to say something else, his eyes flicking sideways for a second, but maybe she'd imagined it, because in the next moment she felt his focus full on her again, and he was smiling and leaning back in his chair. 'Remind me,' he said.

# Chapter Seventeen

*Leni McKenzie memorial page*

*I had never believed in love at first sight until I had to go to a speed awareness driving course, walked in and saw this woman arguing with the teacher that there was no one, absolutely no one, who didn't break the speed limit now and then. I thought – she sounds kind of feisty. And then she turned around and I saw her properly and I swear that the world sort of juddered a bit because I thought, bloody hell, she's gorgeous too. I was smitten, there and then.*

*We hit it off – over a shared hatred for speed awareness courses initially, but then over a shared love of beach holidays, classic sitcoms, Spurs (all right ... maybe that was just me), tennis and curry. So many other things. Our marriage didn't work out in the end, but I'm so happy we were together at all, that I knew her and loved her. The privilege was all mine.*

*Leni, I can't believe you're no longer in the world. Rest in peace, princess.*

*Adam*

★

Up in Oxford, Belinda was quite glad to be in the house alone. Ever since her public breakdown in the swimming baths, she'd felt fragile; an egg liable to be broken by the smallest upset. Tonight, Ray had gone to meet his long-lost son, and she was able to lower herself into her favourite corner of the sofa, a massive glass of wine within reach, and exhale. Sometimes keeping up appearances was bloody exhausting.

She'd always been a cheerful person. You had to be when you worked in social services – it was no place for pessimists – but it was more than that: she loved life, she loved people, she loved being busy. 'You're the most fun I've ever had,' Ray had laughed to her soon after they got together, when they'd been swept up with passion and excitement, off on a new adventure every other week, or so it seemed. And then, of course, life had walloped a curveball at her, right when she least expected it.

Those early weeks of hell, where she'd woken up each morning still living the nightmare, made her shudder to think about now. It hadn't been simply the shock and pain of her own bereavement, it was having to deal with the ripples that kept on coming, the messy business of mopping up after a life lost. Belinda was named as Leni's next of kin and for a while her phone kept ringing with one person or company after another saying apologetically that they'd been unable to get hold of Leni and were contacting Belinda now because this, because that. It had felt like some kind of torture, having to explain the circumstances each time. *She's dead. She's gone. She won't be coming to any more appointments. Yes, you can send me a form to fill in for your wretched system if you must.*

Belinda had dragged herself through it again and again. She'd handled the calls, dealt with the emails, she'd told herself she was coping – *fake it till you make it* had always served her well – right up until the moment when she wasn't coping any more, when faking it was no longer an option, when she had a worried lifeguard squatting in front of her and she couldn't stop crying. Ever since then, it was as if something had cracked inside her, something she couldn't quite fix. She kept experiencing irrational bursts of anger – at the manufacturer of Leni's bike, which had turned out to have a dodgy steering column, at Graham Fenton for popping up again when she'd all but forgotten him, at her own self for failing to be entirely honest about the part he'd played in her life. She'd even sat down and written a heated, blame-throwing letter to Adam, her former son-in-law, telling him that if he'd only been faithful to Leni, if he'd only loved her more, then Leni would probably still be alive. It was all his fault!

She hadn't posted the letter, needless to say. She'd written everything she wanted to say and then she'd burned it over the kitchen sink and washed the black remnants down the plughole. It had felt pretty satisfying getting the anger off her chest, mind you.

Sipping her wine – delicious – she wondered how Alice was getting on, presumably having dinner with Jacob right now (Jacob Murray!! Belinda had adored that boy). Then she remembered her daughter's question about this Josh person, and wished she could think why the name was still ringing a faint bell in her head. *Josh*. Someone had definitely mentioned a Josh to her, but who?

It was the wrong time of day to speak to Will, so she wrote him a long gossipy email instead, full of news about the people who'd come round to look at the house that day (a very nice family, fingers crossed) and how she'd bumped into Will's friend Hattie in town earlier, who sent her love. Then it was time to check in with her eldest daughter, and she topped up her wine in readiness before picking up her phone to call Apolline.

Wait, though – the phone was buzzing in her hand with a new message, and in the next moment, she saw Tony's name on the screen. This time it wasn't a message to the group chat, but one just for her.

*Hi Bel. How are you doing? With a new one on the way and antenatal classes and appointments, I keep finding myself remembering moments with our children when they were tiny – their births, Leni's first word, first Christmases, those exhausting first holidays we somehow made it through. We had some good times, didn't we? Sometimes I look back and think those were the best days of my life. And for many of them – particularly when Leni was a baby – you're the only other person who was there too. I know we've had our differences, I know things didn't work out, but if you ever want to chat about old times, either messaging or in person, I'd love to get together and do that. No agenda! Just for the sake of family ties. Love Tony x*

Belinda nearly choked on her wine. Heavens above. What was she supposed to do with that?

Apolline would know, of course. Her friend had the answer to everything. Although Belinda should probably make it a quick chat this time – her card had been declined in the

191

supermarket earlier that day, which had been mortifying, and when she rang the bank to find out what was going on, the young man who answered said they'd been trying to get in touch with her to authorise a number of recent, large payments. The system had flagged them as suspicious, he said, reading the payment details back to her. They were for Apolline's hotline, needless to say, and she found herself wincing about how much she had spent lately, until remembering that contact with Leni was priceless. Besides, it was nobody else's business.

Some hours later, still comfortably ensconced on the sofa and deep in conversation, with Friday night telly muted in the background, she heard Ray's car outside. 'I'd better go,' she said into the phone, because she and Ray hadn't spoken about Apolline since their last argument on the subject and she didn't want to dredge that up again. She was also keen to find out how he'd got on with Ellis. Ray had bought himself a new shirt for the occasion and got his hair cut, and he'd even jotted down a few topics of conversation so that he wouldn't run out of things to say.

'You've got years to catch up on, you'll be dying to know all about him and his sister,' Belinda had assured him, because she could tell he was getting in a flap. 'You just be yourself, because that is plenty good enough. Show him your hang-gliding photos if you want to impress him.'

She hurried through to the hall at the sound of Ray's key in the front door. 'How did it go? How was he?' she asked as the door opened. Then her eyes widened as she realised that Ray was not alone.

'Here we are, come on in,' he said, walking into the hall, with a tall, mop-haired young man trailing behind.

Ray looked overjoyed, Belinda thought, feeling thrilled for him. 'Hello,' she said warmly to them both. 'You must be Ellis, it's lovely to meet you. I'm Belinda.'

'Gosh, sorry, yes,' Ray gabbled, looking flustered. 'Ellis – Belinda. Belinda – Ellis. You're both so important to me, this feels pretty momentous,' he added, blinking.

Ellis had the same brown eyes as his dad, and a similar smile, albeit a wary, watchful version tonight. He held himself with a rigid stillness as if on his guard within what might yet turn out to be enemy territory. 'Hi,' he said, looming near the door.

'You're very welcome here,' Belinda told him, unable to resist putting a hand on his arm, as if needing to check he was actually real. 'Now – have you two eaten? Can I get either of you a drink? Ellis, there's a loo just along the hall here if you need it and – you're staying the night, I take it?' she interrupted herself.

He was carrying a scuffed blue sports bag and glanced down at it as if uncertain where it had come from. 'Er ... yeah?' he replied, eyeing Ray and then Belinda. 'If you're sure that's okay? It's only for tonight and he – Dad – did say ...'

'Of course it's okay! Absolutely,' Belinda assured him. 'I'll go and make a bed up. Ray, are you sorting out drinks?'

Ray took the cue, and ushered his son down into the kitchen without offering to take his coat first. Never mind. After so long apart, this would not be a deal-breaker, she consoled herself, hurrying upstairs. Her heart thumped with excitement at their unexpected visitor; she wanted everything to be perfect, for him to feel welcome and relaxed while he stayed. She'd win him over with home comforts alone, she vowed, switching on the radiator in Will's old room and stripping the bed linen even though it was clean. Fresh sheets in place, plus a couple of towels; she made sure the bulb in the bedside lamp worked, then left a good thriller she'd just enjoyed on the little table there, in case he, like Belinda, was in the habit of reading a chapter of something before he fell asleep. What else? Would he need pyjamas? A toothbrush? Presumably he had those in that blue sports bag, but she made a note to double-check later. Would it be over the top to put a vase of something on the chest of drawers? Yes, she decided. Plus it was dark outside, and if she went out into the garden and started snipping narcissi and twigs of winter jasmine by torchlight, he'd think his dad had shacked up with a total weirdo.

Okay. Stop fussing. Go down and give that boy some attention and make sure Ray is looking after him properly, she told herself, thudding back downstairs.

'It's just like the old days,' she said, ten minutes later, frying bacon and eggs and a couple of leftover boiled potatoes, now chopped into pieces and sizzling in the pan. 'My son Will would often turn up with a load of friends in tow, who'd want feeding at the drop of a hat – I'd always get the bacon out for them. This takes me right back.' Gosh, she'd forgotten how much she'd loved it when they all bundled in after football, or if they'd been drinking in the park and felt hungry. How important she'd felt, bustling about, providing hot food and a bit of mothering for these lanky, graceless teenage boys with their loud laughs and constant wind-ups. How she had drunk in the compliments like a thirsty plant receiving water. And they'd eaten so much! *You boys, I don't know where you put it!* she'd always marvelled as they tore through loaves of bread in one sitting, as they made short work of a twelve-box of eggs.

Ellis had installed himself at the table, although he hadn't yet let go of the tension about his shoulders. 'Smells great,' he said politely. Then, as the toaster popped up two browned slices, 'Should I butter those?'

So he was well-mannered *and* thoughtful – a good start. Belinda twinkled her eyes at him. 'Yes, please,' she said. 'Thank you, darling. Tell me about yourself, anyway – you're in the area for a job interview, is that right? How did it go?'

Ellis seemed delightful, what with his Welsh twang (Belinda did love a Welsh accent) and his slight shyness, warming up gradually as he tucked into a plateful of food. There was, admittedly, something of a strain to be detected between the two men – Ellis keeping his distance, apparently unwilling to reveal too much too soon, while Ray was perhaps trying a little too hard. Ellis had applied for a trainee management position at a retail park nearby, it transpired, and Belinda tried to flash Ray glances that said *Tone it down* whenever he got over-enthusiastic about his son's prospects. She had to widen her eyes quite warningly at him when he began jotting down the names of a couple of local estate agents for when (if) Ellis needed to find somewhere to live. 'Although, it goes without saying, you're welcome to stay here,' he gushed. 'Right, Bel? For as long as you like.'

'Of course you are,' Belinda told him. 'Absolutely.'

'Thanks, but you're moving, aren't you?' Ellis asked, swishing a square of toast through the puddle of egg yolk on his plate. 'Selling up?'

'Ah. Yes. Not immediately,' Ray assured him. 'I've sold my old flat now and this place is on the market, and we're looking to buy a place together further out of town. Become bumpkins in our old age.'

'Become the owners of a successful B. & B., you mean,' Belinda corrected him, with a wink at Ellis. 'Your dad might be heading for bumpkin-hood, but I'm not ready for that just yet.'

He smiled, but he seemed preoccupied with something. Subdued, even, she thought. Was he worried he'd mucked up the interview, maybe? Having second thoughts about coming here? 'Must be nice,' was all he said.

'If there's anything else I can do that would help, you only have to say,' Ray assured him in the next breath. 'Like – you know, if you want to borrow my car or something, to get around to this job or other interviews. Maybe I could treat you to a really sharp suit that makes you feel extra confident about yourself.' His eyes were pleading, Belinda registered with a twist of empathy. *Let me help,* his face said. *Please, son. Whatever you need, I want to give it to you.* It reminded her of how Tony used to get every now and then, when he realised he'd neglected his kids for the latest woman he'd been after.

'Same goes for Rhiannon,' Ray went on, hands open in front of him as if offering up invisible goods. 'I know I messed up. I know I let you two down, and your mum too. But if there are ways I can start putting that right somehow ...'

Ellis had finished eating and set down his cutlery. 'We're

fine, thanks,' he said, then feigned a yawn. 'This has been really nice, but if it's okay with you, I might just call it a night.'

Ray slumped in his seat as if the air had gone out of him, and Belinda felt an ache of sympathy. Okay, so he had gone off the rails as a young father, he'd said as much himself, but he had turned his life around since then. And he *was* Ellis and Rhiannon's dad, at the end of the day. People could change, couldn't they? Look how Tony had surprised her with his recent efforts.

*Leni thinks you should meet him*, Apolline had said when Belinda had talked through the message she'd received from her ex-husband earlier on, and if it was all right by Leni, then it was all right by Belinda, she'd decided. Besides, Tony was right about there being certain moments that no one else knew about. Presumably he didn't mean the bad ones though.

'Of course,' she said quickly to Ellis now, seeing as Ray still hadn't responded. She glanced up at the clock to see that it was only nine thirty, surely far earlier than anyone in their twenties usually went to bed. 'You must be tired, you've had a long day,' she went on kindly, as much as a reminder to Ray as anything else. *Give him some space. Back off a bit.* The lad did look pale, even after a large plateful of food, and this was a strange, intense situation for him; it was hardly surprising he wanted to retreat. 'Can I run you a bath, or get you anything else? Glass of water to take up with you?'

The chair squawked as he stood up, shaking his head. 'No, thanks. Um . . .'

'Let me show you where you're sleeping,' Ray said, hurrying around the table to lead the way.

'See you in the morning,' Belinda said. 'Lovely to meet you, Ellis.'

'You too,' he said. 'Thanks again.'

Well! She couldn't stop smiling as the door closed behind them. Having Ellis here was not only great for Ray, it made her feel as if she had a purpose again, someone new to look after. And she had missed fussing about over a guest! Will was so far away and Alice didn't come home much any more. But now here was Ellis to bring Ray some optimism for a new father-son relationship. There was so much to discover about him and his sister, so many stories she wanted to coax out. *Death has taken much from you but life will continue to give*, Apolline had said to her that very evening, and she'd been spot on, as ever.

She could hear the tread of footsteps above her head, the low rumble of male voices, and experienced a small charge of happiness inside. Hope, even, about what might yet come to pass. She had almost forgotten what it felt like but there it was, flickering away, a flame that hadn't ever quite died out. 'Thank you,' she whispered into the bright kitchen, grateful for the unexpected gift she'd been handed. 'Thank you for this.'

# Chapter Eighteen

*Leni McKenzie memorial page*

*We lived next door to the McKenzies when I was a little kid and one Easter, I must have been about 4, Leni (a few years older than me) convinced me that Easter eggs were made out of dog poo and if I ate mine, the dogs on the street would know and come and get me in the middle of the night. I totally freaked out and started to cry at this information!! She kindly (or so I thought) offered to take the Easter egg off my hands and I was all too happy to pass it over the fence. We moved away and I forgot all about it until years later I bumped into her in The Old Bookbinders. I said, 'Oi, you owe me an Easter egg' but we had a laugh about it. She bought me a pint so I forgave her.*

    *Liam*

'Tonight,' Sallyanne told the antenatal group, 'we'll be trying a few breathing exercises, and I'll show you mummies some birthing positions that will make the whole beautiful experience more comfortable.'

Seated amidst the enthusiastic parents-to-be, Tony had to clamp his mouth shut so that he didn't let out a snort at the words 'beautiful experience' and 'comfortable'. He was determined to avoid getting himself in trouble this time, not least because he was already in Jackie's bad books. Was it really *that* big a deal that he'd forgotten it was Valentine's Day? Apparently so. Over breakfast that morning, realising his error, he'd tried to make amends, searching online for a restaurant that had spare tables for dinner that evening. This only made her huffier than ever, for overlooking the fact that it was their wretched antenatal class then. According to Jackie, this was yet another sign that he was not as committed to their child as she was. 'I bet you never forgot Valentine's Day for *Belinda*,' she'd muttered, slamming out of the house moments later.

He *had* forgotten, obviously, plenty of times, but that didn't seem to be an argument-clincher. Sometimes you couldn't win, he'd figured, ordering a lavish bouquet of flowers to be sent to her office that morning and almost choking on his toast at the exorbitant cost.

As the group split off into pairs and began the breathing exercises, Jackie didn't seem in a forgiving mood though. Sallyanne had advised the partners that they should encourage the mothers-to-be by breathing along with them but Tony couldn't even get that right – he was too loud, too fast, too annoying, according to his stroppy partner. 'I've got to be a *bit* loud so that you can hear me and tune in with what I'm doing,' he pointed out, wishing they had gone for a Valentine's dinner instead. He tried not to think about the very good

Hereford rib-eye steak he could be tucking into right now; the perfectly cooked chips. A glass of robust red wine to wash it all down.

'I don't *want* to tune in with what you're doing, I can breathe perfectly well without you,' she retorted crossly.

His stomach gurgled, thinking of Béarnaise sauce spooned over his steak; it was an effort to stay focussed. 'Yes, but when you're in the throes of agony, you might appreciate some help, that's the whole point,' he reasoned.

This was met by an irritated exhalation. 'I don't think that telling me I'm going to be in the "throes of agony" is very helpful, actually, Tony,' Jackie snapped, with enough vehemence that a couple of people nearby exchanged looks.

'Seriously? We're trying to be positive over here!' one woman called out, her expression so judgey you'd think he'd just told them that they were all going to die.

'Yes, come on, encouraging words only, please, people,' Sallyanne put in primly.

Tony's teeth were clenched so hard together, he would be grinding down his own jawbone in a minute. Why was it that nobody in this group had the faintest sense of humour? He was starting to wish they *were* all about to die, he thought savagely. From across the room, Gen wrinkled her nose at him sympathetically and he gave her a rueful smile in return, grateful for her comradeship. Yesterday evening, he'd braved it back to the bereavement group, where not only had he managed to say a few words about his own situation, but Gen had talked movingly about losing her brother too, and how difficult his girlfriend was finding it, being left alone

with a small, energetic three-year-old who couldn't understand where his dad had gone. She at least understood that
life could come at you fast; the world could change in the
blink of an eye.

'Shall we try again?' he asked Jackie now, mining his reserves
for extra patience. 'Or have you had enough breathing for
one evening?'

He jinked his eyebrow comically, but she didn't smile at
his feeble quip. 'I'm fine with breathing, it's you I've had
enough of,' she replied. Was she joking? It was hard to tell.

He had a fair idea what had provoked her prickliness; they'd
had a difficult few days, with the Valentine's Day argument the
cherry on the cake. Maybe he shouldn't have confided in her
his worries about his ex-wife after all. Had he been insensitive?
He'd run out of options though. He'd tried calling Alice a
few times after the strange conversation with Ray regarding
Belinda's psychic hotline addiction, but she always seemed to
be on her way out somewhere, or unable to talk. At a loss for
what else to do, he'd messaged Belinda himself about having
a chat, although goodness knows if he'd have the balls to say
anything to her face. Would Jackie have any suggestions? he'd
wondered. Well, nothing ventured . . .

'Can I talk to you about something?' he'd asked her last
night. 'It's to do with Belinda.'

'Oh.' Her face immediately became pinched-looking and
her hands stole to her belly as if protecting their unborn child
from the other woman's presence. 'What is it?'

He'd gone on to describe the peculiar half conversation
he'd heard in the café, and then what Ray had said about

Apolline, the so-called psychic charging Belinda an astronomical amount for a pack of lies. 'It's clearly a crutch, but
not a very healthy one,' he'd said. 'I just don't know what
to do, if anything.' He'd spread his hands helplessly. 'Any
thoughts?'

'Hmm,' she'd replied, typing quickly at her laptop. 'This
is her, I guess. The psychic.' They'd peered at a lurid web
page with a list of phone numbers plus the face of a dark-
haired woman, her hand on a crystal ball, gazing out from
the screen.

Tony pulled a face. 'Christ,' he said. 'It's so ... tacky.' The
thought of vivacious, dynamic Belinda being sucked in by this
rubbish made him feel sad. Angry too. How could anyone set
themselves up to deliberately deceive other people that way?

'Good work, everyone!' Sallyanne said at that moment, and
Tony snapped back to the room, blinking away his concerns.
In hindsight, he probably *had* pissed Jackie off by talking to
her about it. She'd muttered that thing about Belinda and
Valentine's Day at breakfast too; it had clearly been on her
mind. Why did everything have to be so complicated?

'Now, before we take a break, I'd like us to have a group
discussion about managing birth expectations,' Sallyanne went
on. 'So if we could all – yes, Ruth?'

'Sallyanne, I don't want to point the finger, but there seem
to be some very negative attitudes in the class, and I'm finding
it unhelpful,' said Ruth piously. Tony had to try extremely
hard not to groan aloud. This was a dig at him, presumably.
Well, boo-fucking-hoo, Ruth. Get over it!

'I feel *exactly* the same,' put in Reiki Woman, whose name Tony couldn't remember. She flashed him a glare just so that everyone could be quite sure who the villain was. 'It's like ... can't we have some solidarity? Group positivity?'

Jackie snorted. 'Tell me about it,' she muttered. 'You don't have to live with him!'

Tony stared at her, hurt that she could side with these self-righteous strangers. 'Jac!' he protested. 'Steady on.'

'Well, what do you expect, Tony, when you keep banging on about your ex-wife all the time? Even though I'm right here, carrying our baby!'

There was a hiss of sucked-in breaths, an audible cluck of tutting tongues. Was he being paranoid or was the hostility rising? The atmosphere in the room seemed medieval to him suddenly, as if he were a bear being poked with sticks. He could almost hear the crackle of flaming torches and wondered how much more of this he could stand. But then came a different voice.

'Can we give Tony a break, here? You all seem to have made your minds up about him, but most of you don't know that he's a grieving parent. He's lost a child, for heaven's sake!' It was Genevieve, eyes blazing as she glared at every single person there in turn. 'Jackie – I can see you're scared about having a baby –' *Christ*, thought Tony in alarm, 'scared' was pretty much the most inflammatory adjective anybody could ever throw at his partner – 'but please – Tony's scared too. Even I can see that. Wouldn't you be, if you'd already suffered the worst grief a parent can undergo? Wouldn't any of us be terrified?'

She swung her arm around to encompass the entire group

and, one by one, faces fell and their antagonism swiftly turned to guilt. Jackie looked furious but said nothing. Tony too was unable to speak for a moment, partly in horror that Gen had just outed him to the room so bluntly (so much for any bereavement group code of silence) but also because she had come between him and his partner in a way that was undeniably damning for Jackie.

'Tony, I'm extremely sorry to hear that you've experienced something so painful,' Sallyanne said after a moment, eyes glistening with a new compassion behind her glasses.

Her words were echoed by a murmured chorus of similar sentiment. They were sorry, so sorry, their awkward faces said. No, they couldn't imagine how it must feel. Yes, they did all feel quite shit about themselves now. (Okay, so nobody actually said this last thought out loud but he could tell a fair few of them were thinking it. Even Ruth was hanging her head, looking uncomfortable. Good.)

Tony put up his hands wordlessly because there was nothing much to say. He couldn't come back with an easy 'That's okay' or 'It doesn't matter', for instance, because frankly, it wasn't okay and it did matter. Also, if he was honest, because he was rather enjoying knowing that the haters were now absolutely squirming.

'I think we've all learned a lesson today when it comes to not making assumptions about other parents,' Sallyanne went on solemnly. There was always a teaching moment to be found, as Belinda would have said, rolling her eyes. 'Let's all respect one another and acknowledge the fact that it's impossible to know what a person has been through, or might be feeling, based on first impressions alone. Okay! Moving on. This might be a good moment for a break, actually – let's take ten minutes, shall we, to get refreshments or use the loo. And when we come back, we can look at some complications that may arise during the birthing experience – and how you're all going to react calmly and competently in those circumstances.'

Well done, Sallyanne, safely steering them past the car crash and back on track, Tony thought, still avoiding anyone's gaze. There was a subdued feeling in the air as the group broke up, any previous jollity now seemingly on hold following their collective scolding. Tony eyed Jackie, who looked as if she was trying very hard to keep it together. 'You okay?' he asked quietly.

'Sorry,' she muttered, reaching for his hand. 'That was a bit out of order.'

He wasn't completely sure whether she meant she had been out of order, or if she thought Gen had been, for wading in, but then she made a little hiccupping sound and he knew it was the former. 'Hey,' he said, putting an arm around her. 'It's okay. Storm in a teacup.'

She leaned against him. 'I think . . . I think I *am* a bit scared,' she confessed into his shoulder, so low he had to strain to hear her. 'It *is* really fucking scary, all of this.' Her voice was becoming smaller with every word. 'I don't even know if I can do it, let alone if you . . . Well, if you leave me too.'

Ouch. Was that what this was really about? 'I am not about to leave you,' he said. 'It is the biggest regret of my life, not being a better father for my children. I am in this one hundred per cent with you, and with our child. I don't need Valentine's Day to prove how committed I am to the pair of you—' He broke off, registering too late the fact that her insecurities indicated she *did* need this sort of thing. 'Although I'm hearing loud and clear that I need to do better to show you that commitment,' he added in the next breath. 'And I promise I will.'

Over her shoulder he noticed that Genevieve appeared to be getting an ear-bashing from her other half, Penelope, and that they both kept shooting apologetic glances over in his direction. He attempted a *We're okay* face in response before returning to the business in hand, the pep talk he needed to nail.

'As for whether or not you can do this …' He shook his head, because she was the most competent woman he'd ever met and he had no doubts about her abilities himself. 'Jackie Global Director Parker, of *course* you can bloody well do it,' he said, encircling her with both arms now. 'You'll be such a great mum,' he assured her. 'Fun. Energetic. Loving. The best possible role model. And I'm going to be with you every step of the way, I promise.' He rubbed her back bracingly then released her. 'Now – do you want me to get you a special Valentine's cup of peppermint tea? A romantic glass of water?'

She smiled weakly, still leaning against him. 'Sorry, Tony. I felt a bit weirded out, talking about Belinda last night, to be honest,' she confessed, stroking his arm. 'Also, I'm starving. I must have been mad, turning down dinner out tonight. That'll teach me to be pig-headed.'

He kissed the top of her head. 'I'm with *you* now, not Belinda,' he told her. 'And all our favourite restaurants will still be there tomorrow. But in the meantime, let's get a massive takeaway on the way home, yeah?'

# Chapter Nineteen

It was confusing, but ever since she'd met up with Jacob the week before, Alice hadn't been able to stop thinking about him. Having previously filed him in a part of her brain labelled 'History', it had been an unexpected thrill to have her life bump tangentially against his again, dislodging all sorts of memories in the process. She'd found herself remembering what it was to be that young, hopeful Alice, carefree and open to anything. More disturbingly, she'd dreamed one night that she was a teenager again, kissing Jacob amidst the chaos of a house party, only to catch her reflection and discover that she was actually in her thirties and so was he. She'd woken up in an absolute puddle of guilt – he was married! Off limits! – but the dream must have poked a little tendril into her, nevertheless, because when her phone pinged mid-morning and it was a message from him – *Up for Flying Beauties reunion number 2?* – a heady thrill spread through her entire body.

According to Leni's diary, exactly a year ago to this day she'd been in Kiki's, a cocktail bar in Farringdon; a quick search online provided Alice with pictures of her on social media from the night itself. Off-duty Leni, with her hair piled up in a loose chignon, holding an espresso martini with a glint in her eye. Perfect, thought Alice, suggesting it to Jacob. Now here she was, retracing her sister's footsteps as she walked into a dimly lit bar with fairy lights strung from the rafters. There were candles flickering in jars on the tables, a long mustard-yellow banquette running the length of the room, and an old Fleetwood Mac song playing from the speakers. Outside it was raining, the icy sort of rain that was almost sleet, but stepping through the doors of Kiki's was like entering a magical fairy grotto, warm and cosy, spangled with soft lights. *Check it out, Leni,* she thought, spotting Jacob on a high stool at the bar and waving to him. *Look — we're both here, your fellow Flying Beauties. Doing just what you were doing this time last year.*

She and Jacob said hello and had an awkward little hug, and she felt so pleased to see him again, real and solid and smiling, that she was overwhelmed for a second. Who would have thought it, the two of them all grown-up and friends again? 'So,' she went on, glancing up at the cocktail list, chalked above the bar. 'A year ago today, Leni was right here with friends, drinking espresso martinis, so that's what I'm going to have. Can I tempt you?'

'I'm enjoying a very good whisky sour here, but thanks,' he replied, indicating the glass beside him before smiling in what looked like surprise. 'So you're a coffee drinker these days, are you? I remember you hating it back when we were young. In fact, I remember once kissing you after

I'd had a cup and you being disgusted by the taste. Scarred me for life.'

'Oh God, did it really?' she asked, blushing because she'd forgotten this particular moment and it made her feel kind of gauche to have it recounted. Also, having him reference them kissing so soon after her dream felt worryingly as if he could see directly into her head, and knew exactly what her pervy subconscious had been up to.

'Well, years of extensive therapy later, I'm just about over the trauma ...' he teased, eyebrow raised. 'I'm kidding, no need to look so horrified.'

'Ha ha,' she said, defensively. 'And yes, I'm going for it on the drink. Coffee is still the devil's work, but I'm doing it in honour of Leni. One espresso martini, please,' she said as the ginger-goateed bartender appeared in front of her. 'Do you want another of those?' she asked Jacob, who gave her a thumbs up. 'And a whisky sour as well. Thanks.'

They found an empty corner and sat down with their drinks. Alice had painted her nails specially for the occasion – something else that made her think of Leni – and waggled them contentedly under the lights. 'It's so nice to imagine her here,' she said, her voice thick as she mentally conjured up her sister beside them, wearing her favourite blue geometric-print shirt, a big necklace, jeans and army boots. She sipped her drink, only to recoil immediately. Ugh. Coffee.

Jacob must have noticed because he looked as if he was trying not to smirk. 'That good, eh?'

'It's fine!' she said brightly, taking another sip. Yuck. How had Leni drunk this stuff? She set the glass down. 'I wonder how she discovered this place,' she mused. 'I mean, she lived in Acton, and worked at a primary school in Hanwell, so it's not as if she was in the area on a daily basis.'

'I didn't know she was a teacher,' Jacob said. 'Huh. I can see her doing that, actually, but I always figured she'd end up with a more artistic career, like fashion design or . . . I dunno.' He drank his whisky, reflecting. 'How about you, anyway? We spent so long talking about the old days last week, I don't think I know where you're working now.'

'Oh.' She waved a hand dismissively because the thought of letting the dreary details of her nine-to-five at Sage and Golding infiltrate this spangled evening was the last thing she wanted. Although not everything about it was dull, she supposed. She had spent all week hoping to avoid Darren, only to get stuck in the lift with him that morning. Damn it, he still looked sexy even in the too-bright light there, a rain-spattered mac over his crisp suit, his aftershave clean-smelling. He'd smiled at her, cool and composed, while she underwent an agony of awkwardness. 'All right?' he'd said.

'Yep,' she replied, jabbing at the button for her floor and then the Close Doors button, in the hope of speeding things up.

'Fancy going out some other time?' he asked conversationally. 'Maybe even tonight?'

She shook her head, a rigid smile on her face. 'Sorry, I'm busy,' she said, then stared down at her feet. The rest of the journey to her floor had been spent in excruciating silence.

'Nothing very exciting, to be honest,' she said to Jacob, glossing over the subject. 'But going back to Leni, you're right, she did want to be a fashion designer, but it never quite panned out. She had a stall in Spitalfields for a while after she graduated, selling these gorgeous tweedy scarves she made – there was a little piece in *Vogue* about them, can you believe – but it was hard work, slogging over the sewing machine all week, then sitting there on a freezing market stall at the weekend, having to be nice to hipsters who'd try to haggle her prices down …' She'd run out of breath and picked up her drink to refresh herself, only remembering too late that she didn't like it. 'Christ, that's horrible,' she admitted, unable to stop herself pulling a face at the bitter aftertaste.

He burst out laughing at her. 'I'm going to get you another drink, something you actually like,' he said, getting to his feet. 'No arguments. Nostalgia has its limits, Alice, and forcing down a cocktail you actively hate is a step too far.'

She blushed again, unable to argue the case. 'I'll have a Dorset Horn then, please,' she said meekly after a quick glance at the menu. She wouldn't tell him that this too was a tribute to her sister, what with Dorset being the birthplace of the Flying Beauties and all.

He returned with a fresh drink for them both and she found herself telling him about Leni's next job, as a delivery driver, but how she'd got the sack after getting points for speeding – only then, silver lining, she had to go on a speed awareness course and that was where she'd met Adam, who ended up becoming her husband for five years.

'Cupid works in mysterious ways,' he said with a smile. 'How about you, are you married?'

'No,' she said, wrinkling her nose, unable to avoid Leni's words of accusation spiking through the moment. *When are you going to grow up though? What do you know about adult life? Nothing, because you're still acting like a teenager, passively letting stuff happen to you; you've never had the bottle to commit to anything. Lucky you!* The Dorset Horn must have gone to her head because then she blurted out, 'I was dating this guy Noah for a while, but we split up last year after I got into some trouble with the police and ...' For some reason she couldn't stop herself – 'Well, he thought I'd lost it, basically, although in retrospect, I pretty much had, so ...' Now Jacob was staring at her in alarm and she cursed her own big mouth. Shut! Up! Moron! 'Anyway, that's another story,' she said. She briefly considered mentioning Darren before deciding that was an even worse idea. 'So yeah, Leni and Adam had this whirlwind romance and—'

'That sounded pretty bad,' he interrupted. 'Rewind a minute. What happened with the police? Is everything okay? Are *you* okay?'

She stirred her drink vigorously with the straw so that she didn't have to look at his concerned face. Any minute now he would make an excuse and get out of there, then block her number, deciding he didn't have space for a madwoman in his life. When would she learn to rein herself in? 'Oh yeah, I'm fine. It was a fuss about nothing. Not worth repeating.'

He said nothing in response but she could feel the weight of his gaze on her, watchful and concerned. Lana del Rey was singing about summertime sadness in the background, and Alice's face burned as she searched around for a change of subject. 'Anyway!' she said again, with new brightness. 'Where was I?'

'Alice,' he said gently. 'What's going on here? I'm finding this all a bit ... strange.'

She blinked. 'What ... What do you mean?'

'I mean ... Last week we met up for the first time in, what, ten, eleven years and we talked extensively about your sister. Which is fine!' he added quickly as her face changed. 'I can see you need to talk about her and I get that. Totally. But ...' He spread his hands, taking his time to find the next words. 'But I'm not sure I've got anything else to contribute here. I was hoping we could talk more about ourselves tonight, but you keep dodging every personal question I ask you. And dodging them really badly, I have to say. Sorry,' he said, as her face fell.

She hung her head, her face hot. 'Was it that obvious?' she mumbled.

'Well ... yes,' he told her. 'Look, I realise we don't really know each other any more, but you *can* talk to me. It's still me. You don't have to give me the Instagram version of your life, the same as I hope I don't have to pretend that everything's amazing in mine.'

His words stabbed tiny needles of shame into her because she realised in the next moment that she hadn't asked him a single thing about his life, either tonight or the time before. That was rude, wasn't it? She had been on dates like that, when the man had bored on about himself all the time, completely uninterested in her. Had she become this sort of person herself? 'Right,' she said stiffly, before self-defence kicked in. 'I did say it would be nice to meet up and talk about Leni,' she replied. 'I was under the impression you wanted that as well.'

'Yes, but we can do that *and* talk about other stuff too, can't we?' he countered. There was a pause which felt almost as interminable as the lift journey with Darren, and similarly mortifying. 'Or are you not interested in me as a person? Only my memories of Leni?'

She bowed her head, stricken. 'Sorry,' she mumbled, because everything he'd said was on the nail. She couldn't deny a single word of it. 'Sorry, you're right.' She pressed her cold glass against her cheek because her face was so hot. 'I *am* interested in you, of course I am,' she added for good measure. 'I know you're working at UCL and you're married, and have a little boy.'

'That all used to be true,' he said, then put his hands out in front of her. She stared at them, not following, until he said, 'Not married any more,' and she realised he wasn't wearing a ring.

'Oh,' she said, gazing dumbly from his bare fingers up to his face. To think she'd felt a momentary gaucheness earlier – now she was fully appalled at her own bad manners, for not asking him the most basic of questions. For not showing any interest in him at all, in fact. 'Sorry to hear that,' she said, humble with contrition. 'Was it recent? Is she in the UK too?' She sighed, shaking her head. 'Jacob, I've been a really rubbish companion, haven't I? Both last time and tonight, I'm embarrassed. You might not even want to talk about your marriage, but if you do, I'm absolutely going to listen.'

'Don't worry about it,' he said after a moment. 'No harm done. It was a couple of years ago, pretty amicable in the end. Yes, she's in London too, working at King's.'

'She's an academic as well?'

'Yeah. We met at a conference in Zurich eight years ago. She's very smart. We moved to Sweden because she was asked to head up the department at Gothenburg university – we had some very happy years there together.'

'You sound proud of her,' she commented, sipping her drink. He'd had this whole life full of adult things, she marvelled. Marriage. Life in another country. Career glory. A kid. In comparison, she was getting blind drunk and shagging a randomer from work and stuck in a dreary temp job, emotionally stunted; her biggest commitment being a cat who didn't even like her. Leni had been right about her passively letting life just happen to her, she thought dismally. Why was she like this?

'I am,' he said and she imagined him thinking how relieved he was to have managed a proper relationship with an amazing woman after dating car-crash Alice.

'What about your son?' she asked, swallowing the lump in her throat. 'How old is he? Have you got any pictures?'

'Of course,' he said, picking up his phone, and scrolling. There was a small private smile on his face, she noticed; a smile of love for this boy, a smile of gladness that he was a father and had a son. 'Here – this is Max. He's four.'

Max had white-blond hair that fell into his eyes and, with a look of utmost glee, was brandishing a massive stick in a forest. He was wearing a blue coat, unzipped, with mud all over his trousers and a pair of wellies striped yellow and black like a bee. 'Cute,' said Alice, smiling too as she took him in. 'He looks fun.'

'He is *so* much fun,' Jacob replied, taking back the phone. His eyes were soft with fondness, and Alice – ridiculously – felt shut out. Unimportant. She stared down into her drink, wondering if maybe she should have said yes to going out with Darren tonight instead, after all. It would have been a very different evening, conducted on far shallower levels, but at least she'd have felt that they were equals. And maybe that was all she could handle right now?

Later on, coming home and feeding Hamish, Alice knelt beside the cat as he ate, chancing a stroke along his soft, striped back. Embarrassment still tingled through her about how the evening had unfolded, and she cringed as she remembered the moment Jacob had called her out on her unintentional rudeness. The tube journey home had cast a new filter on the evening though, defensiveness increasingly spiking through her with every new station along the line. It wasn't that she wasn't *interested* in him, she argued in her head, it was more the case that her priority was Leni. So sue her!

Conversation had resumed, with her talking about how she had been dragged, kicking and screaming, to a Pilates class with Lou and Celeste the day before – 'I'm surprised they let you in if you were kicking and screaming,' he'd said, mouth twitching in amusement – and then she asked him lots more questions about his life, while successfully deflecting his attempts to go into further detail about her own work. 'Honestly, it's just a temp job and it's deadly dull, there's nothing to say,' she told him, holding up her hand like a stop sign.

'That surprises me,' he'd said. 'I don't want to sound patronising but I always thought you, out of everyone in our sixth form, would go on and do extraordinary things.'

Ugh. Sod off, she thought. Not everyone could get high-flying academic jobs around the world with brilliant brainy spouses. It was on the tip of her tongue to retaliate with tales of previous career glories – great campaigns, promotions, award nominations – but the thought of trying to prove herself in this way seemed demeaning. And what if she told him all of that and he still looked unimpressed? 'That *is* quite patronising,' she retorted instead. 'I feel like I'm one of your students, being badgered about a late essay or something. Any minute now you're going to tell me you're very disappointed in me, in a horribly serious voice.' *Don't you dare*, she thought, her whole body stiffening at the prospect.

'I'm not!' Now it was his turn to hold his hands up. 'I'm absolutely not, Alice. It was meant to be a compliment, although yeah, I'm sorry, it definitely didn't come out how I intended. Anyway, for all I know, you're a secret agent, working undercover and this is all an incredible double bluff.'

'Yeah, you got me,' she said blandly, although soon afterwards, she found herself necking her drink and making an excuse that she needed to go, because the whole conversation about her shortcomings was making her feel uncomfortable. Pissed off, in fact. 'I need to get back to MI5, give them my findings,' she deadpanned. 'Finish that dossier I've been compiling on you.'

She sighed again now, still unsure what to make of his words. *I thought you'd go on and do extraordinary things*, indeed. Did that mean he'd found her a massive downgrade in expectations? He'd even seemed dismayed when he asked if she still made her amazing birthday cakes for people and she'd had to confess no, not since last summer.

Her phone rang and it was Lou, calling for an update on how the evening had gone. 'Badly,' Alice summed up, leaning against the kitchen cupboard, her legs stretched out before her on the lino. 'I think he's actually a bit of a knob.'

'Oh no! What happened?'

Her body felt heavy as she sat there, the floor cold beneath her bottom. 'He just … It wasn't what I was hoping.'

There was a small pause. 'Which was … ? Enlighten me.'

'Well, I wanted to reminisce about Leni – that was the reason I suggested meeting up! – but he kept asking me questions about me, instead.'

'Rude bastard,' said Lou. 'How dare he?'

Alice gave a feeble laugh. 'And then when I did talk a bit about me, he seemed really disappointed, like he thought I'd done nothing with my life.'

Lou whistled. '*What?* Did he say that?'

Alice replayed the conversation in her head for the hundredth time. 'Not exactly, I suppose,' she conceded grudgingly, 'but that was the impression I got. I could tell he thought I was a massive loser.'

'Well, take it from me: you are not,' Lou said heatedly. Then there was a pause. 'Or is this a case of you being hard on yourself?' she asked. 'Because I'm willing to bet he didn't think that at all. Unless he's a total idiot, in which case, forget him.'

'He's not an idiot, worst luck,' Alice replied with a sigh. 'He's the brainiest person I know.'

'He sounds pretty bloody dumb to me.' You couldn't fault Lou on her loyalty, that was for sure. 'Or possibly just emotionally clueless. Maybe he's never had to deal with grief himself, he doesn't know what it looks like. And he was fully expecting you to be the Alice he once knew – go-getting and ambitious and optimistic.'

'As opposed to the miserable version of now,' Alice said, trying not to take offence that her best friend clearly thought she was none of those things any more. 'The version who's stuck in the past and apparently can't move on.'

'Hey, nobody's saying "miserable",' Lou corrected her, although Alice noticed she didn't argue with the bit about her being stuck in the past. 'You're just in a dip, that's all. And if he's too thick to realise that, then that's his lookout.'

Alice took this in, still sitting there on the floor even though Hamish had finished his dinner and long since stalked away. 'I was pretty rude to him,' she confessed. 'The worst conversationalist ever, pretty much.'

'Sounds like he got what he deserved, then,' Lou said. 'Forget him, Alice. It doesn't matter what he thinks. You just do you. There are plenty of us Alice fans still out there in the meantime. Anyway – you *are* moving on. You're doing that pottery thing at the weekend, right?'

'Saturday, yeah,' Alice said, although Lou seemed to have

forgotten that she had booked the *kintsugi* workshop in order to mend Leni's plates. Did it still count as moving on in that case? Probably not. Would she ever move on? Probably not.

'And we're doing Pilates on Tuesday again, yeah? That's another new thing. So you're doing brilliantly, all right? Hang in there.'

# Chapter Twenty

*McKenzies Together group*

**Tony:** *Did we all have a lovely Valentine's Day, then? Jackie and I celebrated with . . . an antenatal class. Who said romance is dead?? This weekend we're off to Blenheim to stay in a posh hotel though, while we still can. Hope you all have nice plans ahead. Will, did you see the Liverpool game? Incredible goals! Love Dad/Tony xx 09.33*

**Alice:** *Romance definitely dead in my life!! All good though. X 11.34*

**Belinda:** *We've had an offer on the house from a lovely family – probably going to accept. If any of you want to come back for a bit of nostalgia in the next few weeks, please do, it might be your last chance. You too, Tony 14.06*

**Tony:** *I'd really like that, Bel. Thank you. Maybe sometime next week? Love Tony x 16.52*

**Belinda:** *How about you, Will, do you think you might be back any time soon? Would be so nice to see you [heart emoji] xxx 17.45*

★

Will read the messages, screwing up his face. *Doubtful*, he typed. *Got quite a lot of work on right now. And – no offence – but Oxford in February vs Thailand in February? Only one winner for me.* Just for good measure, he sent them a beach photo: the sea a sparkling sapphire ribbon splitting the golden sand from the vast, cloudless sky.

He wasn't even lying about the work. He'd moved on recently, having had a serious word with himself: time to get his act together, sharpen up the old sales patter. He'd made an effort socially too, and had been to some brilliant parties up in the hills, dancing until dawn with some of the ex-pats he knew. And then, dazzled with amphetamines and optimism, he'd come to the conclusion that Juno was right, selling flip-flops was a mug's game; it was time to take her up on her suggestion of dealing in more profitable goods. He was on his way to meet her now, having scraped together the last of his savings so that he could pick up a decent stash of weed and pills with which to begin his new career.

His phone buzzed in his pocket and he grimaced, hoping it wasn't Juno, getting in touch to change the arrangements, now that he'd plucked up the courage to go ahead. To his surprise though, he saw a message from an old school friend, Hattie.

*Will! How are you? Hope you're having a good time out there (but also hope you'll be back for September – you know Gaz is getting married, right?? He's been trying to pin you down for his stag – check your DMs!!) Just a quick one to say Sam and I have booked a holiday – to Thailand! Impulse trip – we'll be there at the beginning of March. Still working out an itinerary but would love to see you if possible. Love Hats xxx*

Walking along the street reading this, he stopped dead at the thought of his two worlds colliding, at the idea of Hattie being here. He was almost mown down by a woman pushing a trolley full of water bottles towards a restaurant and had to dodge out of her way.

'Sorry,' he mumbled, but barely heard her annoyed exclamation, the slap of her plastic sandals as she shook her head and marched past, because he was thinking of sweet, lovely Hattie, who he'd known since primary school. She'd been so thoughtful after Leni died, turning up at the funeral to support him, even though she hadn't really known his sister. Lots of people had seemed unsure how to act around him; lots of people, in fact, said nothing at all, because the news was so big, so terrible, where did you begin? Even Molly, the girl he'd been dating, started seeing someone else – 'I didn't think we were exclusive!' she claimed. Hattie had been different – she'd made a concerted effort to be there for him, sending sympathetic messages for days and weeks after Leni's death, making sure he was still invited to everything. Even now, she was trying to include him in Gaz's wedding preparations where he'd cut himself off.

What would she think of him here, with his flat full of fake designer sunglasses, with a stash of pills to sell to hedonistic holidaymakers?

*Don't think about that*, he told himself, walking a little quicker. This was not the time for an existential crisis; he had a job to do.

Juno's apartment was in an area of town he didn't know too well, and as he followed the map on his phone, he found himself becoming disoriented in the heat. These streets were off the tourist trail, quieter and narrow, with blocks of housing three storeys high either side, ropes of washing strung in colourful zigzags above his head. A couple of elderly Thai men playing backgammon watched him from a doorstep; the sound of a baby crying floated down from an upstairs window. He'd brought a backpack with him in which to carry his purchases, currently empty apart from the cash he'd got together, and queasily imagined himself walking back this way with hundreds of pounds' worth of drugs in his possession. It would be all right, wouldn't it? Other people did this. Other people made an absolute ton of money doing it, more to the point.

With an increasing sense of trepidation, he approached her apartment block, noticing too late the two enormous blokes sitting on the wall outside who rose to their feet on seeing him. A sixth sense told him to run, his skin prickling with the premonition of trouble. Both men were squat and muscular, their black T-shirts stretching over their beefy chests; total football-hooligan vibes. 'All right?' Will said, trying to sound casual although his voice became a squeak as they walked towards him, swift and purposeful. 'Er ... I'm here to see Juno?' Did she have bodyguards now? he thought in alarm. Were they about to pat him down for weapons, check him over before letting him in?

Not exactly. In two strides they were either side of him, smelling of sweat and danger, and Will's life flashed before his eyes in a moment of extreme terror. 'Phone,' demanded meathead number one, flicking open a knife and pointing the blade at him, his tone one of menacing intent. The other guy was already tearing at his backpack, almost wrenching Will's arms out of their sockets in an attempt to rip it from his body. 'Hey!' he yelled, stupidly trying to hang on to it – all his money! – but they overpowered him embarrassingly easily, the first guy snatching Will's phone from his puny, clutching fingers for good measure.

Meathead two gave Will a shove that knocked him to the ground and then they both ran, their footsteps thudding as they vanished around the corner. Will's heart pounded, adrenalin pumped uselessly; his wrist and hip throbbed where they'd smashed to the ground. 'Juno!' he called up to the building, dragging himself upright, checking himself for damage. He'd gashed his elbow, he realised dimly. His head felt woozy, his body flooded with shock and hurt. *That's not fair!* They had taken everything from him, he realised. He had his door key in his pocket but that was all he had left. 'Juno!' he yelled again, his voice echoing off the walls around him. He staggered to her door and pressed the buzzer, once and then again. Where was she? 'JUNO!' he shouted for the third time.

A young Thai woman was watching him from the neighbouring building, arms folded. She was wearing a mango-coloured vest top and cut-off blue trousers, her dark hair tied back from her face. 'She gone,' she told him, making walking motions in the air with her fingers. 'Lady gone.'

'Lady gone?' he repeated, confused, because even then he still believed, like the innocent he was; even then he thought

227

he'd been the victim of bad luck, nothing more. He pointed at the door. 'Lady here – gone?'

The woman nodded and shrugged. 'She gone.'

Shell-shocked from the mugging and the heat, his brain struggling to make sense of what had just happened, he ended up getting completely lost on the way home, without his phone to guide him. It made sense, he supposed dazedly. He'd lost everything else, after all: why not his sense of direction too? Then, stumbling round a corner, he blinked to see before him a large red-stone temple with a red and gold triangular-stepped roof, and a row of arched columns decorated with gold paint. Saffron-robed monks sat cross-legged behind the columns, chanting and banging drums, while in a courtyard area at the front of the temple, an ornate white casket was being towed around an unlit pyre on a gleaming gilded cart. It was a funeral, he realised with a jolt, noticing a group of mourners, dressed in black and white, some chanting, some with their heads silently bowed. The mourners all held the same long piece of rope attached to the back of the cart, and followed it in procession.

Will felt unable to turn away, thinking inevitably of Leni's funeral: a day he could hardly remember because he'd been so drunk from start to finish. It was hard to forget the shock on everyone's faces though; the stunned atmosphere of *Is this really happening?* that permeated each row of the crematorium. His mum had been weeping so noisily she'd had to lean on Ray for bodily support when they stood for the hymns. His dad was ashen-faced in a black suit. Alice had given a reading from *Winnie-the-Pooh* – or rather, she'd tried to, but had broken down in sobs, with her friend Lou eventually coming to stand with her at the lectern to help her through the remainder. And then there had been the moment when the crematorium curtains jerkily opened – one lagging behind the other as if it had temporarily become stuck – then the conveyor belt began rolling with an unoiled squeaking, and the coffin trundled backstage into the secret area that nobody wanted to think about. It had all been so neat and tidy, in hindsight. So British. Cover it up, don't think about it, done.

Afterwards, they'd gone to a pub in Headington and he'd got so hammered he ended up falling over in the gents and getting piss all over his smart trousers. He'd had to walk back to his mum's at the end of the night because none of the taxis would take him.

Meanwhile, at this funeral, there were no juddering curtains or squeaky conveyor belt. The casket was being loaded on to the pyre – a tower of wooden pallets – and the mourners were posting flowers and what he guessed were offerings between the slats before putting their hands together in prayer. Stupidly, he felt a shiver of repulsion on realising that they were actually going to light the pyre right there in the open and burn the casket, rather than tucking the scene away behind closed doors. It seemed so medieval somehow, so basic – but then, this was the reality of a cremation, of course. This was what happened behind the curtains.

Feeling as if he were intruding on a private moment, he moved on, searching for landmarks that might help him find his way back to the flat. He really wanted to get home to tend to the throbbing wound on his elbow and work out what the hell he was going to do now that he'd lost all his savings. He still couldn't quite believe that Juno had stitched him up like that. What an idiot he was. What a gullible fool. She'd seen him coming, all right.

He must have been walking blindly around in a circle, because after what felt like ages, he found himself back at the temple again and groaned in dismay. It was like being in a bad dream where he was forced to repeatedly confront death and his own ineptitude. At the funeral, a fire was now alight, flames crackling up through the dry wooden tower. Candles burned at the base of the columns, while floral tributes had been laid on the shallow steps leading up to the main door of the temple, along with large gilt-framed pictures of a man in a suit, presumably the deceased. The mourners sang and prayed; he could smell incense as well as burning wood, and all of a sudden, he felt so overcome by everything that had happened, he found himself raising a hand and clutching one of the painted railings that enclosed the temple courtyard, then leaning his head against it.

Leni's gone, he thought wretchedly, as a new drumbeat started up, slow and sonorous. Leni's really gone and she's not coming back. Not ever. He'd always known that, obviously, but it was as if he'd disguised the truth from himself, shoved it behind a pair of creaking crematorium curtains, conveniently out of sight. He had stepped on to the plane at Heathrow and crossed into a different, self-constructed realm where the pain and reality of death could not touch him. But death was impossible to avoid now as the flames took hold of the pyre, as the singing and drumming grew louder, as the smoke curled and twisted in grey ribbons up against the dense white sky.

In the next moment, it felt as if something was breaking within him. Tears spilled down his face, emotions swelled inside his chest; his own skin suddenly felt too thin to contain his inner self. Everything he had suppressed for so long, everything he had refused to look at, now forced its way seismically to the surface.

'Are you okay?' came an Australian voice from nearby and he turned to see a tall bespectacled woman astride a bike. She was in her late forties, at a guess, with short grey hair, and she had a kindness about her, a mellow art-teacher vibe. Her gaze flicked to the funeral scene behind him. 'Have you lost someone too?' she asked.

'My sister,' he said, gulping a breath. He clenched his fists, trying to control himself. 'Leni. It was last year, nothing to do with this funeral, but . . .'

'But you're remembering her now,' she said gently. 'And it hurts. Of course it hurts.'

'The thing is, it . . . it was my fault she died,' he blurted out. His darkest secret, bursting from him before he could stop it. He knuckled the tears from his eyes, shoulders shaking. 'It was my fault!'

He half expected lightning to strike him for his confession, thunderclouds to boom overhead now that he'd said the words aloud. But instead the woman put a hand on his back and just left it there in solidarity while he wept, unable to control himself any more. 'Sorry,' he said, eventually pulling himself together. 'I'm … It's been …' None of the words seemed right, or enough any more. 'I'm having a really bad day,' he said eventually, and almost wanted to laugh at such a pathetic understatement.

The woman patted his back then reached into a battered wicker basket attached to the front of her bike to retrieve a dented silver water bottle. 'Home-made lemonade,' she told him. 'Try some.'

He accepted gratefully and took a long, cool swig. It was sweet and sharp, insanely refreshing. 'Thank you,' he mumbled, wiping his eyes on his forearm.

'I don't know what happened to your sister, but I can see you're very sorry,' the woman told him kindly. 'And it's especially hard to lose someone when they're young.'

'Yes,' he managed to say.

'In some ways, I think Buddhists have the right idea about death,' she went on, gesturing at the scene before them. 'They see the funeral almost as a staging post before the deceased moves on to a better place. I rather like that, don't you? It's soothing to think the person we love hasn't gone forever; that they still exist in some form or other. Comforting to those of us still here, trying to carry on without them.'

'Yes,' he said again, thankful for her slow, mellifluous voice which felt like a balm to his troubled soul. 'I like that too.' He pushed away the last of his tears, wondering what form Leni might have taken if she had returned. A bird of paradise, maybe, colourful and exotic. A peacock, even – she loved those. Or, of course, a baby, a whole new person, starting the cycle again. He wasn't sure he believed in this theory – he was a scientist, he liked evidence and facts – but the woman was right: the thought itself was consoling regardless.

'Whatever the case, it's good to honour those who go before us,' she said, putting her hands together in prayer and making a neat, respectful bow towards the funeral scene. 'And to allow the grief to flood out when it needs to. At the end of the day, it's another form of love, isn't it? Our tears say: you were important to me, I remember you, I loved you.' She patted him on the arm. 'There's no need to be afraid of your grief. You loved your sister.'

'Thank you,' he stammered, moved beyond words. *You were important to me, I remember you, I loved you.* Yes – that was it exactly. This kind stranger had managed to articulate, within a few clear sentences, the enormity of feeling he had experienced, emotions he hadn't known how to handle. 'And thank you for the lemonade,' he added, giving her back the bottle.

The woman was able to give him directions back to his street and then they said goodbye. His body ached where he'd been knocked to the ground, his throat hurt from the smoke of the funeral pyre, but as he began walking, he felt a new clarity settling on him like quiet flakes of snow. He'd been hiding from everything out here; he'd buried himself on this island far from home in the hope of forgetting his pain and guilt, but it was still there, beating away like an infected wound inside him, wasn't it? And if he ever wanted to scissor it out again, he knew, deep down, that he would have to go home and confront the truth. Look his family in the eye and tell them.

Oh Christ. It was terrifying. But now that he'd lost all his money, now that his life had crashed down around him, he no longer had the luxury of choices. He just had to hope he'd still have a family left once they knew what he'd done.

# Chapter Twenty-One

**Tony:** *If you're sure it's all right for me to come round to the house one last time, how does next Tuesday suit you? I could be there for four o'clock? X 10.25*

**Belinda:** *Sounds good to me. See you then. 11.41*

Belinda's life had suddenly taken a turn for the busier. In the last week she had accepted a good offer on the house from a couple who seemed to genuinely love the property. The thought of leaving the place where her children had grown up was a wrench, but it was for the best, she told herself. Because this was also the house where her marriage had broken down, where the kids had moved out, where she'd had the shattering news about Leni. Buildings could retain echoes of sadness as well as happiness, she'd always thought; as if the very walls were papered with good and bad memories.

Still. Along with the inevitable melancholy of moving on, there had also come an unexpected buffer of solace; that her old home would be loved anew by a different family, that the rooms would once again ring with the sound of children's laughter and songs and play. Far better this, than for it to be purchased by a nameless developer, say. The offer and its acceptance now meant an avalanche of paperwork and solicitor dealings, plus extra impetus in the search for a new home.

Out with the old, in with the ... well, maybe the even older, she thought, when she and Ray returned to see the crumbling doer-upper for a second viewing. Having stormed out on their previous visit, telling the estate agent they weren't interested, she had nonetheless found herself thinking about the house ever since, particularly whenever they had viewed more sensible, ordinary properties. Had she been too hasty, too emotional in her dismissal, she had wondered aloud to Ray, who immediately talked her into a return trip. It turned out he'd been hankering after the place too, and was all too keen to give it another look.

This time, she planned to keep a cooler head, not least because Ellis was back in town and accompanying them for the viewing. A few days ago, he'd got in touch with Ray again to say that he'd been offered the trainee management position, and they had invited him to stay while he looked for a flat to rent. Ellis's job wasn't due to start for another week so he had time on his hands – but despite Ray hoping this might be the launch of a new father-son bonhomie, it hadn't quite worked out that way so far. There was something very guarded about Ellis – watchful, even. You could talk to him for a whole evening and realise that you didn't know him any better; he would deflect and side-step and swerve with all the deftness of a professional footballer. At first Belinda had put it down to shyness, but now she was wondering if the lad was hiding something. Or up to something?

Ray had soft-soaped him today, saying that they'd love his opinion on the house, and so here they were, the three of them roaming the dusty, echoing rooms. The second viewing, Belinda knew, was all about being cold-eyed and realistic, peering into corners, asking the big practical questions – and she indeed felt able to see the place more clearly, knowing that Apolline had assured her of Leni's approval of the property. Unfortunately, rather than being hard-headed and detail-focussed, she was experiencing what could only be described as a rising tide of infatuation for the place, before which any issues regarding damp, wiring or insulation seemed trivial. It would occur to her, for instance, walking through the high-ceilinged hall, that heating costs would be an absolute shocker. (Yes, but the big windows, once cleaned, would let in so much light! replied her inner optimist.) The roof too would surely be a money pit, seeing as it needed a complete overhaul, no doubt running to tens of thousands of pounds. (Yes, but the garden, once they'd pruned and planted and loved it, would be the most wonderful sanctuary on sunny days. They could have chickens! And a vegetable plot! And beautiful statues in unexpected places!)

'So what are you planning, four double rooms for paying guests, is it?' Ellis said, as they tramped around upstairs. For all his reticence about his own affairs, he was certainly taking a great deal of interest in theirs, Belinda couldn't help thinking. 'Have you actually broken down the figures, potential income against expenses, Dad, or is this still a bit of a wish and a promise at the moment?'

Seeming pleased that his son was engaging with the matter, Ray hurried to assure him that yes, they had drawn up a business plan with an accountant friend, before taking him through the details. His whole face lit up whenever he and Ellis spoke, Belinda had noticed, and she felt a pang of envy, wishing that she too could have a lost child returned to her, that she too could be granted a second chance. Ray was such a nice, natural, easy-going dad; whatever demons he'd been in the grip of years earlier had left him now, and the reappearance of his son had given him a new lightness she hadn't seen before.

But, she kept wondering, how did Ellis feel in return? She'd tried to draw him out of himself a few times, but he gave little away. 'Plenty of room for you to stay any time,' she said now, spotting a chance to winkle out some personal information. 'If you wanted to bring a girlfriend, or ... Did you say you had a girlfriend, Ellis? Or someone special?'

He only shrugged and went to peer through the window, as if that was classified information. It had been a perfectly reasonable question though, Belinda thought to herself with renewed suspicion. Why couldn't he answer like any normal person?

They wandered into a bathroom where the ceiling had collapsed into the bath, Belinda's mind still whirring. She didn't want to make presumptions, but couldn't help worrying that Ellis's reasons for being back in Ray's life were ... well, not entirely honourable? Earlier, she'd heard him ask Ray if he could borrow the money for a deposit on a flat, plus a month's rent, and Belinda fervently hoped he could be trusted.

Not that she could articulate this to Ray though, when he had shown nothing but complete faith in his son's intentions from day one. He'd even seemed upset when he noticed her moving her handbag from its usual position in the hall up to their bedroom at night. Just in case.

'What are you . . .? He's not going to steal your credit cards, if that's what you think,' he'd said, spots of indignant colour appearing on his cheeks.

'It's not that,' she'd protested. What Ray seemed to forget sometimes was that she had been a social worker for her entire working life; she had seen a lot of unpleasant behaviour between family members. People could be weak, however much you wanted to see only good there, and that was the unfortunate truth, like it or not. 'But Ray . . . at the end of the day, we don't know him, do we?'

'*I* do,' he'd retorted, turning away but not before she'd seen his hurt expression. 'He's my son, and he's not a thief.'

Ellis almost certainly *wasn't* a thief, and it wasn't as if Belinda had much that was worth nicking in the first place, but all the same, this was what she did when there was anyone she didn't know well in the house: plumbers or builders or the meter reader. 'It was habit more than anything personal,' she'd fretted to Apolline that morning, recounting the exchange. 'The lad seems nice, I've got nothing against him, of course, but . . .'

'But he's a cuckoo in the nest,' Apolline put in. 'You know nothing of his motives.'

'Well . . .'

'And Leni doesn't like him being there,' Apolline went on, which cut Belinda to the quick.

'She doesn't? What did she say?'

'She says not to trust the mouse. She says this will mean something to you.'

'Not to trust the *mouse*?' Belinda tried to transpose Ellis's rather long, lugubrious face with that of a mouse but the image didn't quite work. If you were to call him an animal, he'd be a horse, she found herself thinking, before racking her brain to interpret this mouse business. When she was a child, there had been mice in their family home for a while, that occasionally gnawed through the wires in the cellar, plunging the house into sudden darkness at unexpected moments. She remembered the shock of it, how she and her sister Carolyn would shriek and clutch each other, like something from a horror film. Was Ellis planning to bring darkness into their lives?

She was still musing on this as she wandered into the large, light kitchen that once must have been the heart of the house, with its big stone hearth and windows looking out on to the garden. She wanted to trust Ray's son, but…

'So,' Ray said, appearing behind her just then. 'What are we thinking today?'

For a moment Belinda felt hot with embarrassment, as if he'd been able to see *exactly* what she'd been thinking, until she oriented herself – flagstone floor, dripping tap, dusty windows – and realised that he meant, of course, what was she thinking about the house. This gorgeous, expensive, crumbling wreck that would require plenty of hard work but also offered the bonus of tranquillity, she realised. The space to exhale. She could begin again, in a place where she wouldn't be bumping up against ghosts and memories every moment of every day. They could all come here for Christmas, she thought – Alice and Will, and their partners-yet-to-meet, and maybe one day these corridors would patter with the footsteps of grand-children (yes, she still held out hope), their voices high and excited as they played hide and seek, or came rushing into this same kitchen to bake scones with Grandma. It could be a place of healing for them as a family.

'Well,' she said, as Ray slotted his arm around her and she leaned comfortably against him. 'That is the question.' They stood there for a moment together, considering the grimy old cabinets (oak perhaps, beneath the dirt), along with the broken blinds hanging at drunken angles along the top of the windows (she could make new ones in the space of an after-noon, no problem) and the view through to the walled herb garden beyond (it would be such a suntrap on summer days, she was sure of it). She returned her focus to the kitchen and gestured to the ageing range cooker. 'I bet this would be lovely and cosy on winter days,' she said, her head nestling into the soft space beside his shoulder. 'I'm imagining us cooking in here, getting a stew in the oven or an apple crumble. Friends coming over for raucous dinners, the smell of cakes baking on a Sunday afternoon, a proper larder of food and drink.'

'Not to mention all those bacon and egg breakfasts we'll be frying up for our guests,' he joked, and they both laughed at the image of themselves fussing about in aprons here, making up pots of tea and coffee, cutting toast slices into triangles and wedging them into white china racks. It almost felt as if they would be playing a game, pretending to be hosts; the idea tickled her. Then she forced herself to get a grip on her daydreams.

'We'd have to gut the place, you know that, don't you, if we actually want to reach any health and safety standards,' she said with deliberate sternness. 'New floors, new wiring; I bet the plumbing's ancient. Everything's going to need replacing.' She paused for breath, then her phone chirped with a text from Alice, commenting on the photos she'd sent her. *Wow! Mum, it's incredible. You'd be Lady of the Manor!* Belinda read, and felt herself buoyed by her daughter's words. 'Alice thinks it looks incredible though,' she said, holding the screen in front of him so that he could see.

'How about you?' he prompted, squeezing her gently. 'What do you think?'

He was too kind to remind her of the last time they'd been there, with her flouncing out, saying they didn't want the place. She loved that about him. You could bet your life that if she'd still been married to Tony, he wouldn't have let her histrionics pass without teasing her about them at least twenty times a day.

'I think it's pretty incredible too,' she replied to Ray now. 'And I can't help thinking that once we've knocked it into shape, it will have far more appeal and wow factor to anyone searching online for an Oxfordshire B. & B., won't it?' She'd already sized up the competition on her laptop – a stream of perfectly nice houses on the outskirts of the city, but none as visually appealing as this place. 'I mean, faced with this, or some bland semi on the Woodstock Road, you're always going to pick the gorgeous one, aren't you? We could make it a proper destination for people. Who wouldn't want to stay in a house like this?'

'Well, idiots, that's who,' he said. 'Idiots who we don't want here anyway. So sod 'em!'

'Exactly! And luckily neither of us are scared of hard work, are we?' she went on.

'Like I'd be with you if I was,' he joked.

'Oi!' she cried, elbowing him indignantly, but she knew he didn't mean it. They'd been such a good team in recent weeks, the pair of them decluttering and painting their current home in readiness for selling up. A montage played in her head, of them here together in matching white overalls: up ladders with paint trays, pulling up ancient carpets amidst clouds of dust, cleaning windows simultaneously – one inside, one out, like two characters in a sitcom. Or maybe Laurel and Hardy, she thought, although hopefully a less accident-prone version. 'I'm trying my best to be businesslike and not to fall too hard for this place but ...' She turned her head to smile at him. 'Sod it, I'm in. I love it.'

'Me too,' he said happily. 'And I love you. The two of us, living here ... I think our best days could still be ahead of us, Bel, I really do. Besides, there's nobody with whom I'd rather share the honour of a gargantuan new financial commitment.'

Belinda spluttered with laughter. 'Aww, shucks. You old sweet-talker, you.'

They heard footsteps just then, and turned to see Ellis walking into the room. 'What do you think, son?' Ray asked.

'I mean ... it's a lot of money,' Ellis said dubiously, hands tucked into the pockets of his slouchy grey hoodie. 'Do you really want to be taking on another mortgage at your age? No offence,' he added, more to Belinda than to his dad. 'I mean . . .' He trailed away, apparently unsure how to dig himself out of the implicit insult.

'We really like it,' Ray said, immune to his son's doubts. 'No doubt the survey will throw up all kinds of woes, but hopefully that means we can bargain the price down. The mortgage we're looking at it is a short-term one anyway.'

Belinda eyed Ellis's impassive face. Was his nose out of joint because he was comparing their potential new home to the crummy flats he'd been viewing? He wasn't about to argue that a larger share of Ray's cash should be funnelled into his own living arrangements, was he? 'Anyway, it *is* a lot of money, but we've worked hard for it,' she heard herself saying defensively, but her words must have come out with a sharper edge than intended because Ray's arm tightened around her momentarily and then he was speaking over her.

'I don't think Ellis is implying that we *didn't* work hard for it, love, but—'

'I know! I wasn't saying that,' Belinda interrupted as the boy scuffed at the uneven flooring with a grubby trainer, his expression mulish. Somehow a shadow had fallen across their beautiful moment, the fizz of excitement she'd felt about living here evaporating into the air. 'I just meant—'

'Well, it's none of my business anyway,' Ellis said before she could finish the sentence. His shoulders lifted with a shrug, then he sloped out of the back door without further comment.

Ray went after him and Belinda sighed into the empty room. What had just happened there? She could feel the undercurrents between their triangular dynamic but couldn't quite identify them. Had something changed for Ellis, now that he knew precisely how big a property she and his dad could afford?

Walking over towards the sink, she peered out to see the two men standing on the overgrown patio with their backs to her, heads bowed in conversation, Ray with his arm around his son's shoulders where it had been on Belinda's moments before. Her feelings of mistrust surged like a breaker against a harbour wall and she had to look away, biting her lip. 'What do I do?' she asked the house. 'Why has he come back all of a sudden?'

The house, of course, said nothing, but she put a hand to its scarred worktop nonetheless, seeking reassurance from its stillness. *I've got my eye on you*, she thought, with one final glance through the window.

# Chapter Twenty-Two

*Will: Are you around this weekend? I've decided to head back to the UK and I've got a ticket on the next flight out. It gets in Saturday evening your time, was wondering if I could crash at yours for a bit? X*

*Alice: OMG YES YES YES of course! For as long as you want! Xxx*

Having woken up to the surprise message from her brother on a different number (had he splashed out on a new phone? Talk about living the high life), Alice was now in a large pottery studio in Hackney, tying apron strings around her middle and exchanging shy smiles with the seven other people who'd signed up for the *kintsugi* workshop. They were all seated on high stools at intervals around a central U-shaped workbench with a potter's wheel in one corner and shelves behind them that ran the length of the walls, filled with stacked bowls, plates and pots, presumably made by students. Sunshine poured through the high windows and Alice felt buoyed by it, and by the cardboard box at her feet too, containing the colourful shards of Leni's broken plates. Here she was, about to enact a great big metaphor by transforming the shattered pieces into something new, mended and beautiful. If only it were so easy for people.

Two days had gone by since her second evening out with Jacob, and she still felt disconcerted about the way he'd looked at her, the way he'd talked to her, as if, in his view, she was as damaged as Leni's crockery. She'd mentioned that she was booked in for today's workshop and had explained about *kintsugi*, how it was the centuries-old Japanese art of restoring broken ceramics with a mixture of gold pigment and lacquer. The point was not to hide the imperfections of a piece, but to draw attention to them and beautify them. He'd seemed really interested, until she went on to say that she was hoping to mend some of Leni's plates that way, at which point you could see the light dim in his eyes, his engagement wane. *I always thought you'd go on to do something extraordinary*, she heard him comment again and stiffened at the memory. Get stuffed, Jacob. What right did he have to judge her?

She hadn't wanted to talk about her job because it was nothing to boast about, because she knew he'd glaze over with boredom, all right? Just like she did herself most days, Darren dodges aside. (She hadn't seen him since the lift trauma and wasn't entirely sure whether to be relieved or disappointed.) With four months left on her contract at Sage and Golding, the days passed by with treacly slowness compared to the buzz of working at ReImagine. Just yesterday, she'd noticed that the same line had been used across the company's social media eight days in a row. *Looking for great insurance? Ask your grandad – he knows!*

As a slogan, this would have been laughed out of the door at ReImagine within a millisecond. Was this seriously their attempt at drawing in younger customers, by telling them to ask their grandparents which insurance company they used? On which planet would this ever happen? In Alice's opinion, it would only have an adverse effect: young people didn't like being patronised or advised to consult an older person, and they certainly didn't appreciate sexist old tropes where the grandma didn't get so much as a mention.

'Everything all right over there, Alice?' Tina, her colleague, had asked her yesterday. 'You keep sighing so much, I was starting to think the air conditioning had been turned up.'

Alice had responded with a sheepish smile. 'Sorry. I was just ...Tina, I don't suppose you know who writes the company's social media, do you?'

'The company's social media? What, like Facebook and that?' Tina pursed her lips thoughtfully. She was in her sixties, with neatly shingled salt-and-pepper hair and a penchant for pastel-coloured blouses. Today's was a soft lavender, yesterday's a cool pistachio.

'It would be someone in the comms department,' Alice said. 'Communications,' she added when Tina still looked blank. 'Or marketing?'

'I don't think there *is* a communications department,' Tina replied. *This explained a lot,* thought Alice. 'But marketing's on the fourth floor. Dawn Ellery is the department PA, she's ever so nice. Do you want her number?'

'No thanks,' said Alice, feeling spontaneous. *Maybe I'm not so passive after all*, she thought. *Watch this Flying Beauty go, Leni.* 'I'll pop up there in person.'

Her pulse had quickened as she checked her reflection in the ladies' loos a few moments later, running possible lines of introduction through her head. She would be taking something of a risk by rocking up unannounced to the marketing department, especially when her reason for doing so was that she thought their output was pretty poor and that she could do better. But of course she wouldn't present it to them in those terms. She would smile and be charming and subtle. Plus, given the chance, she might be able to sniff out further information and make a cheeky move. And then, the next time anyone new asked her what she did, she could say, *Well, I was temping at this boring insurance company but then used my initiative and . . .*

Not that it mattered what opinion anyone else had about her life anyway, she'd thought crossly, dismissing Jacob from her mind.

'Good morning, everyone!' said the workshop teacher just then, a young woman called Ichika, whose long black hair was tied in a sleek ponytail down her back. Alice snapped back to attention as Ichika began the session with an introduction to *kintsugi*. Its rise, she told them, could be dated back to the sixteenth and seventeenth centuries, when there was a great tradition of tea-drinking from fashionable tea bowls. Broken bowls would be mended by Japanese lacquer masters using a particular lacquer called *urushi,* made from tree sap. Once the bowls had been stuck back together, the lacquer could take weeks to harden, and then the piece would have to be carefully sanded until the surfaces were perfectly flush. Only then would the lacquer master paint over the seams with gold.

'That is the way a true artisan works,' she smiled to the group, 'but as we only have a three-hour workshop together, we will take some shortcuts so that you can at least finish something today.'

Alice glanced down at the stack of plates she'd brought with her. Ah. Maybe she'd been a tad optimistic, thinking she'd be walking out of the workshop with a fully gilded crockery set and a loving-sister task mentally ticked off. But even one mended plate would be a start, she supposed. She imagined herself proudly showing it to Will when he arrived at her flat. God, she couldn't wait to see him. Her brother, home at last. A piece of the family, a piece of her, about to be fitted back in place. He'd be getting on the plane soon, she calculated, feeling jittery at the thought. She hoped she could keep her envy in check when he told her about all his adventures.

Ichika had brought some broken white saucers for everyone to practise on – 'Nice clean breaks, very straightforward' – and demonstrated how to mix epoxy glue and putty with gold powder as a quicker-drying modern version of the ancient lacquer technique. She went around the tables, distributing the saucers, and when she reached Alice's workstation, Alice hopped off her stool to show her the broken plates she'd brought along. 'I was hoping to work on these,' she said. 'They were my sister's. Would that be okay?'

There was a wobble in Alice's voice which must have been audible, because Ichika's face softened as she glanced down at the bright, shattered crockery pieces, within their newspaper and bubblewrap outerwear. 'Ah,' she said apologetically. 'We do advise on the booking form that it's best not to bring your own materials, as time is so limited in the class, unfortunately.'

'So ... could I make a start on one of these or ... ?' Alice could feel her earlier buoyancy slipping away. She really hadn't thought this through properly.

Ichika picked up a couple of the shards, examining them beneath the light. 'They're really beautiful, aren't they?' she said kindly. 'I can see why you'd want to restore them, rather than throw them away. But I'm afraid it would take even a professional many hours of work to put them back together. Maybe for now you could try with the saucer I have for you and see how you get on? We do hire spaces in the studio if you love *kintsugi* and decide you want to spend the time working on your own crockery – or I could put you in touch with a couple of experts who might be able to help?'

The other woman was doing her best, but Alice felt crushed with disappointment all the same. She knew already she wouldn't be hiring a space in the studio – how could she, when she worked full-time, and had bills to pay? She almost certainly wouldn't be commissioning a professional to repair Leni's crockery either, if it was going to be such a huge job. 'It's fine,' she managed to say. 'I'll use the saucer. Thank you.'

And it *was* fine, in terms of carrying out a calming, mindful activity: mixing her own gold glue and carefully sticking the saucer pieces back together. Piano music tinkled in the background, the group was friendly and chatty, Ichika made them all cups of green tea and produced a plate of dainty little shortbread biscuits decorated with Sakura cherry blossoms. In fact, Alice was surprised to realise towards the end of the workshop that, even though this hadn't been a Leni-centred activity after all, she'd enjoyed herself. It had been deeply relaxing, working with her hands, a chance to let her mind drift. She'd replayed, several times over, the satisfying encounter she'd had with Dawn the marketing PA yesterday, for instance. How, having lavished on her a number of compliments about her jacket and bracelet, Alice had been able to glean that the department had an intern running the social media campaigns – and just between the two of them, Dawn thought he was a bit of a spoiled brat who thought he was a cut above everyone else because he'd been to a posh university. 'I could probably do a better job of it than him,' she'd said, rolling her eyes conspiratorially.

'Well,' Alice had said, taking a deep breath. 'Actually, that's why I'm here ...'

The workshop flew by, with everyone exclaiming their surprise – and disappointment too – when their time was up. The mended saucers needed to be left to dry for forty-eight hours and so Ichika asked everyone to write their names and addresses on stickers that she would use to package and send on the completed pieces. Then, as the class began to disperse, she approached Alice with a smile.

'Have you got a minute?' she asked. 'I've had an idea.'

# Chapter Twenty-Three

Will's plane landed on Saturday night, and as he peered out at the dark runway, the pilot announcing that it was seven forty British time, and two degrees outside, he didn't know whether to laugh or cry. Or whether he should stow away and get himself on the first flight back out of there again, for that matter. Shit. Could he really do this?

Inside the terminal, everyone around him was hurrying towards the baggage reclaim area, but Will lagged behind, in no hurry to be reunited with his battered rucksack and scant possessions, and in even less of a hurry to be reunited with his old life in the UK. He still didn't have a clue what he was going to do with himself now that he was back, how he could start over here. Then his phone beeped and it was a message from Alice. *Thought I'd pick you up! Here in Arrivals waiting for you. Welcome home!*

The bubble he'd formed around himself, the protective shell of foreign distractions, of distance and denial, had been stretching thinner and thinner ever since he'd made his decision to leave Thailand. Alice's cheery message all but undid him. She was here, somewhere in this building, waiting to meet him; it was almost over. Was he ready for this? But in the next moment, he felt a rush of gratitude also – she'd done that for him? He hadn't expected that. He'd envisaged being ejected alone into the melee of Arrivals, having to navigate the journey across London to her flat by himself, tired and broken. The thought of her presence nearby was like a lantern in the darkness.

'Hey! Oh my God! Look at you! Look at your *tan*! Oh, Will, it's really you!' Fifteen minutes later, he was being crushed by her embrace, and he found himself overwhelmed by how unfamiliar and yet exactly the same it felt to have his arms around her, his own sister, once again. He'd noticed her as soon as he emerged through the Arrivals doors, standing a little apart from everyone else, self-contained and watchful in her dark blue coat, a little thinner than he remembered but unmistakably her, his one remaining sibling. Someone who'd known him from the very first day he'd been alive. Was that what it meant to be part of a family, that instant recognition of a person amidst the crowd, knowledge of them imprinted within you like indelible ink?

'Hi,' he said, jet-lagged and emotional, choking on the word as he breathed in the smell of her hair. He'd been so alone, he realised. For months and months, he'd been so lonely, existing in his own safe sphere, cut off from his family and life as he'd once known it. 'It's so good to see you,' he said thickly. 'How are you? Thank you for being here – you didn't have to—'

'Like I was *not* going to meet you, fart-brain,' she said as they finally drew apart. She reached up to ruffle his hair, just as she'd always done when he was a pipsqueak little boy and she was a big cool teenager. 'I couldn't believe it when I got your message. And Mum is absolutely hyped too. Hang on—' She stretched out her arm and took a photo of them both. 'Let me just send this to her ... Okay. My phone will now explode under the weight of all her incoming emojis, you wait. Shall we go?'

It was strange to be back in Alice's car, seeing the familiar British road signs rush by, the rain falling heavily against the windscreen as she drove them across London to her flat. Already he could feel his island life, with all its vivid colours and smells, beginning to recede into the back of his mind, like a mirage once seen. She told him about a pottery workshop she'd been to that day and about her cat, and he in response told her safe things about his life too: a diving trip he'd been on, the party scene, the food. He didn't tell her about the mugging, his failed careers in both drug-dealing and flip-flop selling. He didn't describe the indignity of having to return all the many boxes of unsold goods back to the wholesaler for a last handful of notes so that he could buy his cheap new phone and pay for an airport transfer.

Neither of them mentioned Leni on the journey either, but if he'd thought he could keep this up for long, he'd been kidding himself. As soon as he walked into Alice's flat, it was like stepping into a museum starring their sister, and it was impossible to avoid her. There was Leni's cat, glaring at him and hurrying from the room. Bags of her clothes in one corner. The broken plates Will recognised from her birthday lunch there on the table, along with a pile of paperwork and what looked like a six-week timeline of events pinned up on the wall. Oh God. Was Alice actually all right in the head? he wondered uncertainly as she set about making some pasta and popping open a couple of beers.

'Mind if I have a shower?' he asked, feeling sweat break out on his neck, despite the tepid temperature of her flat. The walls seemed to be closing in; everywhere he turned he was confronted by one picture of Leni or another. He felt as if he had been forced into Guilt Central against his will, with no way out. *Welcome home, sucker. Time to confess your sins!*

'Of course! There are clean towels in the cupboard, help yourself to anything,' she said, handing him a beer. 'Food will be ready in fifteen minutes or so, take your time.'

He escaped into the bathroom, took a massive gulp of cold lager and stared at his crumpled, bloodshot-eyed reflection with what felt increasingly like panic. Fuck. He had the growing conviction that coming back had been a really bad idea. Maybe even his worst yet.

# Chapter Twenty-Four

*Alice:* Hi Mum. Look who I bumped into at the airport!

*Belinda:* [red heart emoji, gold heart emoji, blue heart emoji, green heart emoji, smiling-face emoji, blowing-kiss emoji, heart-eyes emoji] LOOK AT YOU TWO!!!! I just screamed out loud at the picture, nearly gave Ray a heart attack [laughing emoji] I LOVE YOU BOTH!!! XXX

'Come in,' said Belinda on the doorstep, and Tony almost wanted to pinch himself because he couldn't quite believe he was there, back at the old house all these years later. Of course he'd stood outside many times, dropping the children off after weekends and what have you, but it had been a long time since he'd been welcomed over the threshold. *Come over for a last look at the place*, Belinda had suggested, and it had seemed like a good idea at the time, but now that he was stepping inside his former home, a place that held so many memories, good and bad, he was no longer quite so sure.

'Gosh,' he heard himself saying politely, 'it's immaculate. Last time I was here, there were children's paintings all the way up and down the hall and toys crunching under foot. You've done a great job.'

'Amazing how having loads of prospective buyers trooping through your house focusses the mind,' she said drily, leading him through to the kitchen. 'It's just us in, Ray's gone to look at a flat with his son. Coffee?'

'Please.' They were both being very civil and grown-up, he thought, following her into the large sunny room. He had to blink and transpose it over his memories of this space, from the chaos he'd known back then, of there being dolls and games everywhere, school uniforms draped over the radiator to dry, lunchboxes needing to be filled or emptied, half-completed jigsaws on the table, children's party invitations stuck to the fridge with colourful magnets. 'Gosh,' he said again, a lump in his throat that he had once lived within that life, been a part of this house's routines. All the times he'd had breakfast in here before work, the scorched smell as Belinda ironed a shirt for him, the girls squabbling over some toy or other – gone. And yet he still knew exactly how the back door handle would feel in his hand, how the sun sent a shaft of light across the room every morning; the memories contained within this room, this house, were an intrinsic part of him, like woodgrain.

'Two sugars still?' Belinda asked, fussing about with mugs.

'No sugar any more,' he said, smiling a little at her surprise. He wouldn't tell her that he'd given it up when he'd married Tanya, wife number three, he decided. Belinda had liked clean-living, verging-on-pious Tanya possibly least out of all his wives and girlfriends. In hindsight, she'd had a point.

He wandered over to the window to peer into the garden,

only to catch a glimpse of someone in the neighbouring garden, at which point he froze. Old habits died hard, he thought, turning back round. Come on. Those days are gone.

'So how are things? I take it you've spoken to Will?' Belinda's face lit up at his name. 'I can't believe he's back. I'm hoping to get to London in a day or two to see him, how about you?' She put their drinks on the table and went on before he could reply. 'Have a seat. Or would you rather wander round first?'

'I'll sit,' he said, doing just that. Same chairs, he noticed. Same table. He put his hand on its scored pine surface, appreciating how quietly reliable a piece of furniture could be. 'Yes, I'm glad he's back,' he added. 'I can't wait to see him again.' He really was determined to put in some legwork with Will before the baby came along. The two of them had got off to such a difficult start when Will was born – before then, even – and Tony knew he'd never really filled the father space in his son's life afterwards either. It wasn't that he hadn't loved him, more that the relationship had always been ... well, it was complicated.

'Things are okay,' he went on, in answer to Belinda's original question. 'We're into the last six weeks or so before the baby's due, and Jackie's ...' He hesitated, not wanting to betray a confidence. 'Jackie's fine. I've got to say though, Bel, it's all changed since our day. There's this whole new industry around childbirth, you wouldn't believe it. Baby showers and 3D scans and ... and reiki.' He wrinkled his nose, still not entirely sure what reiki actually was. 'I keep thinking of our three being born, how we didn't have any of that business, but how you didn't need it.' He moistened his lips. 'How magnificent you were.'

'Oh, Tony,' she scoffed but he could tell she was pleased by his words. 'I don't know about that.'

There was a pause when he geared up for raising the subject of this psychic hotline – *Someone needs to say something*, Jackie had encouraged him – but Belinda got in first. 'Tony,' she said, looking uncharacteristically nervous, 'I need to ask you a question. On Leni's birthday last year, she mentioned that she'd seen ... um ... Graham. Graham Fenton.'

The name was like a whip-crack in the air; Tony recoiled as if he'd been hit. 'Graham, as in ... ?'

'Yes. He did the Ofsted inspection at her school, recognised her name,' Belinda said. She looked as if she were about to be sick all of a sudden. 'And then when Alice and I were sorting through Leni's things, I found his name and number there on a bit of paper.' She swallowed, staring down at her mug before raising her gaze to him once more. 'Tony, I need to ask you this – did she ever talk to you about him? Did she ... know?'

'So how was Memory Lane?' Alice asked when Tony called her later that evening. He'd already had a full update on Will's return – how his son was uber-tanned, jet-lagged, currently out with mates – and now Alice was handing the conversation baton back to him. 'Did you enjoy your trip back to the old place?'

'Yes, on the whole,' he told her as breezily as he knew how. He was sitting in a room Jackie called 'the snug', a cosy space kitted out with his favourite reclining armchair and a wood-burning stove. She was elsewhere with a friend, so he'd treated himself to a whisky and had lit the fire, the flames leaping mesmerisingly between the logs. 'Funny how your brain can distort things though,' he went on. 'The bedrooms upstairs seemed so much smaller than how I'd remembered them. It all looked so clean – and that posh shower they've put in! Much better than the hold-it-yourself job we had when I was still living there.'

'And things with Mum?' Alice prompted. 'She was nice to you? Didn't give you too much shit about … well, you know. Everything?'

'She was nice,' he confirmed, trying to push from his mind the conversation he'd had with his ex; how complex and emotional it had become. *Did she know?* Belinda had asked him and he'd sighed and said no, nobody knew, he'd kept his promise. She had become tearful and upset, unable to look him in the eye momentarily as she apologised to him all over again. And he had felt … Well, he had felt unhappy himself to be thrust back into that difficult time, a time he had tried very hard not to think about ever since. He had assured her it was water under the bridge now though, that what was done was done, because he knew she was desperate for him to say those words. Even if he wasn't sure he meant them.

Afterwards, he couldn't face broaching the subject of the phone psychic; he'd try again on another day when things weren't so fraught, he'd decided. Changing the subject now, he asked his daughter about her job, which was met by a noise of frustration and then a full-blown rant about what a bunch of stiffs they were at this insurance place.

'So ... can you do anything to shake them up a bit? Give them some of your expert advice?' he suggested. One of the logs gave a loud crack with the heat of the fire; it took him back to scout camps as a boy, the smell of smoke on the night air. There was something so primitively satisfying about watching something burn, he thought.

'Funny you should say that,' she replied, before telling him that she'd wangled herself a meeting with the marketing department the following week, and that she was hoping she could persuade them to let her draw up a plan for their social media strategy on a trial basis. 'But you know, small steps. Making any kind of change in that place would be like trying to turn around a cruise ship with a single piece of bungee cord.'

'Yeah, but you're trying, at least. That's the main thing. Trying to make a difference. And do you know what? They're lucky to have you giving them a kick up the arse. And ...' He hesitated, wondering if she would accept a compliment from him yet, or if she'd throw it back in his face. Sod it, he had to give it a go. 'And I'm proud of you, Ali-cat. Really proud.'

'Oh, Dad!' She sounded so pleased, it absolutely warmed his cockles through. 'Thank you. I'll keep you posted.'

It had been an effort, a sustained campaign of effort for him with his middle daughter, especially as he knew at first he had a lot of ground to make up, but he was starting to think that the two of them were forming a new bond together, their own proper relationship at last. Even getting to use his old nickname for her felt like a win. The strain he'd previously noticed in her voice when they spoke now seemed to have gone; she was starting to confide in him in a way she hadn't done since she was a small girl and worried about Bad Things under the bed. Of course, he was biased, but he really thought she was great: funny, talented, thoughtful. He loved talking to her! He loved hearing about her life – the cat, her friends, the new Pilates class (*Actually quite relaxing, you should try it, Dad*). In return, he told her about the antenatal group, funny stories from his working day, the new restaurant in Broad Street he and Jackie had been to.

Did Alice feel similarly about him? He thought she might. She was taking the piss out of him in a way that seemed affectionate rather than bitter these days; they were laughing and joking more. That had to mean something, right? He hoped so. Their relationship had brought a new layer, new texture to his life. He wasn't only proud of her, he cherished her. Far too much to let her go again, that was for sure.

# Chapter Twenty-Five

'Belinda McKenzie, well I never,' said Graham Fenton after she'd opened the call with a stuttering reintroduction. 'I'd have known your voice anywhere. How are you?'

Belinda swallowed hard, her fingers shaking on the phone. It was strange the way a week could be made up of such completely different elements. Yesterday she'd stepped off the train in Paddington to see Will waiting for her in the concourse, both of them with the biggest smiles on their faces. Joy had filled her from head to foot as she flung her arms around him, not entirely certain she'd ever be able to let him go again. Today, here she was, back at the Park and Ride, the wind buffeting the car with such force that she half expected to find herself spinning up into the air, like Dorothy in *The Wizard of Oz*. (Oh my, Toto!) 'Hello,' she managed to croak.

Ever since the day she and Alice had begun sorting through Leni's possessions, the piece of paper with Graham Fenton's number on it had been squatting at the bottom of Belinda's handbag like an unexploded bomb ominously ticking down to zero. She had waited on tenterhooks for Leni's wrath to come via Apolline, angry accusations of hypocrisy – *how could you, Mum?* – until the suspense had turned her into a nervous wreck. Then she'd made the mistake of asking Tony if he knew anything about Leni's encounter with Graham, only to feel as if she'd uncovered an old wound that still hurt him – and her – all these years later. There was only one thing left to do. Call the number and find out the truth for herself.

'I've got something to ask you,' she said now, cringing in the driver's seat. No turning back.

Graham Fenton had been a naughty little secret at first, a bit of fun. He was the sexy dark-haired man who moved in next door and set Belinda's pulse racing. What a cliché she was! Developing a crush on the good-looking neighbour as a distraction from her mundane life: the juggle of two little girls, housework and a tough job in social work, along with a husband who was frequently away, both emotionally and physically. Not that it was Tony's fault, by any means – he was working all hours as the main breadwinner, as well as dealing with the loss of his parents, one after the other, and trying to sort out the sale of the old family home with his brothers. Nevertheless, she had been lonely. So where was the harm, she'd asked herself, in indulging in some light flirtation over the fence with handsome Graham, as a little pick-me-up at the end of the day? Until he upped the ante considerably, by appearing one evening on her doorstep with a bottle of wine and a suggestively raised eyebrow. Both proved equally hard to resist. And so the affair began.

Caught up in passion, Belinda lost her head. She and Graham became more daring, more reckless, kissing in secluded spots in the garden when the girls were in bed and Tony was glued to the cricketing highlights on TV. Graham kept popping round, supposedly to do odd jobs – creosoting the fence, fixing the guttering on the back wall, digging over a flowerbed – but always ending up in Belinda's bed afterwards. She started wearing perfume for the first time in years, singing in the car, feeling good about her body. Then she found out she was pregnant again, and – the shame of it – had no idea whose baby she might be carrying.

*Oh, Belinda. Now you've gone and done it*, she'd said to herself, her hand shaking with horror as she did three pregnancy tests in a row, just to be sure, only to find them all coming up unmistakably positive. Shit.

'I'm just going to come out and say it,' she began now, trying not to think about how she'd looked at herself in the bathroom mirror back then, wide-eyed with dismay, heart pounding so hard you could almost see it through her dress. Her heart was thudding pretty decisively with this phone conversation, for that matter, she thought, putting a hand to her chest to try and steady herself. 'I know you saw Leni, my daughter, last May. Did you . . . tell her anything?'

She had absolutely no idea how he was going to respond, she realised, watching an empty blue-and-white-striped carrier bag swirl up in a mini tornado, its plastic body ballooning like a pregnant belly before suddenly becoming limp as the wind flung it away out of sight. Graham had been impetuous and hot-headed, with a sexy dynamism lacking in her husband. At the time of their affair, he was a headteacher and, on being offered a prestigious new job in Birmingham, his first thought had been to take Belinda with him. 'How about it?' he'd said. 'We could make a new start together, me and you.'

It was the 'me and you' that had brought Belinda up short. Because obviously there was no 'her', singular; she came as a package along with her two daughters. Plus, of course, this surprise new baby, whose existence was still a complete secret, other than to her and the doctor. Graham's question had changed everything.

'I couldn't believe it when I heard her name,' he said now, sounding amused, and images crashed into Belinda's head, of how he'd looked naked in the bed, the weight of his body against hers. He was so dark and hairy after Tony, so musky-smelling; she would always fling the window open afterwards and change the sheets to try and drive out his scent. It was a wonder the washing machine didn't stage a protest and die, with all the extra laundry she stuffed into it during that time. 'Leni McKenzie, blimey. She looks like you, doesn't she?'

The present tense pressed like a bruise. *Looked, actually, Graham*, she thought, but didn't correct him. One awkward conversation at a time.

'Yes,' she said tightly. 'So – did you? Tell her anything? Only I found your name and number in her things, and ...' *And I've been tying myself in knots wondering ever since if my daughter went to her grave thinking me a liar.*

It had been so awful, when Tony found out. After all their sneaking around, all Belinda's care to keep the secret, the subterfuge was undone by his discovery of a rogue pair of Graham's pants at the end of the bed. The one time she hadn't whipped off the sheets and covered up the evidence!

Afterwards she'd even wondered if Graham had left them there deliberately, trying to provoke a decision out of her. He certainly provoked something, namely the mother of all arguments between Belinda and Tony as the affair exploded into their marriage, culminating in Tony marching next door and punching Graham in the face. (There was dynamism for you, Belinda had been left thinking, but not the sort she'd hankered after.) Graham had moved to Birmingham alone soon afterwards, never knowing about the pregnancy, but she couldn't hide it forever. And of course, when Tony discovered she was expecting, there was only one question uppermost in his mind. 'So whose baby even is it?' he'd asked, devastated.

Oh, Tony. She had done him so wrong, all in all.

'Let me think ... Yeah, she rang me about a week after I'd met her,' Graham said now. 'She left a message saying ... What was it? She'd got my number from the school secretary because she'd mentioned my name to you, and that you'd looked completely freaked out. Something like that. She wondered if I knew of any reason why.'

Belinda swallowed again. She had the worst poker face ever; of course Leni must have been suspicious back then on her birthday. 'And you said ... ?' she prompted, not remotely sure she wanted to hear his reply.

'I didn't ring her back,' he said. 'I just ... Why are you asking now, anyway? This all happened months ago, right? Last summer!'

'So she didn't know,' Belinda said, as much to soothe herself as to him. First Tony, now Graham; neither of them had let slip her worst secret. Tears rushed into her eyes with sheer relief. 'She didn't know about us.'

'Why are you saying "didn't" like that?' he asked, sounding confused. 'Belinda, I don't understand, what—?'

'Sorry, I've got to go,' she said before he could finish his question. 'Thanks, Graham. Goodbye.'

She cut him off, blocked the number and deleted it, then chucked the phone into the passenger seat. Sitting there with her head in her hands, she relived all the guilt and shame she'd felt from that time. How she'd hurt Tony. How she'd damaged their marriage so badly, it had never been able to recover. How she'd gone through her pregnancy feeling sick with doubt the entire time, Tony detached and dispassionate where he'd previously been joyful and excited about her other two. They'd managed to work as a team while Will was unwell as a baby, but it had been very much on practical terms, with none of the shared love and affection from before. And then when they'd split up, when he'd admitted defeat and bowed out of the relationship, she had begged him not to tell the children what she'd done. 'Promise me?' she'd pleaded, practically on her knees. But—

There was a knock at her car window and she jerked back to the present decade, only to be startled almost out of her skin when she saw who was standing there. *'Ray?'* she cried, in astonishment. She opened the car door and began getting out before realising she still had her seat belt on and having to wrestle her way out of it. 'What are you doing here?'

He looked so stern, her brain spun feverishly. 'Are you all right?' she asked. Why had he tracked her down like this? Something must be wrong. 'Is it Ellis? Has something happened?'

'I thought you were going to the dump,' he said, arms folded across his chest. It was still blowing a gale and a tuft of his grey hair flopped up and down comically, although his words were enough to wipe any comic thoughts from Belinda's mind in an instant. 'You told me you were going to the dump.'

'I—'

'I knew you weren't. I knew you were lying. I followed you here and I've been sitting watching you on the phone again. To her, I'm guessing. That bloody woman. Belinda, this has got to stop!'

She opened her mouth to contradict him – *No, actually, Ray!* – only to snap it shut again almost immediately. How could she tell him the truth, that she'd contacted the man with whom she'd had such a shameful affair?

# Chapter Twenty-Six

Alice felt as if change might be in the air at last. Thanks to Dawn, her new contact at work, a meeting had been arranged for her to speak to a couple of marketing people, and she was determined to throw everything at the opportunity. Her gut feeling was that there was a huge area of the market the company simply wasn't looking at, and she hoped to show them, as quickly as possible, how to tempt in this untapped swathe of customers. Humour, she'd decided, was the key. Humour plus the lure of exclusivity. Now she had to prove to them what she could do.

Having set up a social media handle, @GuessWho? with a biography that merely read *Insurance? We've got that covered*, deliberately coined to intrigue, she launched herself into the digital waters and hoped she could make a splash – or, at the very least, a few ripples. And if the whole thing bombed, she reminded herself, nobody ever need know about it.

But it wouldn't bomb! Because she was determined, and she had a plan. Back in her old job at ReImagine, she'd headed up the social media team; she knew her stuff. Of course, in those days, she would have brainstormed extensively with her colleagues before launching a campaign; they'd have dug deep into company research; they'd have run focus groups and consumer panels; they'd have drawn up a list of aspirations, targets to hit. This, by contrast, felt like taking a test flight all alone, without knowing if she could steer the plane, let alone land it any place. Even so, surely she could do a better job than the current intern employed to punt out dreary messages to the brand's few followers?

In her tea break that morning, she pored over what was trending on Twitter, then pounced on a news story about a senior government minister visiting a local primary school who, when trying to show off his sack race skills during PE, had fallen over and cracked his glasses. Alice retweeted a picture of the unfortunate minister, broken specs in hand, and added a caption – *Let's hope you're covered by . . . Guess Who?*, adding the minister's name and hashtag #DontGetTheSack so that it would show up in any searches.

She pursued this approach over the next few days, working with any gossipy news stories that she could bend to the vague theme of insurance. A Premier League footballer, famed for his success at penalty-taking, pranged his expensive sports car on a bollard, prompting a slew of memes and jokes about hitting the wrong target – perfect for Alice's Guess Who? caption purposes. A soap star whose Newfoundland puppy had knocked over (and smashed) her new TV – thank you very much. By now, she'd picked up a modicum of traction, a number of likes and retweets, plus a few follows, although it did feel, at times, as if she were shouting down a well. That was only to be expected though, she reminded herself, and there was nothing wrong with a slow-grow campaign, especially one that kept people guessing. If she could work up enough momentum between now and her meeting with the company marketing team, she could talk to them about building the teasers to a big reveal, with the campaign stretching across all social media networks to maximise reach. Then brainstorm strategies to keep new younger followers on board. It felt so exciting to be working within this sort of creative realm again, as if the synapses in her brain were constantly lighting up with new ideas. If only her sister could be there to cheer her on. Or even admit she'd been wrong about Alice in the first place.

'You know, I've kind of been haunted by this argument I had with Leni on her birthday,' she said to Will on Friday night, having suggested they go out for dinner at a Mexican street food place near her flat. It was an uplifting venue, with cheery mariachi music playing, light bulbs dangling from long cords above red Formica tables and, behind a steel counter, chefs flipping great pans of sizzling peppers for fajitas.

Will's face stiffened a little – *Oh God, here we go*, she saw in his eyes. 'Yeah?' he said, without much enthusiasm.

'Yeah – it was pretty horrible. She laid into me about not growing up, not committing to anything – like, never settling down with a proper boyfriend, all this kind of thing. Letting stuff happen to me passively rather than going out and working for it.' She picked up one of the cheesy nachos from their sharing plate and dug it hungrily into the guacamole, her nose wrinkling as she replayed the scene: Leni's accusing face, her own shocked hurt, how she'd all but run out of the flat to avoid hearing any more of her sister's unkind words. 'And ... well, I'm not saying anything's all *that* different. In fact, Leni might think I've acted even more like a kid, giving up my job, and the whole thing with Dar—' She stopped herself just in time, coughing loudly over the rest of his name. 'But I do feel a bit of a sea change inside, you know. Like – if I can make a go of it as a freelancer, say, then that would be awesome. That would be me standing on my own two feet, properly putting myself out there. And I think ...' She broke off, suddenly awkward, before deciding to say it anyway. 'Yeah, I think she'd be proud of me for it.'

The idea was enough to bring tears to her eyes. For all that Leni had hit her – and hurt her – with that fistful of home truths last year, Alice could admit now that her sister had had a point. Alice had always lived safely, never really sticking out her neck to achieve very much or try something bold. She'd had one not-very-good boyfriend after another because it had been easy to go along with them, as if she didn't deserve better. She'd got an internship at ReImagine straight out of uni and hadn't thought to look anywhere else for work from that moment. Life *had* happened to her, until she'd been forced to start rebuilding things herself. But she was getting there now, wasn't she? How she wished she could tell Leni she was getting there!

She made the mistake of glancing at Will for his reaction, hoping that he might be smiling at her and saying he was proud too. He wasn't. He was staring morosely into his plate of food.

'You don't like me talking about her, do you?' she asked with a sigh.

'Not really,' he mumbled.

She knew this already, of course. He had been awkward around the mention of their sister from the moment he'd arrived in her flat. 'Why've you got all this stuff?' he'd asked on the first night, gesturing to the paperwork and clothes she hadn't yet got around to sorting through. He'd picked up one of Leni's broken plates and looked from it to Alice. 'Wouldn't it be better to chuck these out now?'

'Well, no, actually,' she'd replied, telling him how the *kintsugi* teacher had suggested commissioning a mosaic artist to turn the shattered pieces into a beautiful new piece of art, rather than trying to mend them all individually. (Alice was thrilled by this idea! She was already looking into local creatives who might be able to help her.) Will only shrugged in response though, and she could tell he didn't get it. Maybe he was still jet-lagged, she'd told herself at the time, but in the days that followed, he continued to appear unwilling to engage with the subject of Leni's whereabouts at the end of her life.

'Does it change anything though?' he'd said more than once. 'Like ... this mysterious "A" in her diary. Whatever the "T" was every Tuesday night. Does it matter? Shouldn't we just accept that we can't know everything and get on with our lives?'

'I think you can do both,' she'd countered. 'Try to find out as much as possible *and* get on with our lives.'

Even that morning over breakfast, he'd wanted to deflect

the subject. Alice was still having the same dream where she was searching for Leni in a maze, calling her name, the high green hedges preventing her from seeing further than the next few desperate steps. Once again she'd woken up, frustrated and melancholy. 'I don't think we need Dr Freud to tell us what *that* dream means,' she commented glumly to Will as she made coffee, having recounted the details.

'Mmm,' was all he had to say.

Alice couldn't get her head around this approach. 'I think it's good to bring her into the conversation though,' she argued now. 'I never want to *not* be talking about her.' He said nothing, still not looking in her direction, and her earlier feelings of buoyancy deserted her. 'Will – I think it's important to *try*,' she went on after a moment. 'To remember her out loud as a means of . . . you know, processing everything. Honouring her. It doesn't have to be sad stuff – if you look on her memorial page, there are heaps of funny stories that—'

'I don't want to look on her memorial page,' he said, sounding as if his teeth were gritted. 'I don't *want* to remember her out loud! I just want to—'

He broke off without finishing, his mouth closed up so tight she was reminded of him being a little boy and refusing to eat his vegetables. 'What?' she prompted when he didn't elaborate. 'You want to *forget* her?'

'No! Of course not.' His voice cracked. 'I just wish she was still here.'

'Oh, Will, we all wish that,' she said, reaching over and putting her hand on his arm. He felt stiff and unresponsive beneath her touch; he was holding himself rigidly in the seat, she noticed. 'Every single day, I wish I could ring her up or meet her for a drink or … you know. *Anything*. Some days I still forget that she's gone and grab my phone to message her before I remember all over again.'

He wasn't listening, she could tell. Her words were bouncing off him without hitting the mark. 'No, but Alice, the thing is …' He looked up at her at last and his expression was one of such intense unhappiness, she almost reared back from him. He swallowed, his Adam's apple jerking in his throat. 'The reason I try not to think about her is that …' His voice had sunk almost to a whisper. 'It was my fault she died.'

'What? No, it wasn't,' she argued in surprise. 'It was Ferguson. Callum Ferguson.' She heard the soft *crump* of an egg hitting the window, pictured its slow viscous slide down the glass.

Will shook his head, his expression grim. 'The night she died,' he said, and Alice could tell he was really having to force the words out. 'The night she died, she rang me.'

'She rang me too,' Alice put in eagerly, forgetting his anguished face momentarily because this was news to her. 'Oh God, I wish I'd answered. What did she say?'

'She asked me …' She had never seen him so distraught, she registered with a lurch. 'If I could look at her bike for her. If we could FaceTime so that I could walk her through tightening up the steering column.'

Alice could hardly breathe for a moment because she was remembering the grainy CCTV footage from the coroner's court, the image of her sister weaving wildly across the busy road, apparently losing control of her bike. Her heart thumped as she took in what her brother was saying to her. What he was confessing. 'And you . . .' She faltered, her stomach turning at the look on his face. 'And you said . . . ?'

'I said no.'

# Chapter Twenty-Seven

'Can I ask you a favour, Will?' Leni had asked, and he'd felt irritated by the question because it had seemed like one favour after another in recent months – borrowing money, helping her move into her flat, could he fix this, could he do that? Plus he was still a bit annoyed after her weird birthday lunch when she'd been rude and unfriendly to Molly – *I don't think your sister likes me, babe*, she'd pouted – before freaking out over her broken plates, screaming at them all that they were a shit family. So no, he hadn't been in the maddest of rushes to help her out.

'What?' he'd asked grudgingly.

'There's something wrong with my bike, I think it's the steering column. Would you mind having a look at it?' she'd said.

He had rolled his eyes. Here we go, he'd thought. 'Can you not just take it to your nearest bike shop, get them to sort it out?' he'd asked, exasperated. Everyone else managed to look after themselves and their belongings in this way, after all. Plus – newsflash – he lived out in Swindon, not next door to her. He didn't come to her whining about his stuff, did he? She was eight years older than him and he'd never asked her for a thing, even though he had his own problems: an intimidating landlord and a girlfriend he wasn't entirely sure about, for starters, as well as the growing conviction that he might have thrown away his university place prematurely, and still hadn't found his feet in the world. But did he whinge on to Leni about this? No.

'Yeah, but . . . can't you do it?' she'd wheedled. 'I wanted to go out on it tonight. What if we video call and I show you, and you can give me your advice?'

'No!' he'd said, the word exploding out of him with more force than he'd anticipated. 'I'm busy – I'm meant to be going out in twenty minutes.' It wasn't a complete lie, but the only place he was intending to go was the fried chicken place on the corner and then straight back to his sofa. She didn't have to know that though.

'What, you've finally made some friends there, have you? Thank God!' she responded and he had no idea whether she was being sarcastic or joking – or even if she'd seen through his excuse and was taunting him for it.

Whatever the case, he felt prickly, as if she'd been unkind, so he'd said, 'Oh, sod off,' and hung up on her.

'And that was the last time we spoke,' he told Alice now, staring down at the table. 'My final words to her – *Oh, sod off.* Which makes me feel totally shit.' He couldn't lift his gaze, the weight of shame pressing him down. *Why*, he asked himself for the hundredth time, *couldn't he just have said yes?* He was an engineer, he was good with mechanics, it would have taken him two minutes on a video call to explain what to do. Why couldn't he have given her two minutes?

'Oh, Will,' Alice said wretchedly. 'You should have told me.'

'Why? So you can hate me as much as I hate myself? So you can blame me for her dying too?' He ran a hand wildly through his hair, feeling as if he was falling apart right there and then to the warbling accompaniment of a mariachi band. He thought of the way Belinda had gazed at him in Paddington station the other day, the love shining from her eyes, and imagined how the truth would destroy her if she ever knew; the worst possible slap in the face.

'We all did things we regret, we all said things we wish we hadn't,' Alice replied. 'But—'

'Is everything all right with your food, guys? Do you need anything?' came a voice just then and Will turned to see a smiling dark-haired waiter at their table, wearing an embroidered Mexican-style waistcoat and bootlace tie.

'We're fine, thanks,' he said dutifully.

'Delicious,' echoed Alice in the next breath, because at the end of the day they were still their parents' children, they were still McKenzies with manners, even in the throes of an ultimate confessional breakdown.

'Cool. Enjoy!' the waiter told them, making for the next table.

Their eyes met, and even in the maelstrom of his revelation, they felt the black comedy of the moment cut through – *Cool. Enjoy!* – and pulled wry faces at each other.

'So …' Alice began tentatively.

'Yeah,' he put in. 'You're going to tell me what a wanker I

am, right? And that you hate me and never want to see me again.' He was exaggerating for effect, but all the same, there was a part of him that fully expected her to say *yes, how could you?*

'Oh, Will, of course I'm not,' she said, shaking her head. A moment passed where he saw a whole parade of emotions flash across her face – sadness, regret, resignation – before she returned to him with a new fierceness, as if she'd settled on how to respond. 'You're my *brother*, I don't hate or blame you at all. Not at *all*. That must have been horrible, living with such a massive weight on you for so long.'

He nodded, unable to speak. She didn't blame him? Had he heard that right?

'You must have replayed that conversation a million times, just like I have with all the things I wish I hadn't said or done,' she went on. 'But you didn't force her to go out on the bike, did you? That was her choice, even though she knew it wasn't working properly. You fucking idiot, Leni,' she added, suddenly exasperated. 'Why didn't she just look on YouTube like a normal person? Or get a bloody bus?'

He still wasn't able to say anything. He could hardly breathe with the fact that they were actually talking about this, discussing his secret, after it had been toxic and radioactive inside him for so long.

'Plus,' Alice went on, draining her beer bottle, 'she did ask a *lot* of favours. Loads of favours. She was a nightmare for it sometimes, when she couldn't be bothered to do a thing herself.' She was trying to joke but her mouth was unsteady, her eyes a little too bright. 'And I bet before that night you'd done hundreds of things for her. To be fair, like she did hundreds of things for us in return.'

'Yeah.'

There was a round of cheers at the table behind them as the waiter approached with trays of sizzling fajitas but Alice carried on, caught up in her fervour. 'It's not your fault that the one time you said no to her, this had to happen,' she said. 'I mean it, Will. I'm exonerating you here. Absolutely not your fault. It was just really bad luck. Bad timing. Bad all round. And there's no way I'm going to sit here and blame *you*. Who knows, she might have been ringing to ask *me* how to fix her bike and I didn't even answer the bloody phone. I'm just as responsible!'

Will smiled weakly because Alice was the most impractical member of the family, whom nobody would ever dream of consulting about bike maintenance, and they both knew it. But he appreciated the solidarity. Her sisterliness. 'Thank you,' he said. He put a hand to his chest, aware of the adrenalin still pumping around his body post-confession, giving him a light-headedness, a sense of unreality. Was that really . . . it? After all those months carrying his burden of guilt, was it actually over? 'God, Alice,' he said, suddenly overcome. 'Thank you. I've been so worried about telling you. This has been weighing on me for so long.' He pressed his lips together, emotion getting the better of him. 'I'm glad I've got you.'

'Oh, Will, you big baby,' she scoffed affectionately, an old childhood put-down recast as something entirely more loving. 'You don't ever need to keep secrets from me again, all right? You can always tell me stuff. We've got to stick together, us two, right? Come here.' She reached across the table and hugged him. They held one another and it was as if the rest of the world shrank quite away from them, as if they were the only two people left in the restaurant, the city, the universe. Eventually they parted but he could still feel her warmth against him, still felt imprinted by her love for him.

'Okay,' he said rather shakily, still reeling. Her little speech of togetherness had made all the difference though, he registered, remembering to breathe. His shoulders felt lighter, the world a shade brighter. Already he was a different man to the one who'd walked into this restaurant earlier. 'That's enough about me for a while anyway,' he went on, trying to take it all in. 'How about you? How are things going with Heart-throb Jacob?'

He'd assumed he was on safe ground to tease her when, last he'd heard, she'd been so excited about meeting him. But to his surprise, she pulled a face in response, saying she probably wouldn't see him again.

'How come? Not even as friends?' he replied. Back when he'd first heard Jacob had reappeared in his sister's life, Will had looked him up on social media, messaged him to say hi. 'He said how good it was to catch up with you again,' he added, perhaps unwisely, because Alice's face immediately darkened.

'Well ... good for *him*, maybe,' she muttered.

Will didn't get it. 'What went wrong? I'll go out with him if you don't want to,' he joked, although she didn't smile. 'I thought he was, like, the nicest man in the world. Wasn't he?'

Alice started detailing how Jacob had made her feel bad about herself, but the whole time she was recounting the things he'd said, Will could only hear Jacob being clumsy, rather than unkind. And yet Alice seemed determined to think the worst of him. Sometimes Will wondered if he would ever understand the way women's brains worked. 'Playing devil's advocate here,' he ventured, 'but is it that much of a deal-breaker? I hear you – he hurt your feelings, but you can still be friends, can't you?'

She didn't look convinced. 'I've got enough friends.'

'Yeah, but it's *Jacob.*' He was disappointed for himself, he realised. He'd been looking forward to seeing his substitute big brother again. 'Don't you think life's too short to miss out on a friendship with someone really good?'

'What, like you and that Scottish woman, you mean?' she retaliated, raising an eyebrow as she crammed a loaded nacho into her mouth.

Touché. He was in no place to lecture anyone, he remembered. A moment of understanding passed between them, a moment that said *We're the same*, and he found it surprisingly comforting. 'Okay, you got me,' he admitted, putting his hands up. 'The McKenzie crap-relationship curse strikes again.'

'Fuck the McKenzie crap-relationship curse,' she said grandly. 'Now, do you know what I'm thinking?' she went on. 'I'm thinking Leni would want us to have dessert *and* maybe a cocktail for good measure, don't you? We haven't been able to do this for a long while, after all. Are you in?'

He drained his glass, feeling a rush of love for her and then one for Leni too, who'd never needed an excuse to indulge. 'Too bloody right, I'm in.'

★

Over the weekend, Will found himself at something of a loose end. Alice was tied up with various plans – going to meet a mosaic artist in Walthamstow on the Saturday, catching up with her girlfriends that same evening, and then heading off to Crouch End on Sunday for brunch with Edie, a former colleague. He tried calling his mum but her line was permanently engaged. Even the cat was busy, now that it had the freedom of the newly installed cat flap, and kept barrelling in and out, triumphant with its own agency.

Will had been back in the country a week now and, Leni-confession aside, he'd so far enjoyed a wave of being the new guy in town, the prodigal son returned to his mother, a novelty act with tales of adventure amidst his old friends. But you couldn't inhabit that role forever, he knew. The wave would eventually crash to shore. At some point, he'd have to make a few choices again. How was he going to spend the rest of his life?

*Hi Will*, his dad had messaged rather plaintively a few days ago. *Would love to see you now you're back. Can we meet up for a pint? Dinner? A walk?* Will was yet to reply. He and his dad had never had much of a relationship, and although he could tell Tony was trying hard to rebuild family bridges – Alice certainly seemed to think so – something was stopping Will from falling in with his matey suggestions. Maybe when he'd got his life in order, he might feel more confident about accepting his dad's offers, he told himself.

'You're welcome to stay with us as long as you like, you know that, don't you?' his mum had said the other day, eyes shining, as they had lunch in a Soho diner. She'd put her hand on his arm frequently throughout the meal as if unable to stop checking he was really there, in the flesh. Or maybe she was worried about him taking flight again, and planned to grab him and hold on tight if he tried escaping. 'The new house is going to need a lot of elbow grease, you'd be doing us a favour if you stayed to help.'

'Thanks,' he'd replied, appreciating that she was trying to frame this as him being useful, rather than merely sponging off her. That said, he knew full well that it would feel like a backward step, being under his mum's roof, after living independently for so long.

As he roamed Alice's small flat now, his eye fell on the stack of Leni's paperwork that he'd so far studiously avoided looking at too closely, and he found himself remembering how she'd pivoted in her career, from wannabe artist with her own market stall to primary school teacher; how rewarding she'd found retraining, a new way to work. 'Another year as a student, what's not to love?' she'd said cheerfully. He'd been in sixth form at the time, applying for university places himself, and the link must have occurred to her too because then she was saying, 'Hey, we'll both be at uni together, Will – student buddies!' and high-fiving him.

Only his time up north hadn't quite worked out as he'd thought, after all that. His mum had been so proud when he got into Durham University, but he'd felt out of place from the first moment. Everyone else in his halls seemed to know of each other's expensive, exclusive schools, having competed in the same rugby tournaments and public-speaking competitions, moving in similar circles. Whenever anyone asked him which school he'd gone to and he'd replied with the name of his Oxford comprehensive, you could see their eyes glaze over with disinterest; they seemed to detach from him almost at once, as if decoupling from a train that was heading nowhere. It baffled him until a gobby Mancunian girl on his course decoded the situation. 'It's because they're hoping to meet people who can give them a leg up later on,' she'd said, pulling a face. 'Making connections, networking. Rich-kid bollocks.'

He'd bailed out early; went home for Christmas and never returned. 'Don't let a few posh idiots put you off,' Alice had said sympathetically, but it was too late, he'd already changed his mind about the whole idea and applied for an apprenticeship instead.

Now he wondered if he should have stuck it out rather than quit at the first chance. Or if, like Leni, he could maybe try again, return to university as a mature student, someone who'd be less intimidated by the rich-kid bollocks, as the Mancunian girl had put it. The thought was like a mental thunderclap and he found himself sitting very still, recalibrating, as the idea settled fully into his mind and took shape. He could do that, couldn't he? He pictured himself being back in a physics lab, undertaking some knotty piece of research, and the vision was ... actually pretty tempting. Exciting. Why not?

Okay. So there was one option already, he thought, inspired. And wouldn't his teacher sister have loved 'education' as an answer? 'Thank you,' he said, putting his hands together in a prayer, like the woman at the Buddhist temple had done. See – this was what happened when he took his head out of the sand, when he dared to look at what he'd lost.

He remembered Alice chiding him for not having spent time on their sister's memorial page, and in a burst of resolution, he opened his laptop. Having found the page, he scrolled right up to the top, vowing to read everything. Once and for all, he would face up to Leni's loss. No more pretending and looking away.

To his surprise, the experience proved cathartic. He found himself savouring every story and memory, however small, reading through them slowly and affectionately. He broke off for lunch and coffee at intervals but went back and kept on reading. No longer did it seem a chore or a punishment. With so many different voices on the page, so many fragments of Leni's bright, colourful life sparkling back at him, it felt really bloody lovely, as if he was seeing her again, reconnecting after months of deliberate silence. He was letting her back in.

And then, seeing the small grey diary Alice was obsessed with nearby, something occurred to him, a cog clicking in his brain. *I think where she keeps marking her Tuesday nights T 7.30, it's a therapist appointment*, she'd said to Will, but no, he now believed she was wrong. If he wasn't mistaken, it referred to something else altogether.

Back he scrolled through the comments and messages and anecdotes. Back, back, back, until . . .

He read the entry again. Yes. It must be. He picked up his phone and called her immediately. 'Alice,' he said when she answered. 'Have you got a minute? I think I've found something.'

# Chapter Twenty-Eight

Belinda was walking towards the Westgate Centre, hoping to pick up a few last bits and pieces for Ray's birthday, when her phone rang with an unknown mobile number. She hesitated – it was probably some crook trying to sell her insurance or similar, let's face it – but then a sixth sense made her pick up.

'Belinda? It's Jackie,' she heard, to her surprise. To her dismay, too – damn it, she should have blocked the call, after all. She wasn't keen on her ex-husband's latest partner – too full of herself by half – although in the next moment, she wondered if everything was all right with Tony. Why else would Jackie be calling? 'I don't suppose you're free to meet for a coffee this morning, are you?'

Belinda hesitated, trying to think of a polite way to say no. 'Er …'

'I'll cut to the chase – I've got pre-eclampsia, I'll almost certainly have to go into hospital soon, I'm trying to get everything ticked off my list before I'm plunged into motherhood. Would eleven o'clock suit you?'

It was very hard to argue with a woman using words like pre-eclampsia and hospital as leverage, Belinda thought, grimacing. 'It'll have to be quick,' she replied, rather ungraciously, wondering how on earth she fitted into Jackie's 'list'. Did the other woman want a bitching session about Tony, maybe?

'I can do quick,' Jackie assured her. 'Eleven o'clock at the Art Café – I'll see you there.'

With the prickly, bad-tempered feeling she always got when someone was ordering her around, Belinda reluctantly agreed, and proceeded with her shopping. She was planning to buy Ray a couple of shirts, some of that posh coffee he loved, and the new biography of the rugby star he idolised; apparently Blackwells had signed copies in. Since he'd confronted her in the car park a few days earlier and torn a strip off her for – as he thought – calling Apolline again, there had been an awkwardness between them, a certain coolness. She would make an effort with his birthday presents, and hope it went some way to diminishing her guilty feelings.

At eleven o'clock, she approached the café to see Jackie already sitting outside, frowning at her phone. Her huge bump meant that she was at a slight remove from the table, and she wore a dark grey trouser suit and lilac blouse, her thick glossy hair piled up in a chignon, with make-up so immaculate Belinda wished she'd bothered a bit more with her own that morning.

'Don't get up,' she said as she approached, remembering the indignity of hauling one's body around unnecessarily in the late stages of pregnancy. Perhaps Jackie, like Belinda, didn't take to being told what to do though, because she rose to her feet regardless in order to kiss Belinda politely on the cheek, her spicy perfume making Belinda's nostrils tingle.

They both sat down, then spoke at the same time. 'So,' Jackie began in a businesslike way, just as Belinda said, 'Sorry to hear about the pre-eclampsia. Are you all right?'

Jackie waved a hand. 'One of those things,' she said. 'But yes, I'm fine. And Tony is too, if you were wondering. Although he's worried about you. Which is why I called, because he's been pussyfooting about the subject this whole time, and I thought you'd probably rather just know.'

'Know what?' Belinda asked, taken aback by the abruptness of this opening. The other woman hadn't been exaggerating when she said she could 'do quick'. 'What do you mean, Tony's worried about me?'

'He told me about the psychic hotline you've been ringing,' Jackie went on, so casually it was as if she was chatting about the price of milk.

Belinda's face blazed with the embarrassment of having her precious secret tossed into the open like this, without warning, when until now it had been her private salvation. Embarrassment was swiftly followed by fury. How did *Tony* know? And how dare he gossip about her?

'He's been trying to work up the courage to broach the subject,' Jackie ploughed on, apparently unaware of Belinda's fuming discomfort, 'but . . .'

'It's none of his business,' Belinda interrupted hotly. It was all she could do not to leap up from her chair and march away from this horrible conversation. 'Nor is it yours, for that matter.' A group of people at the next table burst out laughing suddenly and she flinched, imagining they were laughing at her. Did everyone know? she thought wildly, hating the idea of Jackie and Tony talking about her behind her back.

'I found the website and asked one of our legal guys at work to do some digging,' Jackie went on, as if Belinda hadn't spoken. Then her voice softened. 'Look, I'll be straight with you, the findings weren't great. The whole thing is essentially a scam, preying on vulnerable people. The person behind the company is a convicted fraudster; there are links to money laundering and trafficking. It's a really nasty business, Belinda.'

Blood thrummed beneath Belinda's skin as the words attacked her, one by one. The situation felt surreal, as if it couldn't possibly be happening. Like Jackie knew anything about Apolline! 'I trust her,' she said coldly, her chin in the air. *Bore off, Jackie. Take your legal guys and shove them.* 'I believe her. And I—' She was about to say *I need her*, but a ponytailed waitress came over to take their drink orders just then and she had to break off, the words unsaid.

She did need her, Belinda thought, staring doggedly past Jackie to the group of homeless men clustered around the war memorial with cans of extra-strong cider, and the pigeons waddling about, their chest feathers gleaming iridescent pink and green. Without Apolline, how could she go on? It was like an obsession. A compulsion she couldn't ignore.

'Okay, so that's a flat white, a peppermint tea and an apple cake. Is that everything, ladies? I'll be right back,' the waitress said, before bustling away again. Silence fell at the table. A busker outside Marks and Spencer was playing 'Cheek to

Cheek' on the electric guitar and the tune made Belinda remember dancing around the kitchen with Will when he was a toddler, his soft face against hers as she sang to him and whirled him about. *I'm in heaven . . .*

'I'm not trying to be a smart-arse here,' Jackie said after a moment. 'I promise I didn't come here to upset you or make you feel bad.'

Oh really. Like she wasn't absolutely loving rubbing Belinda's nose in it, Belinda thought, humiliation rising. 'You and Tony have had a good old laugh at me, I bet,' she said, her throat tight. 'How did he even know about Apolline anyway?'

'Ray told him. They bumped into each other,' Jackie replied. 'And no one's been laughing at you, I swear. Honestly.'

Belinda chanced a look at the other woman, half expecting to see a crowing contempt on her face, but was brought up short by how sincere Jackie's brown eyes were instead. Compassionate, even. Her head swam, no longer sure what to think, who to believe. Wishing she didn't have to think about this at all. Why couldn't everyone just leave her alone?

'I haven't told Tony what the guys at work uncovered,' Jackie went on. 'This is me talking to you, woman to woman. Nobody else has to be involved. I just thought it was important that . . . well, that *you* knew.'

The waitress reappeared with their drinks and cake, clattering them down on the table. After she'd gone, another weighty silence swelled between them, a silence Belinda didn't know how to fill. She fiddled about adding sweetener to her coffee, stirring so briskly it slopped over the edge of the mug. Jackie, meanwhile, cut the cake in two and put the plate between them. 'Help yourself,' she said. 'I'm meant to be watching my sugar intake but I couldn't resist.'

'Thank you,' Belinda mumbled, taking a piece and nibbling it. Not as good as Alice's, she thought, remembering the spiced apple and walnut Alice had made for her birthday once, the most delicious thing she'd ever tasted. Unfortunately, the family's best baker seemed to have fallen out of love with the whole business; there had been no cakes baked for anyone for almost a year now. *Sorry, I just don't feel like it*, she'd said when Belinda had tentatively put in a request for her last birthday, back in November. Neither of them had mentioned a cake for Ray; Belinda would buy one rather than ask again, she'd decided.

'You've had a horrible time,' Jackie said quietly after several moments had passed. 'The worst. I'm not judging you for anything, I swear I'm not. I can see how ... how comforting it must have felt for you to speak to this woman.' She dabbed up a stray cake crumb with her finger, her gaze lowered. 'I had a couple of miscarriages with my ex-husband,' she went on in a rush. 'And I felt so low for a while afterwards, I could totally imagine myself having done the same as you. Wanting to feel that it wasn't the end.'

Belinda nodded, the words piercing her with their insight. Wasn't that the nub of it, after all, that she just couldn't face it being the end, for her and Leni? 'Sorry to hear about your miscarriages,' she mumbled after another pause.

'And I'm sorry if I've upset you, being too forthright,' Jackie replied. 'You're right, it *is* none of my business, but I hate the thought of anyone being manipulated. Preyed upon.'

A moment passed. Jackie's words about money laundering and trafficking were belatedly making themselves heard in Belinda's brain and she felt a sense of resignation steal over her, as if her last defences were being knocked down. She didn't like the thought of anyone being manipulated either. Not least her own self.

She bowed her head and sighed. 'Okay,' she admitted grudgingly. 'Yes.' It was all she could manage for a second, the acknowledgement like a stone in her throat. 'I . . . I kind of knew,' she muttered when Jackie didn't respond. 'If I'm honest, I kind of did know that it wasn't real. That I was kidding myself.' She exhaled heavily, feeling thoroughly wretched. *There. Happy now, Jackie? Satisfied?* 'But I didn't care because anything from my daughter – even if it wasn't true – felt better than nothing.' She swallowed, the words painful to say. 'It's so hard to accept that there really is nothing left of her. I can't bring myself to believe it. I don't *want* to believe it.' Her heart splintered at the idea that now she would have to forgo this last lifeline of hers, the precious connection she'd valued above all others. But how could she carry on with her phone calls after Jackie had laid out the truth so starkly? She couldn't. It was impossible.

She had a little cry to herself after Jackie had gone, retreating to the Westgate Centre loos, feeling as if she was losing Leni all over again. Feeling stupid and embarrassed too, that it had been Tony's partner of all people who had given her the facts like that. Typical! Sometimes it was as if the whole world was queueing up to poke a stick at you.

But then she blew her nose and pulled her shoulders back,

attempting to rally herself. It was lucky, then, that Belinda McKenzie was made of strong stuff, wasn't it? She would delete Apolline's number, she would move on, she vowed. And – looking on the bright side – hadn't she been hoping to give Ray a great birthday present? Telling him she was giving up the calls would definitely do the job, she supposed, pulling a face at her reflection. Silver lining, Belinda! Even if it didn't feel like much of one right now.

Walking towards the bus stop a few minutes later, no longer in the mood to shop, she was jolted from her thoughts by the surprise sight of Ellis walking quickly ahead of her, his slouchy lope unmistakable. She shouted after him but he didn't hear her and her eyes narrowed with renewed suspicion as she watched him disappear into the crowd. What was Ellis doing here in Oxford? His new job was in Abingdon, eight miles away, and it was still only eleven forty-five, too early for him to have popped over for lunch. This was his second day working there too – surely he shouldn't be wandering around town? Unless he was here for a meeting?

*Unless he's lying to us*, she thought in the next moment, unease churning low in her stomach. *Unless he's playing me and Ray for fools*. Had she been right not to trust him all along?

Back home, after a quick lunch, Belinda had to go over to Summertown with Ray to meet with their solicitor and sign some papers relating to the house sale. Not wanting to ignite another argument, she'd decided not to mention seeing Ellis, but then, when Ray idly commented that he was thinking of giving his son the money for a car so he could get to and from work more easily, Belinda found it impossible to hold back her concerns. 'Is he really working, though?' she blurted out. They were walking up the high street at the time, and he stared at her, so startled by the question that he almost stumbled over a blackboard A-sign outside one of the bakeries.

'What? What do you mean?'

'This job he says he's doing in Abingdon – do you actually have proof of it?' she persisted, quailing a little before his look and hoping she was doing the right thing. Jackie's words echoed in her head – *I thought you'd probably rather just know* – and she forced herself on. 'Only I saw him in town this morning and ... well, it made me wonder, that's all.'

'Made you wonder what?' Ray asked, then went on before she could reply. 'Of course he's working in Abingdon! Why would he lie about that? You must have been mistaken; it must have been someone who looked like him. Didn't you say you'd been meaning to book an optician's appointment?'

Thankfully, they arrived at the solicitor's office at that moment, and Belinda didn't have to answer him. With their attention now taken up with the documents they needed to sign, that might have been the end of the Ellis-in-Oxford mystery. But then, on leaving the building again, Ray checked his phone and made a sudden noise of surprise.

'Everything all right?' Belinda asked warily.

'It's Nicky,' he said, a frown creasing his forehead.

Nicky? His ex-wife never contacted him. Belinda was surprised they even had each other's number. 'Saying what?' she asked.

'That's strange.' Ray passed a hand over his head, still staring at the phone before reading the message aloud. '"We're trying to get hold of Ellis – he hasn't been at home for nearly two weeks. Said he was going to stay with a friend but have just found out that's not true. Have you heard anything from him? Let me know if you do."'

They looked at each other, Belinda's stomach turning slowly over. Something fishy was definitely afoot. *Leni says not to trust the mouse*, she heard Apolline repeat in her head, alarm bells ringing louder than ever, before remembering with a sharp pang that she was not supposed to be caring what Apolline said any more. 'What's that all about, do you think?' she managed to ask.

'Let's find out,' he said grimly, pressing Call and holding the phone to his ear. 'Hi Nicky,' he said. 'It's me. Ellis is here in Oxford. He's okay. I thought you knew?'

# Chapter Twenty-Nine

*Leni McKenzie memorial page*

*One of my happiest memories of Leni was the fuss she made of me for my eighteenth birthday. She sent me a bottle of vodka and some engraved shot glasses on the day, then invited me to stay with her in London, and took me 'out on the town', as she put it, to a really cool Camden bar and then an even cooler Camden club. I was so dazzled by the experience, and felt so grown-up, it was the best gift she could have given me. At the time I remember thinking that it was the best day of my life! When she shone her light in your direction like that, it was always impossible to resist the heady glow it cast around you. I definitely felt a better person in her reflected light, no question.*

*Thanks for being my big sister, Leni. Even though you once tickled me until I wet myself.*

*Love Will x*

That afternoon, Tony had just closed the sale on a top-of-the-range Audi – still got it, he told himself, filing the paperwork with satisfaction – when his phone rang: Jackie's number. 'They're keeping me in,' she said glumly, without preamble. 'Blood pressure through the roof. A ticking off from the midwife for overdoing it.'

'Overdoing it? I thought you were taking things easy today!' he exclaimed in alarm. She'd assured him that very morning – promised him, in fact – that she was taking a duvet day to rest before her antenatal check-up. How could anyone overdo a duvet day?

'Well … as it happened, I had some stuff to sort out. But it's done now.'

She sounded flat and his heart went out to her, knowing how hard she'd found the new restraints of pregnancy, along with its accompanying handmaidens of tiredness and anxiety. 'But the baby's all right? The tests are okay?' His voice rose with worry and he turned away, but not before he noticed his boss, Annabeth, glancing across from her desk in concern.

'We're both fine,' she said. 'There's no immediate worry, you don't have to drop everything and come over. I'm just a bit apprehensive, I guess. I don't think I could bear it if anything went wrong now, Tony. I don't think I could cope if—'

'Nothing's going to go wrong,' he assured her before she had time to finish the sentence. 'Do you hear me? You're in the best place, you'll be well looked after. I'll come over and keep you company after work, and we'll make a plan, okay? We've got this.'

He hung up and sat with his head in his hands for a moment. 'Everything all right, Tone?' Annabeth asked.

'Just going to get some fresh air,' he muttered, striding

across the showroom before she could say anything else. He was remembering the days before Will was born, the stress he had felt as he wondered whose baby his wife was carrying, how dreadfully the question had weighed upon his shoulders in the months spent waiting to find out. In hindsight, he had detached himself there and then from his poor unborn son in an unconscious act of self-protection, dreading seeing Graham fucking Fenton leering back at him from the infant's features. And then Will was born – darling, tiny Will – and he had been so visibly Tony's son with his unmistakable McKenzie nose and long legs, Tony had buckled with relief, right there in the maternity ward. *Oh look, he's overcome*, the midwives had said, smiling. They didn't know the half of it.

It seemed the damage was already done though, an oily mark of doubt staining what should have been a bright and joyful new relationship. He had held his little boy, kissed his small pink face, he had fed and comforted him, he had hung in there for all the months of illness and worry that ensued when Will caught one bug after another, and ping-ponged between home and hospital with exhausting regularity. But still something was missing, the love refusing to simply pour forth for his son the way it had with his daughters. He couldn't forgive Belinda for betraying him, for what she'd put him through. Even after Fenton moved away, whenever Tony glanced through the kitchen window, he still half expected to see the other man lurking in the next-door garden, hoping for a secret tryst with his wife. He had turned away from her and, by association, from his children too. He told himself his exit was for the best, but as a result, his relationship with the children had suffered. Worse, he had taken his eye off the ball, allowed that to happen.

Outside the showroom, he walked across the car park, the wind snatching at his hair and causing him to shiver in his shirtsleeves. He thought about Jackie and the new baby, and then he thought again about Belinda, Graham Fenton and Will, the unholy trinity he had pushed from his mind for all of these years. How could he have let his anger poison the relationship with his own children? The other day when they spoke, Belinda had said she blamed herself for their split, but the only person to blame for Tony's subsequent letting down of their kids was him. He should have done better for them all, particularly for Will, the boy he'd found so hard to love.

The wind blew into his face, causing tears to leak from his eyes. And now here he was, on the verge of it all happening again. Before he became a father for the fourth time, it was imperative that he make amends with Will. If losing Leni had taught him anything, it was that life could be heartbreakingly fragile. More – it had taught him that having a family was too precious a gift to squander.

On impulse, he called his son's number. Why wait a moment longer? 'Will, it's Dad,' he said. 'I'd love to see you. When can I see you?'

Collapsing gratefully into bed that night, Tony could hardly keep his eyes open long enough to turn off the bedside lamp. He'd gone to see his pregnant partner in hospital, loaded up with books, extra pyjamas and her favourite toiletries – she might be there for six weeks, according to the doctors – and he'd finally managed a proper conversation with his son too, where he'd laid his cards on the table. 'I haven't been a great dad and I'm sorry,' he'd said, coming straight to the point. 'But I'm determined to make a better fist of it from now on, if you'll give me another chance.' All being well with Jackie and the baby, Will was going to come and stay that weekend, and Tony was already thinking up a list of father–son activities for them. Nothing would stop him this time.

He was so deeply asleep that he didn't hear his phone at first. He was dreaming that he'd returned to the children's old primary school and found Leni there, a little girl again, her hair in bunches. 'Is it really you?' he asked, astonished with joy. Her face split into a giant smile on seeing him and she jumped up with a shout of 'Daddy!' Then he realised someone was saying his name.

'Tony. *Tony!*'

'Mmm,' he mumbled because he'd been about to scoop Leni up into his arms, his beautiful little girl, and he didn't want this to be taken away from him.

'Tony. *Tony!*' It was his phone, with the ringtone of Jackie's voice that she'd recorded to alert him to her calls. A joke of hers, but he had been too embarrassed to admit he didn't know how to change it back, and now he was stuck with it. 'Tony. *Tony!*' He rolled over, suddenly more alert, and scrabbled to answer the call.

'Hello?' Three thirty in the morning, he registered with a lurch of panic. Was there ever good news at three thirty in the morning?

'It's starting,' his partner said, without so much as a *Good morning.* Fair enough, actually. 'The baby's coming. Oh, Tony, it's too early. I'm so scared!'

'I'm on my way,' he said, already out of bed and heaving on a pair of trousers one-handed. 'I'll be with you as soon as possible, okay? Text me if you think of anything I can bring. It's going to be all right, Jac.'

Fuck. *Would* it be all right though? he thought, blindly throwing on a shirt, finding some socks, almost falling down the stairs in his haste to get going. Last night, they'd been told that the baby would be induced a few weeks earlier than normal, but not this early. 'Premature baby, thirty-four weeks, what is the survival rate, please?' he asked his phone as he started the car engine. His voice caught on the word 'survival' and he squeezed his eyes shut briefly, remembering how blasé he'd been about his older children's births; cavalier, almost. He knew nothing then, obviously. He had no idea that things could go catastrophically wrong.

'Preterm babies born between thirty-one and thirty-four weeks' gestation have a ninety-five per cent chance of survival,' the automated voice told him.

'Thank you,' he said, releasing the handbrake and reversing out of the drive. The road was silent, the night velvety black apart from the dull orange balls of light from the lamp posts. Ninety-five per cent chance of survival – that was good, wasn't it? Good odds. 'Please God, please let them both be okay,' he muttered, voice low.

'I'm sorry, I didn't understand that,' the automated voice replied politely, making him jump.

'Don't worry about it,' he muttered, scrabbling to turn off the app. Then he reached the empty ring road and hit the accelerator. 'I'm coming, Jackie,' he said into the night. 'Hang in there, both of you.'

Three forty in the morning and Belinda was wide awake, fretting. Beside her, Ray snored gently, occasionally making smacking sounds with his lips and, not for the first time, Belinda marvelled at his ability to sleep, even in the most extreme situations. She, meanwhile, couldn't prevent her brain from looping around earlier conversations on repeat.

It had not been the most pleasant of days, overall. After Ray had seen the message from Nicky, he'd called her at once, right there in the street, his face becoming more ashen with every passing moment. According to his ex-wife, there were a number of important details Ellis hadn't thought to share with his dad. Like the fact that his girlfriend back home, Paloma, was pregnant with their child, which had come as a shock to them both – an unwelcome one, by the sound of things. Also that Ellis had walked out on his old job without a word to anyone, apparently vanishing overnight. He seemed to have gone to ground, Nicky said, anguished – except, of course, he hadn't. The blow to Ray's heart was written all over his face as he explained to his ex that Ellis had appeared in Oxford and, in hindsight, might have taken advantage of his father's eagerness for them to be reunited by coming up with stories about a job interview and the subsequent offer. Yes, Ray had been all too quick to believe him. No, of course he hadn't thought to ask many probing questions.

'So you're telling me he's been with you this whole time?' Nicky cried, loud enough for Belinda to hear the snap in her voice. It was the sound of a woman at the end of her tether with worry. 'And you didn't think to *say* anything?'

'I didn't realise he was missing!' Ray replied miserably, his body sagging as if the stuffing had been knocked out of him. Belinda felt her heart break for his crushed face, the realisation that his new-found father–son relationship wasn't actually as good – certainly not as honest – as he'd hoped. 'What do you want me to do when he gets in later?'

'Tell him he needs to ring Paloma, and then ring me, in that order,' came the reply. 'And to come back here and sort his life out, for heaven's sake!'

Ray's hand was trembling on the phone as the call ended. 'You probably heard all that, didn't you?' he said, downcast.

Belinda took Ray's arm and steered him along the pavement. 'I caught most of it,' she replied. 'I'm sorry, Ray. It sounds a bit of a mess.'

'My own son, and he lied to me,' he said, devastated. 'He's lied about everything and I just gobbled it all up like an idiot. Why couldn't he tell me the truth from the start, confide in me? I would have heard him out, I wouldn't have judged him, not for a second. It's not like I've gone through life myself getting everything right, after all.'

Belinda was still holding on to him because he didn't seem all that steady on his feet. 'You mustn't blame yourself,' she said. 'We believe what we want to believe when it comes to our children, because we want to think the best of them. And we want them to love us in return.'

'Yes, but . . .' Ray shook his head. 'What's he been doing all day, when he told us he was at work? Why go through such an elaborate charade?'

*Well*, Belinda felt like saying, *he was in Oxford this morning like I told you*, but she didn't want to rub his nose in it. 'He's obviously troubled,' she said tactfully instead.

'I'll say,' Ray snorted as they started walking again. 'So the night he rang and said he was in the area – that must have been when he heard his girlfriend was pregnant. Nicky said he vanished for a night – sounds like he panicked and just got out of town. Then he went back to Crickhowell, apparently with some story about getting drunk and stopping over at a friend's. But he must have decided all over again that he couldn't cope, which was when he got in touch with me a second time to say he'd got the job. The job he made up, like you suspected.'

There was such anguish in his voice. How Belinda wished she'd been wrong. 'Look, he's completely freaked out, poor lad, at the thought he's going to be a father – which is under-standable, if it was unplanned. But let's be grateful he came to you at all, rather than being on his own, yeah? He turned to you not once but twice, in fact. Even if he wasn't truthful, that's no reflection on you: more that he's been so confused. He saw you as a port in a storm – that's a positive you can take from this. And you didn't let him down, did you? You were there for him.' She squeezed his hand encouragingly. 'We'll talk to him later when he gets home, sort everything out then.'

'This is all my fault,' Ray had groaned. 'If I'd been a better role model in the first place, he wouldn't be so terrified at the prospect of fatherhood; he'd have had the confidence to deal with it.' He turned even paler as something else occurred to him. 'Christ, and this would make me a *grandad*. A grandad, Bel! I'm not that old, surely?'

A thrill passed through Belinda immediately at these words. In all the drama, she hadn't yet put two and two together, but oh heavens, she would definitely be claiming step-grandma rights if Ellis and his girlfriend went ahead and had the baby, just try and stop her. 'I think it would be absolutely lovely!' she cried. Already her mind was racing ahead to how they could turn the box room in their new house into a tiny nursery. Would it be over the top for her to start buying some sweet little baby vests and keeping an eye out for second-hand cots in the nearby charity shops? 'But we can cross that bridge when we come to it,' she added, possibly more to herself than Ray.

That evening when Ellis came home, it all kicked off. Barely had he walked through the door when Ray lost his cool, demanding to know how long his son would have carried on his pretence, and why he hadn't simply been honest. Ellis blanched then leaped straight on the defensive. 'Yeah, you got me,' he said, putting his hands up sarcastically, avoiding eye contact with either of them. 'Turns out I'm a loser, just like you, Dad.' And then he'd stormed out of the house again, slamming the door behind him.

Belinda had rushed after him down the road, still in her socks, begging him to come back and talk the whole thing through properly. It didn't matter, she assured him, they could help in any way he needed. He'd snapped at her to get off his case with such viciousness, though, that she'd come to a forlorn halt there in the street, the freezing pavement numbing the soles of her feet.

He strode off round the corner and out of sight, while she was forced to slink back home, despondent. There she found Ray motionless on the sofa, head in his hands, proving himself to be impervious to all Belinda's words of encouragement as the evening wore on. 'He'll come back, he's just embarrassed and wrong-footed, that's all,' she told him at intervals, but Ray merely shook his head.

'I've lost him again, haven't I?' he kept saying. 'I've blown it now. You heard what he said – he thinks I'm a loser. And he's right. I am.'

'You're not,' she told him staunchly. 'You listen to me now, Ray: you're a good man, and you've been a good dad to him while he's been here. He knows that. He'll be back soon, you wait, and then you can both clear the air and move on.'

But it was the early hours now, and Ellis still wasn't back. *Would* he come back? Was he already well on his way to a new place to hide out and lick his wounds? The wind howled in the chimney and she hoped he was someplace warm, at least.

She stiffened as a new sound reached her ears. A scratching noise – a key in the lock? – followed by the small familiar judder of the front door being opened, where it was swollen and always caught on the floor. Then a muffled thud, which she recognised as the door being closed by someone trying to be quiet. Her handbag was down in the hall but she didn't care. She knew it wasn't a thief. She nudged Ray, who gave a sudden snort as he woke up. 'He's back,' she hissed to him urgently. 'Ellis. He's downstairs. Go and talk to him. Give him a hug, tell him you love him.'

Ray's eyes opened and he blinked a few times, so she said it all over again. He sat up, then reached over and patted her duvet-covered shoulder. 'Thank you,' he murmured, then went and put on his dressing gown, leaving her alone in the bed.

The door creaked behind him and she listened for a little while, ears straining in the darkness, but there were no raised voices to be heard. No shouts, no accusations. She thought she might have detected the hiss of the kettle being boiled but perhaps that was her imagination.

Tiredness crept over her at last and she closed her eyes, meaning merely to rest them for a while until Ray came back to bed, but then her body became heavier, her mind finally slowed and she was out.

# Chapter Thirty

*Leni McKenzie memorial page*

*I only met Leni recently – at a trampolining class! – but she was really fun company and super friendly, suggesting we go for a drink afterwards and taking a genuine interest in everyone. She said she loved trampolining – it made her feel as if she was flying. Leni, you were a beautiful person. Fly free, my friend.*

    *Shanice*


Alice had just emerged from the tube station at St Paul's when she realised her phone was ringing in her bag. *Dad*, she saw on the screen and frowned a little as she swiped to answer it. Calling for a chat at eight forty-five in the morning? This was not his usual style. 'Hi,' she said, walking quickly along the street, the phone pressed to her ear. Up ahead you could see the cathedral, although give it another few weeks and the leaves on the plane trees would be fully out, transforming the view. 'Everything all right?'

She couldn't make out what he was saying at first, partly

because of a bus roaring by in the vicinity but also because he sounded so garbled – was he *crying*? Then she caught a few key phrases: *four pounds, intensive care* – and her brain caught up instantly. 'Jackie's had the baby?'

'A little girl. A beautiful little girl. She's tiny but she's a fighter.' His voice shook again – he *was* crying – then he went on. 'Jackie was amazing. They're both amazing. She – the baby – is in intensive care, she'll need help breathing for a while – but she's got long legs and the McKenzie nose, just like you, Will and Leni.'

'Oh, Dad, congratulations,' she said. A new sister, she thought, feeling a strange twist inside. A tiny new long-legged sister. 'Are *you* all right? Was the labour okay?'

He launched into a lengthy description of what sounded like one stressful complication after another, ending in an emergency C-section for Jackie. He sounded so raw and emotional as he unpacked the story; Alice could hardly bear to hear his vulnerability, especially when she was so many miles away. For the first time in years, she found herself wishing she could give him a hug. 'Sounds like you both did great, Dad,' she assured him. 'So, what are you going to call her, then? My little sister?'

*My little sister.* Words she'd never said before. Words that gave her goosebumps as soon as she heard them aloud. She'd assumed she'd only ever have one sister in her life. Even though she'd known about the baby for months, the idea of an extra sibling had felt more of an abstract concept than reality, the latest nonsense her dad had got himself into. She'd been almost unable to believe in it – in her – until now. But as of this morning, there was a brand new and extremely real person in the world, her baby sister, small, pink and breathing in an incubator, completely unaware that she had marked herself an extra branch on Alice's family tree.

'We're not sure yet,' he said. 'Jackie's a bit out of it at the moment – it's been one hell of a night – but we'll talk properly later. I'll keep you posted.' He cleared his throat and she pictured him there in a hospital corridor, presumably a mixture of adrenalin and emotional exhaustion. 'I'd better go, I need to ring Jackie's sisters and parents, but I'll talk to you again soon, okay?'

'Congratulations, Dad. I'm sending all my love to the three of you. And yeah, whenever it's a good time for a chat, I'm always pleased to hear from you,' she told him.

'Thank you, darling. Love you. Take care.'

'Love you, Dad.' The words rang around her head. *Love you*. Wow. That was nice, wasn't it? Being able to tell your own dad you loved him and to mean it. To hear him say the words himself, moreover, and know that they were sincere. *Did you hear that too, Len?* she thought, bemused, putting her phone away. *I didn't imagine it, did I?*

Feeling dazzled by such intense and unexpected news, she headed towards the office, glancing back at the shopping mall she'd just walked past, wondering if any of the shops there sold baby clothes, already mentally fast-forwarding to her lunch break when she could mooch around the displays, searching for the tiniest of tiny outfits for a very little sister. Her new, hours-old sister, she marvelled again. She wondered, too, how differently she might have felt had Leni still been around. The

314

two of them would probably have expressed to one another the grossness of their ageing dad becoming a father again; there might even have been a certain lacing of resentment in their reaction to the birth announcement, a slight curling of the lip. *Nothing to do with me.*

Instead, the new baby felt totemic to Alice, a chance to start again; it felt like the quiet (or perhaps noisy) turning of a corner into a reshaped family set-up. She even found herself thinking differently towards Jackie – fondly! Gratefully! – for giving her another sibling. An image of *kintsugi* pottery came to mind once more, the broken pieces held together by golden cement, and thereby transcending the original to become something altered but equally beautiful. Beautiful in a new way; she could celebrate that. Maybe all families were *kintsugi* pots at the end of the day. Hers certainly seemed to be piecing itself back together, what with Will's return, and the conviction that they were all trying hard to reconnect.

Moreover, now that Will had unburdened himself of his secret, he seemed less stressed, more willing to talk to her about Leni. Having finally read through her memorial page (and even added to it), he had also solved the puzzle of the Tuesday 'T 7.30' entries, spotting an entry by a woman called Shanice referencing a Tuesday trampolining class Leni had attended. (Hadn't Leni always wanted to fly? Alice loved the image of her bouncing high in the air.) As the moderator of the memorial page, Alice was able to contact Shanice, asking if they could meet. 'Tell me *everything*,' she imagined herself saying the moment this happened.

The street was full of office workers, moving like a tide

along the pavement together, and in the crowd ahead Alice recognised the back of a man's head, the colour of his raincoat. Her heart played a little chord of surprise. Darren? Yes, she thought, as he glanced sideways and she saw his handsome profile. It was him! *Will you just go for it with Baron Darren already?* she imagined Leni encouraging her, and Alice smiled, figuring there might never be a luckier day for her than this, the day when her new baby sister had arrived in the world. Why not? She could just ask him for a drink, couldn't she? Let's face it, he'd asked *her* for a drink a few weeks ago, it wasn't as if he didn't fancy her back. And wasn't she trying to be less passive in her life, to make things happen for herself? They could have a drink, maybe something nice to eat; they could start over. This time she wouldn't become so drunk she couldn't remember getting home, either.

They were nearly at her building now and she decided to make her move, nab him before they went inside. 'Darren!' she called, but a bus wheezed past at that second and she didn't think he'd heard her.

'Darren!' she said again, trying to catch him up. But then, reaching the steps up to the building moments after he did, she realised he wasn't alone. He was holding hands with a woman in a stylish grey coat and then – oh shit – they were embracing and kissing each other, and Alice didn't know where to look.

'Will you be back for dinner, do you think?' she heard the woman asking. 'Only Becca said she might pop round, and—'

The rest of the woman's evening plans were lost in the hoot of a taxi sailing by, but it didn't matter. Alice had heard enough to have already created a whole picture in her head. They were together, Darren and this woman, a couple who lived together, who shared dinner plans and a bed and – well, their lives, basically. Although presumably he hadn't shared the fact that he was partial to one-night stands, and asking out other women in the office lift.

Alice felt a twinge inside – why did people have to be such bullshitters? It was so disappointing! She walked past them, deliberately catching Darren with her elbow as she went by. 'Wanker,' she said for good measure, striding straight ahead. Not before she heard his girlfriend (wife?) ask, 'Did that woman just call you a wanker? Why did she call you a wanker, Daz?'

Sorry, sister, she thought, swiping her company pass on the electronic gates and ducking into a lift, exhaling as the doors slid closed. But take it from me, that's the right word for him. Going up!

You win some, you lose some, she was telling herself by the time she was due at the fourth floor for her meeting in the marketing department. Darren was no real loss to her, at the end of the day, because her emotional balance sheet was far ahead in credit after the earlier bulletin from her father. She felt pretty good as she walked towards the meeting room, optimism swelling inside her. Yes, the universe could trip you up and take from you, but it could reward you too, if you hung on in there and kept trying. She would give this meeting her best shot and cross her fingers that Fate was feeling generous. *Of course you can do this*, she heard her former colleague Edie say in her head. They had met up for brunch the previous weekend, so that Alice could run some of her ideas past her, and she'd received an affectionate, confidence-boosting pep talk into the bargain. *You're good, Alice. We've missed you. So many clients have been asking after you!*

There were three of them waiting for her in the room – two men, one woman, and all of them a good decade her senior. Her heart started pounding as the introductions were made and she set up her PowerPoint presentation. Now that she was here, the implications of what a stepping stone this could be resounded within her. *Do not fuck this up*, she ordered herself.

'I asked to meet with you because I have had over ten years' marketing experience, specialising in social media strategies,' she began. 'And although the company does a brilliant job of serving its loyal, older consumer base, I believe some of your products could be repackaged and sold to a younger demographic in addition.' She was gabbling, her nerves on show, she realised. It was so long since she'd had to do anything like this without a full team backing her up, without having fully chewed over every tiny detail together. Practising in front of her brother plus a disinterested ginger cat was really not the same. Now here she was flying solo, and even though, beforehand, she'd been telling herself how exhilarated she felt, the truth was, she was actually plain old bricking it.

She cleared her throat, forced herself to breathe slower. She thought about Leni, who'd be cheering her on if she could; she thought about her tiny new sister, the raw pink newborn face in the photo her dad had sent. *Come on, you can do this.* 'Until last year, I was heading up the socials team at

ReImagine, an award-winning branding and communications agency,' she went on, 'but as of January, I've been working here, in the claims department, on a maternity cover. Long story,' she added quickly, when she saw the woman's eyebrows rise. It wasn't the moment for all of that. 'I'm passionate about social media, and the rocket boosters it can give to a campaign, so I've been thinking about how I could increase interaction for Sage and Golding's output.'

One of the men was glancing down at his watch; she seemed to be losing him already. Shit. Time to cut to the chase. 'For example, over the last week, I've embarked on a guerrilla campaign in my spare time,' she said. 'Not mentioning the company by name, just trying to build up some interest out there by being nimble, witty and engaged. Creating a bit of mystery. I've started a digital identity called Guess Who? to stir up interest, with the idea being that I – or an interested company – would eventually reveal all with a big fanfare. But as it stands, you don't have to go along with any of this; it's packaged so that any insurance firm could run with it if they chose to.' She paused, hoping her subtext would sink in: if you don't like it, I can take my followers elsewhere.

She clicked on the first slide, and the three of them sat forward in their seats as she explained the thinking behind the name and her simple teasing strategy. Then she took them through her progress so far, showing them a bar chart she'd drawn up, which tracked the rise of engagement throughout the days. There were small increases in numbers but nothing to write home about, and she caught the woman narrowing her eyes as if to say, *Is that it? I gave up half an hour of my day for this?*

'Then,' Alice went on, 'I got a lucky break. Or rather,' she corrected herself, 'the lucky break that comes after you've put yourself in the right place at the right time. I became part of the story.'

It had happened two days ago, when she'd ended up in (digital) conversation with a game-show-winning singer, Liam Frost. Usually famous people ignored advertisers who tried to engage with them, let alone mystery advertisers with hardly any followers, but Frost was something of a maverick, known for occasionally chatting with a fan or follower for no reason other than that he was a bit bored (or, let's face it, a bit pissed). She happened to be scrolling through a list of famous accounts she'd set up Guess Who? to follow when she noticed that he'd recently posted an image of himself with a faceful of make-up, as a promo for his upcoming tour: ruby-red lips, massive false eyelashes, the works. *My oh my!*, she'd written in reply. *Please tell us those gorge eyelashes are fully insured? Because they should be!*

It was only an off-the-cuff remark, a small piece of bread dangled before a very big fish, but to her great surprise, he'd bitten. He replied with a laughing-face emoji. *Eyelash insurance! I knew there was something I'd forgotten to put on my list!*

*Babe,* she wrote back, heart thudding with her own daring, *you wouldn't believe some of the things we have to cover . . . If only I could tell you more!* She'd signed off with the hashtags #GuessWho and #GuessWhat and then, to her immense shock and even bigger joy, he retweeted her comment.

'He retweeted my comment!' she told the marketing panel. 'To his 62,000 followers, with the quote tweet – *Here's a fun guessing game for you all*. And as a result, hundreds of them responded – I'm still getting responses even now – and there was a knock-on effect of a huge spike of new followers for the Guess Who? account.'

She brought up the slide showing Liam's tweet, along with the 5,000 likes and the 600 comments, and the man she'd previously seen glancing at his watch sat up straighter in his seat. 'Gosh!' he said.

'*Would* we insure a person's eyelashes, though?' the other man asked, looking perplexed.

'These are your people,' she went on, clicking the next slide to show a bar chart illustrating the acceleration in interaction. She'd already decided not to show them the actual comments, most of which were decidedly on the smutty side. 'These are your customers, the very consumers it would be good to reach. And this is where I would go from here, if you were interested in working with me.'

She ended with a summing-up of two different approaches available: first, that they could build on the initial success of her Guess Who? account with a full strategy she could draw up for them; or second, that she would dream up an entirely new approach within their existing social media channels that would broaden their output and appeal. 'Either way, there's a huge market out there we could bring into the fold,' she said. 'A huge market that's currently looking elsewhere. I know where they are, and I'd love to help you connect with them.'

She could hear the passion ringing through her voice and hoped it was audible to them too, because she wanted this, so much, and she knew she could deliver on her promises. They went on to ask her a few questions – firstly about how this might dovetail (or not) with her current maternity cover role, and then some light grilling about her experience and previous campaigns she'd worked on. Before she knew it, her time was up, and she was shaking hands with them all, dishing out her newly made business cards and thanking them for their time. Done.

Leaving the room again, she felt light-headed, wondering what they might be saying about her: whether they had genuinely liked her ideas or whether they'd merely been polite. She kept thinking ruefully about the man who'd mused, '*Would we insure a person's eyelashes, though?*', seemingly missing the entire point of what she'd done. Well, she'd tried her best, and if it wasn't their thing, she could keep working up the Guess Who? concept and present it to a different insurance company. Why not? She believed in her own idea; she backed herself as a winner. This was definitely a good outcome.

Once outside, she took her phone off Do Not Disturb and saw that a couple of texts had come in – from her dad and from Lou, both wishing her luck. Also, to her great surprise, there was a message from Jacob.

*Hello Alice,* she read and then she put her hand to her chest as the word 'sorry' leaped out at her. She forced herself to take a deep breath and then read it all the way through properly.

*Hello Alice, hope you're doing okay. I've been thinking about you since our last night out – and thinking too that I didn't exactly behave like a friend should. I'm sorry if I inadvertently trampled on your grief. I don't know why I thought badgering you into hurrying on with your life was a good decision – I could see on your face that it wasn't. Anyway, I'm sorry. No excuses, just sorry. And if you want another Flying Beauties nostalgia trip out, I've thought of the perfect place. Let me know if you're interested. Love Jacob x*

She could feel her heart pounding beneath her fingers but she was smiling too, feeling good. Good about herself. Good about him. Good about the fact that as soon as it was lunch-time, she was going to hit the shops and hunt out the cutest outfit and hat she could find for her new baby sister. Maybe splurge on a bunch of brightly coloured anemones for herself too, just because she had a feeling her luck might be turning at last, that she might finally be clawing her way upwards once more. Sod cheating Darren. He was nothing to her.

*I'm intrigued!* she typed in reply. *Tell me more!*

# Chapter Thirty-One

*Alice: Tell me you haven't been playing Cupid and egging on Jacob to message me?? You didn't, did you? Because he has. And I think I'm going to meet him. Unless I find out you've put him up to it, in which case I might change my mind!*

*Will: Like I've got time to try and sort out YOUR life when I'm trying to get my head round my own?? Don't flatter yourself! PS Definitely meet him*

*DM Will to Jacob: By the way, if Alice asks, I didn't message you about her, all right?*

As Belinda had predicted, the fall-out between Ray and his son had all 'come out in the wash', to coin a phrase from her mum, God rest her soul. Down there in the kitchen, in the wee small hours, Ellis had unburdened himself of the whole story to his dad, truthfully this time, before apologising for his deceit. Ray, in turn, merely hugged him hard and said he understood, and that he was here to listen and help Ellis however he could.

'You were right,' he said to Belinda when he brought her a coffee in bed that morning and got back under the covers beside her. 'Of course I wanted to think he had sought me out for the right reasons, that he wanted to get to know me again.' He pleated the duvet cover between his fingers, before turning back towards her looking tired. 'But I do think he's a good lad at heart, Bel. I do.'

'Oh, without a doubt he is,' she replied. 'He's smashing. A really nice kid.'

'And, you know, nobody's perfect, are they? Especially at that age. Everyone makes mistakes.'

'They do,' said Belinda, suddenly finding she needed to stare into her coffee, hoping he wouldn't notice how pink in the cheeks she'd become. She knew about making mistakes, after all. About how you could learn from them, too. Since Jackie had hit her so bluntly with the truth about Apolline, she hadn't made a single call to the hotline. Like Ray had suggested, maybe there were other people she could talk to instead, professionals trained to help a bereaved mother who was finding it hard to accept a loss. Her fingers itched constantly to pick up her phone, but instead she went back to her crochet hook and wool each time to keep them occupied. She had decided to make herself a long and beautiful scarf for the autumn, and every stitch, every row, felt like a tiny symbol of her progress.

She'd made mistakes with Tony, too, of course, but the two of them had had a long, frank conversation when he'd dropped in at the house that day, and she felt as if they'd each been left with a better understanding of the other. It had been decent of him, for instance, not to tell the children about her affair in all the years since, allowing them to carry on thinking the best of her. Belinda wasn't entirely sure, truth be told, that she'd have managed to be quite so self-sacrificing, had the tables been turned. 'Thank you,' she'd said stiffly, eyes down, at which point he'd put his hand on hers and thanked her in turn for having done the lion's share of the child-raising. She was surprised how much she appreciated him acknowledging this, how deeply sorry he appeared. 'I'll never forgive myself for not giving the kids my full attention when we broke up,' he told her, shamefaced. 'I owe you a lot, Bel.' So they'd both got things right and wrong, in other words. But didn't every parent, at the end of the day?

Ellis went home to Wales that morning, a thorny conversation with his pregnant girlfriend awaiting him. Also on the agenda would be some grovelling to his boss, in the hope that he might still have a job. It turned out he didn't even work in retail, he worked for a young people's charity, sorting out counselling and practical help for those who needed it. 'Sounds wonderful, I bet you're brilliant at that,' Belinda had told him warmly, hugging him goodbye at the train station. In the next moment, though, she'd felt a memory glimmering at the back of her mind, a tiny but important connection that wanted to be made. What was it? There was no time to think because then the train was coming in, and Ellis was thanking her and Ray for their generosity, promising to visit again soon and repeating his offer of help with their house move in ten days' time.

'I'm glad we're part of the same family,' he told Belinda before boarding the train. 'Thanks for being there for Dad.'

'I'm glad too,' she assured him as Ray gave him one last bear hug.

'We both are,' Ray echoed, clapping him on the back.

Once back from the station, Belinda went up to the bedroom to continue packing, in preparation for the big move. She had turned her attention to the more personal items kept at the bottom of her wardrobe, things she treasured, and as she lifted out Leni's laptop in its bright pink case, the flag at the back of her mind started waving again, alerting her to the connection she hadn't quite been able to make before. Something about youth work. Leni's laptop. This Josh that Alice had mentioned before, was he relevant too? She shut her eyes, frowning, trying to piece it all together. Then her phone rang and the sound proved to be the final piece of the puzzle.

'Hi Mum, I'm just calling to pass on Dad's news,' Alice said, only for Belinda to squeak as the laptop slithered off her knees and on to the floor. 'Mum? Everything all right?'

'Sorry! I just . . . Josh, wasn't it, you were asking me about the other week?' Her thoughts whirring, she tucked the phone between her shoulder and ear so that she could unzip the laptop case and switch it on.

Alice seemed confused by the zigzags this conversation was taking. 'What? Oh – Josh? Yes. His name was in Leni's diary. Why, have you remembered something?'

'I think so. It was you ringing that did it. And Ellis talking about youth work.' The laptop seemed to be taking forever to boot up and she jabbed at the mouse pad impatiently. 'Hold on. I'm just ...'

'Mum, I'm not following. What are you—?'

'He was a kid Leni was mentoring. A teenage boy she'd started meeting through a charity. They rang me, back in the summer, wondering why she wasn't returning their calls, but—' She paused to punch in the laptop's PIN; thankfully Leni had been a 1234 girl for all of her passcodes. 'But I had so many calls to deal with back then, so many people and companies I had to tell what had happened, they blurred together after a while. I knew I'd heard the name Josh somewhere though. Here we go,' she said, clicking open the emails. 'Let me check.' She scanned through the list and found one where the charity had arranged the initial meeting between Leni and the boy.

'A teenage boy,' Alice repeated. 'Oh, Leni. Of course he was. Of course she was doing that.'

'Josh, fifteen years old,' Belinda read from the email. 'Excluded from school. Really smart but bored and unmotivated. They thought he and Leni would be a perfect match, apparently.'

'I bet she was great at talking to him,' Alice said wistfully. 'And what a shame that ... Well. That we all lost her, but that he did too. I hope he's all right. I wonder if we could do anything for him?'

They talked about it some more, with Belinda promising to forward Alice details of the charity so that she could contact them herself. Then – 'God! I can't believe it's taken me this long,' Alice said in a rush. 'Jackie's had the baby! A little girl. Tiny and premature but they're both doing okay, Dad said.'

Heavens, the rush of emotions that went through Belinda in that moment! The heady gush of motherly feeling at the thought of a new baby in the world, a burst of affection for Tony and his partner. Love, even. 'A baby girl,' she said, choking up as she remembered, so vividly, hearing those exact words herself, twice over, on the labour ward, and how she'd cried tears of real joy to meet her daughters each time.

And so, having said goodbye to Alice, and returned to her packing, when it happened that the very next thing she took from her box of precious things was the small yellow jacket she'd knitted for the baby Leni didn't have, fresh tears came rolling down her face. Who knew that it was possible to cry because you were sad *and* because you were happy, all at the same time?

She dried her eyes, then put the tiny, soft jacket to her cheek one last time, remembering how she'd poured such hope into its making. Then she set it aside, planning to wrap it carefully in tissue paper as a gift for Tony and Jackie's tiny new daughter. It didn't cost anything to be nice to someone, did it? She was happy for them, besides. 'See how magnanimous I'm getting in my old age, Leni!' she said aloud with a watery smile.

Tony's finger was trembling as he put a hand into the incubator to stroke his baby's soft fragile head. Her skin was rosy pink and downy like a peach. Her eyes were tightly shut. She was four pounds three ounces and had the tiniest fingernails he'd ever seen, plus the most delicate shell-like ears, newly minted. He could hardly breathe as his finger brushed her rounded cheek and her nose twitched in her sleep. She was *beautiful*.

She had passed all of the doctors' medical checks, although babies born this prematurely needed help to breathe and feed, and so she'd have to stay in the NICU for a few weeks, they'd been told. Jackie was on the ward, dozing off the combined assault of surgery, blood loss and a ton of painkillers, and so Tony was tiptoeing between his two sleeping beauties, whispering encouragement at their bedsides until one of them needed him.

'My little girl,' he said now, his voice cracking on the words. He thought back to himself in the babycare shop, dismissive and bored, and that man seemed a world away from this new version of himself, broken open like an egg, emotions spilling everywhere, love swelling above all. 'I'm here,' he told her. 'I'm right here. I'm never going to leave you.' He was already imagining golden, dappled-sunshine days with her in the years ahead: the two of them paddling at the seaside, cycling through woodland, snuggled up with a bedtime story. He could hardly wait for it all to start.

# Chapter Thirty-Two

*McKenzies Together group*

**Tony:** *Morning all. Picture of Amelia Helena McKenzie here — isn't she beautiful? I am besotted. She'll be in intensive care for a little while yet but doing well. Love Dad/Tony xxx 11.33*

**Belinda:** *Gosh, Tony, what a little sweetheart she is! [red heart emoji, baby emoji, baby-bottle emoji, hatching-chick emoji, sunshine emoji] Sending the three of you so much love. I've popped a little parcel in the post but please shout if there's anything I can do that would be a practical help [red heart emoji, pink heart emoji, heart-eyes emoji] xxx 12.15*

**Alice:** *Dad, she is so gorgeous!!!! Lots of love to you and Jackie. And I LOVE that you have given her 'Helena' as a middle name. Perfect. On my way out for the afternoon now but let's catch up later. Love to you all xxx 13.08*

**Will:** *Congrats again, Dad! Can't wait to see you all x 13.27*

\*

In a new spirit of McKenzie togetherness, Will had come to Oxford to stay with his dad. It wasn't the greatest timing, days after the very early birth of Amelia, and Will had braced himself for a Tony McKenzie U-turn, the inevitable let-down change of plan, until the very second he was due to board the train. 'Of course you can still come,' his dad had surprised him by saying though. 'I've been looking forward to it.'

His mum had surprised him too when he mentioned the visit. Throughout his entire childhood, his parents hadn't exactly got on well, to the point where Will was left feeling disloyal towards his mum whenever he'd been to stay with his dad. But something seemed to have changed. 'I'm so glad you two are getting together!' she'd said down the phone. 'You are?' he'd replied, taken aback.

Tony picked him up from the station looking as if he hadn't slept much; his eyes bloodshot, his chin stubbled. He'd had an emotional few days, by the sound of it – his voice wobbling as he described the birth, the baby, Jackie – and Will could see he was struggling to keep himself together. But Tony insisted on them going out to Wolvercote together for a lakeside walk, to 'blow away the cobwebs' as he put it.

It was a crisp, cold day but there were signs of spring everywhere – leaf buds on the trees, pale primroses nestling below their trunks, the blue sky reflected in the still water of the lakes. Will remembered being dragged here for walks with his sisters on the weekends they'd stayed with their dad, and them moaning about being bored, tired, wanting to go home, but today he appreciated the tranquillity. He'd missed the English seasons when he'd been out in Thailand, the change in the air as the year turned.

There was something about walking together that felt companionable too. He'd been apprehensive about how the two of them would get on after so long, but it was surprisingly easy to talk when you were side by side, intermittently pointing out birds of prey or weirdly shaped tree stumps. Will told his dad about how he'd been looking into trying again at university, and it turned out Tony had recently sold a car to a woman who worked at the local further education college who, he claimed, was sure to know all about the university admission process. Will was about to reply that he was pretty confident he'd be able to figure it out for himself, until he realised how chuffed his dad was looking at this opportunity to be helpful. 'That would be great, Dad. Thanks,' he said instead.

Jackie rang at one point and Will could hear the tenderness in his dad's voice as he spoke to her. He thought about the wives that had popped up after his mum – bolshy Isabelle and prissy Tanya; how fake he'd always found them both, how they'd come between the McKenzie kids and their dad like beautiful, cold interruptions. He didn't know Jackie at all but remembered she'd tried to be kind at the funeral, and recognised, moreover, that his dad was speaking to her lovingly now, asking fussy questions about what she might want him to bring her later, checking in on the latest from the doctors.

'You really like her, don't you?' he said when the call was over. It seemed an odd comment to make about his dad's partner, especially when they'd just had a new baby together, but he and Tony had never discussed women or relationships as adult men together. Besides, he too wanted to make the effort, he admitted.

'Jackie? Yeah, she's brilliant,' came the reply. 'I honestly thought I was done with relationships. After me and your mum . . . after our divorce, I made a few mistakes with women. It was all a bit shallow. Ooh – buzzard,' he said suddenly, pointing out the large bird above, gliding on a thermal current. 'But with Jackie – she gives as good as she gets. I've met my match. I think she's absolutely fantastic, to be honest. I love her.'

Will, who'd been expecting broader brushstrokes from him, maybe even something glib, was taken aback by such sincerity. 'Blimey, Dad, I've never heard you talk like that,' he commented, with a sideways glance.

'Yeah, well, when you know, you know,' Tony said. 'And with her . . . well, I just know. I do often wonder what she sees in me, but I'm grateful there's something.' His expression was bashful – for at least two seconds, anyway, before switching the focus away. 'How about you, son? Anyone special on your mind at the moment?'

If you'd told Will when he boarded the Oxford train that morning that he'd end up confiding in his dad about his love life, he'd have laughed his head off. *Yeah, and back on this planet* . . . he'd have scoffed disbelievingly. And yet, in the next minute, he found himself telling his dad about Isla, who he kept thinking of even now.

'So how come you're not up there in Aberdeen, knocking on her door, telling *her* all this?' Tony asked at the end. 'You can pontificate all you like, but sometimes you have to take direct action, do you know what I mean? Especially while you've still got your tan and all. Handsome so-and-so like you, she'd be mad to turn you down.'

'She thinks I'm a closed book, remember,' Will felt compelled to point out. 'She's already turned me down once. And I had a better tan then as well,' he added for good measure.

'Well, then,' his dad said. 'You need to open this closed book, don't you? Show her what you've got. Not like—' He mimed opening a flasher mac and they both laughed. 'Just . . . let her in. Be honest with her.' He clapped Will on the back. 'It's not easy, I get it. At the end of the day, nobody likes feeling vulnerable, putting yourself out there, not knowing what response you're going to get. But you have to be . . . real. Yourself. Honest. That's what I've learned, after three failed marriages; that's my best bit of fatherly wisdom for you, son. Otherwise, what's the point?'

# Chapter Thirty-Three

*Alice: How's it going? Have you seen our new sister yet? Are things okay between you and Big Daddy?*

*Will: New sister alarmingly tiny, luckily for her doesn't look too much like Dad. Things are good — Jackie's house is insanely posh, like luxury hotel. Keep worrying I'm going to break stuff. As for me and Dad ... we're getting on okay. I see what you mean about him having changed. I'm actually enjoying spending time with him. WHO KNEW???!!!*

Alice smiled at her brother's message as she took a seat on the west-bound tube the following day. It had been such a year of reckoning for the McKenzies, she thought. Such a period of readjustment. Without Leni, they'd each had to shuffle into new positions, work out different dynamics between themselves. She felt as if they were all starting again in their own ways, taking steps to reshape their lives accordingly.

She arrived at Holland Park half an hour later, intrigued but also apprehensive. She had no idea what Jacob was planning – all he'd said was that he'd meet her here, Sunday afternoon, and she would find out more in due course. She hoped it wouldn't be weird between them after the last time they'd met.

He was waiting outside the station and she felt a surge of gladness to see him again. Will had been right; he *was* important to her. Too important to let slip away again. 'Hello and welcome to today's Flying Beauties experience: tribute number three,' he said after a brief hug. 'Follow me.'

'This is very mysterious,' she commented as she fell into step beside him. Having previously met up on dark winter evenings, in the Greek restaurant and the cocktail bar, it felt rather nice to be walking along a quiet street with him on an overcast March day, the years vanishing as he smiled down at her. He was wearing a black waterproof coat and jeans, and she remembered the photo he'd shown her of his little boy, wondering if this was his sensible-dad coat, worn for outdoor excursions. The pockets looked as if they might be secretly full of pine cones and small round stones and other interesting finds from his son.

'Well, I'm a very mysterious man, if you hadn't already noticed,' he replied.

'Oh, really?'

'No. Absolutely not. Transparent as a piece of cling film. But I *am* an apologetic man, if not a mysterious one,' he said, glancing over at her, his brown eyes suddenly serious. They paused at the traffic lights and she wondered again where he was taking her. Was this where he lived? she thought, before registering the earnest note in his voice and looking back at him. 'I really am sorry for last time, me trying to browbeat you into conversations you didn't want to have,' he went on.

'Misguidedly trying to push you forward into the future when that wasn't what you needed at the time. I'll go with you to all the Leni-places you want, Alice, if it helps you deal with losing her.'

'Thank you,' she said with a small smile. They crossed the road and walked past some large, elegant houses, set back from the pavement. 'Although, to be fair, you probably had a point. I spoke to some friends about it – I was all indignant, like, "He made out I was stuck in the past!" and they were like, "Um, yep" – which pulled me up a bit. I think I actually *have* been living in the past, quite a lot lately, to be fair. Not really engaging with the rest of my life. But funnily enough, that's all changed this week.'

He gestured up a street on their right. 'This way,' he said. 'So what happened this week then? If you want to talk about it?'

She smiled at him. 'I've had a good few days at work,' she replied, before going on to elaborate with the backstory about Sage and Golding, the meeting she'd requested, and the brilliant news she'd received on Friday. 'The upshot is, the marketing people I spoke to – Emma, Sanjay and Phil – have met with HR, and between them, they've arranged it so that I'll continue the maternity cover for four days a week and then, on Fridays from next week, I'll be working on a free-lance basis, as a social media consultant for their department.'

'Alice! That's brilliant news! We're going in here, by the way. Into the park.'

It really was brilliant news, she thought proudly as they left the street behind and entered the park. Emma, in particular, had been quick to tell her how much they'd loved her ideas and approach for a new digital campaign, and had asked her to work up a full strategy. She'd also indicated that, were things to go well, come the end of Alice's temporary contract, there would almost certainly be the prospect of ongoing freelance work. *The thing about Sage and Golding*, she said, *is that once you're in, you're in. People joke about never leaving but that's because, if they like you, this company are extremely keen to hang on to you.*

'Your business empire starts here,' he said warmly. 'Have you got a name for your new company yet? McKenzie and Associates? Alice McKenzie International?'

'You make me sound like an airport,' she laughed. 'Let me at least have Oxford bus station named after me first.' They were walking around the park, with its mature trees and broad pathways, joggers panting along in Lycra, parents and children, an elderly couple holding hands. 'It's lovely here,' she commented. 'Very peaceful.'

'Yes,' he said. 'And I've taken a bit of gamble today because I'm hoping we'll see something, but we might not. I came here the other day on a recce and saw one, but I gather it's not always guaranteed.'

'You saw one what?' she repeated, intrigued. 'A recce? What are you talking about?'

'It's a surprise,' came his cryptic reply. 'Or rather I hope it will be. Worst comes to the worst, we'll have a walk and then I'll shout you a cup of tea to get over the crushing disappointment of a non-event. But let's head for the Kyoto Garden and keep our fingers crossed in the meantime.'

'The suspense is killing me!' she groaned. 'My brain is absolutely spinning here, trying to work out what you've planned.

I can't cope!' She elbowed him affectionately. 'But thank you for this magical mystery tour anyway, I'm enjoying it so far.'

She remembered to ask him about his week, like a normal person, and he recounted some funny stories about his little boy and told her about the modules he was teaching this year. She responded with news about Will having come to stay with her – 'He sends his love,' she passed on – and how he'd forced her to re-evaluate her approach to Leni. Not only by helping with her investigation of Leni's last few weeks, she explained, but by pointing out what was written at the very end of the diary, details Alice had skimmed over before now.

'Look,' she said, stopping momentarily to retrieve it from her bag. 'I brought it to show you.' She flipped to the last page of the little book, where Leni had written 'NEXT YEAR' at the top of the page, with a list of plans below. *Fall in love,* they both read, heads close together as they leaned in over it. *Have adventures. Girls' holiday! Family get-together. Make a new friend (maybe even two!!) Start an evening class (flamenco??) Get cool haircut. Paint!!! Go to Barcelona on my own. (Or Venice? Both?!) Book theatre tickets. Swim in the sea. Dorset trip with Alice!*

'Wow,' Jacob said. 'She was a dynamo. I can almost hear her saying all of those things with that pure Leni McKenzie *joie de vivre.*'

'Same! Exactly! But do you know what my favourite thing of all is?' Alice asked, pointing to the top of the page. After originally writing 'NEXT YEAR' in black pen, Leni had later added in blue the words '. . . will be amazing!!' 'Isn't that brilliant? *Next year will be amazing.* She was the most optimistic person ever. Even when she'd been through the toughest time of her life.' She put the diary carefully back in her bag. 'Don't laugh at me, because I know this will sound cheesy, but I'm going to try to channel that Leni-spirit from now on. To think – next year will be amazing – and to believe it, too. Because who knows?'

'I love that,' he said. 'And it's not cheesy. Everyone should live with those words in mind. I'm going to try as well. Optimise the optimism! The best days of our lives are yet to come!'

Alice smiled at him. 'I'm absolutely going to get "Optimise the Optimism" put on a T-shirt and I'm going to force you to wear it,' she laughed, glad to have shared Leni's precious words with him, and glad too that he had immediately got on board with the sentiment. More than anything, she was glad to be here at all with him, after Will had made her rethink their friendship.

By now they had reached the Kyoto Garden in the centre of the park, which was very picturesque with a large pond and waterfall, and Japanese planting. She told him about her mum uncovering the mysteries of 'Josh' and how Alice had since contacted the mentoring charity and spoken to someone there. 'They couldn't give me too many details because of confidentiality, but apparently Josh, the boy she was mentoring, is doing well these days. I know Leni would be so pleased about that,' she said, a lump in her throat. 'They also told me that Josh had really liked her.' She broke off, suddenly emotional. 'I felt so ... so proud of her.'

'What a lovely thing to do,' Jacob agreed. 'And what a lovely person she was.'

'I know, right? Will and I were talking about it, saying we

both felt inspired to do something similar in her memory. Passing on that generous spirit of hers, if you know what I mean.'

'That would be amazing. I bet she'd have loved that,' he said. Then he nudged her. 'Aha,' he said, a new note of excitement in his voice as he pointed. 'There. See it?'

She had just noticed a small stone pagoda-like ornament and thought at first he was referring to that, but then she lifted her gaze and saw . . . 'Oh my God,' she said, clapping a hand to her mouth. She almost wanted to rub her eyes and check she was seeing properly. 'No way. Is that . . . real?'

There ahead of them was a *peacock*, an actual peacock strutting slowly across the path. Its blue and green colours gleamed iridescent in the sun, its tiny head bobbing on a long curved neck as its astonishing many-eyed tail feathers swept the ground behind like the train of a wedding dress. 'It's real,' he assured her, and, as if demonstrating that yes, it certainly *was* real, thank you very much, the peacock chose that moment to fan its tail in an exhilarating plumage display. Other people in the vicinity had stopped to see too; you could hear children's voices, high and excited – *Look! Look!* – and Alice found herself joining them from inside her head. *Look, Leni!* she marvelled silently, unable to take her eyes off the extraordinary creature. *Look!*

'Wow,' she breathed, standing motionless as the peacock continued its stately procession across the grass away from them. She briefly considered taking a photo but knew there was no need, because she would remember this moment forever. 'I feel as if I'm in a dream,' she said, a laugh in her voice. 'An incredible dream. Now you're about to tell me you arranged all that, aren't you?'

'To the very last detail,' he replied, pretending to salute the departing bird. 'Cheers, mate. Perfect timing. Oh, and look, he's showing off to his lady friend over there. Must be mating season, I guess.'

He pointed out a peahen almost hidden within the undergrowth towards which the peacock was strutting, its tail wobbling a little with each step. Alice had a visceral memory of pressing the peacock feathers of her 'wings' against her face, feeling how soft and delicate each one was. Then she was remembering the rush of leaping off a bunk bed with her sister. *I think I really did fly a bit just then.* 'Flying Beauties forever,' she said in a shaky voice.

'Flying Beauties forever,' he echoed, putting an arm around her briefly and squeezing her shoulders.

'Thank you,' she said, as the birds vanished into the undergrowth. They continued walking, the vivid scene still replaying in her mind. 'That was the most amazing, wonderful idea. The best thing you could have thought of. I didn't even know there were any peacocks in London, let alone wandering freely around Holland Park like this. I assumed they were all in zoos or on rich people's estates.' She shook her head, still a bit dazed. 'I feel like I'm in some kind of enchanted land, a fairy tale. I don't actually think I've ever seen a real one before now. I wonder if Leni ever did?'

'Well, you've done it for the both of you now, if not,' he replied.

'I have, haven't I?' she marvelled, smiling at him. 'Thank

you, Jay. Honestly. That means so much to me. You've made my week.'

'I think you made your own week, when you sorted out that great bit of work for yourself,' he reminded her. 'But I'm happy to share the credit. And I'll still shout you a cup of tea to toast your success when we get to the café.' They smiled at one another. 'Changing the subject, how come you were working for the insurance company in the first place, if you don't mind me asking? You said something about resigning before Christmas – what happened?'

She would have batted away the question a few weeks ago but was feeling so euphoric from the peacock sighting that she told him the truth: about losing her temper when Nicholas Pearce tried it on, and about the bad old days of her incandescent anger; taking her revenge out on Callum Ferguson, getting escorted home by the police and all the rest of it. She'd become ashamed of her own actions, so ashamed that she'd preferred to bury them away out of sight, but here, in the calm surroundings of the Kyoto Garden where peacocks could appear like magic, she felt a new distance from those dark stormy rages, as if the cool spring breeze had blown them clean away.

He shot her a sympathetic look. 'You've been through such a trauma,' he said. 'A really hard, painful time.'

'Yeah,' she agreed. 'But I'm definitely on the up now. Coming out the other side. Next year will be amazing, and all that. It might even be true.'

'Too right,' he said. 'Do you know, I was listening to a podcast the other day on my way to work,' he went on.

'About rebuilding your life after a traumatic event. And the interviewer referenced an old experiment done with – I can't remember if it was moths or butterflies, actually. Let's say butterflies. Anyway, in the experiment, the butterflies' chrysalises were cut open with a scalpel prematurely, before they were ready to emerge themselves. And each time the butterfly inside would be perfectly formed, with nothing anatomically wrong, except they were completely unable to fly. Every single time. The scientists came to the conclusion that normally a butterfly would push and push and push against the side of the chrysalis in order to break through – and that it was this struggle and this repeated pushing that built up their muscles and ultimately meant they could fly.'

Alice frowned. 'So you're saying—'

'I'm saying, possibly in a heavy-handed way, that sometimes the act of getting through a trauma can give you a strength you didn't have before.'

'The strength to fly,' she said, voice wavering, because yes, she wanted so much to believe in this; hadn't she and Leni always tried so hard to take flight? She gave a little sob and immediately felt embarrassed. 'Oh gosh. That's actually really beautiful. And sort of upsetting at the same time.'

'I'm sorry,' he said. 'I didn't mean—'

'No, it's fine. It's lovely. I'm upset, but in a good way, because . . .' She tried to smile but knew her mouth was going wonky with the emotions she was experiencing. 'Because I feel like I have been bashing against this . . . well, chrysalis, if you like, for so bloody long, and I'm so ready to burst through it, put it behind me, and yet it seems to be going on forever. But I do really want to ...' It was hard to get the word out because it was suddenly loaded with such meaning. 'I do want to fly.'

They had stopped walking and he put his arms around her. 'Oh, Alice,' he said, holding her. 'You will. I know you will.' She shut her eyes because it was so nice to stand there within his embrace, to feel the fabric of his jacket beneath her cheek, to know that he was holding her tight. 'It's going to happen,' he said, his breath warm on her ear. 'I promise you.'

# Chapter Thirty-Four

The time had almost come: this was to be the last week Belinda would ever live in her house, and before Friday, she and Ray had to finish packing and tackle an intimidatingly long list of jobs, big and small. A stressful few days, in other words, which was why Belinda made the executive decision to start Monday with the best stress-buster she knew: swimming. This might be the last chance she had to snatch an hour to herself and she planned to make the most of it.

Once there and changed, she stuffed her shoes and clothes into a locker, smiling indulgently at a little boy wearing Paw Patrol trunks who was capering around his mother's legs while chattering non-stop. *They grow up so fast*, she thought, with a pang for the days when her children had been that size.

Approaching the pool, she eyed up which lane looked emptiest (she did so hate the men who pointedly overtook you with their pathetic competitive zeal) and headed towards the end furthest away, where she could see a single woman in a flowered rubber bathing cap slowly tanking up and down in a relaxed backstroke. Perfect. Even better, today's lifeguard was a beefy bloke rather than the pretty blonde who'd been unfortunate enough to witness Belinda's previous meltdown. But then, as she was nearing the steps, she heard a scuttle of little footsteps behind her, a mischievous high-pitched giggle and a splash.

She almost didn't look round because there were always splashes at this time of day if kids were having lessons, or were here on an inset day. But something urged her to turn – and as she did, she was just in time to catch a glimpse of the little boy with the Paw Patrol trunks disappearing beneath the surface of the water. His mum was nowhere to be seen. The lifeguard's whistle shrieked through the air and he leaped from his chair, and for a millisecond, Belinda thought she was having a flashback to when Leni was a tiny girl and had thrown herself similarly into this very pool. Then her instincts took over.

She jumped in after the boy, whose small flailing body was already sinking towards the tiled bottom, dimly aware of a scream of 'CALEB!' – the poor mum rushing towards them. Hands in a prayer position, Belinda surface-dived down to the child, grabbing a tight hold of his narrow shoulders and hauling him up and out, water raining from his little limbs. He seemed limp, she thought in a panic as the lifeguard appeared at the edge of the pool, followed by the mum, her mouth open in a wail. It must only have been half a second – the longest half second of Belinda's life, it seemed – but then the boy coughed, water spraying from his mouth and nose, and he promptly let out a cry.

'He's okay,' Belinda said, shock pounding through her.

Shock, and relief too, that she had caught him, scooped up into the air like a rebirth. 'You're okay, aren't you, darling?'

She relinquished him to the distraught crouching woman who enfolded him immediately in her arms, her bright pink hair falling over his small bare shoulders. 'Oh, Caleb!' she gasped.

'Are you all right, buddy?' the lifeguard asked the little boy, kneeling on the wet, dimpled concrete tiles. 'Did you bang your head?'

'I just wanted to jump in,' the boy said, pressing himself against the woman.

'And you did, didn't you? While Aunty Gen was still sorting out the locker!' she said, eyes hollow. Goodness, so he wasn't even her son, Belinda thought with a stab of sympathy. Nightmare. 'Thank you,' the woman went on to her, still clutching the child as if she'd never let him go. 'I'm sorry,' she said to the lifeguard. 'I've just had a bit of bad news, I lost my focus.'

Luckily this lifeguard was a lot more understanding than the one who'd yelled at Belinda so many years earlier. 'These things happen,' he said. 'No harm done. And you won't do it again, will you, mate?' he asked Caleb. 'When you're a really good swimmer like me, you can jump in all by yourself, okay? But not before. Understand?'

The boy nodded. Then, shyly lifting his head, he looked at the lifeguard there in his Aertex polo shirt and shorts. 'You've got very big arms,' he said.

'I have, haven't I? Big and strong, so that I can swim really well,' the man said, winking at the two women in a self-deprecating way and flexing his bicep at the boy. He couldn't have been much more than twenty-five, Belinda thought, but there was something really kind about him.

'Sorry,' the pink-haired woman – Aunty Gen – mumbled as the boy reached forward to pat the lifeguard's bicep admiringly. 'He lost his dad last year – my brother. We get this quite a lot with men your age. I hope you don't mind.'

'Not at all,' the lifeguard said, tousling Caleb's hair and rising to his feet. 'Take care of yourself, okay? Remember what I said about learning to be a good swimmer!'

He loped back to his lifeguard chair like a superhero and Belinda rubbed her own, considerably less toned arms self-consciously. 'Sorry to hear about your brother,' she said, because Gen still looked a bit tearful. 'Are you all right?'

The stress of the last few minutes seemed to catch up with the other woman, who shook her head, lips pressed together. 'Not really,' she said. 'We'd just got here and I had a text message from my partner saying she's started bleeding. She's six months pregnant. The midwife said for her to go to hospital and . . . I didn't know what to do. It's my morning to look after this one – I'm trying to help out his mum – but I'm worried about Pen – Penelope, my other half, so . . .'

Belinda was battling to keep up as the words spilled out, on and on. She thought about all the times she'd had to struggle on her own with the kids, lurching from one drama to another – how she'd wished, frequently, that someone would just come to her rescue for once. She could go swimming any time, she figured. They had packers coming in on Wednesday, and both Will and Ellis had offered to muck in too; the work would get done. 'Let me help,' she said, clambering out of the pool.

'I've got my car. I could take you to the hospital, and even sit with little one here, if you need an extra pair of hands. It would be no problem.'

Gen looked as if she might cry with relief. 'Oh my God, really? Are you sure?'

Belinda batted aside thoughts of bubble-wrapping the kitchen crockery and taking cuttings from the garden, as had been her plans for the rest of the day. She would rather put some goodness out into the world, help a stranger whose path had collided so splashily with hers. Wasn't this what living was about, really? Trying to be a good person in society, taking pride in her own actions? 'I'm absolutely sure,' she replied.

# Chapter Thirty-Five

*Two months later*

*Dear Leni,*

*Happy birthday, my darling! I wish we could be celebrating together today, I know you always loved a family occasion. We will do our best without you but you'll be very much on our minds.*

*You would have been thirty-six today. Thirty-six years, and yet I remember your birth as if it were yesterday, the hot rush of love bursting through me when I saw your beautiful face for the first time. I thought, yes, here she is, as if I already knew you. But lucky me, I still had so much to find out, not least what a wonderful, funny, kind daughter you turned out to be. A piece of my heart.*

*So! What's been happening since the last time I wrote? Well, the house is coming along in leaps and bounds – we've moved properly into our bedroom now, curtains and all, and I love it so much. A load of Ray's friends came over last weekend and we got heaps more work done between us – Will and Ellis have been back and forth helping out too. I think we're going to be really happy here, you know. We're beginning work on the first couple of guest bedrooms next week so that we can actually – yikes! – start getting bookings for the summer. Alice and Ray keep teasing me, calling me 'Lady of the Manor', but I have to say, I quite like my new title. There are worse nicknames, right?*

*This is just a quick one as I need to get the roast chicken on, but we'll all be thinking about you today and I'll write again soon to let you know how it all went. And if there's any gossip, obviously!!*

*Love you so much. Miss you every day. Thank you for being a light in my life for thirty-five years, my gorgeous, precious birthday girl.*

*Mum xx*

It was mid-May, and Oxford was bursting into bloom: the trees along the river in full leaf, the stately old college buildings pale yellow in the sunshine, boat races up and down the river cheered on by students and passers-by alike. Two weeks ago, the bells had rung from the Magdalen College tower to see in the month, the choristers serenading the city from the rooftop, and Morris dancers had paraded their jingling way through to Radcliffe Square. Now everyone had settled into the late spring warmth with an eye on summer just around the corner.

Out in her Oxfordshire home – newly rewired, with working plumbing and a kitchen so recently decorated you could still smell the paint – Belinda was basting a roast chicken. She was looking forward to having the whole family under her roof for the day, together again for the first time since Leni's funeral. Today would have been Leni's thirty-sixth birthday – seven short words that added up to one of the saddest sentences she could think of – but the McKenzies were coming together to mark the occasion, to hold each other up through the day. *Leni's death has left you in great pain, but it's important that you allow yourself to feel it*, her new counsellor Rachel had told her during one of their sessions. *Over time, the pain will lessen, your wounds will heal, and life will reshape itself around the loss of your daughter, like a stream flowing around a rock. Be gentle with yourself in the meantime.*

What on earth had she done before Rachel? Kind, wise, non-judgemental Rachel, who listened to Belinda with great empathy, passed her tissues whenever she needed them (frequently) and who seemed to be holding a lantern for her to follow through the darkness, as she stumbled towards acceptance. It had been Rachel's idea for Belinda to write letters to Leni whenever she wanted to say something, and it had proved both comforting and cathartic. Rachel had also put her in touch with a support group of other bereaved parents who met every fortnight in a neighbouring village to reminisce and encourage and commiserate. How wonderful it was to meet people who understood what you were going through, who indulged you with compassion while you showed them your favourite photos, then squeezed your arm if you started tearing up. Apolline was in Belinda's past now, where she belonged – although it had made her feel gratifyingly less of an idiot, hearing that a couple of other grieving parents within the group had taken similar paths themselves while in the depths of heartbroken denial. 'And who can blame us?' one of the women had said. 'Wouldn't we all give anything for one more conversation with them? One more day?'

All in all, Belinda felt as if she was starting to live again. The house move had been a huge distraction, keeping her busy for many weeks, but it was a positive busyness; she loved being in their new space, painting and unpacking, making curtains and flinging open the windows so that the spring sunshine and fresh air could pour in. Day by day, unpacked box by unpacked box, she and Ray were turning the old neglected building into their home, with August earmarked as the B. & B.'s grand opening. And yes, although she hadn't dared say as much, you bet she had secretly earmarked a small upstairs room for a grandchild's bedroom. You bet she had already spent some time planning a soft cream colour palette with rosebud-print curtains. Or maybe a sweet farm-animal print, or … Well, whatever, she'd make it gorgeous and cosy by the time Ellis and Paloma had their little one in October, that was for sure. Was it terrible to admit that she was very much hoping for a Christmas visit from them? She and Ray had gone over to Crickhowell a fortnight ago for a weekend break, and Paloma seemed a sweet girl, with Ellis much happier and more relaxed now that he was home. Ellis turned out to be something of an adrenalin junkie like his dad, suggesting he and Ray go off for a gliding session in the Black Mountains, which they both seemed to love. Best of all for Ray was the fact that Rhiannon, his estranged daughter, had consented to see him for the first time in years as well, and after an initial slow burn, they were getting on like the proverbial house on fire.

'My children! And a new little mouse to look forward to!' Ray had said the other evening when they'd been looking over some photos Ellis had sent.

Sitting on the sofa, Belinda had jerked in surprise. The word 'mouse' was ringing a bell in her head and she couldn't think why. 'A new little mouse?' she repeated, looking at him quizzically.

'Oh! It was what we used to call Ellis when he was born, Mouse. Mouseling, sometimes.' He had the fond smile of one remembering a happy time. 'I'm getting used to the idea of being a grandad. Having a tiny new mouseling to look after and love.'

*Mouse. Ellis.* There was definitely something there, the bell in her head continuing to jangle, but Belinda couldn't think, for the life of her, of the connection. It would come to her, she assured herself, smiling back.

In the meantime, it was a privilege to be party to his happiness, and to get to know these fine young people, and to feel that her own life was a touch richer, a touch warmer, for them being in it. And today she was thankful for her own two children, yes, and her ex-husband as well, who would be joining her and Ray here today. She couldn't wait for them all to be around her table, in the hope that any happiness they could share, any reminiscences, would be something to celebrate.

Tony was yet to see the new house – he had his hands full, with Jackie and the baby only recently out of hospital, and a few extra grey hairs to show for the stressful time they'd all had – but Alice and Will had both come over several times already. In fact, Will, bless him, had not only helped on the day of the move but had stayed for a few days afterwards too, heaving furniture around with Ray, cleaning and unpacking. It had been so nice to see him and Ellis get to know one another, the two of them really hitting it off. She and the boys had rather ganged up on Ray, joking that any unlabelled boxes must be more of Ray's 'extensive wardrobe' – the punchline being, of course, that Ray only had about four T-shirts and two pairs of jeans to his name. You could tell Ray absolutely loved the ribbing though. What was a family, after all, if they couldn't take the mick out of one another at all times?

As she was smiling to herself about this, the fashionista himself came in from the garden, where he'd mown the lawn, set up the patio table and chairs, and hung bunting between the ancient apple trees that had surprised them both by flowering with the most exquisite blossom. 'Can I do anything?' he asked. 'What are you smiling about?' he added suspiciously, noticing her expression.

'Just thinking how much I love you,' she said, sliding the bronzed chicken back into the oven, then walking over to hug him. By now, she'd come clean about the whole Graham Fenton business and, to her relief, he'd told her it made absolutely no difference to the way he felt about her. *You think that's bad? I'm glad you didn't see me in my youth, put it like that*, he'd told her, holding her tightly. *We all make mistakes, right?*

Just then the doorbell rang and her heart swelled with joyful anticipation. 'Ah!' she said, disentangling herself from him. 'Who's first, I wonder?'

★

Tony stood on the doorstep, a bunch of white roses in his arms, as well as a bottle of fizz and a somewhat belated New Home card for his ex-wife and Ray. He glanced down at himself, checking for baby-sick patches on his shirt (nope) and also to make sure his flies were done up (thankfully yes). Ever since Jackie and baby Amelia had been allowed home, he hadn't been getting very much sleep. Small, previously mundane things – doing up his trousers properly, brushing his teeth regularly, managing to wear matching socks, getting dressed before midday – had been far more difficult to keep on top of lately. He had got in the car the other day, and stared blankly in front of him, wondering what had happened to the steering wheel, before realising he was actually sitting in the passenger seat. Then he'd wondered if perhaps he was too tired to even consider driving at all.

But they had made it this far, he kept telling himself. After a fairly nail-biting start to life, Amelia – or Mimi, as they'd soon switched to calling her – had thrived in the intensive care unit, quickly putting on weight and gradually becoming more animated and alert. 'The doctors are hopeful she'll have no serious health repercussions as a result of her prematurity,' he'd been able to update friends and family, faint with relief every time.

Jackie, however, had been less fortunate. She'd somehow picked up an infection after the birth that had developed, frighteningly fast, into full-blown sepsis, leaving her very ill for almost a month. There had been a few dark times when it seemed Tony was staring right into the abyss, with no glimmer of light on the horizon: times when he thought he might fall apart. Except then he'd go to see his tiny girl in her incubator and he'd feel such strength of will, it gave him the fuel to keep going each time. Will stayed on for moral support, and Tony was grateful to have him there. Alice too had been a godsend, popping back and forth between London and Oxford whenever she could manage it. She'd had tears in her eyes the first time she met Amelia, and Tony had found himself welling up too, so emotionally charged had the moment been. Seeing Alice hold her new sister, stroke her tiny round cheek, tell her about all the fun the two of them were going to have together ... Tony felt love waterfall into him at the sight; the most soothing balm against old scars. It was no magical cure-all to give his daughter a new sister when she was still grieving the loss of Leni, but he could see that there was a comfort to be had, the consolation of tiny Amelia, nestled in the crook of her arms. A brand new love unfolding before his eyes.

Outside the two spheres of home and hospital, normality was suspended meanwhile. His boss, Annabeth, herself the doting aunty of twins born prematurely, was understanding, rearranging his workload to reduce pressure, reminding him to take care of himself. Friends of theirs had offered help and advice. The antenatal group rallied with support and small kindnesses (Reiki Woman of all people turned out to make a cracking vegetable lasagne, as he discovered when she dropped round with it one evening). And the bereavement group were there for him too, listening and helping with practical suggestions. Gen insisted on taking him for a pint and chat after their last session, not least because she and Pen were now the proud parents of hefty ten-pounder Otto. In the run-up to his birth, Pen had suffered a couple of worrying bleeds, but she'd carried Otto to term, and both she and Gen were besotted with their boy. Tony was glad. Who would have thought, a year ago, he'd have a confidante like Gen? He was grateful for her, and all the other good people in his life.

And now Jackie and Amelia were home at last, the three of them trying out family life for size. Jackie was understandably still shaky and traumatised by her experience, worried that she had lost out on precious bonding time with their daughter and upset that she'd missed her chance to breastfeed. But she was alive and recovering a little more every day. Tony had taken a month's paternity leave, starting from when Amelia had been allowed home, and had thrown himself into fatherhood and caring; doing everything for them all, badly at first, admittedly, but he was learning on the hoof. He took care of the laundry; he washed, fed and changed Amelia; he organised supermarket deliveries, dealt with household bills and cleaned everything, so thoroughly and energetically that their existing cleaner clucked at him, complaining he was doing her out of a job. That was fine, though, because it meant he was on top of things; he was pulling his weight. Wasn't this proof that he was a committed partner, a proper dad?

It was all good, in other words, although, God, it was exhausting too. He had somehow overlooked the sheer fatigue of living with a tiny baby, however delightful, who needed feeding and winding and washing and wiping at frequent intervals. Now that he was no longer pumped so full of adrenalin, he could feel tiredness filling him like insulation foam from an aerosol can, expanding into every corner. He had known nothing of what Belinda had gone through with their children together, he'd realised. Absolutely nothing. But all of the slog was worth it now, to have his new daughter in the world. Every single bit.

It had been with a strange mixture of feelings that he'd left Jackie and Amelia behind half an hour ago, to travel around the ring road to Belinda and Ray's new place. They'd been invited too, but Jackie sensed that this might be better as a McKenzies-only day, and wanted to give them space to reminisce. 'I'll come along next time,' she'd said, hugging him goodbye. 'Give everyone my love.' She was probably right, but as he parked in Belinda's posh new driveway and tried to get himself together in readiness for what was sure to be an intensely moving reunion, he found himself unsure if he could manage this alone. Leni's birthday, and she wasn't alive to be with them. How could it be anything other than awful?

'Tony,' said Belinda as she opened the door and saw him standing there looking emotional. 'Are you all right?'

He looked back at her, momentarily overcome, because of course he didn't have to manage this alone. Here was Belinda, a woman he'd once loved more than anyone, the woman who'd given him three wonderful children. She was so important to him, after everything, and it had taken a tragedy to make him appreciate her. Instinctively, he stepped forward and put his arms around her, slightly crushing the bouquet he'd brought, but never mind. 'Thanks, Bel,' he said, his throat tight with sentiment. What a strange, beautiful, wild day it had been, when Leni came into the world and changed their lives forever by making them parents. 'Thanks for everything,' he said. 'With all my heart.'

She embraced him, then stepped back with an air of puzzled concern before her eyes narrowed. 'You haven't slept, have you?' she said knowingly. 'And you're mad with tiredness, aren't you? I can tell. Come in. Lunch will be another half an hour, why don't you have a quick kip upstairs before the others get here?'

He staggered as he crossed the threshold; the past few months catching up on him in a single moment, overwhelming him body and soul. 'That,' he managed to say, choking back his gratitude, 'is the best offer I've had all year.'

# Chapter Thirty-Six

Will shoved his bag up on to the luggage rack, then slid into the window seat, waiting for the train to depart. He'd flown down from Aberdeen to Bristol the day before, spending the night with an old friend who'd lived there since university, then today he'd set off for Oxford. Now he was on the last leg of the journey, on the small stopping train headed to the village station nearest his mum's new place.

*It would have been Leni's birthday today*, he typed into the memorial page. Ever since Alice had encouraged him to be a part of it, he had found real solace in adding to it frequently. *One of my earliest memories was a birthday party of hers – her twelfth, possibly, which would make me nearly four. The house was full of these enormous loud girls wearing shiny clothes, dancing to music in the living room, balloons bobbing everywhere. I remember being transfixed by the sight of my sisters with Leni's friends, as if they were briefly transformed into princesses or goddesses who had taken over the house. That, and the fact that they all screamed 'A boy! A boy!' whenever I tried to join in the games. (In hindsight, this explained a lot about my love life in later years.)*

*Another memory is of her coming back really pissed on her six-teen birthday, where she'd gone out to the park with friends, taking with her a buttercream-iced cake that Mum had slaved and sworn over, but also, it later emerged, with several dodgy-looking bottles of alcohol nicked from Mum's collection. I was fast asleep in bed but got woken by the front door banging when she crashed in after dark, followed by unmissable, prolonged vomiting in the downstairs toilet. When I crept on to the landing to peer down through the banisters, there was Leni staggering around the hall with what looked like handfuls of buttercream in her hair, being held up by an extremely cross-looking Mum. Cross, because Leni had had a cake fight after all Mum's hard work, I guessed as an innocent seven-year-old, thrilled at such naughtiness, but the next morning at breakfast, Mum made a few tart remarks about Leni's hangover and yes, she did have to go to school, actually, and I had to think again.*

*Happy birthday, Leni, you buttercream-haired legend and total party animal. Definitely going to raise a glass or two in your honour later (but might hold back on the cake fights). Will*

He posted the message only to see a reply from Alice appear almost immediately.

*Oh my God, yes, I'd forgotten that!! She was in SO MUCH TROUBLE! I absolutely loved it!!!*

He smiled, and then again as a message appeared from Belinda. *The work I put into that cake!!! Ungrateful little minx. I've only JUST forgiven you, Leni, love Mum xxx*

'Have you thought about doing something positive to honour her memory, like a legacy?' Isla had asked one time when the subject of Leni came up during his stay. Will had booked the cheapest room of the cheapest hotel when he went up to Aberdeen, but a mere two hours into their first evening out together – that truly wonderful, fun, joyful first evening – she'd cocked her head at him and said, 'Why don't you come back to mine tonight?' Which was where he'd stayed the entire fortnight, as things turned out. (There was a distinct possibility that it had been the greatest fortnight of his life, truth be told.)

'Actually, I've found this charity that teaches people how to mend and care for their bikes up and down the country,' he had replied, turning pink with sudden self-consciousness. 'I was thinking I might volunteer for them, just so that ...' He couldn't get the words out. 'You know. So that other people like Leni could learn that sort of stuff.'

Isla got it immediately, of course. 'That's such a good idea,' she'd said, folding her slender fingers around his hand. By then he'd abandoned the closed-book approach and told her all about his secret guilt around his sister, and now they were draped cosily along her sofa together, music playing, both of them full after a takeaway curry. Her red hair smelled like jasmine flowers and he felt a moment of supreme happiness that he was there at all; certain that he had done the right thing in facing up to both his past and his future. *I've changed*, he'd messaged her on Facebook when he first got back in touch, his dad's words about being honest ringing in his ears. *I've thought about what you said and you were right. I was massively in denial. But I'm back in the UK and I'm dealing with everything, and trying to put a new life together for myself. Would you like to meet up?*

Thank God she'd said yes. She'd been thinking about him

too. She'd come to pick him up from Aberdeen airport and they'd had a moment of recognition – attraction, definitely – and then she'd thrown her arms around him. 'It's good to see you, Will,' she said huskily in his ear and he'd almost exploded with lust, right there in the Arrivals area.

He felt, at last, as if he had something to offer her, as if there was some substance to him, other than light-hearted charm. He'd made the decision to reapply to university and, to his surprise, the woman at the FE college his dad had put him in touch with proved to be fantastically helpful when it came to making that happen. With her assistance, he'd been able to organise meetings with a couple of different universities, Glasgow and Birmingham, both of whom had ended up offering him a place on their Physics courses for September. 'Come on, it's got to be Glasgow, surely?' Isla said on hearing about this, just as he'd hoped she would. 'We're going to give this a shot, right?'

His heart had stuttered a little with joy at her question. 'I would love to give me and you a shot,' he replied.

In the months before he moved up to Scotland, he had a few things to be getting on with. He'd have to return to his old textbooks, for one, in order to swot up on some of the content he'd forgotten over time, but he was looking forward to reimmersing himself in the subject. He also needed to earn some money over the summer to buffer himself through the penny-pinching student years. He had a meeting lined up next week with the bike-repair charity, plus he'd looked into the mentoring charity Leni had worked for, contacting their Glasgow office to say he'd love to get involved with the programme if possible. Life was shaping up pretty well, all in all.

'We are now approaching Pearbridge,' the automated voice announced at that moment. 'Pearbridge will be your next station stop in approximately two minutes.'

The hedgerows outside were full of flowers as the train rattled past them, the fields lush and verdant. Will stood up and heaved down his bag, feeling ready for the next chapter in his life.

# Chapter Thirty-Seven

Later on, after the roast chicken had been polished off, Alice produced her contribution: a chocolate cake with three layers and white chocolate icing. It had been the first time she'd baked anything for over a year and she found herself holding her breath as her mum plunged the knife in, to *Ooh*s and *Aah*s. Before now, she'd always taken pride in baking birthday cakes for family and friends, but she'd felt so terrible, not making the effort for Leni last May, she'd fallen out of love with the idea for a while. This was her way of redeeming herself for the supermarket brownies the year before. She just wished her sister could have had a slice too.

'Amazing, Alice,' her mum said warmly, licking chocolate off her fingers.

'That is *good*,' agreed Will, going in for a second piece.

'A triumph,' Tony declared, scraping up the last crumbs with his fork.

The four of them were out in the garden, drinking champagne and swapping old memories. Ray had made a tactful exit, claiming he needed to sort out some paperwork, but really, Alice knew it was so that the McKenzies could fully abandon themselves to the retelling of old family tales, with all the in-jokes, bad impressions and other shortcuts enjoyed by people who'd been there.

Alice had been dreading this day, there were no two ways about it. She'd woken that morning, tried (and failed) to interest Hamish in a loving embrace – he was still having none of it – before leafing through an album of Leni photos, smiling one moment and feeling like bursting into tears the next. 'I wish you were here,' she murmured to different versions of her sister – in a gold bikini and aviator shades on a beach in Ibiza; looking effortlessly glamorous in front of the Eiffel Tower in a trench coat and red lipstick; laughing her head off at someone's house party in a glittering silver dress with a short-lived bleached-hair experiment. 'I bloody wish you were here, mate.'

Her phone had been pinging away – her dad and Will, saying they were looking forward to seeing her later. Belinda, sounding frazzled, asking her to bring various bits and bobs – a tablecloth, some champagne glasses – because hers were still packed up in boxes somewhere, as well as a further message about driving carefully and checking her tyres (old habits died hard). There had also been a couple of messages from her friends – Celeste saying, *Hope it all goes well today. Thinking of you*, and Lou saying, *Have a good day. Let's have a pint after dance class next week and you can tell us all about it.* She'd added a second message: *Just like real dancers do, I bet*, with several pint glass emojis and a laughing face.

Alice smiled because, despite her earlier doubts, she had

come to enjoy her friends' monthly challenges. After some drizzly netball sessions in March, they'd tried aqua aerobics in April (hilarious) and now they were learning street dance at a studio in King's Cross. It was so hard! And made her feel so uncoordinated and unfit! But thankfully Lou was even more uncoordinated than she was, and so far, every week they'd ended up limp with breathless giggles at the back of the class. The three of them were off to Palma for a long weekend at the end of the month and Lou was already suggesting they bust out their new moves in the clubs there. Alice knew for a fact it would take *mucha cerveza* for her to be persuaded to join in, but stranger things had happened, after all. Sometimes you had to say yes and sod the consequences, right?

As she lay in bed, not sure she quite wanted the day to start yet, Alice's eye fell on the mosaic now taking pride of place on the wall opposite. Last Saturday, she had returned to Walthamstow to pick up the piece she'd commissioned, an image of a peacock (what else?), made from the broken shards of Leni's crockery set. The plates were unrecognisable in their new form: teal and green and purple pieces nestling alongside one another to create the bird's gleaming body, its tail, its crown, all held in place with cement. Alice had hugged the mosaic artist, in awe of what she'd created. 'It's perfect,' she said, gently stroking the dazzling surface. 'Absolutely perfect.'

It had made what was always going to be a tough week more bearable, the spur to get her out of bed that morning, showered, dressed and eventually on to the motorway, putting on the radio and smiling to hear an old Pixies song playing, one of Leni's favourite bands. Having arrived at her mum's, she'd found the others already there: Belinda chopping mint from the garden to sprinkle over the buttered new potatoes. Her dad, dazed and a little crumpled-looking where he'd just had an impromptu nap. Will, full of tales from his Scottish trip and walking tall. 'Will's in *lurrrvvve*,' Alice teased him, because embarrassing your little brother was never not fun.

To her surprise, their get-together had so far been a thoroughly jolly occasion. For long periods of the lunch, Leni barely got a look-in as they caught up on each other's news. Tony proudly showed everyone the latest pictures of Amelia (did he realise that he'd forgotten to shave that morning though, Alice wondered, hiding a smile), while Ray provided cheerful updates on how things were going with his son and daughter (swimmingly, in a word). Will talked enthusiastically about his university plans ('Finally!' cried Belinda) and what a great time he'd had in Aberdeen with Isla ('Finally!' echoed Alice with a grin). As for Alice herself, she had plenty of her own good news to share.

The first thing was that she already felt as if she had proved her worth in her new extracurricular ròle at Sage and Golding. Having officially taken over responsibility for the company's social media output, she had suggested a strategy based around the slogan *We get you. We've got you*, cleverly showing how the company both understood and looked after a broad range of people. The accompanying visuals were humorous and deliberately diverse, carefully avoiding stereotypes. The focus groups had loved them and now that the campaign was under way, there had been a noticeable uptick in engagement online, with the stats showing that enquiries from new customers had similarly risen. *We get you, we've got you – you've got this!* Emma had emailed her jokily. *We're all delighted, Alice.*

With her maternity cover contract due to end in another six weeks, she'd been busily networking with other possible clients, as well as contacting a few familiar faces at companies she knew from her ReImagine days. She had a number of meetings in the pipeline thanks to further intel from her friend Edie, too. 'I don't want to tempt fate,' she said now, swiftly touching the wooden table as she spoke, 'but it's going pretty well. I'm excited!'

Things were going pretty well with Jacob, too, she thought, her eye falling on a cabbage-white butterfly touring her mum's garden, its papery wings translucent in the sun. Since the peacock day in Holland Park, they'd gone on to spend more and more time together, ostensibly for Flying Beauties nostalgia and chat, until it dawned on her, one Saturday lunchtime in a Brick Lane café, that they hadn't so much as mentioned Leni's name, and that, actually, this had become something more than a mere nostalgia trip. They'd gone out for dinner in all of Leni's favourite places by now, and made a few new favourites of their own. He'd taken her to the climbing centre he went to (exhilarating!); they'd hired a boat on the Serpentine one sunny April afternoon; they'd taken a one-day wine-tasting course together and got hilariously sozzled. Best of all, they'd talked and talked, about the big stuff and the small stuff: life, friends, dreams, love, the latest trashy TV show they were both obsessed with.

She loved seeing him, she loved having him back in her life. Her mum was totally right: he'd always been number one in terms of the best boyfriend she'd ever had, and he'd grown up into this lovely, funny, clever, kind man. A little bit uncool with his dad coat and crumpled shirts, but after all the shallow, vain boys she'd dated since him, this could only be a good thing. *Transparent as a piece of cling film*, he'd joked to her on the way to Holland Park, but thank goodness for that, after years of faking and posturing in other relationships. She'd take Sincere over Cool, any day.

All of these feelings had rushed up inside her that day in Brick Lane, as they ate lunch in an outdoor café. 'Jacob,' she said, interrupting him because she couldn't wait a second longer, not even for him to finish his sentence. She was done with passivity, after all. 'Are you feeling this too? Me and you, I mean. I'm not imagining it, am I? We . . .' Then she broke off, unsure how to say the words. All she could think about was his lovely expressive mouth and how much she wanted to kiss him. So then she gave up on words entirely and, instead, impulsively leaned forward to do just that.

'Oh,' he mumbled in surprise as her lips landed on his. Then they drew apart, looked at one another wordlessly and mutually went in for another. *'Oh,'* he repeated afterwards. 'Where did that come from? Was the anecdote about my boss *that* erotic, or . . . ?'

'Sorry,' she said, giddy at her own daring. She had forgotten what a good kisser he was. How they had kissed for hours on end as teenagers, until their lips became swollen. 'I suddenly felt like I couldn't contain myself any more. I felt compelled to pounce on you. Was that – is that – okay?'

He moved a tomato-shaped ketchup bottle out of the way

so that he could take her hand across the table. 'Is it *okay*?' he repeated. 'I've wanted that to happen since approximately Christmas Eve twelve years ago when you dumped me. Yes, it's okay, Alice. It's better than okay. It's . . .' He looked overcome for a moment. 'It's good.'

'What do you mean, you've wanted that to happen? You didn't have to wait!' She laughed. 'Newsflash: you could have done something about it yourself.'

He gave her the side-eye. 'Yeah, like that's not the ultimate dick move: take advantage of a grieving woman,' he scoffed. 'Although . . .' He screwed up his face. 'Well, okay, there were times when I nearly *did* do that, if I'm honest,' he admitted with a laugh. 'It's been killing me, Alice. Getting to know you second time around . . . hand on my heart, I've been quietly falling in love with you all over again. Maybe even more than before. Seeing you is always the best bit of my week. I just . . . love being with you. In fact, I knew, right from the sixth-form Christmas disco, that you were something special.' He smiled at her, eyes soulful. 'Can we give it another go, do you think? You and me, the star-crossed lovers beneath the glitterball?'

'Oh, Jay,' she said, overwhelmed by his words. *Something special.* She had spent so many months last year feeling as if life had lost its gloss, and as if she had too; free-falling through the darkness all alone. For someone as good and true as he was to be saying these things, to see her as special, made her glow inside with such unalloyed pleasure. 'I love being with you too. And even though we don't have a glitterball right now, I'm saying a million per cent yes, let's absolutely give it another go.' It was almost impossible to manage her feelings any more;

they were swelling inside her, overflowing. She couldn't stop smiling. 'I never thought I'd feel happy again,' she blurted out. Losing Leni had been like having all the light blotted out from her life, as if the sun would never shine again. Somehow her friends and family – and Jacob – had brought her out of the shadows. 'But you make me happy,' she told him.

They kissed some more, their lunches growing colder by the second, and she felt her whole body quickening towards him, the enchanted princess waking from a spell. She leaned her head against his shoulder, then smiled to herself. 'Hey, you know who's going to be really delighted about this, don't you?'

'Well, *I'm* feeling pretty delighted . . .'

'My mum! Because you've always been the OG boyfriend, according to her; the greatest of all time. She will be *buzzing* when I tell her.'

He laughed. 'Oh God, mine too. She was so excited about us getting back in touch. Every time I've spoken to her on the phone since February, it's been her first question – *And how's that lovely Alice doing?* – like it's some kind of soap opera she's following.'

'We should send them selfies of us snogging, it'll blow their minds,' Alice giggled. And then they were grinning at one another and kissing again, lunches stone cold and congealing by now, but who cared? She was here with her first love, the best of all men, certain that he was the real deal. 'Oh wow,' she said, as something occurred to her. 'Does this mean I get to meet your little boy?'

'Of course!' he said. 'You'll love him. And if you swot up on your dinosaur knowledge beforehand, there's a strong chance it'll be mutual.' He quirked an eyebrow. 'The big question is, do I get to meet Hamish?'

She burst out laughing. 'I'm afraid you'll have to lower your expectations on a warm welcome, but yes, you definitely get to meet him. It's meeting my friends you *really* have to worry about. Spoiler alert: they're already pumped and dying to grill you.'

Since then, Alice had met Max (adorable) and managed to win him over, drawing him a comic strip featuring his dinosaurs ('My daddy can't draw *anything*,' he'd said, impressed), and both she and Jacob had met each other's friends. 'Oh my days, what an absolute doll,' Lou had swooned to Alice in the pub loos during a grilling break. 'And you *dumped* him?' Celeste put in, sounding appalled. 'Jesus, Alice. Imagine if you'd never found him again!'

Jacob had also become a frequent visitor to her flat and, miracle of all miracles, Hamish had not only allowed Jacob to stroke him but had also produced a rusty old purr, the first Alice had heard from him. 'Oh, right, like that, is it? Prefer him to me, do you, Hamish, you traitor?' she'd complained, rolling her eyes. Secretly she was delighted though. Surely this, above anything, was a stamp of approval – proof that Jacob was the right one?

He had certainly put some kind of spell on her, as well as on her cat, she figured now as the butterfly twirled and spun through the sweet-smelling apple blossom. Because not only was she feeling happier, as if there were spots of warmth and brightness spangled liberally through her life again, but she'd also gained a little perspective on the past year. Sorted out some unfinished business at long last. It had been Jacob who'd persuaded her that getting in touch with Callum Ferguson might be a kind of closure for her, a means of turning the page on a difficult period in her life. 'And say what?' she'd asked, initially panicked at the suggestion. 'Don't ask me to say "I forgive you" to him, because I just can't.'

He'd shrugged, replying that it was up to her, and that he wasn't going to try and put words in her mouth. 'It's only a thought,' he said, before changing the subject.

She'd mulled it over afterwards and decided that it wouldn't be any skin off her nose to say sorry for the way she'd gone after him. Imagine how shit you'd feel, accidentally knocking a woman off her bike and killing her. Imagine how it would haunt you. And then, for the woman's sister to track you down and come to your house, incoherent with distress and hell-bent on punishing you for what had happened ... She felt sorry for him, if anything. The anger had quietly trickled away and now she felt pity. It wasn't his fault. He'd suffered too.

It had taken her a while to find the right words but eventually she'd managed to compose a short letter, apologising for her behaviour. *I realise this must have been awful for you as well*, she wrote. *I'm sorry that I made it worse. I hope you're doing okay.*

She wasn't expecting to hear back from him – she was half dreading a visit from his antagonistic son, if anything *(What part of 'leave him alone' don't you understand?)* – but a week later, a response came.

*Thank you, Alice, for your kind letter. I appreciate it more than I can say. I don't blame you for being angry, I would have felt exactly the same way. I'm so sorry for what happened and will have to live with it for the rest of my life. Whenever I dream about that night, I manage to swerve away just in time and she cycles on down the road. I wish with all my heart that this is what had happened.*

His words had been more eloquent and moving than she could ever have anticipated. She found it comforting, the thought of Leni cycling on down the road in Callum Ferguson's dreams. Carrying on to her audition, singing the words under her breath as she pedalled ... Alice sat a little straighter in her chair, remembering that this was something she'd meant to tell the others. It had felt too big a deal to drop into a phone conversation; she'd deliberately waited until they were here together. This was the moment. 'Oh! By the way,' she said to them. 'I found out where Leni was going the night she died.'

She explained how Will had made the connection with the mysterious 'T' in Leni's diary being her trampolining class, when it had been there in plain sight on the memorial page the whole time.

'And so I messaged this Shanice woman and asked if I could meet her, because it was the first I'd heard of any trampolining – did you know Leni had enrolled on a course?' Her parents shook their heads blankly. 'Anyway, Shanice said, sure, come over.'

Shanice was a nurse in her late thirties with two young girls, and she'd immediately invited Alice round on hearing who she was. Making Alice tea in a small colourful kitchen adorned with childish drawings and paintings, she confessed she'd taken up a trampolining class because she'd loved bouncing with her daughters in their local trampoline park, and wanted to learn some skills to keep up with them.

'I felt a bit shy at first – it's ages since I've done anything like that, with people I don't know, but your sister was really lovely to me from the start, saying hello and chatting away. She said she'd been in the doldrums lately – split up with her husband or something? – but was trying to throw herself into the world again.' Shanice smiled sadly, pouring boiling water into mugs. 'That was her exact phrase – throw myself into the world again.'

The words made Alice smile in return, although she had mixed feelings to hear this second-hand, from a woman her sister had barely known. 'This is all news to me,' she admitted, her mouth twisting. 'We'd had an argument at the time. We weren't speaking much.' She accepted the mug of tea, warming her hands around it. 'I'm glad she was feeling on the up though.'

'Oh, she was. And she loved trampolining, so much. She used to say, *I've always wanted to fly and this is the closest I've ever got to it* – with this big smile on her face. Real euphoria, you know.'

Alice did know. She could easily imagine her sister leaping for joy on the trampoline, just as she'd leaped off their grandma's old bunk bed all those years before, her face alight with the thrill. *I think I really did fly a bit just then. Did you see?*

'Was there anything else? Was she planning other ways to "throw herself back into the world"?' she asked, suddenly greedy for every one of this woman's memories, however banal. Her mind jumped to the list of ideas Leni had written in the back of her diary. *Paint! Fall in love! Make a new friend!* She'd done the last one, at least, Alice thought to herself.

Shanice's face fell. 'Well ... Yes. There was something,' she said. 'I mentioned singing in a choir and she was really interested – said how happy singing made her and what a lovely thing to do. So I suggested she audition to join us.' Now it was her turn to drop her gaze. 'Alice ... I hate to say this, but I think that she died coming to the audition that night. Because I'd arranged to see her there and she never showed up.'

The air seemed to leave Alice's lungs for a second. 'She died ... on her way to the audition, you think?' And then she remembered the Cherry House listing, how there had been a Thursday evening choir. A for Audition – of course. 'Was this at Cherry House, by any chance?'

Shanice nodded miserably. 'Yes. The choir leader said she'd hear Leni and a couple of other try-outs before the main session, only Leni never came.' Her eyes clouded. 'We'd chatted the day before – she said she'd been practising her audition song all week. She'd picked the song from *La La Land* – it's actually called "Audition", the one Emma Stone sings at the end? And that evening, she texted me saying she was excited about seeing me later, only ...' Her words trailed away. 'Afterwards, when I saw the news on Facebook, I couldn't help feeling it was my fault. I shouldn't have suggested—'

'No!' said Alice immediately. 'No, Shanice. You mustn't think that. Not for a minute.'

'She would have been alive if it wasn't for me though, wouldn't she? She would still be coming trampolining every week, and getting on with being your sister and everyone's friend, and—'

'You weren't to know! How could you possibly have known?' Alice could see how distraught the other woman looked; clearly this had been preying on her mind. She seized Shanice's hands. 'Please. Please don't feel bad, at all. You did a really nice thing, inviting her along. A lovely thing. And actually—' Her mind filled with an image of Leni cycling along, no doubt mentally giving it her best Emma Stone in her head, chords rising, blissfully unaware of the traffic around her. 'It's still awful but I'm glad at least that she was singing.' Emotions rose inside her. 'That she was happy.'

'She was so happy and excited,' Shanice said. There was a pause and then she added, 'I thought you must know about this, otherwise I'd have got in touch before. She said she was going to call you that night, you see. She said, *my sister's like Dutch courage in human form.* I remember thinking how lucky the two of you were to have each other.'

Alice had to swallow down the lump in her throat. 'She did call me. I never answered,' she replied, her voice barely more than a croak. How she loved that Leni had said that about her – *Dutch courage in human form* – but oh, how she wished she could have picked up the call, so that Leni could have excitedly told her about the audition. Knowing her sister, she'd have asked if she could practise her song down the phone for good measure. What Alice would give to go back in time and answer the phone, to hear her sing! 'I didn't give her any Dutch courage,' she added, feeling hollow inside.

Now it was Shanice who was squeezing Alice's hands. 'She

loved you,' she said simply. 'Focus on that. She loved you, she was happy, she was singing. And the end, when it came, would have been fast. She wouldn't have felt a moment's pain.'

'Oh my goodness,' Belinda said, putting a hand to her chest as Alice finished telling them. 'I like to think she was happy that day. I can't believe how nice that is to hear.'

They all had a wobbly few moments thinking about Leni singing on her bike and had to hug each other and blow their noses. Alice, for her part, had found peace in knowing, at last, Leni's last moments and her frame of mind, and since finding this out from Shanice, she'd stopped dreaming about chasing through the maze after her sister. Well, almost. She'd dreamed about the maze a few nights ago, actually, and it had started out like all of the other dreams, with Alice running and running, desperate for a glimpse of Leni, trying her best to catch her up. Until she'd rounded a corner of the maze in her dream and there she was, standing waiting, with a huge smile on her face.

*Leni!* Alice had cried, overjoyed. *You're here!*

*I've been here all along, you dozy fart*, Leni laughed, then came over and hugged Alice so tightly, Alice thought she might combust with sheer happiness. She could smell her sister's perfume, feel the solid warmth of her body, their faces pressed against each other.

*I love you*, she said. *I've missed you so much.*

*I love you too*, Leni said. *But I'm okay, you know. I'm actually really busy. And I'm happy!*

In her dream, Alice had burst out laughing – she might even have laughed out loud for real because suddenly she was awake, lying there in the darkness, and she was all alone. 'Did I just dream you?' she whispered aloud. 'Or were we together for real?' In some ways it didn't matter, because she'd had that moment regardless; she'd felt their togetherness. And it was so very Leni to be busying around in the afterlife, wasn't it? Knowing her, she'd probably already drawn up a new *Next year will be amazing!* plan for herself and was going about ticking it off, Alice had thought, smiling as she fell back to sleep.

Belinda got up now and started stacking the empty cake plates together. 'If I open another bottle of fizz, will anyone help me drink it?' she asked, and everyone agreed that it would be a good idea, even Tony, who was driving and not drinking. Alice and Will were going to stay over for the night and, as the family's collective sadness receded once more, a conviction took hold inside Alice that they were in for a really memorable evening together. It seemed that Belinda thought the same.

'This feels truly special,' she said, lifting her glass in a little salute once she'd poured everyone new drinks. 'I'm so glad you're all here. I've just been talking to Ray in the kitchen – he's going to come out and join us again in a bit – and we would like to have an ongoing family open house, on the first Sunday of every month, for a roast lunch and a get-together. You're all welcome – partners and babies too, of course,' she said, twinkling her eyes at Tony, and then at the other two. 'And Ray's family as well. Because it's important, this, isn't it? Us being together. It's so precious to me, spending time with you all. I know Leni thought so too.'

'Mum, I love that idea,' Alice said warmly. 'Thank you.'

'Obviously I'm hoping Jacob will come with you,' she said at once. 'And Will, I'm desperate to meet Isla—'

'Here we go, I knew there was an ulterior motive,' he groaned, but you could tell he was pleased all the same.

'And it goes without saying, I can't wait to get my hands on little Amelia – and to get to know Jackie properly too,' Belinda went on, which had Alice and Will exchanging surprised looks. A new matiness seemed to have sprung up between their mum and Jackie in recent weeks, and neither of them quite knew where it had come from. But some mysteries could be appreciated without being fully understood, Alice figured. 'We can be this evolving, organic family, can't we?' Belinda continued. 'McKenzies United – and the ones we love too.'

'McKenzies United,' Tony echoed, clinking his glass against hers. 'The very best team.'

'Hear hear,' Alice said, a new lump forming in her throat at the sight of her parents so amicable with one another. It felt so nice, she thought, smiling at them both and then Will. Then she reached down to the bag she'd brought with her, pulling it on to her lap. 'And in that spirit of family togetherness, I've got something for you all here. You know the memorial page up on Facebook? So many people have left lovely stories and memories of Leni there, I wanted to make a permanent record of them, for us to keep. So . . .' She dipped a hand into the bag and pulled out four white-covered books. 'I had these printed up, one each,' she said, passing them around.

It had been a labour of love, collating and typesetting the many stories, arranged in roughly biographical order, so that they began with recollections of Leni as a little girl, through teenage shenanigans, university life and onwards. Alice hadn't been able to read it all the way through herself yet without choking up – or cracking up – at one story or another, and she already knew it would be a precious object for her, for the rest of her life: a kaleidoscope featuring over a hundred bright, funny, memorable slices of her sister's life, recaptured by a host of different voices. They had known her. They had loved her. They remembered her.

Peace fell for a moment as everyone leafed through the pages, before Belinda punctured the silence with a snort.

'Oh goodness.' She had her hand to her mouth. 'I've just read the Easter egg story. I'd forgotten all about that.'

'Oh, from Liam-next-door?' Alice sniggered. 'I love that one.'

Tony and Will were also flicking through their copies. 'The driving test story, Christ, how come this is the first I've heard about it?' Tony said, looking appalled. 'How did she get away with that? She could have been arrested!'

Belinda had gone misty-eyed again. 'She was a one-off, wasn't she?'

'Some might think that's a good thing,' Will said, raising both eyebrows at the page he'd just read. 'Like that poor bloke in the ice cream van, here.' He'd seen the story before, of course, but it still brought a smile to his face. 'I mean, what the hell?'

Alice laughed because she knew exactly which driving test and which ice cream van they were referring to. A delicious giddy feeling began to unfurl in her, the pleasure of being here, with these people, on this warm May afternoon. 'What a privilege to have known her,' she said, raising her glass in the air. A second white butterfly had joined the first – sisters? she wondered tipsily – then she clinked glasses with her mum, her dad and her brother. 'How lucky we are to have had her in our lives.'

There was so much love in the garden in that moment as they chorused Leni's name and raised their glasses. Sadness and heartache and regret, yes, of course, but a great force of love too, as pure and golden as the beams of sunlight shining down on them. *We are broken crockery, glued back together*, Alice thought, her mouth full of cold, bubbling champagne. *Different and still broken, weakened and yet strong. We're together and we're all going to live happily ever after, with the best yet to come*. She, for one, was ready to break through, take a leap . . . and fly.

# Acknowledgements

A book is a true team effort and I'm lucky enough to have a really great team behind this one. Huge thanks to the Quercus superstars, in particular Cassie Browne, editor extraordinaire, for enthusiasm, creativity and precision red-penning – it's so brilliant to work with you! This book is a hundred times better for your input. Thanks also to Milly Reid, Kat Burdon, Bethan Ferguson, Ellie Nightingale, Dave Murphy and the entire sales team. Take a bow, Micaela Alcaino, for your artistic cover wizardry and thanks to everyone in design and production for turning my pages of words into another truly beautiful book. Sharona Selby deserves a medal for pin-sharp proofreading and attention to detail.

Many thanks as ever to the David Higham dream team – first and foremost Lizzy Kremer, the best in the business, plus Kay Begum, Maddalena Cavaciuti, Emma Jamison, Margaux Vialleron, Alice Howe, Johanna Clarke, Sam Norman, Ilaria Albani and Imogen Bovill. Thanks also to my foreign publishers around the world for all your fantastic work.

I'm immensely grateful to Amy Stobie and Emilie Hawes

from Agency UK in Bath – thank you both so much for brainstorming ideas with me around Alice's storyline and for giving me your time, imagination and marketing expertise. I loved talking to you both and hope I've done your advice justice (obviously any mistakes are entirely mine).

Lots of love to my author friends, for always brightening up my day with your humour, kindness and generosity – especially Ronnie, Milly, Harriet, Cally, Mimi, Jo, Rachel, Emma and Jill. Thanks also to Hayley, Kate, Fran, Cath and Cath for friendship and awesomeness.

Thank you to the booksellers and festivals who have supported me this year, and the readers who have got in touch with kind messages about my books or left lovely reviews. Your words always give me such a boost and are very much appreciated (even if I am hopeless at replying promptly – apologies).

Finally, last but never least, my wonderful family – Martin, Hannah, Tom and Holly, as well as my mum and dad, Phil, Ellie, Fiona, Ian and Julian. I am so very lucky to have you all.

# About the Author

**Lucy Diamond** grew up in Nottingham and has lived in Leeds, London, Oxford and Brighton. She now lives in Bath with her family. Lucy is the *Sunday Times* bestselling author of seventeen novels including *The Beach Café*, *An Almost Perfect Holiday* and *Anything Could Happen*. *The Best Days of Our Lives* is her eighteenth novel.

**Discover more from Lucy Diamond in this joyful story of love, family and second chances**

'The book we all need – full of escapism, romance, hope and kindness'
Milly Johnson

*Out now in paperback, eBook and audio*

**Discover more from *Sunday Times*
bestselling author**

Visit www.lucydiamond.co.uk for:

About Lucy

★

FAQs for Aspiring Writers

★

And to contact Lucy

To sign up to Lucy's newsletter,
scan the QR code here:

Follow Lucy on social media:

 @LDiamondAuthor

 @LucyDiamondAuthor

 @lucydiamondwrites